MW01519571

R. M. Ballantyne

The Coral Island & The Gorilla Hunters

e-artnow 2020

R. M. Ballantyne

The Coral Island & The Gorilla Hunters

Adventure Classics: A Tale of the Pacific Ocean & A Tale of the Wilds of Africa

e-artnow, 2020
Contact: info@e-artnow.org

ISBN 978-80-273-0720-3

Contents

The Coral Island

CHAPTER ONE

Beginning-My early life and character —I thirst for adventure in foreign lands, and go to sea.

Roving has always been, and still is, my ruling passion, the joy of my heart, the very sunshine of my existence. In childhood, in boyhood, and in man's estate I have been a rover; not a mere rambler among the woody glens and upon the hill-tops of my own native land, but an enthusiastic rover throughout the length and breadth of the wide, wide world.

It was a wild, black night of howling storm, the night on which I was born on the foaming bosom of the broad Atlantic Ocean. My father was a sea-captain; my grandfather was a sea-captain; my great-grandfather had been a marine. Nobody could tell positively what occupation *his* father had followed; but my dear mother used to assert that he had been a midshipman, whose grandfather, on the mother's side, had been an admiral in the Royal Navy. At any rate, we knew that as far back as our family could be traced, it had been intimately connected with the great watery waste. Indeed, this was the case on both sides of the house; for my mother always went to sea with my father on his long voyages, and so spent the greater part of her life upon the water.

Thus it was, I suppose, that I came to inherit a roving disposition. Soon after I was born, my father, being old, retired from a seafaring life, purchased a small cottage in a fishing village on the west coast of England, and settled down to spend the evening of his life on the shores of that sea which had for so many years been his home. It was not long after this that I began to show the roving spirit that dwelt within me. For some time past my infant legs had been gaining strength, so that I came to be dissatisfied with rubbing the skin off my chubby knees by walking on them, and made many attempts to stand up and walk like a man-all of which attempts, however, resulted in my sitting down violently and in sudden surprise. One day I took advantage of my dear mother's absence to make another effort; and, to my joy, I actually succeeded in reaching the doorstep, over which I tumbled into a pool of muddy water that lay before my father's cottage door. Ah, how vividly I remember the horror of my poor mother when she found me sweltering in the mud amongst a group of cackling ducks, and the tenderness with which she stripped off my dripping clothes and washed my dirty little body! From this time forth my rambles became more frequent and, as I grew older, more distant, until at last I had wandered far and near on the shore and in the woods around our humble dwelling, and did not rest content until my father bound me apprentice to a coasting-vessel and let me go to sea.

For some years I was happy in visiting the seaports, and in coasting along the shores, of my native land. My Christian name was Ralph; and my comrades added to this the name of Rover, in consequence of the passion which I always evinced for travelling. Rover was not my real name; but as I never received any other, I came at last to answer to it as naturally as to my proper name. And as it is not a bad one, I see no good reason why I should not introduce myself to the reader as Ralph Rover. My shipmates were kind, good-natured fellows, and they and I got on very well together. They did, indeed, very frequently make game of and banter me, but not unkindly; and I overheard them sometimes saying that Ralph Rover was a "queer, old-fashioned fellow." This, I must confess, surprised me much; and I pondered the saying long, but could come at no satisfactory conclusion as to that wherein my old-fashionedness lay. It is true I was a quiet lad, and seldom spoke except when spoken to. Moreover, I never could understand the jokes of my companions even when they were explained to me, which dulness in apprehension occasioned me much grief. However, I tried to make up for it by smiling and looking pleased when I observed that they were laughing at some witticism which I had failed to detect. I was also very fond of inquiring into the nature of things and their causes, and often fell into fits of abstraction while thus engaged in my mind. But in all this I saw nothing that did not seem to be exceedingly natural, and could by no means understand why my comrades should call me "an old-fashioned fellow."

Now, while engaged in the coasting trade I fell in with many seamen who had travelled to almost every quarter of the globe; and I freely confess that my heart glowed ardently within me as they recounted their wild adventures in foreign lands-the dreadful storms they had weathered, the appalling dangers they had escaped, the wonderful creatures they had seen both on the land and in the sea, and the interesting lands and strange people they had visited. But of all the places of which they told me, none captivated and charmed my imagination so much as the Coral Islands of the Southern Seas. They told me of thousands of beautiful, fertile islands that had been formed by a small creature called the coral insect, where summer reigned nearly all the year round, where the trees were laden with a constant harvest of luxuriant fruit, where the climate was almost perpetually delightful; yet where, strange to say, men were wild, bloodthirsty savages, excepting in those favoured isles to which the Gospel of our Saviour had been conveyed. These exciting accounts had so great an effect upon my mind that, when I reached the age of fifteen, I resolved to make a voyage to the South Seas.

I had no little difficulty, at first, in prevailing on my dear parents to let me go; but when I urged on my father that he would never have become a great captain had he remained in the coasting trade, he saw the truth of what I said and gave his consent. My dear mother, seeing that my father had made up his mind, no longer offered opposition to my wishes. "But, oh Ralph!" she said on the day I bade her adieu, "come back soon to us, my dear boy; for we are getting old now, Ralph, and may not have many years to live."

I will not take up my readers' time with a minute account of all that occurred before I took my final leave of my dear parents. Suffice it to say that my father placed me under the charge of an old messmate of his own, a merchant captain, who was on the point of sailing to the South Seas in his own ship, the *Arrow*. My mother gave me her blessing and a small Bible; and her last request was that I would never forget to read a chapter every day and say my prayers, which I promised, with tears in my eyes, that I would certainly do.

Soon afterwards I went on board the *Arrow*, which was a fine, large ship, and set sail for the islands of the Pacific Ocean.

CHAPTER TWO

The departure-The sea-My companions-Some account of the wonderful sights we saw on the great deep —A dreadful storm and a frightful wreck.

It was a bright, beautiful, warm day when our ship spread her canvas to the breeze and sailed for the regions of the south. Oh, how my heart bounded with delight as I listened to the merry chorus of the sailors while they hauled at the ropes and got in the anchor! The captain shouted; the men ran to obey; the noble ship bent over to the breeze, and the shore gradually faded from my view; while I stood looking on, with a kind of feeling that the whole was a delightful dream.

The first thing that struck me as being different from anything I had yet seen during my short career on the sea, was the hoisting of the anchor on deck and lashing it firmly down with ropes, as if we had now bid adieu to the land for ever and would require its services no more.

"There, lass!" cried a broad-shouldered jack-tar, giving the fluke of the anchor a hearty slap with his hand after the housing was completed —"there, lass, take a good nap now, for we sha'n't ask you to kiss the mud again for many a long day to come!"

And so it was. That anchor did not "kiss the mud" for many long days afterwards; and when at last it did, it was for the last time!

There were a number of boys in the ship, but two of them were my special favourites. Jack Martin was a tall, strapping, broad-shouldered youth of eighteen, with a handsome, good-humoured, firm face. He had had a good education, was clever and hearty and lion-like in his actions, but mild and quiet in disposition. Jack was a general favourite, and had a peculiar fondness for me. My other companion was Peterkin Gay. He was little, quick, funny, decidedly mischievous, and about fourteen years old. But Peterkin's mischief was almost always harmless, else he could not have been so much beloved as he was.

"Hallo, youngster!" cried Jack Martin, giving me a slap on the shoulder the day I joined the ship, "come below and I'll show you your berth. You and I are to be messmates; and I think we shall be good friends, for I like the look o' you."

Jack was right. He and I, and Peterkin afterwards, became the best and staunchest friends that ever tossed together on the stormy waves.

I shall say little about the first part of our voyage. We had the usual amount of rough weather and calm; also we saw many strange fish rolling in the sea, and I was greatly delighted one day by seeing a shoal of flying-fish dart out of the water and skim through the air about a foot above the surface. They were pursued by dolphins, which feed on them; and one flying-fish, in its terror, flew over the ship, struck on the rigging, and fell upon the deck. Its wings were just fins elongated; and we found that they could never fly far at a time, and never mounted into the air like birds, but skimmed along the surface of the sea. Jack and I had it for dinner, and found it remarkably good.

When we approached Cape Horn, at the southern extremity of America, the weather became very cold and stormy, and the sailors began to tell stories about the furious gales and the dangers of that terrible cape.

"Cape Horn," said one, "is the most horrible headland I ever doubled. I've sailed round it twice already, and both times the ship was a'most blow'd out o' the water."

"I've been round it once," said another; "an' that time the sails were split, and the ropes frozen in the blocks so that they wouldn't work, and we wos all but lost."

"An' I've been round it five times," cried a third; "an' every time wos wuss than another, the gales wos so tree-mendous!"

"And I've been round it, no times at all," cried Peterkin with an impudent wink in his eye, "an' that time I wos blow'd inside out!"

Nevertheless we passed the dreaded cape without much rough weather, and in the course of a few weeks afterwards were sailing gently, before a warm tropical breeze, over the Pacific

Ocean. Thus we proceeded on our voyage-sometimes bounding merrily before a fair breeze; at other times floating calmly on the glassy wave and fishing for the curious inhabitants of the deep, all of which, although the sailors thought little of them, were strange, and interesting, and very wonderful to me.

At last we came among the Coral Islands of the Pacific; and I shall never forget the delight with which I gazed-when we chanced to pass one-at the pure white, dazzling shores, and the verdant palm-trees, which looked bright and beautiful in the sunshine. And often did we three long to be landed on one, imagining that we should certainly find perfect happiness there! Our wish was granted sooner than we expected.

One night, soon after we entered the tropics, an awful storm burst upon our ship. The first squall of wind carried away two of our masts, and left only the foremast standing. Even this, however, was more than enough, for we did not dare to hoist a rag of sail on it. For five days the tempest raged in all its fury. Everything was swept off the decks, except one small boat. The steersman was lashed to the wheel lest he should be washed away, and we all gave ourselves up for lost. The captain said that he had no idea where we were, as we had been blown far out of our course; and we feared much that we might get among the dangerous coral reefs which are so numerous in the Pacific. At daybreak on the sixth morning of the gale we saw land ahead; it was an island encircled by a reef of coral, on which the waves broke in fury. There was calm water within this reef, but we could see only one narrow opening into it. For this opening we steered; but ere we reached it a tremendous wave broke on our stern, tore the rudder completely off, and left us at the mercy of the winds and waves.

"It's all over with us now, lads!" said the captain to the men. "Get the boat ready to launch; we shall be on the rocks in less than half-an-hour."

The men obeyed in gloomy silence, for they felt that there was little hope of so small a boat living in such a sea.

"Come, boys," said Jack Martin, in a grave tone, to me and Peterkin, as we stood on the quarter-deck awaiting our fate —"come, boys; we three shall stick together. You see it is impossible that the little boat can reach the shore, crowded with men. It will be sure to upset, so I mean rather to trust myself to a large oar. I see through the telescope that the ship will strike at the tail of the reef, where the waves break into the quiet water inside; so if we manage to cling to the oar till it is driven over the breakers, we may perhaps gain the shore. What say you? Will you join me?"

We gladly agreed to follow Jack, for he inspired us with confidence-although I could perceive, by the sad tone of his voice, that he had little hope; and indeed, when I looked at the white waves that lashed the reef and boiled against the rocks as if in fury, I felt that there was but a step between us and death. My heart sank within me; but at that moment my thoughts turned to my beloved mother, and I remembered those words, which were among the last that she said to me: "Ralph, my dearest child, always remember, in the hour of danger, to look to your Lord and Saviour Jesus Christ. He alone is both able and willing to save your body and your soul." So I felt much comforted when I thought thereon.

The ship was now very near the rocks. The men were ready with the boat, and the captain beside them giving orders, when a tremendous wave came towards us. We three ran towards the bow to lay hold of our oar, and had barely reached it when the wave fell on the deck with a crash like thunder. At the same moment the ship struck; the foremast broke off close to the deck and went over the side, carrying the boat and men along with it. Our oar got entangled with the wreck, and Jack seized an axe to cut it free; but owing to the motion of the ship, he missed the cordage and struck the axe deep into the oar. Another wave, however, washed it clear of the wreck. We all seized hold of it, and the next instant we were struggling in the wild sea. The last thing I saw was the boat whirling in the surf, and all the sailors tossed into the foaming waves. Then I became insensible.

On recovering from my swoon I found myself lying on a bank of soft grass, under shelter of an overhanging rock, with Peterkin on his knees by my side, tenderly bathing my temples with water, and endeavouring to stop the blood that flowed from a wound in my forehead.

CHAPTER THREE

The Coral Island-Our first cogitations after landing and the result of them-We conclude that the island is uninhabited.

There is a strange and peculiar sensation experienced in recovering from a state of insensibility which is almost indescribable: a sort of dreamy, confused consciousness; a half-waking, half-sleeping condition, accompanied with a feeling of weariness, which, however, is by no means disagreeable. As I slowly recovered, and heard the voice of Peterkin inquiring whether I felt better, I thought that I must have overslept myself, and should be sent to the masthead for being lazy; but before I could leap up in haste, the thought seemed to vanish suddenly away, and I fancied that I must have been ill. Then a balmy breeze fanned my cheek; and I thought of home, and the garden at the back of my father's cottage with its luxuriant flowers, and the sweet-scented honeysuckle that my dear mother trained so carefully upon the trellised porch. But the roaring of the surf put these delightful thoughts to flight, and I was back again at sea, watching the dolphins and the flying-fish, and reefing topsails off the wild and stormy Cape Horn. Gradually the roar of the surf became louder and more distinct. I thought of being wrecked far, far away from my native land, and slowly opened my eyes to meet those of my companion Jack, who, with a look of intense anxiety, was gazing into my face.

"Speak to us, my dear Ralph!" whispered Jack tenderly. "Are you better now?"

I smiled and looked up, saying, "Better! Why, what do you mean, Jack? I'm quite well."

"Then what are you shamming for, and frightening us in this way?" said Peterkin, smiling through his tears; for the poor boy had been really under the impression that I was dying.

I now raised myself on my elbow, and putting my hand to my forehead, found that it had been cut pretty severely, and that I had lost a good deal of blood.

"Come, come, Ralph," said Jack, pressing me gently backward, "lie down, my boy; you're not right yet. Wet your lips with this water; it's cool and clear as crystal. I got it from a spring close at hand. There, now, don't say a word-hold your tongue," he said, seeing me about to speak. "I'll tell you all about it, but you must not utter a syllable till you have rested well."

"Oh, don't stop him from speaking, Jack!" said Peterkin, who, now that his fears for my safety were removed, busied himself in erecting a shelter of broken branches in order to protect me from the wind-which, however, was almost unnecessary, for the rock beside which I had been laid completely broke the force of the gale. "Let him speak, Jack; it's a comfort to hear that he's alive after lying there stiff and white and sulky for a whole hour, just like an Egyptian mummy. —Never saw such a fellow as you are, Ralph-always up to mischief. You've almost knocked out all my teeth and more than half-choked me, and now you go shamming dead! It's very wicked of you, indeed it is."

While Peterkin ran on in this style my faculties became quite clear again, and I began to understand my position. "What do you mean by saying I half-choked you, Peterkin?" said I.

"What do I mean? Is English not your mother-tongue? or do you want me to repeat it in French by way of making it clearer? Don't you remember?"

"I remember nothing," said I, interrupting him, "after we were thrown into the sea."

"Hush, Peterkin!" said Jack; "you're exciting Ralph with your nonsense. —I'll explain it to you. You recollect that, after the ship struck, we three sprang over the bow into the sea? Well, I noticed that the oar struck your head and gave you that cut on the brow which nearly stunned you, so that you grasped Peterkin round the neck without knowing apparently what you were about. In doing so, you pushed the telescope-which you clung to as if it had been your life-against Peterkin's mouth —"

"Pushed it against his mouth!" interrupted Peterkin; "say crammed it down his throat! Why, there's a distinct mark of the brass rim on the back of my gullet at this moment!"

"Well, well, be that as it may," continued Jack, "you clung to him, Ralph, till I feared you really would choke him. But I saw that he had a good hold of the oar; so I exerted myself to the utmost to push you towards the shore, which we luckily reached without much trouble, for the water inside the reef is quite calm."

"But the captain and crew, what of them?" I inquired anxiously.

Jack shook his head.

"Are they lost?"

"No, they are not lost, I hope; but, I fear, there is not much chance of their being saved. The ship struck at the very tail of the island on which we are cast. When the boat was tossed into the sea it fortunately did not upset, although it shipped a good deal of water, and all the men managed to scramble into it; but before they could get the oars out, the gale carried them past the point and away to leeward of the island. After we landed I saw them endeavouring to pull towards us; but as they had only one pair of oars out of the eight that belonged to the boat, and as the wind was blowing right in their teeth, they gradually lost ground. Then I saw them put about and hoist some sort of sail —a blanket, I fancy, for it was too small for the boat-and in half-an-hour they were out of sight."

"Poor fellows!" I murmured sorrowfully.

"But the more I think about it I've better hope of them," continued Jack in a more cheerful tone. "You see, Ralph, I've read a great deal about these South Sea Islands, and I know that in many places they are scattered about in thousands over the sea, so they're almost sure to fall in with one of them before long."

"I'm sure I hope so," said Peterkin earnestly. "But what has become of the wreck, Jack? I saw you clambering up the rocks there while I was watching Ralph. Did you say she had gone to pieces?"

"No, she has not gone to pieces; but she has gone to the bottom," replied Jack. "As I said before, she struck on the tail of the island and stove in her bow; but the next breaker swung her clear, and she floated away to leeward. The poor fellows in the boat made a hard struggle to reach her, but long before they came near her she filled and went down. It was after she had foundered that I saw them trying to pull to the island."

There was a long silence after Jack had ceased speaking, and I have no doubt that each was revolving in his mind our extraordinary position. For my part, I cannot say that my reflections were very agreeable. I knew that we were on an island, for Jack had said so; but whether it was inhabited or not, I did not know. If it should be inhabited, I felt certain, from all I had heard of South Sea Islanders, that we should be roasted alive and eaten. If it should turn out to be uninhabited, I fancied that we should be starved to death. "Oh," thought I, "if the ship had only struck on the rocks we might have done pretty well, for we could have obtained provisions from her, and tools to enable us to build a shelter; but now-alas! alas! we are lost!" These last words I uttered aloud in my distress.

"Lost, Ralph!" exclaimed Jack, while a smile overspread his hearty countenance. "Saved, you should have said. Your cogitations seem to have taken a wrong road, and led you to a wrong conclusion."

"Do you know what conclusion I have come to?" said Peterkin. "I have made up my mind that it's capital-first-rate-the best thing that ever happened to us, and the most splendid prospect that ever lay before three jolly young tars. We've got an island all to ourselves. We'll take possession in the name of the king. We'll go and enter the service of its black inhabitants. Of course we'll rise, naturally, to the top of affairs: white men always do in savage countries. You shall be king, Jack; Ralph, prime minister; and I shall be —"

"The court-jester," interrupted Jack.

"No," retorted Peterkin; "I'll have no title at all. I shall merely accept a highly responsible situation under government; for you see, Jack, I'm fond of having an enormous salary and nothing to do."

"But suppose there are no natives?"

"Then we'll build a charming villa, and plant a lovely garden round it, stuck all full of the most splendiferous tropical flowers; and we'll farm the land, plant, sow, reap, eat, sleep, and be merry."

"But to be serious," said Jack, assuming a grave expression of countenance-which, I observed, always had the effect of checking Peterkin's disposition to make fun of everything —"we are really in rather an uncomfortable position. If this is a desert island, we shall have to live very much like the wild beasts; for we have not a tool of any kind-not even a knife."

"Yes, we have *that*," said Peterkin, fumbling in his trousers pocket, from which he drew forth a small penknife with only one blade, and that was broken.

"Well, that's better than nothing. —But come," said Jack, rising; "we are wasting our time in *talking* instead of *doing*. —You seem well enough to walk now, Ralph. —Let us see what we have got in our pockets; and then let us climb some hill and ascertain what sort of island we have been cast upon, for, whether good or bad, it seems likely to be our home for some time to come."

CHAPTER FOUR

We examine into our personal property, and make a happy discovery-Our island described-Jack proves himself to be learned and sagacious above his fellows-Curious discoveries-Natural lemonade!

We now seated ourselves upon a rock, and began to examine into our personal property. When we reached the shore after being wrecked, my companions had taken off part of their clothes and spread them out in the sun to dry; for although the gale was raging fiercely, there was not a single cloud in the bright sky. They had also stripped off most part of my wet clothes and spread them also on the rocks. Having resumed our garments, we now searched all our pockets with the utmost care, and laid their contents out on a flat stone before us; and now that our minds were fully alive to our condition, it was with no little anxiety that we turned our several pockets inside out in order that nothing might escape us. When all was collected together, we found that our worldly goods consisted of the following articles:

First, a small penknife with a single blade, broken off about the middle and very rusty, besides having two or three notches on its edge. (Peterkin said of this, with his usual pleasantry, that it would do for a saw as well as a knife, which was a great advantage.) Second, an old German-silver pencil-case without any lead in it. Third, a piece of whip-cord about six yards long. Fourth, a sailmaker's needle of a small size. Fifth, a ship's telescope, which I happened to have in my hand at the time the ship struck, and which I had clung to firmly all the time I was in the water; indeed, it was with difficulty that Jack got it out of my grasp when I was lying insensible on the shore. I cannot understand why I kept such a firm hold of this telescope. They say that a drowning man will clutch at a straw. Perhaps it may have been some such feeling in me, for I did not know that it was in my hand at the time we were wrecked. However, we felt some pleasure in having it with us now-although we did not see that it could be of much use to us, as the glass at the small end was broken to pieces. Our sixth article was a brass ring which Jack always wore on his little finger. I never understood why he wore it; for Jack was not vain of his appearance, and did not seem to care for ornaments of any kind. Peterkin said, "it was in memory of the girl he left behind him!" But as he never spoke of this girl to either of us, I am inclined to think that Peterkin was either jesting or mistaken. In addition to these articles, we had a little bit of tinder and the clothes on our backs. These last were as follows:

Each of us had on a pair of stout canvas trousers and a pair of sailors' thick shoes. Jack wore a red flannel shirt, a blue jacket, and a red Kilmarnock bonnet or nightcap, besides a pair of worsted socks, and a cotton pocket-handkerchief with sixteen portraits of Lord Nelson printed on it and a union-jack in the middle. Peterkin had on a striped flannel shirt-which he wore outside his trousers and belted round his waist, after the manner of a tunic-and a round black straw hat. He had no jacket, having thrown it off just before we were cast into the sea; but this was not of much consequence, as the climate of the island proved to be extremely mild-so much so, indeed, that Jack and I often preferred to go about without our jackets. Peterkin had also a pair of white cotton socks and a blue handkerchief with white spots all over it. My own costume consisted of a blue flannel shirt, a blue jacket, a black cap, and a pair of worsted socks, besides the shoes and canvas trousers already mentioned. This was all we had, and besides these things we had nothing else; but when we thought of the danger from which we had escaped, and how much worse off we might have been had the ship struck on the reef during the night, we felt very thankful that we were possessed of so much, although, I must confess, we sometimes wished that we had had a little more.

While we were examining these things and talking about them, Jack suddenly started and exclaimed:

"The oar! We have forgotten the oar!"

"What good will that do us?" said Peterkin. "There's wood enough on the island to make a thousand oars."

"Ay, lad," replied Jack; "but there's a bit of hoop-iron at the end of it, and that may be of much use to us."

"Very true," said I; "let us go fetch it." And with that we all three rose and hastened down to the beach. I still felt a little weak from loss of blood, so that my companions soon began to leave me behind; but Jack perceived this, and, with his usual considerate good-nature, turned back to help me. This was now the first time that I had looked well about me since landing, as the spot where I had been laid was covered with thick bushes, which almost hid the country from our view. As we now emerged from among these and walked down the sandy beach together, I cast my eyes about, and truly my heart glowed within me and my spirits rose at the beautiful prospect which I beheld on every side. The gale had suddenly died away, just as if it had blown furiously till it dashed our ship upon the rocks, and had nothing more to do after accomplishing that. The island on which we stood was hilly, and covered almost everywhere with the most beautiful and richly coloured trees, bushes, and shrubs, none of which I knew the names of at that time-except, indeed, the cocoa-nut palms, which I recognised at once from the many pictures that I had seen of them before I left home. A sandy beach of dazzling whiteness lined this bright-green shore, and upon it there fell a gentle ripple of the sea. This last astonished me much, for I recollected that at home the sea used to fall in huge billows on the shore long after a storm had subsided. But on casting my glance out to sea the cause became apparent. About a mile distant from the shore I saw the great billows of the ocean rolling like a green wall, and falling with a long, loud roar upon a low coral reef, where they were dashed into white foam and flung up in clouds of spray. This spray sometimes flew exceedingly high, and every here and there a beautiful rainbow was formed for a moment among the falling drops. We afterwards found that this coral reef extended quite round the island, and formed a natural breakwater to it. Beyond this, the sea rose and tossed violently from the effects of the storm; but between the reef and the shore it was as calm and as smooth as a pond.

My heart was filled with more delight than I can express at sight of so many glorious objects, and my thoughts turned suddenly to the contemplation of the Creator of them all. I mention this the more gladly, because at that time, I am ashamed to say, I very seldom thought of my Creator, although I was constantly surrounded by the most beautiful and wonderful of His works. I observed, from the expression of my companion's countenance, that he too derived much joy from the splendid scenery, which was all the more agreeable to us after our long voyage on the salt sea. There the breeze was fresh and cold; but here it was delightfully mild, and when a puff blew off the land it came laden with the most exquisite perfume that can be imagined. While we thus gazed we were startled by a loud "Huzza!" from Peterkin, and on looking towards the edge of the sea we saw him capering and jumping about like a monkey, and ever and anon tugging with all his might at something that lay upon the shore.

"What an odd fellow he is, to be sure!" said Jack, taking me by the arm and hurrying forward. "Come, let us hasten to see what it is."

"Here it is, boys-hurrah! Come along! Just what we want!" cried Peterkin as we drew near, still tugging with all his power. "First-rate; just the very ticket!"

I need scarcely say to my readers that my companion Peterkin was in the habit of using very remarkable and peculiar phrases. And I am free to confess that I did not well understand the meaning of some of them-such, for instance, as "the very ticket;" but I think it my duty to recount everything relating to my adventures with a strict regard to truthfulness in as far as my memory serves me, so I write, as nearly as possible, the exact words that my companions spoke. I often asked Peterkin to explain what he meant by "ticket," but he always answered me by going into fits of laughter. However, by observing the occasions on which he used it, I came to understand that it meant to show that something was remarkably good or fortunate.

On coming up we found that Peterkin was vainly endeavouring to pull the axe out of the oar into which, it will be remembered, Jack struck it while endeavouring to cut away the cordage among which it had become entangled at the bow of the ship. Fortunately for us, the axe had remained fast in the oar, and even now all Peterkin's strength could not draw it out of the cut.

"Ah, that is capital indeed!" cried Jack, at the same time giving the axe a wrench that plucked it out of the tough wood. "How fortunate this is! It will be of more value to us than a hundred knives, and the edge is quite new and sharp."

"I'll answer for the toughness of the handle, at any rate!" cried Peterkin; "my arms are nearly pulled out of the sockets. But see here, our luck is great. There is iron on the blade." He pointed to a piece of hoop-iron as he spoke, which had been nailed round the blade of the oar to prevent it from splitting.

This also was a fortunate discovery. Jack went down on his knees, and with the edge of the axe began carefully to force out the nails. But as they were firmly fixed in, and the operation blunted our axe, we carried the oar up with us to the place where we had left the rest of our things, intending to burn the wood away from the iron at a more convenient time.

"Now, lads," said Jack after we had laid it on the stone which contained our little all, "I propose that we should go to the tail of the island, where the ship struck, which is only a quarter of a mile off; and see if anything else has been thrown ashore. I don't expect anything, but it is well to see. When we get back here it will be time to have our supper and prepare our beds."

"Agreed!" cried Peterkin and I together, as, indeed, we would have agreed to any proposal that Jack made; for, besides his being older and much stronger and taller than either of us, he was a very clever fellow, and, I think, would have induced people much older than himself to choose him for their leader, especially if they required to be led on a bold enterprise.

Now as we hastened along the white beach, which shone so brightly in the rays of the setting sun that our eyes were quite dazzled by its glare, it suddenly came into Peterkin's head that we had nothing to eat except the wild berries which grew in profusion at our feet.

"What shall we do, Jack?" said he with a rueful look. "Perhaps they may be poisonous!"

"No fear," replied Jack confidently. "I have observed that a few of them are not unlike some of the berries that grow wild on our own native hills. Besides, I saw one or two strange birds eating them just a few minutes ago, and what won't kill the birds won't kill us. But look up there, Peterkin," continued Jack, pointing to the branched head of a cocoa-nut palm. "There are nuts for us in all stages."

"So there are!" cried Peterkin, who, being of a very unobservant nature, had been too much taken up with other things to notice anything so high above his head as the fruit of a palm-tree. But whatever faults my young comrade had, he could not be blamed for want of activity or animal spirits. Indeed, the nuts had scarcely been pointed out to him when he bounded up the tall stem of the tree like a squirrel, and in a few minutes returned with three nuts, each as large as a man's fist.

"You had better keep them till we return," said Jack. "Let us finish our work before eating."

"So be it, captain; go ahead!" cried Peterkin, thrusting the nuts into his trousers pocket. "In fact, I don't want to eat just now; but I would give a good deal for a drink. Oh, that I could find a spring! but I don't see the smallest sign of one hereabouts. I say, Jack, how does it happen that you seem to be up to everything? You have told us the names of half-a-dozen trees already, and yet you say that you were never in the South Seas before."

"I'm not up to everything, Peterkin, as you'll find out ere long," replied Jack with a smile; "but I have been a great reader of books of travel and adventure all my life, and that has put me up to a good many things that you are, perhaps, not acquainted with."

"Oh, Jack, that's all humbug! If you begin to lay everything to the credit of books, I'll quite lose my opinion of you," cried Peterkin with a look of contempt. "I've seen a lot o' fellows that were *always* poring over books, and when they came to try to *do* anything, they were no better than baboons!"

"You are quite right," retorted Jack; "and I have seen a lot of fellows, who never looked into books at all, who knew nothing about anything except the things they had actually seen, and very little they knew even about these. Indeed, some were so ignorant that they did not know that cocoa-nuts grew on cocoa-nut trees!"

I could not refrain from laughing at this rebuke, for there was much truth in it as to Peterkin's ignorance.

"Humph! maybe you're right," answered Peterkin; "but I would not give *tuppence* for a man of books if he had nothing else in him."

"Neither would I," said Jack; "but that's no reason why you should run books down, or think less of me for having read them. Suppose, now, Peterkin, that you wanted to build a ship, and I were to give you a long and particular account of the way to do it, would not that be very useful?"

"No doubt of it," said Peterkin, laughing.

"And suppose I were to write the account in a letter instead of telling you in words, would that be less useful?"

"Well-no, perhaps not."

"Well, suppose I were to print it and send it to you in the form of a book, would it not be as good and useful as ever?"

"Oh, bother! Jack, you're a philosopher, and that's worse than anything!" cried Peterkin with a look of pretended horror.

"Very well, Peterkin, we shall see," returned Jack, halting under the shade of a cocoa-nut tree. "You said you were thirsty just a minute ago. Now jump up that tree and bring down a nut-not a ripe one; bring a green, unripe one."

Peterkin looked surprised, but seeing that Jack was in earnest, he obeyed.

"Now cut a hole in it with your penknife and clap it to your mouth, old fellow," said Jack.

Peterkin did as he was directed, and we both burst into uncontrollable laughter at the changes that instantly passed over his expressive countenance. No sooner had he put the nut to his mouth, and thrown back his head in order to catch what came out of it, than his eyes opened to twice their ordinary size with astonishment, while his throat moved vigorously in the act of swallowing. Then a smile and a look of intense delight overspread his face, except, indeed, the mouth, which, being firmly fixed to the hole in the nut, could not take part in the expression; but he endeavoured to make up for this by winking at us excessively with his right eye. At length he stopped, and drawing a long breath, exclaimed:

"Nectar! perfect nectar! —I say, Jack, you're a Briton-the best fellow I ever met in my life- Only taste that!" said he, turning to me and holding the nut to my mouth. I immediately drank, and certainly I was much surprised at the delightful liquid that flowed copiously down my throat. It was extremely cool, and had a sweet taste, mingled with acid; in fact, it was the likest thing to lemonade I ever tasted, and was most grateful and refreshing. I handed the nut to Jack, who, after tasting it, said, "Now, Peterkin, you unbeliever! I never saw or tasted a cocoa-nut in my life before, except those sold in shops at home; but I once read that the green nuts contain that stuff; and you see it is true."

"And, pray," asked Peterkin, "what sort of 'stuff' does the ripe nut contain?"

"A hollow kernel," answered Jack, "with a liquid like milk in it; but it does not satisfy thirst so well as hunger. It is very wholesome food, I believe."

"Meat and drink on the same tree!" cried Peterkin; "washing in the sea, lodging on the ground-and all for nothing! My dear boys, we're set up for life! It must be the ancient Paradise- hurrah!" and Peterkin tossed his straw hat in the air and ran along the beach, hallooing like a madman with delight.

We afterwards found, however, that these lovely islands were very unlike Paradise in many things. But more of this in its proper place.

We had now come to the point of rocks on which the ship had struck, but did not find a single article, although we searched carefully among the coral rocks, which at this place jutted out so far as nearly to join the reef that encircled the island. Just as we were about to return, however, we saw something black floating in a little cove that had escaped our observation. Running forward, we drew it from the water, and found it to be a long, thick, leather boot, such as fishermen at home wear; and a few paces farther on, we picked up its fellow. We at once recognised these as having belonged to our captain, for he had worn them during the whole of the storm in order to guard his legs from the waves and spray that constantly washed over our decks. My first thought on seeing them was that our dear captain had been drowned; but Jack soon put my mind more at rest on that point by saying that if the captain had been drowned with the boots on, he would certainly have been washed ashore along with them, and that he had no doubt whatever he had kicked them off while in the sea that he might swim more easily.

Peterkin immediately put them on; but they were so large that, as Jack said, they would have done for boots, trousers, and vest too. I also tried them; but although I was long enough in the legs for them, they were much too large in the feet for me. So we handed them to Jack, who was anxious to make me keep them; but as they fitted his large limbs and feet as if they had been made for him, I would not hear of it, so he consented at last to use them. I may remark, however, that Jack did not use them often, as they were extremely heavy.

It was beginning to grow dark when we returned to our encampment; so we put off our visit to the top of a hill till next day, and employed the light that yet remained to us in cutting down a quantity of boughs and the broad leaves of a tree of which none of us knew the name. With these we erected a sort of rustic bower, in which we meant to pass the night. There was no absolute necessity for this, because the air of our island was so genial and balmy that we could have slept quite well without any shelter; but we were so little used to sleeping in the open air that we did not quite relish the idea of lying down without any covering over us. Besides, our bower would shelter us from the night-dews or rain, if any should happen to fall. Having strewed the floor with leaves and dry grass, we bethought ourselves of supper.

But it now occurred to us, for the first time, that we had no means of making a fire.

"Now, there's a fix! What shall we do?" said Peterkin, while we both turned our eyes to Jack, to whom we always looked in our difficulties. Jack seemed not a little perplexed.

"There are flints enough, no doubt, on the beach," said he; "but they are of no use at all without a steel. However, we must try." So saying, he went to the beach, and soon returned with two flints. On one of these he placed the tinder, and endeavoured to ignite it; but it was with great difficulty that a very small spark was struck out of the flints, and the tinder, being a bad, hard piece, would not catch. He then tried the bit of hoop-iron, which would not strike fire at all; and after that the back of the axe, with no better success. During all these trials Peterkin sat with his hands in his pockets, gazing with a most melancholy visage at our comrade, his face growing longer and more miserable at each successive failure.

"Oh dear!" he sighed; "I would not care a button for the cooking of our victuals-perhaps they don't need it-but it's so dismal to eat one's supper in the dark, and we have had such a capital day that it's a pity to finish off in this glum style. Oh, I have it!" he cried, starting up: "the spy-glass —the big glass at the end is a burning-glass!"

"You forget that we have no sun," said I.

Peterkin was silent. In his sudden recollection of the telescope he had quite overlooked the absence of the sun.

"Ah, boys, I've got it now!" exclaimed Jack, rising and cutting a branch from a neighbouring bush, which he stripped of its leaves. "I recollect seeing this done once at home. Hand me the bit of whip-cord." With the cord and branch Jack soon formed a bow. Then he cut a piece about three inches long off the end of a dead branch, which he pointed at the two ends. Round this he passed the cord of the bow, and placed one end against his chest, which was protected from its point by a chip of wood; the other point he placed against the bit of tinder, and then began to saw vigorously with the bow, just as a blacksmith does with his drill while boring a hole in a piece of iron. In a few seconds the tinder began to smoke; in less than a minute it caught fire; and in less than a quarter of an hour we were drinking our lemonade and eating cocoa-nuts round a fire that would have roasted an entire sheep, while the smoke, flames, and sparks flew up among the broad leaves of the overhanging palm-trees, and cast a warm glow upon our leafy bower.

That night the starry sky looked down through the gently rustling trees upon our slumbers, and the distant roaring of the surf upon the coral reef was our lullaby.

CHAPTER FIVE

Morning, and cogitations connected therewith-We luxuriate in the sea, try our diving powers, and make enchanting excursions among the coral groves at the bottom of the ocean-The wonders of the deep enlarged upon.

What a joyful thing it is to awaken on a fresh, glorious morning, and find the rising sun staring into your face with dazzling brilliancy! to hear the birds twittering in the bushes, and to hear the murmuring of a rill, or the soft, hissing ripples as they fall upon the seashore! At any time, and in any place, such sights and sounds are most charming; but more especially are they so when one awakens to them, for the first time, in a novel and romantic situation, with the soft, sweet air of a tropical climate mingling with the fresh smell of the sea, and stirring the strange leaves that flutter overhead and around one, or ruffling the plumage of the stranger birds that fly inquiringly around as if to demand what business we have to intrude uninvited on their domains. When I awoke on the morning after the shipwreck, I found myself in this most delightful condition; and as I lay on my back upon my bed of leaves, gazing up through the branches of the cocoa-nut trees into the clear blue sky, and watched the few fleecy clouds that passed slowly across it, my heart expanded more and more with an exulting gladness, the like of which I had never felt before. While I meditated, my thoughts again turned to the great and kind Creator of this beautiful world, as they had done on the previous day when I first beheld the sea and the coral reef, with the mighty waves dashing over it into the calm waters of the lagoon.

While thus meditating, I naturally bethought me of my Bible, for I had faithfully kept the promise which I gave at parting to my beloved mother-that I would read it every morning; and it was with a feeling of dismay that I remembered I had left it in the ship. I was much troubled about this. However, I consoled myself with reflecting that I could keep the second part of my promise to her-namely, that I should never omit to say my prayers. So I rose quietly lest I should disturb my companions, who were still asleep, and stepped aside into the bushes for this purpose.

On my return I found them still slumbering, so I again lay down to think over our situation. Just at that moment I was attracted by the sight of a very small parrot, which Jack afterwards told me was called a paroquet. It was seated on a twig that overhung Peterkin's head, and I was speedily lost in admiration of its bright-green plumage, which was mingled with other gay colours. While I looked I observed that the bird turned its head slowly from side to side and looked downwards, first with the one eye and then with the other. On glancing downwards I observed that Peterkin's mouth was wide open, and that this remarkable bird was looking into it. Peterkin used to say that I had not an atom of fun in my composition, and that I never could understand a joke. In regard to the latter, perhaps he was right; yet I think that, when they were explained to me, I understood jokes as well as most people. But in regard to the former, he must certainly have been wrong, for this bird seemed to me to be extremely funny; and I could not help thinking that if it should happen to faint, or slip its foot, and fall off the twig into Peterkin's mouth, he would perhaps think it funny too! Suddenly the paroquet bent down its head and uttered a loud scream in his face. This awoke him, and with a cry of surprise, he started up, while the foolish bird flew precipitately away.

"Oh, you monster!" cried Peterkin, shaking his fist at the bird. Then he yawned, and rubbed his eyes, and asked what o'clock it was.

I smiled at this question, and answered that, as our watches were at the bottom of the sea, I could not tell, but it was a little past sunrise.

Peterkin now began to remember where we were. As he looked up into the bright sky, and snuffed the scented air, his eyes glistened with delight, and he uttered a faint "Hurrah!" and yawned again. Then he gazed slowly round, till, observing the calm sea through an opening in the bushes, he started suddenly up as if he had received an electric shock, uttered a vehement shout, flung off his garments, and rushing over the white sands, plunged into the water. The cry awoke Jack, who rose on his elbow with a look of grave surprise; but this was followed by a quiet smile of intelligence on seeing Peterkin in the water. With an energy that he only gave way to in moments of excitement, Jack bounded to his feet, threw off his clothes, shook back his hair, and with a lion-like spring, dashed over the sands and plunged into the sea with such force as quite to envelop Peterkin in a shower of spray. Jack was a remarkably good swimmer and diver, so that after his plunge we saw no sign of him for nearly a minute, after which he suddenly emerged, with a cry of joy, a good many yards out from the shore. My spirits were so much raised by seeing all this that I, too, hastily threw off my garments and endeavoured to imitate Jack's vigorous bound; but I was so awkward that my foot caught on a stump, and I fell to the ground. Then I slipped on a stone while running over the sand and nearly fell again, much to the amusement of Peterkin, who laughed heartily and called me a "slow coach;" while Jack cried out, "Come along, Ralph, and I'll help you!" However, when I got into the water I managed very well; for I was really a good swimmer and diver too. I could not, indeed, equal Jack, who was superior to any Englishman I ever saw; but I infinitely surpassed Peterkin, who could only swim a little, and could not dive at all.

While Peterkin enjoyed himself in the shallow water and in running along the beach, Jack and I swam out into the deep water and occasionally dived for stones. I shall never forget my surprise and delight on first beholding the bottom of the sea. As I have before stated, the water within the reef was as calm as a pond; and as there was no wind, it was quite clear from the surface to the bottom, so that we could see down easily even at a depth of twenty or thirty yards. When Jack and I dived into shallower water we expected to have found sand and stones, instead of which we found ourselves in what appeared really to be an enchanted garden. The whole of the bottom of the lagoon, as we called the calm water within the reef, was covered with coral of every shape, size, and hue. Some portions were formed like large mushrooms; others appeared like the brain of a man, having stalks or necks attached to them; but the most common kind was a species of branching coral, and some portions were of a lovely pale-pink colour, others were pure white. Among this there grew large quantities of seaweed of the richest hues imaginable, and of the most graceful forms; while innumerable fishes-blue, red, yellow, green, and striped-sported in and out amongst the flower-beds of this submarine garden, and did not appear to be at all afraid of our approaching them.

On darting to the surface for breath after our first dive, Jack and I rose close to each other.

"Did you ever in your life, Ralph, see anything so lovely?" said Jack as he flung the spray from his hair.

"Never," I replied. "It appears to me like fairy realms. I can scarcely believe that we are not dreaming."

"Dreaming!" cried Jack. "Do you know, Ralph, I'm half-tempted to think that we really are dreaming! But if so, I am resolved to make the most of it and dream another dive; so here goes-down again, my boy!"

We took the second dive together, and kept beside each other while under water; and I was greatly surprised to find that we could keep down much longer than I ever recollect having done in our own seas at home. I believe that this was owing to the heat of the water, which was so warm that we afterwards found we could remain in it for two and three hours at a time without feeling any unpleasant effects such as we used to experience in the sea at home. When Jack reached the bottom, he grasped the coral stems and crept along on his hands and knees, peeping under the seaweed and among the rocks. I observed him, also, pick up one or two large oysters and retain them in his grasp, as if he meant to take them up with him; so I also gathered a few. Suddenly he made a grasp at a fish with blue and yellow stripes on its back, and actually touched its tail, but did not catch it. At this he turned towards me and attempted to smile; but no sooner had he done so than he sprang like an arrow to the surface, where, on following him, I found him gasping and coughing and spitting water from his mouth. In a few minutes he recovered, and we both turned to swim ashore.

"I declare, Ralph," said he, "that I actually tried to laugh under water!"

"So I saw," I replied; "and I observed that you very nearly caught that fish by the tail. It would have done capitally for breakfast, if you had."

"Breakfast enough here," said he, holding up the oysters as we landed and ran up the beach. — "Hallo, Peterkin! Here you are, boy! split open these fellows while Ralph and I put on our clothes. They'll agree with the cocoa-nuts excellently, I have no doubt."

Peterkin, who was already dressed, took the oysters and opened them with the edge of our axe, exclaiming, "Now, that's capital! There's nothing I'm so fond of."

"Ah! that's lucky," remarked Jack. "I'll be able to keep you in good order now, Master Peterkin. You know you can't dive any better than a cat. So, sir, whenever you behave ill you shall have no oysters for breakfast."

"I'm very glad that our prospect of breakfast is so good," said I, "for I'm very hungry."

"Here, then, stop your mouth with that, Ralph," said Peterkin, holding a large oyster to my lips. I opened my mouth and swallowed it in silence, and really it was remarkably good.

We now set ourselves earnestly about our preparations for spending the day. We had no difficulty with the fire this morning as our burning-glass was an admirable one; and while we roasted a few oysters and ate our cocoa-nuts, we held a long, animated conversation about our plans for the future. What those plans were, and how we carried them into effect, the reader shall see hereafter.

CHAPTER SIX

An excursion into the interior in which we make many valuable and interesting dis-
coveries-We get a dreadful fright-The bread-fruit tree-Wonderful peculiarity of some
of the fruit-trees —Signs of former inhabitants.

Our first care, after breakfast, was to place the few articles we possessed in the crevice of a
rock at the farther end of a small cave which we discovered near our encampment. This cave,
we hoped, might be useful to us afterwards as a storehouse. Then we cut two large clubs off a
species of very hard tree which grew near at hand. One of these was given to Peterkin, the other
to me, and Jack armed himself with the axe. We took these precautions because we purposed
to make an excursion to the top of the mountains of the interior, in order to obtain a better
view of our island. Of course we knew not what dangers might befall us by the way, so thought
it best to be prepared.

Having completed our arrangements and carefully extinguished our fire, we sallied forth and
walked a short distance along the sea-beach till we came to the entrance of a valley, through
which flowed the rivulet before mentioned. Here we turned our backs on the sea and struck
into the interior.

The prospect that burst upon our view on entering the valley was truly splendid. On either
side of us there was a gentle rise in the land, which thus formed two ridges, about a mile apart,
on each side of the valley. These ridges-which, as well as the low grounds between them, were
covered with trees and shrubs of the most luxuriant kind-continued to recede inland for about
two miles, when they joined the foot of a small mountain. This hill rose rather abruptly from
the head of the valley, and was likewise entirely covered, even to the top, with trees-except on
one particular spot near the left shoulder, where was a bare and rocky place of a broken and
savage character. Beyond this hill we could not see, and we therefore directed our course up
the banks of the rivulet towards the foot of it, intending to climb to the top, should that be
possible-as, indeed, we had no doubt it was.

Jack, being the wisest and boldest among us, took the lead, carrying the axe on his shoulder.
Peterkin, with his enormous club, came second, as he said he should like to be in a position to
defend me if any danger should threaten. I brought up the rear; but having been more taken up
with the wonderful and curious things I saw at starting than with thoughts of possible danger, I
had very foolishly left my club behind me. Although, as I have said, the trees and bushes were
very luxuriant, they were not so thickly crowded together as to hinder our progress among
them. We were able to wind in and out, and to follow the banks of the stream quite easily,
although, it is true, the height and thickness of the foliage prevented us from seeing far ahead.
But sometimes a jutting-out rock on the hillsides afforded us a position whence we could enjoy
the romantic view and mark our progress towards the foot of the hill. I was particularly struck,
during the walk, with the richness of the undergrowth in most places, and recognised many
berries and plants that resembled those of my native land, especially a tall, elegantly formed
fern, which emitted an agreeable perfume. There were several kinds of flowers, too; but I did
not see so many of these as I should have expected in such a climate. We also saw a great variety
of small birds of bright plumage, and many paroquets similar to the one, that awoke Peterkin
so rudely in the morning.

Thus we advanced to the foot of the hill without encountering anything to alarm us, except,
indeed, once, when we were passing close under a part of the hill which was hidden from our
view by the broad leaves of the banana-trees, which grew in great luxuriance in that part. Jack
was just preparing to force his way through this thicket when we were startled and arrested by
a strange pattering or rumbling sound, which appeared to us quite different from any of the
sounds we had heard during the previous part of our walk.

"Hallo!" cried Peterkin, stopping short, and grasping his club with both hands; "what's that?"

Neither of us replied; but Jack seized his axe in his right hand, while with the other he pushed aside the broad leaves and endeavoured to peer amongst them.

"I can see nothing," he said after a short pause. "I think it —"

Again the rumbling sound came, louder than before, and we all sprang back and stood on the defensive. For myself, having forgotten my club, and not having taken the precaution to cut another, I buttoned my jacket, doubled my fists, and threw myself into a boxing attitude. I must say, however, that I felt somewhat uneasy; and my companions afterwards confessed that their thoughts at this moment had been instantly filled with all they had ever heard or read of wild beasts and savages, torturings at the stake, roastings alive, and such-like horrible things. Suddenly the pattering noise increased with tenfold violence. It was followed by a fearful crash among the bushes, which was rapidly repeated, as if some gigantic animal were bounding towards us. In another moment an enormous rock came crashing through the shrubbery, followed by a cloud of dust and small stones, and flew close past the spot where we stood, carrying bushes and young trees along with it.

"Pooh! is that all?" exclaimed Peterkin, wiping the perspiration off his forehead. "Why, I thought it was all the wild men and beasts in the South Sea Islands, galloping on in one grand charge to sweep us off the face of the earth, instead of a mere stone tumbling down the mountain-side!"

"Nevertheless," remarked Jack, "if that same stone had hit any of us it would have rendered the charge you speak of quite unnecessary, Peterkin."

This was true, and I felt very thankful for our escape. On examining the spot more narrowly, we found that it lay close to the foot of a very rugged precipice, from which stones of various sizes were always tumbling at intervals. Indeed, the numerous fragments lying scattered all round might have suggested the cause of the sound had we not been too suddenly alarmed to think of anything.

We now resumed our journey, resolving that, in our future excursions into the interior, we would be careful to avoid this dangerous precipice.

Soon afterwards we arrived at the foot of the hill, and prepared to ascend it. Here Jack made a discovery which caused us all very great joy. This was a tree of a remarkably beautiful appearance, which Jack confidently declared to be the celebrated bread-fruit tree.

"Is it celebrated?" inquired Peterkin with a look of great simplicity.

"It is," replied Jack.

"That's odd, now," rejoined Peterkin; "I never heard of it before."

"Then it's not so celebrated as I thought it was," returned Jack, quietly squeezing Peterkin's hat over his eyes; "but listen, you ignorant boobie! and hear of it now."

Peterkin readjusted his hat, and was soon listening with as much interest as myself while Jack told us that this tree is one of the most valuable in the islands of the south; that it bears two, sometimes three, crops of fruit in the year; that the fruit is very like wheaten bread in appearance, and that it constitutes the principal food of many of the islanders.

"So," said Peterkin, "we seem to have everything ready prepared to our hands in this wonderful island-lemonade ready bottled in nuts, and loaf-bread growing on the trees!"

Peterkin, as usual, was jesting; nevertheless, it is a curious fact that he spoke almost the literal truth.

"Moreover," continued Jack, "the bread-fruit tree affords a capital gum, which serves the natives for pitching their canoes; the bark of the young branches is made by them into cloth; and of the wood, which is durable and of a good colour, they build their houses. So you see, lads, that we have no lack of material here to make us comfortable, if we are only clever enough to use it."

"But are you sure that that's it?" asked Peterkin.

"Quite sure," replied Jack; "for I was particularly interested in the account I once read of it, and I remember the description well. I am sorry, however that I have forgotten the descriptions of many other trees which I am sure we have seen to-day, if we could but recognise them. So you see, Peterkin, I'm not up to everything yet."

"Never mind, Jack," said Peterkin with a grave, patronising expression of countenance, patting his tall companion on the shoulder —"never mind, Jack; you know a good deal for your age. You're a clever boy, sir —a promising young man; and if you only go on as you have begun, sir, you will —"

The end of this speech was suddenly cut short by Jack tripping up Peterkin's heels and tumbling him into a mass of thick shrubs, where, finding himself comfortable, he lay still, basking in the sunshine, while Jack and I examined the bread-fruit tree.

We were much struck with the deep, rich green colour of its broad leaves, which were twelve or eighteen inches long, deeply indented, and of a glossy smoothness, like the laurel. The fruit, with which it was loaded, was nearly round, and appeared to be about six inches in diameter, with a rough rind, marked with lozenge-shaped divisions. It was of various colours, from light pea-green to brown and rich yellow. Jack said that the yellow was the ripe fruit. We afterwards found that most of the fruit-trees on the island were evergreens, and that we might, when we wished, pluck the blossom and the ripe fruit from the same tree. Such a wonderful difference from the trees of our own country surprised us not a little. The bark of the tree was rough and light-coloured; the trunk was about two feet in diameter, and it appeared to be twenty feet high, being quite destitute of branches up to that height, where it branched off into a beautiful and umbrageous head. We noticed that the fruit hung in clusters of twos and threes on the branches; but as we were anxious to get to the top of the hill, we refrained from attempting to pluck any at that time.

Our hearts were now very much cheered by our good fortune, and it was with light and active steps that we clambered up the steep sides of the hill. On reaching the summit a new, and if possible a grander, prospect met our gaze. We found that this was not the highest part of the island, but that another hill lay beyond, with a wide valley between it and the one on which we stood. This valley, like the first, was also full of rich trees-some dark and some light green, some heavy and thick in foliage, and others light, feathery, and graceful, while the beautiful blossoms on many of them threw a sort of rainbow tint over all, and gave to the valley the appearance of a garden of flowers. Among these we recognised many of the bread-fruit trees, laden with yellow fruit, and also a great many cocoa-nut palms. After gazing our fill we pushed down the hillside, crossed the valley, and soon began to ascend the second mountain. It was clothed with trees nearly to the top; but the summit was bare, and in some places broken.

While on our way up we came to an object which filled us with much interest. This was the stump of a tree that had evidently been cut down with an axe! So, then, we were not the first who had viewed this beautiful isle. The hand of man had been at work there before us. It now began to recur to us again that perhaps the island was inhabited, although we had not seen any traces of man until now. But a second glance at the stump convinced us that we had not more reason to think so now than formerly; for the surface of the wood was quite decayed and partly covered with fungus and green matter, so that it must have been cut many years ago.

"Perhaps," said Peterkin, "some ship or other has touched here long ago for wood, and only taken one tree."

We did not think this likely, however, because, in such circumstances, the crew of a ship would cut wood of small size and near the shore; whereas this was a large tree, and stood near the top of the mountain. In fact, it was the highest large tree on the mountain, all above it being wood of very recent growth.

"I can't understand it," said Jack, scratching the surface of the stump with his axe. "I can only suppose that the savages have been here and cut it for some purpose known only to themselves. But, hallo! what have we here?"

As he spoke Jack began carefully to scrape away the moss and fungus from the stump, and soon laid bare three distinct traces of marks, as if some inscription or initials had been cut thereon. But although the traces were distinct, beyond all doubt, the exact form of the letters could not be made out. Jack thought they looked like JS, but we could not be certain. They had apparently been carelessly cut, and long exposure to the weather had so broken them up that we could not make out what they were. We were exceedingly perplexed at this discovery, and stayed a long time at the place conjecturing what these marks could have been, but without avail; so, as the day was advancing, we left it, and quickly reached the top of the mountain.

We found this to be the highest point of the island, and from it we saw our kingdom lying, as it were, like a map around us. As I have always thought it impossible to get a thing properly into one's understanding without comprehending it, I shall beg the reader's patience for a little while I describe our island, thus, shortly:

It consisted of two mountains: the one we guessed at five hundred feet; the other, on which we stood, at one thousand. Between these lay a rich, beautiful valley, as already said. This valley crossed the island from one end to the other, being high in the middle and sloping on each side towards the sea. The large mountain sloped, on the side farthest from where we had been wrecked, gradually towards the sea; but although, when viewed at a glance, it had thus a regular sloping appearance, a more careful observation showed that it was broken up into a multitude of very small vales-or, rather, dells and glens-intermingled with little rugged spots and small but abrupt precipices here and there, with rivulets tumbling over their edges and wandering down the slopes in little white streams, sometimes glistening among the broad leaves of the bread-fruit and cocoa-nut trees, or hiding altogether beneath the rich underwood. At the base of this mountain lay a narrow bright-green plain or meadow, which terminated abruptly at the shore. On the other side of the island, whence we had come, stood the smaller hill, at the foot of which diverged three valleys-one being that which we had ascended, with a smaller vale on each side of it, and separated from it by the two ridges before mentioned. In these smaller valleys there were no streams, but they were clothed with the same luxuriant vegetation.

The diameter of the island seemed to be about ten miles, and as it was almost circular in form, its circumference must have been thirty miles-perhaps a little more, if allowance be made for the numerous bays and indentations of the shore. The entire island was belted by a beach of pure white sand, on which laved the gentle ripples of the lagoon. We now also observed that the coral reef completely encircled the island; but it varied its distance from it here and there-in some places being a mile from the beach, in others a few hundred yards, but the average distance was half-a-mile. The reef lay very low, and the spray of the surf broke quite over it in many places. This surf never ceased its roar; for, however calm the weather might be, there is always a gentle swaying motion in the great Pacific, which, although scarce noticeable out at sea, reaches the shore at last in a huge billow. The water within the lagoon, as before said, was perfectly still. There were three narrow openings in the reef: one opposite each end of the valley which I have described as crossing the island; the other opposite our own valley, which we afterwards named the Valley of the Wreck. At each of these openings the reef rose into two small green islets, covered with bushes, and having one or two cocoa-nut palms on each. These islets were very singular, and appeared as if planted expressly for the purpose of marking the channel into the lagoon. Our captain was making for one of these openings the day we were wrecked-and would have reached it, too, I doubt not, had not the rudder been torn away. Within the lagoon were several pretty, low coral islands, just opposite our encampment; and immediately beyond these, out at sea, lay about a dozen other islands, at various distances, from half-a-mile to ten miles-all of them, as far as we could discern, smaller than ours and apparently uninhabited. They seemed to be low coral islands, raised but little above the sea, yet covered with cocoa-nut trees.

All this we noted, and a great deal more, while we sat on the top of the mountain. After we had satisfied ourselves we prepared to return; but here, again, we discovered traces of the presence of man. These were a pole or staff, and one or two pieces of wood which had been squared with an axe. All of these were, however, very much decayed, and they had evidently not been touched for many years.

Full of these discoveries, we returned to our encampment. On the way we fell in with the traces of some four-footed animal, but whether old or of recent date none of us were able to guess. This also tended to raise our hopes of obtaining some animal food on the island; so we reached home in good spirits, quite prepared for supper, and highly satisfied with our excursion.

After much discussion, in which Peterkin took the lead, we came to the conclusion that the island was uninhabited, and went to bed.

CHAPTER SEVEN

Jack's ingenuity-We get into difficulties about fishing, and get out of them by a method which gives us a cold bath-Horrible encounter with a shark.

For several days after the excursion related in the last chapter we did not wander far from our encampment, but gave ourselves up to forming plans for the future and making our present abode comfortable.

There were various causes that induced this state of comparative inaction. In the first place, although everything around us was so delightful, and we could without difficulty obtain all that we required for our bodily comfort, we did not quite like the idea of settling down here for the rest of our lives, far away from our friends and our native land. To set energetically about preparations for a permanent residence seemed so like making up our minds to saying adieu to home and friends for ever that we tacitly shrank from it, and put off our preparations, for one reason and another, as long as we could. Then there was a little uncertainty still as to there being natives on the island, and we entertained a kind of faint hope that a ship might come and take us off. But as day after day passed, and neither savages nor ships appeared, we gave up all hope of an early deliverance, and set diligently to work at our homestead.

During this time, however, we had not been altogether idle. We made several experiments in cooking the cocoa-nut, most of which did not improve it. Then we removed our goods and took up our abode in the cave, but found the change so bad that we returned gladly to the bower. Besides this, we bathed very frequently, and talked a great deal-at least Jack and Peterkin did; I listened. Among other useful things, Jack, who was ever the most active and diligent, converted about three inches of the hoop-iron into an excellent knife. First, he beat it quite flat with the axe; then he made a rude handle, and tied the hoop-iron to it with our piece of whip-cord, and ground it to an edge on a piece of sandstone. When it was finished he used it to shape a better handle, to which he fixed it with a strip of his cotton handkerchief-in which operation he had, as Peterkin pointed out, torn off one of Lord Nelson's noses. However, the whip-cord, thus set free, was used by Peterkin as a fishing-line. He merely tied a piece of oyster to the end of it. This the fish were allowed to swallow, and then they were pulled quickly ashore. But as the line was very short and we had no boat, the fish we caught were exceedingly small.

One day Peterkin came up from the beach, where he had been angling, and said in a very cross tone, "I'll tell you what, Jack, I'm not going to be humbugged with catching such contemptible things any longer. I want you to swim out with me on your back, and let me fish in deep water!"

"Dear me, Peterkin!" replied Jack; "I had no idea you were taking the thing so much to heart, else I would have got you out of that difficulty long ago. Let me see;" and Jack looked down at a piece of timber, on which he had been labouring, with a peculiar gaze of abstraction which he always assumed when trying to invent or discover anything.

"What say you to building a boat?" he inquired, looking up hastily.

"Take far too long," was the reply; "can't be bothered waiting. I want to begin at once!"

Again Jack considered. "I have it!" he cried. "We'll fell a large tree and launch the trunk of it in the water, so that when you want to fish you've nothing to do but to swim out to it."

"Would not a small raft do better?" said I.

"Much better; but we have no ropes to bind it together with. Perhaps we may find something hereafter that will do as well, but in the meantime let us try the tree."

This was agreed on; so we started off to a spot, not far distant, where we knew of a tree that would suit us which grew near the water's edge. As soon as we reached it Jack threw off his coat, and wielding the axe with his sturdy arms, hacked and hewed at it for a quarter of an hour without stopping. Then he paused, and while he sat down to rest I continued the work. Then Peterkin made a vigorous attack on it; so that when Jack renewed his powerful blows, a few minutes' cutting brought it down with a terrible crash.

"Hurrah! Now for it!" cried Jack. "Let us off with its head!"

So saying, he began to cut through the stem again at about six yards from the thick end. This done, he cut three strong, short poles or levers from the stout branches, with which to roll the log down the beach into the sea; for, as it was nearly two feet thick at the large end, we could not move it without such helps. With the levers, however, we rolled it slowly into the sea.

Having been thus successful in launching our vessel, we next shaped the levers into rude oars or paddles, and then attempted to embark. This was easy enough to do; but after seating ourselves astride the log, it was with the utmost difficulty we kept it from rolling round and plunging us into the water. Not that we minded that much; but we preferred, if possible, to fish in dry clothes. To be sure, our trousers were necessarily wet, as our legs were dangling in the water on each side of the log; but as they could be easily dried, we did not care. After half-an-hour's practice, we became expert enough to keep our balance pretty steadily. Then Peterkin laid down his paddle, and having baited his line with a whole oyster, dropped it into deep water.

"Now, then, Jack," said he, "be cautious; steer clear o' that seaweed. There! that's it; gently, now-gently. I see a fellow at least a foot long down there coming to — Ha! that's it! Oh bother! he's off!"

"Did he bite?" said Jack, urging the log onwards a little with his paddle.

"Bite? Ay! he took it into his mouth, but the moment I began to haul he opened his jaws and let it out again."

"Let him swallow it next time," said Jack, laughing at the melancholy expression of Peterkin's visage.

"There he's again!" cried Peterkin, his eyes flashing with excitement. "Look out! Now, then! No! Yes! No! Why, the brute *won't* swallow it!"

"Try to haul him up by the mouth, then!" cried Jack. "Do it gently."

A heavy sigh and a look of blank despair showed that poor Peterkin had tried and failed again.

"Never mind, lad," said Jack in a voice of sympathy; "we'll move on and offer it to some other fish." So saying, Jack plied his paddle; but scarcely had he moved from the spot when a fish with an enormous head and a little body darted from under a rock and swallowed the bait at once.

"Got him this time-that's a fact!" cried Peterkin, hauling in the line. "He's swallowed the bait right down to his tail, I declare! Oh, what a thumper!"

As the fish came struggling to the surface we leaned forward to see it, and overbalanced the log. Peterkin threw his arms round the fish's neck, and in another instant we were all floundering in the water!

A shout of laughter burst from us as we rose to the surface, like three drowned rats, and seized hold of the log. We soon recovered our position, and sat more warily; while Peterkin secured the fish, which had well-nigh escaped in the midst of our struggles. It was little worth having, however. But, as Peterkin remarked, it was better than the smouts he had been catching for the last two or three days; so we laid it on the log before us, and having re-baited the line, dropped it in again for another.

Now, while we were thus intent upon our sport, our attention was suddenly attracted by a ripple on the sea, just a few yards away from us. Peterkin shouted to us to paddle in that direction, as he thought it was a big fish and we might have a chance of catching it. But Jack, instead of complying, said, in a deep, earnest tone of voice, which I never before heard him use, "Haul up your line, Peterkin; seize your paddle. Quick-it's a shark!"

The horror with which we heard this may well be imagined; for it must be remembered that our legs were hanging down in the water, and we could not venture to pull them up without upsetting the log. Peterkin instantly hauled up the line, and grasping his paddle, exerted himself to the utmost, while we also did our best to make for shore. But we were a good way off, and the log being, as I have before said, very heavy, moved but slowly through the water. We now saw the shark quite distinctly swimming round and round us, its sharp fin every now and then protruding above the water. From its active and unsteady motions, Jack knew it was making up its mind to attack us; so he urged us vehemently to paddle for our lives, while he himself set us the example. Suddenly he shouted, "Look out! there he comes!" and in a second we saw the monstrous fish dive close under us and turn half-over on his side. But we all made a great commotion with our paddles, which, no doubt, frightened it away for that time, as we saw it immediately after circling round us as before.

"Throw the fish to him!" cried Jack in a quick, suppressed voice; "we'll make the shore in time yet if we can keep him off for a few minutes."

Peterkin stopped one instant to obey the command, and then plied his paddle again with all his might. No sooner had the fish fallen on the water than we observed the shark to sink. In another second we saw its white breast rising; for sharks always turn over on their sides when about to seize their prey, their mouths being not at the point of their heads like those of other fish, but, as it were, under their chins. In another moment his snout rose above the water; his wide jaws, armed with a terrific double row of teeth, appeared; the dead fish was engulfed, and the shark sank out of sight. But Jack was mistaken in supposing that it would be satisfied. In a very few minutes it returned to us, and its quick motions led us to fear that it would attack us at once.

"Stop paddling!" cried Jack suddenly. "I see it coming up behind us. Now, obey my orders *quickly*. Our lives may depend on it. Ralph-Peterkin-do your best to *balance the log*. Don't look out for the shark. Don't glance behind you. Do nothing but balance the log."

Peterkin and I instantly did as we were ordered, being only too glad to do anything that afforded us a chance or a hope of escape, for we had implicit confidence in Jack's courage and wisdom. For a few seconds, that seemed long minutes to my mind, we sat thus silently; but I could not resist glancing backward, despite the orders to the contrary. On doing so, I saw Jack sitting rigid like a statue, with his paddle raised, his lips compressed, and his eyebrows bent over his eyes, which glared savagely from beneath them down into the water.

I also saw the shark, to my horror, quite close under the log, in the act of darting towards Jack's foot. I could scarce suppress a cry on beholding this. In another moment the shark rose. Jack drew his leg suddenly from the water and threw it over the log. The monster's snout rubbed against the log as it passed, and revealed its hideous jaws, into which Jack instantly plunged the paddle and thrust it down its throat. So violent was this act that Jack rose to his feet in performing it; the log was thereby rolled completely over, and we were once more plunged into the water. We all rose, spluttering and gasping, in a moment.

"Now, then, strike out for shore!" cried Jack. —"Here, Peterkin, catch hold of my collar, and kick out with a will!"

Peterkin did as he was desired, and Jack struck out with such force that he cut through the water like a boat; while I, being free from all encumbrance, succeeded in keeping up with him. As we had by this time drawn pretty near to the shore, a few minutes more sufficed to carry us into shallow water; and finally, we landed in safety, though very much exhausted, and not a little frightened, by our terrible adventure.

CHAPTER EIGHT

The beauties of the bottom of the sea tempt Peterkin to dive-How he did it-More difficulties overcome-The water garden-Curious creatures of the sea-The tank-Candles missed very much, and the candle-nut tree discovered-Wonderful account of Peterkin's first voyage-Cloth found growing on a tree —A plan projected, and arms prepared for offence and defence —A dreadful cry.

Our encounter with the shark was the first great danger that had befallen us since landing on this island; and we felt very seriously affected by it, especially when we considered that we had so often unwittingly incurred the same danger before while bathing. We were now forced to take to fishing again in the shallow water until we should succeed in constructing a raft. What troubled us most, however, was that we were compelled to forego our morning swimming-excursions. We did, indeed, continue to enjoy our bathe in the shallow water; but Jack and I found that one great source of our enjoyment was gone when we could no longer dive down among the beautiful coral groves at the bottom of the lagoon. We had come to be so fond of this exercise, and to take such an interest in watching the formations of coral and the gambols of the many beautiful fish amongst the forest of red and green seaweeds, that we had become quite familiar with the appearance of the fish and the localities that they chiefly haunted. We had also become expert divers. But we made it a rule never to stay long under water at a time. Jack told me that to do so often was bad for the lungs, and instead of affording us enjoyment, would ere long do us a serious injury. So we never stayed at the bottom as long as we might have done, but came up frequently to the top for fresh air, and dived down again immediately. Sometimes, when Jack happened to be in a humorous frame, he would seat himself at the bottom of the sea on one of the brain-corals, as if he were seated on a large paddock-stool, and then make faces at me in order, if possible, to make me laugh under water. At first, when he took me unawares, he nearly succeeded, and I had to shoot to the surface in order to laugh; but afterwards I became aware of his intentions, and being naturally of a grave disposition, I had no difficulty in restraining myself. I used often to wonder how poor Peterkin would have liked to be with us; and he sometimes expressed much regret at being unable to join us. I used to do my best to gratify him, poor fellow, by relating all the wonders that we saw; but this, instead of satisfying, seemed only to whet his curiosity the more, so one day we prevailed on him to try to go down with us. But although a brave boy in every other way, Peterkin was very nervous in the water; and it was with difficulty we got him to consent to be taken down, for he could never have managed to push himself down to the bottom without assistance. But no sooner had we pulled him down a yard or so into the deep, clear water than he began to struggle and kick violently; so we were forced to let him go, when he rose out of the water like a cork, gave a loud gasp and a frightful roar, and struck out for the land with the utmost possible haste.

Now all this pleasure we were to forego, and when we thought thereon, Jack and I felt very much depressed in our spirits. I could see, also, that Peterkin grieved and sympathised with us; for, when talking about this matter, he refrained from jesting and bantering us upon it.

As, however, a man's difficulties usually set him upon devising methods to overcome them, whereby he often discovers better things than those he may have lost, so this our difficulty induced us to think of searching for a large pool among the rocks, where the water should be deep enough for diving, yet so surrounded by rocks as to prevent sharks from getting at us. And such a pool we afterwards found, which proved to be very much better than our most sanguine hopes anticipated. It was situated not more than ten minutes' walk from our camp, and was in the form of a small, deep bay or basin, the entrance to which, besides being narrow, was so shallow that no fish so large as a shark could get in-at least, not unless he should be a remarkably thin one.

Inside of this basin, which we called our Water Garden, the coral formations were much more wonderful, and the seaweed plants far more lovely and vividly coloured, than in the lagoon itself.

And the water was so clear and still that, although very deep, you could see the minutest object at the bottom. Besides this, there was a ledge of rock which overhung the basin at its deepest part, from which we could dive pleasantly, and whereon Peterkin could sit and see not only all the wonders I had described to him, but also see Jack and me creeping amongst the marine shrubbery at the bottom, like-as he expressed it —"two great white sea-monsters." During these excursions of ours to the bottom of the sea we began to get an insight into the manners and customs of its inhabitants, and to make discoveries of wonderful things, the like of which we never before conceived. Among other things, we were deeply interested with the operations of the little coral insect, which, I was informed by Jack, is supposed to have entirely constructed many of the numerous islands in the Pacific Ocean. And certainly, when we considered the great reef which these insects had formed round the island on which we were cast, and observed their ceaseless activity in building their myriad cells, it did at first seem as if this might be true; but then, again, when I looked at the mountains of the island, and reflected that there were thousands of such (many of them much higher) in the South Seas, I doubted that there must be some mistake here. But more of this hereafter.

I also became much taken up with the manners and appearance of the anemones, and starfish, and crabs, and sea-urchins, and such-like creatures; and was not content with watching those I saw during my dives in the Water Garden, but I must needs scoop out a hole in the coral rock close to it, which I filled with salt water, and stocked with sundry specimens of anemones and shell-fish, in order to watch more closely how they were in the habit of passing their time. Our burning-glass, also, now became a great treasure to me, as it enabled me to magnify, and so to perceive more clearly, the forms and actions of these curious creatures of the deep.

Having now got ourselves into a very comfortable condition, we began to talk of a project which we had long had in contemplation-namely, to travel entirely round the island, in order, first, to ascertain whether it contained any other productions which might be useful to us; and, second, to see whether there might be any place more convenient and suitable for our permanent residence than that on which we were now encamped. Not that we were in any degree dissatisfied with it. On the contrary, we entertained quite a home-feeling to our bower and its neighbourhood; but if a better place did exist, there was no reason why we should not make use of it. At any rate, it would be well to know of its existence.

We had much earnest talk over this matter. But Jack proposed that, before undertaking such an excursion, we should supply ourselves with good defensive arms; for, as we intended not only to go round all the shore, but to descend most of the valleys, before returning home, we should be likely to meet in with-he would not say *dangers* —but at least with everything that existed on the island, whatever that might be.

"Besides," said Jack, "it won't do for us to live on cocoa-nuts and oysters always. No doubt they are very excellent in their way, but I think a little animal food now and then would be agreeable as well as good for us; and as there are many small birds among the trees, some of which are probably very good to eat, I think it would be a capital plan to make bows and arrows, with which we could easily knock them over."

"First-rate!" cried Peterkin. "You will make the bows, Jack, and I'll try my hand at the arrows. The fact is, I'm quite tired of throwing stones at the birds. I began the very day we landed, I think, and have persevered up to the present time, but I've never hit anything yet."

"You forget," said I, "you hit me one day on the shin."

"Ah, true!" replied Peterkin; "and a precious shindy you kicked up in consequence. But you were at least four yards away from the impudent paroquet I aimed at, so you see what a horribly bad shot I am."

"But, Jack," said I, "you cannot make three bows and arrows before to-morrow; and would it not be a pity to waste time, now that we have made up our minds to go on this expedition? — Suppose that you make one bow and arrow for yourself, and we can take our clubs?"

"That's true, Ralph. The day is pretty far advanced, and I doubt if I can make even one bow before dark. To be sure, I might work by firelight after the sun goes down."

We had, up to this time, been in the habit of going to bed with the sun, as we had no pressing call to work o' nights; and, indeed, our work during the day was usually hard enough-what between fishing, and improving our bower, and diving in the Water Garden, and rambling in the woods-so that when night came we were usually very glad to retire to our beds. But now that we had a desire to work at night, we felt a wish for candles.

"Won't a good blazing fire give you light enough?" inquired Peterkin.

"Yes," replied Jack, "quite enough; but then it will give us a great deal more than enough of heat in this warm climate of ours."

"True," said Peterkin; "I forgot that. It would roast us."

"Well, as you're always doing that at any rate," remarked Jack, "we could scarcely call it a change. But the fact is, I've been thinking over this subject before. There is a certain nut growing in these islands which is called the candle-nut, because the natives use it instead of candles; and I know all about it, and how to prepare it for burning —"

"Then why don't you do it?" interrupted Peterkin. "Why have you kept us in the dark so long, you vile philosopher?"

"Because," said Jack, "I have not seen the tree yet, and I'm not sure that I should know either the tree or the nuts if I did see them. You see, I forget the description."

"Ah! that's just the way with me," said Peterkin with a deep sigh. "I never could keep in my mind for half-an-hour the few descriptions I ever attempted to remember. The very first voyage I ever made was caused by my mistaking a description-or forgetting it, which is the same thing. And a horrible voyage it was. I had to fight with the captain the whole way out, and made the homeward voyage by swimming!"

"Come, Peterkin," said I, "you can't get even *me* to believe that."

"Perhaps not, but it's true notwithstanding," returned Peterkin, pretending to be hurt at my doubting his word.

"Let us hear how it happened," said Jack, while a good-natured smile overspread his face.

"Well, you must know," began Peterkin, "that the very day before I went to sea I was greatly taken up with a game at hockey, which I was playing with my old school-fellows for the last time before leaving them. —You see I was young then, Ralph." Peterkin gazed, in an abstracted and melancholy manner, out to sea. —"Well, in the midst of the game, my uncle, who had taken all the bother and trouble of getting me bound 'prentice and rigged out, came and took me aside, and told me that he was called suddenly away from home, and would not be able to see me aboard, as he had intended. 'However,' said he, 'the captain knows you are coming, so that's not of much consequence; but as you'll have to find the ship yourself, you must remember her name and description. D'ye hear, boy?' I certainly did hear, but I'm afraid I did not understand; for my mind was so taken up with the game, which I saw my side was losing, that I began to grow impatient, and the moment my uncle finished his description of the ship and bade me good-bye I bolted back to my game, with only a confused idea of three masts, and a green-painted taffrail, and a gilt figurehead of Hercules with his club at the bow. Next day I was so much cast down with everybody saying good-bye, and a lot o' my female friends cryin' horribly over me, that I did not start for the harbour, where the ship was lying among a thousand others, till it was almost too late. So I had to run the whole way. When I reached the pier, there were so many masts, and so much confusion, that I felt quite humble-bumbled in my faculties. 'Now,' said I to myself, 'Peterkin, you're in a fix.' Then I fancied I saw a gilt figurehead and three masts belonging to a ship just about to start; so I darted on board, but speedily jumped on shore again when I found that two of the masts belonged to another vessel and the figurehead to a third! At last I caught sight of what I made sure was it —a fine large vessel just casting off her moorings. The taffrail was green. Three masts-yes, that must be it-and the gilt figurehead of Hercules. To be sure, it had a three-pronged pitchfork in its hand instead of a club; but that might be my uncle's mistake, or perhaps Hercules sometimes varied his weapons. 'Cast off!' roared a voice from the quarter-deck. 'Hold on!' cried I, rushing frantically through the crowd. 'Hold on! hold on!' repeated some of the bystanders, while the men at the ropes delayed for a minute. This threw the captain into a frightful rage; for some of his friends had come down to see him off, and having his orders contradicted so flatly was too much for him. However, the delay was sufficient. I took a race and a good leap; the ropes were cast off; the steam-tug gave a puff, and we started. Suddenly the captain walks up to me: 'Where did you come from, you scamp, and what do you want here?'

"'Please, sir,' said I, touching my cap, 'I'm your new 'prentice come aboard.'

"'New 'prentice!' said he, stamping; 'I've got no new 'prentice. My boys are all aboard already. This is a trick, you young blackguard! You've run away, you have!' And the captain stamped about the deck and swore dreadfully; for, you see, the thought of having to stop the ship and lower a boat and lose half-an-hour, all for the sake of sending a small boy ashore, seemed to make him very angry. Besides, it was blowin' fresh outside the harbour, so that to have let the steamer alongside to put me into it was no easy job. Just as we were passing the pier-head, where several boats were rowing into the harbour, the captain came up to me.

"'You've run away, you blackguard!' he said, giving me a box on the ear.

"'No, I haven't!' said I angrily, for the box was by no means a light one.

"'Hark'ee, boy, can you swim?'

"'Yes,' said I.

"'Then do it!' and seizing me by my trousers and the nape of my neck, he tossed me over the side into the sea. The fellows in the boats at the end of the pier backed their oars on seeing this; but observing that I could swim, they allowed me to make the best of my way to the pier-head. —So you see, Ralph, that I really did swim my first homeward voyage."

Jack laughed, and patted Peterkin on the shoulder.

"But tell us about the candle-nut tree," said I. "You were talking about it."

"Very true," said Jack; "but I fear I can remember little about it. I believe the nut is about the size of a walnut; and I think that the leaves are white, but I am not sure."

"Eh! ha! hum!" exclaimed Peterkin; "I saw a tree answering to that description this very day."

"Did you?" cried Jack. "Is it far from this?"

"No, not half-a-mile."

"Then lead me to it," said Jack, seizing his axe.

In a few minutes we were all three pushing through the underwood of the forest, headed by Peterkin.

We soon came to the tree in question, which, after Jack had closely examined it, we concluded must be the candle-nut tree. Its leaves were of a beautiful silvery white, and formed a fine contrast to the dark-green foliage of the surrounding trees. We immediately filled our pockets with the nuts, after which Jack said:

"Now, Peterkin, climb that cocoa-nut tree and cut me one of the long branches."

This was soon done; but it cost some trouble, for the stem was very high, and as Peterkin usually pulled nuts from the younger trees, he was not much accustomed to climbing the high ones. The leaf or branch was a very large one, and we were surprised at its size and strength. Viewed from a little distance, the cocoa-nut tree seems to be a tall, straight stem, without a single branch except at the top, where there is a tuft of feathery-looking leaves that seem to wave like soft plumes in the wind. But when we saw one of these leaves or branches at our feet, we found it to be a strong stalk, about fifteen feet long, with a number of narrow, pointed leaflets ranged alternately on each side. But what seemed to us the most wonderful thing about it was a curious substance resembling cloth, which was wrapped round the thick end of the stalk where it had been cut from the tree. Peterkin told us that he had the greatest difficulty in separating the branch from the stem on account of this substance, as it was wrapped quite round the tree, and, he observed, round all the other branches, thus forming a strong support to the large leaves while exposed to high winds. When I call this substance cloth I do not exaggerate. Indeed, with regard to all the things I saw during my eventful career in the South Seas, I have been exceedingly careful not to exaggerate, or in any way to mislead or deceive my readers. This cloth, I say, was remarkably like to coarse brown cotton cloth. It had a seam or fibre down the centre of it, from which diverged other fibres, about the size of a bristle. There were two layers of these fibres, very long and tough, the one layer crossing the other obliquely, and the whole was cemented together with a still finer fibrous and adhesive substance. When we regarded it attentively, we could with difficulty believe that it had not been woven by human hands. This remarkable piece of cloth we stripped carefully off, and found it to be above two feet long by a foot broad, and we carried it home with us as a great prize.

Jack now took one of the leaflets, and cutting out the central spine or stalk, hurried back with it to our camp. Having made a small fire, he baked the nuts slightly and then peeled off the husks. After this he wished to bore a hole in them, which, not having anything better at hand at the time, he did with the point of our useless pencil-case. Then he strung them on the cocoa-nut spine, and on putting a light to the topmost nut we found, to our joy, that it burned with a clear, beautiful flame, upon seeing which Peterkin sprang up and danced round the fire for at least five minutes in the excess of his satisfaction.

"Now, lads," said Jack, extinguishing our candle, "the sun will set in an hour, so we have no time to lose. I shall go and cut a young tree to make my bow out of, and you had better each of you go and select good strong sticks for clubs, and we'll set to work at them after dark."

So saying, he shouldered his axe and went off; followed by Peterkin; while I took up the piece of newly discovered cloth, and fell to examining its structure. So engrossed was I in this that I was still sitting in the same attitude and occupation when my companions returned.

"I told you so!" cried Peterkin with a loud laugh. —"Oh Ralph, you're incorrigible! See, there's a club for you. I was sure, when we left you looking at that bit of stuff, that we would find you poring over it when we came back, so I just cut a club for you as well as for myself."

"Thank you, Peterkin," said I. "It was kind of you to do that instead of scolding me for a lazy fellow, as I confess I deserve."

"Oh, as to that," returned Peterkin, "I'll blow you up yet if you wish it; only it would be of no use if I did, for you're a perfect mule!"

As it was now getting dark we lighted our candle, and placing it in a holder made of two crossing branches inside of our bower, we seated ourselves on our leafy beds and began to work.

"I intend to appropriate the bow for my own use," said Jack, chipping the piece of wood he had brought with his axe. "I used to be a pretty fair shot once. —But what's that you're doing?" he added, looking at Peterkin, who had drawn the end of a long pole into the tent, and was endeavouring to fit a small piece of the hoop-iron to the end of it.

"I'm going to enlist into the Lancers," answered Peterkin. "You see, Jack, I find the club rather an unwieldy instrument for my delicately formed muscles, and I flatter myself I shall do more execution with a spear."

"Well, if length constitutes power," said Jack, "you'll certainly be invincible."

The pole which Peterkin had cut was full twelve feet long, being a very strong but light and tough young tree, which merely required thinning at the butt to be a serviceable weapon.

"That's a very good idea," said I.

"Which—this?" inquired Peterkin, pointing to the spear.

"Yes," I replied.

"Humph!" said he; "you'd find it a pretty tough and matter-of-fact idea if you had it stuck through your gizzard, old boy!"

"I mean the idea of making it is a good one," said I, laughing. "And, now I think of it, I'll change my plan too. I don't think much of a club, so I'll make me a sling out of this piece of cloth. I used to be very fond of slinging, ever since I read of David slaying Goliath the Philistine, and I was once thought to be expert at it."

So I set to work to manufacture a sling. For a long time we all worked very busily without speaking. At length Peterkin looked up. "I say, Jack, I'm sorry to say I must apply to you for another strip of your handkerchief to tie on this rascally head with. It's pretty well torn at any rate, so you won't miss it."

Jack proceeded to comply with this request, when Peterkin suddenly laid his hand on his arm and arrested him.

"Hist, man!" said he; "be tender! You should never be needlessly cruel if you can help it. Do try to shave past Lord Nelson's mouth without tearing it, if possible! Thanks. There are plenty more handkerchiefs on the cocoa-nut trees."

Poor Peterkin! with what pleasant feelings I recall and record his jests and humorous sayings now!

While we were thus engaged we were startled by a distant, but most strange and horrible, cry. It seemed to come from the sea, but was so far away that we could not clearly distinguish its precise direction. Rushing out of our bower, we hastened down to the beach and stayed to listen. Again it came, quite loud and distinct on the night air —a prolonged, hideous cry, something like the braying of an ass. The moon had risen, and we could see the islands in and beyond the lagoon quite plainly; but there was no object visible to account for such a cry. A strong gust of wind was blowing from the point whence the sound came, but this died away while we were gazing out to sea.

"What can it be?" said Peterkin in a low whisper, while we all involuntarily crept closer to each other.

"Do you know," said Jack, "I have heard that mysterious sound twice before, but never so loud as to-night. Indeed, it was so faint that I thought I must have merely fancied it; so, as I did not wish to alarm you, I said nothing about it."

We listened for a long time for the sound again; but as it did not come, we returned to the bower and resumed our work.

"Very strange!" said Peterkin quite gravely. —"Do you believe in ghosts, Ralph?"

"No," I answered, "I do not. Nevertheless, I must confess that strange, unaccountable sounds, such as we have just heard, make me feel a little uneasy."

"What say you to it, Jack?"

"I neither believe in ghosts nor feel uneasy," he replied. "I never saw a ghost myself, and I never met with any one who had; and I have generally found that strange and unaccountable things have almost always been accounted for, and found to be quite simple, on close examination. I certainly can't imagine what *that* sound is; but I'm quite sure I shall find out before long, and if it's a ghost I'll —I'll —"

"Eat it!" cried Peterkin.

"Yes, I'll eat it! —Now, then, my bow and two arrows are finished; so, if you're ready, we had better turn in."

By this time Peterkin had thinned down his spear, and tied an iron point very cleverly to the end of it; I had formed a sling, the lines of which were composed of thin strips of the cocoa-nut cloth, plaited; and Jack had made a stout bow, nearly five feet long, with two arrows, feathered with two or three large plumes which some bird had dropped. They had no barbs; but Jack said that if arrows were well feathered they did not require iron points, but would fly quite well if merely sharpened at the point, which I did not know before.

"A feathered arrow without a barb," said he, "is a good weapon, but a barbed arrow without feathers is utterly useless."

The string of the bow was formed of our piece of whip-cord, part of which, as he did not like to cut it, was rolled round the bow.

Although thus prepared for a start on the morrow we thought it wise to exercise ourselves a little in the use of our weapons before starting, so we spent the whole of the next day in practising. And it was well we did so, for we found that our arms were very imperfect, and that we were far from perfect in the use of them. First, Jack found that the bow was much too strong, and he had to thin it. Also the spear was much too heavy, and so had to be reduced in thickness, although nothing would induce Peterkin to have it shortened. My sling answered very well; but I had fallen so much out of practice that my first stone knocked off Peterkin's hat, and narrowly missed making a second Goliath of him. However, after having spent the whole day in diligent practice, we began to find some of our former expertness returning, at least Jack and I did. As for Peterkin, being naturally a neat-handed boy, he soon handled his spear well, and could run full tilt at a cocoa-nut, and hit it with great precision once out of every five times.

But I feel satisfied that we owed much of our rapid success to the unflagging energy of Jack, who insisted that since we had made him captain, we should obey him; and he kept us at work from morning till night, perseveringly, at the same thing. Peterkin wished very much to run about and stick his spear into everything he passed; but Jack put up a cocoa-nut, and would not let him leave off running at that for a moment except when he wanted to rest. We laughed at Jack for this, but we were both convinced that it did us much good.

That night we examined and repaired our arms ere we lay down to rest, although we were much fatigued, in order that we might be in readiness to set out on our expedition at daylight on the following morning.

CHAPTER NINE

Prepare for a journey round the island-Sagacious reflections-Mysterious appearances and startling occurrences.

Scarcely had the sun shot its first ray across the bosom of the broad Pacific when Jack sprang to his feet, and hallooing in Peterkin's ear to awaken him, ran down the beach to take his customary dip in the sea. We did not, as was our wont, bathe that morning in our Water Garden, but in order to save time, refreshed ourselves in the shallow water just opposite the bower. Our breakfast was also despatched without loss of time, and in less than an hour afterwards all our preparations for the journey were completed.

In addition to his ordinary dress, Jack tied a belt of cocoa-nut cloth round his waist, into which he thrust the axe. I was also advised to put on a belt and carry a short cudgel or bludgeon in it, for, as Jack truly remarked, the sling would be of little use if we should chance to come to close quarters with any wild animal. As for Peterkin, notwithstanding that he carried such a long and, I must add, frightful-looking spear over his shoulder, we could not prevail on him to leave his club behind; "for," said he, "a spear at close quarters is not worth a button." I must say that it seemed to me that the club was, to use his own style of language, not worth a button-hole; for it was all knotted over at the head, something like the club which I remember to have observed in picture-books of Jack the Giant-killer, besides being so heavy that he required to grasp it with both hands in order to wield it at all. However, he took it with him, and in this manner we set out upon our travels.

We did not consider it necessary to carry any food with us, as we knew that wherever we went we should be certain to fall in with cocoa-nut trees-having which we were amply supplied, as Peterkin said, with meat and drink and pocket-handkerchiefs! I took the precaution, however, to put the burning-glass into my pocket lest we should want fire.

The morning was exceedingly lovely. It was one of that very still and peaceful sort which made the few noises that we heard seem to be quiet noises (I know no other way of expressing this idea) —noises which, so far from interrupting the universal tranquillity of earth, sea, and sky, rather tended to reveal to us how quiet the world round us really was. Such sounds as I refer to were the peculiar, melancholy-yet, it seemed to me, cheerful-plaint of sea-birds floating on the glassy waters or sailing in the sky; also the subdued twittering of little birds among the bushes, the faint ripples on the beach, and the solemn boom of the surf upon the distant coral reef. We felt very glad in our hearts as we walked along the sands, side by side. For my part, I felt so deeply overjoyed that I was surprised at my own sensations, and fell into a reverie upon the causes of happiness. I came to the conclusion that a state of profound peace and repose, both in regard to outward objects and within the soul, is the happiest condition in which man can be placed; for although I had many a time been most joyful and happy when engaged in bustling, energetic, active pursuits or amusements, I never found that such joy or satisfaction was so deep or so pleasant to reflect upon as that which I now experienced. And I was the more confirmed in this opinion when I observed-and, indeed, as told by himself-that Peterkin's happiness was also very great; yet he did not express this by dancing, as was his wont, nor did he give so much as a single shout, but walked quietly between us with his eye sparkling and a joyful smile upon his countenance. My reader must not suppose that I thought all this in the clear and methodical manner in which I have set it down here. These thoughts did indeed pass through my mind; but they did so in a very confused and indefinite manner, for I was young at that time and not much given to deep reflections. Neither did I consider that the peace whereof I write is not to be found in this world-at least in its perfection-although I have since learned that, by religion, a man may attain to a very great degree of it.

I have said that Peterkin walked along the sands between us. We had two ways of walking together about our island. When we travelled through the woods we always did so in single file, as by this method we advanced with greater facility, the one treading in the other's footsteps.

In such cases Jack always took the lead, Peterkin followed, and I brought up the rear. But when we travelled along the sands, which extended almost in an unbroken line of glistening white round the island, we marched abreast, as we found this method more sociable and every way more pleasant. Jack, being the tallest, walked next the sea, and Peterkin marched between us, as by this arrangement either of us could talk to him or he to us, while if Jack and I happened to wish to converse together we could conveniently do so over Peterkin's head. Peterkin used to say, in reference to this arrangement, that had he been as tall as either of us, our order of march might have been the same; for, as Jack often used to scold him for letting everything we said to him pass in at one ear and out at the other, his head could, of course, form no interruption to our discourse.

We were now fairly started. Half-a-mile's walk conveyed us round a bend in the land which shut out our bower from view, and for some time we advanced at a brisk pace without speaking, though our eyes were not idle, but noted everything-in the woods, on the shore, or in the sea-that was interesting. After passing the ridge of land that formed one side of our valley-the Valley of the Wreck-we beheld another small vale lying before us in all the luxuriant loveliness of tropical vegetation. We had indeed seen it before from the mountain-top, but we had no idea that it would turn out to be so much more lovely when we were close to it. We were about to commence the exploration of this valley when Peterkin stopped us, and directed our attention to a very remarkable appearance in advance along the shore.

"What's yon, think you?" said he, levelling his spear as if he expected an immediate attack from the object in question, though it was full half-a-mile distant.

As he spoke, there appeared a white column above the rocks, as if of steam or spray. It rose upwards to a height of several feet, and then disappeared. Had this been near the sea, we would not have been so greatly surprised, as it might in that case have been the surf, for at this part of the coast the coral reef approached so near to the island that in some parts it almost joined it. There was, therefore, no lagoon between, and the heavy surf of the ocean beat almost up to the rocks. But this white column appeared about fifty yards inland. The rocks at the place were rugged, and they stretched across the sandy beach into the sea. Scarce had we ceased expressing our surprise at this sight when another column flew upwards for a few seconds, not far from the spot where the first had been seen, and disappeared; and so, at long, irregular intervals, these strange sights recurred. We were now quite sure that the columns were watery, or composed of spray; but what caused them we could not guess, so we determined to go and see.

In a few minutes we gained the spot, which was very rugged and precipitous, and, moreover, quite damp with the falling of the spray. We had much ado to pass over dry-shod. The ground, also, was full of holes here and there. Now, while we stood anxiously waiting for the reappearance of these waterspouts, we heard a low, rumbling sound near us, which quickly increased to a gurgling and hissing noise, and a moment afterwards a thick spout of water burst upwards from a hole in the rock and spouted into the air with much violence, and so close to where Jack and I were standing that it nearly touched us. We sprang aside, but not before a cloud of spray descended and drenched us both to the skin.

Peterkin, who was standing farther off, escaped with a few drops, and burst into an uncontrollable fit of laughter on beholding our miserable plight.

"Mind your eye!" he shouted eagerly; "there goes another!" The words were scarcely out of his mouth when there came up a spout from another hole, which served us exactly in the same manner as before.

Peterkin now shrieked with laughter; but his merriment was abruptly put a stop to by the gurgling noise occurring close to where he stood.

"Where'll it spout this time, I wonder?" he said, looking about with some anxiety and preparing to run. Suddenly there came a loud hiss or snort; a fierce spout of water burst up between Peterkin's legs, blew him off his feet, enveloped him in its spray, and hurled him to the ground. He fell with so much violence that we feared he must have broken some of his bones, and ran anxiously to his assistance; but fortunately he had fallen on a clump of tangled herbage, in which he lay sprawling in a most deplorable condition.

It was now our turn to laugh; but as we were not yet quite sure that he was unhurt, and as we knew not when or where the next spout might arise, we assisted him hastily to jump up and hurry from the spot.

I may here add that, although I am quite certain that the spout of water was very strong, and that it blew Peterkin completely off his legs, I am not quite certain of the exact height to which it lifted him, being somewhat startled by the event, and blinded partially by the spray, so that my power of observation was somewhat impaired for the moment.

"What's to be done now?" asked Peterkin ruefully.

"Make a fire, lad, and dry ourselves," replied Jack.

"And here is material ready to our hand," said I, picking up a dried branch of a tree as we hurried up to the woods.

In about an hour after this mishap our clothes were again dried. While they were hanging up before the fire we walked down to the beach, and soon observed that these curious spouts took place immediately after the fall of a huge wave, never before it; and, moreover, that the spouts did not take place excepting when the billow was an extremely large one. From this we concluded that there must be a subterraneous channel in the rock into which the water was driven by the larger waves, and finding no way of escape except through these small holes, was thus forced up violently through them. At any rate, we could not conceive any other reason for these strange waterspouts, and as this seemed a very simple and probable one, we forthwith adopted it.

"I say, Ralph, what's that in the water? Is it a shark?" said Jack just as we were about to quit the place.

I immediately ran to the overhanging ledge of rock, from which he was looking down into the sea, and bent over it. There I saw a very faint, pale object of a greenish colour, which seemed to move slightly while I looked at it.

"It's like a fish of some sort," said I.

"Hallo, Peterkin!" cried Jack. "Fetch your spear; here's work for it!"

But when we tried to reach the object, the spear proved to be too short.

"There, now," said Peterkin with a sneer; "you were always telling me it was too long."

Jack now drove the spear forcibly towards the object, and let go his hold. But although it seemed to be well aimed, he must have missed, for the handle soon rose again; and when the spear was drawn up, there was the pale-green object in exactly the same spot, slowly moving its tail.

"Very odd!" said Jack.

But although it was undoubtedly very odd, and although Jack and all of us plunged the spear at it repeatedly, we could neither hit it nor drive it away, so we were compelled to continue our journey without discovering what it was. I was very much perplexed at this strange appearance in the water, and could not get it out of my mind for a long time afterwards. However, I quieted myself by resolving that I would pay a visit to it again at some more convenient season.

CHAPTER TEN

Make discovery of many excellent roots and fruits-The resources of the coral island gradually unfolded-The banyan tree-Another tree which is supported by natural planks-Water-fowl found —A very remarkable discovery, and a very peculiar murder-We luxuriate on the fat of the land.

Our examination of the little valley proved to be altogether most satisfactory. We found in it not only similar trees to those we had already seen in our own valley, but also one or two others of a different species. We had also the satisfaction of discovering a peculiar vegetable, which, Jack concluded, must certainly be that of which he had read as being very common among the South Sea Islanders, and which was named taro. Also we found a large supply of yams, and another root like a potato in appearance. As these were all quite new to us, we regarded our lot as a most fortunate one, in being thus cast on an island which was so prolific and so well stored with all the necessaries of life. Long afterwards we found out that this island of ours was no better in these respects than thousands of other islands in those seas. Indeed, many of them were much richer and more productive; but that did not render us the less grateful for our present good fortune. We each put one of these roots in our pocket, intending to use them for our supper-of which more hereafter. We also saw many beautiful birds here, and traces of some four-footed animal again. Meanwhile the sun began to descend; so we returned to the shore and pushed on, round the spouting rocks, into the next valley. This was that valley of which I have spoken as running across the entire island. It was by far the largest and most beautiful that we had yet looked upon. Here were trees of every shape and size and hue which it is possible to conceive of, many of which we had not seen in the other valleys; for, the stream in this valley being larger, and the mould much richer than in the Valley of the Wreck, it was clothed with a more luxuriant growth of trees and plants. Some trees were dark, glossy green; others of a rich and warm hue, contrasting well with those of a pale, light green, which were everywhere abundant. Among these we recognised the broad, dark heads of the bread-fruit, with its golden fruit; the pure, silvery foliage of the candle-nut, and several species which bore a strong resemblance to the pine; while here and there, in groups and in single trees, rose the tall forms of the cocoa-nut palms, spreading abroad, and waving their graceful plumes high above all the rest, as if they were a superior race of stately giants keeping guard over these luxuriant forests. Oh, it was a most enchanting scene! and I thanked God for having created such delightful spots for the use of man.

Now, while we were gazing around us in silent admiration, Jack uttered an exclamation of surprise, and pointing to an object a little to one side of us, said:

"That's a banyan tree."

"And what's a banyan tree?" inquired Peterkin as we walked towards it.

"A very curious one, as you shall see presently," replied Jack. "It is called the *aoa* here, if I recollect rightly, and has a wonderful peculiarity about it. What an enormous one it is, to be sure!"

"*It!*" repeated Peterkin. "Why, there are dozens of banyans here! What do you mean by talking bad grammar? Is your philosophy deserting you, Jack?"

"There is but one tree here of this kind," returned Jack, "as you will perceive if you will examine it." And, sure enough, we did find that what we had supposed was a forest of trees was in reality only one. Its bark was of a light colour, and had a shining appearance, the leaves being lance-shaped, small, and of a beautiful pea-green. But the wonderful thing about it was that the branches, which grew out from the stem horizontally, sent down long shoots or fibres to the ground, which, taking root, had themselves become trees, and were covered with bark like the tree itself. Many of these fibres had descended from the branches at various distances, and thus supported them on natural pillars, some of which were so large and strong that it was not easy at first to distinguish the offspring from the parent stem. The fibres were of all sizes and in all states of advancement, from the pillars we have just mentioned to small cords which hung down and were about to take root, and thin brown threads still far from the ground, which swayed about with every motion of wind. In short, it seemed to us that, if there were only space afforded to it, this single tree would at length cover the whole island.

Shortly after this we came upon another remarkable tree, which, as its peculiar formation afterwards proved extremely useful to us, merits description. It was a splendid chestnut, but its proper name Jack did not know. However, there were quantities of fine nuts upon it, some of which we put in our pockets. But its stem was the most wonderful part of it. It rose to about twelve feet without a branch, and was not of great thickness; on the contrary, it was remarkably slender for the size of the tree. But to make up for this, there were four or five wonderful projections in this stem, which I cannot better describe than by asking the reader to suppose that five planks of two inches thick and three feet broad had been placed round the trunk of the tree, with their *edges* closely fixed to it, from the ground up to the branches, and that these planks had been covered over with the bark of the tree and incorporated with it. In short, they were just natural buttresses, without which the stem could not have supported its heavy and umbrageous top. We found these chestnuts to be very numerous. They grew chiefly on the banks of the stream, and were of all sizes.

While we were examining a small tree of this kind Jack chipped a piece off a buttress with his axe, and found the wood to be firm and easily cut. He then struck the axe into it with all his force, and very soon split it off close to the tree-first, however, having cut it across transversely above and below. By this means he satisfied himself that we could now obtain short planks, as it were all ready sawn, of any size and thickness that we desired, which was a very great discovery indeed-perhaps the most important we had yet made.

We now wended our way back to the coast, intending to encamp near the beach, as we found that the mosquitoes were troublesome in the forest. On our way we could not help admiring the birds which flew and chirped around us. Among them we observed a pretty kind of paroquet, with a green body, a blue head, and a red breast; also a few beautiful turtle-doves, and several flocks of wood-pigeons. The hues of many of these birds were extremely vivid-bright green, blue, and scarlet being the prevailing tints. We made several attempts throughout the day to bring down one of these, both with the bow and the sling-not for mere sport, but to ascertain whether they were good for food. But we invariably missed, although once or twice we were very near hitting. As evening drew on however, a flock of pigeons flew past. I slung a stone into the midst of them at a venture, and had the good fortune to kill one. We were startled soon after by a loud whistling noise above our heads, and on looking up, saw a flock of wild ducks making for the coast. We watched these, and observing where they alighted, followed them up until we came upon a most lovely blue lake, not more than two hundred yards long, embosomed in verdant trees. Its placid surface, which reflected every leaf and stem as if in a mirror, was covered with various species of wild ducks, feeding among the sedges and broad-leaved water-plants which floated on it, while numerous birds like water-hens ran to and fro most busily on its margin. These all, with one accord, flew tumultuously away the instant we made our appearance. While walking along the margin we observed fish in the water, but of what sort we could not tell.

Now, as we neared the shore, Jack and I said we would go a little out of our way to see if we could procure one of those ducks; so, directing Peterkin to go straight to the shore and kindle a fire, we separated, promising to rejoin him speedily. But we did not find the ducks, although we made a diligent search for half-an-hour. We were about to retrace our steps when we were arrested by one of the strangest sights that we had yet beheld.

Just in front of us, at the distance of about ten yards, grew a superb tree, which certainly was the largest we had yet seen on the island. Its trunk was at least five feet in diameter, with a smooth, grey bark; above this the spreading branches were clothed with light-green leaves, amid which were clusters of bright-yellow fruit, so numerous as to weigh down the boughs with their great weight. This fruit seemed to be of the plum species, of an oblong form, and a good deal larger than the magnum bonum plum. The ground at the foot of this tree was thickly strewn with the fallen fruit, in the midst of which lay sleeping, in every possible attitude, at least twenty hogs of all ages and sizes, apparently quite surfeited with a recent banquet.

Jack and I could scarce restrain our laughter as we gazed at these coarse, fat, ill-looking animals while they lay groaning and snoring heavily amid the remains of their supper.

"Now, Ralph," said Jack in a low whisper, "put a stone in your sling —a good big one-and let fly at that fat fellow with his back toward you. I'll try to put an arrow into yon little pig."

"Don't you think we had better put them up first?" I whispered. "It seems cruel to kill them while asleep."

"If I wanted *sport*, Ralph, I would certainly set them up; but as we only want *pork*, we'll let them lie. Besides, we're not sure of killing them; so, fire away."

Thus admonished, I slung my stone with so good an aim that it went bang against the hog's flank as if against the head of a drum; but it had no other effect than that of causing the animal to start to its feet, with a frightful yell of surprise, and scamper away. At the same instant Jack's bow twanged, and the arrow pinned the little pig to the ground by the ear.

"I've missed, after all!" cried Jack, darting forward with uplifted axe; while the little pig uttered a loud squeal, tore the arrow from the ground, and ran away with it, along with the whole drove, into the bushes and disappeared, though we heard them screaming long afterwards in the distance.

"That's very provoking, now," said Jack, rubbing the point of his nose.

"Very," I replied, stroking my chin.

"Well, we must make haste and rejoin Peterkin," said Jack; "it's getting late." And without further remark, we threaded our way quickly through the woods towards the shore.

When we reached it we found wood laid out, the fire lighted and beginning to kindle up, with other signs of preparation for our encampment; but Peterkin was nowhere to be found. We wondered very much at this; but Jack suggested that he might have gone to fetch water, so he gave a shout to let him know that we had arrived, and sat down upon a rock, while I threw off my jacket and seized the axe, intending to split up one or two billets of wood. But I had scarce moved from the spot when, in the distance, we heard a most appalling shriek, which was followed up by a chorus of yells from the hogs, and a loud hurrah.

"I do believe," said I, "that Peterkin has met with the hogs."

"When Greek meets Greek," said Jack, soliloquising, "then comes the tug of —"

"Hurrah!" shouted Peterkin in the distance.

We turned hastily towards the direction whence the sound came, and soon descried Peterkin walking along the beach towards us with a little pig transfixed on the end of his long spear!

"Well done, my boy!" exclaimed Jack, slapping him on the shoulder when he came up. "You're the best shot amongst us."

"Look here, Jack!" cried Peterkin as he disengaged the animal from his spear. "Do you recognise that hole?" said he, pointing to the pig's ear; "and are you familiar with this arrow, eh?"

"Well, I declare!" said Jack.

"Of course you do," interrupted Peterkin; "but, pray, restrain your declarations at this time, and let's have supper-for I'm uncommonly hungry, I can tell you. And it's no joke to charge a whole herd of swine with their great-grandmother bristling like a giant porcupine, at the head of them!"

We now set about preparing supper; and, truly, a good display of viands we made when all was laid out on a flat rock in the light of the blazing fire. There was, first of all, the little pig; then there were the taro-root, and the yam, and the potato, and six plums; and lastly, the wood-pigeon. To these Peterkin added a bit of sugar-cane, which he had cut from a little patch of that plant which he had found not long after separating from us; "and," said he, "the patch was somewhat in a square form, which convinces me it must have been planted by man."

"Very likely," replied Jack. "From all we have seen, I'm inclined to think that some of the savages must have dwelt here long ago."

We found no small difficulty in making up our minds how we were to cook the pig. None of us had ever cut up one before, and we did not know exactly how to begin; besides, we had nothing but the axe to do it with, our knife having been forgotten. At last Jack started up and said:

"Don't let us waste more time talking about it, boys. —Hold it up, Peterkin. There, lay the hind leg on this block of wood-so;" and he cut it off; with a large portion of the haunch, at a single blow of the axe. "Now the other-that's it." And having thus cut off the two hind legs, he made several deep gashes in them, thrust a sharp-pointed stick through each, and stuck them up before the blaze to roast. The wood-pigeon was then split open, quite flat, washed clean in salt water, and treated in a similar manner. While these were cooking we scraped a hole in the sand and ashes under the fire, into which we put our vegetables and covered them up.

The taro-root was of an oval shape, about ten inches long and four or five thick. It was of a mottled-grey colour, and had a thick rind. We found it somewhat like an Irish potato, and exceedingly good. The yam was roundish, and had a rough brown skin. It was very sweet and well flavoured. The potato, we were surprised to find, was quite sweet and exceedingly palatable, as also were the plums-and, indeed, the pork and pigeon too-when we came to taste them. Altogether, this was decidedly the most luxurious supper we had enjoyed for many a day. Jack said it was out-of-sight better than we ever got on board ship; and Peterkin said he feared that if we should remain long on the island he would infallibly become a glutton or an epicure, whereat Jack remarked that he need not fear that, for he was both already! And so, having eaten our fill, not forgetting to finish off with a plum, we laid ourselves comfortably down to sleep, upon a couch of branches, under the overhanging ledge of a coral rock.

CHAPTER ELEVEN

Effects of overeating, and reflections thereon-Humble advice regarding cold water-The "horrible cry" accounted for-The curious birds called penguins-Peculiarity of the cocoa-nut palm-Questions on the formation of coral islands-Mysterious footsteps-Strange discoveries and sad sights.

When we awoke on the following morning we found that the sun was already a good way above the horizon, so I came to the conclusion that a heavy supper is not conducive to early rising. Never-the-less, we felt remarkably strong and well, and much disposed to have our breakfast. First, however, we had our customary morning bathe, which refreshed us greatly.

I have often wondered very much in after years that the inhabitants of my own dear land did not make more frequent use of this most charming element, water —I mean in the way of cold bathing. Of course, I have perceived that it is not convenient for them to go into the sea or the rivers in winter, as we used to do on the Coral Island; but then I knew from experience that a large washing-tub and a sponge do form a most pleasant substitute. The feelings of freshness, of cleanliness, of vigour, and extreme hilarity that always followed my bathes in the sea-and even, when in England, my ablutions in the wash-tub —were so delightful that I would sooner have gone without my breakfast than without my bathe in cold water. My readers will forgive me for asking whether they are in the habit of bathing thus every morning; and if they answer "No", they will pardon me for recommending them to begin at once. Of late years, since retiring from the stirring life of adventure which I have led so long in foreign climes, I have heard of a system called the cold-water cure. Now, I do not know much about that system; so I do not mean to uphold it, neither do I intend to run it down. Perhaps, in reference to it, I may just hint that there may be too much of a good thing —I know not. But of this I am quite certain, that there may also be too little of a good thing; and the great delight I have had in cold bathing during the course of my adventurous career inclines me to think that it is better to risk taking too much than to content one's self with too little. Such is my opinion, derived from much experience; but I put it before my readers with the utmost diffidence and with profound modesty, knowing that it may possibly jar with their feelings of confidence in their own ability to know and judge as to what is best and fittest in reference to their own affairs. But to return from this digression, for which I humbly crave forgiveness.

We had not advanced on our journey much above a mile or so, and were just beginning to feel the pleasant glow that usually accompanies vigorous exercise, when, on turning a point that revealed to us a new and beautiful cluster of islands, we were suddenly arrested by the appalling cry which had so alarmed us a few nights before. But this time we were by no means so much alarmed as on the previous occasion, because, whereas at that time it was night, now it was day; and I have always found, though I am unable to account for it, that daylight banishes many of the fears that are apt to assail us in the dark.

On hearing the sound, Peterkin instantly threw forward his spear.

"Now, what can it be?" said he, looking round at Jack. "I tell you what it is: if we are to go on being pulled up in a constant state of horror and astonishment, as we have been for the last week, the sooner we're out o' this island the better, notwithstanding the yams and lemonade, and pork and plums!"

Peterkin's remark was followed by a repetition of the cry, louder than before.

"It comes from one of these islands," said Jack.

"It must be the ghost of a jackass, then," said Peterkin, "for I never heard anything so like."

We all turned our eyes towards the cluster of islands, where, on the largest, we observed curious objects moving on the shore.

"Soldiers they are-that's flat!" cried Peterkin, gazing at them in the utmost amazement.

And, in truth, Peterkin's remark seemed to me to be correct; for at the distance from which we saw them, they appeared to be an army of soldiers. There they stood, rank and file, in lines and in squares, marching and counter-marching, with blue coats and white trousers. While we were looking at them the dreadful cry came again over the water, and Peterkin suggested that it must be a regiment sent out to massacre the natives in cold blood. At this remark Jack laughed and said:

"Why, Peterkin, they are penguins!"

"Penguins?" repeated Peterkin.

"Ay, penguins, Peterkin, penguins-nothing more or less than big sea-birds, as you shall see one of these days when we pay them a visit in our boat, which I mean to set about building the moment we return to our bower."

"So, then, our dreadful yelling ghosts and our murdering army of soldiers," remarked Peterkin, "have dwindled down to penguins-big sea-birds! Very good. Then I propose that we continue our journey as fast as possible, lest our island should be converted into a dream before we get completely round it."

Now, as we continued on our way, I pondered much over this new discovery and the singular appearance of these birds, of which Jack could only give us a very slight and vague account; and I began to long to commence our boat, in order that we might go and inspect them more narrowly. But by degrees these thoughts left me, and I began to be much taken up again with the interesting peculiarities of the country which we were passing through.

The second night we passed in a manner somewhat similar to the first-at about two-thirds of the way round the island, as we calculated-and we hoped to sleep on the night following at our bower. I will not here note so particularly all that we said and saw during the course of this second day, as we did not make any further discoveries of great importance. The shore along which we travelled, and the various parts of the woods through which we passed, were similar to those which have been already treated of. There were one or two observations that we made, however, and these were as follows:

We saw that, while many of the large fruit-bearing trees grew only in the valleys, and some of them only near the banks of the streams, where the soil was peculiarly rich, the cocoa-nut palm grew in every place whatsoever-not only on the hillsides, but also on the seashore, and even, as has been already stated, on the coral reef itself, where the soil, if we may use the name, was nothing better than loose sand mingled with broken shells and coral rock. So near to the sea, too, did this useful tree grow, that in many places its roots were washed by the spray from the breakers. Yet we found the trees growing thus on the sands to be quite as luxuriant as those growing in the valleys, and the fruit as good and refreshing also. Besides this, I noticed that on the summit of the high mountain, which we once more ascended at a different point from our first ascent, were found abundance of shells and broken coral formations, which, Jack and I agreed, proved either that this island must have once been under the sea, or that the sea must once have been above the island: in other words, that as shells and coral could not possibly climb to the mountain-top, they must have been washed upon it while the mountain-top was on a level with the sea. We pondered this very much; and we put to ourselves the question, "What raised the island to its present height above the sea?" But to this we could by no means give to ourselves a satisfactory reply. Jack thought it might have been blown up by a volcano; and Peterkin said he thought it must have jumped up of its own accord! We also noticed, what had escaped us before, that the solid rocks of which the island was formed were quite different from the live coral rocks on the shore, where, the wonderful little insects were continually working. They seemed, indeed, to be of the same material —a substance like limestone; but while the coral rocks were quite full of minute cells in which the insects lived, the other rocks inland were hard and solid, without the appearance of cells at all. Our thoughts and conversations on this subject were sometimes so profound that Peterkin said we should certainly get drowned in them at last, even although we were such good divers! Nevertheless, we did not allow his pleasantry on this and similar points to deter us from making our notes and observations as we went along.

We found several more droves of hogs in the woods, but abstained from killing any of them, having more than sufficient for our present necessities. We saw, also, many of their footprints in this neighbourhood. Among these we also observed the footprints of a smaller animal, which we examined with much care, but could form no certain opinion as to them. Peterkin thought they were those of a little dog, but Jack and I thought differently. We became very curious on this matter, the more so that we observed these footprints to lie scattered about in one locality, as if the animal which had made them was wandering round about in a very irregular manner and without any object in view. Early in the forenoon of our third day we observed these footprints to be much more numerous than ever, and in one particular spot they diverged off into the woods in a regular beaten track, which was, however, so closely beset with bushes that we pushed through it with difficulty. We had now become so anxious to find out what animal this was, and where it went to, that we determined to follow the track and, if possible, clear up the mystery. Peterkin said, in a bantering tone, that he was sure it would be cleared up, as usual, in some frightfully simple way, and prove to be no mystery at all!

The beaten track seemed much too large to have been formed by the animal itself, and we concluded that some larger animal had made it, and that the smaller one made use of it. But everywhere the creeping plants and tangled bushes crossed our path, so that we forced our way along with some difficulty. Suddenly, as we came upon an open space, we heard a faint cry, and observed a black animal standing in the track before us.

"A wild cat!" cried Jack, fitting an arrow to his bow, and discharging it so hastily that he missed the animal, and hit the earth about half-a-foot to one side of it. To our surprise, the wild cat did not fly, but walked slowly towards the arrow and snuffed at it.

"That's the most comical wild cat I ever saw!" cried Jack.

"It's a tame wild cat, I think," said Peterkin, levelling his spear to make a charge.

"Stop!" cried I, laying my hand on his shoulder. "I do believe the poor beast is blind. See, it strikes against the branches as it walks along. It must be a very old one;" and I hastened towards it.

"Only think," said Peterkin with a suppressed laugh, "of a superannuated wild cat!"

We now found that the poor cat was not only blind, or nearly so, but extremely deaf, as it did not hear our footsteps until we were quite close behind it. Then it sprang round, and, putting up its back and tail, while the black hair stood all on end, uttered a hoarse mew and a fuff.

Poor thing said Peterkin, gently extending his hand and endeavouring to pat the cat's head. "Poor pussy! chee, chee, chee! puss, puss, puss! cheetie pussy!"

No sooner did the cat hear these sounds than all signs of anger fled, and advancing eagerly to Peterkin, it allowed itself to be stroked, and rubbed itself against his legs, purring loudly all the time, and showing every symptom of the most extreme delight.

"It's no more a wild cat than I am!" cried Peterkin, taking it in his arms; "it's quite tame. — Poor pussy! cheetie pussy!"

We now crowded around Peterkin, and were not a little surprised-and, to say truth, a good deal affected-by the sight of the poor animal's excessive joy. It rubbed its head against Peterkin's cheek, licked his chin, and thrust its head almost violently into his neck, while it purred more loudly than I ever heard a cat purr before, and appeared to be so much overpowered by its feelings that it occasionally mewed and purred almost in the same breath. Such demonstrations of joy and affection led us at once to conclude that this poor cat must have known man before, and we conjectured that it had been left either accidentally or by design on the island many years ago, and was now evincing its extreme joy at meeting once more with human beings. While we were fondling the cat and talking about it, Jack glanced round the open space in the midst of which we stood.

"Hallo!" exclaimed he; "this looks something like a clearing. The axe has been at work here. Just look at these tree-stumps."

We now turned to examine these, and without doubt we found trees that had been cut down here and there, also stumps and broken branches-all of which, however, were completely covered over with moss, and bore evidence of having been in this condition for some years. No human footprints were to be seen either on the track or among the bushes, but those of the cat were found everywhere. We now determined to follow up the track as far as it went, and Peterkin put the cat down; but it seemed to be so weak, and mewed so very pitifully, that he took it up again and carried it in his arms, where in a few minutes it fell sound asleep.

About ten yards farther on, the felled trees became more numerous, and the track, diverging to the right, followed for a short space the banks of a stream. Suddenly we came to a spot where once must have been a rude bridge, the stones of which were scattered in the stream, and those on each bank entirely covered over with moss. In silent surprise and expectancy we continued to advance, and a few yards farther on, beheld, under the shelter of some bread-fruit trees, a small hut or cottage. I cannot hope to convey to my readers a very correct idea of the feelings that affected us on witnessing this unexpected sight. We stood for a long time in silent wonder, for there was a deep and most melancholy stillness about the place that quite overpowered us; and when we did at length speak, it was in subdued whispers, as if we were surrounded by some awful or supernatural influence. Even Peterkin's voice, usually so quick and lively on all occasions, was hushed now; for there was a dreariness about this silent, lonely, uninhabited cottage-so strange in its appearance, so far away from the usual dwellings of man, so old, decayed, and deserted in its aspect that fell upon our spirits like a thick cloud, and blotted out as with a pall the cheerful sunshine that had filled us since the commencement of our tour round the island.

The hut or cottage was rude and simple in its construction. It was not more than twelve feet long by ten feet broad, and about seven or eight feet high. It had one window, or rather a small frame in which a window might perhaps once have been, but which was now empty. The door was exceedingly low, and formed of rough boards, and the roof was covered with broad cocoa-nut and plantain leaves. But every part of it was in a state of the utmost decay. Moss and green matter grew in spots all over it. The woodwork was quite perforated with holes; the roof had nearly fallen in, and appeared to be prevented from doing so altogether by the thick matting of creeping plants and the interlaced branches which years of neglect had allowed to cover it almost entirely; while the thick, luxuriant branches of the bread-fruit and other trees spread above it, and flung a deep, sombre shadow over the spot, as if to guard it from the heat and the light of day; We conversed long and in whispers about this strange habitation ere we ventured to approach it; and when at length we did so, it was, at least on my part, with feelings of awe.

At first Jack endeavoured to peep in at the window; but from the deep shadow of the trees already mentioned, and the gloom within, he could not clearly discern objects, so we lifted the latch and pushed open the door. We observed that the latch was made of iron, and almost eaten away with rust. In the like condition were also the hinges, which creaked as the door swung back. On entering, we stood still and gazed around us, while we were much impressed with the dreary stillness of the room. But what we saw there surprised and shocked us not a little. There was no furniture in the apartment save a little wooden stool and an iron pot, the latter almost eaten through with rust. In the corner farthest from the door was a low bedstead, on which lay two skeletons, embedded in a little heap of dry dust. With beating hearts we went forward to examine them. One was the skeleton of a man; the other that of a dog, which was extended close beside that of the man, with its head resting on his bosom.

Now we were very much concerned about this discovery, and could scarce refrain from tears on beholding these sad remains. After some time we began to talk about what we had seen, and to examine in and around the hut, in order to discover some clue to the name or history of this poor man, who had thus died in solitude, with none to mourn his loss save his cat and his faithful dog. But we found nothing-neither a book nor a scrap of paper. We found, however, the decayed remnants of what appeared to have been clothing, and an old axe. But none of these things bore marks of any kind, and indeed they were so much decayed as to convince us that they had lain in the condition in which we found them for many years.

This discovery now accounted to us for the tree-stump at the top of the mountain with the initials cut on it; also for the patch of sugar-cane and other traces of man which we had met with in the course of our rambles over the island. And we were much saddened by the reflection that the lot of this poor wanderer might possibly be our own, after many years' residence on the island, unless we should be rescued by the visit of some vessel or the arrival of natives. Having no clue whatever to account for the presence of this poor human being in such a lonely spot, we fell to conjecturing what could have brought him there. I was inclined to think that he must have been a shipwrecked sailor, whose vessel had been lost here, and all the crew been drowned except himself and his dog and cat. But Jack thought it more likely that he had run away from his vessel, and had taken the dog and cat to keep him company. We were also much occupied in our minds with the wonderful difference between the cat and the dog. For here we saw that while the one perished like a loving friend by its master's side, with its head resting on his bosom, the other had sought to sustain itself by prowling abroad in the forest, and had lived in solitude to a good old age. However, we did not conclude from this that the cat was destitute of affection, for we could not forget its emotions on first meeting with us; but we saw from this that the dog had a great deal more of generous love in its nature than the cat, because it not only found it impossible to live after the death of its master, but it must needs, when it came to die, crawl to his side and rest its head upon his lifeless breast.

While we were thinking on these things, and examining into everything about the room, we were attracted by an exclamation from Peterkin.

"I say, Jack," said he, "here is something that will be of use to us."

"What is it?" said Jack, hastening across the room.

"An old pistol," replied Peterkin, holding up the weapon, which he had just pulled from under a heap of broken wood and rubbish that lay in a corner.

"That, indeed, might have been useful," said Jack, examining it, "if we had any powder; but I suspect the bow and the sling will prove more serviceable."

"True, I forgot that," said Peterkin; "but we may as well take it with us, for the flint will serve to strike fire with when the sun does not shine."

After having spent more than an hour at this place without discovering anything of further interest, Peterkin took up the old cat, which had lain very contentedly asleep on the stool whereon he had placed it, and we prepared to take our departure. In leaving the hut, Jack stumbled heavily against the door-post, which was so much decayed as to break across, and the whole fabric of the hut seemed ready to tumble about our ears. This put it into our heads that we might as well pull it down, and so form a mound over the skeleton. Jack, therefore, with his axe, cut down the other door-post, which, when it was done, brought the whole hut in ruins to the ground, and thus formed a grave to the bones of the poor recluse and his dog. Then we left the spot, having brought away the iron pot, the pistol, and the old axe, as they might be of much use to us hereafter.

During the rest of this day we pursued our journey, and examined the other end of the large valley, which we found to be so much alike to the parts already described that I shall not recount the particulars of what we saw in this place. I may, however, remark that we did not quite recover our former cheerful spirits until we arrived at our bower, which we did late in the evening, and found everything just in the same condition as we had left it three days before.

CHAPTER TWELVE

Something wrong with the tank-Jack's wisdom and Peterkin's impertinence-Wonderful behaviour of a crab-Good wishes for those who dwell far from the sea-Jack commences to build a little boat.

Rest is sweet, as well for the body as for the mind. During my long experience, amid the vicissitudes of a chequered life, I have found that periods of profound rest at certain intervals, in addition to the ordinary hours of repose, are necessary to the well-being of man. And the nature, as well as the period, of this rest varies according to the different temperaments of individuals and the peculiar circumstances in which they may chance to be placed. To those who work with their minds, bodily labour is rest; to those who labour with the body, deep sleep is rest; to the downcast, the weary, and the sorrowful, joy and peace are rest. Nay, further, I think that to the gay, the frivolous, the reckless, when sated with pleasures that cannot last, even sorrow proves to be rest of a kind, although, perchance, it were better that I should call it relief than rest. There is, indeed, but one class of men to whom rest is denied-there is no rest to the wicked. At this I do but hint, however, as I treat not of that rest which is spiritual, but more particularly of that which applies to the mind and to the body.

Of this rest we stood much in need on our return home, and we found it exceedingly sweet when we indulged in it after completing the journey just related. It had not, indeed, been a very long journey; nevertheless, we had pursued it so diligently that our frames were not a little prostrated. Our minds were also very much exhausted in consequence of the many surprises, frequent alarms, and much profound thought to which they had been subjected; so that when we lay down, on the night of our return, under the shelter of the bower, we fell immediately into very deep repose. I can state this with much certainty; for Jack afterwards admitted the fact, and Peterkin, although he stoutly denied it, I heard snoring loudly at least two minutes after lying down. In this condition we remained all night and the whole of the following day without awaking once, or so much as moving our positions. When we did awake it was near sunset, and we were all in such a state of lassitude that we merely rose to swallow a mouthful of food. As Peterkin remarked, in the midst of a yawn, we took breakfast at tea-time, and then went to bed again, where we lay till the following forenoon.

After this we arose very greatly refreshed, but much alarmed lest we had lost count of a day. I say we were much alarmed on this head; for we had carefully kept count of the days, since we were cast upon our island, in order that we might remember the Sabbath-day, which day we had hitherto, with one accord, kept as a day of rest, and refrained from all work whatsoever. However, on considering the subject, we all three entertained the same opinion as to how long we had slept, and so our minds were put at ease.

We now hastened to our Water Garden to enjoy a bathe, and to see how did the animals which I had placed in the tank. We found the garden more charming, pellucid, and inviting than ever; and Jack and I plunged into its depths and gambolled among its radiant coral groves, while Peterkin wallowed at the surface, and tried occasionally to kick us as we passed below. Having dressed, I then hastened to the tank; but what was my surprise and grief to find nearly all the animals dead, and the water in a putrid condition! I was greatly distressed at this, and wondered what could be the cause of it.

"Why, you precious humbug!" said Peterkin, coming up to me, "how could you expect it to be otherwise? When fishes are accustomed to live in the Pacific Ocean, how can you expect them to exist in a hole like that?"

"Indeed, Peterkin," I replied, "there seems to be truth in what you say. Nevertheless, now I think of it, there must be some error in your reasoning; for if I put in but a few very small animals, they will bear the same proportion to this pond that the millions of fish bear to the ocean."

"I say, Jack!" cried Peterkin, waving his hand; "come here, like a good fellow. Ralph is actually talking philosophy. Do come to our assistance, for he's out o' sight beyond me already!"

"What's the matter?" inquired Jack, coming up, while he endeavoured to scrub his long hair dry with a towel of cocoa-nut cloth.

I repeated my thoughts to Jack, who, I was happy to find, quite agreed with me. "The best plan," he said, "will be to put very few animals at first into your tank, and add more as you find it will bear them. And look here," he added, pointing to the sides of the tank, which, for the space of two inches above the water-level, were encrusted with salt, "you must carry your philosophy a little further, Ralph. That water has evaporated so much that it is too salt for anything to live in. You will require to add *fresh* water now and then, in order to keep it at the same degree of saltness as the sea."

"Very true, Jack; that never struck me before," said I.

"And, now I think of it," continued Jack, "it seems to me that the surest way of arranging your tank so as to get it to keep pure and in good condition will be to *imitate* the ocean in it; in fact, make it a miniature Pacific. I don't see how you can hope to succeed unless you do that."

"Most true," said I, pondering what my companion said. "But I fear that that will be very difficult."

"Not at all," cried Jack, rolling his towel up into a ball and throwing it into the face of Peterkin, who had been grinning and winking at him during the last five minutes —"not at all. Look here. There is water of a certain saltness in the sea; well, fill your tank with sea-water, and keep it at that saltness by marking the height at which the water stands on the sides. When it evaporates a little, pour in *fresh* water from the brook till it comes up to the mark, and then it will be right, for the salt does not evaporate with the water. Then there's lots of seaweed in the sea; well, go and get one or two bits of seaweed and put them into your tank. Of course the weed must be alive, and growing to little stones; or you can chip a bit off the rocks with the weed sticking to it. Then, if you like, you can throw a little sand and gravel into your tank, and the thing's complete."

"Nay, not quite," said Peterkin, who had been gravely attentive to this off-hand advice —"not quite. You must first make three little men to dive in it before it can be said to be perfect; and that would be rather difficult, I fear, for two of them would require to be philosophers. But hallo! what's this? —I say, Ralph, look here! There's one o' your crabs up to something uncommon. It's performing the most remarkable operation for a crab I ever saw-taking off its coat, I do believe, before going to bed!"

We hastily stooped over the tank, and certainly were not a little amused at the conduct of one of the crabs which still survived its companions. It was one of the common small crabs, like to those that are found running about everywhere on the coast of England. While we gazed at it we observed its back to split away from the lower part of its body, and out of the gap thus formed came a soft lump which moved and writhed unceasingly. This lump continued to increase in size until it appeared like a bunch of crab's legs; and, indeed, such it proved in a very few minutes to be, for the points of the toes were at length extricated from the hole in its back, the legs spread out, the body followed, and the crab walked away quite entire, even to the points of its nipper-claws, leaving a perfectly entire shell behind it, so that, when we looked, it seemed as though there were two complete crabs instead of one.

"Well," exclaimed Peterkin, drawing a long breath, "I've *heard* of a man jumping out of his skin and sitting down in his skeleton in order to cool himself, but I never expected to *see* a crab do it!"

We were, in truth, much amazed at this spectacle, and the more so when we observed that the new crab was larger than the crab that it came out of. It was also quite soft, but by next morning its skin had hardened into a good shell. We came thus to know that crabs grow in this way, and not by the growing of their shells, as we had always thought before we saw this wonderful operation.

Now I considered well the advice which Jack had given me about preparing my tank, and the more I thought of it the more I came to regard it as very sound and worthy of being acted on. So I forthwith put his plan in execution, and found it to answer excellently well-indeed, much beyond my expectation; for I found that after a little experience had taught me the proper proportion of seaweed and animals to put into a certain amount of water, the tank needed no further attendance. And, moreover, I did not require ever afterwards to renew or change the sea-water, but only to add a very little fresh water from the brook, now and then, as the other evaporated. I therefore concluded that if I had been suddenly conveyed, along with my tank, into some region where there was no salt sea at all, my little sea and my sea-fish would have continued to thrive and to prosper notwithstanding. This made me greatly to desire that those people in the world who live far inland might know of my wonderful tank, and by having materials like to those of which it was made conveyed to them, thus be enabled to watch the habits of those most mysterious animals that reside in the sea, and examine with their own eyes the wonders of the great deep.

For many days after this, while Peterkin and Jack were busily employed in building a little boat out of the curious natural planks of the chestnut-tree, I spent much of my time in examining with the burning-glass the marvellous operations that were constantly going on in my tank. Here I saw those anemones which cling, like little red, yellow, and green blobs of jelly, to the rocks, put forth, as it were, a multitude of arms and wait till little fish or other small animalcules unwarily touched them, when they would instantly seize them, fold arm after arm round their victims, and so engulf them in their stomachs. Here I saw the ceaseless working of those little coral insects whose efforts have encrusted the islands of the Pacific with vast rocks, and surrounded them with enormous reefs; and I observed that many of these insects, though extremely minute, were very beautiful, coming out of their holes in a circle of fine threads, and having the form of a shuttlecock. Here I saw curious little barnacles opening a hole in their backs and constantly putting out a thin, feathery hand, with which, I doubt not, they dragged their food into their mouths. Here, also, I saw those crabs which have shells only on the front of their bodies, but no shell whatever on their remarkably tender tails, so that, in order to find a protection to them, they thrust them into the empty shells of whelks, or some such fish, and when they grow too big for one, change into another. But, most curious of all, I saw an animal which had the wonderful power, when it became ill, of casting its stomach and its teeth away from it, and getting an entirely new set in the course of a few months! All this I saw, and a great deal more, by means of my tank and my burning-glass; but I refrain from setting down more particulars here, as I have still much to tell of the adventures that befell us while we remained on this island.

CHAPTER THIRTEEN

Notable discovery at the spouting cliffs-The mysterious green monster explained-We are thrown into unutterable terror by the idea that Jack is drowned-The diamond cave.

"Come, Jack," cried Peterkin one morning about three weeks after our return from our long excursion, "let's be jolly to-day, and do something vigorous. I'm quite tired of hammering and bammering, hewing and screwing, cutting and butting at that little boat of ours, that seems as hard to build as Noah's ark. Let us go on an excursion to the mountain-top, or have a hunt after the wild ducks, or make a dash at the pigs. I'm quite flat-flat as bad ginger-beer —flat as a pancake; in fact, I want something to rouse me-to toss me up, as it were. Eh! what do you say to it?"

"Well," answered Jack, throwing down the axe with which he was just about to proceed towards the boat, "if that's what you want, I would recommend you to make an excursion to the waterspouts. The last one we had to do with tossed you up a considerable height; perhaps the next will send you higher-who knows? —if you're at all reasonable or moderate in your expectations!"

"Jack, my dear boy," said Peterkin gravely, "you are really becoming too fond of jesting. It's a thing I don't at all approve of; and if you don't give it up, I fear that, for our mutual good, we shall have to part."

"Well, then, Peterkin," replied Jack with a smile, "what would you have?"

"Have?" said Peterkin. "I would *have* nothing. I didn't say I wanted to *have*; I said that I wanted to *do*."

"By the bye," said I, interrupting their conversation, "I am reminded by this that we have not yet discovered the nature of yon curious appearance that we saw near the waterspouts on our journey round the island. Perhaps it would be well to go for that purpose."

"Humph!" ejaculated Peterkin, "I know the nature of it well enough."

"What was it?" said I.

"It was of a *mysterious* nature, to be sure!" said he with a wave of his hand, while he rose from the log on which he had been sitting and buckled on his belt, into which he thrust his enormous club.

"Well, then, let us away to the waterspouts," cried Jack, going up to the bower for his bow and arrows. —"And bring your spear, Peterkin; it may be useful."

We now, having made up our minds to examine into this matter, sallied forth eagerly in the direction of the waterspout rocks, which, as I have before mentioned, were not far from our present place of abode. On arriving there we hastened down to the edge of the rocks and gazed over into the sea, where we observed the pale-green object still distinctly visible, moving its tail slowly to and fro in the water.

"Most remarkable!" said Jack.

"Exceedingly curious!" said I.

"Beats everything!" said Peterkin. —"Now, Jack," he added, "you made such a poor figure in your last attempt to stick that object that I would advise you to let me try it. If it has got a heart at all, I'll engage to send my spear right through the core of it; if it hasn't got a heart, I'll send it through the spot where its heart ought to be."

"Fire away, then, my boy," replied Jack with a laugh.

Peterkin immediately took the spear, poised it for a second or two above his head, then darted it like an arrow into the sea. Down it went straight into the centre of the green object, passed quite through it, and came up immediately afterwards, pure and unsullied, while the mysterious tail moved quietly as before!

"Now," said Peterkin gravely, "that brute is a heartless monster; I'll have nothing more to do with it."

"I'm pretty sure now," said Jack, "that it is merely a phosphoric light; but I must say I'm puzzled at its staying always in that exact spot."

I also was much puzzled, and inclined to think with Jack that it must be phosphoric light, of which luminous appearance we had seen much while on our voyage to these seas. "But," said I, "there is nothing to hinder us from diving down to it, now that we are sure it is not a shark."

"True," returned Jack, stripping off his clothes. "I'll go down, Ralph, as I'm better at diving than you are. —Now, then, Peterkin, out o' the road!" Jack stepped forward, joined his hands above his head, bent over the rocks, and plunged into the sea. For a second or two the spray caused by his dive hid him from view; then the water became still, and we saw him swimming far down in the midst of the green object. Suddenly he sank below it, and vanished altogether from our sight! We gazed anxiously down at the spot where he had disappeared for nearly a minute, expecting every moment to see him rise again for breath; but fully a minute passed and still he did not reappear. Two minutes passed! and then a flood of alarm rushed in upon my soul when I considered that, during all my acquaintance with him, Jack had never stayed under water more than a minute at a time-indeed, seldom so long.

"Oh Peterkin!" I said in a voice that trembled with increasing anxiety, "something has happened. It is more than three minutes now." But Peterkin did not answer; and I observed that he was gazing down into the water with a look of intense fear mingled with anxiety, while his face was overspread with a deadly paleness. Suddenly he sprang to his feet and rushed about in a frantic state, wringing his hands, and exclaiming, "Oh Jack! Jack! He is gone! It must have been a shark, and he is gone for ever!"

For the next five minutes I know not what I did; the intensity of my feelings almost bereft me of my senses. But I was recalled to myself by Peterkin seizing me by the shoulders and staring wildly into my face, while he exclaimed, "Ralph! Ralph! perhaps he has only fainted! Dive for him, Ralph!"

It seemed strange that this did not occur to me sooner. In a moment I rushed to the edge of the rocks, and without waiting to throw off my garments, was on the point to spring into the waves when I observed something black rising up through the green object. In another moment Jack's head rose to the surface, and he gave a wild shout, flinging back the spray from his locks, as was his wont after a dive. Now we were almost as much amazed at seeing him reappear, well and strong, as we had been at first at his non-appearance; for, to the best of our judgment, he had been nearly ten minutes under water-perhaps longer-and it required no exertion of our reason to convince us that this was utterly impossible for mortal man to do and retain his strength and faculties. It was, therefore, with a feeling akin to superstitious awe that I held down my hand and assisted him to clamber up the steep rocks. But no such feeling affected Peterkin. No sooner did Jack gain the rocks and seat himself on one, panting for breath, than he threw his arms round his neck and burst into a flood of tears. "Oh Jack! Jack!" said he, "where were you? What kept you so long?"

After a few moments Peterkin became composed enough to sit still and listen to Jack's explanation, although he could not restrain himself from attempting to wink every two minutes at me in order to express his joy at Jack's safety. I say he attempted to wink, but I am bound to add that he did not succeed; for his eyes were so much swollen with weeping that his frequent attempts only resulted in a series of violent and altogether idiotical contortions of the face, that were very far from expressing what he intended. However, I knew what the poor fellow meant by it; so I smiled to him in return, and endeavoured to make believe that he was winking.

"Now, lads," said Jack when we were composed enough to listen to him, "yon green object is not a shark; it is a stream of light issuing from a cave in the rocks. Just after I made my dive, I observed that this light came from the side of the rock above which we are now sitting; so I struck out for it, and saw an opening into some place or other that appeared to be luminous within. For one instant I paused to think whether I ought to venture. Then I made up my mind and dashed into it; for you see, Peterkin, although I take some time to tell this, it happened in the space of a few seconds, so that I knew I had wind enough in me to serve to bring me out o' the hole and up to the surface again. Well, I was just on the point of turning-for I began to feel a little uncomfortable in such a place-when it seemed to me as if there was a faint light right above me. I darted upwards, and found my head out of water. This relieved me greatly, for I now felt that I could take in air enough to enable me to return the way I came. Then it all at once occurred to me that I might not be able to find the way out again; but on glancing downwards, my mind was put quite at rest by seeing the green light below me streaming into the cave, just like the light that we had seen streaming out of it, only what I now saw was much brighter.

"At first I could scarcely see anything as I gazed around me, it was so dark; but gradually my eyes became accustomed to it, and I found that I was in a huge cave, part of the walls of which I observed on each side of me. The ceiling just above me was also visible, and I fancied that I could perceive beautiful, glittering objects there; but the farther end of the cave was shrouded in darkness. While I was looking around me in great wonder, it came into my head that you two would think I was drowned; so I plunged down through the passage again in a great hurry, rose to the surface, and-here I am!"

When Jack concluded his recital of what he had seen in this remarkable cave, I could not rest satisfied till I had dived down to see it; which I did, but found it so dark, as Jack had said, that I could scarcely see anything. When I returned we had a long conversation about, it, during which I observed that Peterkin had a most lugubrious expression on his countenance.

"What's the matter, Peterkin?" said I.

"The matter?" he replied. "It's all very well for you two to be talking away like mermaids about the wonders of this cave; but you know I must be content to hear about it, while you are enjoying yourselves down there like mad dolphins. It's really too bad!"

"I'm very sorry for you, Peterkin-indeed I am," said Jack; "but we cannot help you. If you would only learn to dive —"

"Learn to fly, you might as well say!" retorted Peterkin in a very sulky tone.

"If you would only consent to keep still," said I, "we would take you down with us in ten seconds."

"Hum!" returned Peterkin; "suppose a salamander was to propose to you 'only to keep still' and he would carry you through a blazing fire in a few seconds, what would you say?"

We both laughed and shook our heads, for it was evident that nothing was to be made of Peterkin in the water. But we could not rest satisfied till we had seen more of this cave; so, after further consultation, Jack and I determined to try if we could take down a torch with us, and set fire to it in the cavern. This we found to be an undertaking of no small difficulty, but we accomplished it at last by the following means: First, we made a torch of a very inflammable nature out of the bark of a certain tree, which we cut into strips, and after twisting, cemented together with a kind of resin or gum, which we also obtained from another tree; neither of which trees, however, was known by name to Jack. This, when prepared, we wrapped up in a great number of plies of cocoa-nut cloth, so that we were confident it could not get wet during the short time it should be under water. Then we took a small piece of the tinder, which we had carefully treasured up lest we should require it, as before said, when the sun should fail us; also, we rolled up some dry grass and a few chips, which, with a little bow and drill, like those described before, we made into another bundle and wrapped it up in cocoa-nut cloth. When all was ready we laid aside our garments, with the exception of our trousers, which, as we did not know what rough scraping against the rocks we might be subjected to, we kept on.

Then we advanced to the edge of the rocks-Jack carrying one bundle, with the torch; I the other, with the things for producing fire.

"Now don't weary for us, Peterkin, should we be gone some time," said Jack. "We'll be sure to return in half-an-hour at the very latest, however interesting the cave should be, that we may relieve your mind."

"Farewell!" said Peterkin, coming up to us with a look of deep but pretended solemnity, while he shook hands and kissed each of us on the cheek —"farewell! And while you are gone I shall repose my weary limbs under the shelter of this bush, and meditate on the changefulness of all things earthly, with special reference to the forsaken condition of a poor shipwrecked sailor-boy!" So saying, Peterkin waved his hand, turned from us, and cast himself upon the ground with a look of melancholy resignation, which was so well feigned that I would have thought it genuine had he not accompanied it with a gentle wink. We both laughed, and springing from the rocks together, plunged head first into the sea.

We gained the interior of the submarine cave without difficulty, and on emerging from the waves, supported ourselves for some time by treading water, while we held the two bundles above our heads. This we did in order to let our eyes become accustomed to the obscurity. Then, when we could see sufficiently, we swam to a shelving rock, and landed in safety. Having wrung the water from our trousers, and dried ourselves as well as we could under the circumstances, we proceeded to ignite the torch. This we accomplished without difficulty in a few minutes; and no sooner did it flare up than we were struck dumb with the wonderful objects that were revealed to our gaze. The roof of the cavern just above us seemed to be about ten feet high, but grew higher as it receded into the distance until it was lost in darkness. It seemed to be made of coral, and was supported by massive columns of the same material. Immense icicles (as they appeared to us) hung from it in various places. These, however, were formed, not of ice, but of a species of limestone, which seemed to flow in a liquid form towards the point of each, where it became solid. A good many drops fell, however, to the rock below, and these formed little cones, which rose to meet the points above. Some of them had already met, and thus we saw how the pillars were formed, which at first seemed to us as if they had been placed there by some human architect to support the roof. As we advanced farther in we saw that the floor was composed of the same material as the pillars, and it presented the curious appearance of ripples such as are formed on water when gently ruffled by the wind. There were several openings on either hand in the walls that seemed to lead into other caverns, but these we did not explore at this time. We also observed that the ceiling was curiously marked in many places, as if it were the fretwork of a noble cathedral; and the walls, as well as the roof, sparkled in the light of our torch, and threw back gleams and flashes as if they were covered with precious stones. Although we proceeded far into this cavern, we did not come to the end of it; and we were obliged to return more speedily than we would otherwise have done, as our torch was nearly expended. We did not observe any openings in the roof, or any indications of places whereby light might enter; but near the entrance to the cavern stood an immense mass of pure-white coral rock, which caught and threw back the little light that found an entrance through the cave's mouth, and thus produced, we conjectured, the pale-green object which had first attracted our attention. We concluded, also, that the reflecting power of this rock was that which gave forth the dim light that faintly illumined the first part of the cave.

Before diving through the passage again we extinguished the small piece of our torch that remained, and left it in a dry spot-conceiving that we might possibly stand in need of it if, at any future time, we should chance to wet our torch while diving into the cavern. As we stood for a few minutes after it was out, waiting till our eyes became accustomed to the gloom, we could not help remarking the deep, intense stillness and the unutterable gloom of all around us; and as I thought of the stupendous dome above, and the countless gems that had sparkled in the torchlight a few minutes before, it came into my mind to consider how strange it is that God should make such wonderful and exquisitely beautiful works never to be seen at all-except, indeed, by chance visitors such as ourselves.

I afterwards found that there were many such caverns among the islands of the South Seas, some of them larger and more beautiful than the one I have just described.

"Now, Ralph, are you ready?" said Jack in a low voice, that seemed to echo up into the dome above.

"Quite ready."

"Come along, then," said he; and plunging off the ledge of the rock into the water, we dived through the narrow entrance. In a few seconds we were panting on the rocks above, and receiving the congratulations of our friend Peterkin.

CHAPTER FOURTEEN

Strange peculiarity of the tides-Also of the twilight-Peterkin's remarkable conduct in embracing a little pig and killing a big sow-Sage remarks on jesting-Also on love.

It was quite a relief to us to breathe the pure air and to enjoy the glad sunshine after our long ramble in the Diamond Cave, as we named it; for although we did not stay more than half-an-hour away, it seemed to us much longer. While we were dressing, and during our walk home, we did our best to satisfy the curiosity of poor Peterkin, who seemed to regret, with lively sincerity, his inability to dive.

There was no help for it, however, so we condoled with him as we best could. Had there been any great rise or fall in the tide of these seas, we might perhaps have found it possible to take him down with us at low water; but as the tide never rose or fell more than eighteen inches or two feet, this was impossible.

This peculiarity of the tide-its slight rise and fall-had not attracted our observation till some time after our residence on the island. Neither had we observed another curious circumstance until we had been some time there. This was the fact that the tide rose and fell with constant regularity, instead of being affected by the changes of the moon as in our own country, and as it is in most other parts of the world-at least, in all those parts with which I am acquainted. Every day and every night, at twelve o'clock precisely, the tide is at the full; and at six o'clock, every morning and evening, it is ebb. I can speak with much confidence on this singular circumstance, as we took particular note of it, and never found it to alter. Of course I must admit we had to guess the hour of twelve midnight, and I think we could do this pretty correctly; but in regard to twelve noon we are quite positive, because we easily found the highest point that the sun reached in the sky by placing ourselves at a certain spot whence we observed the sharp summit of a cliff resting against the sky, just where the sun passed.

Jack and I were surprised that we had not noticed this the first few days of our residence here, and could only account for it by our being so much taken up with the more obvious wonders of our novel situation. I have since learned, however, that this want of observation is a sad and very common infirmity of human nature, there being hundreds of persons before whose eyes the most wonderful things are passing every day who nevertheless, are totally ignorant of them. I therefore have to record my sympathy with such persons, and to recommend to them a course of conduct which I have now for a long time myself adopted-namely, the habit of forcing my attention upon all things that go on around me, and of taking some degree of interest in them whether I feel it naturally or not. I suggest this the more earnestly, though humbly, because I have very frequently come to know that my indifference to a thing has generally been caused by my ignorance in regard to it.

We had much serious conversation on this subject of the tides; and Jack told us, in his own quiet, philosophical way, that these tides did great good to the world in many ways, particularly in the way of cleansing the shores of the land, and carrying off the filth that was constantly poured into the sea therefrom-which, Peterkin suggested, was remarkably tidy of it to do. Poor Peterkin could never let slip an opportunity to joke, however inopportune it might be, which at first we found rather a disagreeable propensity, as it often interrupted the flow of very agreeable conversation-and, indeed, I cannot too strongly record my disapprobation of this tendency in general; but we became so used to it at last that we found it no interruption whatever. Indeed, strange to say, we came to feel that it was a necessary part of our enjoyment (such is the force of habit), and found the sudden outbursts of mirth, resulting from his humorous disposition, quite natural and refreshing to us in the midst of our more serious conversations. But I must not misrepresent Peterkin. We often found, to our surprise, that he knew many things which we did not; and I also observed that those things which he learned from experience were never forgotten. From all these things I came at length to understand that things very opposite and dissimilar in themselves, when united, do make an agreeable whole; as, for example, we three on this our island, although most unlike in many things, when united, made a trio so harmonious that I question if there ever met before such an agreeable triumvirate. There was, indeed, no note of discord whatever in the symphony we played together on that sweet Coral Island; and I am now persuaded that this was owing to our having been all tuned to the same key-namely, that of *love*! Yes, we loved one another with much fervency while we lived on that island; and, for the matter of that, we love each other still.

And while I am on this subject, or rather the subject that just preceded it-namely, the tides — I may here remark on another curious natural phenomenon. We found that there was little or no twilight in this island. We had a distinct remembrance of the charming long twilight at home, which some people think the most delightful part of the day-though, for my part, I have always preferred sunrise; and when we first landed, we used to sit down on some rocky point or eminence, at the close of our day's work, to enjoy the evening breeze, but no sooner had the sun sunk below the horizon than all became suddenly dark. This rendered it necessary that we should watch the sun when we happened to be out hunting; for to be suddenly left in the dark while in the woods was very perplexing, as, although the stars shone with great beauty and brilliancy, they could not pierce through the thick umbrageous boughs that interlaced above our heads.

But to return. After having told all we could to Peterkin about the Diamond Cave under Spouting Cliff, as we named the locality, we were wending our way rapidly homewards when a grunt and a squeal were borne down by the land breeze to our ears.

"That's the ticket!" was Peterkin's remarkable exclamation as he started convulsively and levelled his spear.

"Hist!" cried Jack; "these are your friends, Peterkin. They must have come over expressly to pay you a friendly visit, for it is the first time we have seen them on this side of the island."

"Come along!" cried Peterkin, hurrying towards the wood; while Jack and I followed, smiling at his impatience.

Another grunt and half-a-dozen squeals, much louder than before, came down the valley. At this time we were just opposite the small vale which lay between the Valley of the Wreck and Spouting Cliff.

"I say, Peterkin!" cried Jack in a hoarse whisper.

"Well, what is't?"

"Stay a bit, man! These grunters are just up there on the hillside. If you go and stand with Ralph in the lee of yon cliff I'll cut round behind and drive them through the gorge, so that you'll have a better chance of picking out a good one. Now, mind you pitch into a fat young pig, Peterkin!" added Jack as he sprang into the bushes.

"Won't I, just!" said Peterkin, licking his lips, as we took our station beside the cliff. "I feel quite a tender affection for young pigs in my heart. Perhaps it would be more correct to say in my tum —"

"There they come!" cried I as a terrific yell from Jack sent the whole herd screaming down the hill. Now Peterkin, being unable to hold back, crept a short way up a very steep grassy mound in order to get a better view of the hogs before they came up; and just as he raised his head above its summit, two little pigs, which had outrun their companions, rushed over the top with the utmost precipitation. One of these brushed close past Peterkin's ear; the other, unable to arrest its headlong flight, went, as Peterkin himself afterwards expressed it, 'bash' into his arms with a sudden squeal, which was caused more by the force of the blow than the will of the animal, and both of them rolled violently down to the foot of the mound. No sooner was this reached than the little pig recovered its feet, tossed up its tail, and fled shrieking from the spot. But I slung a large stone after it, which, being fortunately well aimed, hit it behind the ear and felled it to the earth.

"Capital, Ralph! that's your sort!" cried Peterkin, who, to my surprise and great relief, had risen to his feet apparently unhurt, though much dishevelled. He rushed frantically towards the gorge, which the yells of the hogs told us they were now approaching. I had made up my mind that I would abstain from killing another, as, if Peterkin should be successful, two were more than sufficient for our wants at the present time. Suddenly they all burst forth-two or three little round ones in advance, and an enormous old sow with a drove of hogs at her heels.

"Now, Peterkin," said I, "there's a nice little fat one; just spear it."

But Peterkin did not move; he allowed it to pass unharmed. I looked at him in surprise, and saw that his lips were compressed and his eyebrows knitted, as if he were about to fight with some awful enemy.

"What is it?" I inquired with some trepidation.

Suddenly he levelled his spear, darted forward, and with a yell that nearly froze the blood in my veins, stabbed the old sow to the heart. Nay, so vigorously was it done that the spear went in at one side and came out at the other!

"Oh Peterkin!" said I, going up to him, "what have you done?"

"Done? I've killed their great-great-grandmother, that's all," said he, looking with a somewhat awestruck expression at the transfixed animal.

"Hallo! what's this?" said Jack as he came up. "Why, Peterkin, you must be fond of a tough chop. If you mean to eat this old hog, she'll try your jaws, I warrant. What possessed you to stick *her*, Peterkin?"

"Why, the fact is, I want a pair of shoes."

"What have your shoes to do with the old hog?" said I, smiling.

"My present shoes have certainly nothing to do with her," replied Peterkin; "nevertheless, she will have a good deal to do with my future shoes. The fact is, when I saw you floor that pig so neatly, Ralph, it struck me that there was little use in killing another. Then I remembered all at once that I had long wanted some leather or tough substance to make shoes of, and this old grandmother seemed so tough that I just made up my mind to stick her-and you see I've done it!"

"That you certainly have, Peterkin," said Jack as he was examining the transfixed animal.

We now considered how we were to carry our game home, for, although the distance was short, the hog was very heavy. At length we hit on the plan of tying its four feet together, and passing the spear-handle between them. Jack took one end on his shoulder, I took the other on mine, and Peterkin carried the small pig.

Thus we returned in triumph to our bower, laden, as Peterkin remarked, with the glorious spoils of a noble hunt. As he afterwards spoke in similarly glowing terms in reference to the supper that followed, there is every reason to believe that we retired that night to our leafy beds in a high state of satisfaction.

CHAPTER FIFTEEN

Boat-building extraordinary-Peterkin tries his hand at cookery, and fails most signally-The boat finished-Curious conversation with the cat, and other matters.

For many days after this, Jack applied himself with unremitting assiduity to the construction of our boat, which at length began to look something like one. But those only who have had the thing to do can entertain a right idea of the difficulty involved in such an undertaking, with no other implements than an axe, a bit of hoop-iron, a sail-needle, and a broken penknife. But Jack did it. He was of that disposition which *will* not be conquered. When he believed himself to be acting rightly, he overcame all obstacles. I have seen Jack, when doubtful whether what he was about to do were right or wrong, as timid and vacillating as a little girl; and I honour him for it!

As this boat was a curiosity in its way, a few words here relative to the manner of its construction may not be amiss.

I have already mentioned the chestnut-tree with its wonderful buttresses or planks. This tree, then, furnished us with the chief part of our material. First of all, Jack sought out a limb of a tree of such a form and size as, while it should form the keel, a bend at either end should form the stem and stern-posts. Such a piece, however, was not easy to obtain; but at last he procured it by rooting up a small tree which had a branch growing at the proper angle about ten feet up its stem, with two strong roots growing in such a form as enabled him to make a flat-sterned boat. This placed, he procured three branching roots of suitable size, which he fitted to the keel at equal distances, thus forming three strong ribs. Now the squaring and shaping of these, and the cutting of the grooves in the keel, was an easy enough matter, as it was all work for the axe, in the use of which Jack was become wonderfully expert; but it was quite a different affair when he came to nailing the ribs to the keel, for we had no instrument capable of boring a large hole, and no nails to fasten them with. We were, indeed, much perplexed here; but Jack at length devised an instrument that served very well. He took the remainder of our hoop-iron and beat it into the form of a pipe or cylinder, about as thick as a man's finger. This he did by means of our axe and the old rusty axe we had found at the house of the poor man at the other side of the island. This, when made red hot, bored slowly through the timbers; and the better to retain the heat, Jack shut up one end of it and filled it with sand. True, the work was very slowly done; but it mattered not-we had little else to do. Two holes were bored in each timber, about an inch and a half apart, and also down into the keel, but not quite through. Into these were placed stout pegs made of a tree called iron-wood, and when they were hammered well home, the timbers were as firmly fixed as if they had been nailed with iron. The gunwales, which were very stout, were fixed in a similar manner. But besides the wooden nails, they were firmly lashed to the stem and stern-posts and ribs by means of a species of cordage which we had contrived to make out of the fibrous husk of the cocoa-nut. This husk was very tough, and when a number of the threads were joined together they formed excellent cordage. At first we tied the different lengths together; but this was such a clumsy and awkward complication of knots that we contrived, by careful interlacing of the ends together before twisting, to make good cordage of any size or length we chose. Of course it cost us much time and infinite labour; but Jack kept up our spirits when we grew weary, and so all that we required was at last constructed.

Planks were now cut off the chestnut-trees of about an inch thick. These were dressed with the axe-but clumsily, for an axe is ill-adapted for such work. Five of these planks on each side were sufficient; and we formed the boat in a very rounded, barrel-like shape, in order to have as little twisting of the planks as possible, for although we could easily bend them, we could not easily twist them. Having no nails to rivet the planks with, we threw aside the ordinary fashion of boat-building and adopted one of our own. The planks were therefore placed on each other's edges, and sewed together with the tough cordage already mentioned; they were also thus sewed to the stem, the stern, and the keel. Each stitch or tie was six inches apart, and was formed thus: Three holes were bored in the upper plank and three in the lower, the holes being above each other-that is, in a vertical line. Through these holes the cord was passed, and when tied, formed a powerful stitch of three-ply. Besides this, we placed between the edges of the planks layers of cocoa-nut fibre, which, as it swelled when wetted, would, we hoped, make our little vessel water-tight. But in order further to secure this end, we collected a large quantity of pitch from the bread-fruit tree, with which, when boiled in our old iron pot, we paid the whole of the inside of the boat, and while it was yet hot, placed large pieces of cocoa-nut cloth on it, and then gave it another coat above that. Thus the interior was covered with a tough, water-tight material; while the exterior, being uncovered, and so exposed to the swelling action of the water, was, we hoped, likely to keep the boat quite dry. I may add that our hopes were not disappointed.

While Jack was thus engaged, Peterkin and I sometimes assisted him; but as our assistance was not much required, we more frequently went a-hunting on the extensive mud-flats at the entrance of the long valley which lay nearest to our bower. Here we found large flocks of ducks of various kinds, some of them bearing so much resemblance to the wild ducks of our own country that I think they must have been the same. On these occasions we took the bow and the sling, with both of which we were often successful, though I must confess that I was the least so. Our suppers were thus pleasantly varied, and sometimes we had such a profusion spread out before us that we frequently knew not with which of the dainties to begin.

I must also add that the poor old cat which we had brought home had always a liberal share of our good things; and so well was it looked after, especially by Peterkin, that it recovered much of its former strength, and seemed to improve in sight as well as hearing.

The large flat stone, or rock of coral, which stood just in front of the entrance to our bower, was our table. On this rock we had spread out the few articles we possessed the day we were shipwrecked; and on the same rock, during many a day afterwards, we spread out the bountiful supply with which we had been blessed on our Coral Island. Sometimes we sat down at this table to a feast consisting of hot rolls-as Peterkin called the newly baked bread-fruit —a roast pig, roast duck, boiled and roasted yams, cocoa-nuts, taro, and sweet potatoes; which we followed up with a dessert of plums, apples, and plantains-the last being a large-sized and delightful fruit, which grew on a large shrub or tree not more than twelve feet high, with light-green leaves of enormous length and breadth. These luxurious feasts were usually washed down with cocoa-nut lemonade.

Occasionally Peterkin tried to devise some new dish —"a conglomerate," as he used to say; but these generally turned out such atrocious compounds that he was ultimately induced to give up his attempts in extreme disgust-not forgetting, however, to point out to Jack that his failure was a direct contradiction to the proverb which he (Jack) was constantly thrusting down his throat-namely, that "where there's a will there's a way." For he had a great will to become a cook, but could by no means find a way to accomplish that end.

One day, while Peterkin and I were seated beside our table, on which dinner was spread, Jack came up from the beach, and flinging down his axe, exclaimed:

"There, lads, the boat's finished at last! So we've nothing to do now but shape two pair of oars, and then we may put to sea as soon as we like."

This piece of news threw us into a state of great joy; for although we were aware that the boat had been gradually getting near its completion, it had taken so long that we did not expect it to be quite ready for at least two or three weeks. But Jack had wrought hard and said nothing, in order to surprise us.

"My dear fellow," cried Peterkin, "you're a perfect trump! But why did you not tell us it was so nearly ready? Won't we have a jolly sail to-morrow, eh?"

"Don't talk so much, Peterkin," said Jack; "and, pray, hand me a bit of that pig."

"Certainly, my dear," cried Peterkin, seizing the axe. "What part will you have? A leg, or a wing, or a piece of the breast-which?"

"A hind leg, if you please," answered Jack; "and, pray, be so good as to include the tail."

"With all my heart," said Peterkin, exchanging the axe for his hoop-iron knife, with which he cut off the desired portion. "I'm only too glad, my dear boy, to see that your appetite is so wholesale, and there's no chance whatever of its dwindling down into re-tail again-at least, in so far as this pig is concerned. —Ralph, lad, why don't you laugh, eh?" he added, turning suddenly to me with a severe look of inquiry.

"Laugh!" said I. "What at, Peterkin? Why should I laugh?"

Both Jack and Peterkin answered this inquiry by themselves laughing so immoderately that I was induced to believe I had missed noticing some good joke, so I begged that it might be explained to me; but as this only produced repeated roars of laughter, I smiled and helped myself to another slice of plantain.

"Well, but," continued Peterkin, "I was talking of a sail to-morrow. Can't we have one, Jack?"

"No," replied Jack, "we can't have a sail; but I hope we shall have a row, as I intend to work hard at the oars this afternoon, and if we can't get them finished by sunset, we'll light our candle-nuts, and turn them out of hands before we turn into bed."

"Very good," said Peterkin, tossing a lump of pork to the cat, who received it with a mew of satisfaction. "I'll help you, if I can."

"Afterwards," continued Jack, "we will make a sail out of the cocoa-nut cloth, and rig up a mast; and then we shall be able to sail to some of the other islands, and visit our old friends the penguins."

The prospect of being so soon in a position to extend our observations to the other islands, and enjoy a sail over the beautiful sea, afforded us much delight, and after dinner we set about making the oars in good earnest. Jack went into the woods and blocked them roughly out with the axe, and I smoothed them down with the knife, while Peterkin remained in the bower spinning, or rather twisting, some strong, thick cordage with which to fasten them to the boat.

We worked hard and rapidly, so that when the sun went down Jack and I returned to the bower with four stout oars, which required little to be done to them save a slight degree of polishing with the knife. As we drew near we were suddenly arrested by the sound of a voice. We were not a little surprised at this-indeed, I may almost say alarmed; for although Peterkin was undoubtedly fond of talking, we had never, up to this time, found him talking to himself. We listened intently, and still heard the sound of a voice as if in conversation. Jack motioned me to be silent, and advancing to the bower on tiptoe, we peeped in.

The sight that met our gaze was certainly not a little amusing. On the top of a log which we sometimes used as a table sat the black cat with a very demure expression on its countenance, and in front of it, sitting on the ground with his legs extended on either side of the log, was Peterkin. At the moment we saw him he was gazing intently into the cat's face, with his nose about four inches from it, his hands being thrust into his breeches pockets.

"Cat," said Peterkin, turning his head a little on one side, "I love you!"

There was a pause, as if Peterkin awaited a reply to this affectionate declaration. But the cat said nothing.

"Do you hear me?" cried Peterkin sharply. "I love you —I do! Don't you love me?"

To this touching appeal the cat said "mew" faintly.

"Ah, that's right! You're a jolly old rascal! Why did you not speak at once, eh?" and Peterkin put forward his mouth and kissed the cat on the nose!

"Yes," continued Peterkin after a pause, "I love you. D'you think I'd say so if I didn't, you black villain? I love you because I've got to take care of you, and to look after you, and to think about you, and to see that you don't die —"

"Mew, me-a-w!" said the cat.

"Very good," continued Peterkin; "quite true, I have no doubt. But you've no right to interrupt me, sir. Hold your tongue till I have done speaking. Moreover, cat, I love you because you came to me the first time you ever saw me, and didn't seem to be afraid, and appeared to be fond of me, though you didn't know that I wasn't going to kill you. Now that was brave, that was bold, and very jolly, old boy, and I love you for it —I do!"

Again there was a pause of a few minutes, during which the cat looked placid, and Peterkin dropped his eyes upon its toes as if in contemplation. Suddenly he looked up.

"Well, cat, what are you thinking about now? Won't speak, eh? Now tell me: don't you think it's a monstrous shame that those two scoundrels, Jack and Ralph, should keep us waiting for our supper so long?"

Here the cat arose, put up its back and stretched itself, yawned slightly, and licked the point of Peterkin's nose!

"Just so, old boy; you're a clever fellow. —I really do believe the brute understands me!" said Peterkin, while a broad grin overspread his face as he drew back and surveyed the cat.

At this point Jack burst into a loud fit of laughter. The cat uttered an angry fuff and fled, while Peterkin sprang up and exclaimed:

"Bad luck to you, Jack! You've nearly made the heart jump out of my body, you have!"

"Perhaps I have," replied Jack, laughing, as we entered the bower; "but as I don't intend to keep you or the cat any longer from your supper, I hope that you'll both forgive me."

Peterkin endeavoured to turn this affair off with a laugh. But I observed that he blushed very deeply at the time we discovered ourselves, and he did not seem to relish any allusion to the subject afterwards; so we refrained from remarking on it ever after, though it tickled us not a little at the time.

After supper we retired to rest, and to dream of wonderful adventures in our little boat and distant voyages upon the sea.

CHAPTER SIXTEEN

The boat launched-We visit the coral reef-The great breaker that never goes down-Coral insects-The way in which coral islands are made-The boats sail-We tax our ingenuity to form fish-hooks —Some of the fish we saw-And a monstrous whale-Wonderful shower of little fish-Waterspouts.

It was a bright, clear, beautiful morning when we first launched our little boat and rowed out upon the placid waters of the lagoon. Not a breath of wind ruffled the surface of the deep. Not a cloud spotted the deep-blue sky. Not a sound that was discordant broke the stillness of the morning, although there were many sounds-sweet, tiny, and melodious-that mingled in the universal harmony of nature. The sun was just rising from the Pacific's ample bosom, and tipping the mountain-tops with a red glow. The sea was shining like a sheet of glass, yet heaving with the long, deep swell that, all the world round, indicates the life of Ocean; and the bright seaweeds and the brilliant corals shone in the depths of that pellucid water, as we rowed over it, like rare and precious gems. Oh, it was a sight fitted to stir the soul of man to its profoundest depths! and if he owned a heart at all, to lift that heart in adoration and gratitude to the great Creator of this magnificent and glorious universe!

At first, in the strength of our delight, we rowed hither and thither without aim or object. But after the effervescence of our spirits was abated, we began to look about us and to consider what we should do.

"I vote that we row to the reef," cried Peterkin.

"And I vote that we visit the islands within the lagoon," said I.

"And I vote we do both," cried Jack; "so pull away, boys!"

As I have already said, we had made four oars; but our boat was so small that only two were necessary. The extra pair were reserved in case any accident should happen to the others. It was therefore only needful that two of us should row, while the third steered by means of an oar-and relieved the rowers occasionally.

First we landed on one of the small islands and ran all over it, but saw nothing worthy of particular notice. Then we landed on a larger island, on which were growing a few cocoa-nut trees. Not having eaten anything that morning, we gathered a few of the nuts and breakfasted. After this we pulled straight out to sea, and landed on the coral reef.

This was indeed a novel and interesting sight to us. We had now been so long on shore that we had almost forgotten the appearance of breakers, for there were none within the lagoon. But now, as we stood beside the foam-crested billow of the open sea, all the enthusiasm of the sailor was awakened in our breasts; and as we gazed on the widespread ruin of that single magnificent breaker that burst in thunder at our feet, we forgot the Coral Island behind us, we forgot our bower and the calm repose of the scented woods, we forgot all that had passed during the last few months, and remembered nothing but the storms, the calms, the fresh breezes, and the surging billows of the open sea.

This huge, ceaseless breaker, to which I have so often alluded, was a much larger and more sublime object than we had at all imagined it to be. It rose many yards above the level of the sea, and could be seen approaching at some distance from the reef. Slowly and majestically it came on, acquiring greater volume and velocity as it advanced, until it assumed the form of a clear watery arch, which sparkled in the bright sun. On it came with resistless and solemn majesty, the upper edge lipped gently over, and it fell with a roar that seemed as though the heart of Ocean were broken in the crash of tumultuous water, while the foam-clad coral reef appeared to tremble beneath the mighty shock!

We gazed long and wonderingly at this great sight, and it was with difficulty we could tear ourselves away from it. As I have once before mentioned, this wave broke in many places over the reef and scattered some of its spray into the lagoon; but in most places the reef was sufficiently broad and elevated to receive and check its entire force. In many places the coral rocks were covered with vegetation-the beginning, as it appeared to us, of future islands. Thus, on this reef, we came to perceive how most of the small islands of those seas are formed. On one part we saw the spray of the breaker washing over the rocks, and millions of little, active, busy creatures continuing the work of building up this living rampart. At another place, which was just a little too high for the waves to wash over it, the coral insects were all dead; for we found that they never did their work above water. They had faithfully completed the mighty work which their Creator had given them to do, and they were now all dead. Again, in other spots the ceaseless lashing of the sea had broken the dead coral in pieces, and cast it up in the form of sand. Here sea-birds had alighted, little pieces of seaweed and stray bits of wood had been washed up, seeds of plants had been carried by the wind, and a few lovely blades of bright green had already sprung up, which, when they died, would increase the size and fertility of these emeralds of Ocean. At other places these islets had grown apace, and were shaded by one or two cocoa-nut trees, which grew literally in the sand, and were constantly washed by the ocean spray-yet, as I have before remarked, their fruit was most refreshing and sweet to our taste.

Again, at this time Jack and I pondered the formation of the large coral islands. We could now understand how the low ones were formed; but the larger islands cost us much consideration, yet we could arrive at no certain conclusion on the subject.

Having satisfied our curiosity, and enjoyed ourselves during the whole day in our little boat, we returned, somewhat wearied, and withal rather hungry, to our bower.

"Now," said Jack, "as our boat answers so well we will get a mast and sail made immediately."

"So we will!" cried Peterkin as we all assisted to drag the boat above high-water mark. "We'll light our candle and set about it this very night. Hurrah, my boys, pull away!"

As we dragged our boat, we observed that she grated heavily on her keel; and as the sands were in this place mingled with broken coral rocks, we saw portions of the wood being scraped off.

"Hallo!" cried Jack on seeing this, "that won't do. Our keel will be worn off in no time at this rate."

"So it will," said I, pondering deeply as to how this might be prevented. But I am not of a mechanical turn naturally, so I could conceive no remedy save that of putting a plate of iron on the keel; but as we had no iron, I knew not what was to be done. "It seems to me, Jack," I added, "that it is impossible to prevent the keel being worn off thus."

"Impossible?" cried Peterkin. "My dear Ralph, you are mistaken; there is nothing so easy."

"How?" I inquired in some surprise.

"Why, by not using the boat at all!" replied Peterkin.

"Hold your impudent tongue, Peterkin!" said Jack as he shouldered the oars. "Come along with me, and I'll give you work to do. In the first place, you will go and collect coca-nut fibre, and set to work to make sewing-twine with it —"

"Please, captain," interrupted Peterkin, "I've got lots of it made already-more than enough, as a little friend of mine used to be in the habit of saying every day after dinner."

"Very well," continued Jack; "then you'll help Ralph to collect cocoa-nut cloth and cut it into shape, after which we'll make a sail of it. I'll see to getting the mast and the gearing; so let's to work."

And to work we went right busily, so that in three days from that time we had set up a mast and sail, with the necessary rigging, in our little boat. The sail was not, indeed, very handsome to look at, as it was formed of a number of oblong patches of cloth; but we had sewed it well by means of our sail-needle, so that it was strong, which was the chief point. —Jack had also overcome the difficulty about the keel by pinning to it a *false* keel. This was a piece of tough wood, of the same length and width as the real keel, and about five inches deep. He made it of this depth because the boat would be thereby rendered not only much more safe, but more able to beat against the wind-which, in a sea where the trade-winds blow so long and so steadily in one direction, was a matter of great importance. This piece of wood was pegged very firmly to the keel; and we now launched our boat with the satisfaction of knowing that when the false keel should be scraped off we could easily put on another, —whereas, should the real keel have been scraped away, we could not have renewed it without taking our boat to pieces, which Peterkin said made his "marrow quake to think upon."

The mast and sail answered excellently; and we now sailed about in the lagoon with great delight, and examined with much interest the appearance of our island from a distance. Also, we gazed into the depths of the water, and watched for hours the gambols of the curious and bright-coloured fish among the corals and seaweed. Peterkin also made a fishing-line; and Jack constructed a number of hooks, some of which were very good, others remarkably bad. Some of these hooks were made of iron-wood —which did pretty well, the wood being extremely hard-and Jack made them very thick and large. Fish there are not particular. Some of the crooked bones in fish-heads also answered for this purpose pretty well. But that which formed our best and most serviceable hook was the brass finger-ring belonging to Jack. It gave him not a little trouble to manufacture it. First he cut it with the axe, then twisted it into the form of a hook. The barb took him several hours to cut. He did it by means of constant sawing with the broken penknife. As for the point, an hour's rubbing on a piece of sandstone made an excellent one.

It would be a matter of much time and labour to describe the appearance of the multitudes of fish that were day after day drawn into our boat by means of the brass hook. Peterkin always caught them-for we observed that he derived much pleasure from fishing-while Jack and I found ample amusement in looking on, also in gazing down at the coral groves, and in baiting the hook. Among the fish that we saw, but did not catch, were porpoises and swordfish, whales and sharks. The porpoises came frequently into our lagoon in shoals, and amused us not a little by their bold leaps into the air and their playful gambols in the sea. The swordfish were wonderful creatures-some of them apparently ten feet in length, with an ivory spear six or eight feet long projecting from their noses. We often saw them darting after other fish, and no doubt they sometimes killed them with their ivory swords. Jack remembered having heard once of a swordfish attacking a ship, which seemed strange indeed; but as they are often in the habit of attacking whales, perhaps it mistook the ship for one. This swordfish ran against the vessel with such force that it drove its sword quite through the thick planks; and when the ship arrived in harbour, long afterwards, the sword was found still sticking in it!

Sharks did not often appear; but we took care never again to bathe in deep water without leaving one of our number in the boat, to give us warning if he should see a shark approaching. As for the whales, they never came into our lagoon; but we frequently saw them spouting in the deep water beyond the reef. I shall never forget my surprise the first day I saw one of these huge monsters close to me. We had been rambling about on the reef during the morning, and were about to re-embark in our little boat to return home, when a loud blowing sound caused us to wheel rapidly round. We were just in time to see a shower of spray falling, and the flukes or tail of some monstrous fish disappear in the sea a few hundred yards off. We waited some time to see if he would rise again. As we stood, the sea seemed to open up at our very feet; an immense spout of water was sent with a snort high into the air, and the huge, blunt head of a sperm-whale rose before us. It was so large that it could easily have taken our little boat, along with ourselves, into its mouth! It plunged slowly back into the sea, like a large ship foundering, and struck the water with its tail so forcibly as to cause a sound like a cannon-shot.

We also saw a great number of flying-fish, although we caught none; and we noticed that they never flew out of the water except when followed by their bitter foe the dolphin, from whom they thus endeavoured to escape. But of all the fish that we saw, none surprised us so much as those that we used to find in shallow pools after a shower of rain; and this not on account of their appearance, for they were ordinary-looking and very small, but on account of their having descended in a shower of rain! We could account for them in no other way, because the pools in which we found these fish were quite dry before the shower, and at some distance above high-water mark. Jack, however, suggested a cause which seemed to me very probable. We used often to see waterspouts in the sea. A waterspout is a whirling body of water, which rises from the sea like a sharp-pointed pillar. After rising a good way, it is met by a long tongue, which comes down from the clouds; and when the two have joined, they look something like an hour-glass. The waterspout is then carried by the wind-sometimes gently, sometimes with violence-over the sea, sometimes up into the clouds; and then, bursting asunder, it descends in a deluge. This often happens over the land as well as over the sea; and it sometimes does much damage, but frequently it passes gently away. Now, Jack thought that the little fish might perhaps have been carried up in a waterspout, and so sent down again in a shower of rain. But we could not be certain as to this point, yet we thought it likely.

During these delightful fishing and boating excursions we caught a good many eels, which we found to be very good to eat. We also found turtles among the coral rocks, and made excellent soup in our iron kettle. Moreover, we discovered many shrimps and prawns, so that we had no lack of variety in our food; and, indeed, we never passed a week without making some new and interesting discovery of some sort or other, either on the land or in the sea.

CHAPTER SEVENTEEN

> A monster wave and its consequences-The boat lost and found-Peterkin's terrible accident-Supplies of food for a voyage in the boat-We visit Penguin Island, and are amazed beyond measure-Account of the penguins.

One day, not long after our little boat was finished, we were sitting on the rocks at Spouting Cliff, and talking of an excursion which we intended to make to Penguin Island the next day.

"You see," said Peterkin, "it might be all very well for a stupid fellow like me to remain here and leave the penguins alone; but it would be quite inconsistent with your characters as philosophers to remain any longer in ignorance of the habits and customs of these birds, so the sooner we go the better."

"Very true," said I. "There is nothing I desire so much as to have a closer inspection of them."

"And I think," said Jack, "that you had better remain at home, Peterkin, to take care of the cat; for I'm sure the hogs will be at it in your absence, out of revenge for your killing their great-grandmother so recklessly."

"Stay at home!" cried Peterkin. "My dear fellow, you would certainly lose your way, or get upset, if I were not there to take care of you."

"Ah, true!" said Jack gravely; "that did not occur to me. No doubt you must go. Our boat does require a good deal of ballast; and all that you say, Peterkin, carries so much weight with it that we won't need stones if you go."

Now, while my companions were talking, a notable event occurred, which, as it is not generally known, I shall be particular in recording here.

While we were talking, as I have said, we noticed a dark line, like a low cloud or fog-bank, on the seaward horizon. The day was a fine one, though cloudy, and a gentle breeze was blowing; but the sea was not rougher, or the breaker on the reef higher, than usual. At first we thought that this looked like a thundercloud, and as we had had a good deal of broken weather of late, accompanied by occasional peals of thunder, we supposed that a storm must be approaching. Gradually, however, this line seemed to draw nearer without spreading up over the sky, as would certainly have been the case if it had been a storm-cloud. Still nearer it came, and soon we saw that it was moving swiftly towards the island; but there was no sound till it reached the islands out at sea. As it passed these islands we observed, with no little anxiety, that a cloud of white foam encircled them, and burst in spray into the air; it was accompanied by a loud roar. This led us to conjecture that the approaching object was an enormous wave of the sea; but we had no idea how large it was till it came near to ourselves. When it approached the outer reef, however, we were awestruck with its unusual magnitude; and we sprang to our feet, and clambered hastily up to the highest point of the precipice, under an indefinable feeling of fear.

I have said before that the reef opposite Spouting Cliff was very near to the shore, while just in front of the bower it was at a considerable distance out to sea. Owing to this formation, the wave reached the reef at the latter point before it struck at the foot of Spouting Cliff. The instant it touched the reef we became aware, for the first time, of its awful magnitude. It burst completely over the reef at all points with a roar that seemed louder to me than thunder, and this roar continued for some seconds while the wave rolled gradually along towards the cliff on which we stood. As its crest reared before us we felt that we were in great danger, and turned to flee; but we were too late. With a crash that seemed to shake the solid rock, the gigantic billow fell, and instantly the spouting-holes sent up a gush of waterspouts with such force that they shrieked on issuing from their narrow vents. It seemed to us as if the earth had been blown up with water. We were stunned and confused by the shock, and so drenched and blinded with spray that we knew not for a few moments whither to flee for shelter. At length we all three gained an eminence beyond the reach of the water. But what a scene of devastation met our gaze as we looked along the shore! This enormous wave not only burst over the reef, but continued its way across the lagoon, and fell on the sandy beach of the island with such force that it passed completely over it and dashed into the woods, levelling the smaller trees and bushes in its headlong course.

On seeing this, Jack said he feared our bower must have been swept away, and that the boat, which was on the beach, must have been utterly destroyed. Our hearts sank within us as we thought of this, and we hastened round through the woods towards our home. On reaching it we found, to our great relief of mind, that the force of the wave had been expended just before reaching the bower; but the entrance to it was almost blocked up by the torn-up bushes and tangled heaps of seaweed. Having satisfied ourselves as to the bower, we hurried to the spot where the boat had been left; but no boat was there. The spot on which it had stood was vacant, and no sign of it could we see on looking around us.

"It may have been washed up into the woods," said Jack, hurrying up the beach as he spoke. Still no boat was to be seen, and we were about to give ourselves over to despair when Peterkin called to Jack and said:

"Jack, my friend, you were once so exceedingly sagacious and wise as to make me acquainted with the fact that cocoa-nuts grow upon trees. Will you now be so good as to inform me what sort of fruit that is growing on the top of yonder bush? for I confess to being ignorant, or at least doubtful, on the point."

We looked towards the bush indicated, and there, to our surprise, beheld our little boat snugly nestled among the leaves. We were very much overjoyed at this, for we would have suffered any loss rather than the loss of our boat. We found that the wave had actually borne the boat on its crest from the beach into the woods, and there launched it into the heart of this bush, which was extremely fortunate; for had it been tossed against a rock or a tree, it would have been dashed to pieces, whereas it had not received the smallest injury. It was no easy matter, however, to get it out of the bush and down to the sea again. This cost us two days of hard labour to accomplish.

We had also much ado to clear away the rubbish from before the bower, and spent nearly a week in constant labour ere we got the neighbourhood to look as clean and orderly as before; for the uprooted bushes and seaweed that lay on the beach formed a more dreadfully confused-looking mass than one who had not seen the place after the inundation could conceive.

Before leaving the subject I may mention, for the sake of those who interest themselves in the curious natural phenomena of our world, that this gigantic wave occurs regularly on some of the islands of the Pacific once, and sometimes twice, in the year. I heard this stated by the missionaries during my career in those seas. They could not tell me whether it visited all of the islands, but I was certainly assured that it occurred periodically in some of them.

After we had got our home put to rights, and cleared of the débris of the inundation, we again turned our thoughts to paying the penguins a visit. The boat was therefore overhauled and a few repairs done. Then we prepared a supply of provisions, for we intended to be absent at least a night or two-perhaps longer. This took us some time to do; for, while Jack was busy with the boat, Peterkin was sent into the woods to spear a hog or two, and had to search long, sometimes, ere he found them. Peterkin was usually sent on this errand when we wanted a pork chop (which was not seldom), because he was so active and could run so wonderfully fast that he found no difficulty in overtaking the hogs; but being dreadfully reckless, he almost invariably tumbled over stumps and stones in the course of his wild chase, and seldom returned home without having knocked the skin off his shins. Once, indeed, a more serious accident happened to him. He had been out all the morning alone, and did not return at the usual time to dinner. We wondered at this, for Peterkin was always very punctual at the dinner-hour. As supper-time drew near we began to be anxious about him, and at length sallied forth to search the woods. For a long time we sought in vain; but a little before dark we came upon the tracks of the hogs, which we followed up until we came to the brow of a rather steep bank or precipice. Looking over this, we beheld Peterkin lying in a state of insensibility at the foot, with his cheek resting on the snout of a little pig, which was pinned to the earth by the spear. We were dreadfully alarmed, but hastened to bathe his forehead with water, and had soon the satisfaction of seeing him revive. After we had carried him home, he related to us how the thing had happened.

"You must know," said he, "I walked about all the forenoon, till I was as tired as an old donkey, without seeing a single grunter-not so much as a track of one; but as I was determined not to return empty-handed, I resolved to go without my dinner, and —"

"What!" exclaimed Jack, "did you *really* resolve to do that?"

"Now, Jack, hold your tongue," returned Peterkin. "I say that I resolved to forego my dinner and to push to the head of the small valley, where I felt pretty sure of discovering the hogs. I soon found that I was on the right scent, for I had scarcely walked half-a-mile in the direction of the small plum-tree we found there the other day when a squeak fell on my ear. 'Ho, ho,' said I, 'there you go, my boys;' and I hurried up the glen. I soon started them, and singling out a fat pig, ran tilt at him. In a few seconds I was up with him, and stuck my spear right through his dumpy body. Just as I did so, I saw that we were on the edge of a precipice-whether high or low, I knew not; but I had been running at such a pace that I could not stop, so the pig and I gave a howl in concert and went plunging over together. I remembered nothing more after that till I came to my senses, and found you bathing my temples, and Ralph wringing his hands over me."

But although Peterkin was often unfortunate in the way of getting tumbles, he was successful on the present occasion in hunting, and returned before evening with three very nice little hogs. I also was successful in my visit to the mud-flats, where I killed several ducks. So that when we launched and loaded our boat at sunrise the following morning, we found our store of provisions to be more than sufficient. Part had been cooked the night before, and on taking note of the different items, we found the account to stand thus:

10 Bread-fruits (two baked, eight unbaked).
20 Yams (six roasted, the rest raw).
6 Taro-roots.
50 Fine large plums.
6 Cocoa-nuts, ripe.
6 Ditto, green (for drinking).
4 Large ducks and two small ones, raw.
3 Cold roast pigs, with stuffing.

I may here remark that the stuffing had been devised by Peterkin specially for the occasion. He kept the manner of its compounding a profound secret, so I cannot tell what it was; but I can say, with much confidence, that we found it to be atrociously bad, and after the first tasting, scraped it carefully out and threw it overboard. We calculated that this supply would last us for several days; but we afterwards found that it was much more than we required, especially in regard to the cocoa-nuts, of which we found large supplies wherever we went. However, as Peterkin remarked, it was better to have too much than too little, as we knew not to what straits we might be put during our voyage.

It was a very calm, sunny morning when we launched forth and rowed over the lagoon towards the outlet in the reef, and passed between the two green islets that guarded the entrance. We experienced some difficulty and no little danger in passing the surf of the breaker, and shipped a good deal of water in the attempt; but once past the billow, we found ourselves floating placidly on the long, oily swell that rose and fell slowly as it rolled over the wide ocean.

Penguin Island lay on the other side of our own island, at about a mile beyond the outer reef, and we calculated that it must be at least twenty miles distant by the way we should have to go. We might, indeed, have shortened the way by coasting round our island inside of the lagoon, and going out at the passage in the reef nearly opposite to Penguin Island; but we preferred to go by the open sea-first, because it was more adventurous, and secondly, because we should have the pleasure of again feeling the motion of the deep, which we all loved very much, not being liable to sea-sickness.

"I wish we had a breeze," said Jack.

"So do I," cried Peterkin, resting on his oar and wiping his heated brow; "pulling is hard work. Oh dear, if we could only catch a hundred or two of these gulls, tie them to the boat with long strings, and make them fly as we want them, how capital it would be!"

"Or bore a hole through a shark's tail and reeve a rope through it, eh?" remarked Jack. "But, I say, it seems that my wish is going to be granted, for here comes a breeze. Ship your oar, Peterkin. —Up with the mast, Ralph; I'll see to the sail. Mind your helm; look out for squalls!"

This last speech was caused by the sudden appearance of a dark-blue line on the horizon, which, in an incredibly short space of time, swept down on us, lashing up the sea in white foam as it went. We presented the stern of the boat to its first violence, and in a few seconds it moderated into a steady breeze, to which we spread our sail and flew merrily over the waves. Although the breeze died away soon afterwards, it had been so stiff while it lasted that we were carried over the greater part of our way before it fell calm again; so that when the flapping of the sail against the mast told us that it was time to resume the oars, we were not much more than a mile from Penguin Island.

"There go the soldiers!" cried Peterkin as we came in sight of it. "How spruce their white trousers look this morning! I wonder if they will receive us kindly? —D'you think they are hospitable, Jack?"

"Don't talk, Peterkin, but pull away, and you shall see shortly."

As we drew near to the island, we were much amused by the manoeuvres and appearance of these strange birds. They seemed to be of different species: for some had crests on their heads, while others had none; and while some were about the size of a goose, others appeared nearly as large as a swan. We also saw a huge albatross soaring above the heads of the penguins. It was followed and surrounded by numerous flocks of sea-gulls. Having approached to within a few yards of the island, which was a low rock, with no other vegetation on it than a few bushes, we lay on our oars and gazed at the birds with surprise and pleasure, they returning our gaze with interest. We now saw that their soldierlike appearance was owing to the stiff erect manner in which they sat on their short legs —"bolt-upright," as Peterkin expressed it. They had black heads, long, sharp beaks, white breasts, and bluish backs. Their wings were so short that they looked more like the fins of a fish, and indeed we soon saw that they used them for the purpose of swimming under water. There were no quills on these wings, but a sort of scaly feathers, which also thickly covered their bodies. Their legs were short, and placed so far back that the birds, while on land, were obliged to stand quite upright in order to keep their balance; but in the water they floated like other water-fowl. At first we were so stunned with the clamour which they and other sea-birds kept up around us that we knew not which way to look, for they covered the rocks in thousands; but as we continued to gaze, we observed several quadrupeds (as we thought) walking in the midst of the penguins.

"Pull in a bit," cried Peterkin, "and let's see what these are. They must be fond of noisy company to consort with such creatures."

To our surprise, we found that these were no other than penguins which had gone down on all fours, and were crawling among the bushes on their feet and wings, just like quadrupeds. Suddenly one big old bird, that had been sitting on a point very near to us, gazing in mute astonishment, became alarmed, and scuttling down the rocks, plumped or fell, rather than ran, into the sea. It dived in a moment, and, a few seconds afterwards, came out of the water far ahead with such a spring, and such a dive back into the sea again, that we could scarcely believe it was not a fish that had leaped in sport.

"That beats everything!" said Peterkin, rubbing his nose, and screwing up his face with an expression of exasperated amazement. "I've heard of a thing being neither fish, flesh, nor fowl; but I never did expect to live to see a brute that was all three together-at once-in one! But look there!" he continued, pointing with a look of resignation to the shore —"look there! there's no end to it. What has that brute got under its tail?"

We turned to look in the direction pointed out, and there saw a penguin walking slowly and very sedately along the shore with an egg under its tail. There were several others, we observed, burdened in the same way; and we found afterwards that these were a species of penguin that always carried their eggs so. Indeed, they had a most convenient cavity for the purpose, just between the tail and the legs. We were very much impressed with the regularity and order of this colony. The island seemed to be apportioned out into squares, of which each penguin possessed one, and sat in stiff solemnity in the middle of it, or took a slow march up and down the spaces between. Some were hatching their eggs, but others were feeding their young ones in a manner that caused us to laugh not a little. The mother stood on a mound or raised rock, while the young one stood patiently below her on the ground. Suddenly the mother raised her head and uttered a series of the most discordant cackling sounds.

"She's going to choke," cried Peterkin.

But this was not the case, although, I confess, she looked like it. In a few seconds she put down her head and opened her mouth, into which the young one thrust its beak and seemed to suck something from her throat. Then the cackling was renewed, the sucking continued, and so the operation of feeding was carried on till the young one was satisfied; but what she fed her little one with we could not tell.

"Now, just look yonder!" said Peterkin in an excited tone. "If that isn't the most abominable piece of maternal deception I ever saw! That rascally old lady penguin has just pitched her young one into the sea, and there's another about to follow her example."

This indeed seemed to be the case, for on the top of a steep rock close to the edge of the sea we observed an old penguin endeavouring to entice her young one into the water; but the young one seemed very unwilling to go, and notwithstanding the enticements of its mother, moved very slowly towards her. At last she went gently behind the young bird and pushed it a little towards the water, but with great tenderness, as much as to say, "Don't be afraid, darling; I won't hurt you, my pet!" But no sooner did she get it to the edge of the rock, where it stood looking pensively down at the sea, than she gave it a sudden and violent push, sending it headlong down the slope into the water, where its mother left it to scramble ashore as it best could. We observed many of them employed in doing this, and we came to the conclusion that this is the way in which old penguins teach their children to swim.

Scarcely had we finished making our remarks on this, when we were startled by about a dozen of the old birds hopping in the most clumsy and ludicrous manner towards the sea. The beach here was a sloping rock, and when they came to it some of them succeeded in hopping down in safety, but others lost their balance and rolled and scrambled down the slope in the most helpless manner. The instant they reached the water, however, they seemed to be in their proper element. They dived, and bounded out of it and into it again with the utmost agility; and so, diving and bounding and sputtering-for they could not fly-they went rapidly out to sea.

On seeing this, Peterkin turned with a grave face to us and said, "It's my opinion that these birds are all stark, staring mad, and that this is an enchanted island. I therefore propose that we should either put about ship and fly in terror from the spot, or land valorously on the island and sell our lives as dearly as we can."

"I vote for landing; so pull in, lads!" said Jack, giving a stroke with his oar that made the boat spin. In a few seconds we ran the boat into a little creek, where we made her fast to a projecting piece of coral, and running up the beach, entered the ranks of the penguins, armed with our cudgels and our spear. We were greatly surprised to find that instead of attacking us, or showing signs of fear at our approach, these curious birds did not move from their places until we laid hands on them, and merely turned their eyes on us in solemn, stupid wonder as we passed. There was one old penguin, however, that began to walk slowly towards the sea; and Peterkin took it into his head that he would try to interrupt its progress, so he ran between it and the sea and brandished his cudgel in its face. But this proved to be a resolute old bird. It would not retreat; nay, more, it would not cease to advance, but battled with Peterkin bravely, and drove him before it until it reached the sea. Had Peterkin used his club he could easily have felled it, no doubt; but as he had no wish to do so cruel an act merely out of sport, he let the bird escape.

We spent fully three hours on this island in watching the habit of these curious birds; but when we finally left them, we all three concluded, after much consultation, that they were the most wonderful creatures we had ever seen, and further, we thought it probable that they were the most wonderful creatures in the world!

CHAPTER EIGHTEEN

An awful storm and its consequences-Narrow escape —A rock proves a sure foundation —A fearful night and a bright morning-Deliverance from danger.

It was evening before we left the island of the penguins. As we had made up our minds to encamp for the night on a small island whereon grew a few cocoa-nut trees, which was about two miles off, we lay-to our oars with some energy. But a danger was in store for us which we had not anticipated. The wind, which had carried us so quickly to Penguin Island, freshened as evening drew on to a stiff breeze, and before we had made half the distance to the small island, it became a regular gale. Although it was not so directly against us as to prevent our rowing in the course we wished to go, yet it checked us very much; and although the force of the sea was somewhat broken by the island, the waves soon began to rise and to roll their broken crests against our small craft, so that she began to take in water, and we had much ado to keep ourselves afloat. At last the wind and sea together became so violent that we found it impossible to make the island; so Jack suddenly put the head of the boat round, and ordered Peterkin and me to hoist a corner of the sail, intending to run back to Penguin Island.

"We shall at least have the shelter of the bushes," he said as the boat flew before the wind, "and the penguins will keep us company."

As Jack spoke, the wind suddenly shifted and blew so much against us that we were forced to hoist more of the sail in order to beat up for the island, being by this change thrown much to leeward of it. What made matters worse was that the gale came in squalls, so that we were more than once nearly upset.

"Stand by, both of you!" cried Jack in a quick, earnest tone. "Be ready to deuce the sail. I very much fear we won't make the island after all."

Peterkin and I were so much in the habit of trusting everything to Jack that we had fallen into the way of not considering things, especially such things as were under Jack's care. We had, therefore, never doubted for a moment that all was going well, so that it was with no little anxiety that we heard him make the above remark. However, we had no time for question or surmise, for at the moment he spoke a heavy squall was bearing down upon us, and as we were then flying with our lee gunwale dipping occasionally under the waves, it was evident that we should have to lower our sail altogether. In a few seconds the squall struck the boat; but Peterkin and I had the sail down in a moment, so that it did not upset us. But when it was past we were more than half-full of water. This I soon bailed out, while Peterkin again hoisted a corner of the sail. But the evil which Jack had feared came upon us. We found it quite impossible to make Penguin Island. The gale carried us quickly past it towards the open sea, and the terrible truth flashed upon us that we should be swept out and left to perish miserably in a small boat in the midst of the wide ocean.

This idea was forced very strongly upon us, because we saw nothing in the direction whither the wind was blowing us save the raging billows of the sea; and indeed we trembled as we gazed around us, for we were now beyond the shelter of the islands, and it seemed as though any of the huge billows, which curled over in masses of foam, might swallow us up in a moment. The water also began to wash in over our sides, and I had to keep constantly bailing; for Jack could not quit the helm, nor Peterkin the sail, for an instant, without endangering our lives. In the midst of this distress Jack uttered an exclamation of hope, and pointed towards a low island or rock which lay directly ahead. It had been hitherto unobserved, owing to the dark clouds that obscured the sky and the blinding spray that seemed to fill the whole atmosphere.

As we neared this rock we observed that it was quite destitute of trees and verdure, and so low that the sea broke completely over it. In fact, it was nothing more than the summit of one of the coral formations, which rose only a few feet above the level of the water, and was, in stormy weather, all but invisible. Over this island the waves were breaking in the utmost fury, and our hearts sank within us as we saw that there was not a spot where we could thrust our little boat without its being dashed to pieces.

"Show a little bit more sail!" cried Jack as we swept past the weather side of the rock with fearful speed.

"Ay, ay!" answered Peterkin, hoisting about a foot more of our sail.

Little though the addition was, it caused the boat to lie over and creak so loudly, as we cleft the foaming waves, that I expected to be upset every instant; and I blamed Jack in my heart for his rashness. But I did him injustice; for although during two seconds the water rushed inboard in a torrent, he succeeded in steering us sharply round to the leeward side of the rock, where the water was comparatively calm and the force of the breeze broken.

"Out your oars now, lads! That's well done! Give way!" We obeyed instantly. The oars splashed into the waves together. One good, hearty pull, and we were floating in a comparatively calm creek that was so narrow as to be barely able to admit our boat. Here we were in perfect safety, and as we leaped on shore and fastened our cable to the rocks, I thanked God in my heart for our deliverance from so great danger. But although I have said we were now in safety, I suspect that few of my readers would have envied our position. It is true we had no lack of food; but we were drenched to the skin; the sea was foaming round us, and the spray flying over our heads, so that we were completely enveloped, as it were, in water; the spot on which we had landed was not more than twelve yards in diameter, and from this spot we could not move without the risk of being swept away by the storm. At the upper end of the creek was a small hollow or cave in the rock, which sheltered us from the fury of the winds and waves; and as the rock extended in a sort of ledge over our heads, it prevented the spray from falling upon us.

"Why," said Peterkin, beginning to feel cheery again, "it seems to me that we have got into a mermaid's cave, for there is nothing but water all round us; and as for earth and sky, they are things of the past."

Peterkin's idea was not inappropriate, for what with the sea roaring in white foam up to our very feet, and the spray flying in white sheets continually over our heads, and the water dripping heavily from the ledge above like a curtain in front of our cave, it did seem to us very much more like being below than above water.

"Now, boys," cried Jack, "bestir yourselves, and let's make ourselves comfortable. —Toss out our provisions, Peterkin; and here, Ralph, lend a hand to haul up the boat. Look sharp!"

"Ay, ay, captain!" we cried as we hastened to obey, much cheered by the hearty manner of our comrade.

Fortunately the cave, although not very deep, was quite dry, so that we succeeded in making ourselves much more comfortable than could have been expected. We landed our provisions, wrung the water out of our garments, spread our sail below us for a carpet, and after having eaten a hearty meal, began to feel quite cheerful. But as night drew on our spirits sank again, for with the daylight all evidence of our security vanished away. We could no longer see the firm rock on which we lay, while we were stunned with the violence of the tempest that raged around us. The night grew pitchy dark as it advanced, so that we could not see our hands when we held them up before our eyes, and were obliged to feel each other occasionally to make sure that we were safe, for the storm at last became so terrible that it was difficult to make our voices audible. A slight variation of the wind, as we supposed, caused a few drops of spray ever and anon to blow into our faces; and the eddy of the sea, in its mad boiling, washed up into our little creek until it reached our feet and threatened to tear away our boat. In order to prevent this latter calamity, we hauled the boat farther up and held the cable in our hands. Occasional flashes of lightning shone with a ghastly glare through the watery curtains around us, and lent additional horror to the scene. Yet we longed for those dismal flashes, for they were less appalling than the thick blackness that succeeded them. Crashing peals of thunder seemed to tear the skies in twain, and fell upon our ears through the wild yelling of the hurricane as if it had been but a gentle summer breeze; while the billows burst upon the weather side of the island until we fancied that the solid rock was giving way, and in our agony we clung to the bare ground, expecting every moment to be whirled away and whelmed in the black, howling sea. Oh, it was a night of terrible anxiety! and no one can conceive the feelings of intense gratitude and relief with which we at last saw the dawn of day break through the vapoury mists around us.

For three days and three nights we remained on this rock, while the storm continued to rage with unabated fury. On the morning of the fourth day it suddenly ceased, and the wind fell altogether; but the waves still ran so high that we did not dare to put off in our boat. During the greater part of this period we scarcely slept above a few minutes at a time; but on the third night we slept soundly, and awoke early on the fourth morning to find the sea very much down, and the sun shining brightly again in the clear blue sky.

It was with light hearts that we launched forth once more in our little boat and steered away for our island home, which, we were overjoyed to find, was quite visible on the horizon, for we had feared that we had been blown out of sight of it altogether. As it was a dead calm, we had to row during the greater part of the day; but towards the afternoon a fair breeze sprang up, which enabled us to hoist our sail. We soon passed Penguin Island and the other island which we had failed to reach on the day the storm commenced; but as we had still enough of provisions, and were anxious to get home, we did not land-to the great disappointment of Peterkin, who seemed to entertain quite an affection for the penguins.

Although the breeze was pretty fresh for several hours, we did not reach the outer reef of our island till nightfall; and before we had sailed more than a hundred yards into the lagoon, the wind died away altogether, so that we had to take to our oars again. It was late, and the moon and stars were shining brightly when we arrived opposite the bower and leaped upon the strand. So glad were we to be safe back again on our beloved island that we scarcely took time to drag the boat a short way up the beach, and then ran up to see that all was right at the bower. I must confess, however, that my joy was mingled with a vague sort of fear lest our home had been visited and destroyed during our absence; but on reaching it we found everything just as it had been left, and the poor black cat curled up, sound asleep, on the coral table in front of our humble dwelling.

CHAPTER NINETEEN

Shoemaking-The even tenor of our way suddenly interrupted-An unexpected visit and an appalling battle-We all become warriors, and Jack proves himself to be a hero.

For many months after this we continued to live on our island in uninterrupted harmony and happiness. Sometimes we went out a-fishing in the lagoon, and sometimes went a-hunting in the woods, or ascended to the mountain-top by way of variety, although Peterkin always asserted that we went for the purpose of hailing any ship that might chance to heave in sight. But I am certain that none of us wished to be delivered from our captivity, for we were extremely happy; and Peterkin used to say that as we were very young, we should not feel the loss of a year or two. Peterkin, as I have said before, was thirteen years of age, Jack eighteen, and I fifteen. But Jack was very tall, strong, and manly for his age, and might easily have been mistaken for twenty.

The climate was so beautiful that it seemed to be a perpetual summer, and as many of the fruit-trees continued to bear fruit and blossom all the year round, we never wanted for a plentiful supply of food. The hogs, too, seemed rather to increase than diminish, although Peterkin was very frequent in his attacks on them with his spear. If at any time we failed in finding a drove, we had only to pay a visit to the plum-tree before mentioned, where we always found a large family of them asleep under its branches.

We employed ourselves very busily during this time in making various garments of cocoa-nut cloth, as those with which we had landed were beginning to be very ragged. Peterkin also succeeded in making excellent shoes out of the skin of the old hog in the following manner: He first cut a piece of the hide, of an oblong form, a few inches longer than his foot. This he soaked in water, and while it was wet he sewed up one end of it so as to form a rough imitation of that part of the heel of a shoe where the seam is. This done, he bored a row of holes all round the edge of the piece of skin, through which a tough line was passed. Into the sewed-up part of this shoe he thrust his heel; then, drawing the string tight, the edges rose up and overlapped his foot all round. It is true there were a great many ill-looking puckers in these shoes; but we found them very serviceable notwithstanding, and Jack came at last to prefer them to his long boots. We also made various other useful articles, which added to our comfort, and once or twice spoke of building us a house; but we had so great an affection for the bower, and withal found it so serviceable, that we determined not to leave it, nor to attempt the building of a house, which in such a climate might turn out to be rather disagreeable than useful.

We often examined the pistol that we had found in the house on the other side of the island, and Peterkin wished much that we had powder and shot, as it would render pig-killing much easier; but, after all, we had become so expert in the use of our sling and bow and spear that we were independent of more deadly weapons.

Diving in the Water Garden also continued to afford us as much pleasure as ever, and Peterkin began to be a little more expert in the water from constant practice. As for Jack and me, we began to feel as if water were our native element, and revelled in it with so much confidence and comfort that Peterkin said he feared we would turn into fish some day and swim off and leave him, adding that he had been for a long time observing that Jack was becoming more and more like a shark every day. Whereupon Jack remarked that if he (Peterkin) were changed into a fish, he would certainly turn into nothing better or bigger than a shrimp. Poor Peterkin did not envy us our delightful excursions under water-except, indeed, when Jack would dive down to the bottom of the Water Garden, sit down on a rock, and look up and make faces at him. Peterkin did feel envious then, and often said he would give anything to be able to do that. I was much amused when Peterkin said this; for if he could only have seen his own face when he happened to take a short dive, he would have seen that Jack's was far surpassed by it-the great difference being, however, that Jack made faces on purpose, Peterkin couldn't help it!

Now, while we were engaged with these occupations and amusements, an event occurred one day which was as unexpected as it was exceedingly alarming and very horrible.

Jack and I were sitting, as we were often wont to do, on the rocks at Spouting Cliff, and Peterkin was wringing the water from his garments, having recently fallen by accident into the sea —a thing he was constantly doing-when our attention was suddenly arrested by two objects which appeared on the horizon.

"What are yon, think you?" I said, addressing Jack.

"I can't imagine," answered he. "I've noticed them for some time, and fancied they were black sea-gulls; but the more I look at them, the more I feel convinced they are much larger than gulls."

"They seem to be coming towards us," said I.

"Hallo! what's wrong?" inquired Peterkin, coming up.

"Look there," said Jack.

"Whales!" cried Peterkin, shading his eyes with his hand. "No-eh-can they be boats, Jack?"

Our hearts beat with excitement at the very thought of seeing human faces again.

"I think you are about right, Peterkin. But they seem to me to move strangely for boats," said Jack in a low tone, as if he were talking to himself.

I noticed that a shade of anxiety crossed Jack's countenance as he gazed long and intently at the two objects, which were now nearing us fast. At last he sprang to his feet. "They are canoes, Ralph! whether war-canoes or not, I cannot tell; but this I know-that all the natives of the South Sea Islands are fierce cannibals, and they have little respect for strangers. We must hide if they land here, which I earnestly hope they will not do."

I was greatly alarmed at Jack's speech; but I confess I thought less of what he said than of the earnest, anxious manner in which he said it, and it was with very uncomfortable feelings that Peterkin and I followed him quickly into the woods.

"How unfortunate," said I as we gained the shelter of the bushes, "that we have forgotten our arms!"

"It matters not," said Jack; "here are clubs enough and to spare." As he spoke, he laid his hand on a bundle of stout poles of various sizes, which Peterkin's ever-busy hands had formed, during our frequent visits to the cliff, for no other purpose, apparently, than that of having something to do.

We each selected a stout club according to our several tastes and lay down behind a rock, whence we could see the canoes approach without ourselves being seen. At first we made an occasional remark on their appearance; but after they entered the lagoon and drew near the beach, we ceased to speak, and gazed with intense interest at the scene before us.

We now observed that the foremost canoe was being chased by the other, and that it contained a few women and children as well as men-perhaps forty souls altogether-while the canoe which pursued it contained only men. They seemed to be about the same in number, but were better armed, and had the appearance of being a war-party. Both crews were paddling with all their might, and it seemed as if the pursuers exerted themselves to overtake the fugitives ere they could land. In this, however, they failed. The foremost canoe made for the beach close beneath the rocks behind which we were concealed. Their short paddles flashed like meteors in the water, and sent up a constant shower of spray. The foam curled from the prow, and the eyes of the rowers glistened in their black faces as they strained every muscle of their naked bodies. Nor did they relax their efforts till the canoe struck the beach with a violent shock; then, with a shout of defiance, the whole party sprang, as if by magic, from the canoe to the shore. Three women, two of whom carried infants in their arms, rushed into the woods; and the men crowded to the water's edge, with stones in their hands, spears levelled, and clubs brandished, to resist the landing of their enemies.

The distance between the two canoes had been about half-a-mile, and at the great speed they were going, this was soon passed. As the pursuers neared the shore, no sign of fear or hesitation was noticeable. On they came, like a wild charger-received, but recked not of, a shower of stones. The canoe struck, and with a yell that seemed to issue from the throats of incarnate fiends, they leaped into the water and drove their enemies up the beach.

The battle that immediately ensued was frightful to behold. Most of the men wielded clubs of enormous size and curious shapes, with which they dashed out each other's brains. As they were almost entirely naked, and had to bound, stoop, leap, and run in their terrible hand-to-hand encounters, they looked more like demons than human beings. I felt my heart grow sick at the sight of this bloody battle, and would fain have turned away; but a species of fascination seemed to hold me down and glue my eyes upon the combatants. I observed that the attacking party was led by a most extraordinary being, who, from his size and peculiarity, I concluded was a chief. His hair was frizzed out to an enormous extent, so that it resembled a large turban. It was of a light-yellow hue, which surprised me much, for the man's body was as black as coal, and I felt convinced that the hair must have been dyed. He was tattooed from head to foot; and his face, besides being tattooed, was besmeared with red paint and streaked with white. Altogether, with his yellow turban-like hair, his Herculean black frame, his glittering eyes, and white teeth, he seemed the most terrible monster I ever beheld. He was very active in the fight, and had already killed four men.

Suddenly the yellow-haired chief was attacked by a man quite as strong and large as himself. He flourished a heavy club, something like an eagle's beak at the point. For a second or two these giants eyed each other warily, moving round and round, as if to catch each other at a disadvantage; but seeing that nothing was to be gained by this caution, and that the loss of time might effectually turn the tide of battle either way, they apparently made up their minds to attack at the same instant, for, with a wild shout and simultaneous spring, they swung their heavy clubs, which met with a loud report. Suddenly the yellow-haired savage tripped, his enemy sprang forward, the ponderous club was swung; but it did not descend, for at that moment the savage was felled to the ground by a stone from the hand of one who had witnessed his chief's danger. This was the turning-point in the battle. The savages who landed first turned and fled towards the bush on seeing the fall of their chief. But not one escaped; they were all overtaken and felled to the earth. I saw, however, that they were not all killed. Indeed, their enemies, now that they were conquered, seemed anxious to take them alive; and they succeeded in securing fifteen, whom they bound hand and foot with cords, and carrying them up into the woods, laid them down among the bushes. Here they left them, for what purpose I knew not, and returned to the scene of the late battle, where the remnant of the party were bathing their wounds.

Out of the forty blacks that composed the attacking party only twenty-eight remained alive, two of whom were sent into the bush to hunt for the women and children. Of the other party, as I have said, only fifteen survived, and these were lying bound and helpless on the grass.

Jack and Peterkin and I now looked at each other, and whispered our fears that the savages might clamber up the rocks to search for fresh water, and so discover our place of concealment; but we were so much interested in watching their movements that we agreed to remain where we were-and indeed we could not easily have risen without exposing ourselves to detection. One of the savages now went up to the woods and soon returned with a bundle of firewood, and we were not a little surprised to see him set fire to it by the very same means used by Jack the time we made our first fire-namely, with the bow and drill. When the fire was kindled, two of the party went again to the woods and returned with one of the bound men. A dreadful feeling of horror crept over my heart as the thought flashed upon me that they were going to burn their enemies. As they bore him to the fire my feelings almost overpowered me. I gasped for breath, and seizing my club, endeavoured to spring to my feet; but Jack's powerful arm pinned me to the earth. Next moment one of the savages raised his club and fractured the wretched creature's skull. He must have died instantly; and, strange though it may seem, I confess to a feeling of relief when the deed was done, because I now knew that the poor savage could not be burned alive. Scarcely had his limbs ceased to quiver when the monsters cut slices of flesh from his body, and after roasting them slightly over the fire, devoured them.

Suddenly there arose a cry from the woods, and in a few seconds the two savages hastened towards the fire, dragging the three women and their two infants along with them. One of these women was much younger than her companions, and we were struck with the modesty of her demeanour and the gentle expression of her face, which, although she had the flattish nose and thick lips of the others, was of a light-brown colour, and we conjectured that she must be of a different race. She and her companions wore short petticoats, and a kind of tippet on their shoulders. Their hair was jet black, but instead of being long, was short and curly-though not woolly-somewhat like the hair of a young boy. While we gazed with interest and some anxiety at these poor creatures, the big chief advanced to one of the elder females and laid his hand upon the child. But the mother shrank from him, and clasping the little one to her bosom, uttered a wail of fear. With a savage laugh, the chief tore the child from her arms and tossed it into the sea. A low groan burst from Jack's lips as he witnessed this atrocious act and heard the mother's shriek as she fell insensible on the sand. The rippling waves rolled the child on the beach, as if they refused to be a party in such a foul murder, and we could observe that the little one still lived.

The young girl was now brought forward, and the chief addressed her; but although we heard his voice and even the words distinctly, of course we could not understand what he said. The girl made no answer to his fierce questions, and we saw by the way in which he pointed to the fire that he threatened her life.

"Peterkin," said Jack in a hoarse whisper, "have you got your knife?"

"Yes," replied Peterkin, whose face was pale as death.

"That will do. Listen to me, and do my bidding quick. —Here is the small knife, Ralph. Fly, both of you, through the bush, cut the cords that bind the prisoners, and set them free! There! quick, ere it be too late!" Jack sprang up and seized a heavy but short bludgeon, while his strong frame trembled with emotion, and large drops rolled down his forehead.

At this moment the man who had butchered the savage a few minutes before advanced towards the girl with his heavy club. Jack uttered a yell that rang like a death-shriek among the rocks. With one bound he leaped over a precipice full fifteen feet high, and before the savages had recovered from their surprise, was in the midst of them, while Peterkin and I dashed through the bushes towards the prisoners. With one blow of his staff Jack felled the man with the club; then turning round with a look of fury he rushed upon the big chief with the yellow hair. Had the blow which Jack aimed at his head taken effect, the huge savage would have needed no second stroke; but he was agile as a cat, and avoided it by springing to one side, while at the same time he swung his ponderous club at the head of his foe. It was now Jack's turn to leap aside; and well was it for him that the first outburst of his blind fury was over, else he had become an easy prey to his gigantic antagonist. But Jack was cool now. He darted his blows rapidly and well, and the superiority of his light weapon was strikingly proved in this combat; for while he could easily evade the blows of the chief's heavy club, the chief could not so easily evade those of his light one. Nevertheless, so quick was he, and so frightfully did he fling about the mighty weapon, that although Jack struck him almost every blow, the strokes had to be delivered so quickly that they wanted force to be very effectual.

It was lucky for Jack that the other savages considered the success of their chief in this encounter to be so certain that they refrained from interfering. Had they doubted it, they would have probably ended the matter at once by felling him. But they contented themselves with awaiting the issue.

The force which the chief expended in wielding his club now began to be apparent. His movements became slower, his breath hissed through his clenched teeth, and the surprised savages drew nearer in order to render assistance. Jack observed this movement. He felt that his fate was sealed, and resolved to cast his life upon the next blow. The chief's club was again about to descend on his head. He might have evaded it easily, but instead of doing so, he suddenly shortened his grasp of his own club, rushed in under the blow, struck his adversary right between the eyes with all his force, and fell to the earth, crushed beneath the senseless body of the chief. A dozen clubs flew high in air, ready to descend on the head of Jack; but they hesitated a moment, for the massive body of the chief completely covered him. That moment saved his life. Ere the savages could tear the chief's body away, seven of their number fell prostrate beneath the clubs of the prisoners whom Peterkin and I had set free, and two others fell under our own hand. We could never have accomplished this had not our enemies been so engrossed with the fight between Jack and their chief that they had failed to observe us until we were upon them. They still outnumbered our party by three; but we were flushed with victory, while they were taken by surprise and dispirited by the fall of their chief. Moreover, they were awestruck by the sweeping fury of Jack, who seemed to have lost his senses altogether, and had no sooner shaken himself free of the chief's body than he rushed into the midst of them, and in three blows equalised our numbers. Peterkin and I flew to the rescue, the savages followed us, and in less than ten minutes the whole of our opponents were knocked down or made prisoners, bound hand and foot, and extended side by side upon the seashore.

CHAPTER TWENTY

> Intercourse with the savages-Cannibalism prevented-The slain are buried and the survivors depart, leaving us again alone on our Coral Island.

After the battle was over, the savages crowded round us and gazed at us in surprise, while they continued to pour upon us a flood of questions, which, being wholly unintelligible, of course we could not answer. However, by way of putting an end to it, Jack took the chief (who had recovered from the effects of his wound) by the hand and shook it warmly. No sooner did the blacks see that this was meant to express good-will than they shook hands with us all round. After this ceremony was gone through Jack went up to the girl, who had never once moved from the rock where she had been left, but had continued an eager spectator of all that had passed. He made signs to her to follow him, and then, taking the chief by the hand, was about to conduct him to the bower when his eye fell on the poor infant which had been thrown into the sea and was still lying on the shore. Dropping the chief's hand he hastened towards it, and, to his great joy, found it to be still alive. We also found that the mother was beginning to recover slowly.

"Here, get out o' the way," said Jack, pushing us aside as we stooped over the poor woman and endeavoured to restore her; "I'll soon bring her round." So saying, he placed the infant on her bosom and laid its warm cheek on hers. The effect was wonderful. The woman opened her eyes, felt the child, looked at it, and with a cry of joy, clasped it in her arms, at the same time endeavouring to rise-for the purpose, apparently, of rushing into the woods.

"There, that's all right," said Jack, once more taking the chief by the hand. —"Now, Ralph and Peterkin, make the women and these fellows follow me to the bower. We'll entertain them as hospitably as we can."

In a few minutes the savages were all seated on the ground in front of the bower, making a hearty meal off a cold roast pig, several ducks, and a variety of cold fish, together with an unlimited supply of cocoa-nuts, bread-fruits, yams, taro, and plums-with all of which they seemed to be quite familiar and perfectly satisfied.

Meanwhile we three, being thoroughly knocked up with our day's work, took a good draught of cocoa-nut lemonade, and throwing ourselves on our beds, fell fast asleep. The savages, it seems, followed our example, and in half-an-hour the whole camp was buried in repose.

How long we slept I cannot tell; but this I know-that when we lay down the sun was setting, and when we awoke it was high in the heavens. I awoke Jack, who started up in surprise, being unable at first to comprehend our situation. "Now, then," said he, springing up, "let's see after breakfast. —Hallo, Peterkin, lazy fellow! how long do you mean to lie there?"

Peterkin yawned heavily. "Well," said he, opening his eyes and looking up after some trouble, "if it isn't to-morrow morning, and me thinking it was to-day all this time-Hallo, Venus! where did you come from? You seem tolerably at home, anyhow. Bah! might as well speak to the cat as to you-better, in fact, for it understands me, and you don't."

This remark was called forth by the sight of one of the elderly females, who had seated herself on the rock in front of the bower, and having placed her child at her feet, was busily engaged in devouring the remains of a roast pig.

By this time the natives outside were all astir, and breakfast in an advanced state of preparation. During the course of it we made sundry attempts to converse with the natives by signs, but without effect. At last we hit upon a plan of discovering their names. Jack pointed to his breast and said "Jack" very distinctly; then he pointed to Peterkin and to me, repeating our names at the same time. Then he pointed to himself again and said "Jack," and laying his finger on the breast of the chief, looked inquiringly into his face. The chief instantly understood him, and said "Tararo" twice distinctly. Jack repeated it after him, and the chief, nodding his head approvingly, said "Chuck," on hearing which Peterkin exploded with laughter. But Jack turned, and with a frown rebuked him, saying, "I must look even more indignantly at you than I feel,

Peterkin, you rascal, for these fellows don't like to be laughed at." Then turning towards the youngest of the women, who was seated at the door of the bower, he pointed to her; whereupon the chief said "Avatea," and pointing towards the sun, raised his finger slowly towards the zenith, where it remained steadily for a minute or two.

"What can that mean, I wonder?" said Jack, looking puzzled.

"Perhaps," said Peterkin, "the chief means she is an angel come down to stay here for a while. If so, she's an uncommonly black one!"

We did not feel quite satisfied with this explanation, so Jack went up to her and said "Avatea." The woman smiled sadly and nodded her head, at the same time pointing to her breast and then to the sun in the same manner as the chief had done. We were much puzzled to know what this could signify; but as there was no way of solving our difficulty, we were obliged to rest content.

Jack now made signs to the natives to follow him, and taking up his axe, he led them to the place where the battle had been fought. Here we found the prisoners, who had passed the night on the beach, having been totally forgotten by us, as our minds had been full of our guests, and were ultimately overcome by sleep. They did not seem the worse for their exposure, however, as we judged by the hearty appetite with which they devoured the breakfast that was soon after given to them. Jack then began to dig a hole in the sand, and after working a few seconds, he pointed to it and to the dead bodies that lay exposed on the beach. The natives immediately perceived what he wanted, and running for their paddles, dug a hole in the course of half-an-hour that was quite large enough to contain all the bodies of the slain. When it was finished, they tossed their dead enemies into it with so much indifference that we felt assured they would not have put themselves to this trouble had we not asked them to do so. The body of the yellow-haired chief was the last thrown in. This wretched man would have recovered from the blow with which Jack felled him, and indeed he did endeavour to rise during the *mêlée* that followed his fall; but one of his enemies, happening to notice the action, dealt him a blow with his club that killed him on the spot.

While they were about to throw the sand over this chief, one of the savages stooped over him, and with a knife, made apparently of stone, cut a large slice of flesh from his thigh. We knew at once that he intended to make use of this for food, and could not repress a cry of horror and disgust.

"Come, come, you blackguard!" cried Jack, starting up and seizing the man by the arm, "pitch that into the hole. Do you hear?"

The savage, of course, did not understand the command; but he perfectly understood the look of disgust with which Jack regarded the flesh, and his fierce gaze as he pointed towards the hole. Nevertheless, he did not obey. Jack instantly turned to Tararo and made signs to him to enforce obedience. The chief seemed to understand the appeal; for he stepped forward, raised his club, and was on the point of dashing out the brains of his offending subject when Jack sprang forward and caught his uplifted arm.

"Stop, you blockhead!" he shouted. "I don't want you to kill the man!" He then pointed again to the flesh and to the hole. The chief uttered a few words, which had the desired effect; for the man threw the flesh into the hole, which was immediately filled up. This man was of a morose, sulky disposition, and during all the time he remained on the island, regarded us-especially Jack-with a scowling visage. His name, we found, was Mahine.

The next three or four days were spent by the savages in mending their canoe, which had been damaged by the violent shock it had sustained on striking the shore. This canoe was a very curious structure. It was about thirty feet long, and had a high, towering stern. The timbers of which it was partly composed were fastened much in the same way as those of our little boat were put together; but the part that seemed most curious to us was a sort of outrigger, or long plank, which was attached to the body of the canoe by means of two stout cross-beams. These beams kept the plank parallel with the canoe, but not in contact with it, for it floated in the water with an open space between-thus forming a sort of double canoe. This, we found, was intended to prevent the upsetting of the canoe, which was so narrow that it could not have maintained an upright position without the outrigger. We could not help wondering both at the ingenuity and the clumsiness of this contrivance.

When the canoe was ready, we assisted the natives to carry the prisoners into it, and helped them to load it with provisions and fruit. Peterkin also went to the plum-tree for the purpose of making a special onslaught upon the hogs, and killed no less than six of them. These we baked and presented to our friends, on the day of their departure. On that day Tararo made a great many energetic signs to us, which, after much consideration, we came to understand were proposals that we should go away with him to his island; but having no desire to do so, we shook our heads very decidedly. However, we consoled him by presenting him with our rusty axe, which we thought we could spare, having the excellent one which had been so providentially washed ashore to us the day we were wrecked. We also gave him a piece of wood with our names carved on it, and a piece of string to hang it round his neck as an ornament.

In a few minutes more we were all assembled on the beach. Being unable to speak to the savages, we went through the ceremony of shaking hands, and expected they would depart; but before doing so, Tararo went up to Jack and rubbed noses with him, after which he did the same with Peterkin and me! Seeing that this was their mode of salutation, we determined to conform to their custom; so we rubbed noses heartily with the whole party, women and all! The only disagreeable part of the process was when we came to rub noses with Mahine; and Peterkin afterwards said that when he saw his wolfish eyes glaring so close to his face, he felt much more inclined to *bang* than to *rub* his nose. Avatea was the last to take leave of us, and we experienced a feeling of real sorrow when she approached to bid us farewell. Besides her modest air and gentle manners, she was the only one of the party who exhibited the smallest sign of regret at parting from us. Going up to Jack, she put out her flat little nose to be rubbed, and thereafter paid the same compliment to Peterkin and me.

An hour later the canoe was out of sight; and we, with an indefinable feeling of sadness creeping round our hearts, were seated in silence beneath the shadow of our bower, meditating on the wonderful events of the last few days.

CHAPTER TWENTY ONE

Sagacious and moral remarks in regard to life —A sail! —An unexpected salute-The end of the black cat —A terrible dive-An incautious proceeding and a frightful catastrophe.

Life is a strange compound. Peterkin used to say of it that it beat a druggist's shop all to sticks; for whereas the first is a compound of good and bad, the other is a horrible compound of all that is utterly detestable. And indeed the more I consider it, the more I am struck with the strange mixture of good and evil that exists, not only in the material earth, but in our own natures. In our own Coral Island we had experienced every variety of good that a bountiful Creator could heap on us. Yet on the night of the storm we had seen how almost, in our case-and altogether, no doubt, in the case of others less fortunate-all this good might be swept away for ever. We had seen the rich fruit-trees waving in the soft air, the tender herbs shooting upwards under the benign influence of the bright sun; and the next day we had seen these good and beautiful trees and plants uprooted by the hurricane, crushed and hurled to the ground in destructive devastation. We had lived for many months in a clime, for the most part, so beautiful that we had often wondered whether Adam and Eve had found Eden more sweet; and we had seen the quiet solitudes of our paradise suddenly broken in upon by ferocious savages, and the white sands stained with blood and strewed with lifeless forms, yet among these cannibals we had seen many symptoms of a kindly nature. I pondered these things much, and while I considered them there recurred to my memory those words which I had read in my Bible: "The works of God are wonderful, and His ways past finding out."

After these poor savages had left us we used to hold long and frequent conversations about them, and I noticed that Peterkin's manner was now much altered. He did not, indeed, jest less heartily than before, but he did so less frequently; and often there was a tone of deep seriousness in his manner, if not in his words, which made him seem to Jack and me as if he had grown two years older within a few days. But indeed I was not surprised at this when I reflected on the awful realities which we had witnessed so lately. We could by no means shake off a tendency to gloom for several weeks afterwards; but as time wore away, our usual good spirits returned somewhat, and we began to think of the visit of the savages with feelings akin to those with which we recall a terrible dream.

One day we were all enjoying ourselves in the Water Garden preparatory to going on a fishing excursion, for Peterkin had kept us in such constant supply of hogs that we had become quite tired of pork and desired a change. Peterkin was sunning himself on the ledge of rock, while we were creeping among the rocks below. Happening to look up, I observed Peterkin cutting the most extraordinary capers and making violent gesticulations for us to come up; so I gave Jack a push and rose immediately.

"A sail! a sail-Ralph, look-Jack, away on the horizon there, just over the entrance to the lagoon!" cried Peterkin as we scrambled up the rocks.

"So it is-and a schooner, too!" said Jack as he proceeded hastily to dress.

Our hearts were thrown into a terrible flutter by this discovery, for if it should touch at our island, we had no doubt the captain would be happy to give us a passage to some of the civilised islands, where we could find a ship sailing for England or some other part of Europe. Home, with all its associations, rushed in upon my heart like a flood; and much though I loved the Coral Island and the bower which had now been our home so long, I felt that I could have quitted all at that moment without a sigh. With joyful anticipations we hastened to the highest point of rock near our dwelling and awaited the arrival of the vessel, for we now perceived that she was making straight for the island under a steady breeze.

In less than an hour she was close to the reef, where she rounded-to and backed her topsails in order to survey the coast. Seeing this, and fearing that they might not perceive us, we all three waved pieces of cocoa-nut cloth in the air, and soon had the satisfaction of seeing them beginning to lower a boat and bustle about the decks as if they meant to land. Suddenly a flag was run up to the peak, a little cloud of white smoke rose from the schooner's side, and before we could guess their intentions, a cannon-shot came crashing through the bushes, carried away several cocoa-nut trees in its passage, and burst in atoms against the cliff a few yards below the spot on which we stood.

With feelings of terror we now observed that the flag at the schooner's peak was black, with a Death's-head and cross-bones upon it. As we gazed at each other in blank amazement, the word "pirate" escaped our lips simultaneously.

"What is to be done?" cried Peterkin as we observed a boat shoot from the vessel's side and make for the entrance of the reef. "If they take us off the island, it will either be to throw us overboard for sport or to make pirates of us."

I did not reply, but looked at Jack, as being our only resource in this emergency. He stood with folded arms, and his eyes fixed with a grave, anxious expression on the ground. "There is but one hope," said he, turning with a sad expression of countenance to Peterkin. "Perhaps, after all, we may not have to resort to it. If these villains are anxious to take us, they will soon overrun the whole island. But come, follow me."

Stopping abruptly in his speech, Jack bounded into the woods, and led us by a circuitous route to Spouting Cliff. Here he halted, and advancing cautiously to the rocks, glanced over their edge. We were soon by his side, and saw the boat, which was crowded with armed men, just touching the shore. In an instant the crew landed, formed line, and rushed up to our bower.

In a few seconds we saw them hurrying back to the boat, one of them swinging the poor cat round his head by the tail. On reaching the water's edge he tossed it far into the sea, and joined his companions, who appeared to be holding a hasty council.

"You see what we may expect," said Jack bitterly. "The man who will wantonly kill a poor brute for sport will think little of murdering a fellow-creature. Now, boys, we have but one chance left-the Diamond Cave."

"The Diamond Cave!" cried Peterkin. "Then my chance is a poor one, for I could not dive into it if all the pirates on the Pacific were at my heels."

"Nay, but," said I, "we will take you down, Peterkin, if you will only trust us."

As I spoke, we observed the pirates scatter over the beach, and radiate, as if from a centre, towards the woods and along shore.

"Now, Peterkin," said Jack in a solemn tone, "you must make up your mind to do it, or we must make up our minds to die in your company."

"Oh Jack, my dear friend!" cried Peterkin, turning pale, "leave me; I don't believe they'll think it worth while to kill me. Go, you and Ralph, and dive into the cave."

"That will not I," answered Jack quietly, while he picked up a stout cudgel from the ground. —"So now, Ralph, we must prepare to meet these fellows. Their motto is 'No quarter.' If we can manage to floor those coming in this direction, we may escape into the woods for a while."

"There are five of them," said I; "we have no chance."

"Come, then!" cried Peterkin, starting up and grasping Jack convulsively by the arm; "let us dive. I will go."

Those who are not naturally expert in the water know well the feelings of horror that over-whelm them, when in it, at the bare idea of being held down even for a few seconds-that spasmodic, involuntary recoil from compulsory immersion which has no connection whatever with cowardice; and they will understand the amount of resolution that it required in Peterkin to allow himself to be dragged down to a depth of ten feet, and then, through a narrow tunnel, into an almost pitch-dark cavern. But there was no alternative. The pirates had already caught sight of us, and were now within a short distance of the rocks.

Jack and I seized Peterkin by the arms.

"Now, keep quite still-no struggling," said Jack, "or we are lost!"

Peterkin made no reply; but the stern gravity of his marble features, and the tension of his muscles, satisfied us that he had fully made up his mind to go through with it. Just as the pirates gained the foot of the rocks, which hid us for a moment from their view, we bent over the sea and plunged down together, head foremost. Peterkin behaved like a hero. He floated passively between us like a log of wood, and we passed the tunnel and rose into the cave in a shorter space of time than I had ever done it before.

Peterkin drew a long, deep breath on reaching the surface, and in a few seconds we were all standing on the ledge of rock in safety. Jack now searched for the tinder and torch which always lay in the cave. He soon found them, and lighting the torch, revealed to Peterkin's wondering gaze the marvels of the place. But we were too wet to waste much time in looking about us. Our first care was to take off our clothes and wring them as dry as we could. This done, we proceeded to examine into the state of our larder, for, as Jack truly remarked, there was no knowing how long the pirates might remain on the island.

"Perhaps," said Peterkin, "they may take it into their heads to stop here altogether, and so we shall be buried alive in this place."

"Don't you think, Peterkin, that it's the nearest thing to being drowned alive that you ever felt?" said Jack with a smile. "But I have no fear of that. These villains never stay long on shore. The sea is their home, so you may depend upon it that they won't stay more than a day or two at the furthest."

We now began to make arrangements for spending the night in the cavern. At various periods Jack and I had conveyed cocoa-nuts and other fruits, besides rolls of cocoa-nut cloth, to this submarine cave, partly for amusement, and partly from a feeling that we might possibly be driven one day to take shelter here from the savages. Little did we imagine that the first savages who would drive us into it would be white savages-perhaps our own countrymen! We found the cocoa-nuts in good condition, and the cooked yams; but the bread-fruits were spoiled. We also found the cloth where we had left it, and on opening it out, there proved to be sufficient to make a bed-which was important, as the rock was damp. Having collected it all together, we spread out our bed, placed our torch in the midst of us, and ate our supper. It was indeed a strange chamber to feast in; and we could not help remarking on the cold, ghastly appearance of the walls, and the black water at our side with the thick darkness beyond, and the sullen sound of the drops that fell at long intervals from the roof of the cavern into the still water, and the strong contrast between all this and our bed and supper, which, with our faces, were lit up with the deep-red flame of the torch.

We sat long over our meal, talking together in subdued voices, for we did not like the dismal echoes that rang through the vault above when we happened to raise them. At last the faint light that came through the opening died away, warning us that it was night and time for rest. We therefore put out our torch and lay down to sleep.

On awaking, it was some time ere we could collect our faculties so as to remember where we were, and we were in much uncertainty as to whether it was early or late. We saw by the faint light that it was day, but could not guess at the hour; so Jack proposed that he should dive out and reconnoitre.

"No, Jack," said I; "do you rest here. You've had enough to do during the last few days. Rest yourself now, and take care of Peterkin, while I go out to see what the pirates are about. I'll be very careful not to expose myself, and I'll bring you word again in a short time."

"Very well, Ralph," answered Jack; "please yourself. But don't be long. And if you'll take my advice, you'll go in your clothes; for I would like to have some fresh cocoa-nuts, and climbing trees without clothes is uncomfortable-to say the least of it."

"The pirates will be sure to keep a sharp lookout," said Peterkin; "so, pray, be careful."

"No fear," said I. "Good-bye."

"Good-bye," answered my comrades.

And while the words were yet sounding in my ears, I plunged into the water, and in a few seconds found myself in the open air. On rising, I was careful to come up gently and to breathe softly, while I kept close in beside the rocks; but as I observed no one near me, I crept slowly out and ascended the cliff, a step at a time, till I obtained a full view of the shore. No pirates were to be seen-even their boat was gone; but as it was possible they might have hidden themselves, I did not venture too boldly forward. Then it occurred to me to look out to sea, when, to my surprise, I saw the pirate schooner sailing away almost hull down on the horizon! On seeing this I uttered a shout of joy. Then my first impulse was to dive back to tell my companions the good news; but I checked myself, and ran to the top of the cliff in order to make sure that the vessel I saw was indeed the pirate schooner. I looked long and anxiously at her, and giving vent to a deep sigh of relief, said aloud, "Yes, there she goes; the villains have been balked of their prey this time at least!"

"Not so sure of that!" said a deep voice at my side, while at the same moment a heavy hand grasped my shoulder and held it as if in a vice.

CHAPTER TWENTY TWO

I fall into the hands of pirates-How they treated me, and what I said to them-The result of the whole ending in a melancholy separation and in a most unexpected gift.

My heart seemed to leap into my throat at the words; and turning round, I beheld a man of immense stature and fierce aspect regarding me with a smile of contempt. He was a white man-that is to say, he was a man of European blood, though his face, from long exposure to the weather, was deeply bronzed. His dress was that of a common seaman, except that he had on a Greek skull-cap, and wore a broad shawl of the richest silk round his waist. In this shawl were placed two pairs of pistols and a heavy cutlass. He wore a beard and moustache, which, like the locks on his head, were short, curly, and sprinkled with grey hairs.

"So, youngster," he said with a sardonic smile, while I felt his grasp tighten on my shoulder, "the villains have been balked of their prey, have they? We shall see-we shall see. Now, you whelp, look yonder!" As he spoke, the pirate uttered a shrill whistle. In a second or two it was answered, and the pirate boat rowed round the point at the Water Garden and came rapidly towards us. "Now, go make a fire on that point; and hark'ee, youngster, if you try to run away I'll send a quick and sure messenger after you," and he pointed significantly at his pistols.

I obeyed in silence; and as I happened to have the burning-glass in my pocket, a fire was speedily kindled, and a thick smoke ascended into the air. It had scarcely appeared for two minutes when the boom of a gun rolled over the sea, and looking up, I saw that the schooner was making for the island again. It now flashed across me that this was a ruse on the part of the pirates, and that they had sent their vessel away, knowing that it would lead us to suppose that they had left altogether. But there was no use of regret now. I was completely in their power; so I stood helplessly beside the pirate, watching the crew of the boat as they landed on the beach. For an instant I contemplated rushing over the cliff into the sea; but this, I saw, I could not now accomplish, as some of the men were already between me and the water.

There was a good deal of jesting at the success of their scheme, as the crew ascended the rocks and addressed the man who had captured me by the title of "Captain". They were a ferocious set of men, with shaggy beards and scowling brows. All of them were armed with cutlasses and pistols, and their costumes were, with trifling variations, similar to that of the captain. As I looked from one to the other, and observed the low, scowling brows that never unbent even when the men laughed, and the mean, rascally expression that sat on each face, I felt that my life hung by a hair.

"But where are the other cubs?" cried one of the men with an oath that made me shudder. "I'll swear to it there were three at least, if not more."

"You hear what he says, whelp: where are the other dogs?" said the captain.

"If you mean my companions," said I in a low voice, "I won't tell you."

A loud laugh burst from the crew at this answer.

The pirate captain looked at me in surprise. Then drawing a pistol from his belt, he cocked it and said, "Now, youngster, listen to me. I've no time to waste here. If you don't tell me all you know, I'll blow your brains out! Where are your comrades?"

For an instant I hesitated, not knowing what to do in this extremity. Suddenly a thought occurred to me.

"Villain," said I, shaking my clenched fist in his face, "to blow my brains out would make short work of me, and be soon over; death by drowning is as sure, and the agony prolonged. Yet I tell you to your face, if you were to toss me over yonder cliff into the sea, I would not tell you where my companions are; and I dare you to try me!"

The pirate captain grew white with rage as I spoke. "Say you so?" cried he, uttering a fierce oath. —"Here, lads, take him by the legs and heave him in-quick!"

The men, who were utterly silenced with surprise at my audacity, advanced and seized me; and as they carried me towards the cliff, I congratulated myself not a little on the success of my scheme, for I knew that once in the water I should be safe, and could rejoin Jack and Peterkin in the cave. But my hopes were suddenly blasted by the captain crying out, "Hold on, lads, hold on! We'll give him a taste of the thumb-screws before throwing him to the sharks. Away with him into the boat. Look alive! the breeze is freshening."

The men instantly raised me shoulder-high, and hurrying down the rocks, tossed me into the bottom of the boat, where I lay for some time stunned with the violence of my fall.

On recovering sufficiently to raise myself on my elbow, I perceived that we were already outside the coral reef and close alongside the schooner, which was of small size and clipper-built. I had only time to observe this much when I received a severe kick on the side from one of the men, who ordered me, in a rough voice, to jump aboard. Rising hastily, I clambered up the side. In a few minutes the boat was hoisted on deck, the vessel's head put close to the wind, and the Coral Island dropped slowly astern as we beat up against a head sea.

Immediately after coming aboard, the crew were too busily engaged in working the ship and getting in the boat to attend to me; so I remained leaning against the bulwarks close to the gangway, watching their operations. I was surprised to find that there were no guns or carronades of any kind in the vessel, which had more the appearance of a fast-sailing trader than a pirate. But I was struck with the neatness of everything. The brass-work of the binnacle and about the tiller, as well as the copper belaying-pins, were as brightly polished as if they had just come from the foundry. The decks were pure white and smooth. The masts were clean-scraped and varnished, except at the cross-trees and truck, which were painted black. The standing and running rigging was in the most perfect order, and the sails white as snow. In short, everything, from the single narrow red stripe on her low, black hull to the trucks on her tapering masts, evinced an amount of care and strict discipline that would have done credit to a ship of the Royal Navy. There was nothing lumbering or unseemly about the vessel, excepting, perhaps, a boat, which lay on the deck with its keel up between the fore and main masts. It seemed disproportionately large for the schooner; but when I saw that the crew amounted to between thirty and forty men, I concluded that this boat was held in reserve in case of any accident compelling the crew to desert the vessel.

As I have before said, the costumes of the men were similar to that of the captain. But in head-gear they differed, not only from him, but from each other-some wearing the ordinary straw hat of the merchant service, while others wore cloth caps and red worsted nightcaps. I observed that all their arms were sent below, the captain only retaining his cutlass and a single pistol in the folds of his shawl. Although the captain was the tallest and most powerful man in the ship, he did not strikingly excel many of his men in this respect; and the only difference that an ordinary observer would have noticed was a certain degree of open candour, straightforward daring, in the bold, ferocious expression of his face, which rendered him less repulsive than his low-browed associates, but did not by any means induce the belief that he was a hero. This look was, however, the indication of that spirit which gave him the pre-eminence among the crew of desperadoes who called him captain. He was a lion-like villain, totally devoid of personal fear, and utterly reckless of consequences, and therefore a terror to his men, who individually hated him, but unitedly felt it to be to their advantage to have him at their head.

But my thoughts soon reverted to the dear companions whom I had left on shore; and as I turned towards the Coral Island, which was now far away to leeward, I sighed deeply, and the tears rolled slowly down my cheeks as I thought that I might never see them more.

"So you're blubbering, are you, you obstinate whelp?" said the deep voice of the captain as he came up and gave me a box on the ear that nearly felled me to the deck. "I don't allow any such weakness aboard o' this ship. So clap a stopper on your eyes, or I'll give you something to cry for."

I flushed with indignation at this rough and cruel treatment, but felt that giving way to anger would only make matters worse; so I made no reply, but took out my handkerchief and dried my eyes.

"I thought you were made of better stuff," continued the captain angrily. "I'd rather have a mad bulldog aboard than a water-eyed puppy. But I'll cure you, lad, or introduce you to the sharks before long. Now go below, and stay there till I call you."

As I walked forward to obey, my eye fell on a small keg standing by the side of the mainmast, on which the word *gunpowder* was written in pencil. It immediately flashed across me that as we were beating up against the wind, anything floating in the sea would be driven on the reef encircling the Coral Island. I also recollected-for thought is more rapid than the lightning-that my old companions had a pistol. Without a moment's hesitation, therefore, I lifted the keg from the deck and tossed it into the sea! An exclamation of surprise burst from the captain and some of the men who witnessed this act of mine.

Striding up to me, and uttering fearful imprecations, the captain raised his hand to strike me, while he shouted, "Boy! whelp! what mean you by that?"

"If you lower your hand," said I in a loud voice, while I felt the blood rush to my temples, "I'll tell you. Until you do so, I'm dumb."

The captain stepped back and regarded me with a look of amazement.

"Now," continued I, "I threw that keg into the sea because the wind and waves will carry it to my friends on the Coral Island, who happen to have a pistol but no powder. I hope that it will reach them soon; and my only regret is that the keg was not a bigger one. Moreover, pirate, you said just now that you thought I was made of better stuff. I don't know what stuff I am made of—I never thought much about that subject; but I'm quite certain of this-that I am made of such stuff as the like of you shall never tame, though you should do your worst!"

To my surprise, the captain, instead of flying into a rage, smiled, and thrusting his hand into the voluminous shawl that encircled his waist, turned on his heel and walked aft, while I went below.

Here, instead of being rudely handled, as I had expected, the men received me with a shout of laughter; and one of them, patting me on the back, said, "Well done, lad! You're a brick, and I have no doubt will turn out a rare cove. Bloody Bill there was just such a fellow as you are, and he's now the biggest cut-throat of us all."

"Take a can of beer, lad," cried another, "and wet your whistle after that speech o' your'n to the captain. If any one o' us had made it, youngster, he would have had no whistle to wet by this time."

"Stop your clapper, Jack!" vociferated a third. "Give the boy a junk o' meat. Don't you see he's a'most goin' to kick the bucket?"

"And no wonder," said the first speaker with an oath, "after the tumble you gave him into the boat! I guess it would have broke your neck if you had got it."

I did indeed feel somewhat faint, which was owing, doubtless, to the combined effects of ill-usage and hunger; for it will be recollected that I had dived out of the cave that morning before breakfast, and it was now near midday. I therefore gladly accepted a plate of boiled pork and a yam, which were handed to me by one of the men from the locker on which some of the crew were seated eating their dinner. But I must add that the zest with which I ate my meal was much abated in consequence of the frightful oaths and the terrible language that flowed from the lips of these godless men, even in the midst of their hilarity and good-humour. The man who had been alluded to as Bloody Bill was seated near me, and I could not help wondering at the moody silence he maintained among his comrades. He did indeed reply to their questions in a careless, off-hand tone, but he never volunteered a remark. The only difference between him and the others was his taciturnity and his size, for he was nearly, if not quite, as large a man as the captain.

During the remainder of the afternoon I was left to my own reflections, which were anything but agreeable; for I could not banish from my mind the threat about the thumbscrews, of the nature and use of which I had a vague but terrible conception. I was still meditating on my unhappy fate when, just after nightfall, one of the watch on deck called down the hatchway:

"Hallo, there! One o' you tumble up and light the cabin lamp, and send that boy aft to the captain-sharp!"

"Now, then, do you hear, youngster? the captain wants you. Look alive!" said Bloody Bill, raising his huge frame from the locker on which he had been asleep for the last two hours. He sprang up the ladder, and I instantly followed him, and going aft, was shown into the cabin by one of the men, who closed the door after me.

A small silver lamp which hung from a beam threw a dim, soft light over the cabin, which was a small apartment, and comfortably but plainly furnished. Seated on a camp-stool at the table, and busily engaged in examining a chart of the Pacific, was the captain, who looked up as I entered, and in a quiet voice bade me be seated, while he threw down his pencil, and rising from the table, stretched himself on a sofa at the upper end of the cabin.

"Boy," said he, looking me full in the face, "what is your name?"

"Ralph Rover," I replied.

"Where did you come from, and how came you to be on that island? How many companions had you on it? Answer me, now, and mind you tell no lies."

"I never tell lies," said I firmly.

The captain received this reply with a cold, sarcastic smile, and bade me answer his questions.

I then told him the history of myself and my companions from the time we sailed till the day of his visit to the island-taking care, however, to make no mention of the Diamond Cave. After I had concluded, he was silent for a few minutes; then looking up, he said, "Boy, I believe you."

I was surprised at this remark, for I could not imagine why he should not believe me. However, I made no reply.

"And what," continued the captain, "makes you think that this schooner is a pirate?"

"The black flag," said I, "showed me what you are; and if any further proof were wanting, I have had it in the brutal treatment I have received at your hands."

The captain frowned as I spoke; but, subduing his anger, he continued, "Boy, you are too bold. I admit that we treated you roughly, but that was because you made us lose time and gave us a good deal of trouble. As to the black flag, that is merely a joke that my fellows play off upon people sometimes in order to frighten them. It is their humour, and does no harm. I am no pirate, boy, but a lawful trader—a rough one, I grant you; but one can't help that in these seas, where there are so many pirates on the water and such murderous blackguards on the land. I carry on a trade in sandal-wood with the Feejee Islands; and if you choose, Ralph, to behave yourself and be a good boy, I'll take you along with me and give you a good share of the profits. You see, I'm in want of an honest boy like you to look after the cabin, and keep the log, and superintend the traffic on shore sometimes. What say you, Ralph: would you like to become a sandal-wood trader?"

I was much surprised by this explanation, and a good deal relieved to find that the vessel, after all, was not a pirate; but instead of replying, I said, "If it be as you state, then why did you take me from my island, and why do you not now take me back?"

The captain smiled as he replied, "I took you off in anger, boy, and I'm sorry for it. I would even now take you back, but we are too far away from it. See, there it is," he added, laying his finger on the chart; "and we are now here-fifty miles, at least. It would not be fair to my men to put about now, for they have all an interest in the trade."

I could make no reply to this; so, after a little more conversation, I agreed to become one of the crew-at least, until we could reach some civilised island where I might be put ashore. The captain assented to this proposition; and after thanking him for the promise, I left the cabin and went on deck with feelings that ought to have been lighter, but which were, I could not tell why, marvellously heavy and uncomfortable still.

CHAPTER TWENTY THREE

Bloody Bill-Dark surmises —A strange sail, and a strange crew, and a still stranger cargo-New reasons for favouring missionaries —A murderous massacre, and thoughts thereon.

Three weeks after the conversation narrated in the last chapter I was standing on the quarter-deck of the schooner, watching the gambols of a shoal of porpoises that swam round us. It was a dead calm-one of those still, hot, sweltering days so common in the Pacific, when nature seems to have gone to sleep, and the only thing in water or in air that proves her still alive is her long, deep breathing in the swell of the mighty sea. No cloud floated in the deep blue above, no ripple broke the reflected blue below. The sun shone fiercely in the sky, and a ball of fire blazed with almost equal power from out the bosom of the water. So intensely still was it, and so perfectly transparent was the surface of the deep, that had it not been for the long swell already alluded to, we might have believed the surrounding universe to be a huge, blue, liquid ball, and our little ship the one solitary material speck in all creation floating in the midst of it.

No sound broke on our ears save the soft puff now and then of a porpoise, the slow creak of the masts as we swayed gently on the swell, the patter of the reef-points, and the occasional flap of the hanging sails. An awning covered the fore and after parts of the schooner, under which the men composing the watch on deck lolled in sleepy indolence, overcome with excessive heat. Bloody Bill, as the men invariably called him, was standing at the tiller; but his post for the present was a sinecure, and he whiled away the time by alternately gazing in dreamy abstraction at the compass in the binnacle and by walking to the taffrail in order to spit into the sea. In one of these turns he came near to where I was standing, and leaning over the side, looked long and earnestly down into the blue wave.

This man, although he was always taciturn and often surly, was the only human being on board with whom I had the slightest desire to become better acquainted. The other men, seeing that I did not relish their company, and knowing that I was a protégé of the captain, treated me with total indifference. Bloody Bill, it is true, did the same; but as this was his conduct to every one else, it was not peculiar in reference to me. Once or twice I tried to draw him into conversation, but he always turned away after a few cold monosyllables. As he now leaned over the taffrail, close beside me, I said to him:

"Bill, why is it that you are so gloomy? Why do you never speak to any one?"

Bill smiled slightly as he replied, "Why, I s'pose it's because I hain't got nothin' to say!"

"That's strange," said I musingly. "You look like a man that could think, and such men can usually speak."

"So they can, youngster," rejoined Bill somewhat sternly; "and I could speak too if I had a mind to, but what's the use o' speakin' here? The men only open their mouths to curse and swear, and they seem to find it entertainin'; but I don't, so I hold my tongue."

"Well, Bill, that's true, and I would rather not hear you speak at all than hear you speak like the other men. But I don't swear, Bill; so you might talk to me sometimes, I think. Besides, I'm weary of spending day after day in this way, without a single soul to say a pleasant word to. I've been used to friendly conversation, Bill, and I really would take it kind if you would talk with me a little now and then."

Bill looked at me in surprise, and I thought I observed a sad expression pass across his sun-burned face.

"An' where have you been used to friendly conversation?" said Bill, looking down again into the sea. "Not on that Coral Island, I take it?"

"Yes, indeed," said I energetically. "I have spent many of the happiest months in my life on that Coral Island;" and without waiting to be further questioned, I launched out into a glowing account of the happy life that Jack and Peterkin and I had spent together, and related minutely every circumstance that befell us while on the island.

"Boy, boy," said Bill in a voice so deep that it startled me, "this is no place for you!"

"That's true," said I. "I am of little use on board, and I don't like my comrades; but I can't help it, and at any rate I hope to be free again soon."

"Free?" said Bill, looking at me in surprise.

"Yes, free," returned I. "The captain said he would put me ashore after this trip was over."

"*This trip*! Hark'ee, boy," said Bill, lowering his voice, "what said the captain to you the day you came aboard?"

"He said that he was a trader in sandal-wood, and no pirate, and told me that if I would join him for this trip he would give me a good share of the profits, or put me on shore in some civilised island if I chose."

Bill's brows lowered savagely as he muttered, "Ay, he said truth when he told you he was a sandal-wood trader, but he lied when—"

"Sail ho!" shouted the lookout at the masthead.

"Where away?" cried Bill, springing to the tiller; while the men, startled by the sudden cry, jumped up and gazed round the horizon.

"On the starboard quarter, hull down, sir," answered the lookout.

At this moment the captain came on deck, and mounting into the rigging, surveyed the sail through the glass. Then sweeping his eye round the horizon, he gazed steadily at the particular point.

"Take in topsails!" shouted the captain, swinging himself down on the deck by the main-back stay.

"Take in topsails!" roared the first mate.

"Ay, ay, sir—r—r!" answered the men as they sprang into the rigging and went aloft like cats.

Instantly all was bustle on board the hitherto quiet schooner. The topsails were taken in and stowed, the men stood by the sheets and halyards, and the captain gazed anxiously at the breeze, which was now rushing towards us like a sheet of dark blue. In a few seconds it struck us. The schooner trembled, as if in surprise at the sudden onset, while she fell away; then, bending gracefully to the wind, as though in acknowledgment of her subjection, she cut through the waves with her sharp prow like a dolphin, while Bill directed her course towards the strange sail.

In half-an-hour we neared her sufficiently to make out that she was a schooner, and from the clumsy appearance of her masts and sails we judged her to be a trader. She evidently did not like our appearance, for the instant the breeze reached her she crowded all sail and showed us her stern. As the breeze had moderated a little, our topsails were again shaken out; and it soon became evident-despite the proverb, "A stern chase is a long one" —that we doubled her speed, and would overhaul her speedily. When within a mile we hoisted British colours, but receiving no acknowledgment, the captain ordered a shot to be fired across her bows. In a moment, to my surprise, a large portion of the bottom of the boat amidships was removed, and in the hole thus exposed appeared an immense brass gun. It worked on a swivel, and was elevated by means of machinery. It was quickly loaded and fired. The heavy ball struck the water a few yards ahead of the chase, and ricochetting into the air, plunged into the sea a mile beyond it.

This produced the desired effect. The strange vessel backed her topsails and hove-to, while we ranged up and lay-to about a hundred yards off.

"Lower the boat!" cried the captain.

In a second the boat was lowered and manned by a part of the crew, who were all armed with cutlasses and pistols. As the captain passed me to get into it he said, "Jump into the stern-sheets, Ralph; I may want you." I obeyed, and in ten minutes more we were standing on the stranger's deck. We were all much surprised at the sight that met our eyes. Instead of a crew of such sailors as we were accustomed to see, there were only fifteen blacks, standing on the quarter-deck, and regarding us with looks of undisguised alarm. They were totally unarmed, and most of them unclothed. One or two, however, wore portions of European attire. One had on a pair of duck trousers, which were much too large for him, and stuck out in a most ungainly manner; another wore nothing but the common, scanty, native garment round the loins and a black beaver hat; but the most ludicrous personage of all, and one who seemed to be chief, was a tall, middle-aged man, of a mild, simple expression of countenance, who wore a white cotton shirt, a swallow-tailed coat, and a straw hat, while his black, brawny legs were totally uncovered below the knees.

"Where's the commander of this ship?" inquired our captain, stepping up to this individual.

"I is cap'in," he answered, taking off his straw hat and making a low bow.

"You!" said our captain in surprise. "Where do you come from, and where are you bound? What cargo have you aboard?"

"We is come," answered the man with the swallow-tail, "from Aitutaki; we was go for Raro-tonga. We is native miss'nary ship; our name is de *Olive Branch*; an' our cargo is two tons cocoa-nuts, seventy pigs, twenty cats, and de Gosp'l."

This announcement was received by the crew of our vessel with a shout of laughter, which, however, was peremptorily checked by the captain, whose expression instantly changed from one of severity to that of frank urbanity as he advanced towards the missionary and shook him warmly by the hand.

"I am very glad to have fallen in with you," said he, "and I wish you much success in your missionary labours. Pray take me to your cabin, as I wish to converse with you privately."

The missionary immediately took him by the hand, and as he led him away I heard him saying, "me most glad to find you trader; we t'ought you be pirate. You very like one 'bout the masts."

What conversation the captain had with this man I never heard; but he came on deck again in a quarter of an hour, and shaking hands cordially with the missionary, ordered us into our boat and returned to the schooner, which was immediately put before the wind. In a few minutes the *Olive Branch* was left far behind us.

That afternoon, as I was down below at dinner, I heard the men talking about this curious ship.

"I wonder," said one, "why our captain looked so sweet on yon swallow-tailed supercargo o' pigs and Gospels? If it had been an ordinary trader, now, he would have taken as many o' the pigs as he required and sent the ship with all on board to the bottom."

"Why, Dick, you must be new to these seas if you don't know that!" cried another. "The captain cares as much for the Gospel as you do (an' that's precious little); but he knows, and everybody knows, that the only place among the southern islands where a ship can put in and get what she wants in comfort is where the Gospel has been sent to. There are hundreds o' islands, at this blessed moment, where you might as well jump straight into a shark's maw as land without a band o' thirty comrades armed to the teeth to back you."

"Ay," said a man with a deep scar over his right eye. "Dick's new to the work. But if the captain takes us for a cargo o' sandal-wood to the Feejees, he'll get a taste o' these black gentry in their native condition. For my part, I don't know, and I don't care, what the Gospel does to them; but I know that when any o' the islands chance to get it, trade goes all smooth and easy. But where they ha'n't got it, Beelzebub himself could hardly desire better company."

"Well, you ought to be a good judge," cried another, laughing, "for you've never kept any company but the worst all your life!"

"Ralph Rover!" shouted a voice down the hatchway; "captain wants you, aft."

Springing up the ladder, I hastened to the cabin, pondering as I went the strange testimony borne by these men to the effect of the Gospel on savage natures-testimony which, as it was perfectly disinterested, I had no doubt whatever was strictly true.

On coming again on deck I found Bloody Bill at the helm, and as we were alone together, I tried to draw him into conversation. After repeating to him the conversation in the forecastle about the missionaries, I said:

"Tell me, Bill: is this schooner really a trader in sandal-wood?"

"Yes, Ralph, she is; but she's just as really a pirate. The black flag you saw flying at the peak was no deception."

"Then how can you say she's a trader?" asked I.

"Why, as to that, she trades when she can't take by force; but she takes by force when she can, in preference. Ralph," he added, lowering his voice, "if you had seen the bloody deeds that I have witnessed done on these decks, you would not need to ask if we were pirates. But you'll find it out soon enough. As for the missionaries, the captain favours them because they are useful to him. The South Sea Islanders are such incarnate fiends that they are the better of being tamed, and the missionaries are the only men who can do it."

Our track after this lay through several clusters of small islets, among which we were becalmed more than once. During this part of our voyage the watch on deck and the lookout at the masthead were more than usually vigilant, as we were not only in danger of being attacked by the natives (who, I learned from the captain's remarks, were a bloody and deceitful tribe at this group), but we were also exposed to much risk from the multitudes of coral reefs that rose up in the channels between the islands-some of them just above the surface, others a few feet below it. Our precautions against the savages, I found, were indeed necessary.

One day we were becalmed among a group of small islands, most of which appeared to be uninhabited. As we were in want of fresh water, the captain sent the boat ashore to bring off a cask or two. But we were mistaken in thinking there were no natives; for scarcely had we drawn near to the shore when a band of naked blacks rushed out of the bush and assembled on the beach, brandishing their clubs and spears in a threatening manner. Our men were well armed, but refrained from showing any signs of hostility, and rowed nearer in order to converse with the natives; and I now found that more than one of the crew could imperfectly speak dialects of the language peculiar to the South Sea Islanders. When within forty yards of the shore we ceased rowing, and the first mate stood up to address the multitude; but instead of answering us, they replied with a shower of stones, some of which cut the men severely. Instantly our muskets were levelled, and a volley was about to be fired when the captain hailed us in a loud voice from the schooner, which lay not more than five or six hundred yards off the shore.

"Don't fire!" he shouted angrily. "Pull off to the point ahead of you!"

The men looked surprised at this order, and uttered deep curses as they prepared to obey; for their wrath was roused, and they burned for revenge. Three or four of them hesitated, and seemed disposed to mutiny.

"Don't distress yourselves, lads," said the mate, while a bitter smile curled his lip. "Obey orders. The captain's not the man to take an insult tamely. If Long Tom does not speak presently, I'll give myself to the sharks."

The men smiled significantly as they pulled from the shore, which was now crowded with a dense mass of savages, amounting probably to five or six hundred. We had not rowed off above a couple of hundred yards when a loud roar thundered over the sea, and the big brass gun sent a withering shower of grape point-blank into the midst of the living mass, through which a wide lane was cut; while a yell, the like of which I could not have imagined, burst from the miserable survivors as they fled to the woods. Amongst the heaps of dead that lay on the sand just where they had fallen, I could distinguish mutilated forms writhing in agony; while ever and anon one and another rose convulsively from out the mass, endeavoured to stagger towards the wood, and ere they had taken a few steps, fell and wallowed on the bloody sand. My blood curdled within me as I witnessed this frightful and wanton slaughter; but I had little time to think, for the captain's deep voice came again over the water towards us: "Pull ashore, lads, and fill your water-casks!" The men obeyed in silence, and it seemed to me as if even their hard hearts were shocked by the ruthless deed. On gaining the mouth of the rivulet at which we intended to take in water, we found it flowing with blood; for the greater part of those who were slain had been standing on the banks of the stream, a short way above its mouth. Many of the wretched creatures had fallen into it; and we found one body, which had been carried down, jammed between two rocks, with the staring eyeballs turned towards us, and his black hair waving in the ripples of the blood-red stream. No one dared to oppose our landing now, so we carried our casks to a pool above the murdered group, and having filled them, returned on board. Fortunately a breeze sprang up soon afterwards, and carried us away from the dreadful spot; but it could not waft me away from the memory of what I had seen.

"And this," thought I, gazing in horror at the captain, who, with a quiet look of indifference, leaned upon the taffrail, smoking a cigar and contemplating the fertile green islets as they passed like a lovely picture before our eyes —"this is the man who favours the missionaries because they are useful to him and can tame the savages better than any one else can do it!" Then I wondered in my mind whether it were possible for any missionary to tame *him*!

CHAPTER TWENTY FOUR

> Bloody Bill is communicative and sagacious-Unpleasant prospects-Retrospective meditations interrupted by volcanic agency-The pirates negotiate with a Feejee chief-Various etceteras that are calculated to surprise and horrify.

It was many days after the events just narrated ere I recovered a little of my wonted spirits. I could not shake off the feeling for a long time that I was in a frightful dream, and the sight of our captain filled me with so much horror that I kept out of his way as much as my duties about the cabin would permit. Fortunately he took so little notice of me that he did not observe my changed feelings towards him, otherwise it might have been worse for me.

But I was now resolved that I would run away the very first island we should land at, and commit myself to the hospitality of the natives rather than remain an hour longer than I could help in the pirate schooner. I pondered this subject a good deal, and at last made up my mind to communicate my intention to Bloody Bill; for during several talks I had had with him of late, I felt assured that he too would willingly escape if possible. When I told him of my design he shook his head. "No, no, Ralph," said he; "you must not think of running away here. Among some of the groups of islands you might do so with safety; but if you tried it here, you would find that you had jumped out of the fryin'-pan into the fire."

"How so, Bill?" said I. "Would the natives not receive me?"

"That they would, lad; but they would eat you too."

"Eat me!" said I in surprise. "I thought the South Sea Islanders never ate anybody except their enemies."

"Humph!" ejaculated Bill. "I 'spose 'twas yer tender-hearted friends in England that put that notion into your head. There's a set o' soft-hearted folk at home that I knows on who don't like to have their feelin's ruffled; and when you tell them anything they don't like-that shocks them, as they call it-no matter how true it be, they stop their ears and cry out, 'Oh, that is *too* horrible! We can't believe that!' An' they say truth. They can't believe it, 'cause they won't believe it. Now, I believe there's thousands o' the people in England who are sich born drivellin' *won't believers* that they think the black fellows hereaways, at the worst, eat an enemy only now an' then out o' spite; whereas I know for certain, and many captains of the British and American navies know as well as me, that the Feejee Islanders eat not only their enemies but one another-and they do it not for spite, but for pleasure. It's a *fact* that they prefer human flesh to any other. But they don't like white men's flesh so well as black; they say it makes them sick."

"Why, Bill," said I, "you told me just now that they would eat *me* if they caught me!"

"So I did, and so I think they would. I've only heard some o' them say they don't like white men *so well* as black; but if they was hungry they wouldn't be particular. Anyhow, I'm sure they would kill you. You see, Ralph, I've been a good while in them parts, and I've visited the different groups of islands oftentimes as a trader. And thorough-goin' blackguards some o' them traders are-no better than pirates, I can tell you. One captain that I sailed with was not a chip better than the one we're with now. He was trading with a friendly chief one day aboard his vessel. The chief had swam off to us with the things for trade tied atop of his head, for them chaps are like otters in the water. Well, the chief was hard on the captain, and would not part with some o' his things. When their bargainin' was over they shook hands, and the chief jumped overboard to swim ashore; but before he got forty yards from the ship, the captain seized a musket and shot him dead. He then hove up anchor and put to sea, and as we sailed along the shore he dropped six black fellows with his rifle, remarkin' that 'that would spoil the trade for the next-comers.' But, as I was sayin', I'm up to the ways o' these fellows. One o' the laws o' the country is that every shipwrecked person who happens to be cast ashore, be he dead or alive, is doomed to be roasted and eaten. There was a small tradin' schooner wrecked off one of these islands when we were lyin' there in harbour during a storm. The crew was lost-all but three men, who swam ashore. The moment they landed, they were seized by the natives and carried up into the woods. We knew pretty well what their fate would be; but we could not help them, for our crew was small, and if we had gone ashore they would likely have killed us all. We never saw the three men again. But we heard frightful yelling and dancing and merrymaking that night; and one of the natives, who came aboard to trade with us next day, told us that the *long pigs*, as he called the men, had been roasted and eaten, and their bones were to be converted into sail-needles. He also said that white men were bad to eat, and that most o' the people on shore were sick."

I was very much shocked and cast down in my mind at this terrible account of the natives, and asked Bill what he would advise me to do. Looking round the deck to make sure that we were not overheard, he lowered his voice and said, "There are two or three ways that we might escape, Ralph, but none o' them's easy. If the captain would only sail for some o' the islands near Tahiti we might run away there well enough, because the natives are all Christians; an' we find that wherever the savages take up with Christianity they always give over their bloody ways, and are safe to be trusted. I never cared for Christianity myself," he continued in a soliloquising voice, "and I don't well know what it means; but a man with half-an-eye can see what it does for these black critters. However, the captain always keeps a sharp lookout after us when we get to these islands, for he half-suspects that one or two o' us are tired of his company. Then we might manage to cut the boat adrift some fine night when it's our watch on deck, and clear off before they discovered that we were gone. But we would run the risk o' bein' caught by the blacks. I wouldn't like to try that plan. But you and I will think over it, Ralph, and see what's to be done. In the meantime it's our watch below, so I'll go and turn in."

Bill then bade me good-night and went below, while a comrade took his place at the helm; but feeling no desire to enter into conversation with him, I walked aft, and leaning over the stern, looked down into the phosphorescent waves that gurgled around the rudder, and streamed out like a flame of blue light in the vessel's wake. My thoughts were very sad, and I could scarce refrain from tears as I contrasted my present wretched position with the happy, peaceful time I had spent on the Coral Island with my dear companions. As I thought upon Jack and Peterkin, anxious forebodings crossed my mind, and I pictured to myself the grief and dismay with which they would search every nook and corner of the island in a vain attempt to discover my dead body; for I felt assured that if they did not see any sign of the pirate schooner or boat when they came out of the cave to look for me, they would never imagine that I had been carried away. I wondered, too, how Jack would succeed in getting Peterkin out of the cave without my assistance; and I trembled when I thought that he might lose presence of mind, and begin to kick when he was in the tunnel! These thoughts were suddenly interrupted and put to flight by a bright-red blaze, which lighted up the horizon to the southward and cast a crimson glow far over the sea. This appearance was accompanied by a low growling sound, as of distant thunder, and at the same time the sky above us became black, while a hot, stifling wind blew around us in fitful gusts.

The crew assembled hastily on deck, and most of them were under the belief that a frightful hurricane was pending; but the captain, coming on deck, soon explained the phenomena.

"It's only a volcano," said he. "I knew there was one hereabouts, but thought it was extinct. — Up, there, and furl topgallant sails! We'll likely have a breeze, and it's well to be ready."

As he spoke, a shower began to fall, which, we quickly observed, was not rain, but fine ashes. As we were many miles distant from the volcano, these must have been carried to us from it by the wind. As the captain had predicted, a stiff breeze soon afterwards sprang up, under the influence of which we speedily left the volcano far behind us; but during the greater part of the night we could see its lurid glare and hear its distant thunder. The shower did not cease to fall for several hours, and we must have sailed under it for nearly forty miles-perhaps farther. When we emerged from the cloud, our decks and every part of the rigging were completely covered with a thick coat of ashes. I was much interested in this, and recollected that Jack had often spoken of many of the islands of the Pacific as being volcanoes, either active or extinct, and had said that the whole region was more or less volcanic, and that some scientific men were of opinion that the islands of the Pacific were nothing more or less than the mountain-tops of a huge continent which had sunk under the influence of volcanic agency.

Three days after passing the volcano, we found ourselves a few miles to windward of an island of considerable size and luxuriant aspect. It consisted of two mountains, which seemed to be nearly four thousand feet high. They were separated from each other by a broad valley, whose thick-growing trees ascended a considerable distance up the mountain-sides; and rich, level plains or meadow-land spread round the base of the mountains, except at the point immediately opposite the large valley, where a river seemed to carry the trees, as it were, along with it down to the white, sandy shore. The mountain-tops, unlike those of our Coral Island, were sharp, needle-shaped, and bare, while their sides were more rugged and grand in outline than anything I had yet seen in those seas. Bloody Bill was beside me when the island first hove in sight.

"Ah!" he exclaimed, "I know that island well. They call it Emo."

"Have you been there before, then?" I inquired.

"Ay, that I have, often, and so has this schooner. 'Tis a famous island for sandal-wood. We have taken many cargoes of it already-and have paid for them, too, for the savages are so numerous that we dared not try to take it by force. But our captain has tried to cheat them so often that they're beginnin' not to like us overmuch now. Besides, the men behaved ill the last time we were here, and I wonder the captain is not afraid to venture. But he's afraid o' nothin' earthly, I believe."

We soon ran inside the barrier coral reef, and let go our anchor in six fathoms water, just opposite the mouth of a small creek, whose shores were densely covered with mangroves and tall umbrageous trees. The principal village of the natives lay about half-a-mile from this point. Ordering the boat out, the captain jumped into it, and ordered me to follow him. The men, fifteen in number, were well armed; and the mate was directed to have Long Tom ready for emergencies.

"Give way, lads!" cried the captain.

The oars fell into the water at the word, the boat shot from the schooner's side, and in a few minutes reached the shore. Here, contrary to our expectation, we were met with the utmost cordiality by Romata, the principal chief of the island, who conducted us to his house and gave us mats to sit upon. I observed in passing that the natives, of whom there were two or three thousand, were totally unarmed.

After a short preliminary palaver, a feast of baked pigs and various roots was spread before us, of which we partook sparingly, and then proceeded to business. The captain stated his object in visiting the island, regretted that there had been a slight misunderstanding during the last visit, and hoped that no ill-will was borne by either party, and that a satisfactory trade would be accomplished.

Romata answered that he had forgotten there had been any differences between them, protested that he was delighted to see his friends again, and assured them they should have every assistance in cutting and embarking the wood. The terms were afterwards agreed on, and we rose to depart. All this conversation was afterwards explained to me by Bill, who understood the language pretty well.

Romata accompanied us on board, and explained that a great chief from another island was then on a visit to him, and that he was to be ceremoniously entertained on the following day. After begging to be allowed to introduce him to us, and receiving permission, he sent his canoe ashore to bring him off. At the same time he gave orders to bring on board his two favourites, a cock and a paroquet. While the canoe was gone on this errand, I had time to regard the savage chief attentively. He was a man of immense size, with massive but beautifully moulded limbs and figure, only parts of which-the broad chest and muscular arms-were uncovered; for although the lower orders generally wore no other clothing than a strip of cloth called *maro* round their loins, the chief, on particular occasions, wrapped his person in voluminous folds of a species of native cloth made from the bark of the Chinese paper-mulberry. Romata wore a magnificent black beard and moustache, and his hair was frizzed out to such an extent that it resembled a large turban, in which was stuck a long wooden pin! I afterwards found that this pin served for scratching the head, for which purpose the fingers were too short without disarranging the hair. But Romata put himself to much greater inconvenience on account of his hair; for we found that he slept with his head resting on a wooden pillow, in which was cut a hollow for the neck, so that the hair of the sleeper might not be disarranged.

In ten minutes the canoe returned, bringing the other chief, who certainly presented a most extraordinary appearance, having painted one half of his face red and the other half yellow, besides ornamenting it with various designs in black! Otherwise he was much the same in appearance as Romata, though not so powerfully built. As this chief had never seen a ship before-except, perchance, some of the petty traders that at long intervals visit these remote islands-he was much taken up with the neatness and beauty of all the fittings of the schooner. He was particularly struck with a musket which was shown to him, and asked where the white men got hatchets hard enough to cut the tree of which the barrel was made! While he was thus engaged, his brother-chief stood aloof, talking with the captain, and fondling a superb cock and a little blue-headed paroquet-the favourites of which I have before spoken. I observed that all the other natives walked in a crouching posture while in the presence of Romata. Before our guests left us, the captain ordered the brass gun to be uncovered and fired for their gratification; and I have every reason to believe he did so for the purpose of showing our superior power, in case the natives should harbour any evil designs against us. Romata had never seen this gun before, as it had not been uncovered on previous visits, and the astonishment with which he viewed it was very amusing. Being desirous of knowing its power, he begged that the captain would fire it; so a shot was put into it. The chiefs were then directed to look at a rock about two miles out at sea, and the gun was fired. In a second the top of the rock was seen to burst asunder, and to fall in fragments into the sea.

Romata was so delighted with the success of this shot that he pointed to a man who was walking on the shore, and begged the captain to fire at him, evidently supposing that his permission was quite sufficient to justify the captain in such an act. He was therefore surprised, and not a little annoyed, when the captain refused to fire at the native and ordered the gun to be housed.

Of all the things, however, that afforded matter of amusement to these savages, that which pleased Romata's visitor most was the ship's pump. He never tired of examining it and pumping up the water. Indeed, so much was he taken up with this pump that he could not be prevailed on to return on shore, but sent a canoe to fetch his favourite stool, on which he seated himself, and spent the remainder of the day in pumping the bilge-water out of the ship!

Next day the crew went ashore to cut sandal-wood, while the captain, with one or two men, remained on board, in order to be ready, if need be, with the brass gun, which was unhoused and conspicuously elevated, with its capacious muzzle directed point-blank at the chief's house. The men were fully armed, as usual; and the captain ordered me to go with them, to assist in the work. I was much pleased with this order, for it freed me from the captain's company, which I could not now endure, and it gave me an opportunity of seeing the natives.

As we wound along in single file through the rich, fragrant groves of banana, cocoa-nut, bread-fruit, and other trees, I observed that there were many of the plum and banyan trees, with which I had become familiar on the Coral Island. I noticed, also, large quantities of taro-roots, yams, and sweet potatoes growing in enclosures. On turning into an open glade of the woods, we came abruptly upon a cluster of native houses. They were built chiefly of bamboos, and were thatched with the large, thick leaves of the pandanus; but many of them had little more than a sloping roof and three sides with an open front, being the most simple shelter from the weather that could well be imagined. Within these and around them were groups of natives-men, women, and children-who all stood up to gaze at us as we marched along, followed by the party of men whom the chief had sent to escort us. About half-a-mile inland we arrived at the spot where the sandal-wood grew, and while the men set to work I clambered up an adjoining hill to observe the country.

About midday the chief arrived with several followers, one of whom carried a baked pig on a wooden platter, with yams and potatoes on several plantain leaves, which he presented to the men, who sat down under the shade of a tree to dine. The chief sat down to dine also; but, to my surprise, instead of feeding himself, one of his wives performed that office for him! I was seated beside Bill, and asked him the reason of this.

"It is beneath his dignity, I believe, to feed himself," answered Bill; "but I dare say he's not particular, except on great occasions. They've a strange custom among them, Ralph, which is called *tabu*, and they carry it to great lengths. If a man chooses a particular tree for his god, the fruit o' that tree is tabued to him; and if he eats it, he is sure to be killed by his people-and eaten, of course, for killing means eating hereaway. Then, you see that great mop o' hair on the chief's head? Well, he has a lot o' barbers to keep it in order; and it's a law that whoever touches the head of a living chief or the body of a dead one, his hands are tabued. So in that way the barbers' hands are always tabued, and they daren't use them for their lives, but have to be fed like big babies-as they are, sure enough!"

"That's odd, Bill. But look there," said I, pointing to a man whose skin was of a much lighter colour than the generality of the natives. "I've seen a few of these light-skinned fellows among the Feejeeans. They seem to me to be of quite a different race."

"So they are," answered Bill. "These fellows come from the Tongan Islands, which lie a long way to the eastward. They come here to build their big war-canoes; and as these take two, and sometimes four, years to build, there's always some o' the brown-skins among the black sarpents o' these islands."

"By the way, Bill," said I, "your mentioning serpents reminds me that I have not seen a reptile of any kind since I came to this part of the world."

"No more there are any," said Bill, "if ye except the niggers themselves. There's none on the islands but a lizard or two, and some sich harmless things; but I never seed any myself. If there's none on the land, however, there's more than enough in the water; and that reminds me of a wonderful brute they have here. But come, I'll show it to you." So saying, Bill arose, and leaving the men still busy with the baked pig, led me into the forest. After proceeding a short distance we came upon a small pond of stagnant water. A native lad had followed us, to whom we called and beckoned him to come to us. On Bill saying a few words to him, which I did not understand, the boy advanced to the edge of the pond and gave a low, peculiar whistle. Immediately the water became agitated, and an enormous eel thrust its head above the surface and allowed the youth to touch it. It was about twelve feet long, and as thick round the body as a man's thigh.

"There!" said Bill, his lip curling with contempt; "what do you think of that for a god, Ralph? This is one o' their gods, and it has been fed with dozens o' livin' babies already. How many more it'll get afore it dies is hard to say."

"Babies!" said I with an incredulous look.

"Ay, babies," returned Bill. "Your soft-hearted folk at home would say, 'Oh, horrible! Impossible!' to that, and then go away as comfortable and unconcerned as if their sayin' 'Horrible! impossible!' had made it a lie. But I tell you, Ralph, it's a *fact*. I've seed it with my own eyes the last time I was here; an' mayhap, if you stop awhile at this accursed place and keep a sharp lookout, you'll see it too. They don't feed it regularly with livin' babies, but they give it one now and then as a treat. —Bah, you brute!" cried Bill in disgust, giving the reptile a kick on the snout with his heavy boot that sent it sweltering back in agony into its loathsome pool. I thought it lucky for Bill-indeed for all of us-that the native youth's back happened to be turned at the time, for I am certain that if the poor savages had come to know that we had so rudely handled their god we should have had to fight our way back to the ship. As we retraced our steps I questioned my companion further on this subject.

"How comes it, Bill, that the mothers allow such a dreadful thing to be done?"

"Allow it? the mothers *do* it! It seems to me that there's nothing too fiendish or diabolical for these people to do. Why, in some of the islands they have an institution called the *Areoi*, and the persons connected with that body are ready for any wickedness that mortal man can devise. In fact, they stick at nothing; and one o' their customs is to murder their infants the moment they are born. The mothers agree to it, and the fathers do it. And the mildest ways they have of murdering them is by sticking them through the body with sharp splinters of bamboo, strangling them with their thumbs, or burying them alive and stamping them to death while under the sod."

I felt sick at heart while my companion recited these horrors.

"But it's a curious fact," he continued after a pause, during which we walked in silence towards the spot where we had left our comrades —"it's a curious fact that wherever the missionaries get a footin' all these things come to an end at once, an' the savages take to doin' each other good and singin' psalms, just like Methodists."

"God bless the missionaries," said I, while a feeling of enthusiasm filled my heart so that I could speak with difficulty. "God bless and prosper the missionaries till they get a footing in every island of the sea!"

"I would say Amen to that prayer, Ralph, if I could," said Bill, in a deep, sad voice; "but it would be a mere mockery for a man to ask a blessing for others who dare not ask one for himself. But, Ralph," he continued, "I've not told you half o' the abominations I have seen durin' my life in these seas. If we pull long together, lad, I'll tell you more; and if times have not changed very much since I was here last, it's like that you'll have a chance o' seeing a little for yourself before long."

CHAPTER TWENTY FIVE

The sandal-wood party-Native children's games somewhat surprising-Desperate amusements suddenly and fatally brought to a close-An old friend recognised-News-Romata's mad conduct.

Next day the wood-cutting party went ashore again, and I accompanied them as before. During the dinner-hour I wandered into the woods alone, being disinclined for food that day. I had not rambled far when I found myself unexpectedly on the seashore, having crossed a narrow neck of land which separated the native village from a large bay. Here I found a party of the islanders busy with one of their war-canoes, which was almost ready for launching. I stood for a long time watching this party with great interest, and observed that they fastened the timbers and planks to each other very much in the same way in which I had seen Jack fasten those of our little boat. But what surprised me most was its immense length, which I measured carefully, and found to be a hundred feet long; and it was so capacious that it could have held three hundred men. It had the unwieldy outrigger and enormously high stern-posts which I had remarked on the canoe that came to us while I was on the Coral Island. Observing some boys playing at games a short way along the beach, I resolved to go and watch them; but as I turned from the natives who were engaged so busily and cheerfully at their work, I little thought of the terrible event that hung on the completion of that war-canoe.

Advancing towards the children, who were so numerous that I began to think this must be the general playground of the village, I sat down on a grassy bank under the shade of a plantain-tree to watch them. And a happier or more noisy crew I have never seen. There were at least two hundred of them, both boys and girls, all of whom were clad in no other garments than their own glossy little black skins, except the maro, or strip of cloth, round the loins of the boys, and a very short petticoat or kilt on the girls. They did not all play at the same game, but amused themselves in different groups.

One band was busily engaged in a game exactly similar to our blind man's buff. Another set were walking on stilts, which raised the children three feet from the ground. They were very expert at this amusement, and seldom tumbled. In another place I observed a group of girls standing together, and apparently enjoying themselves very much; so I went up to see what they were doing, and found that they were opening their eyelids with their fingers till their eyes appeared of an enormous size, and then thrusting pieces of straw between the upper and lower lids, across the eyeball, to keep them in that position! This seemed to me, I must confess, a very foolish as well as dangerous amusement. Nevertheless, the children seemed to be greatly delighted with the hideous faces they made. I pondered this subject a good deal, and thought that if little children knew how silly they seemed to grown-up people when, they make faces, they would not be so fond of doing it. In another place were a number of boys engaged in flying kites; and I could not help wondering that some of the games of those little savages should be so like to our own, although they had never seen us at play. But the kites were different from ours in many respects, being of every variety of shape. They were made of very thin cloth, and the boys raised them to a wonderful height in the air by means of twine made from the cocoa-nut husk. Other games there were, some of which showed the natural depravity of the hearts of these poor savages, and made me wish fervently that missionaries might be sent out to them. But the amusement which the greatest number of the children of both sexes seemed to take chief delight in was swimming and diving in the sea, and the expertness which they exhibited was truly amazing. They seemed to have two principal games in the water, one of which was to dive off a sort of stage which had been erected near a deep part of the sea, and chase each other in the water. Some of them went down to an extraordinary depth; others skimmed along the surface, or rolled over and over like porpoises, or diving under each other, came up unexpectedly and pulled each other down by a leg or an arm. They never seemed to tire of this sport, and from the great heat of the water in the South Seas, they could remain in it nearly all day without feeling chilled. Many of these children were almost infants, scarce able to walk; yet they staggered down the beach, flung their round, fat little black bodies fearlessly into deep water, and struck out to sea with as much confidence as ducklings.

The other game to which I have referred was swimming in the surf. But as this is an amusement in which all engage, from children of ten to grey-headed men of sixty, and as I had an opportunity of witnessing it in perfection the day following, I shall describe it more minutely.

I suppose it was in honour of their guest that this grand swimming-match was got up, for Romata came and told the captain that they were going to engage in it, and begged him to "come and see."

"What sort of amusement is this surf-swimming?" I inquired of Bill as we walked together to a part of the shore on which several thousands of the natives were assembled.

"It's a very favourite lark with these 'xtr'or'nary critters," replied Bill, giving a turn to the quid of tobacco that invariably bulged out of his left cheek. "Ye see, Ralph, them fellows take to the water as soon a'most as they can walk, an' long before they can do that anything respectably, so that they are as much at home in the sea as on the land. Well, ye see, I 'spose they found swimmin' for miles out to sea, and divin' fathoms deep, wasn't excitin' enough, so they invented this game o' swimmin' on the surf. Each man and boy, as you see, has got a short board or plank, with which he swims out for a mile or more to sea, and then, gettin' on the top o' yon thunderin' breaker, they come to shore on the top of it, yellin' and screechin' like fiends. It's a marvel to me that they're not dashed to shivers on the coral reef, for sure an' sart'in am I that if any o' us tried it, we wouldn't be worth the fluke of a broken anchor after the wave fell. But there they go!"

As he spoke, several hundreds of the natives, amongst whom we were now standing, uttered a loud yell, rushed down the beach, plunged into the surf, and were carried off by the seething foam of the retreating wave.

At the point where we stood, the encircling coral reef joined the shore, so that the magnificent breakers, which a recent stiff breeze had rendered larger than usual, fell in thunder at the feet of the multitudes who lined the beach. For some time the swimmers continued to strike out to sea, breasting over the swell like hundreds of black seals. Then they all turned, and watching an approaching billow, mounted its white crest, and each laying his breast on the short, flat board, came rolling towards the shore, careering on the summit of the mighty wave, while they and the onlookers shouted and yelled with excitement. Just as the monster wave curled in solemn majesty to fling its bulky length upon the beach, most of the swimmers slid back into the trough behind; others, slipping off their boards, seized them in their hands, and plunging through the watery waste, swam out to repeat the amusement; but a few, who seemed to me the most reckless, continued their career until they were launched upon the beach and enveloped in the churning foam and spray. One of these last came in on the crest of the wave most manfully, and landed with a violent bound almost on the spot where Bill and I stood. I saw by his peculiar head-dress that he was the chief whom the tribe entertained as their guest. The sea-water had removed nearly all the paint with which his face had been covered, and as he rose panting to his feet, I recognised, to my surprise, the features of Tararo, my old friend of the Coral Island!

Tararo at the same moment recognised me, and advancing quickly, took me round the neck and rubbed noses, which had the effect of transferring a good deal of the moist paint from his nose to mine. Then, recollecting that this was not the white man's mode of salutation, he grasped me by the hand and shook it violently.

"Hallo, Ralph!" cried Bill in surprise, "that chap seems to have taken a sudden fancy to you, or he must be an old acquaintance."

"Right, Bill," I replied; "he is indeed an old acquaintance." And I explained, in a few words, that he was the chief whose party Jack and Peterkin and I had helped to save.

Tararo having thrown away his surf-board, entered into an animated conversation with Bill, pointing frequently during the course of it to me, whereby I concluded he must be telling him about the memorable battle and the part we had taken in it. When he paused I begged of Bill to ask him about the woman Avatea, for I had some hope that she might have come with Tararo on this visit. "And ask him," said I, "who she is, for I am persuaded she is of a different race from the Feejeeans." On the mention of her name the chief frowned darkly, and seemed to speak with much anger.

"You're right, Ralph," said Bill when the chief had ceased to talk; "she's not a Feejee girl, but a Samoan. How she ever came to this place the chief does not very clearly explain; but he says she was taken in war, and that he got her three years ago, an' kept her as his daughter ever since. Lucky for her, poor girl, else she'd have been roasted and eaten like the rest."

"But why does Tararo frown and look so angry?" said I.

"Because the girl's somewhat obstinate, like most o' the sex, an' won't marry the man he wants her to. It seems that a chief of some other island came on a visit to Tararo and took a fancy to her; but she wouldn't have him on no account, bein' already in love, and engaged to a young chief whom Tararo hates, and she kicked up a desperate shindy. So, as he was goin' on a war-expedition in his canoe, he left her to think about it, sayin' he'd be back in six months or so, when he hoped she wouldn't be so obstropolous. This happened just a week ago; an' Tararo says that if she's not ready to go, when the chief returns, as his bride, she'll be sent to him as a *long pig.*"

"As a long pig!" I exclaimed in surprise. "Why, what does he mean by that?"

"He means somethin' very unpleasant," answered Bill with a frown. "You see, these black-guards eat men an' women just as readily as they eat pigs; and as baked pigs and baked men are very like each other in appearance, they call men *long* pigs. If Avatea goes to this fellow as a long pig, it's all up with her, poor thing!"

"Is she on the island now?" I asked eagerly.

"No; she's at Tararo's island."

"And where does it lie?"

"About fifty or sixty miles to the south'ard o' this," returned Bill; "but I —"

At this moment we were startled by the cry of "mao! mao —a shark! a shark!" which was immediately followed by a shriek that rang clear and fearfully loud above the tumult of cries that arose from the savages in the water and on the land. We turned hastily towards the direction whence the cry came, and had just time to observe the glaring eyeballs of one of the swimmers as he tossed his arms in the air. Next instant he was pulled under the waves. A canoe was instantly launched, and the hand of the drowning man was caught; but only half of his body was dragged from the maw of the monster, which followed the canoe until the water became so shallow that it could scarcely swim. The crest of the next billow was tinged with red as it rolled towards the shore.

In most countries of the world this would have made a deep impression on the spectators; but the only effect it had upon these islanders was to make them hurry with all speed out of the sea, lest a similar fate should befall some of the others. But so utterly reckless were they of human life that it did not for a moment suspend the progress of their amusements. It is true the surf-swimming ended for that time somewhat abruptly, but they immediately proceeded with other games. Bill told me that sharks do not often attack the surf-swimmers, being frightened away by the immense numbers of men and boys in the water, and by the shouting and splashing that they make. "But," said he, "such a thing as you have seen just now don't frighten them much. They'll be at it again to-morrow or next day, just as if there wasn't a single shark between Feejee and Nova Zembla."

After this the natives had a series of wrestling and boxing matches; and being men of im-mense size and muscle, they did a good deal of injury to each other, especially in boxing, in which not only the lower orders but several of the chiefs and priests engaged. Each bout was very quickly terminated; for they did not pretend to a scientific knowledge of the art, and wasted, no time in sparring, but hit straight out at each other's heads, and their blows were delivered with great force. Frequently one of the combatants was knocked down with a single blow, and one gigantic fellow hit his adversary so severely that he drove the skin entirely off his forehead. This feat was hailed with immense applause by the spectators.

During these exhibitions, which were very painful to me, though I confess I could not refrain from beholding them, I was struck with the beauty of many of the figures and designs that were tattooed on the persons of the chiefs and principal men. One figure, that seemed to me very elegant, was that of a palm-tree tattooed on the back of a man's leg, the roots rising, as it were, from under his heel, the stem ascending the tendon of the ankle, and the graceful head branching out upon the calf. I afterwards learned that this process of tattooing is very painful, and takes long to do, commencing at the age of ten, and being continued at intervals up to the age of thirty. It is done by means of an instrument made of bone, with a number of sharp teeth, with which the skin is punctured. Into these punctures a preparation made from the kernel of the candle-nut, mixed with cocoa-nut oil, is rubbed, and the mark thus made is indelible. The operation is performed by a class of men whose profession it is, and they tattoo as much at a time as the person on whom they are operating can bear, which is not much, the pain and inflammation caused by tattooing being very great-sometimes causing death. Some of the chiefs were tattooed with an ornamental stripe down the legs, which gave them the appearance of being clad in tights; others had marks round the ankles and insteps, which looked like tight-fitting and elegant boots. Their faces were also tattooed, and their breasts were very profusely marked with every imaginable species of device-muskets, dogs, birds, pigs, clubs, and canoes, intermingled with lozenges, squares, circles, and other arbitrary figures.

The women were not tattooed so much as the men, having only a few marks on their feet and arms. But I must say, however objectionable this strange practice may be, it nevertheless had this good effect-that it took away very much from their appearance of nakedness.

Next day, while we were returning from the woods to our schooner, we observed Romata rushing about in the neighbourhood of his house, apparently mad with passion.

"Ah!" said Bill to me, "there he's at his old tricks again. That's his way when he gets drink. The natives make a sort of drink o' their own, and it makes him bad enough; but when he gets brandy he's like a wild tiger. The captain, I suppose, has given him a bottle, as usual, to keep him in good-humour. After drinkin' he usually goes to sleep, and the people know it well, and keep out of his way for fear they should waken him. Even the babies are taken out of earshot; for when he's waked up he rushes out, just as you see him now, and spears or clubs the first person he meets."

It seemed at the present time, however, that no deadly weapon had been in his way, for the infuriated chief was raging about without one. Suddenly he caught sight of an unfortunate man who was trying to conceal himself behind a tree. Rushing towards him, Romata struck him a terrible blow on the head, which knocked out the poor man's eye and also dislocated the chief's finger. The wretched creature offered no resistance; he did not even attempt to parry the blow. Indeed, from what Bill said, I found that he might consider himself lucky in having escaped with his life, which would certainly have been forfeited had the chief been possessed of a club at the time.

"Have these wretched creatures no law among themselves," said I, "which can restrain such wickedness?"

"None," replied Bill. "The chief's word is law. He might kill and eat a dozen of his own subjects any day for nothing more than his own pleasure, and nobody would take the least notice of it."

This ferocious deed took place within sight of our party as we wended our way to the beach, but I could not observe any other expression on the faces of the men than that of total indifference or contempt. It seemed to me a very awful thing that it should be possible for men to come to such hardness of heart and callousness to the sight of bloodshed and violence; but, indeed, I began to find that such constant exposure to scenes of blood was having a slight effect upon myself, and I shuddered when I came to think that I too was becoming callous.

I thought upon this subject much that night while I walked up and down the deck during my hours of watch, and I came to the conclusion that if I, who hated, abhorred, and detested such bloody deeds as I had witnessed within the last few weeks, could so soon come to be less sensitive about them, how little wonder that these poor, ignorant savages, who were born and bred in familiarity therewith, should think nothing of them at all, and should hold human life in so very slight esteem!

CHAPTER TWENTY SIX

Mischief brewing-My blood is made to run cold-Evil consultations and wicked re-
solves-Bloody Bill attempts to do good, and fails-The attack-Wholesale murder-The
flight-The escape.

Next morning I awoke with a feverish brow and a feeling of deep depression at my heart; and
the more I thought on my unhappy fate, the more wretched and miserable did I feel.

I was surrounded on all sides by human beings of the most dreadful character, to whom
the shedding of blood was mere pastime. On shore were the natives, whose practices were so
horrible that I could not think of them without shuddering. On board were none but pirates
of the blackest dye, who, although not cannibals, were foul murderers, and more blameworthy
even than the savages, inasmuch as they knew better. Even Bill, with whom I had, under the
strange circumstances of my lot, formed a kind of intimacy, was so fierce in his nature as to
have acquired the title of "Bloody" from his vile companions. I felt very much cast down the
more I considered the subject and the impossibility of delivery, as it seemed to me-at least,
for a long time to come. At last, in my feeling of utter helplessness, I prayed fervently to the
Almighty that He would deliver me out of my miserable condition; and when I had done so
I felt some degree of comfort.

When the captain came on deck, before the hour at which the men usually started for the
woods, I begged of him to permit me to remain aboard that day, as I did not feel well; but
he looked at me angrily, and ordered me, in a surly tone, to get ready to go on shore as usual.
The fact was that the captain had been out of humour for some time past. Romata and he had
had some differences, and high words had passed between them, during which the chief had
threatened to send a fleet of his war-canoes, with a thousand men, to break up and burn the
schooner; whereupon the captain smiled sarcastically, and going up to the chief, gazed sternly
in his face while he said, "I have only to raise my little finger just now, and my big gun will
blow your whole village to atoms in five minutes!" Although the chief was a bold man, he
quailed before the pirate's glance and threat, and made no reply; but a bad feeling had been
raised, and old sores had been opened.

I had, therefore, to go with the woodcutters that day. Before starting, however, the captain
called me into the cabin and said:

"Here, Ralph; I've got a mission for you, lad. That blackguard Romata is in the dumps, and
nothing will mollify him but a gift; so do you go up to his house and give him these whale's
teeth, with my compliments. Take with you one of the men who can speak the language."

I looked at the gift in some surprise, for it consisted of six white whale's teeth, and two of
the same dyed bright red, which seemed to me very paltry things. However, I did not dare to
hesitate, or to ask any questions; so gathering them up, I left the cabin, and was soon on my
way to the chief's house, accompanied by Bill. On expressing my surprise at the gift, he said:

"They're paltry enough to you or me, Ralph, but they're considered of great value by them
chaps. They're a sort o' cash among them. The red ones are the most prized, one of them
bein' equal to twenty o' the white ones. I suppose the only reason for their bein' valuable is
that there ain't many of them, and they're hard to be got."

On arriving at the house we found Romata sitting on a mat, in the midst of a number of large
bales of native cloth and other articles, which had been brought to him as presents from time to
time by inferior chiefs. He received us rather haughtily; but on Bill explaining the nature of our
errand, he became very condescending, and his eyes glistened with satisfaction when he received
the whale's teeth, although he laid them aside with an assumption of kingly indifference.

"Go," said he with a wave of the hand — "go tell your captain that he may cut wood to-day,
but not to-morrow. He must come ashore; I want to have a palaver with him."

As we left the house to return to the woods, Bill shook his head.

"There's mischief brewin' in that black rascal's head. I know him of old. But what comes here?"

As he spoke, we heard the sound of laughter and shouting in the wood, and presently there issued from it a band of savages, in the midst of whom were a number of men bearing burdens on their shoulders. At first I thought that these burdens were poles with something rolled round them, the end of each pole resting on a man's shoulder; but on a nearer approach I saw that they were human beings, tied hand and foot, and so lashed to the poles that they could not move. I counted twenty of them as they passed.

"More murder!" said Bill in a voice that sounded between a hoarse laugh and a groan.

"Surely they are not going to murder them?" said I, looking anxiously into Bill's face.

"I don't know, Ralph," replied Bill, "what they're goin' to do with them; but I fear they mean no good when they tie fellows up in that way."

As we continued our way towards the woodcutters, I observed that Bill looked anxiously over his shoulder in the direction where the procession had disappeared. At last he stopped, and turning abruptly on his heel, said:

"I tell ye what it is, Ralph: I must be at the bottom o' that affair. Let us follow these black scoundrels and see what they're goin' to do."

I must say I had no wish to pry further into their bloody practices; but Bill seemed bent on it, so I turned and went. We passed rapidly through the bush, being guided in the right direction by the shouts of the savages. Suddenly there was a dead silence, which continued for some time, while Bill and I involuntarily quickened our pace until we were running at the top of our speed across the narrow neck of land previously mentioned. As we reached the verge of the wood we discovered the savages surrounding the large war-canoe, which they were apparently on the point of launching. Suddenly the multitude put their united strength to the canoe; but scarcely had the huge machine begun to move when a yell, the most appalling that ever fell upon my ear, rose high above the shouting of the savages. It had not died away when another and another smote upon my throbbing ear, and then I saw that these inhuman monsters were actually launching their canoe over the living bodies of their victims. But there was no pity in the breasts of these men. Forward they went in ruthless indifference, shouting as they went, while high above their voices rang the dying shrieks of those wretched creatures as, one after another, the ponderous canoe passed over them, burst the eyeballs from their sockets, and sent the life-blood gushing from their mouths. Oh reader, this is no fiction! I would not, for the sake of thrilling you with horror, invent so terrible a scene. It was witnessed. It is true-true as that accursed sin which has rendered the human heart capable of such diabolical enormities!

When it was over I turned round and fell upon the grass with a deep groan; but Bill seized me by the arm, and lifting me up as if I had been a child, cried:

"Come along, lad; let's away!" And so, staggering and stumbling over the tangled underwood, we fled from the fatal spot.

During the remainder of that day I felt as if I were in a horrible dream. I scarce knew what was said to me, and was more than once blamed by the men for idling my time. At last the hour to return aboard came. We marched down to the beach, and I felt relief for the first time when my feet rested on the schooner's deck.

In the course of the evening I overheard part of a conversation between the captain and the first mate, which startled me not a little. They were down in the cabin, and conversed in an undertone; but the skylight being off; I overhead every word that was said.

"I don't half-like it," said the mate. "It seems to me that we'll only have hard fightin' and no pay."

"No pay!" repeated the captain in a voice of suppressed anger. "Do you call a good cargo all for nothing no pay?"

"Very true," returned the mate; "but we've got the cargo aboard. Why not cut your cable and take French leave o' them? What's the use o' tryin' to kill the blackguards when it'll do us no manner o' good?"

"Mate," said the captain in a low voice, "you talk like a fresh-water sailor. I can only attribute this shyness to some strange delusion, for surely," —his voice assumed a slightly sneering tone as he said this —"surely I am not to suppose that you have become soft-hearted! Besides, you are wrong in regard to the cargo being aboard; there's a good quarter of it lying in the woods, and that blackguard chief knows it, and won't let me take it off. He defied us to do our worst yesterday."

"Defied us! did he?" cried the mate with a bitter laugh. "Poor, contemptible thing!"

"And yet he seems not so contemptible but that you are afraid to attack him."

"Who said I was afraid?" growled the mate sulkily. "I'm as ready as any man in the ship. But, captain, what is it that you intend to do?"

"I intend to muffle the sweeps and row the schooner up to the head of the creek there, from which point we can command the pile of sandal-wood with our gun. Then I shall land with all the men except two, who shall take care of the schooner and be ready with the boat to take us off. We can creep through the woods to the head of the village, where these cannibals are always dancing round their suppers of human flesh; and if the carbines of the men are loaded with a heavy charge of buck-shot, we can drop forty or fifty at the first volley. After that the thing will be easy enough. The savages will take to the mountains in a body, and we shall take what we require, up anchor, and away."

To this plan the mate at length agreed. As he left the cabin, I heard the captain say:

"Give the men an extra glass of grog, and don't forget the buck-shot."

The reader may conceive the horror with which I heard this murderous conversation. I immediately repeated it to Bill, who seemed much perplexed about it. At length he said:

"I'll tell you what I'll do, Ralph. I'll swim ashore after dark and fix a musket to a tree not far from the place where we'll have to land, and I'll tie a long string to the trigger, so that when our fellows cross it they'll let it off, and so alarm the village in time to prevent an attack, but not in time to prevent us gettin' back to the boat. —So, Master Captain," added Bill with a smile that, for the first time, seemed to me to be mingled with good-natured cheerfulness, "you'll be balked at least for once in your life by Bloody Bill."

After it grew dark, Bill put this resolve in practice. He slipped over the side with a musket in his left hand, while with his right he swam ashore and entered the woods. He soon returned, having accomplished his purpose, and got on board without being seen, I being the only one on deck.

When the hour of midnight approached, the men were mustered on deck, the cable was cut, and the muffled sweeps got out. These sweeps were immensely large oars, each requiring a couple of men to work it. In a few minutes we entered the mouth of the creek, which was indeed the mouth of a small river, and took about half-an-hour to ascend it, although the spot where we intended to land was not more than six hundred yards from the mouth, because there was a slight current against us, and the mangroves which narrowed the creek impeded the rowers in some places. Having reached the spot, which was so darkened by overhanging trees that we could see with difficulty, a small kedge-anchor attached to a thin line was let softly down over the stern.

"Now, lads," whispered the captain as he walked along the line of men, who were all armed to the teeth, "don't be in a hurry, aim low, and don't waste your first shots."

He then pointed to the boat, into which the men crowded in silence. There was no room to row; but oars were not needed, as a slight push against the side of the schooner sent the boat gliding to the shore.

"There's no need of leaving two in the boat," whispered the mate as the men stepped out; "we shall want all our hands. Let Ralph stay."

The captain assented, and ordered me to stand in readiness with the boat-hook, to shove ashore at a moment's notice if they should return, or to shove off if any of the savages should happen to approach. He then threw his carbine into the hollow of his arm, and glided through the bushes, followed by his men. With a throbbing heart I awaited the result of our plan. I knew the exact locality where the musket was placed, for Bill had described it to me, and I kept my straining eyes fixed upon the spot. But no sound came, and I began to fear that either they had gone in another direction or that Bill had not fixed the string properly. Suddenly I heard a faint click, and observed one or two bright sparks among the bushes. My heart immediately sank within me, for I knew at once that the trigger had indeed been pulled, but that the priming had not caught. The plan, therefore, had utterly failed. A feeling of dread now began to creep over me as I stood in the boat, in that dark, silent spot, awaiting the issue of this murderous expedition. I shuddered as I glanced at the water that glided past like a dark reptile. I looked back at the schooner; but her hull was just barely visible, while her tapering masts were lost among the trees which overshadowed her. Her lower sails were set, but so thick was the gloom that they were quite invisible.

Suddenly I heard a shot. In a moment a thousand voices raised a yell in the village; again the cry rose on the night air, and was followed by broken shouts as of scattered parties of men bounding into the woods. Then I heard another shout, loud and close at hand; it was the voice of the captain cursing the man who had fired the premature shot. Then came the order, "Forward!" followed by a wild hurrah of our men as they charged the savages. Shots now rang in quick succession, and at last a loud volley startled the echoes of the woods. It was followed by a multitude of wild shrieks, which were immediately drowned in another hurrah from the men, the distance of the sound proving that they were driving their enemies before them towards the sea.

While I was listening intently to these sounds, which were now mingled in confusion, I was startled by the rustling of the leaves not far from me. At first I thought it was a party of savages who had observed the schooner, but I was speedily undeceived by observing a body of natives-apparently several hundreds, as far as I could guess in the uncertain light-bounding through the woods towards the scene of battle. I saw at once that this was a party who had outflanked our men, and would speedily attack them in the rear. And so it turned out; for in a short time the shouts increased tenfold, and among them I thought I heard a death-cry uttered by voices familiar to my ear.

At length the tumult of battle ceased, and from the cries of exultation that now arose from the savages, I felt assured that our men had been conquered. I was immediately thrown into dreadful consternation. What was I now to do? To be taken by the savages was too horrible to be thought of; to flee to the mountains was hopeless, as I should soon be discovered; and to take the schooner out of the creek without assistance was impossible. I resolved, however, to make the attempt, as being my only hope, and was on the point of pushing off, when my hand was stayed and my blood chilled by an appalling shriek, in which I recognised the voice of one of the crew. It was succeeded by a shout from the savages. Then came another and another shriek of agony, making my ears to tingle, as I felt convinced they were murdering the pirate crew in cold blood. With a bursting heart and my brain whirling as if on fire, I seized the boat-hook to push from shore when a man sprang from the bushes.

"Stop! Ralph, stop! There, now, push off!" he cried, and bounded into the boat so violently as nearly to upset her. It was Bill's voice! In another moment we were on board-the boat made fast, the line of the anchor cut, and the sweeps run out. At the first stroke of Bill's giant arm the schooner was nearly pulled ashore, for in his haste he forgot that I could scarcely move the unwieldy oar. Springing to the stern, he lashed the rudder in such a position as that, while it aided me, it acted against him, and so rendered the force of our strokes nearly equal. The schooner now began to glide quickly down the creek; but before we reached its mouth, a yell from a thousand voices on the bank told that we were discovered. Instantly a number of the savages plunged into the water and swam towards us; but we were making so much way that they could not overtake us. One, however, an immensely powerful man, succeeded in laying hold of the cut rope that hung from the stern, and clambered quickly upon deck. Bill caught sight of him the instant his head appeared above the taffrail. But he did not cease to row, and did not appear even to notice the savage until he was within a yard of him; then dropping the sweep, he struck him a blow on the forehead with his clenched fist that felled him to the deck. Lifting him up, he hurled him overboard, and resumed the oar. But now a greater danger awaited us; for the savages had outrun us on the bank, and were about to plunge into the water ahead of the schooner. If they succeeded in doing so, our fate was sealed. For one moment Bill stood irresolute. Then drawing a pistol from his belt, he sprang to the brass gun, held the pan of his pistol over the touch-hole, and fired. The shot was succeeded by the hiss of the cannon's priming; then the blaze and the crashing thunder of the monstrous gun burst upon the savages with such deafening roar that it seemed as if their very mountains had been rent asunder.

This was enough. The moment of surprise and hesitation caused by the unwonted sound gave us time to pass the point; a gentle breeze, which the dense foliage had hitherto prevented us from feeling, bulged out our sails; the schooner bent before it, and the shouts of the disappointed savages grew fainter and fainter in the distance as we were slowly wafted out to sea.

CHAPTER TWENTY SEVEN

Reflections-The wounded man-The squall-True consolation-Death.

There is a power of endurance in human beings, both in their bodies and in their minds, which, I have often thought, seems to be wonderfully adapted and exactly proportioned to the circumstances in which individuals may happen to be placed —a power which, in most cases, is sufficient to carry a man through and over every obstacle that may happen to be thrown in his path through life, no matter how high or how steep the mountain may be, but which often forsakes him the moment the summit is gained, the point of difficulty passed, and leaves him prostrated, with energies gone, nerves unstrung, and a feeling of incapacity pervading the entire frame that renders the most trifling effort almost impossible.

During the greater part of that day I had been subjected to severe mental and much physical excitement, which had almost crushed me down by the time I was relieved from duty in the course of the evening. But when the expedition whose failure has just been narrated was planned, my anxieties and energies had been so powerfully aroused that I went through the protracted scenes of that terrible night without a feeling of the slightest fatigue. My mind and body were alike active and full of energy. No sooner was the last thrilling fear of danger past, however, than my faculties were utterly relaxed; and when I felt the cool breezes of the Pacific playing around my fevered brow, and heard the free waves rippling at the schooner's prow, as we left the hated island behind us, my senses forsook me, and I fell in a swoon upon the deck.

From this state I was quickly aroused by Bill, who shook me by the arm, saying:

"Hallo, Ralph, boy! Rouse up, lad; we're safe now! Poor thing! I believe he's fainted." And raising me in his arms he laid me on the folds of the gaff-topsail, which lay upon the deck near the tiller. "Here, take a drop o' this; it'll do you good, my boy," he added in a voice of tenderness which I had never heard him use before, while he held a brandy-flask to my lips.

I raised my eyes gratefully as I swallowed a mouthful; next moment my head sank heavily upon my arm, and I fell fast asleep. I slept long, for when I awoke the sun was a good way above the horizon. I did not move on first opening my eyes, as I felt a delightful sensation of rest pervading me, and my eyes were riveted on and charmed with the gorgeous splendour of the mighty ocean that burst upon my sight. It was a dead calm; the sea seemed a sheet of undulating crystal, tipped and streaked with the saffron hues of sunrise, which had not yet merged into the glowing heat of noon; and there was a deep calm in the blue dome above that was not broken even by the usual flutter of the sea-fowl. How long I would have lain in contemplation of this peaceful scene I know not, but my mind was recalled suddenly and painfully to the past and the present by the sight of Bill, who was seated on the deck at my feet, with his head reclining, as if in sleep, on his right arm, which rested on the tiller. As he seemed to rest peacefully, I did not mean to disturb him; but the slight noise I made in raising myself on my elbow caused him to start and look round.

"Well, Ralph, awake at last, my boy? You have slept long and soundly," he said, turning towards me.

On beholding his countenance I sprang up in anxiety. He was deadly pale, and his hair, which hung in dishevelled locks over his face, was clotted with blood. Blood also stained his hollow cheeks and covered the front of his shirt, which, with the greater part of his dress, was torn and soiled with mud.

"Oh Bill!" said I with deep anxiety, "what is the matter with you? You are ill. You must have been wounded."

"Even so, lad," said Bill in a deep, soft voice, while he extended his huge frame on the couch from which I had just risen. "I've got an ugly wound, I fear; and I've been waiting for you to waken to ask you to get me a drop o' brandy and a mouthful o' bread from the cabin lockers. You seemed to sleep so sweetly, Ralph, that I didn't like to disturb you. But I don't feel up to much just now."

I did not wait till he had done talking, but ran below immediately, and returned in a few seconds with a bottle of brandy and some broken biscuit. He seemed much refreshed after eating a few morsels and drinking a long draught of water mingled with a little of the spirits. Immediately afterwards he fell asleep, and I watched him anxiously until he awoke, being desirous of knowing the nature and extent of his wound.

"Ha!" he exclaimed on awaking suddenly, after a slumber of an hour; "I'm the better of that nap, Ralph. I feel twice the man I was;" and he attempted to rise, but sank back again immediately with a deep groan.

"Nay, Bill, you must not move, but lie still while I look at your wound. I'll make a comfortable bed for you here on deck, and get you some breakfast. After that you shall tell me how you got it. Cheer up, Bill!" I added, seeing that he turned his head away; "you'll be all right in a little, and I'll be a capital nurse to you, though I'm no doctor."

I then left him, and lighted a fire in the caboose. While it was kindling, I went to the steward's pantry and procured the materials for a good breakfast, with which, in little more than half-an-hour, I returned to my companion. He seemed much better, and smiled kindly on me as I set before him a cup of coffee and a tray with several eggs and some bread on it.

"Now, then, Bill," said I cheerfully, sitting down beside him on the deck, "let's fall to. I'm very hungry myself, I can tell you. But —I forgot-your wound," I added, rising; "let me look at it."

I found that the wound was caused by a pistol-shot in the chest. It did not bleed much, and as it was on the right side, I was in hopes that it might not be very serious. But Bill shook his head. "However," said he, "sit down, Ralph, and I'll tell you all about it.

"You see, after we left the boat an' began to push through the bushes, we went straight for the line of my musket, as I had expected. But by some unlucky chance it didn't explode, for I saw the line torn away by the men's legs, and heard the click o' the lock; so I fancy the priming had got damp and didn't catch. I was in a great quandary now what to do, for I couldn't concoct in my mind, in the hurry, any good reason for firin' off my piece. But they say necessity's the mother of invention; so just as I was giving it up and clinchin' my teeth to bide the worst o't and take what should come, a sudden thought came into my head. I stepped out before the rest, seemin' to be awful anxious to be at the savages, tripped my foot on a fallen tree, plunged head foremost into a bush, an' ov coorse my carbine exploded! Then came such a screechin' from the camp as I never heard in all my life. I rose at once, and was rushin' on with the rest when the captain called a halt.

"'You did that a purpose, you villain!' he said with a tremendous oath, and drawin' a pistol from his belt, let fly right into my breast. I fell at once, and remembered no more till I was startled and brought round by the most awful yell I ever heard in my life-except, maybe, the shrieks o' them poor critters that were crushed to death under yon big canoe. Jumpin' up, I looked round, and through the trees saw a fire gleamin' not far off; the light of which showed me the captain and men tied hand and foot, each to a post, and the savages dancin' round them like demons. I had scarce looked for a second when I saw one o' them go up to the captain flourishing a knife, and before I could wink he plunged it into his breast, while another yell, like the one that roused me, rang upon my ear. I didn't wait for more, but bounding up, went crashing through the bushes into the woods. The black fellows caught sight of me, however, but not in time to prevent me jumpin' into the boat, as you know."

Bill seemed to be much exhausted after this recital, and shuddered frequently during the narrative; so I refrained from continuing the subject at that time, and endeavoured to draw his mind to other things.

"But now, Bill," said I, "it behoves us to think about the future, and what course of action we shall pursue. Here we are, on the wide Pacific, in a well-appointed schooner, which is our own-at least, no one has a better claim to it than we have-and the world lies before us. Moreover, here comes a breeze, so we must make up our minds which way to steer."

"Ralph, boy," said my companion, "it matters not to me which way we go. I fear that my time is short now. Go where you will; I'm content."

"Well, then, Bill, I think we had better steer to the Coral Island and see what has become of my dear old comrades, Jack and Peterkin. I believe the island has no name, but the captain once pointed it out to me on the chart, and I marked it afterwards; so, as we know pretty well our position just now, I think I can steer to it. Then, as to working the vessel, it is true I cannot hoist the sails single-handed, but luckily we have enough of sail set already; and if it should come on to blow a squall, I could at least drop the peaks of the main and fore sails, and clew them up partially without help, and throw her head close into the wind, so as to keep her all shaking till the violence of the squall is past. And if we have continued light breezes, I'll rig up a complication of blocks and fix them to the topsail halyards, so that I shall be able to hoist the sails without help. 'Tis true I'll require half-a-day to hoist them, but we don't need to mind that. Then I'll make a sort of erection on deck to screen you from the sun, Bill; and if you can only manage to sit beside the tiller and steer for two hours every day, so as to let me get a nap, I'll engage to let you off duty all the rest of the twenty-four hours. And if you don't feel able for steering, I'll lash the helm and heave-to while I get you your breakfasts and dinners; and so we'll manage famously, and soon reach the Coral Island."

Bill smiled faintly as I ran on in this strain.

"And what will you do," said he, "if it comes on to blow a storm?"

This question silenced me, while I considered what I should do in such a case. At length I laid my hand on his arm and said, "Bill, when a man has done all that he can do, he ought to leave the rest to God."

"Oh Ralph," said my companion in a faint voice, looking anxiously into my face, "I wish that I had the feelin's about God that you seem to have, at this hour. I'm dyin', Ralph; yet I, who have braved death a hundred times, am afraid to die. I'm afraid to enter the next world. Something within tells me there will be a reckoning when I go there. But it's all over with me, Ralph. I feel that there's no chance o' my bein' saved."

"Don't say that, Bill," said I in deep compassion; "don't say that. I'm quite sure there's hope even for you, but I can't remember the words of the Bible that make me think so. Is there not a Bible on board, Bill?"

"No; the last that was in the ship belonged to a poor boy that was taken aboard against his will. He died, poor lad —I think through ill-treatment and fear. After he was gone, the captain found his Bible and flung it overboard."

I now reflected, with great sadness and self-reproach, on the way in which I had neglected my Bible, and it flashed across me that I was actually, in the sight of God, a greater sinner than this blood-stained pirate; for, thought I, he tells me that he never read the Bible and was never brought up to care for it, whereas I was carefully taught to read it by my own mother, and had read it daily as long as I possessed one, yet to so little purpose that I could not now call to mind a single text that would meet this poor man's case and afford him the consolation he so much required. I was much distressed, and taxed my memory for a long time. At last a text did flash into my mind, and I wondered much that I had not thought of it before.

"Bill," said I in a low voice, "'Believe on the Lord Jesus Christ, and thou shalt be saved.'"

"Ay, Ralph, I've heard the missionaries say that before now; but what good can it do me? It's not for me, that; it's not for the likes o' me."

I knew not now what to say, for although I felt sure that that word was for him as well as for me, I could not remember any other word whereby I could prove it.

After a short pause, Bill raised his eyes to mine and said, "Ralph, I've led a terrible life. I've been a sailor since I was a boy, and I've gone from bad to worse ever since I left my father's roof. I've been a pirate three years now. It is true I did not choose the trade, but I was inveigled aboard this schooner and kept here by force till I became reckless and at last joined them. Since that time my hand has been steeped in human blood again and again. Your young heart would grow cold if I —But why should I go on? 'Tis of no use, Ralph; my doom is fixed."

"Bill," said I, "'Though your sins be red like crimson, they shall be white as snow.' Only believe."

"Only believe!" cried Bill, starting up on his elbow. "I've heard men talk o' believing as if it was easy. Ha! 'tis easy enough for a man to point to a rope and say, 'I believe that would bear my weight;' but 'tis another thing for a man to catch hold o' that rope and swing himself by it over the edge of a precipice!"

The energy with which he said this, and the action with which it was accompanied, were too much for Bill. He sank back with a deep groan. As if the very elements sympathised with this man's sufferings, a low moan came sweeping over the sea.

"Hist, Ralph!" said Bill, opening his eyes; "there's a squall coming, lad! Look alive, boy! Clew up the foresail! Drop the mainsail peak! Them squalls come quick sometimes."

I had already started to my feet, and saw that a heavy squall was indeed bearing down on us. It had hitherto escaped my notice, owing to my being so much engrossed by our conversation. I instantly did as Bill desired, for the schooner was lying motionless on the glassy sea. I observed with some satisfaction that the squall was bearing down on the larboard bow, so that it would strike the vessel in the position in which she would be best able to stand the shock. Having done my best to shorten sail, I returned aft, and took my stand at the helm.

"Now, boy," said Bill in a faint voice, "keep her close to the wind."

A few seconds afterwards he said, "Ralph, let me hear those two texts again."

I repeated them.

"Are ye sure, lad, ye saw them in the Bible?"

"Quite sure," I replied.

Almost before the words had left my lips the wind burst upon us, and the spray dashed over our decks. For a time the schooner stood it bravely, and sprang forward against the rising sea like a war-horse. Meanwhile clouds darkened the sky, and the sea began to rise in huge billows. There was still too much sail on the schooner, and as the gale increased, I feared that the masts would be torn out of her or carried away, while the wind whistled and shrieked through the strained rigging. Suddenly the wind shifted a point, a heavy sea struck us on the bow, and the schooner was almost laid on her beam-ends, so that I could scarcely keep my legs. At the same moment Bill lost his hold of the belaying-pin which had served to steady him, and he slid with stunning violence against the skylight. As he lay on the deck close beside me, I could see that the shock had rendered him insensible; but I did not dare to quit the tiller for an instant, as it required all my faculties, bodily and mental, to manage the schooner. For an hour the blast drove us along, while, owing to the sharpness of the vessel's bow and the press of canvas, she dashed through the waves instead of breasting over them, thereby drenching the decks with water fore and aft. At the end of that time the squall passed away, and left us rocking on the bosom of the agitated sea.

My first care, the instant I could quit the helm, was to raise Bill from the deck and place him on the couch. I then ran below for the brandy-bottle, and rubbed his face and hands with it, and endeavoured to pour a little down his throat. But my efforts, although I continued them long and assiduously, were of no avail; as I let go the hand which I had been chafing, it fell heavily on the deck. I laid my hand over his heart, and sat for some time quite motionless; but there was no flutter there-the pirate was dead!

CHAPTER TWENTY EIGHT

Alone on the deep-Necessity the mother of invention —A valuable book discovered-Natural phenomenon —A bright day in my history.

It was with feelings of awe, not unmingled with fear, that I now seated myself on the cabin skylight and gazed upon the rigid features of my late comrade, while my mind wandered over his past history and contemplated with anxiety my present position. Alone in the midst of the wide Pacific, having a most imperfect knowledge of navigation, and in a schooner requiring at least eight men as her proper crew! But I will not tax the reader's patience with a minute detail of my feelings and doings during the first few days that followed the death of my companion. I will merely mention that I tied a cannon-ball to his feet, and with feelings of the deepest sorrow, consigned him to the deep.

For fully a week after that a steady breeze blew from the east, and as my course lay west and by north, I made rapid progress towards my destination. I could not take an observation, which I very much regretted, as the captain's quadrant was in the cabin; but from the day of setting sail from the island of the savages I had kept a dead reckoning, and as I knew pretty well now how much leeway the schooner made, I hoped to hit the Coral Island without much difficulty. In this I was the more confident that I knew its position on the chart-which, I understood, was a very good one-and so had its correct bearings by compass.

As the weather seemed now quite settled and fine, and as I had got into the trade-winds, I set about preparations for hoisting the topsails. This was a most arduous task, and my first attempts were complete failures, owing, in a great degree, to my reprehensible ignorance of mechanical forces. The first error I made was in applying my apparatus of blocks and pulleys to a rope which was too weak, so that the very first heave I made broke it in two, and sent me staggering against the after-hatch, over which I tripped, and striking against the main-boom, tumbled down the companion-ladder into the cabin. I was much bruised and somewhat stunned by this untoward accident. However, I considered it fortunate that I was not killed. In my next attempt I made sure of not coming by a similar accident, so I unreeved the tackling and fitted up larger blocks and ropes. But although the principle on which I acted was quiet correct, the machinery was now so massive and heavy that the mere friction and stiffness of the thick cordage prevented me from moving it at all. Afterwards, however, I came to proportion things more correctly; but I could not avoid reflecting at the time how much better it would have been had I learned all this from observation and study, instead of waiting till I was forced to acquire it through the painful and tedious lessons of experience.

After the tackling was prepared and in good working order, it took me the greater part of a day to hoist the main topsail. As I could not steer and work at this at the same time, I lashed the helm in such a position that, with a little watching now and then, it kept the schooner in her proper course. By this means I was enabled, also, to go about the deck and down below for things that I wanted as occasion required; also to cook and eat my victuals. But I did not dare to trust to this plan during the three hours of rest that I allowed myself at night, as the wind might have shifted, in which case I should have been blown far out of my course ere I awoke. I was, therefore, in the habit of heaving-to during those three hours-that is, fixing the rudder and the sails in such a position as that, by acting against each other, they would keep the ship stationary. After my night's rest, therefore, I had only to make allowance for the leeway she had made, and so resume my course.

Of course I was, to some extent, anxious lest another squall should come; but I made the best provision I could in the circumstances, and concluded that by letting go the weather-braces of the topsails and the topsail halyards at the same time, I should thereby render these sails almost powerless. Besides this, I proposed to myself to keep a sharp lookout on the barometer in the cabin; and if I observed at any time a sudden fall in it, I resolved that I would instantly set about my multiform appliances for reducing sail, so as to avoid being taken unawares. Thus I sailed prosperously for two weeks, with a fair wind, so that I calculated I must be drawing near to the Coral Island, at the thought of which my heart bounded with joyful expectation.

The only book I found on board, after a careful search, was a volume of Captain Cook's voyages. This, I suppose, the pirate captain had brought with him in order to guide him, and to furnish him with information regarding the islands of these seas. I found this a most delightful book indeed; and I not only obtained much interesting knowledge about the sea in which I was sailing, but I had many of my own opinions, derived from experience, corroborated, and not a few of them corrected. Besides the reading of this charming book, and the daily routine of occupations, nothing of particular note happened to me during this voyage-except once, when on rising one night, after my three hours' nap, while it was yet dark, I was amazed and a little alarmed to find myself floating in what appeared to be a sea of blue fire! I had often noticed the beautiful appearance of phosphorescent light, but this far exceeded anything of the sort I ever saw before. The whole sea appeared somewhat like milk, and was remarkably luminous.

I rose in haste, and letting down a bucket into the sea, brought some of the water on board and took it down to the cabin to examine it; but no sooner did I approach the light than the strange appearance disappeared, and when I removed the cabin lamp the luminous light appeared again. I was much puzzled with this, and took up a little of the water in the hollow of my hand and then let it run off, when I found that the luminous substance was left behind on my palm. I ran with it to the lamp, but when I got there it was gone. I found, however, that when I went into the dark my hand shone again; so I took the large glass of the ship's telescope and examined my hand minutely, when I found that there were on it one or two small patches of a clear, transparent substance like jelly, which were so thin as to be almost invisible to the naked eye. Thus I came to know that the beautiful phosphoric light, which I had so often admired before, was caused by animals; for I had no doubt that these were of the same kind as the medusa or jelly-fish, which are seen in all parts of the world.

On the evening of my fourteenth day I was awakened out of a nap into which I had fallen by a loud cry, and starting up, I gazed around me. I was surprised and delighted to see a large albatross soaring majestically over the ship. I immediately took it into my head that this was the albatross I had seen at Penguin Island. I had, of course, no good reason for supposing this; but the idea occurred to me, I know not why, and I cherished it, and regarded the bird with as much affection as if he had been an old friend. He kept me company all that day, and left me as night fell.

Next morning, as I stood motionless and with heavy eyes at the helm-for I had not slept well —I began to weary anxiously for daylight, and peered towards the horizon, where I thought I observed something like a black cloud against the dark sky. Being always on the alert for squalls, I ran to the bow. There could be no doubt it was a squall, and as I listened I thought I heard the murmur of the coming gale. Instantly I began to work might and main at my cumbrous tackle for shortening sail, and in the course of an hour and a half had the most of it reduced-the topsail yards down on the caps, the topsails clewed up, the sheets hauled in, the main and fore peaks lowered, and the flying-jib down. While thus engaged, the dawn advanced, and I cast an occasional furtive glance ahead in the midst of my labour. But now that things were prepared for the worst, I ran forward again and looked anxiously over the bow. I now heard the roar of the waves distinctly; and as a single ray of the rising sun gleamed over the ocean, I saw-what! could it be that I was dreaming? —that magnificent breaker with its ceaseless roar-that mountain-top! Yes, once more I beheld the Coral Island!

CHAPTER TWENTY NINE

The effect of a cannon-shot —A happy reunion of a somewhat moist nature-Retrospect and explanations-An awful dive-New plans-The last of the Coral Island.

I almost fell upon the deck with the tumult of mingled emotions that filled my heart as I gazed ardently towards my beautiful island. It was still many miles away, but sufficiently near to enable me to trace distinctly the well-remembered outlines of the two mountains. My first impulse was to utter an exclamation of gratitude for being carried to my former happy home in safety; my second, to jump up, clap my hands, shout, and run up and down the deck, with no other object in view than that of giving vent to my excited feelings. Then I went below for the telescope, and spent nearly ten minutes of the utmost impatience in vainly trying to get a focus, and in rubbing the skin nearly off my eyes, before I discovered that having taken off the large glass to examine the phosphoric water with, I had omitted to put it on again.

After that I looked up impatiently at the sails, which I now regretted having lowered so hastily, and for a moment thought of hoisting the main topsail again; but recollecting that it would take me full half-a-day to accomplish, and that, at the present rate of sailing, two hours would bring me to the island, I immediately dismissed the idea.

The remainder of the time I spent in making feverish preparations for arriving and seeing my dear comrades. I remembered that they were not in the habit of rising before six, and as it was now only three, I hoped to arrive before they were awake. Moreover, I set about making ready to let go the anchor, resolving in my own mind that as I knew the depth of water in the passage of the reef and within the lagoon, I would run the schooner in and bring up opposite the bower. Fortunately the anchor was hanging at the cat-head, otherwise I should never have been able to use it. Now I had only to cut the tackling, and it would drop of its own weight. After searching among the flags, I found the terrible black one, which I ran up to the peak. While I was doing this a thought struck me. I went to the powder-magazine, brought up a blank cartridge, and loaded the big brass gun, which, it will be remembered, was unhoused when we set sail; and as I had no means of housing it, there it had stood, bristling alike at fair weather and foul all the voyage. I took care to grease its mouth well, and before leaving the fore part of the ship, thrust the poker into the fire.

All was now ready. A steady five-knot breeze was blowing, so that I was now not more than quarter of a mile from the reef. I was soon at the entrance; and as the schooner glided quickly through, I glanced affectionately at the huge breaker as if it had been the same one I had seen there when I bade adieu, as I feared for ever, to the island. On coming opposite the Water Garden, I put the helm hard down. The schooner came round with a rapid, graceful bend, and lost way just opposite the bower. Running forward, I let go the anchor, caught up the red-hot poker, applied it to the brass gun, and saluted the mountains with a *bang* such as had only once before broke their slumbering echoes!

Effective although it was, however, it was scarcely equal to the bang with which, instantly after, Peterkin bounded from the bower, in scanty costume, his eyeballs starting from his head with surprise and terror. One gaze he gave, one yell, and then fled into the bushes like a wild cat. The next moment Jack went through exactly the same performance, the only difference being that his movements were less like those of Jack-in-the-box, though not less vigorous and rapid than those of Peterkin.

"Hallo!" I shouted, almost mad with joy. "What ho! Peterkin! Jack! hallo! it's *me!*"

My shout was just in time to arrest them. They halted and turned round, and the instant I repeated the cry I saw that they recognised my voice by both of them running at full speed towards the beach. I could no longer contain myself. Throwing off my jacket, I jumped overboard at the same moment that Jack bounded into the sea. In other moment we met in deep water, clasped each other round the neck, and sank, as a matter of course, to the bottom! We were well-nigh choked, and instantly struggled to the surface, where Peterkin was spluttering about like a wounded duck, laughing and crying by turns, and choking himself with salt water!

It would be impossible to convey to my reader, by description, an adequate conception of the scene that followed my landing on the beach, as we stood embracing each other indiscriminately in our dripping garments, and giving utterance to incoherent rhapsodies, mingled with wild shouts. It can be more easily imagined than described; so I will draw a curtain over this part of my history, and carry the reader forward over an interval of three days.

During the greater part of that period Peterkin did nothing but roast pigs, taro, and bread-fruit, and ply me with plantains, plums, potatoes, and cocoa-nuts, while I related to him and Jack the terrible and wonderful adventures I had gone through since we last met. After I had finished the account, they made me go all over it again; and when I had concluded the second recital I had to go over it again, while they commented upon it piecemeal. They were much affected by what I told them of the probable fate of Avatea, and Peterkin could by no means brook the idea of the poor girl being converted into a *long pig*! As for Jack, he clenched his teeth, and shook his fist towards the sea, saying at the same time that he was sorry he had not broken Tararo's head, and he only hoped that one day he should be able to plant his knuckles on the bridge of that chief's nose! After they had 'pumped me dry,' as Peterkin said, I begged to be informed of what had happened to them during my long absence, and particularly as to how they got out of the Diamond Cave.

"Well, you must know," began Jack, "after you had dived out of the cave, on the day you were taken away from us, we waited very patiently for half-an-hour, not expecting you to return before the end of that time. Then we began to upbraid you for staying so long when you knew we would be anxious; but when an hour passed we became alarmed, and I resolved at all hazards to dive out and see what had become of you, although I felt for poor Peterkin, because, as he truly said, 'If you never come back, I'm shut up here for life.' However, I promised not to run any risk, and he let me go—which, to say truth, I thought very courageous of him!"

"I should just think it was," interrupted Peterkin, looking at Jack over the edge of a monstrous potato which he happened to be devouring at the time.

"Well," continued Jack, "you may guess my consternation when you did not answer to my halloo. At first I imagined that the pirates must have killed you, and left you in the bush or thrown you into the sea; then it occurred to me that this would have served no end of theirs, so I came to the conclusion that they must have carried you away with them. As this thought struck me, I observed the pirate schooner standing away to the nor'ard, almost hull down on the horizon, and I sat down on the rocks to watch her as she slowly sank from my sight. And I tell you, Ralph, my boy, that I shed more tears that time at losing you than I have done, I verily believe, all my life before —"

"Pardon me, Jack, for interrupting," said Peterkin; "surely you must be mistaken in that. You've often told me that when you were a baby you used to howl and roar from morning to —"

"Hold your tongue, Peterkin!" cried Jack. —"Well, after the schooner had disappeared, I dived back into the cave, much to Peterkin's relief, and told him what I had seen. We sat down and had a long talk over this matter, and then we agreed to make a regular, systematic search through the woods, so as to make sure at least that you had not been killed. But now we thought of the difficulty of getting out of the cave without your help. Peterkin became dreadfully nervous when he thought of this; and I must confess I felt some alarm, for, of course, I could not hope alone to take him out so quickly as we two together had brought him in. And he himself vowed that if we had been a moment longer with him that time, he would have had to take a breath of salt water. However, there was no help for it, and I endeavoured to calm his fears as well as I could; 'for,' said I, 'you can't live here, Peterkin,' to which he replied, 'Of course not, Jack; I can only die here, and as that's not at all desirable, you had better propose something.' So I suggested that he should take a good, long breath, and trust himself to me.

"'Might we not make a large bag of cocoa-nut cloth, into which I could shove my head, and tie it tight round my neck?' he asked with a haggard smile. 'It might let me get one breath under water!'

"'No use,' said I; 'it would fill in a moment and suffocate you. I see nothing for it, Peterkin, if you really can't keep your breath so long, but to let me knock you down, and carry you out while in a state of insensibility.'

"But Peterkin didn't relish this idea. He seemed to fear that I would not be able to measure the exact force of the blow, and might, on the one hand, hit him so softly as to render a second or third blow necessary, which would be very uncomfortable; or, on the other hand, give him such a smash as would entirely spoil his figurehead, or mayhap knock the life out of him altogether! At last I got him persuaded to try to hold his breath, and commit himself to me; so he agreed, and down we went. But I had not got half-way through when he began to struggle and kick like a wild bull, burst from my grasp, and hit against the roof of the tunnel. I was therefore obliged to force him violently back into the cave again, where he, rose panting to the surface. In short, he had lost his presence of mind, and —"

"Nothing of the sort!" cried Peterkin indignantly; "I only lost my wind, and if I had not had presence of mind enough to kick as I did, I should have bu'st in your arms!"

"Well, well, so be it," resumed Jack with a smile. —"But the upshot of it was that we had to hold another consultation on the point; and I really believe that had it not been for a happy thought of mine, we should have been consulting there yet."

"I wish we had!" again interrupted Peterkin with a sigh. —"I'm sure, Ralph, if I had thought that you were coming back again I would willingly have awaited your return for months rather than have endured the mental agony which I went through. —But proceed."

"The thought was this," continued Jack —"that I should tie Peterkin's hands and feet with cords, and then lash him firmly to a stout pole about five feet long, in order to render him quite powerless and keep him straight and stiff. You should have seen his face of horror, Ralph, when I suggested this! But he came to see that it was his only chance, and told me to set about it as fast as I could; 'for,' said he, 'this is no jokin', Jack, *I* can tell you, and the sooner it's done the better.' I soon procured the cordage and a suitable pole, with which I returned to the cave, and lashed him as stiff and straight as an Egyptian mummy; and, to say truth, he was no bad representation of what an English mummy would be, if there were such things, for he was as white as a dead man.

"'Now,' said Peterkin in a tremulous voice, 'swim with me as near to the edge of the hole as you can before you dive; then let me take a long breath; and as I sha'n't be able to speak after I've taken it, you'll watch my face, and the moment you see me wink-dive! And oh,' he added earnestly, 'pray don't be long!'

"I promised to pay the strictest attention to his wishes, and swam with him to the outlet of the cave. Here I paused. 'Now, then,' said I, 'pull away at the wind, lad.'

"Peterkin drew in a breath so long that I could not help thinking of the frog in the fable, that wanted to swell itself as big as the ox. Then I looked into his face earnestly. Slap went the lid of his right eye; down went my head, and up went my heels. We shot through the passage like an arrow, and rose to the surface of the open sea before you could count twenty.

"Peterkin had taken in such an awful load of wind that, on reaching the free air, he let it out with a yell loud enough to have been heard a mile off; and then the change in his feelings was so sudden and great that he did not wait till we landed, but began, tied up as he was, to shout and sing for joy as I supported him with my left arm to the shore. However, in the middle of a laugh that a hyena might have envied, I let him accidentally slip, which extinguished him in a moment.

"After this happy deliverance, we immediately began our search for your dead body, Ralph; and you have no idea how low our hearts sank as we set off, day after day, to examine the valleys and mountain-sides with the utmost care. In about three weeks we completed the survey of the whole island, and had at least the satisfaction of knowing that you had not been killed.

But it occurred to us that you might have been thrown into the sea; so we examined the sands and the lagoon carefully, and afterwards went all round the outer reef. One day, while we were upon the reef, Peterkin espied a small, dark object lying among the rocks, which seemed to be quite different from the surrounding stones. We hastened towards the spot, and found it to be a small keg. On knocking out the head we discovered that it was gunpowder."

"It was I who sent you that, Jack," said I with a smile.

"Fork out!" cried Peterkin energetically, starting to his feet and extending his open hand to Jack. "Down with the money, sir, else I'll have you shut up for life in a debtor's prison the moment we return to England!"

"I'll give you an I.O.U. in the meantime," returned Jack, laughing, "so sit down and be quiet. —The fact is, Ralph, when we discovered this keg of powder Peterkin immediately took me a bet of a thousand pounds that you had something to do with it, and I took him a bet of ten thousand that you had not."

"Peterkin was right, then," said I, explaining how the thing had occurred.

"Well, we found it very useful," continued Jack, "although some of it had got a little damp; and we furbished up the old pistol, with which Peterkin is a crack shot now. But to continue. We did not find any other vestige of you on the reef, and finally gave up all hope of ever seeing you again. After this the island became a dreary place to us, and we began to long for a ship to heave in sight and take us off. But now that you're back again, my dear fellow, it looks as bright and cheerful as it used to do, and I love it as much as ever.

"And now," continued Jack, "I have a great desire to visit some of the other islands of the South Seas. Here we have a first-rate schooner at our disposal, so I don't see what should hinder us."

"Just the very thing I was going to propose!" cried Peterkin. "I vote for starting at once."

"Well, then," said Jack, "it seems to me that we could not do better than shape our course for the island on which Avatea lives, and endeavour to persuade Tararo to let her marry the black fellow to whom she is engaged instead of making a 'long pig' of her. If he has a spark of gratitude in him, he'll do it. Besides, having become champions for this girl once before, it behoves us, as true knights, not to rest until we set her free; at least, all the heroes in all the story-books I have ever read would count it foul disgrace to leave such a work unfinished."

"I'm sure I don't know or care what your knights in story-books would do," said Peterkin; "but I'm certain that it would be capital fun, so I'm your man whenever you want me."

This plan of Jack's was quite in accordance with his romantic, impulsive nature; and having made up his mind to save this black girl, he could not rest until the thing was commenced.

"But there may be great danger in this attempt," he said at the end of a long consultation on the subject. "Will you, lads, go with me in spite of this?"

"Go with you!" we repeated in the same breath.

"Can you doubt it?" said I.

"For a moment?" added Peterkin.

I need scarcely say that having made up our minds to go on this enterprise, we lost no time in making preparations to quit the island; and as the schooner was well laden with stores of every kind for a long cruise, we had little to do except to add to our abundant supply a quantity of cocoa-nuts, bread-fruit, taro, yams, plums, and potatoes, chiefly with the view of carrying the fragrance of our dear island along with us as long as we could.

When all was ready, we paid a farewell visit to the different familiar spots where most of our time had been spent. We ascended the mountain-top, and gazed for the last time at the rich green foliage in the valleys, the white sandy beach, the placid lagoon, and the barrier coral reef with its crested breakers. Then we descended to Spouting Cliff, and looked down at the pale-green monster which we had made such fruitless efforts to spear in days gone by. From this we hurried to the Water Garden, and took a last dive into its clear waters and a last gambol amongst its coral groves. I hurried out before my companions, and dressed in haste, in order to have a long examination of my tank, which Peterkin, in the fulness of his heart, had tended with the utmost care, as being a vivid remembrancer of me rather than out of love for natural history. It was in superb condition: the water as clear and pellucid as crystal; the red and green seaweed of the most brilliant hues; the red, purple, yellow, green, and striped anemones fully expanded, and stretching out their arms as if to welcome and embrace their former master; the starfish, zoophytes, sea-pens, and other innumerable marine insects, looking fresh and beautiful; and the crabs, as Peterkin said, looking as wide-awake, impertinent, rampant, and pugnacious as ever. It was, indeed, so lovely and so interesting that I would scarcely allow myself to be torn away from it.

Last of all, we returned to the bower and collected the few articles we possessed-such as the axe, the pencil-case, the broken telescope, the penknife, the hook made from the brass ring, and the sail-needle, with which we had landed on the island; also the long boots and the pistol, besides several curious articles of costume which we had manufactured from time to time.

These we conveyed on board in our little boat, after having carved our names on a chip of iron-wood, thus:

Jack Martin
Ralph Rover
Peterkin Gay

This we fixed up inside of the bower. The boat was then hoisted on board and the anchor weighed, which latter operation cost us great labour and much time, as the anchor was so heavy that we could not move it without the aid of my complex machinery of blocks and pulleys. A steady breeze was blowing off-shore when we set sail, at a little before sunset. It swept us quickly past the reef and out to sea. The shore grew rapidly more indistinct as the shades of evening fell, while our clipper bark bounded lightly over the waves. Slowly the mountain-top sank on the horizon until it became a mere speck. In another moment the sun and the Coral Island sank together into the broad bosom of the Pacific.

CHAPTER THIRTY

> The voyage-The island, and a consultation in which danger is scouted as a thing unworthy of consideration-Rats and cats-The native teacher-Awful revelations-Wonderful effects of Christianity.

Our voyage during the next two weeks was most interesting and prosperous. The breeze continued generally fair, and at all times enabled us to lie our course; for being, as I have said before, clipper-built, the pirate schooner could lie very close to the wind and make little leeway. We had no difficulty now in managing our sails, for Jack was heavy and powerful, while Peterkin was active as a kitten. Still, however, we were a very insufficient crew for such a vessel; and if any one had proposed to us to make such a voyage in it before we had been forced to go through so many hardships from necessity, we would have turned away with pity from the individual making such proposal as from a madman. I pondered this a good deal, and at last concluded that men do not know how much they are capable of doing till they try, and that we should never give way to despair in any undertaking, however difficult it may seem-always supposing, however, that our cause is a good one, and that we can ask the Divine blessing on it.

Although, therefore, we could now manage our sails easily, we nevertheless found that my pulleys were of much service to us in some things, though Jack did laugh heartily at the uncouth arrangement of ropes and blocks, which had, to a sailor's eye, a very lumbering and clumsy appearance. But I will not drag my reader through the details of this voyage. Suffice it to say that, after an agreeable sail of about three weeks, we arrived off the island of Mango, which I recognised at once from the description that the pirate Bill had given me of it during one of our conversations.

As soon as we came within sight of it, we hove the ship to and held a council of war.

"Now, boys," said Jack as we seated ourselves beside him on the cabin skylight, "before we go further in this business we must go over the pros and cons of it; for although you have so generously consented to stick by me through thick and thin, it would be unfair did I not see that you thoroughly understand the danger of what we are about to attempt."

"Oh, bother the danger!" cried Peterkin. "I wonder to hear you, Jack, talk of danger! When a fellow begins to talk about it, he'll soon come to magnify it to such a degree that he'll not be fit to face it when it comes-no more than a suckin' baby."

"Nay, Peterkin," replied Jack gravely, "I won't be jested out of it. I grant you that when we've once resolved to act, and have made up our minds what to do, we should think no more of danger. But before we have so resolved, it behoves us to look it straight in the face, and examine into it, and walk round it; for if we flinch at a distant view, we're sure to run away when the danger is near. —Now, I understand from you, Ralph, that the island is inhabited by thorough-going, out-and-out cannibals, whose principal law is, 'Might is right, and the weakest goes to the wall?'"

"Yes," said I; "so Bill gave me to understand. He told me, however, that at the southern side of it the missionaries had obtained a footing amongst an insignificant tribe. A native teacher had been sent there by the Wesleyans, who had succeeded in persuading the chief at that part to embrace Christianity. But instead of that being of any advantage to our enterprise, it seems the very reverse; for the chief Tararo is a determined heathen, and persecutes the Christians-who are far too weak in numbers to offer any resistance-and looks with dislike upon all white men, whom he regards as propagators of the new faith."

"'Tis a pity," said Jack, "that the Christian tribe is so small, for we shall scarcely be safe under their protection, I fear. If Tararo takes it into his head to wish for our vessel, or to kill ourselves, he could take us from them by force. You say that the native missionary talks English?"

"So I believe."

"Then, what I propose is this," said Jack. "We will run round to the south side of the island, and cast anchor off the Christian village. We are too far away just now to have been descried by any of the savages, so we shall get there unobserved, and have time to arrange our plans before the heathen tribes know of our presence. But in doing this we run the risk of being captured by the ill-disposed tribes, and being very ill-used, if not —a —"

"Roasted alive and eaten!" cried Peterkin. "Come, out with it, Jack! According to your own showing, it's well to look the danger straight in the face."

"Well, that *is* the worst of it, certainly. Are you prepared, then, to take your chance of that?"

"I've been prepared and had my mind made up long ago," cried Peterkin, swaggering about the deck with his hands thrust into his breeches pockets. "The fact is, Jack, I don't believe that Tararo will be so ungrateful as to eat us, and I'm quite sure that he'll be too happy to grant us whatever we ask; so the sooner we go in and win the better."

Peterkin was wrong, however, in his estimate of savage gratitude, as the sequel will show.

The schooner was now put before the wind, and after making a long run to the southward, we put about and beat up for the south side of Mango, where we arrived before sunset, and hove-to off the coral reef. Here we awaited the arrival of a canoe, which immediately put off on our rounding-to. When it arrived, a mild-looking native, of apparently forty years of age, came on board, and taking off his straw hat, made us a low bow. He was clad in a respectable suit of European clothes; and the first words he uttered, as he stepped up to Jack and shook hands with him, were:

"Good-day, gentlemen. We are happy to see you at Mango. You are heartily welcome."

After returning his salutation, Jack exclaimed, "You must be the native missionary teacher of whom I have heard-are you not?"

"I am. I have the joy to be a servant of the Lord Jesus at this station."

"You're the very man I want to see, then," replied Jack; "that's lucky. Come down to the cabin, friend, and have a glass of wine. I wish particularly to speak with you. My men there" — pointing to Peterkin and me —"will look after your people."

"Thank you," said the teacher as he followed Jack to the cabin; "I do not drink wine or any strong drink."

"Oh! then there's lots of water, and you can have biscuit."

"Now, 'pon my word, that's cool!" said Peterkin; "his *men*, forsooth! Well, since we are to be men, we may as well come it as strong over these black chaps as we can. —Hallo, there!" he cried to the half-dozen of natives who stood upon the deck, gazing in wonder at all they saw, "here's for you;" and he handed them a tray of broken biscuit and a can of water. Then thrusting his hands into his pockets, he walked up and down the deck with an enormous swagger, whistling vociferously.

In about half-an-hour Jack and the teacher came on deck, and the latter, bidding us a cheerful good-evening, entered his canoe and paddled to the shore. When he was gone, Peterkin stepped up to Jack, and touching his cap, said:

"Well, captain, have you any communications to make to your *men?*"

"Yes," cried Jack: "ready about, mind the helm, and clew up your tongue, while I con the schooner through the passage in the reef. The teacher, who seems a first-rate fellow, says it's quite deep, and good anchorage within the lagoon close to the shore."

While the vessel was slowly advancing to her anchorage, under a light breeze, Jack explained to us that Avatea was still on the island, living amongst the heathens; that she had expressed a strong desire to join the Christians; but Tararo would not let her, and kept her constantly in close confinement.

"Moreover," continued Jack, "I find that she belongs to one of the Samoan Islands, where Christianity had been introduced long before her capture by the heathens of a neighbouring island; and the very day after she was taken she was to have joined the church which had been planted there by that excellent body, the London Missionary Society. The teacher tells me, too, that the poor girl has fallen in love with a Christian chief, who lives on an island some fifty miles or so to the south of this one, and that she is meditating a desperate attempt at escape. So, you see, we have come in the nick of time. —I fancy that this chief is the fellow whom you heard of, Ralph, at the island of Emo. —Besides all this, the heathen savages are at war among themselves, and there's to be a battle fought the day after to-morrow, in which the principal leader is Tararo; so that we'll not be able to commence our negotiations with the rascally chief till the day after."

The village off which we anchored was beautifully situated at the head of a small bay, from the margin of which trees of every description peculiar to the tropics rose in the richest luxuriance to the summit of a hilly ridge, which was the line of demarcation between the possessions of the Christians and those of the neighbouring heathen chief.

The site of the settlement was an extensive plot of flat land, stretching in a gentle slope from the sea to the mountain. The cottages stood several hundred yards from the beach, and were protected from the glare of the sea by the rich foliage of rows of large Barringtonia and other trees which girt the shore. The village was about a mile in length, and perfectly straight, with a wide road down the middle, on either side of which were rows of the tufted-topped ti-tree, whose delicate and beautiful blossoms, hanging beneath their plume-crested tops, added richness to the scene. The cottages of the natives were built beneath these trees, and were kept in the most excellent order, each having a little garden in front, tastefully laid out and planted, while the walks were covered with black and white pebbles.

Every house had doors and Venetian windows, painted partly with lamp-black made from the candle-nut, and partly with red ochre, which contrasted powerfully with the dazzling coral lime that covered the walls. On a prominent position stood a handsome church, which was quite a curiosity in its way. It was a hundred feet long by fifty broad, and was seated throughout to accommodate upwards of two thousand persons. It had six large folding-doors, and twelve windows with Venetian blinds; and although a large and substantial edifice, it had been built, we were told by the teacher: in the space of two months! There was not a single iron nail in the fabric, and the natives had constructed it chiefly with their stone and bone axes and other tools, having only one or two axes or tools of European manufacture. Everything around this beautiful spot wore an aspect of peace and plenty; and as we dropped our anchor within a stone's-cast of the substantial coral wharf, I could not avoid contrasting it with the wretched village of Emo, where I had witnessed so many frightful scenes. When the teacher afterwards told me that the people of this tribe had become converts only a year previous to our arrival, and that they had been living before that in the practice of the most bloody system of idolatry, I could not refrain from exclaiming, "What a convincing proof that Christianity is of God!"

On landing from our little boat we were received with a warm welcome by the teacher and his wife, the latter being also a native, clothed in a simple European gown and a straw bonnet. The shore was lined with hundreds of natives, whose persons were all more or less clothed with native cloth. Some of the men had on a kind of poncho formed of this cloth, their legs being uncovered; others wore clumsily fashioned trousers, and no upper garment except hats made of straw and cloth. Many of the dresses, both of women and men, were grotesque enough, being very bad imitations of the European garb; but all wore a dress of some sort or other. They seemed very glad to see us, and crowded round us as the teacher led the way to his dwelling, where we were entertained, in the most sumptuous manner, on baked pig and all the varieties of fruits and vegetables that the island produced. We were much annoyed, however, by the rats: they seemed to run about the house like domestic animals. As we sat at table, one of them peeped up at us over the edge of the cloth, close to Peterkin's elbow, who floored it with a blow on the snout from his knife, exclaiming as he did so:

"I say, Mister Teacher, why don't you set traps for these brutes? Surely you are not fond of them!"

"No," replied the teacher with a smile. "We would be glad to get rid of them if we could; but if we were to trap all the rats on the island, it would occupy our whole time."

"Are they, then, so numerous?" inquired Jack.

"They swarm everywhere. The poor heathens on the north side eat them, and think them very sweet. So did my people formerly; but they do not eat so many now, because the missionary who was last here expressed disgust at it. The poor people asked if it was wrong to eat rats; and he told them that it was certainly not wrong, but that the people of England would be much disgusted were they asked to eat rats."

We had not been an hour in the house of this kind-hearted man when we were convinced of the truth of his statement as to their numbers; for the rats ran about the floors in dozens, and during our meal two men were stationed at the table to keep them off!

"What a pity you have no cats!" said Peterkin; and he aimed a blow at another reckless intruder, and missed it.

"We would indeed be glad to have a few," rejoined the teacher, "but they are difficult to be got. The hogs, we find, are very good rat-killers; but they do not seem to be able to keep the numbers down. I have heard that they are better than cats."

As the teacher said this, his good-natured black face was wrinkled with a smile of merriment. Observing that I had noticed it, he said:

"I smiled just now when I remembered the fate of the first cat that was taken to Rarotonga. This is one of the stations of the London Missionary Society. It, like our own, is infested with rats, and a cat was brought at last to the island. It was a large black one. On being turned loose, instead of being content to stay among men, the cat took to the mountains and lived in a wild state, sometimes paying visits during the night to the houses of the natives; some of whom, living at a distance from the settlement, had not heard of the cat's arrival, and were dreadfully frightened in consequence, calling it a 'monster of the deep,' and flying in terror away from it. One night the cat-feeling a desire for company, I suppose-took its way to the house of a chief who had recently been converted to Christianity, and had begun to learn to read and pray. The chief's wife, who was sitting awake at his side while he slept, beheld with horror two fires glistening in the doorway, and heard with surprise a mysterious voice. Almost petrified with fear, she awoke her husband, and began to upbraid him for forsaking his old religion and burning his god, who, she declared, was now come to be avenged of them. 'Get up and pray! get up and pray!' she cried. The chief arose, and on opening his eyes, beheld the same glaring lights and heard the same ominous sound. Impelled by the extreme urgency of the case, he commenced, with all possible vehemence, to vociferate the alphabet, as a prayer to God to deliver them from the vengeance of Satan! On hearing this, the cat, as much alarmed as themselves, fled precipitately away, leaving the chief and his wife congratulating themselves on the efficacy of their prayer."

We were much diverted with this anecdote, which the teacher related in English so good that we certainly could not have supposed him a native but for the colour of his face and the foreign accent in his tone. Next day we walked out with this interesting man, and were much entertained and instructed by his conversation as we rambled through the cool, shady groves of bananas, citrons, limes, and other trees, or sauntered among the cottages of the natives, and watched them while they laboured diligently in the taro-beds or manufactured the tapa, or native cloth. To some of these Jack put questions, through the medium of the missionary; and the replies were such as to surprise us at the extent of their knowledge. Indeed, Peterkin very truly remarked that "they seemed to know a considerable deal more than Jack himself."

Among other pieces of interesting information that we obtained was the following, in regard to coral formations:

"The islands of the Pacific," said our friend, "are of three different kinds or classes. Those of the first class are volcanic, mountainous, and wild-some shooting their jagged peaks into the clouds at an elevation of ten and fifteen thousand feet. Those of the second class are of crystallised limestone, and vary in height from one hundred to five hundred feet. The hills on these are not so wild or broken as those of the first class, but are richly clothed with vegetation, and very beautiful. I have no doubt that the Coral Island on which you were wrecked was one of this class. They are supposed to have been upheaved from the bottom of the sea by volcanic agency; but they are not themselves volcanic in their nature, neither are they of coral formation.

Those of the third class are the low coralline islands, usually having lagoons of water in their midst. They are very numerous.

"As to the manner in which coral islands and reefs are formed, there are various opinions on this point. I will give you what seems to me the most probable theory—a theory, I may add, which is held by some of the good and scientific missionaries. It is well known that there is much lime in salt water; it is also known that coral is composed of lime. It is supposed that the polypes, or coral insects, have the power of attracting this lime to their bodies, and with this material they build their little cells or habitations. They choose the summit of a volcano, or the top of a submarine mountain, as a foundation on which to build, for it is found that they never work at any great depth below the surface. On this they work. The polypes on the mountain-top, of course, reach the surface first; then those at the outer edges reach the top sooner than the others between them and the centre, thus forming the coral reef surrounding the lagoon of water and the central island. After that, the insects within the lagoon cease working. When the surface of the water is reached, these myriads of wonderful creatures die. Then birds visit the spot, and seeds are thus conveyed thither, which take root and spring up and flourish. Thus are commenced those coralline islets of which you have seen so many in these seas. The reefs round the large islands are formed in a similar manner. When we consider," added the missionary, "the smallness of the architects used by our heavenly Father in order to form those lovely and innumerable islands, we are filled with much of that feeling which induced the ancient king to exclaim, 'How manifold, O Lord, are Thy works! in wisdom hast Thou made them all.'"

We all heartily agreed with the missionary in this sentiment, and felt not a little gratified to find that the opinions which Jack and I had been led to form, from personal observation on our Coral Island, were thus to a great extent corroborated.

The missionary also gave us an account of the manner in which Christianity had been introduced among them. He said: "When missionaries were first sent here, three years ago, a small vessel brought them; and the chief, who is now dead, promised to treat well the two native teachers who were left with their wives on the island. But scarcely had the boat which landed them returned to the ship than the natives began to maltreat their guests, taking away all they possessed, and offering them further violence, so that when the boat was sent in haste to fetch them away, the clothes of both men and women were torn nearly off their backs.

"Two years after this the vessel visited them again, and I, being in her, volunteered to land alone, without any goods whatever, begging that my wife might be brought to me the following year-that is, *this* year; and, as you see, she is with me. But the surf was so high that the boat could not land me; so with nothing on but my trousers and shirt, and with a few catechisms and a Bible, besides some portions of the Scripture translated into the Mango tongue, I sprang into the sea, and swam ashore on the crest of a breaker. I was instantly dragged up the beach by the natives; who, on finding I had nothing worth having upon me, let me alone. I then made signs to my friends in the ship to leave me, which they did. At first the natives listened to me in silence, but laughed at what I said while I preached the Gospel of our blessed Saviour Jesus Christ to them. Afterwards they treated me ill, sometimes; but I persevered, and continued to dwell among them, and dispute, and exhort them to give up their sinful ways of life, burn their idols, and come to Jesus.

"About a month after I landed, I heard that the chief was dead. He was the father of the present chief, who is now a most consistent member of the Church. It is a custom here that when a chief dies his wives are strangled and buried with him. Knowing this, I hastened to his house to endeavour to prevent such cruelty if possible. When I arrived, I found two of the wives had already been killed, while another was in the act of being strangled. I pleaded hard for her, but it was too late; she was already dead. I then entreated the son to spare the fourth wife, and after much hesitation, my prayer was granted; but in half-an-hour afterwards this poor woman repented of being unfaithful, as she termed it, to her husband, and insisted on being strangled, which was accordingly done.

"All this time the chief's son was walking up and down before his father's house with a brow black as thunder. When he entered I went in with him, and found, to my surprise, that his father was *not* dead! The old man was sitting on a mat in a corner, with an expression of placid resignation on his face.

"'Why,' said I, 'have you strangled your father's wives before he is dead?'

"To this the son replied, 'He is dead. That is no longer my father. He is as good as dead now. He is to be *buried alive.*'

"I now remembered having heard that it is a custom among the Feejee Islanders that when the reigning chief grows old and infirm, the heir to the chieftainship has a right to depose his father, in which case he is considered as dead, and is buried alive. The young chief was now about to follow this custom, and despite my earnest entreaties and pleadings, the old chief was buried that day before my eyes in the same grave with his four strangled wives! Oh, my heart groaned when I saw this! and I prayed to God to open the hearts of these poor creatures, as He had already opened mine, and pour into them the light and the love of the Gospel of Jesus. My prayer was answered very soon. A week afterwards the son, who was now chief of the tribe, came to me, bearing his god on his shoulders, and groaning beneath its weight. Flinging it down at my feet, he desired me to burn it!

"You may conceive how overjoyed I was at this. I sprang up and embraced him, while I shed tears of joy. Then we made a fire and burned the god to ashes, amid an immense concourse of the people, who seemed terrified at what was being done, and shrank back when we burned the god, expecting some signal vengeance to be taken upon us; but seeing that nothing happened, they changed their minds, and thought that our God must be the true one after all. From that time the mission prospered steadily; and now, while there is not a single man in the tribe who has not burned his household gods and become a convert to Christianity, there are not a few, I hope, who are true followers of the Lamb, having been plucked as brands from the burning by Him who can save unto the uttermost. I will not tell you more of our progress at this time; but you see," he said, waving his hand around him, "the village, and the church did not exist a year ago!"

We were indeed much interested in this account, and I could not help again in my heart praying to God to prosper those missionary societies that send such inestimable blessings to these islands of dark and bloody idolatry. The teacher also added that the other tribes were very indignant at this one for having burned its gods, and threatened to destroy it altogether; but they had done nothing yet. "And if they should," said the teacher, "the Lord is on our side; of whom shall we be afraid?"

"Have the missionaries many stations in these seas?" inquired Jack.

"Oh yes. The London Missionary Society have a great many in the Tahiti group, and other islands in that quarter. Then the Wesleyans have the Feejee Islands all to themselves, and the Americans have many stations in other groups. But still, my friend, there are hundreds of islands here, the natives of which have never heard of Jesus, or the good word of God, or the Holy Spirit; and thousands are living and dying in the practice of those terrible sins and bloody murders of which you have already heard. —I trust, my friends," he added, looking earnestly into our faces —"I trust that if you ever return to England, you will tell your Christian friends that the horrors which they hear of in regard to these islands are *literally true,* and that when they have heard the worst, the '*half has not been told them;*' for there are perpetrated here foul deeds of darkness of which man may not speak. You may also tell them," he said, looking around with a smile, while a tear of gratitude trembled in his eye and rolled down his coal-black cheek —"tell them of the blessings that the Gospel has wrought *here!*"

We assured our friend that we would certainly not forget his request. On returning towards the village, about noon, we remarked on the beautiful whiteness of the cottages.

"That is owing to the lime with which they are plastered," said the teacher. "When the natives were converted, as I have described, I set them to work to build cottages for themselves, and also this handsome church which you see. When the framework and other parts of the house were up, I sent the people to fetch coral from the sea. They brought immense quantities. Then I made them cut wood, and piling the coral above it, set it on fire.

"'Look! look!' cried the poor people in amazement; 'what wonderful people the Christians are! He is roasting stones! We shall not need taro or bread-fruit any more; we may eat stones!'

"But their surprise was still greater when the coral was reduced to a fine, soft, white powder. They immediately set up a great shout, and mingling the lime with water, rubbed their faces and their bodies all over with it, and ran through the village screaming with delight. They were also much surprised at another thing they saw me do. I wished to make some household furniture, and constructed a turning-lathe to assist me. The first thing that I turned was the leg of a sofa, which was no sooner finished than the chief seized it with wonder and delight, and ran through the village exhibiting it to the people, who looked upon it with great admiration. The chief then, tying a string to it, hung it round his neck as an ornament! He afterwards told me that if he had seen it before he became a Christian, he would have made it his god!"

As the teacher concluded this anecdote we reached his door. Saying that he had business to attend to, he left us to amuse ourselves as we best could.

"Now, lads," said Jack, turning abruptly towards us, and buttoning up his jacket as he spoke, "I'm off to see the battle. I've no particular fondness for seein' bloodshed; but I must find out the nature o' these fellows and see their customs with my own eyes, so that I may be able to speak of it again, if need be, authoritatively. It's only six miles off, and we don't run much more risk than that of getting a rap with a stray stone or an overshot arrow. Will you go?"

"To be sure we will," said Peterkin.

"If they chance to see us, we'll cut and run for it," added Jack.

"Dear me!" cried Peterkin; "*you* run! I thought you would scorn to run from any one."

"So I would, if it were my duty to fight," returned Jack coolly; "but as I don't want to fight, and don't intend to fight, if they offer to attack us I'll run away, like the veriest coward that ever went by the name of Peterkin. So come along."

CHAPTER THIRTY ONE

A strange and bloody battle-The lion bearded in his den-Frightful scenes of cruelty, and fears for the future.

We had ascertained from the teacher the direction to the spot on which the battle was to be fought, and after a walk of two hours, reached it. The summit of a bare hill was the place chosen; for, unlike most of the other islanders, who are addicted to bush-fighting, those of Mango are in the habit of meeting on open ground. We arrived before the two parties had commenced the deadly struggle, and creeping as close up as we dared among the rocks, we lay and watched them.

The combatants were drawn up face to face, each side ranged in rank four deep. Those in the first row were armed with long spears; the second with clubs to defend the spearmen; the third row was composed of young men with slings; and the fourth consisted of women, who carried baskets of stones for the slingers, and clubs and spears with which to supply the warriors. Soon after we arrived, the attack was made with great fury. There was no science displayed. The two bodies of savages rushed headlong upon each other and engaged in a general mêlée, and a more dreadful set of men I have never seen. They wore grotesque war-caps, made of various substances and decorated with feathers. Their faces and bodies were painted so as to make them look as frightful as possible; and as they brandished their massive clubs, leaped, shouted, yelled, and dashed each other to the ground, I thought I had never seen men look so like demons before.

We were much surprised at the conduct of the women, who seemed to be perfect furies, and hung about the heels of their husbands in order to defend them. One stout young woman we saw, whose husband was hard pressed and about to be overcome: she lifted a large stone, and throwing it at his opponent's head, felled him to the earth. But the battle did not last long. The band most distant from us gave way and were routed, leaving eighteen of their comrades dead upon the field. These the victors brained as they lay; and putting some of their brains on leaves, went off with them, we were afterwards informed, to their temples to present them to their gods as an earnest of the human victims who were soon to be brought there.

We hastened back to the Christian village with feelings of the deepest sadness at the sanguinary conflict which we had just witnessed.

Next day, after breakfasting with our friend the teacher, we made preparations for carrying out our plan. At first the teacher endeavoured to dissuade us.

"You do not know," said he, turning to Jack, "the danger you run in venturing amongst these ferocious savages. I feel much pity for poor Avatea; but you are not likely to succeed in saving her, and you may die in the attempt."

"Well," said Jack quietly, "I am not afraid to die in a good cause."

The teacher smiled approvingly at him as he said this, and after a little further conversation, agreed to accompany us as interpreter-saying that although Tararo was unfriendly to him, he had hitherto treated him with respect.

We now went on board the schooner, having resolved to sail round the island and drop anchor opposite the heathen village. We manned her with natives, and hoped to overawe the savages by displaying our brass gun to advantage. The teacher soon after came on board, and setting our sails, we put to sea. In two hours more we made the cliffs reverberate with the crash of the big gun, which we fired by way of salute, while we ran the British ensign up to the peak and cast anchor. The commotion on shore showed us that we had struck terror into the hearts of the natives; but seeing that we did not offer to molest them, a canoe at length put off and paddled cautiously towards us. The teacher showed himself, and explaining that we were friends and wished to palaver with the chief, desired the native to go and tell him to come on board.

We waited long and with much impatience for an answer. During this time the native teacher conversed with us again, and told us many things concerning the success of the Gospel among

139

those islands; and perceiving that we were by no means so much gratified as we ought to have been at the hearing of such good news, he pressed us more closely in regard to our personal interest in religion, and exhorted us to consider that our souls were certainly in as great danger as those of the wretched heathen whom we pitied so much if we had not already found salvation in Jesus Christ. "Nay, further," he added, "if such be your unhappy case, you are, in the sight of God, much worse than these savages-forgive me, my young friends, for saying so-for they have no knowledge, no light, and do not profess to believe; while you, on the contrary, have been brought up in the light of the blessed Gospel and call yourselves Christians. These poor savages are indeed the enemies of our Lord; but you, if ye be not true believers, are traitors!"

I must confess that my heart condemned me while the teacher spoke in this earnest manner, and I knew not what to reply. Peterkin, too, did not seem to like it, and, I thought, would willingly have escaped. But Jack seemed deeply impressed, and wore an anxious expression on his naturally grave countenance, while he assented to the teacher's remarks, and put to him many earnest questions. Meanwhile the natives who composed our crew, having nothing particular to do, had squatted down on the deck and taken out their little books containing the translated portions of the New Testament, along with hymns and spelling-books, and were now busily engaged-some vociferating the alphabet, others learning prayers off by heart, while a few sang hymns-all of them being utterly unmindful of our presence. The teacher soon joined them, and soon afterwards they all engaged in a prayer, which was afterwards translated to us, and proved to be a petition for the success of our undertaking and for the conversion of the heathen.

While we were thus engaged a canoe put off from shore, and several savages leaped on deck, one of whom advanced to the teacher and informed him that Tararo could not come on board that day, being busy with some religious ceremonies before the gods, which could on no account be postponed. He was also engaged with a friendly chief, who was about to take his departure from the island, and therefore begged that the teacher and his friends would land and pay a visit to him. To this the teacher returned answer that we would land immediately.

"Now, lads," said Jack as we were about to step into our little boat, "I'm not going to take any weapons with me, and I recommend you to take none either. We are altogether in the power of these savages; and the utmost we could do, if they were to attack us, would be to kill a few of them before we were ourselves overpowered. I think that our only chance of success lies in mild measures. Don't you think so?"

To this I assented gladly; and Peterkin replied by laying down a huge bell-mouthed blunder-buss, and divesting himself of a pair of enormous horse-pistols, with which he had purposed to overawe the natives! We then jumped into our boat and rowed ashore.

On reaching the beach we were received by a crowd of naked savages, who shouted a rude welcome, and conducted us to a house or shed where a baked pig and a variety of vegetables were prepared for us. Having partaken of these, the teacher begged to be conducted to the chief; but there seemed some hesitation, and after some consultation among themselves, one of the men stood forward and spoke to the teacher.

"What says he?" inquired Jack when the savage had concluded.

"He says that the chief is just going to the temple of his god, and cannot see us yet; so we must be patient, my friend."

"Well," cried Jack, rising, "if he won't come to see me, I'll e'en go and see him. Besides, I have a great desire to witness their proceedings at this temple of theirs. Will you go with me, friend?"

"I cannot," said the teacher, shaking his head. "I must not go to the heathen temples and witness their inhuman rites, except for the purpose of condemning their wickedness and folly."

"Very good," returned Jack; "then I'll go alone, for I cannot condemn their doings till I have seen them."

Jack arose, and we, having determined to go also, followed him through the banana-groves to a rising ground immediately behind the village, on the top of which stood the Buré, or temple, under the dark shade of a group of iron-wood trees. As we went through the village I was again led to contrast the rude huts and sheds, and their almost naked, savage-looking inhabitants, with the natives of the Christian village, who, to use the teacher's scriptural expression, were now "clothed and in their right mind."

As we turned into a broad path leading towards the hill, we were arrested by the shouts of an approaching multitude in the rear. Drawing aside into the bushes, we awaited their coming up; and as they drew near, we observed that it was a procession of the natives, many of whom were dancing and gesticulating in the most frantic manner. They had an exceedingly hideous aspect, owing to the black, red, and yellow paints with which their faces and naked bodies were bedaubed. In the midst of these came a band of men carrying three or four planks, on which were seated, in rows, upwards of a dozen men. I shuddered involuntarily as I recollected the sacrifice of human victims at the island of Emo, and turned with a look of fear to Jack as I said:

"Oh Jack! I have a terrible dread that they are going to commit some of their cruel practices on these wretched men. We had better not go to the temple. We shall only be horrified without being able to do any good, for I fear they are going to kill them."

Jack's face wore an expression of deep compassion as he said in a low voice, "No fear, Ralph; the sufferings of these poor fellows are over long ago."

I turned with a start as he spoke, and glancing at the men, who were now quite near to the spot where we stood, saw that they were all dead. They were tied firmly with ropes in a sitting posture on the planks, and seemed, as they bent their sightless eyeballs and grinning mouths over the dancing crew below, as if they were laughing in ghastly mockery at the utter inability of their enemies to hurt them now. These, we discovered afterwards, were the men who had been slain in the battle of the previous day, and were now on their way to be first presented to the gods and then eaten. Behind these came two men leading between them a third, whose hands were pinioned behind his back. He walked with a firm step, and wore a look of utter indifference on his face as they led him along, so that we concluded he must be a criminal who was about to receive some slight punishment for his faults. The rear of the procession was brought up by a shouting crowd of women and children, with whom we mingled and followed to the temple.

Here we arrived in a few minutes. The temple was a tall, circular building, open at one side. Around it were strewn heaps of human bones and skulls. At a table inside sat the priest, an elderly man with a long grey beard. He was seated on a stool, and before him lay several knives, made of wood, bone, and splinters of bamboo, with which he performed his office of dissecting dead bodies. Farther in lay a variety of articles that had been dedicated to the god, and among them were many spears and clubs. I observed among the latter some with human teeth sticking in them, where the victims had been clubbed in their mouths.

Before this temple the bodies, which were painted with vermilion and soot, were arranged in a sitting posture; and a man called a "dan-vosa" (orator) advanced, and laying his hands on their heads, began to chide them, apparently, in a low, bantering tone. What he said we knew not, but as he went on he waxed warm, and at last shouted to them at the top of his lungs, and finally finished by kicking the bodies over and running away, amid the shouts and laughter of the people, who now rushed forward. Seizing the bodies by a leg or an arm, or by the hair of the head, they dragged them over stumps and stones and through sloughs until they were exhausted. The bodies were then brought back to the temple and dissected by the priest, after which they were taken out to be baked.

Close to the temple a large fire was kindled, in which stones were heated red hot. When ready these were spread out on the ground, and a thick coating of leaves strewn over them to slack the heat. On this "lovo," or oven, the bodies were then placed, covered over, and left to bake.

The crowd now ran with terrible yells towards a neighbouring hill or mound, on which we observed the framework of a house lying ready to be erected. Sick with horror, yet fascinated by curiosity, we staggered after them mechanically, scarce knowing where we were going or what we did, and feeling a sort of impression that all we saw was a dreadful dream.

Arrived at the place, we saw the multitude crowding round a certain spot. We pressed forward, and obtained a sight of what they were doing. A large wooden beam or post lay on the ground, beside the other parts of the framework of the house, and close to the end of it was a hole about seven feet deep and upwards of two feet wide. While we looked, the man whom we had before observed with his hands pinioned was carried into the circle. His hands were now free, but his legs were tightly strapped together. The post of the house was then placed in the hole, and the man put in beside it. His head was a good way below the surface of the hole, and his arms were clasped round the post. Earth was now thrown in until all was covered over and stamped down; and this, we were afterwards told, was a ceremony usually performed at the dedication of a new temple or the erection of a chief's house!

"Come, come," cried Jack on beholding this horrible tragedy; "we have seen enough, enough—far more than enough! Let us go."

Jack's face looked ghastly pale and haggard as we hurried back to rejoin the teacher; and I have no doubt that he felt terrible anxiety when he considered the number and ferocity of the savages, and the weakness of the few arms which were ready indeed to essay, but impotent to effect, Avatea's deliverance from these ruthless men.

CHAPTER THIRTY TWO

An unexpected discovery, and a bold, reckless defiance, with its consequences-Plans of escape, and heroic resolves.

When we returned to the shore and related to our friend what had passed, he was greatly distressed, and groaned in spirit; but we had not sat long in conversation when we were interrupted by the arrival of Tararo on the beach, accompanied by a number of followers bearing baskets of vegetables and fruits on their heads.

We advanced to meet him, and he expressed, through our interpreter, much pleasure in seeing us.

"And what, is it that my friends wish to say to me?" he inquired.

The teacher explained that we came to beg that Avatea might be spared.

"Tell him," said Jack, "that I consider that I have a right to ask this of him, having not only saved the girl's life, but the lives of his own people also; and say that I wish her to be allowed to follow her own wishes, and join the Christians."

While this was being translated the chief's brow lowered, and we could see plainly that our request met with no favourable reception. He replied with considerable energy and at some length.

"What says he?" inquired Jack.

"I regret to say that he will not listen to the proposal. He says he has pledged his word to his friend that the girl shall be sent to him, and a deputy even now on this island awaiting the fulfilment of the pledge."

Jack bit his lip in suppressed anger. "Tell Tararo," he exclaimed with a flashing eye, "that if he does not grant my demand it will be worse for him. Say I have a big gun on board my schooner that will blow his village into the sea if he does not give up the girl."

"Nay, my friend," said the teacher gently, "I will not tell him that. We must 'overcome evil with good.'"

"What does my friend say?" inquired the chief, who seemed nettled by Jack's looks of defiance.

"He is displeased," replied the teacher.

Tararo turned away with a smile of contempt, and walked towards the men who carried the baskets of vegetables, and who had now emptied the whole on the beach in an enormous pile.

"What are they doing there?" I inquired.

"I think that they are laying out a gift which they intend to present to some one," said the teacher.

At this moment a couple of men appeared, leading a young girl between them, and going towards the heap of fruits and vegetables, placed her on top of it. We started with surprise and fear, for in the young female before us we recognised the Samoan girl, Avatea.

We stood rooted to the earth with surprise and thick-coming fears.

"Oh my dear young friend!" whispered the teacher in a voice of deep emotion; while he seized Jack by the arm, "she is to be made a sacrifice even now!"

"Is she?" cried Jack with a vehement shout, spurning the teacher aside, and dashing over two natives who stood in his way, while he rushed towards the heap, sprang up its side, and seized Avatea by the arm. In another moment he dragged her down, placed her back to a large tree, and wrenching a war-club from the hand of a native who seemed powerless and petrified with surprise, whirled it above his head, and yelled, rather than shouted, while his face blazed with fury, "Come on, the whole nation of you, an ye like it, and do your worst!"

It seemed as though the challenge had been literally accepted; for every savage on the ground ran precipitately at Jack with club and spear, and doubtless would speedily have poured out his brave blood on the sod had not the teacher rushed in between them, and raising his voice to its utmost, cried:

"Stay your hands, warriors! It is not your part to judge in this matter! It is for Tararo, the chief, to say whether or not the young man shall live or die!"

The natives were arrested; and I know not whether it was the gratifying acknowledgment of his superiority thus made by the teacher, or some lingering feeling of gratitude for Jack's former aid in time of need, that influenced Tararo, but he stepped forward, and waving his hand, said to his people, "Desist. The young man's life is mine." Then turning to Jack, he said, "You have forfeited your liberty and life to me. Submit yourself, for we are more numerous than the sand upon the shore. You are but one: why should you die?"

"Villain!" exclaimed Jack passionately. "I may die, but assuredly I shall not perish alone! I will not submit until you promise that this girl shall not be injured!"

"You are very bold," replied the chief haughtily, "but very foolish. Yet I will say that Avatea shall not be sent away-at least, for three days."

"You had better accept these terms," whispered the teacher entreatingly. "If you persist in this mad defiance, you will be slain and Avatea will be lost. Three days are worth having."

Jack hesitated a moment, then lowered his club, and throwing it moodily to the ground, crossed his arms on his breast and hung down his head in silence.

Tararo seemed pleased by his submission, and told the teacher to say that he did not forget his former services, and therefore would leave him free as to his person, but that the schooner would be detained till he had further considered the matter.

While the teacher translated this, he approached as near to where Avatea was standing as possible without creating suspicion, and whispered to her a few words in the native language. Avatea, who, during the whole of the foregoing scene, had stood leaning against the tree perfectly passive, and seemingly quite uninterested in all that was going on, replied by a single rapid glance of her dark eye, which was instantly cast down again on the ground at her feet.

Tararo now advanced, and taking the girl by the hand, led her unresistingly away; while Jack, Peterkin, and I returned with the teacher on board the schooner.

On reaching the deck we went down to the cabin, where Jack threw himself, in a state of great dejection, on a couch; but the teacher seated himself by his side, and laying his hand upon his shoulder, said:

"Do not give way to anger, my young friend. God has given us three days, and we must use the means that are in our power to free this poor girl from slavery. We must not sit in idle disappointment; we must act —"

"Act!" cried Jack, raising himself and tossing back his hair wildly. "It is mockery to talk of acting when one is bound hand and foot. How can I act? I cannot fight a whole nation of savages single-handed. Yes," he said with a bitter smile, "I *can* fight them; but I cannot conquer them, or save Avatea."

"Patience, my friend: your spirit is not a good one just now. You cannot expect that blessing which alone can ensure success unless you are more submissive. I will tell you my plans if you will listen."

"Listen!" cried Jack eagerly. "Of course I will, my good fellow! I did not know you had any plans. Out with them! I only hope you will show me how I can get the girl on board of this schooner, and I'd up anchor and away in no time. But proceed with your plans."

The teacher smiled sadly. "Ah, my friend, if one fathom of your anchor-chain were to rattle as you drew it in, a thousand warriors would be standing on your deck! No, no; that could not be done. Even now your ship would be taken from you were it not that Tararo has some feeling of gratitude towards you. But I know Tararo well. He is a man of falsehood, as all the unconverted savages are. The chief to whom he has promised this girl is very powerful, and Tararo *must* fulfil his promise. He has told you that he would do nothing to the girl for three days, but that is because the party who are to take her away will not be ready to start for three days. Still, as he might have made you a prisoner during those three days, I say that God has given them to us."

"Well, but what do you propose to do?" said Jack impatiently.

"My plan involves much danger; but I see no other, and I think you have courage to brave it. It is this. There is an island about fifty miles to the south of this, the natives of which are Christians, and have been so for two years or more, and the principal chief is Avatea's lover. Once there, Avatea would be safe. Now, I suggest that you should abandon your schooner. Do you think that you can make so great a sacrifice?"

"Friend," replied Jack, "when I make up my mind to go through with a thing of importance, I can make any sacrifice."

The teacher smiled. "Well, then, the savages could not conceive it possible that for the sake of a girl you would voluntarily lose your fine vessel; therefore, as long as she lies here, they think they have you all safe. So I suggest that we get a quantity of stores conveyed to a sequestered part of the shore, provide a small canoe, put Avatea on board, and you three would paddle to the Christian island."

"Bravo!" cried Peterkin, springing up and seizing the teacher's hand. "Missionary, you're a regular brick! I didn't think you had so much in you!"

"As for me," continued the teacher, "I will remain on board till they discover that you are gone. Then they will ask me where you are gone to, and I will refuse to tell."

"And what'll be the result of that?" inquired Jack.

"I know not. Perhaps they will kill me; but," he added, looking at Jack with a peculiar smile, "I too am not afraid to die in a good cause!"

"But how are we to get hold of Avatea?" inquired Jack.

"I have arranged with her to meet us at a particular spot, to which I will guide you to-night. We shall then arrange about it. She will easily manage to elude her keepers, who are not very strict in watching her, thinking it impossible that she could escape from the island. Indeed, I am sure that such an idea will never enter their heads. But, as I have said, you run great danger. Fifty miles in a small canoe, on the open sea, is a great voyage to make. You may miss the island, too, in which case there is no other in that direction for a hundred miles or more; and if you lose your way and fall among other heathens, you know the law of Feejee —a castaway who gains the shore is doomed to die. You must count the cost, my young friend."

"I have counted it," replied Jack. "If Avatea consents to run the risk, most certainly I will; and so will my comrades also. Besides," added Jack, looking seriously into the teacher's face, "your Bible-our Bible-tells of *One* who delivers those who call on Him in the time of trouble; who holds the winds in His fists, and the waters in the hollow of His hand."

We now set about active preparations for the intended voyage: collected together such things as we should require, and laid out on the deck provisions sufficient to maintain us for several weeks, purposing to load the canoe with as much as she could hold consistently with speed and safety. These we covered with a tarpaulin, intending to convey them to the canoe only a few hours before starting. When night spread her sable curtain over the scene, we prepared to land; but first kneeling along with the natives and the teacher, the latter implored a blessing on our enterprise. Then we rowed quietly to the shore and followed our sable guide, who led us by a long détour in order to avoid the village, to the place of rendezvous. We had not stood more than five minutes under the gloomy shade of the thick foliage when a dark figure glided noiselessly up to us.

"Ah, here you are!" said Jack as Avatea approached. —"Now, then, tell her what we've come about, and don't waste time."

"I understan' leetl' English," said Avatea in a low voice.

"Why, where did you pick up English?" exclaimed Jack in amazement. "You were dumb as a stone when I saw you last."

"She has learned all she knows of it from me," said the teacher, "since she came to the island."

We now gave Avatea a full explanation of our plans, entering into all the details, and concealing none of the danger, so that she might be fully aware of the risk she ran. As we had anticipated, she was too glad of the opportunity thus afforded her to escape from her persecutors to think of the danger or risk.

"Then you're willing to go with us, are you?" said Jack.

"Yis, I willing to go."

"And you're not afraid to trust yourself out on the deep sea so far?"

"No, I not 'fraid to go. Safe with Christian."

After some further consultation the teacher suggested that it was time to return, so we bade Avatea good-night; and having appointed to meet at the cliff where the canoe lay on the following night, just after dark, we hastened away-we to row back to the schooner with muffled oars, Avatea to glide back to her prison-hut among the Mango savages.

CHAPTER THIRTY THREE

The flight-The pursuit-Despair and its results-The lion bearded in his den again-Awful danger threatened and wonderfully averted —A terrific storm.

As the time for our meditated flight drew near, we became naturally very fearful lest our purpose should be discovered, and we spent the whole of the following day in a state of nervous anxiety. We resolved to go ashore and ramble about the village, as if to observe the habits and dwellings of the people, as we thought that an air of affected indifference to the events of the previous day would be more likely than any other course of conduct to avert suspicion as to our intentions. While we were thus occupied, the teacher remained on board with the Christian natives, whose powerful voices reached us ever and anon as they engaged in singing hymns or in prayer.

At last the long and tedious day came to a close, the sun sank into the sea, and the short-lived twilight of those regions, to which I have already referred, ended abruptly in a dark night. Hastily throwing a few blankets into our little boat, we stepped into it, and whispering farewell to the natives in the schooner, rowed gently over the lagoon, taking care to keep as near to the beach as possible. We rowed in the utmost silence and with muffled oars, so that had any one observed us at the distance of a few yards, he might have almost taken us for a phantom boat or a shadow on the dark water. Not a breath of air was stirring; but fortunately the gentle ripple of the sea upon the shore, mingled with the soft roar of the breaker on the distant reef, effectually drowned the slight plash that we unavoidably made in the water by the dipping of our oars.

A quarter of an hour sufficed to bring us to the overhanging cliff under whose black shadow our little canoe lay, with her bow in the water, ready to be launched, and most of her cargo already stowed away. As the keel of our little boat grated on the sand, a hand was laid upon the bow, and a dim form was seen.

"Ha!" said Peterkin in a whisper as he stepped upon the beach; "is that you, Avatea?"

"Yis, it am me," was the reply.

"All right-Now, then, gently-Help me to shove off the canoe," whispered Jack to the teacher. —"And, Peterkin, do you shove these blankets aboard; we may want them before long. —Avatea, step into the middle: that's right."

"Is all ready?" whispered the teacher.

"Not quite," replied Peterkin. —"Here, Ralph, lay hold o' this pair of oars, and stow them away if you can. I don't like paddles. After we're safe away, I'll try to rig up rowlocks for them."

"Now, then, in with you and shove off!"

One more earnest squeeze of the kind teacher's hand, and with his whispered blessing yet sounding in our ears, we shot like an arrow from the shore, sped over the still waters of the lagoon, and paddled as swiftly as strong arms and willing hearts could urge us over the long swell of the open sea.

All that night and the whole of the following day we plied our paddles in almost total silence and without a halt, save twice to recruit our failing energies with a mouthful of food and a draught of water. Jack had taken the bearing of the island just after starting, and laying a small pocket-compass before him, kept the head of the canoe due south, for our chance of hitting the island depended very much on the faithfulness of our steersman in keeping our tiny bark exactly and constantly on its proper course. Peterkin and I paddled in the bow, and Avatea worked untiringly in the middle.

As the sun's lower limb dipped on the gilded edge of the sea Jack ceased working, threw down his paddle, and called a halt.

"There!" he cried, heaving a deep, long-drawn sigh; "we've put a considerable breadth of water between us and these black rascals, so now we'll have a hearty supper and a sound sleep."

"Hear, hear!" cried Peterkin. "Nobly spoken, Jack! —Hand me a drop of water, Ralph. —Why, girl, what's wrong with you? You look just like a black owl blinking in the sunshine!"

Avatea smiled. "I sleepy," she said; and as if to prove the truth of this, she laid her head on the edge of the canoe and fell fast asleep.

"That's uncommon sharp practice," said Peterkin with a broad grin. "Don't you think we should awake her to make her eat something first? Or perhaps," he added with a grave, meditative look —"perhaps we might put some food in her mouth, which is so elegantly open at the present moment, and see if she'd swallow it while asleep. —If so, Ralph, you might come round to the front here and feed her quietly, while Jack and I are tucking into the victuals. It would be a monstrous economy of time."

I could not help smiling at Peterkin's idea, which indeed, when I pondered it, seemed remarkably good in theory; nevertheless, I declined to put it in practice, being fearful of the result should the victuals chance to go down the wrong throat. But on suggesting this to Peterkin, he exclaimed:

"Down the wrong throat, man! Why, a fellow with half-an-eye might see that if it went down Avatea's throat it could not go down the wrong throat! —unless, indeed, you have all of a sudden become inordinately selfish, and think that all the throats in the world are wrong ones except your own. However, don't talk so much, and hand me the pork before Jack finishes it. I feel myself entitled to at least one minute morsel."

"Peterkin, you're a villain —a paltry little villain!" said Jack quietly as he tossed the hind legs (including the tail) of a cold roast pig to his comrade; "and I must again express my regret that unavoidable circumstances have thrust your society upon me, and that necessity has compelled me to cultivate your acquaintance. Were it not that you are incapable of walking upon the water, I would order you, sir, out of the canoe!"

"There! you've awakened Avatea with your long tongue," retorted Peterkin, with a frown, as the girl gave vent to a deep sigh. "No," he continued, "it was only a snore. Perchance she dreameth of her black Apollo. —I say, Ralph, do leave just one little slice of that yam! Between you and Jack I run a chance of being put on short allowance, if not-yei-a-a-ow!"

Peterkin's concluding remark was a yawn of so great energy that Jack recommended him to postpone the conclusion of his meal till next morning —a piece of advice which he followed so quickly that I was forcibly reminded of his remark, a few minutes before, in regard to the sharp practice of Avatea.

My readers will have observed, probably, by this time, that I am much given to meditation: they will not, therefore, be surprised to learn that I fell into a deep reverie on the subject of sleep, which was continued without intermission into the night, and prolonged without interruption into the following morning. But I cannot feel assured that I actually slept during that time, although I am tolerably certain that I was not awake.

Thus we lay, like a shadow, on the still bosom of the ocean, while the night closed in, and all around was calm, dark, and silent.

A thrilling cry of alarm from Peterkin startled us in the morning, just as the grey dawn began to glimmer in the east.

"What's wrong?" cried Jack, starting up.

Peterkin replied by pointing, with a look of anxious dread, towards the horizon; and a glance sufficed to show us that one of the largest-sized war-canoes was approaching us!

With a groan of mingled despair and anger, Jack seized his paddle, glanced at the compass, and in a suppressed voice commanded us to "Give way!" But we did not require to be urged. Already our four paddles were glancing in the water, and the canoe bounded over the glassy sea like a dolphin, while a shout from our pursuers told that they had observed our motions.

"I see something like land ahead," said Jack in a hopeful tone. "It seems impossible that we could have made the island yet; still, if it is so, we may reach it before these fellows can catch us, for our canoe is light and our muscles are fresh."

No one replied; for, to say truth, we felt that in a long chase we had no chance whatever with a canoe which held nearly a hundred warriors. Nevertheless, we resolved to do our utmost to escape, and paddled with a degree of vigour that kept us well in advance of our pursuers.

The war-canoe was so far behind us that it seemed but a little speck on the sea, and the shouts to which the crew occasionally gave vent came faintly towards us on the morning breeze. We therefore hoped that we should be able to keep in advance for an hour or two, when we might perhaps reach the land ahead. But this hope was suddenly crushed by the supposed land, not long after, rising up into the sky, thus proving itself to be a fog-bank!

A bitter feeling of disappointment filled each heart, and was expressed on each countenance, as we beheld this termination to our hopes. But we had little time to think of regret. Our danger was too great and imminent to permit of a moment's relaxation from our exertions. No hope now animated our bosoms; but a feeling of despair, strange to say, lent us power to work, and nerved our arms with such energy that it was several hours ere the savages overtook us. When we saw that there was indeed no chance of escape, and that paddling any longer would only serve to exhaust our strength without doing any good, we turned the side of our canoe towards the approaching enemy and laid down our paddles.

Silently, and with a look of bitter determination on his face, Jack lifted one of the light boat-oars that we had brought with us, and resting it on his shoulder, stood up in an attitude of bold defiance. Peterkin took the other oar and also stood up, but there was no anger visible on his countenance: when not sparkling with fun, it usually wore a mild, sad expression, which was deepened on the present occasion as he glanced at Avatea, who sat with her face resting in her hands upon her knees. Without knowing very well what I intended to do, I also arose and grasped my paddle with both hands.

On came the large canoe like a war-horse of the deep, with the foam curling from its sharp bow, and the spear-heads of the savages glancing in the beams of the rising sun. Perfect silence was maintained on both sides; and we could hear the hissing water, and see the frowning eyes of the warriors, as they came rushing on. When about twenty yards distant, five or six of the savages in the bow rose, and laying aside their paddles, took up their spears. Jack and Peterkin raised their oars, while, with a feeling of madness whirling in my brain, I grasped my paddle and prepared for the onset. But before any of us could strike a blow, the sharp prow of the war-canoe struck us like a thunderbolt on the side and hurled us into the sea!

What occurred after this I cannot tell, for I was nearly drowned; but when I recovered from the state of insensibility into which I had been thrown, I found myself stretched on my back, bound hand and foot, between Jack and Peterkin, in the bottom of the large canoe.

In this condition we lay the whole day, during which time the savages only rested one hour. When night came they rested again for another hour, and appeared to sleep just as they sat. But we were neither unbound nor allowed to speak to each other during the voyage, nor was a morsel of food or a draught of water given to us. For food, however, we cared little; but we would have given much for a drop of water to cool our parched lips. And we would have been glad, too, had they loosened the cords that bound us; for they were tightly fastened, and occasioned us much pain. The air, also, was unusually hot-so much so that I felt convinced that a storm was brewing. This also added to our sufferings. However, these were at length relieved by our arrival at the island from which we had fled.

While we were being led ashore, we caught a glimpse of Avatea, who was seated in the hinder part of the canoe. She was not fettered in any way. Our captors now drove us before them towards the hut of Tararo, at which we speedily arrived, and found the chief seated with an expression on his face that boded us no good. Our friend the teacher stood beside him, with a look of anxiety on his mild features.

"How comes it," said Tararo, turning to the teacher, "that these youths have abused our hospitality?"

"Tell him," replied Jack, "that we have not abused his hospitality, for his hospitality has not been extended to us. I came to the island to deliver Avatea, and my only regret is that I have failed to do so. If I get another chance, I will try to save her yet."

The teacher shook his head. "Nay, my young friend, I had better not tell him that: it will only incense him."

"I care not," replied Jack. "If you don't tell him that, you'll tell him nothing, for I won't say anything softer."

On hearing Jack's speech, Tararo frowned, and his eye flashed with anger.

"Go, presumptuous boy!" he said. "My debt to you cancelled. You and your companions shall die!"

As he spoke he rose and signed to several of attendants, who seized Jack and Peterkin and violently by the collars, and dragging us from the house of the chief, led us through the wood to the outskirts of the village. Here they thrust us into a species of natural cave in a cliff, and having barricaded the entrance, left us in total darkness.

After feeling about for some time-for our legs were unshackled, although our wrists were still bound with thongs-we found a low ledge of rock running along one side of the cavern. On this we seated ourselves, and for a long time maintained unbroken silence.

At last I could restrain my feelings no longer. "Alas! dear Jack and Peterkin," said I, "what is to become of us? I fear that we are doomed to die."

"I know not," replied Jack in a tremulous voice —"I know not. Ralph, I regret deeply the hastiness of my violent temper, which, I must confess, has been the chief cause of our being brought to this sad condition. Perhaps the teacher may do something for us. But I have little hope."

"Ah no!" said Peterkin with a heavy sigh; "I am sure he can't help us. Tararo doesn't care more for him than for one of his dogs."

"Truly," said I, "there seems no chance of deliverance, unless the Almighty puts forth His arm to save us. Yet I must say I have great hope, my comrades; for we have come to this dark place by no fault of ours-unless it be a fault to try to succour a woman in distress."

I was interrupted in my remarks by a noise at the entrance to the cavern, which was caused by the removal of the barricade. Immediately after three men entered, and taking us by the collars of our coats, led us away through the forest. As we advanced we heard much shouting and beating of native drums in the village, and at first we thought that our guards were conducting us to the hut of Tararo again. But in this we were mistaken. The beating of drums gradually increased, and soon after we observed a procession of the natives coming towards us. At the head of this procession we were placed, and then we all advanced together towards the temple where human victims were wont to be sacrificed!

A thrill of horror ran through my heart as I recalled to mind the awful scenes that I had before witnessed at that dreadful spot. But deliverance came suddenly from a quarter whence we little expected it. During the whole of that day there had been an unusual degree of heat in the atmosphere, and the sky assumed that lurid aspect which portends a thunderstorm. Just as we were approaching the horrid temple, a growl of thunder burst overhead, and heavy drops of rain began to fall.

Those who have not witnessed gales and storms in tropical regions can form but a faint conception of the fearful hurricane that burst upon the island of Mango at this time. Before we reached the temple the storm burst upon us with a deafening roar; and the natives, who knew too well the devastation that was to follow, fled right and left through the woods in order to save their property, leaving us alone in the midst of the howling storm. The trees around us bent before the blast like willows, and we were about to flee in order to seek shelter when the teacher ran toward us with a knife in his hand.

"Thank the Lord," he said, cutting our bonds, "I am in time! Now, seek the shelter of the nearest rock."

This we did without a moment's hesitation, for the whistling wind burst, ever and anon, like thunderclaps among the trees, and tearing them from their roots, hurled them with violence to the ground. Rain cut across the land in sheets, and lightning played like forked serpents in the air, while high above the roar of the hissing tempest the thunder crashed and burst and rolled in awful majesty.

In the village the scene was absolutely appalling. Roofs were blown completely off the houses in many cases, and in others the houses themselves were levelled with the ground. In the midst of this the natives were darting to and fro-in some instances saving their goods, but in many others seeking to save themselves from the storm of destruction that whirled around them. But terrific although the tempest was on land, it was still more tremendous on the mighty ocean. Billows sprang, as it were, from the great deep, and while their crests were absolutely scattered into white mist, they fell upon the beach with a crash that seemed to shake the solid land. But they did not end there. Each successive wave swept higher and higher on the beach until the ocean lashed its angry waters among the trees and bushes, and at length, in a sheet of white, curdled foam, swept into the village and upset and carried off, or dashed into wreck, whole rows of the native dwellings! It was a sublime, an awful scene, calculated, in some degree at least, to impress the mind of beholders with the might and majesty of God.

We found shelter in a cave that night and all the next day, during which time the storm raged in fury. But on the night following, it abated somewhat; and in the morning we went to the village to seek for food, being so famished with hunger that we lost all feeling of danger and all wish to escape in our desire to satisfy the cravings of nature. But no sooner had we obtained food than we began to wish that we had rather endeavoured to make our escape into the mountains. This we attempted to do soon afterwards; but the natives were now able to look after us, and on our showing a disposition to avoid observation and make towards the mountains, we were seized by three warriors, who once more bound our wrists and thrust us into our former prison.

It is true Jack made a vigorous resistance, and knocked down the first savage who seized him with a well-directed blow of his fist, but he was speedily overpowered by others. Thus we were again prisoners, with the prospect of torture and a violent death before us.

CHAPTER THIRTY FOUR

Imprisonment-Sinking hopes-Unexpected freedom to more than one, and in more
senses than one.

For a long, long month we remained in our dark and dreary prison, during which dismal time
we did not see the face of a human being except that of the silent savage who brought us our
daily food.

There have been one or two seasons in my life during which I have felt as if the darkness of
sorrow and desolation that crushed my inmost heart could never pass away until death should
make me cease to feel. The present was such a season.

During the first part of our confinement we felt a cold chill at our hearts every time we
heard a footfall near the cave, dreading lest it should prove to be that of our executioner. But
as time dragged heavily on we ceased to feel this alarm, and began to experience such a deep,
irrepressible longing for freedom that we chafed and fretted in our confinement like tigers.
Then a feeling of despair came over us, and we actually longed for the time when the savages
would take us forth to die. But these changes took place very gradually, and were mingled
sometimes with brighter thoughts; for there were times when we sat, in that dark cavern on
our ledge of rock, and conversed almost pleasantly about the past until we well-nigh forgot the
dreary present. But we seldom ventured to touch upon the future.

A few decayed leaves and boughs formed our bed, and a scanty supply of yams and taro,
brought to us once a day, constituted our food.

"Well, Ralph, how have you slept?" said Jack in a listless tone on rising one morning from
his humble couch. "Were you much disturbed by the wind last night?"

"No," said I. "I dreamed of home all night, and I thought that my mother smiled upon me
and beckoned me to go to her; but I could not, for I was chained."

"And I dreamed too," said Peterkin; "but it was of our happy home on the Coral Island. I
thought we were swimming in the Water Garden. Then the savages gave a yell, and we were
immediately in the cave at Spouting Cliff, which, somehow or other changed into this gloomy
cavern; and I awoke to find it true."

Peterkin's tone was so much altered by the depressing influence of his long imprisonment
that, had I not known it was he who spoke, I should scarcely have recognised it, so sad was it,
and so unlike to the merry, cheerful voice we had been accustomed to hear. I pondered this
much, and thought of the terrible decline of happiness that may come on human beings in so
short a time; how bright the sunshine in the sky at one time, and in a short space bow dark
the overshadowing cloud! I had no doubt that the Bible would have given me much light and
comfort on this subject if I had possessed one, and I once more had occasion to regret deeply
having neglected to store my memory with its consoling truths.

While I meditated thus, Peterkin again broke the silence of the cave by saying, in a melancholy
tone, "Oh, I wonder if we shall ever see our dear island more!"

His voice trembled, and covering his face with both hands, he bent down his head and wept.
It was an unusual sight for me to see our once joyous companion in tears, and I felt a burning
desire to comfort him; but, alas! what could I say? I could hold out no hope; and although
I essayed twice to speak, the words refused to pass my lips. While I hesitated Jack sat down
beside him and whispered a few words in his ear, while Peterkin threw himself on his friend's
breast and rested his head on his shoulder.

Thus we sat for some time in deep silence. Soon after we heard footsteps at the entrance of
the cave, and immediately our jailer entered. We were so much accustomed to his regular visits,
however, that we paid little attention to him, expecting that he would set down our meagre
fare as usual and depart. But, to our surprise, instead of doing so, he advanced towards us with
a knife in his hand, and going up to Jack, he cut the thongs that bound his wrists; then he did

the same to Peterkin and me! For fully five minutes we stood in speechless amazement, with our freed hands hanging idly by our sides. The first thought that rushed into my mind was that the time had come to put us to death; and although, as I have said before, we actually wished for death in the strength of our despair, now that we thought it drew really near I felt all the natural love of life revive in my heart, mingled with a chill of horror at the suddenness of our call.

But I was mistaken. After cutting our bonds the savage pointed to the cave's mouth, and we marched, almost mechanically, into the open air. Here, to our surprise, we found the teacher standing under a tree, with his hands clasped before him, and the tears trickling down his dark cheeks. On seeing Jack, who came out first, he sprang towards him, and clasping him in his arms, exclaimed:

"Oh my dear young friend, through the great goodness of God you are free!"

"Free?" cried Jack.

"Ay, free!" repeated the teacher, shaking us warmly by the hands again and again —"free to go and come as you will. The Lord has unloosed the bonds of the captive, and set the prisoners free. A missionary has been sent to us, and Tararo has embraced the Christian religion! The people are even now burning their gods of wood! Come, my dear friends, and see the glorious sight!"

We could scarcely credit our senses. So long had we been accustomed, in our cavern, to dream of deliverance, that we imagined for a moment this must surely be nothing more than another vivid dream. Our eyes and minds were dazzled, too, by the brilliant sunshine, which almost blinded us after our long confinement to the gloom of our prison, so that we felt giddy with the variety of conflicting emotions that filled our throbbing bosoms; but as we followed the footsteps of our sable friend, and beheld the bright foliage of the trees, and heard the cries of the paroquets, and smelt the rich perfume of the flowering shrubs, the truth-that we were really delivered from prison and from death-rushed with overwhelming power into our souls, and with one accord, while tears sprang to our eyes, we uttered a loud, long cheer of joy.

It was replied to by a shout from a number of the natives who chanced to be near. Running towards us, they shook us by the hand with every demonstration of kindly feeling. They then fell behind, and forming a sort of procession, conducted us to the dwelling of Tararo.

The scene that met our eyes here was one that I shall never forget. On a rude bench in front of his house sat the chief. A native stood on his left hand, who from his dress seemed to be a teacher. On his right stood an English gentleman, who I at once, and rightly, concluded was a missionary. He was tall, thin, and apparently past forty, with a bald forehead and thin grey hair. The expression of his countenance was the most winning I ever saw, and his clear grey eyes beamed with a look that was frank, fearless, loving, and truthful. In front of the chief was an open space, in the centre of which lay a pile of wooden idols, ready to be set on fire; and around these were assembled thousands of natives, who had come to join in or to witness the unusual sight. A bright smile overspread the missionary's face as he advanced quickly to meet us, and he shook us warmly by the hands.

"I am overjoyed to meet you, my dear young friends," he said. "My friend and *your* friend, the teacher, has told me your history; and I thank our Father in heaven with all my heart, that He has guided me to this island and made me the instrument of saving you."

We thanked the missionary most heartily, and asked him, in some surprise, how he had succeeded in turning the heart of Tararo in our favour.

"I will tell you that at a more convenient time," he answered, "meanwhile we must not forget the respect due to the chief. He waits to receive you."

In the conversation that immediately followed between us and Tararo, the latter said that the light of the Gospel of Jesus Christ had been sent to the island, and that to it we were indebted for our freedom. Moreover, he told us that we were at liberty to depart in our schooner whenever we pleased, and that we should be supplied with as much provision as we required. He concluded by shaking hands with us warmly, and performing the ceremony of rubbing noses.

This was indeed good news to us, and we could hardly find words to express our gratitude to the chief and to the missionary.

"And what of Avatea?" inquired Jack.

The missionary replied by pointing to a group of natives, in the midst of whom the girl stood. Beside her was a tall, strapping fellow, whose noble mien and air of superiority bespoke him a chief of no ordinary kind. "That youth is her lover. He came this very morning in his war-canoe to treat with Tararo for Avatea. He is to be married in a few days, and afterwards returns to his island home with his bride."

"That's capital!" said Jack as he stepped up to the savage and gave him a hearty shake of the hand. "I wish you joy, my lad! —And you too, Avatea!"

As Jack spoke, Avatea's lover took him by the hand and led him to the spot where Tararo and the missionary stood, surrounded by most of the chief men of the tribe. The girl herself followed and stood on his left hand, while her lover stood on his right, and commanding silence, made the following speech, which was translated by the missionary:

"Young friend, you have seen few years, but your head is old. Your heart, also, is large and very brave. I and Avatea are your debtors; and we wish, in the midst of this assembly, to acknowledge our debt, and to say that it is one which we can never repay. You have risked your life for one who was known to you only for a few days. But she was a woman in distress, and that was enough to secure to her the aid of a Christian man. We, who live in these islands of the sea, know that the true Christians always act thus. Their religion is one of love and kindness. We thank God that so many Christians have been sent here: we hope many more will come. Remember that I and Avatea will think of you, and pray for you and your brave comrades, when you are far away."

To this kind speech Jack returned a short, sailor-like reply, in which he insisted that he had only done for Avatea what he would have done for any woman under the sun. But Jack's forte did not lie in speech-making, so he terminated rather abruptly by seizing the chief's hand and shaking it violently, after which he made a hasty retreat.

"Now, then, Ralph and Peterkin," said Jack as we mingled with the crowd, "it seems to me that, the object we came here for having been satisfactorily accomplished, we have nothing more to do but get ready for sea as fast as we can, and hurrah for old England!"

"That's my idea precisely," said Peterkin, endeavouring to wink; but he had wept so much of late, poor fellow, that he found it difficult. "However, I'm not going away till I see these fellows burn their gods."

Peterkin had his wish, for in a few minutes afterwards fire was put to the pile, the roaring flames, ascended, and amid the acclamations of the assembled thousands, the false gods of Mango were reduced to ashes!

CHAPTER THIRTY FIVE

Conclusion.

To part is the lot of all mankind. The world is a scene of constant leave-taking, and the hands that grasp in cordial greeting to-day are doomed ere long to unite for the last time when the quivering lips pronounce the word "Farewell." It is a sad thought, but should we on that account exclude it from our minds? May not a lesson worth learning be gathered in the contemplation of it? May it not, perchance, teach us to devote our thoughts more frequently and attentively to that land where we meet but part no more?

How many do we part from in this world with a light good-bye whom we never see again! Often do I think, in my meditations on this subject, that if we realised more fully the shortness of the fleeting intercourse that we have in this world with many of our fellow-men, we would try more earnestly to do them good, to give them a friendly smile, as it were, in passing (for the longest intercourse on earth is little more than a passing word and glance), and show that we have sympathy with them in the short, quick struggle of life by our kindly words and looks and actions.

The time soon drew near when we were to quit the islands of the South Seas; and strange though it may appear, we felt deep regret at parting with the natives of the island of Mango, for after they embraced the Christian faith, they sought, by showing us the utmost kindness, to compensate for the harsh treatment we had experienced at their hands. And we felt a growing affection for the native teachers and the missionary, and especially for Avatea and her husband.

Before leaving we had many long and interesting conversations with the missionary, in one of which he told us that he had been making for the island of Rarotonga when his native-built sloop was blown out of its course, during a violent gale, and driven to this island. At first the natives refused to listen to what he had to say; but after a week's residence among them, Tararo came to him and said that he wished to become a Christian and would burn his idols. He proved himself to be sincere, for, as we have seen, he persuaded all his people to do likewise. I use the word "persuaded" advisedly, for, like all the other Feejee chiefs, Tararo was a despot, and might have commanded obedience to his wishes; but he entered so readily into the spirit of the new faith that he perceived at once the impropriety of using constraint in the propagation of it. He set the example, therefore; and that example was followed by almost every man of the tribe.

During the short time that we remained at the island repairing our vessel and getting her ready for sea, the natives had commenced building a large and commodious church under the superintendence of the missionary, and several rows of new cottages were marked out; so that the place bid fair to become, in a few months, as prosperous and beautiful as the Christian village at the other end of the island.

After Avatea was married, she and her husband were sent away loaded with presents, chiefly of an edible nature. One of the native teachers went with them, for the purpose of visiting still more distant islands of the sea, and spreading, if possible, the light of the glorious Gospel there.

As the missionary intended to remain for several weeks longer in order to encourage and confirm his new converts, Jack and Peterkin and I held a consultation in the cabin of our schooner-which we found just as we had left her, for everything that had been taken out of her was restored. We now resolved to delay our departure no longer. The desire to see our beloved native land was strong upon us, and we could not wait.

Three natives volunteered to go with us to Tahiti, where we thought it likely that we should be able to procure a sufficient crew of sailors to man our vessel; so we accepted their offer gladly.

It was a bright, clear morning when we hoisted the snow-white sails of the pirate schooner and left the shores of Mango. The missionary and thousands of the natives came down to bid us God-speed and to see us sail away. As the vessel bent before a light, fair wind, we glided quickly over the lagoon under a cloud of canvas.

Just as we passed through the channel in the reef the natives gave us a loud cheer; and as the missionary waved his hat, while he stood on a coral rock with his grey hairs floating in the wind, we heard the single word "Farewell" borne faintly over the sea.

That night, as we sat on the taffrail gazing out upon the wide sea and up into the starry firmament, a thrill of joy, strangely mixed with sadness, passed through our hearts; for we were at length "homeward bound" and were gradually leaving far behind us the beautiful, bright-green coral islands of the Pacific Ocean.

The Gorilla Hunters

CHAPTER ONE
In which the hunters are introduced.

It was five o'clock in the afternoon. There can be no doubt whatever as to that. Old Agnes may say what she pleases-she has a habit of doing so-but I know for certain (because I looked at my watch not ten minutes before it happened) that it was exactly five o'clock in the afternoon when I received a most singular and every way remarkable visit —a visit which has left an indelible impression on my memory, as well it might; for, independent of its singularity and unexpectedness, one of its results was the series of strange adventures which are faithfully detailed in this volume.

It happened thus: —

I was seated in an armchair in my private study in a small town on the west coast of England. It was a splendid afternoon, and it was exactly five o'clock. Mark that. Not that there is anything singular about the mere fact, neither is it in any way mixed up with the thread of this tale; but old Agnes is very obstinate-singularly positive-and I have a special desire that she should see it in print, that I have not given in on that point. Yes, it was five precisely, and a beautiful evening. I was ruminating, as I frequently do, on the pleasant memories of bygone days, especially the happy days that I spent long ago among the coral islands of the Pacific, when a tap at the door aroused me.

"Come in."

"A veesiter, sir," said old Agnes (my landlady), "an' he'll no gie his name."

Old Agnes, I may remark, is a Scotchwoman.

"Show him in," said I.

"Maybe he's a pickpocket," suggested Agnes.

"I'll take my chance of that."

"Ay! that's like 'ee. Cares for naethin'. Losh, man, what if he cuts yer throat?"

"I'll take my chance of that too; only *do* show him in, my good woman," said I, with a gesture of impatience that caused the excellent (though obstinate) old creature to depart, grumbling.

In another moment a quick step was heard on the stair, and a stranger burst into the room, shut the door in my landlady's face as she followed him, and locked it.

I was naturally surprised, though not alarmed, by the abrupt and eccentric conduct of my visitor, who did not condescend to take off his hat, but stood with his arms folded on his breast, gazing at me and breathing hard.

"You are agitated, sir; pray be seated," said I, pointing to a chair.

The stranger, who was a little man and evidently a gentleman, made no reply, but, seizing a chair, placed it exactly before me, sat down on it as he would have seated himself on a horse, rested his arms on the back, and stared me in the face.

"You are disposed to be facetious," said I, smiling (for I never take offence without excessively good reason).

"Not at all, by no means," said he, taking off his hat and throwing it recklessly on the floor. "You are Mr Rover, I presume?"

"The same, sir, at your service."

"Are you? oh, that's yet to be seen! Pray, is your Christian name Ralph?"

"It is," said I, in some surprise at the coolness of my visitor.

"Ah! just so. Christian name Ralph, t'other name Rover-Ralph Rover. Very good. Age twenty-two yesterday, eh?"

"My birthday *was* yesterday, and my age *is* twenty-two. You appear to know more of my private history than I have the pleasure of knowing of yours. Pray, sir, may I —but, bless me! are you unwell?"

I asked this in some alarm, because the little man was rolling about in his seat, holding his sides, and growing very red in the face.

"Oh no! not at all; perfectly well-never was better in my life," he said, becoming all at once preternaturally grave. "You were once in the Pacific-lived on a coral island —"

"I did."

"Oh, don't trouble yourself to answer. Just shut up for a minute or two. You were rather a soft green youth then, and you don't seem to be much harder or less verdant now."

"Sir!" I exclaimed, getting angry.

"Just so," continued he, "and you knew a young rascal there —"

"I know a rascal *here*," I exclaimed, starting up, "whom I'll kick —"

"What!" cried the little stranger, also starting up and capsizing the chair; "Ralph Rover, has time and sunburning and war so changed my visage that you cannot recognise Peterkin?"

I almost gasped for breath.

"Peterkin-Peterkin Gay!" I exclaimed.

I am not prone to indulge in effeminate demonstration, but I am not ashamed to confess that when I gazed on the weather-beaten though ruddy countenance of my old companion, and observed the eager glance of his bright blue eyes, I was quite overcome, and rushed violently into his arms. I may also add that until that day I had had no idea of Peterkin's physical strength; for during the next five minutes he twisted me about and spun me round and round my own room until my brain began to reel, and I was fain to cry him mercy.

"So, you're all right-the same jolly, young old wiseacre in whiskers and long coat," cried Peterkin. "Come now, Ralph, sit down if you can. I mean to stay with you all evening, and all night, and all to-morrow, and all next day, so we'll have lots of time to fight our battles o'er again. Meanwhile compose yourself, and I'll tell you what I've come about. Of course, my first and chief reason was to see your face, old boy; but I have another reason too —a very peculiar reason. I've a proposal to make and a plan to unfold, both of 'em stunners; they'll shut you up and screw you down, and altogether flabbergast you when you hear 'em, so sit down and keep quiet-do."

I sat down accordingly, and tried to compose myself; but, to say truth, I was so much over-joyed and excited by the sight of my old friend and companion that I had some difficulty at first in fixing my attention on what he said, the more especially that he spoke with extreme volubility, and interrupted his discourse very frequently, in order to ask questions or to explain.

"Now, old fellow," he began, "here goes, and mind you don't interrupt me. Well, I mean to go, and I mean you to go with me, to-but, I forgot, perhaps you won't be able to go. What are you?"

"What am I?"

"Ay, your profession, your calling; lawyer, M.D., scrivener-which?"

"I am a naturalist."

"A what?"

"A naturalist."

"Ralph," said Peterkin slowly, "have you been long troubled with that complaint?"

"Yes," I replied, laughing; "I have suffered from it from my earliest infancy, more or less."

"I thought so," rejoined my companion, shaking his head gravely. "I fancied that I observed the development of that disease when we lived together on the coral island. It don't bring you in many thousands a year, does it?"

"No," said I, "it does not. I am only an amateur, having a sufficiency of this world's goods to live on without working for my bread. But although my dear father at his death left me a small fortune, which yields me three hundred a year, I do not feel entitled to lead the life of an idler in this busy world, where so many are obliged to toil night and day for the bare necessaries of life. I have therefore taken to my favourite studies as a sort of business, and flatter myself that I have made one or two not unimportant discoveries, and added a few mites to the sum of human knowledge. A good deal of my time is spent in scientific roving expeditions throughout the country, and in contributing papers to several magazines."

While I was thus speaking I observed that Peterkin's face was undergoing the most remarkable series of changes of expression, which, as I concluded, merged into a smile of beaming delight, as he said, —"Ralph, you're a trump!"

"Possibly," said I, "you are right; but, setting that question aside for the present, let me remind you that you have not yet told me where you mean to go to."

"I mean," said Peterkin slowly, placing both hands on his knees and looking me steadily in the face —"I mean to go a-hunting in-but I forgot. You don't know that I'm a hunter, a somewhat famous hunter?"

"Of course I don't. You are so full of your plans and proposals that you have not yet told me where you have been or what doing these six years. And you ye never written to me once all that time, shabby fellow. I thought you were dead."

"Did you go into mourning for me, Ralph?"

"No, of course not."

"A pretty fellow you are to find fault. You thought that I, your oldest and best friend, was dead, and you did not go into mourning. How could I write to you when you parted from me without giving me your address? It was a mere chance my finding you out even now. I was taking a quiet cup of coffee in the commercial room of a hotel not far distant, when I overheard a stranger speaking of his friend 'Ralph Rover, the philosopher,' so I plunged at him promiscuously, and made him give me your address. But I've corresponded with Jack ever since we parted on the pier at Dover."

"What! Jack-Jack Martin?" I exclaimed, as a warm gush of feeling filled my heart at the sound of his well-remembered name. "Is Jack alive?"

"Alive! I should think so. If possible, he's more alive than ever; for I should suppose he must be full-grown now, which he was not when we last met. He and I have corresponded regularly. He lives in the north of England, and by good luck happens to be just now within thirty miles of this town. You don't mean to say, Ralph, that you have never met!"

"Never. The very same mistake that happened with you occurred between him and me. We parted vowing to correspond as long as we should live, and three hours after I remembered that we had neglected to exchange our addresses, so that we could not correspond. I have often, often made inquiries both for you and him, but have always failed. I never heard of Jack from the time we parted at Dover till to-day."

"Then no doubt you thought us both dead, and yet you did not go into mourning for either of us! O Ralph, Ralph, I had entertained too good an opinion of you."

"But tell me about Jack," said I, impatient to hear more concerning my dear old comrade.

"Not just now, my boy; more of him in a few minutes. First let us return to the point. What was it? Oh! a —about my being a celebrated hunter. A very Nimrod-at least a miniature copy. Well, Ralph, since we last met I have been all over the world, right round and round it. I'm a lieutenant in the navy now-at least I was a week ago. I've been fighting with the Kaffirs and the Chinamen, and been punishing the rascally sepoys in India, and been hunting elephants in Ceylon and tiger-shooting in the jungles, and harpooning whales in the polar seas, and shooting lions at the Cape; oh, you've no notion where all I've been. It's a perfect marvel I've turned up here alive. But there's one beast I've not yet seen, and I'm resolved to see him and shoot him too —"

"But," said I, interrupting, "what mean you by saying that you were a lieutenant in the navy a week ago?"

"I mean that I've given it up. I'm tired of the sea. I only value it as a means of getting from one country to another. The land, the land for me! You must know that an old uncle, a rich old uncle of mine, whom I never saw, died lately and left me his whole fortune. Of course he died in India. All old uncles who die suddenly and leave unexpected fortunes to unsuspecting nephews are old Indian uncles, and mine was no exception to the general rule. So I'm independent, like you, Ralph, only I've got three or four thousand a year instead of hundreds, I believe; but I'm not sure and don't care-and I'm determined now to go on a long hunting expedition. What think ye of all that, my boy?"

"In truth," said I, "it would puzzle me to say what I think, I am so filled with surprise by all you tell me. But you forget that you have not yet told me to which part of the world you mean to go, and what sort of beast it is you are so determined to see and shoot if you can."

"If I can!" echoed Peterkin, with a contemptuous curl of the lip. "Did not I tell you that I was a *celebrated* hunter? Without meaning to boast, I may tell you that there is no peradventure in my shooting. If I only get there and see the brute within long range, I'll-ha! won't I!"

"Get *where*, and see *what*?"

"Get to Africa and see the gorilla!" cried Peterkin, while a glow of enthusiasm lighted up his eyes. "You've heard of the gorilla, Ralph, of course-the great ape-the enormous puggy-the huge baboon-the man monkey, that we've been hearing so much of for some years back, and that the niggers on the African coast used to dilate about till they caused the very hair of my head to stand upon end? I'm determined to shoot a gorilla, or prove him to be a myth. And I mean you to come and help me, Ralph; he's quite in your way. A bit of natural history, I suppose, although he seems by all accounts to be a very unnatural monster. And Jack shall go too —I'm resolved on that; and we three shall roam the wild woods again, as we did in days of yore, and —"

"Hold, Peterkin," said I, interrupting. "How do you know that Jack will go?"

"How do I know? Intuitively, of course. I shall write to him to-night; the post does not leave till ten. He'll get it to-morrow at breakfast, and will catch the forenoon coach, which will bring him down here by two o'clock, and then we'll begin our preparations at once, and talk the matter over at dinner. So you see it's all cut and dry. Give me a sheet of paper and I'll write at once. Ah! here's a bit; now a pen. Bless me, Ralph, haven't you got a quill? Who ever heard of a philosophical naturalist writing with steel. Now, then, here goes: — 'B'luv'd Jack,' —will that do to begin with, eh? I'm afraid it's too affectionate; he'll think it's from a lady friend. But it can't be altered, —'Here I am, and here's Ralph-Ralph Rover!!!!!! think of that,' (I say, Ralph, I've put six marks of admiration there); 'I've found him out. Do come to see us. Excruciatingly important business. Ever thine-Peterkin Gay.' Will that bring him, d'ye think?"

"I think it will," said I, laughing.

"Then off with it, Ralph," cried my volatile friend, jumping up and looking hastily round for the bell-rope. Not being able to find it, my bell-pull being an unobtrusive knob and not a rope, he rushed to the door, unlocked it, darted out, and uttered a tremendous roar, which was followed by a clatter and a scream from old Agnes, whom he had upset and tumbled over.

It was curious to note the sudden change that took place in Peterkin's face, voice, and manner, as he lifted the poor old woman, who was very thin and light, in his arms, and carrying her into the room, placed her in my easy-chair. Real anxiety was depicted in his countenance, and he set her down with a degree of care and tenderness that quite amazed me. I was myself very much alarmed at first.

"My poor dear old *woman*," said Peterkin, supporting my landlady's head; "my stupid haste I fear you are hurt."

"Hech! it's nae hurt-it's deed I am, fair deed; killed be a whaumlskamerin' young blagyird. Oh, ma puir heed!"

The manner and tone in which this was said convinced me that old Agnes was more frightened than injured. In a few minutes the soothing tones and kind manner of my friend had such an effect upon her that she declared she was better, and believed after all that she was only a "wee bit frichtened." Nay, so completely was she conciliated, that she insisted on conveying the note to the post-office, despite Peterkin's assurance that he would not hear of it. Finally she hobbled out of the room with the letter in her hand.

It is interesting to note how that, in most of the affairs of humanity, things turn out very different, often totally different, from what we had expected or imagined. During the remainder of that evening Peterkin and I talked frequently and much of our old friend Jack Martin. We recalled his manly yet youthful countenance, his bold, lion-like courage, his broad shoulders and winning gentle smile, and although we knew that six years must have made an immense difference in his personal appearance-for he was not much more than eighteen when we last parted-we could not think of him except as a hearty, strapping sailor-boy. We planned, too, how we would meet him at the coach; how we would stand aside in the crowd until he began to look about for us in surprise, and then one of us would step forward and ask if he wished to be directed to any particular part of the town, and so lead him on and talk to him as a stranger for some time before revealing who we were. And much more to the same effect. But when next day came our plans and our conceptions were utterly upset.

A little before two we sauntered down to the coach-office, and waited impatiently for nearly twenty minutes. Of course the coach was late; it always is on such occasions.

"Suppose he does not come," said I.

"What a fellow you are," cried Peterkin, "to make uncomfortable suppositions! Let us rather suppose that he does come."

"Oh, then, it would be all right; but if he does not come, what then?"

"Why, then, it would be all wrong, and we should have to return home and eat our dinner in the sulks, that's all."

As my companion spoke we observed the coach come sweeping round the turn of the road about half a mile distant. In a few seconds it dashed into the town at full gallop, and finally drew up abruptly opposite the door of the inn, where were assembled the usual group of hostlers and waiters and people who expected friends by the coach.

"He's not there," whispered Peterkin, in deep disappointment —"at least he's not on the outside, and Jack would never travel inside of a coach even in bad weather, much less in fine. That's not him on the back-seat beside the fat old woman with the blue bundle, surely! It's very like him, but too young, much too young. There's a great giant of a man on the box-seat with a beard like a grenadier's shako, and a stout old gentleman behind him with gold spectacles. That's all, except two boys farther aft, and three ladies in the cabin. Oh, *what* a bore!"

Although deeply disappointed at the non-arrival of Jack, I could with difficulty refrain from smiling at the rueful and woe-begone countenance of my poor companion. It was evident that he could not bear disappointment with equanimity, and I was on the point of offering some consolatory remarks, when my attention was attracted by the little old woman with the blue bundle, who went up to the gigantic man with the black beard, and in the gentlest possible tone of voice asked if he could direct her to the white house.

"No, madam," replied the big man hastily; "I'm a stranger here."

The little old woman was startled by his abrupt answer. "Deary me, sir, no offence, I hope."

She then turned to Peterkin and put the same question, possibly under a vague sort of impression that if a gigantic frame betokened a gruff nature, diminutive stature must necessarily imply extreme amiability. If so, she must have been much surprised as well as disappointed, for Peterkin, rendered irascible by disappointment, turned short round and said sharply, "Why, madam, how can *I* tell you where the white house is, unless you say which white house you want? Half the houses of the town are white-at least they're *dirty* white," he added bitterly, as he turned away.

"I think I can direct you, ma'am," said I, stepping quickly up with a bland smile, in order to counteract, if possible, my companion's rudeness.

"Thank you, sir, kindly," said the little old woman; "I'm glad to find *some* little civility in the town."

"Come with me, ma'am; I am going past the white house, and will show you the way."

"And pray, sir," said the big stranger, stepping up to me as I was about to move away, "can you recommend me to a good hotel?"

I replied that I could; that there was one in the immediate vicinity of the white house, and that if he would accompany me I would show him the way. All this I did purposely in a very affable and obliging tone and manner; for I hold that example is infinitely better than precept, and always endeavour, if possible, to overcome evil with good. I offered my arm to the old woman, who thanked me and took it.

"What!" whispered Peterkin, "you don't mean me to take this great ugly gorilla in tow?"

"Of course," replied I, laughing, as I led the way.

Immediately I entered into conversation with my companion, and I heard "the gorilla" attempt to do so with Peterkin; but from the few sharp cross replies that reached my ear, I became aware that he was unsuccessful. In the course of a few minutes, however, he appeared to have overcome his companion's ill-humour, for I overheard their voices growing louder and more animated as they walked behind me.

Suddenly I heard a shout, and turning hastily round, observed Peterkin struggling in the arms of the gorilla! Amazed beyond measure at the sight, and firmly persuaded that a cowardly assault had been made upon my friend, I seized the old woman's umbrella, as the only available weapon, and flew to the rescue.

"Jack, my boy! can it be possible?" gasped Peterkin.

"I believe it is," replied Jack, laughing. —"Ralph, my dear old fellow, how are you?"

I stood petrified. I believed that I was in a dream.

I know not what occurred during the next five minutes. All I could remember with anything like distinctness was a succession of violent screams from the little old woman, who fled shouting thieves and murder at the full pitch of her voice. We never saw that old woman again, but I made a point of returning her umbrella to the "white house."

Gradually we became collected and sane.

"Why, Jack, how did you find us out?" cried Peterkin, as we all hurried on to my lodgings, totally forgetful of the little old woman, whom, as I have said, we never saw again, but who, I sincerely trust, arrived at the white house in safety.

"Find you out! I knew you the moment I set eyes on you. Ralph puzzled me for a second, he has grown so much stouter; but I should know your nose, Peterkin, at a mile off."

"Well, Jack, I did not know you," retorted Peterkin, "but I'm safe never again to forget you. Such a great hairy Cossack as you have become! Why, what do you mean by it?"

"I couldn't help it, please," pleaded Jack; "I grew in spite of myself; but I think I've stopped now."

"It's time," remarked Peterkin.

Jack had indeed grown to a size that men seldom attain to without losing in grace infinitely more than they gain in bulk, but he had retained all the elegance of form and sturdy vigour of action that had characterised him as a boy. He was fully six feet two inches in his stockings, but so perfect were his proportions that his great height did not become apparent until you came close up to him. Full half of his handsome manly face was hid by a bushy black beard and moustache, and his curly hair had been allowed to grow luxuriantly, so that his whole aspect was more like to the descriptions we have of one of the old Scandinavian Vikings than a gentleman of the present time. In whatever company he chanced to be he towered high above every one else, and I am satisfied that, had he walked down Whitechapel, the Horse Guards would have appeared small beside him, for he possessed not only great length of limb but immense breadth of chest and shoulders.

During our walk to my lodgings Peterkin hurriedly stated his "plan and proposal," which caused Jack to laugh very much at first, but in a few minutes he became grave, and said slowly, "That will just suit-it will do exactly."

"What will do exactly? Do be more explicit, man," said Peterkin, with some impatience.

"I'll go with you, my boy."

"Will you?" cried Peterkin, seizing his hand and shaking it violently; "I knew you would. I said it; didn't I, Ralph? And now we shall be sure of a gorilla, if there's one in Africa, for I'll use you as a stalking-horse."

"Indeed!" exclaimed Jack.

"Yes; I'll put a bear-skin or some sort of fur on your shoulders, and tie a lady's boa to you for a tail, and send you into the woods. The gorillas will be sure to mistake you for a relative until you get quite close; then you'll take one pace to the left with the left foot (as the volunteers say), I'll take one to the front with the right-at fifty yards, ready-present-bang, and down goes the huge puggy with a bullet right between its two eyes! There. And Ralph's agreed to go too."

"O Peterkin, I've done nothing of the sort. You *proposed* it."

"Well, and isn't that the same thing? I wonder, Ralph that you can give way to such mean-spirited prevarication. What? 'It's not prevarication!' Don't say that now; you know it is. Ah! you may laugh, my boy, but you have promised to go with me and Jack to Africa, and go you shall."

And so, reader, it was ultimately settled, and in the course of two weeks more we three were on our way to the land of the slave, the black savage, and the gorilla.

CHAPTER TWO
Life in the wild woods.

One night, about five or six weeks after our resolution to go to Africa on a hunting expedition was formed, I put to myself the question, "Can it be possible that we are actually here, in the midst of it?"

"Certainly, my boy, in the very thick of it," answered Peterkin, in a tone of voice which made Jack laugh, while I started and exclaimed —

"Why, Peterkin, how did you come to guess my thoughts?"

"Because, Ralph, you have got into a habit of thinking aloud, which may do very well as long as you have no secrets to keep but it may prove inconvenient some day, so I warn you in time."

Not feeling disposed at that time to enter into a bantering conversation with my volatile companion, I made no reply, but abandoned myself again to the pleasing fancies and feelings which were called up by the singular scene in the midst of which I found myself.

It seemed as if it were but yesterday when we drove about the crowded streets of London making the necessary purchases for our intended journey, and now, as I gazed around, every object that met my eye seemed strange, and wild, and foreign, and romantic. We three were reclining round an enormous wood fire in the midst of a great forest, the trees and plants of which were quite new to me, and totally unlike those of my native land. Rich luxuriance of vegetation was the feature that filled my mind most. Tall palms surrounded us, throwing their broad leaves overhead and partially concealing the starlit sky. Thick tough limbs of creeping plants and wild vines twisted and twined round everything and over everything, giving to the woods an appearance of tangled impenetrability; but the beautiful leaves of some, and the delicate tendrils of others, half concealed the sturdy limbs of the trees, and threw over the whole a certain air of wild grace, as might a semi-transparent and beautiful robe if thrown around the form of a savage.

The effect of a strong fire in the woods at night is to give to surrounding space an appearance of ebony blackness, against which dark ground the gnarled stems and branches and pendent foliage appear as if traced out in light and lovely colours, which are suffused with a rich warm tone from the blaze.

We were now in the wilds of Africa, although, as I have said, I found it difficult to believe the fact. Jack and I wore loose brown shooting coats and pantaloons; but we had made up our minds to give up waistcoats and neckcloths, so that our scarlet flannel shirts with turned-down collars gave to us quite a picturesque and brigand-like appearance as we encircled the blaze-Peterkin smoking vigorously, for he had acquired that bad and very absurd habit at sea. Jack smoked too, but he was not so inveterate as Peterkin.

Jack was essentially moderate in his nature. He did nothing violently or in a hurry; but this does not imply that he was slow or lazy. He was leisurely in disposition, and circumstances seldom required him to be otherwise. When Peterkin or I had to lift heavy weights, we were obliged to exert our utmost strength and agitate our whole frames; but Jack was so powerful that a comparatively slight effort was all that he was usually obliged to make. Again, when we two were in a hurry we walked quickly, but Jack's long limbs enabled him to keep up with us without effort. Nevertheless there were times when he was called upon to act quickly and with energy. On those occasions he was as active as Peterkin himself, but his movements were tremendous. It was, I may almost say, awful to behold Jack when acting under powerful excitement. He was indeed a splendid fellow, and not by any means deserving of the name of gorilla, which Peterkin had bestowed on him.

But to continue my description of our costume. We all wore homespun grey trousers of strong material. Peterkin and Jack wore leggings in addition, so that they seemed to have on what are now termed knickerbockers. Peterkin, however, had no coat. He preferred a stout grey flannel shirt hanging down to his knees and belted round his waist in the form of a tunic. Our tastes in headdress were varied. Jack wore a pork-pie cap; Peterkin and I had wide-awakes.

My facetious little companion said that I had selected this species of hat because I was always more than half asleep! Being peculiar in everything, Peterkin wore his wide-awake in an unusual manner-namely, turned up at the back, down at the front, and curled very much up at the sides.

We were so filled with admiration of Jack's magnificent beard and moustache, that Peterkin and I had resolved to cultivate ours while in Africa; but I must say that, as I looked at Peterkin's face, the additional hair was not at that time an improvement, and I believe that much more could not have been said for myself. The effect on my little comrade was to cause the lower part of his otherwise good-looking face to appear extremely dirty.

"I wonder," said Peterkin, after a long silence, "if we shall reach the niggers' village in time for the hunt to-morrow. I fear that we have spent too much time in this wild-goose chase."

"Wild-goose chase, Peterkin!" I exclaimed. "Do you call hunting the gorilla by such a term?"

"*Hunting* the gorilla? no, certainly; but *looking* for the gorilla in a part of the woods where no such beast was ever heard of since Adam was a schoolboy —"

"Nay, Peterkin," interrupted Jack; "we are getting very near to the gorilla country, and you must make allowance for the enthusiasm of a naturalist."

"Ah! we shall see where the naturalist's enthusiasm will fly to when we actually do come face to face with the big puggy."

"Well," said I, apologetically, "I won't press you to go hunting again; I'll be content to follow."

"Press me, my dear Ralph!" exclaimed Peterkin hastily, fearing that he had hurt my feelings; "why, man, I do but jest with you-you are so horridly literal. I'm overjoyed to be pressed to go on the maddest wild-goose chase that ever was invented. My greatest delight would be to go gorilla-hunting down Fleet Street, if you were so disposed. —But to be serious, Jack, do you think we shall be in time for the elephant-hunt to-morrow?"

"Ay, in capital time, if you don't knock up."

"What! *I* knock up! I've a good mind to knock you down for suggesting such an egregious impossibility."

"That's an impossibility anyhow, Peterkin, because I'm down already," said Jack, yawning lazily and stretching out his limbs in a more comfortable and *dégagé* manner.

Peterkin seemed to ponder as he smoked his pipe for some time in silence.

"Ralph," said he, looking up suddenly, "I don't feel a bit sleepy, and yet I'm tired enough."

"You are smoking too much, perhaps," I suggested.

"It's not that," cried Jack; "he has eaten too much supper."

"Base insinuation!" retorted Peterkin.

"Then it must be the monkey. That's it. Roast monkey does not agree with you."

"Do you know, I shouldn't wonder if you were right; and it's a pity, too, for we shall have to live a good deal on such fare, I believe. However, I suppose we shall get used to it. —But I say, boys, isn't it jolly to be out here living like savages? I declare it seems to me like a dream or a romance. —Just look, Ralph, at the strange wild creepers that are festooned overhead, and the great tropical leaves behind us, and the clear sky above, with the moon-ah! the moon; yes, that's one comfort-the moon is unchanged. The same moon that smiles down upon us through a tangled mesh-work of palm-leaves and wild vines and monkeys' tails, is peeping down the chimney-pots of London and Edinburgh and Dublin!"

"Why, Peterkin, you must have studied hard in early life to be so good a geographer."

"Rather," observed Peterkin.

"Yes; and look at the strange character of the tree-stems," said I, unwilling to allow the subject to drop. "See those huge palmettoes like-like —"

"Overgrown cabbages," suggested Peterkin; and he continued, "Observe the quaint originality of form in the body and limbs of that bloated old spider that is crawling up your leg, Ralph!"

I started involuntarily, for there is no creature of which I have a greater abhorrence than a spider.

"Where is it? oh! I see," and the next moment I secured my prize and placed it with loathing, but interest, in my entomological box.

At that moment a hideous roar rang through the woods, seemingly close behind us. We all started to our feet, and seizing our rifles, which lay beside us ready loaded, cocked them and drew close together round the fire.

"This won't do, lads," said Jack, after a few minutes' breathless suspense, during which the only sound we could hear was the beating of our own hearts; "we have allowed the fire to get too low, and we've forgotten to adopt our friend the trader's advice, and make two fires."

So saying, Jack laid down his rifle, and kicking the logs with his heavy boot, sent up such a cloud of bright sparks as must certainly have scared the wild animal, whatever it was, away; for we heard no more of it that night.

"You're right, Jack," remarked Peterkin; "so let us get up a blaze as fast as we can, and I'll take the first watch, not being sleepy. Come along."

In a few minutes we cut down with our axes a sufficient quantity of dry wood to keep two large fires going all night; we then kindled our second fire at a few yards distant from the first, and made our camp between them. This precaution we took in order to scare away the wild animals whose cries we heard occasionally during the night. Peterkin, having proposed to take the first watch-for we had to watch by turns all the night through-lighted his pipe and sat down before the cheerful fire with his back against the stem of a palm-tree, and his rifle lying close to his hand, to be ready in case of a surprise. There were many natives wandering about in that neighbourhood, some of whom might be ignorant of our having arrived at their village on a peaceful errand. If these should have chanced to come upon us suddenly, there was no saying what they might do in their surprise and alarm, so it behoved us to be on our guard.

Jack and I unrolled the light blankets that we carried strapped to our shoulders through the day, and laying ourselves down side by side with our feet to the fire and our heads pillowed on a soft pile of sweet-scented grass, we addressed ourselves to sleep. But sleep did not come so soon as we expected. I have often noted with some surprise and much interest the curious phases of the phenomenon of sleep. When I have gone to bed excessively fatigued and expecting to fall asleep almost at once, I have been surprised and annoyed to find that the longer I wooed the drowsy god the longer he refused to come to me; and at last, when I have given up the attempt in despair, he has suddenly laid his gentle hand upon my eyes and carried me into the land of Nod. Again, when I have been exceedingly anxious to keep awake, I have been attacked by sleep with such irresistible energy that I have been utterly unable to keep my eyelids open or my head erect, and have sat with my eyes blinking like those of an owl in the sunshine, and my head nodding like that of a Chinese mandarin.

On this our first night in the African bush, at least our first night on a hunting expedition-we had been many nights in the woods on our journey to that spot-on this night, I say, Jack and I could by no means get to sleep for a very long time after we lay down, but continued to gaze up through the leafy screen overhead at the stars, which seemed to wink at us, I almost fancied, jocosely. We did not speak to each other, but purposely kept silence. After a time, however, Jack groaned, and said softly —

"Ralph, are you asleep?"

"No," said I, yawning.

"I'm quite sure that Peterkin is," added Jack, raising his head and looking across the fire at the half-recumbent form of our companion.

"Is he?" said Peterkin in a low tone. "Just about as sound as a weasel!"

"Jack," said I.

"Well?"

"I can't sleep a wink. Ye-a-ow! isn't it odd?"

"No more can I. Do you know, Ralph, I've been counting the red berries in that tree above me for half an hour, in the hope that the monotony of the thing would send me off; but I was interrupted by a small monkey who has been sitting up among the branches and making faces at me for full twenty minutes. There it is yet, I believe. Do you see it?"

"No; where?"

"Almost above your head."

I gazed upward intently for a few minutes, until I thought I saw the monkey, but it was very indistinct. Gradually, however, it became more defined; then to my surprise it turned out to be the head of an elephant! I was not only amazed but startled at this.

"Get your rifle, Jack!" said I, in a low whisper.

Jack made some sort of reply, but his voice sounded hollow and indistinct. Then I looked up again, and saw that it was the head of a hippopotamus, not that of an elephant, which was looking down at me. Curiously enough, I felt little or no surprise at this, and when in the course of a few minutes I observed a pair of horns growing out of the creature's eyes and a bushy tail standing erect on the apex of its head, I ceased to be astonished at the sight altogether, and regarded it as quite natural and commonplace. The object afterwards assumed the appearance of a lion with a crocodile's bail, and a serpent with a monkey's head, and lastly of a gorilla, without producing in me any other feeling than that of profound indifference. Gradually the whole scene vanished, and I became totally oblivious.

This state of happy unconsciousness had scarcely lasted-it seemed to me-two minutes, when I was awakened by Peterkin laying his hand on my shoulder and saying —

"Now then, Ralph, it's time to rouse up."

"O Peterkin," said I, in a tone of remonstrance, "how could you be so unkind as to waken me when I had just got to sleep? Shabby fellow!"

"Just got to sleep, say you? You've been snoring like an apoplectic alderman for exactly two hours."

"You don't say so!" I exclaimed, getting into a sitting posture.

"Indeed you have. I'm sorry to rouse you, but time's up, and I'm sleepy; so rub your eyes, man, and try to look a little less like an astonished owl if you can. I have just replenished both the fires, so you can lean your back against that palm-tree and take it easy for three-quarters of an hour or so. After that you'll have to heap on more wood."

I looked at Jack, who was now lying quite unconscious, breathing with the slow, deep regularity of profound slumber, and with his mouth wide open.

"What a chance for some waggish baboon to drop a nut or a berry in!" said Peterkin, winking at me with one eye as he lay down in the spot from which I had just risen.

He was very sleepy, poor fellow, and could hardly smile at his own absurd fancy. He was asleep almost instantly. In fact, I do not believe that he again opened the eye with which he had winked at me, but that he merely shut the other and began to slumber forthwith.

I now began to feel quite interested in my responsible position as guardian of the camp. I examined my rifle to see that it was in order and capped; then leaning against the palm-tree, which was, as it were, my sentry-box, I stood erect and rubbed my hands and took off my cap, so that the pleasant night air might play about my temples, and more effectually banish drowsiness.

In order to accomplish this more thoroughly I walked round both fires and readjusted the logs, sending up showers of sparks as I did so. Then I went to the edge of the circle of light, in the centre of which our camp lay, and peered into the gloom of the dark forest.

There was something inexpressibly delightful yet solemn in my feelings as I gazed into that profound obscurity where the great tree-stems and the wild gigantic foliage nearest to me appeared ghost-like and indistinct, and the deep solitudes of which were peopled, not only with the strange fantastic forms of my excited fancy, but, as I knew full well, with real wild creatures, both huge and small, such as my imagination at that time had not fully conceived. I felt awed, almost oppressed, with the deep silence around, and, I must confess, looked somewhat nervously over my shoulder as I returned to the fire and sat down to keep watch at my post.

CHAPTER THREE
Wherein I mount guard, and how I did it, etcetera.

Now it so happened that the battle which I had to fight with myself after taking my post was precisely the converse of that which I fought during the earlier part of that night. Then, it was a battle with wakefulness; now, it was a struggle with sleep; and of the two fights the latter was the more severe by far.

I began by laying down my rifle close by my side, leaning back in a sitting posture against the palm-tree, and resigning myself to the contemplation of the fire, which burned merrily before me, while I pondered with myself how I should best employ my thoughts during the three long hours of my watch. But I had not dwelt on that subject more than three minutes, when I was rudely startled by my own head falling suddenly and heavily forward on my chest. I immediately roused myself. "Ah! Ralph, Ralph," said I to myself in a whisper, "this won't do, lad. To sleep at your post! shame on you! Had you been a sentinel in time of war that nod would have cost you your life, supposing you to have been caught in the act."

Soliloquising thus, I arose and shook myself. Then I slapped my chest several times and pulled my nose and sat down again. Only a few minutes elapsed before the same thing occurred to me again, so I leaped up, and mended the fires, and walked to and fro, until I felt thoroughly awake, but in order to make sure that it should not occur again, I walked to the edge of the circle of light and gazed for some time into the dark forest, as I had done before. While standing thus I felt my knees give way, as if they had been suddenly paralysed, and I awoke just in time to prevent myself falling to the ground. I must confess I was much amazed at this, for although I had often read of soldiers falling asleep standing at their posts, I had never believed the thing possible.

I now became rather anxious, "for," thought I, "if I go to sleep and the fires die down, who knows but wild beasts may come upon us and kill us before we can seize our arms." For a moment or two I meditated awaking Jack and begging him to keep me company, but when I reflected that his watch was to come immediately after mine, I had not the heart to do it. "No!" said I (and I said it aloud for the purpose of preventing drowsiness) —"no; I will fight this battle alone! I will repeat some stanzas from my favourite authors. Yes, I will try to remember a portion of 'A Midsummer-Night's Dream.' It will be somewhat appropriate to my present circumstances."

Big with this resolve, I sat down with my face to the fire and my back to the palm-tree, and-fell sound asleep instantly!

How long I lay in this condition I know not, but I was suddenly awakened by a yell so appalling that my heart leaped as if into my throat, and my nerves thrilled with horror. For one instant I was paralysed; then my blood seemed to rebound on its course. I sprang up and attempted to seize my rifle.

The reader may judge of my state of mind when I observed that it was gone! I leaped towards the fire, and grasping a lighted brand, turned round and glared into the woods in the direction whence the yell came.

It was grey dawn, and I could see things pretty distinctly; but the only living object that met my gaze was Peterkin, who stood with my rifle in his hand laughing heartily!

I immediately turned to look at Jack, who was sitting up in the spot where he had passed the night, with a sleepy smile on his countenance.

"Why, what's the meaning of this?" I inquired.

"The meaning of it?" cried Peterkin, as he advanced and restored the rifle to its place. "A pretty fellow you are to mount guard! we might have been all murdered in our sleep by niggers or eaten alive by gorillas, for all that you would have done to save us."

"But, Peterkin," said I gravely, "you ought not to have startled me so; you gave me a terrible fright. People have been driven mad before now, I assure you, by practical jokes."

"My dear fellow," cried Peterkin, with much earnestness, "I know that as well as you. But, in the first place, you were guilty of so heinous a crime that I determined to punish you, and at the same time to do it in a way that would impress it forcibly on your memory; and in the second place, I would not have done it at all had I not known that your nerves are as strong as those of a dray-horse. You ought to be taking shame to yourself on account of your fault rather than objecting to your punishment."

"Peterkin is right, my boy," said Jack, laughing, "though I must say he had need be sure of the nerves of any one to whom he intends to administer such a ferocious yell as that. Anyhow, I have no reason to complain; for you have given me a good long sleep, although I can't say exactly that you have taken my watch. It will be broad daylight in half an hour, so we must be stirring, comrades."

On considering the subject I admitted the force of these remarks, and felt somewhat crest-fallen. No doubt, my companions had treated the thing jocularly, and, to say truth, there was much that was comical in the whole affair; but the more I thought of it, the more I came to perceive how terrible might have been the consequences of my unfaithfulness as a sentinel. I laid the lesson to heart, and I can truly say that from that day to this I have never again been guilty of the crime of sleeping at my post.

We now busied ourselves in collecting together the dying embers of our fire and in preparing breakfast, which consisted of tea, hard biscuit, and cold monkey. None of us liked the monkey; not that its flesh was bad-quite the contrary-but it looked so like a small roasted baby that we could not relish it at all. However, it was all we had; for we had set off on this hunting excursion intending to live by our rifles, but had been unfortunate, having seen nothing except a monkey or two.

The kettle was soon boiled, and we sat down to our meagre fare with hearty appetites. While we are thus engaged, I shall turn aside for a little and tell the reader, in one or two brief sentences, how we got to this place.

We shipped in a merchant ship at Liverpool, and sailed for the west coast of Africa. Arrived there we found a party, under the command of a Portuguese trader, about to set off to the interior. He could speak a little English; so we arranged to go with him as far as he intended to proceed, learn as much of the native language as possible while in his company, and then obtain a native guide to conduct us to the country in which the gorillas are found. To this native guide, we arranged, should be explained by the trader our object in visiting the country, so that he might tell the tribes whom we intended to visit. This, we found, was an absolutely needful precaution, on the following ground.

The natives of Africa have a singular and very bad style of carrying on trade with the white men who visit their shores. The traffic consists chiefly of ivory, barwood (a wood much used in dyeing), and indiarubber. The natives of the far interior are not allowed to convey these commodities directly to the coast, but by the law of the land (which means the law of the strongest, for they are absolute savages) are obliged to deliver their goods to the care of the tribe next to them; these pass them on to the next tribe; and so on they go from tribe to tribe till they reach the coast, where they are sold by the tribe there. The price obtained, which usually consists of guns, powder and shot, looking-glasses, cloth, and sundry other articles and trinkets useful to men in a savage state, is returned to the owners in the far interior through the same channel; but as each tribe deducts a percentage for its trouble, the price dwindles down as it goes, until a mere trifle, sometimes nothing at all, remains to be handed over to the unfortunate people of the tribe who originally sent off the goods for sale. Of course, such a system almost paralyses trade. But the intermediate tribes between the coast and the interior being the gainers by this system, are exceedingly jealous of anything like an attempt to carry on direct trade. They are ready to go to war with the tribes of the interior, should they attempt it, and they throw all the opposition they can in the way of the few white men who ever penetrate the interior for such a purpose.

It will thus be seen that our travels would be hindered very much, if not stopped altogether, and ourselves be regarded with jealousy, or perhaps murdered, if our motives in going inland were not fully and satisfactorily explained to the different tribes as we passed through their lands. And we therefore proposed to overcome the difficulty by taking a native guide with us from the tribe with which we should chance to be residing when obliged to separate from the Portuguese trader.

We had now reached this point. The day before that on which we encamped in the woods, as above related, we arrived at a native village, and had been received kindly by the king. Almost immediately after our arrival we heard so many stories about gorillas that I felt persuaded we should fall in with one if we went a-hunting, and being exceedingly anxious to add one to my collection of animals-for I had a small museum at home —I prevailed on Jack and Peterkin to go one day's journey into the bush to look for them. They laughed very much at me indeed, and said that we were still very far away from the gorilla country; but I had read in some work on Africa a remark to the effect that there is no cordillera, or mountain range, extending across the whole continent to limit the *habitat* of certain classes of animals, and I thought that if any animal in Africa would not consent to remain in one region when it wished to go to another, that animal must be the ferocious gorilla. The trader also laughed at me, and said that he had never seen any himself in that region, and that we would have to cross the desert before seeing them. Still, I felt a disposition to try; besides, I felt certain that we should at least fall in with some sort of animals or plants or minerals that would be worth collecting; so it was agreed that we should go out for a single day, and be back in time for a great elephant-hunt which was about to take place.

But to return from this digression. Having finished breakfast, we made three bundles or packages of our blankets, provisions, and camp equipage; strapped them on our backs; and then, shouldering our rifles, set out on our return to the negro village.

Of course we gave Jack the largest and heaviest bundle to carry. Peterkin's and mine were about equal, for although I was taller than Peterkin, I was not by any means so powerful or active. I often wondered at the great strength that lay in the little frame of my friend. To look at him, no one would believe that he was such a tough, wiry, hardy little fellow. He was the same hearty, jovial creature that I had lived with so pleasantly when he and Jack and I were cast away on the coral island. With the exception of a small scrap of whisker on each cheek, a scar over the right eye, and a certain air of manliness, there was little change in my old comrade.

"Ralph," said Jack, as we strode along through the forest, "do you remember how we three used to wander about together in the woods of our coral island?"

"Remember!" I cried with enthusiasm, for at that moment the thought occurred to my own mind; "how can I ever forget it, Jack? It seems to me just like yesterday. I can hardly believe that six long years have passed since we drank that delicious natural lemonade out of the green cocoa-nuts, and wandered on the coral beach, and visited Penguin Island, and dived into the cave to escape the pirates. The whole scene rises up before me so vividly that I could fancy we were still there. Ah! these were happy times."

"So they were," cried Peterkin; "but don't you go and become sentimentally sad, Ralph, when you talk of those happy days. If we were happy there, are we not happy *here*? —There's no change in us-except, indeed, that Jack has become a gorilla."

"Ay, and you a monkey," retorted Jack.

"True; and Ralph a naturalist, which is the strangest beast of all," added Peterkin. —"Can you tell me, Ralph, by the way, what tree that is?"

"I'm sure I cannot tell. Never saw or heard of one like it before," I replied, looking at the tree referred to with some interest. It was a fine tree, but the great beauty about it was the gorgeous fruit with which it was laden. It hung in the form of bunches of large grapes, and was of the brightest scarlet colour. The glowing bunches seemed like precious gems glittering amongst the green foliage, and I observed that a few monkeys and several parrots were peeping at us through the branches.

"It seems good for food," said Jack. "You'd better climb up, Peterkin, and pull a few bunches. The puggies won't mind you, of course, being one of themselves."

"Ralph," said Peterkin, turning to me, and deigning no reply to Jack, "you call yourself a naturalist; so I suppose you are acquainted with the habits of monkeys, and can turn your knowledge to practical account."

"Well," I replied, "I know something about the monkey tribes, but I cannot say that at this moment I remember any particular habit of which we might avail ourselves."

"Do you not? Well, now, that's odd. I'm a student of nature myself, and I have picked up a little useful knowledge in the course of my travels. Did you ever travel so far as the Zoological Gardens in London?"

"Of course I have done so, often."

"And did you ever observe a peculiar species of monkey, which, when you made a face at it, instantly flew into a towering passion, and shook the bars of its cage until you expected to see them broken?"

"Yes," said I, laughing; "what then?"

"Look here, you naturalist, and I'll put a wrinkle on your horn. Yonder hangs a magnificent bunch of fruit that I very much desire to possess."

"But it's too high to reach," said I.

"But there's a monkey sitting beside it," said Peterkin.

"I see. You don't expect him to pull it and throw it down, do you?"

"Oh no, certainly not; but —" Here Peterkin stepped up to the tree, and looking up at the monkey, said, "O-o-o-oo-o!" angrily.

"*O-o-o-oo-o!*" replied the monkey, stretching out its neck and looking down with an expression of surprise and indignation, as if to say, "What on earth do you mean by that?"

"Oo-o-o-oo-o!" roared Peterkin.

Hereupon the monkey uttered a terrific shriek of passion, exposed all its teeth and gums, glared at its adversary like a little fiend, and seizing the branch with both hands, shook it with all its might. The result was, that not only did the coveted bunch of fruit fall to the ground, but a perfect shower of bunches came down, one of which hit Jack on the forehead, and, bursting there, sent its fragrant juice down his face and into his beard, while the parrots and all the other monkeys took to flight, shrieking with mingled terror and rage.

"You see I'm a practical man," observed Peterkin quietly, as he picked up the fruit and began to eat it. "Knowledge is power, my boy. A man with a philosophical turn of mind like yourself ought to have been up to a dodge of this sort. How capital this fruit is, to be sure! —Does it make good pomade, Jack?"

"Excellent; but as I'm not in the habit of using pomade, I shall wash this out of my beard as quickly as possible."

While Jack went to a brook that ran close to where we stood, I tasted the fruit, and found it most excellent, the pulp being juicy, with a very pleasant flavour.

While we were thus engaged a wild pig ran grunting past us.

"Doesn't that remind you of some of our doings on the coral island, Ralph?" said Peterkin.

Before I could reply a herd of lovely small gazelles flew past. Our rifles were lying on the ground, and before either of us could take aim the swift creatures were lost sight of in the thick underwood. Peterkin fired one shot at a venture, but without any result.

We were still deploring our stupidity in not having our rifles handy, when a strange sound was heard in the distance. By this time Jack had come up, so we all three seized our rifles and listened intently. The sound was evidently approaching. It was a low, dull, booming roar, which at one moment seemed to be distant thunder, at another the cry of some huge animal in rage or pain. Presently the beating of heavy hoofs on the turf and the crash of branches were heard. Each of us sprang instinctively towards a tree, feeling that if danger were near its trunk would afford us some protection.

Being ignorant, as yet, of the cries of the various wild beasts inhabiting those woods, we were greatly at a loss to determine what creature it could be that approached at such headlong speed. That its mad career was caused by fear soon became apparent, for the tones of terror either in man or beast, when distinctly heard, cannot be mistaken.

Immediately in front of the spot where we stood was an open space or glade of considerable extent. Towards this the animal approached, as was evident from the increasing loudness of its wild roar, which was almost continuous. In another moment the thick wall of underwood at its farther extremity was burst asunder with a crash, and a wild buffalo bull bounded into the plain and dashed madly across. On its neck was crouched a leopard, which had fixed its claws and teeth deep in the flesh of the agonised animal. In vain did the bull bound and rear, toss and plunge. At one moment it ran like the wind; the next it stopped with such violence as to tear up the turf and scatter it around. Then it reared, almost falling back; anon it plunged and rushed on again, with the foam flying from its mouth, and its bloodshot eyes glaring with the fire of rage and terror, while the woods seemed to tremble with its loud and deep-toned bellowing. Twice in its passage across the open glade it ran, in its blind fury, straight against a tree, almost beating in its skull, and for a moment arresting its progress; but it instantly recovered the shock and burst away again as madly as ever. But no effort that it was capable of making could relieve the poor creature from its deadly burden, or cause the leopard in the slightest degree to relax its fatal gripe.

It chanced that the wild bull's mad gallop was in a direction that brought it within a few yards of the spot where we stood, so we prepared to put an end to its misery. As it drew near, Jack, who was in advance, raised his rifle. I, being only a short distance from him, also made ready to fire, although I confess that in the agitation of the moment I could not make up my mind whether I should fire at the buffalo or the leopard. As far as I can recall my rapid and disjointed thoughts on that exciting occasion, I reasoned thus: "If I shoot the leopard the bull will escape, and if I shoot the bull the leopard will escape." It did not occur to me at that trying moment, when self-possession and decision were so necessary, that I might shoot the bull with one barrel, and the leopard with the other. Still less did it occur to me that I might miss bull and leopard altogether.

While I was engaged in this hurried train of troubled thought, Jack fired both barrels of his rifle, one after the other, as quickly as possible. The bull stumbled forward upon its knees. In order to make assurance doubly sure, I aimed at its head and fired both barrels at once. Instantly the bull rose, with a hideous bellow, and stood for one moment irresolute, glaring at its new enemies. The leopard, I observed, was no longer on its back. At this moment I heard an exclamation of anger, and looking round I observed Peterkin struggling violently in the grasp of one of the wild vines or thorny plants which abound in some parts of the African forests and render them almost impassable. It seems that as the bull drew near, Peterkin, who, like Jack and me, was preparing to shoot, found that a dense thicket came between him and the game, so as to prevent his firing. He leaped nimbly over a bush, intending to run to another spot, whence he could more conveniently take aim, but found himself, as I have related, suddenly entangled among the thorns in such a way that the more he struggled the more firmly he became ensnared. Being of an impatient disposition, he did struggle violently, and it was this, probably, that attracted the attention of the bull and decided its future course and its ultimate fate; for after remaining one moment, as I have stated, in an irresolute attitude, it turned suddenly to the left and rushed, with its head down and its tail up, straight at Peterkin.

I cannot describe the sensations that overwhelmed me on observing the imminent danger of my friend. Horror almost overwhelmed me as I gazed with a stare of fascination at the frightful brute, which with flashing eyes and bloody foam dripping from its mouth charged into the thicket, and crashed through the tough boughs and bushes as if they were grass. A film came over my eyes. I tried to reload my rifle, but my trembling hand refused to act, and I groaned with mingled shame and despair on finding myself thus incapable of action in the hour of extreme peril. At that moment I felt I would joyfully have given my own life to have saved that of Peterkin. It takes me long to describe it, but the whole scene passed with the rapidity almost of a flash of light.

Jack did not even attempt to load, but uttering a fearful cry, he sprang towards our friend with a bound like that of an enraged tiger. A gleam of hope flashed through my soul as I beheld his gigantic form dash through the underwood. It seemed to me as if no living creature could withstand such a furious onset. Alas for Peterkin, had his life depended on Jack, strong and lion-like though he was! His aid could not have been in time. A higher Power nerved his arm and steeled his heart at that terrible moment. As I gazed helplessly at Peterkin, I observed that he suddenly ceased his struggles to get free, and throwing forward the muzzle of his piece, stood boldly up and awaited the onset with calm self-possession. The bull was on him almost in an instant. One stride more and he would have been lost, but that stride was never taken. His rifle poured its deadly charge into the skull of the wild bull, which fell a mass of dead flesh, literally at his feet.

It were vain to attempt to describe the state of our feelings on this memorable occasion-the fervour with which we thanked our heavenly Father for our friend's deliverance-the delight with which we shook his hands, again and again, and embraced him. It was with considerable difficulty that we extricated Peterkin from his entanglement. When this was accomplished we proceeded to examine our prize.

We were not a little puzzled on discovering that only three bullets had struck the bull. For my part, I fired straight at its forehead, and had felt certain at the time that my shots had taken effect; yet there was but one ball in the animal's head, and that was undoubtedly Peterkin's, for the hair all round the hole was singed off, so near had it been to him when he fired. The other two shots were rather wide apart-one in the shoulder, the other in the neck. Both would have proved mortal in the long run, but neither was sufficiently near to a vital spot to kill speedily.

"Now, Ralph, my boy," said Jack, after our excitement was in some degree abated, "you and I must divide the honour of these two shots, for I fear we can't tell which of us fired them. Peterkin only fired once, and that was pretty effectual."

"Yes," I replied, "it is rather perplexing; for although I have no objection whatever to your having all the honour of those two shots, still one likes to know with certainty who actually made them."

"You'd better toss for them," suggested Peterkin, who was seated on the trunk of a fallen tree, examining, with a somewhat rueful countenance, the tattered condition of his garments.

"There would not be much satisfaction in that," replied Jack, laughing.

"It is probable," said I, "that each of us hit with one barrel and missed with the other."

"And it is possible," added Jack, "that one of us hit with both, and the other missed with both. All that I can positively affirm is that I fired both barrels at his shoulder-one after the other."

"And all that I am certain of," said I, "is that I fired both barrels at his forehead, and that I discharged them both at once."

"Did you?" said Peterkin, looking up quickly; "then, Ralph, I'm afraid you must give all the honour to Jack, for you have missed altogether."

"How do you know that?" I asked, in a somewhat piqued tone.

"Simply enough. If you fired both shots together at so short a distance, they would have been found close together wherever they had struck, whereas the two shots in the neck and shoulder are more than two feet apart."

I was compelled to admit that there was much truth in the observation, but still felt unwilling to give up all claim to having assisted in slaying our first buffalo. I pondered the subject a good deal during the remainder of the time we spent in cutting up and packing part of the buffalo meat, and in preparing to continue our journey, but could come at no satisfactory conclusion in my own mind, and, to say truth, I felt not a little crestfallen at my conduct in the whole affair.

While wandering in this mood near the spot where the buffalo had been first wounded, I received a sudden and severe start on observing the leopard crouching within a couple of yards of me. I saw it through the bushes quite distinctly, but could not make quite sure of its attitude. With a mingled cry of alarm and astonishment I sprang back to the place where I had left my rifle.

Jack and Peterkin instantly ran up with their pieces cocked.

"Where is it?" they cried in a breath.

"There, crouching just behind that bush."

Jack darted forward.

"Crouching!" he cried, with a loud laugh, seizing the animal by the tail and dragging it forth; "why, it's dead-stone dead."

"Dead as mutton," said Peterkin. "Hallo! what's this?" he added in surprise. "Two holes close together in its forehead, I do declare! Hooray! Ralph, my boy, give us your paw! You've missed the bull and hit the leopard! If you haven't been and put two bullets right between its two eyes, I'm a Dutchman!"

And so, in truth, it turned out. I had aimed at the bull and hit the leopard. So I left that spot not a little pleased with my bad aim and my good fortune.

CHAPTER FOUR
Wherein will be found much that is philosophical.

Having skinned the leopard and cut off as much of the buffalo meat as we could carry, we started for the negro village at a round pace, for we had already lost much time in our last adventure. As we walked along I could not help meditating on the uncertainty of this life, and the terrible suddenness with which we might at any unexpected moment be cut off. These thoughts led me naturally to reflect how important a matter it is that every one, no matter how young, should be in a state of preparedness to quit this world.

I also reflected, and not without a feeling of shame, on my want of nerve, and was deeply impressed with the importance of boys being inured from childhood to trifling risks and light dangers of every possible description, such as tumbling into ponds and off trees, etcetera, in order to strengthen their nervous system. I do not, of course, mean to say that boys ought deliberately to tumble into ponds or climb trees until they fall off; but they ought not to avoid the risk of such mishaps. They ought to encounter such risks and many others perpetually. They ought to practise leaping off heights into deep water. They ought never to hesitate to cross a stream on a narrow unsafe plank *for fear of a ducking*. They ought never to decline to climb up a tree to pull fruit merely because there is a *possibility* of their falling off and breaking their necks. I firmly believe that boys were intended to encounter all kinds of risks, in order to prepare them to meet and grapple with the risks and dangers incident to man's career with cool, cautious self-possession —a self-possession founded on experimental knowledge of the character and powers of their own spirits and muscles. I also concluded that this reasoning applies to some extent to girls as well as boys, for they too are liable through life to occasional encounters with danger-such as meeting with mad bulls, being run away with on horseback, being upset in boats, being set on fire by means of crinoline; in all of which cases those who have been trained to risk slight mishaps during early life will find their nerves equal to the shock, and their minds cool and collected enough to look around and take hasty advantage of any opportunity of escape that may exist; while those who have been unhappily nurtured in excessive delicacy, and advised from the earliest childhood to "take care of themselves and carefully avoid all risks," will probably fall victims to their nervous alarms and the kind but injudicious training of parents or guardians.

The more I pondered this subject the more deeply impressed did I become with its great importance to the well-being of mankind, and I was so profoundly engrossed with it that my companions utterly failed to engage me in general conversation as we walked briskly along through the forest. Jack again and again attempted to draw my attention to the splendour of the curious specimens of tropical foliage and vegetation through which we passed; but I could not rouse myself to take interest therein. In vain did Peterkin jest and rally me, and point out the monkeys that grinned at us ever and anon as we passed beneath them, or the serpents that glided more than once from our path, I was fascinated with my train of meditation, and as I could not then give it up until I had thought it out, so now I cannot pass from the subject until I have at least endeavoured to guard myself from misconception.

I beg, then, that it will be understood that I do not by any means inculcate hare-brained recklessness, or a course of training that will foster that state of mind. On the contrary, the course of training which I should like to see universally practised would naturally tend to counteract recklessness, for it would enable a boy to judge correctly as to what he could and could not do. Take an illustration. A naturally bold boy has been unwisely trained to be exceedingly careful of himself. He does not know the extent of his own courage, or the power and agility of his own muscles; he knows these things to some extent indeed, but owing to restraint he does not know them fully. Hence he is liable both to over and under estimate them.

This bold boy-we shall call him Tom-takes a walk into the country with a friend, whom we shall name Pat. Pat is a bad boy, but he has been permitted to train his muscles as he pleased, and his natural disposition has led him to do difficult and sometimes slightly dangerous things.

"You can't jump over that river, Tom," says Pat.

"Perhaps not," replies Tom: "I never tried such a jump, because my mother tells me never to go where I am likely to tumble into the water."

"Oh, your mother's a muff!" cries Pat.

"Pat," says Tom, flushing with indignation and confronting his friend, "don't you ever say that again, else the friendship between you and me will come to an end. I know you don't really mean what you say; but I won't allow you to speak disrespectfully of my mother."

"Well, I won't," says Pat, "but *you're* a muff, anyhow."

"Perhaps I am," replies Tom.

"Of course you are, because you're afraid to jump over that river, and I'm not. So here goes."

Pat thereupon jumps the river (he is a splendid leaper), and Tom hesitates.

"Come along, Tom; don't be a hen."

Tom gives way, alas! to a disobedient impulse, and dashing at the leap comes to the edge, when he finds, somehow, that he has not got the proper foot first for the spring-almost every boy knows the feeling I allude to; his heart fails, and he balks.

"O Tom, what a nimini-pimini muff you are, to be sure!"

Tom, as I have said, is a bold boy. His blood boils at this; he rushes wildly at the bank, hurls himself recklessly into the air, barely reaches the opposite side with a scramble, and falls souse into the river, from which he issues, as Pat says amid peals of laughter, "like a half-drowned rat."

Now, had Tom been permitted to follow the bent of his own bold impulses, he would have found out, years ago, how far and how high he could leap, and how far exactly he could depend on his own courage in certain circumstances; and he would either, on the one hand, have measured the leap with an accustomed eye, and declined to take it with a good-humoured admission that it was beyond his powers, or, on the other hand, he would calmly have collected his well and oft tried energies for the spring. The proper foot, from long experience, would have come to the ground at the right time. His mind, freed from all anxiety as to what he could accomplish, would have received a beneficial impulse from his friend's taunt. No nervous dread of a ducking would have checked the completeness of his bound, because he would have often been ducked before, and would have discovered that in most cases, if the clothes be changed at once, a ducking is not worth mentioning-from a hydropathic point of view is, in fact, beneficial-and he would have cleared the river with comfort to himself and confusion to his friend, and without a ducking or the uneasiness of conscience caused by the knowledge that he had disobeyed his mother. Had Peterkin not been trained to encounter danger, his natural boldness alone would never have enabled him to stand the charge of that buffalo bull.

There are muffs in this world. I do not refer to those hairy articles of female apparel in which ladies are wont to place their hands, handkerchiefs, and scent-bottles. Although not given to the use of slang, I avail myself of it on this occasion, the word "muff" being eminently expressive of a certain class of boys, big as well as little, old as well as young. There are three distinct classes of boys-namely, muffs, sensible fellows, and boasters. I say there are three distinct classes, but I do not say that every boy belongs to one or other of those classes. Those who have studied chemistry know that nature's elements are few. Nearly all kinds of matter, and certainly all varieties of mind, are composite. There are no pure and simple muffs. Most boasters have a good deal of the muff in them, and many muffs are boasters; while sensible fellows are occasionally tinged with a dash of both the bad qualities-they are, if I may be allowed to coin a word, *sensible-boasto-muffers*! Still, for the sake of lucidity, I will maintain that there are three distinct phases of character in boys.

The muff is a boy who from natural disposition, or early training, or both, is mild, diffident, and gentle. So far he is an estimable character. Were this all, he were not a muff. In order to deserve that title he must be timid and unenthusiastic. He must refuse to venture anything that will subject him to danger, however slight. He must be afraid of a shower of rain; afraid of dogs in general, good and bad alike; disinclined to try bold things; indifferent about learning to swim. He must object to the game called "dumps," because the blows from the ball are sometimes severe; and be a sworn enemy to single-stick, because the whacks are uncommonly painful. So feeling and acting, he will, when he becomes a man, find himself unable to act in the common emergencies of life-to protect a lady from insolence, to guard his house from robbery, or to save his own child should it chance to fall into the water. The muff is addicted to boasting sometimes, especially when in the company of girls; but when on the playground he hangs on the skirts of society, and sings very small. There are many boys, alas! who are made muffs by injudicious training, who would have grown up to be bold, manly fellows had they been otherwise treated. There are also many kinds of muffs. Some are good-hearted, amiable muffs; others are petty, sneaking muffs.

With many of the varieties I have a strong sympathy, and for their comfort I would say that muffs may cure themselves if they choose to try energetically.

Courage and cowardice are not two distinct and entirely antagonistic qualities. To a great extent those qualities are the result of training. Every courageous man has a slight amount of cowardice in his composition, and all cowards have a certain infusion of courage. The matador stands before the infuriated bull, and awaits its charge with unflinching firmness, not because he has more courage than his comrades in the ring who run away, but because long training has enabled him to make almost certain of killing the bull. He knows what he has done before, he feels that he can do it again, therefore he stands like a hero. Were a doubt of his capacity to cross his mind for an instant, his cheek would blanch, his hand would tremble, and, ten to one, he would turn and flee like the rest.

Let muffs, therefore, learn to swim, to leap, and to run. Let them wrestle with boys bigger than themselves, regardless of being thrown. Let them practise "jinking" with their compan- ions, so that if even they be chased by a mad bull, they will, if unable to get out of his way by running, escape perhaps by jinking. Let them learn to leap off considerable heights into deep water, so that, if ever called on to leap off the end of a pier or the side of a ship to save a fellow-creature, they may do so with confidence and promptitude. Let them even put on "the gloves," and become regardless of a swelled nose, in order that they may be able to defend themselves or others from sudden assault. So doing they will become sensible fellows, whose character I have thus to some extent described. Of course, I speak of sensible fellows only with reference to this one subject of training the nerves and muscles. Let it never be forgotten that there are men who, although sensible in this respect, are uncommonly senseless in regard to other things of far higher moment.

As to boasters, I will dismiss them with a few words. They are too easily known to merit particular description. They are usually loud and bold in the drawing-room, but rather mild in the field. They are desperately egotistical, fond of exaggeration, and prone to depreciate the deeds of their comrades. They make bad soldiers and sailors, and are usually held in contempt by others, whatever they may think of themselves. I may wind up this digression-into which I have been tempted by an earnest desire to warn my fellow-men against the errors of nervous and muscular education, which, in my case, led to the weak conduct of which I had been guilty that day —I may wind up this digression, I say, by remarking that the boys who are most loved in this world are those who are lambs, *almost* muffs, in the drawing-room, but lions in the field.

How long I should have gone on pondering this subject I know not, but Peterkin somewhat rudely interrupted me by uttering a wild scream, and beginning to caper as if he were a madman. I was much alarmed as well as surprised at this course of conduct; for although my friend was an inveterate joker, he was the very reverse of what is termed a buffoon, and never indulged in personally grotesque actions with a view to make people laugh-such as making faces, a practice which, in ninety-nine cases out of a hundred, causes the face-makers to look idiotical rather than funny, and induces beholders to pity them, and to feel very uncomfortable sensations.

Peterkin's yells, instead of ceasing, continued and increased.

"Why, what's wrong?" I cried, in much alarm.

Instead of answering, Peterkin darted away through the wood like a maniac, tearing off his clothes as he went. At the same moment Jack began to roar like a bull, and became similarly distracted. It now flashed across me that they must have been attacked by an army of the Bashikouay ant, a species of ant which is so ferocious as to prove a perfect scourge to the parts of the country over which it travels. The thought had scarcely occurred to me when I was painfully convinced of its accuracy. The ants suddenly came to me, and in an instant I was covered from head to foot by the passionate creatures, which hit me so severely that I also began to scream and to tear off my garments; for I had been told by the trader who accompanied us to this part of the country that this was the quickest method of getting rid of them.

We all three fled, and soon left the army of Bashikouay ants behind us, undressing, as we ran, in the best way we could; and when we at length came to a halt we found ourselves almost in a state of nudity. Hastily divesting ourselves of the remainder of our apparel, we assisted each other to clear away the ants, though we could not rid ourselves of the painful effects of the bites with which we were covered.

"What dreadful villains!" gasped Peterkin, as he busied himself in hastily picking off the furious creatures from his person.

"It would be curious to observe the effect of an army of soldiers stepping into an army of Bashikouays," said Jack. "They would be routed instantly. No discipline or courage could hold them together for two minutes after they were attacked."

I was about to make some reply, when our attention was attracted by a shout at no great distance, and in a few seconds we observed, to our confusion, the trader and a band of negroes approaching us. We hurried on our clothes as rapidly as possible, and were a little more presentable when they arrived. They had a good laugh at us, of course, and the naked blacks seemed to be much tickled with the idea that we had been compelled to divest ourselves, even for a short time, of what they considered our unnecessary covering.

"We thought you were lost," said the trader, "and I began to blame myself for letting you away into the woods, where so many dangers may be encountered, without a guide. But what have you got there? meat of some kind? Your guns seem to have done service on this your first expedition."

"Ay, that they have," answered Jack. "We've killed a buffalo bull, and if you send your black fellows back on our track for some hours they'll come to the carcass, of which we could not, of course, bring very much away on our shoulders, which are not accustomed yet to heavy loads."

"Besides," added Peterkin, "we were anxious to get back in time for your elephant-hunt, else we should have brought more meat with us. But Jack has not mentioned what I consider our chief prize, the honour of shooting which belongs to my friend Ralph Rover. —Come, Ralph, unfasten your pack and let them see it."

Although unwilling to put off more time, I threw down my pack, and untying it, displayed my leopard skin. The shout of delight and surprise which the sight of it drew from the negroes was so enthusiastic that I at once perceived I was considered to have secured a great prize.

"Why, Mr Rover, you're in luck," said the trader, examining the skin; "it's not every day that one falls in with such a fine leopard as that. And you have already made a reputation as a daring hunter, for the niggers consider it a bold and dangerous thing to attack these critters; they're so uncommon fierce."

"Indeed I do not by any means deserve such a reputation," said I, refastening my pack, "for the shot was entirely accidental; so I pray you, good sir, to let the negroes know that, as I have no desire to go under a false flag, as my friend Peterkin would say —"

"Go under a false flag!" exclaimed Peterkin, in contempt. "Sail under false colours, man! That's what you should have said. Whatever you do, Ralph, never misquote a man. Go under a false flag! ha, ha! Why, you might just as well have said, 'progress beneath assumed bunting.'"

"Well, accidental or otherwise," said the trader, "you've got credit for the deed, and your fame will be spread among the tribe whether you will or not; for these fellows are such incorrigible liars themselves that they will never believe you if you tell them the shot was accidental. They will only give you credit for some strange though unknown motive in telling such a falsehood."

While the trader was speaking I observed that the negroes were talking with the eager looks and gesticulations that are peculiar to the Africans when excited, and presently two or three of them came forward and asked several questions, while their eyes sparkled eagerly and their black faces shone with animation as they pointed into the woods in the direction whence we had come.

"They want to know where you have left the carcass of the leopard, and if you have taken away the brains," said the trader, turning to me. "I daresay you know-if not you'll soon come to find out-that all the nigger tribes in Africa are sunk in gross and cruel superstitions. They have more fetishes, and greegrees, and amulets, and wooden gods, and charms, than they know what to do with, and have surrounded themselves with spiritual mysteries that neither themselves nor anybody else can understand. Among other things, they attach a very high value to the brains of the leopard, because they imagine that he who possesses them will be rendered extraordinarily bold and successful in hunting. These fellows are in hopes that, being ignorant of the value of leopard brains, you have left them in the carcass, and are burning with anxiety to be off after them."

"Poor creatures!" said I, "they are heartily welcome to the brains; and the carcass lies not more than four hours' march from this spot, I should think, —Is it not so, Jack?"

My friend nodded assent, and the trader, turning to the expectant crowd of natives, gave them the information they desired. No sooner had he finished than with loud cries they turned and darted away, tossing their arms wildly in the air, and looking more like to a band of scared monkeys than to human beings.

"They're queer fellows," remarked Peterkin.

"So they are," replied the trader, "and they're kindly fellows too-jovial and good-humoured, except when under the influence of their abominable superstitions. Then they become incarnate fiends, and commit deeds of cruelty that make one's blood run cold to think of."

I felt much saddened by these remarks, and asked the trader if the missionaries accomplished any good among them.

"Oh yes," he replied, "they do much good, such of them at least as really are missionaries; for it does not follow that every one who wears a black coat and white neck-cloth, and goes abroad, is a missionary. But what can a few men scattered along the coast here and there, however earnest they be, do among the thousands upon thousands of savages that wander about in the interior of Africa? No good will ever be done in this land, to any great extent, until traders and missionaries go hand in hand into the interior, and the system of trade is entirely remodelled."

"From what you remark," said I, feeling much interested, "I should suppose that you have given this subject a good deal of attention."

"I have. But there are people in this world who, supposing that because I am a trader I am therefore prone to exalt trade to an equality with religion, do not give me credit for disinterestedness when I speak. Perhaps you are one of these."

"Not I, in truth," said I, earnestly. "My chief desire in conversing with mankind is to acquire knowledge; I therefore listen with attention and respect to the opinions of others, instead of endeavouring to assert my own. In the present instance, being ignorant, I have no opinions to assert."

"I wish there were more people in your country," replied the trader, "who felt as you do. I would tell them that, although a trader, I regard the salvation of men's souls as the most important work in this world. I would argue that until you get men to listen, you cannot preach the gospel to them; that the present system of trade in Africa is in itself antagonistic to religion, being based upon dishonesty, and that, therefore, the natives will not listen to missionaries-of course, in some cases they will; for I believe that the gospel, when truly preached, is never preached in vain-but they will throw every possible impediment in their way. I would tell them that in order to make the path of the missionary practicable, the system of trade must be inverted, the trader and the missionary must go hand in hand, and commerce and religion-although incomparably different in their nature and ends-must act the part of brother and sister if anything *great* is to be done for the poor natives of Africa."

Conversing thus we beguiled the time pleasantly while we proceeded rapidly on our way, for the day was drawing to a close, and we were still at a considerable distance from the native village.

CHAPTER FIVE
Preparations for a grand hunt.

All was bustle, noise, and activity in the village, or, more correctly speaking, in the native town of his Majesty King Jambai, early in the morning after our arrival. A great elephant-hunt had been resolved on. The hunters were brushing up their spears and old guns-all of which latter were flint-locks that had been procured from traders, and were not worth more than a few shillings. The women were busy preparing breakfast, and the children were playing around their huts.

These huts were of the simplest construction-made of bamboo, roofed with large palm-leaves, and open in front. The wants of savages are generally few; their household furniture is very plain, and there is little of it. A large hut near to that of his sable majesty had been set apart for the trader and his party during our residence at the town. In this we had spent the night as pleasantly as we could, but the mosquitoes kept up an unceasing warfare upon us, so that daylight was welcomed gladly when it came.

On going to the hut of King Jambai, who had invited us to breakfast with him, we found the Princess Oninga alone, seated in the king's armchair and smoking her pipe with uncommon gusto. She had spent the early part of the morning in preparing breakfast for her father and ourselves, and was now resting from her labours.

"You are early astir, Princess Oninga," said the trader as we entered and took our seats round the fire, for at that hour the air felt chilly.

The princess took her pipe from her lips and admitted that she was, blowing a long thin cloud of smoke into the air with a sigh of satisfaction.

"We are ready for breakfast," added the trader. "Is the king at home?"

"He is in the woods, but will be back quickly." With this remark the princess rose, and knocking the ashes out of her pipe, left the tent.

"Upon my word, she's a cool beauty," said Peterkin.

"I should rather say a black one," remarked Jack.

"Perhaps an odd one would be the most appropriate term," said I. "Did you ever see such a headdress?"

The manner in which the Princess Oninga had seen fit to dress her head was indeed peculiar, I may say ludicrous. Her woolly hair had been arranged in the form of a cocked hat, with a horn projecting in front, and at a short distance off it might easily have been mistaken for the headpiece of a general officer minus the feathers. There was little in the way of artificial ornament about it, but the princess wore a number of heavy brass rings on her arms and ankles. Those on the latter reached half-way up to her knees, and they were so heavy that her walk was little better than a clumsy waddle. Before we could pass further comment on her appearance, King Jambai entered, and saluted us by taking us each separately and rubbing noses with us. This done, he ordered in breakfast, which consisted of roast and boiled plantains, ground nuts, roast fowl, and roast pig; so we fell to at once, and being exceedingly hungry after our long walk of the day before, made a hearty meal.

"Now, sir," said Jack, when our repast was about concluded, "as you are going to leave us soon, you had better arrange with the king about getting us an interpreter and supplying us with a few men to carry our goods. I think you said there was once a man in the tribe who spoke a little English. Have you found out whether he is alive?"

"Yes; I have heard that he is alive and well, and is expected in every day from a hunting expedition. He is a splendid hunter and a capital fellow. His name is Makarooroo, and if you get him you will be fortunate."

"Then ask his black majesty," said Peterkin, "as quick as you please, for, to say truth, I'm rather anxious on this point. I feel that we should never get on without a good interpreter."

To our satisfaction we found that the king was quite willing to do all that we wished and a great deal more. In fact, we soon perceived that he felt highly honoured by our visit, and had boasted not a little of "*his white men*" to the chiefs of neighbouring tribes, some of whom had come a considerable distance to see us.

"You have made quite a conquest, gentlemen, of worthy Jambai," said the trader, after translating the king's favourable reply. "The fact is he is pleased with the liberality you have shown towards him in the way of gifts, and is proud of the confidence you have placed in him. Had you been bent on a trading expedition, he would have opposed your further progress; but knowing that you are simply hunters, he is anxious to assist you by all the means at his command. He is surprised, indeed, at your taking so much trouble and coming so far merely to kill wild animals, for he cannot understand the idea of sporting. He himself hunts for the sake of procuring meat."

"Can he not understand," said Peterkin, "that *we* hunt for fun?"

"No, he don't quite see through that. He said to me a few minutes ago, 'Have these men no meat at home, that they come all this long way to get it?' I told him that you had plenty, and then endeavoured to explain your idea of hunting 'for fun.' But he shook his head, and I think he does not believe you."

At this point in our conversation the king rose and gave the signal to set out on the hunting expedition. Instantly the whole population of the town turned out and rushed to the banks of the river, near which it stood, where canoes were prepared for us. Suddenly there arose a great shout, and the name "Makarooroo, Makarooroo," passed from mouth to mouth. Presently a fine, tall, deep-chested and broad-shouldered negro stepped up to the king and laid a leopard skin at his feet, while the people shouted and danced with delight at the success of their companion; for, as I have already stated, it is deemed a bold feat to attack and slay a leopard single-handed.

While the commotion caused by this event was going on, I said to the trader —

"How comes it that Makarooroo can speak English?"

"He spent a couple of years on the coast, in the service of a missionary, and during that time attended the missionary school, where he picked up a smattering of English and a trifle of geography and arithmetic; but although a stout, sturdy hunter, and an intelligent man, he was a lazy student, and gave the good missionary much trouble to hammer the little he knows into his thick skull. At last he grew tired of it, and returned to his tribe; but he brought his Bible with him, and I am told is very diligent in the study of it. His education has gained for him a great reputation as a fetishman, or doctor of mysteries, among his people. I used often to see him at school hammering away at m-a, ma-b-a, ba, and so on, amid a group of children. He used to sit beside the king —"

"The king!" said I, in surprise.

"Ay; the king of that district became a Christian, and he and the queen, with one or two others of the royal household, used to attend school with the children every day, and their diligence in studying the A B C was beyond all praise. But they were terribly stupid. The children beat them easily, showing how true is the saying that 'youth is the time to learn.' The king was always booby, and Makarooroo was always beside him."

As the trader spoke, Makarooroo came forward and shook hands with him in the English fashion. He was then introduced to us, and expressed his willingness to become our interpreter in somewhat curious but quite comprehensible English. As I looked at his intelligent, good-natured countenance, I could not help thinking that the trader had underrated his intellectual powers.

"He's a funny dog that Makarooroo," said Peterkin, as our interpreter hastened away to fetch his rusty old gun and spears; for he meant to join our hunting expedition, although he had only that moment arrived from a long and fatiguing chase.

"Do you think so?" said Jack.

"I don't agree with you," said I; "to me he seems rather of a grave and quiet disposition."

"O Ralph, what a bat you are! He was grave enough just now, truly; but did you not observe the twinkle in his eye when he spoke to us in English? Depend on it he's a funny dog."

"There must be freemasonry, then, among funny dogs," I retorted, "for Jack and I don't perceive it."

"Is this our canoe?" inquired Jack of the trader.

"It is."

"Then let's jump in."

In a few seconds the river was crowded with a fleet of small canoes, and we all paddled quickly up the stream, which was sluggish at that part. We did not intend to proceed more than a few miles by water, as the place where game was expected was at some distance from the river. I felt some regret at this, for the trip up the river was to me most enchanting.

Every yard we advanced new beauties of scenery were revealed to view. The richness of the tropical vegetation seemed in this place to culminate, it was so rank and gorgeous. The day was fine, too, and all the strange-looking creatures-ugly and beautiful, large and small-peculiar to those regions, seemed to have resolved on a general peace in order to bask in the sunshine and enjoy the glorious weather. Man alone was bent on war, and our track, alas! was marked with blood wherever we passed along. I pondered much on this subject, and wondered at the bloodthirsty spirit which seems to be natural to man in all conditions and climes. Then I thought of the difficulty these poor Africans have at times in procuring food, the frequency with which they are reduced almost to a state of starvation, and I ceased to wonder that they shot and speared everything that came in their way.

We proceeded up the left bank of the river, keeping close in to the shore in order to obtain the protection of the overhanging boughs and foliage; for the sun soon began to grow hot, and in the middle of the day became so intense that I sometimes feared that I or my companions would receive a sunstroke. I confess that the subject of health often caused me much anxiety; for although I knew that we were all old experienced travellers-though young in years-and had become in a great degree inured to hardships, I feared that the deadly climate of Central Africa might prove too much for our European constitutions. By the free use of quinine, however, and careful attention to the roles of health as far as circumstances would permit, we were fortunate enough to keep in excellent health and spirits during the whole course of our sojourn there; for which, when I thought of the hundreds of Europeans who had perished on that deadly coast without even venturing into the interior, I felt very thankful. One of our chief delights, to which I in a great degree attribute our uninterrupted health, was bathing daily in the streams and ponds with which we fell in, or on which we paddled during our travels. On these occasions we were fain, however, to be exceeding careful in the selection of our bathing-pool, as crocodiles and alligators, and I know not what other hideous animals, were constantly on the lookout for prey, and I make no doubt would have been very ready to try the flavour of a morsel of English food had we given them the chance.

On these occasions, when we had made sure of our pool, we were wont to paddle about in the cool refreshing stream, and recall to mind the splendid dips we had had together six years before in the clear waters of the coral island. Since that time Peterkin had learned to swim well, which was not only a source of much satisfaction and gratification to himself now, but, he told me, had been the means of preserving not only his own life on more than one occasion, but the life of a little child which he had the good fortune to rescue from drowning when cruising off the island of Madagascar.

Peterkin used to speak very strongly when talking on this subject, and I observed, from the unusual seriousness of his manner, that he felt deeply too.

"Ralph," he said to me one day, "half the world is mad —I am not sure that I might not say three-quarters of the world is mad-and I'm quite certain that all the *ladies* in the world are mad with the exception of the brown ladies of the South Seas, and a few rare specimens elsewhere; they're all mad together in reference to the matter of swimming. Now that I have learned it nothing is so easy, and any one who is not as blind as a rheumatic owl must see that nothing is more important; for every one almost is subject to being pitched now and then into deep water, and if he can't swim it's all up with him. Why, every time an angler goes out to *fish* he runs the chance of slipping and being swept into a deep hole, where, if he cannot swim, he is certain to be drowned. And yet five strokes would save his life. *Good* swimming is by no means what is wanted; swimming of any kind, however poor, is all that is desiderated. Every time a lady goes to have a row on a lake she is liable to be upset by the clumsiness of those who accompany her, and although it may be close to shore, if she cannot swim, down she goes to the bottom. And *floating* won't do. Some ladies delude themselves with the idea that floating is of great value. In nine cases out of ten it is of no value at all; for unless water be perfectly smooth and still, a person cannot float so as to keep the waves from washing over the face, in which case choking is the certain result. There is no excuse for not learning to swim. In most large cities there are swimming-baths; if the sea is not available, a river is, everywhere. I tell you what it is, Ralph: people who don't learn to swim are-are —I was going to say asses, but that would be an insult to the much-maligned long-eared animal; and parents who don't teach their offspring to swim deserve to be drowned in butter-milk; and I wish I saw-no, I *don't* quite wish I saw them all drowned in that way, but I do wish that I could impress upon mankind over the length and breadth of this rotund world the great, the immense, the intense importance of boys *and girls* being taught to swim."

"You make use of strong language," said I.

"Quite a powerful orator," added Jack, laughing.

"Bah!" exclaimed Peterkin; "your reception of this grand truth is but a type of the manner in which it will be received by the pig-headed world. What's the use of preaching common sense? I'm a perfect donkey!"

"Nay, Peterkin," said Jack; "I appreciate what you say, and have no doubt whatever that your remarks, if made public, would create quite a revolution in the juvenile world, and convert them speedily into aquatic animals. Did you ever think of sending your views on that subject to the *Times*?"

"The *Times*!" cried Peterkin.

"Yes, the *Times*; why not?"

"Because," said Peterkin slowly, "I once sent a letter to that great but insolent periodical, and what do you think it did?"

"Can't tell, I'm sure."

"*Took no notice of it whatever!*" said Peterkin, with a look of ineffable disgust.

But to return from this digression. I was much struck with the splendid contrast of colours that met my eye everywhere here. The rich variety of greens in the different trees harmonised with the bright pink plums and scarlet berries, and these latter were almost dimmed in their lustre by the bright plumage of the birds, which I felt intense longing to procure, many of them being quite new to me, and, I am certain, totally unknown to naturalists, while others I recognised with delight as belonging to several of the species of which I had read in ornitholog-ical works. I tried hard to shoot several of these lovely creatures, intending to stuff them, but, to my regret, was utterly unable to hit them. Seeing this, Peterkin took pity on me, and sitting down in the bow of our canoe, picked off all the birds I pointed out to him as we passed, with unerring precision. Most of them fell into the water, and were easily secured, while one or two toppled off the branches into the canoe. Several of them he shot on the wing —a feat which even filled Jack with surprise, and so astounded the natives that they surrounded our canoe at last, and gazed open-mouthed at my friend, whom they evidently regarded as the greatest fetishman that had ever come amongst them.

He was obliged to stop at last and lay down his gun in order to make the natives cease from crowding round us and delaying our voyage. A number of iguanas were observed on the branches of the trees that overhung the stream. They dropped into the water as we approached; but the natives succeeded in spearing a good many, and I afterwards found that they considered them excellent food.

If I was charmed with the birds, Peterkin was no less delighted with the monkeys that chat-tered at us as we passed along. I never saw a man laugh as he did that day. He almost became hysterical, so much was he tickled with their antics; and the natives, who have a keen sense of the ludicrous, seemed quite to sympathise with his spirit, although, of course, what amused him could not have similarly affected them, seeing that they were used to monkeys from infancy.

"There's something new!" exclaimed Jack, as we rounded a bend in the river and came in view of an open flat where it assumed somewhat the aspect of a pond or small lake. He pointed to a flock of birds standing on a low rock, which I instantly recognised to be pelicans.

"Surely," said I, "pelicans are not new to you!"

"Certainly not; but if you look a little more attentively, I think you will find material for your note-book."

Jack was right. I observed a very fine fish-hawk circling over the head of one of the pelicans. Its head and neck were white, and its body was of a reddish chocolate colour. Just as we came in sight, the pelican caught a fine fish, which it stowed away safe in the pouch under its chin. The sly hawk, which had been watching for this, immediately made a descent towards its victim, making a considerable noise with its wings as it came down. Hearing this, the pelican looked hastily up, and supposing that a terrible and deadly assault was about to be made, opened its mouth and screamed in terror. This was just what the hawk wanted. The open bill revealed the fish in the pouch. Down he swooped, snatched it out, and then soared away with his ill-gotten gains in his talons.

"Oh, what a thief!" exclaimed Peterkin.

"And the pelican seems to take his loss in a remarkably philosophical manner," observed Jack.

To my surprise the great stupid bird, instead of flying away, as I had expected, quietly resumed his fishing as if nothing had happened. No doubt he was well pleased to find himself still alive, and it is not improbable that the hawk made several more meals at the expense of his long-beaked friend after we had passed by.

We soon put him to flight, however, by landing near the spot where he stood, this being the place where we were to quit our canoes and pass through the jungle on foot. The hunters now prepared themselves for action, for the recent tracks of elephants were seen on the bank of the stream, and the natives said they could not be far off. Jack and Peterkin were armed with immensely heavy rifles, which carried balls of the weight of six-ounces. I carried my trusty, double-barrelled fowling-piece, which is of the largest size, and which I preferred to a rifle, because, not being a good shot, I resolved, on all occasions, to reserve my fire until we should come to close quarters with game, leaving my more expert comrades to take the longer shots. We had also two natives-one being our guide, Makarooroo, who carried Jack and Peterkin's double-barrelled guns as a reserve. These were loaded, of course, with ball.

"This looks something like business," said Jack, as he leaned on his heavy rifle and looked at the natives, who were selecting their spears and otherwise making preparations.

"It does," replied Peterkin. "Are you loaded?"

"Ay, and I have just examined the caps to see that they are dry; for it's not like grouse-shooting on the Scottish hills this African hunting, depend upon it. A snapping cap might cost us our lives, —Ralph, my boy, you must keep well in rear. I don't want to hurt your feelings, but it won't do to go in front when you cannot depend on your nerves."

I experienced a feeling of sadness not unmingled with shame as my friend said this, but I could not question the justness of his remark, and I knew well that he would not have made it at all, but for his anxiety lest I should run recklessly into danger, which I might find myself, when too late, unable to cope with. I was careful, however, to conceal my feelings as I replied with a smile —

"You are right, Jack. I shall act the part of a support, while you and Peterkin skirmish in advance."

"And be careful," said Peterkin, solemnly, "that you don't fire into us by mistake."

Somewhat of Peterkin's own spirit came over me as I replied, "Indeed, I have been thinking of that, and I'm not sure that I can restrain myself when I see a chimpanzee monkey and a gorilla walking through the woods before me."

"I think we'd better take his gun from him," suggested Jack.

At this moment the king gave the signal to advance, so we shouldered our weapons and joined him. As we walked rapidly along, Jack suggested that we should allow the natives to kill any elephants we might fall in with in their own way, so as to observe how they managed it, rather than try to push ourselves forward on this our first expedition. We all agreed to this, and shortly after we came to the place which elephants were known to frequent.

Here great preparations had evidently been made for them. A space of more than a mile was partially enclosed by what might be termed a vine wall. The huge, thorny, creeping vines had been torn down from the trees and woven into a rude sort of network, through which it was almost impossible for any animal except an elephant to break. This was intended-not to stop the elephant altogether, but to entangle and retard him in his flight, until the hunters could kill him with their spears. The work, we were given to understand, was attended with considerable danger, for some of the natives were occasionally caught by the thorny vines when flying from the charge of the infuriated animal, and were instantly stamped to death by his ponderous feet.

I felt a new and powerful excitement creep over me as I saw the natives extend themselves in a wide semicircle of nearly two miles in extent, and begin to advance with loud shouts and cries, in order to drive the game towards the vines, and the flashing eyes and compressed lips of my two companions showed that they were similarly affected. We determined to keep together and follow close on that part of the line where the king was.

"You no be 'fraid?" said Makarooroo, looking down at Peterkin, who, he evidently supposed, was neither mentally nor physically adapted for an African hunter.

Peterkin was so tickled with the question that he suddenly began to tremble like an aspen leaf, and to chatter with his teeth and display all the symptoms of abject terror. Pointing over Makarooroo's shoulder into the bush behind him, he gasped, "The leopard!"

The negro uttered a hideous yell, and springing nearly his own height into the air, darted behind a tree with the agility of a wild-cat.

Instantly Peterkin resumed his composure, and turning round with a look of cool surprise, said —

"What! you're not afraid, Makarooroo?" The good-humoured fellow burst into a loud laugh on perceiving the practical joke that had been passed on him, and it was evident that the incident, trifling though it was, had suddenly raised his estimation of Peterkin to a very exalted pitch.

We now began to draw near to the enclosure, and I was beginning to fear that our hunt was to prove unsuccessful that day. A considerable quantity of small game had passed us, alarmed by the cries of the natives; but we purposely withheld our fire, although I saw that Jack was sorely tempted once or twice, when several beautiful gazelles and one or two wild pigs ran past within shot. Presently we heard a shrill trumpeting sound, which Peterkin, who had hunted in the forests of Ceylon, told us, in an excited voice, was the cry of the elephant. We hastened forward with our utmost speed, when suddenly we were brought to a stand by hearing a tremendous roar close in front of us. Immediately after, a large male lion bounded from among the bushes, and with one stroke of his enormous paw struck down a negro who stood not twenty yards from us. The terrible brute stood for an instant or two, lashing his sides with his tail and glaring defiance. It chanced that I happened to be nearest to him, and that the position of the tangled underwood prevented my companions from taking good aim; so without waiting for them, being anxious to save, if possible, the life of the prostrate negro, I fired both barrels into the lion's side. Giving utterance to another terrible roar, he bounded away into the bush, scattering the negroes who came in his way, and made his escape, to our great disappointment.

We found, to our horror, on going up to the fallen hunter, that he was quite dead. His skull had been literally smashed in, as if it had received a blow from a sledge-hammer.

I cannot describe my feelings on beholding thus, for the first time, the king of beasts in all the savage majesty of strength and freedom, coupled with the terrible death of a human being. My brain was in a whirl of excitement; I scarce knew what I was doing. But I had no time to think, for almost immediately after firing the shots at the lion, two elephants came crashing through the bushes. One was between ten and eleven feet high, the other could not have been less than twelve feet. I had never seen anything like this in the menageries of England, and their appearance, as they burst thus suddenly on my vision, was something absolutely appalling.

Those who have only seen the comparatively small and sluggish animals that are wont to ring their bells to attract attention, and to feed on gingerbread nuts from the hands of little boys, can form no idea of the terrible appearance of the gigantic monsters of Africa as they go tearing in mad fury through the forests with their enormous ears, and tails, and trunks erect, their ponderous tusks glistening in the sunshine, and their wicked little eyes flashing like balls of fire as they knock down, rend asunder, and overturn all that comes in their way.

The two that now approached us in full career were flying before a crowd of negroes who had already fixed a number of spears in their sides, from which the blood was flowing copiously. To say that the bushes went down before them like grass would not give a correct idea of the ponderous rush of these creatures. Trees of three and four inches diameter were run against and snapped off like twigs, without proving in any degree obstructive.

By this time the negroes had crowded in from all sides, and as the elephants approached the place where we stood, a perfect cloud of spears and javelins descended on their devoted sides. I observed that many of the active natives had leaped up into the trees and discharged their spears from above, while others, crouching behind fallen trees or bushes, threw them from below, so that in a few seconds dozens of spears entered their bodies at every conceivable angle, and they appeared as if suddenly transformed into monstrous porcupines or hedgehogs. There was something almost ludicrous in this, but the magnitude and aspect of the animals were too terrible, and our danger was too imminent, to permit anything like comic ideas to enter our brains. I observed, too, that the natives were perfectly wild with excitement. Their black faces worked convulsively, and their white eyes and teeth glittered as they leaped and darted about in a state of almost perfect nudity, so that their aspect was quite demoniacal.

The suddenness and violence of the attack made near to us had the effect of turning the elephants aside, and the next instant they were tearing and wrenching themselves through the meshes of the tough and thorny vines. The natives closed in with wild cries and with redoubled energy. Nothing surprised me so much as to observe the incredible number of spears that were sticking all over these creatures, and the amount of blood that they lost, without any apparent diminution of strength resulting. It seemed as if no human power could kill them, and at that moment I almost doubted Peterkin's assertion that he had, while in Ceylon, actually killed elephants with a single ball.

While Jack and Peterkin and I were gazing in deep interest and surprise at the curious struggle going on before us, and holding ourselves in readiness to act, should there be any chance of our game escaping, the larger of the two elephants succeeded in disentangling himself by backing out of the snare. He then wheeled round and charged straight at King Jambai, who stood close to us, with incredible fury. The beast, as it came on with the bristling spears all over it, the blood spirting from its innumerable wounds, and trumpeting shrill with rage, seemed to me like some huge unearthly phantom. It was with difficulty I could believe the whole scene other than a hideous dream. Jambai launched his javelin into the animal's chest, and then turned and fled. The other natives also darted and scattered hither and thither, so that the elephant could not make up its mind on which of its enemies to wreak its vengeance. We, too, turned and took to our heels at once with right good will. All at once I heard Jack utter a wild shout or yell, very unlike to anything I ever heard from him before. I looked back, and saw that his foot had got entangled in a thorny shrub, and that the elephant was making at him.

To this day I have never been able to account for the remarkable condition of mind and body that ensued on this occasion. Instead of being paralysed as I had been when Peterkin was in imminent danger, all sensation of fear or hesitancy seemed to vanish on thine instant. I felt my nerves and muscles strung, as it were, and rendered firm as a rock, and with calm deliberation, yet with the utmost rapidity of which I was capable, I turned round, sprang between Jack and the enraged beast, and presented my piece at his head.

"Right in the centre of his forehead," gasped Jack, as he endeavoured to wrench his foot from the entanglement.

At that moment I observed Peterkin leap to my side; the next instant the report of both our guns rang through the woods; the elephant bounded completely over Jack, as Peterkin and I leaped to either side to let it pass, and fell to the ground with such violence that a tree about six inches thick, against which it struck, went down before it like a willow wand.

We immediately assisted Jack to extricate himself; but we had no time to congratulate ourselves on our narrow escape, for mingled shouts and yells from the men in the bushes ahead apprised us that some new danger menaced them in that direction.

Reloading as fast as we could, we hastened forward, and soon gained the new scene of battle. Here stood the other elephant, trying to break down a small tree up which King Jambai had climbed, partly for safety and partly in order to dart a javelin down on the brute as it passed.

This was a common custom of the natives; but the king, who was a bold, reckless man, had neglected to take the very necessary precaution of selecting a strong tree. The elephant seemed actually to have observed this, for instead of passing on, it suddenly rushed headlong against the tree and began to break it down. When we came up the beast was heaving and straining with all its might, the stout tree was cracking and rending fearfully, so that the king could scarcely retain his position on it. The natives were plying their spears with the utmost vigour; but although mortally wounded, it was evident that in a few more seconds the elephant would succeed in throwing down the tree and trample the king to death.

Peterkin instantly sprang forward, but Jack laid his hand on his shoulder.

"It's my turn this time, lad," he cried, and leaping towards the monster, he placed the muzzle of his rifle close to its shoulder and sent a six-ounce ball right through its heart.

The effect was instantaneous. The elephant fell to the ground, a mountain of dead flesh.

The delight of the negroes at this happy termination of the battle was excessive. They leaped and laughed and danced like insane men, and we had much ado to prevent them seizing us in their arms and rubbing noses with us.

As we had not commenced the hunt until well on in the day, evening was now closing in; so the king gave orders to encamp on a dry rising ground not far distant, where the jungle was less dense, and thither we all repaired, the natives bringing in all the game, and cutting up the elephants in a very short space of time.

"Your shot was not such a bad one this time, Ralph," observed Peterkin, as we three stood looking at the large elephant which the natives were cutting up. "There they are, just above the proboscis. But let me warn you never again to venture on such a foolhardy thing as to fire in the face of a charging elephant unless you are a dead shot."

"Thank you, Peterkin, for your advice, which, however, I will not take when a comrade's life may depend on my doing so."

"I give you full credit for the excellence of your intention," rejoined my friend; "but if Jack's life had depended on those two shots from your double-barrel, he would have been but a dead man now. There is only one vulnerable spot in the front of an elephant's head; that is, exactly in the centre of the forehead. The spot is not bigger than a saucer, and the bone is comparatively thin there. If you cannot make *sure* of hitting that, you simply face certain death. I would not have tried it on any account whatever, had I not seen that both you and Jack would have been killed had I not done so."

On examination we found that the heavy ball from Peterkin's rifle had indeed penetrated the exact spot referred to, and had been the means of killing the elephant, while my two bullets were found embedded in the bone.

The tusks of this animal were magnificent. I do not know what their exact weight was, not having the means wherewith to weigh them. They were probably worth a considerable sum of money in the British market. Of course we did not lay claim to any part of the spoil of that day, with the exception of a few of the beautiful birds shot on the voyage up the river, which were of no value to the natives, although priceless to me. Alas! when I came to examine them next morning, I found that those destructive creatures the white ants had totally destroyed the greater part of them, and the few that were worth stuffing were very much damaged.

Experience is a good though sometimes a severe teacher. Never again did I, after that, put off the stuffing of any valuable creature till the next day. I always stuffed it in the evening of the day on which it was killed; and thus, although the practice cost me many a sleepless night, I preserved, and ultimately brought home, many specimens of rare and beautiful birds and beasts, which would otherwise have been destroyed by those rapacious insects.

That night the scene of our camp was indescribably romantic and wild. Numerous huge fires were lighted, and round these the negroes circled and cooked elephant and venison steaks, while they talked over the events of the day or recounted the adventures of former hunts with noisy volubility and gesticulation.

The negro has a particular love for a fire. The nights in his warm climate are chill to him, though not so to Europeans, and he luxuriates in the heat of a fire as a cat does in the rays of the sun. The warm blaze seems to draw out his whole soul, and causes his eyes to sparkle with delight. A good supper and a warm fire render him almost perfectly happy. There is but one thing wanting to render him supremely so, and that is — a pipe! No doubt, under similar circumstances, the white man also is in a state of enviable felicity, but he does not show his joy like the negro, who seems to forget his cares and sorrows, the miseries which his gross superstitions entail on him, the frequency with which he is exposed to sudden destruction; everything, in short, is forgotten save the present, and he enjoys himself with unmitigated fervour.

It really did my heart good as I sat with my comrades beside our fire and looked around me on their happy faces, which were rendered still happier by the gift from us of a small quantity of tobacco, with which we had taken care to provide ourselves for this very purpose.

I could scarcely believe that the jovial, kindly, hearty fellows were the very men who are well-known to be such cruel, bloodthirsty fiends when under the influence of their dreadful superstitions, and who, but a few hours before, had been darting through the woods besmeared with blood and yelling like maniacs or demons. In fact, the whole scene before me, and the day's proceedings, seemed to me, at that time, like a vivid dream instead of a reality. Moreover, after I lay down, the reality became a dream, and I spent that night, as I had spent the day, shooting gazelles, lions, wild pigs, and elephants in imagination.

CHAPTER SIX
Dreaming and feeding and bloody work enlarged upon.

The first object of which my senses became cognisant on awaking next morning was my friend Peterkin, who had evidently awakened just a moment or two before me, for he was in the act of yawning and rubbing his eyes.

I have all my life been a student of character, and the most interesting yet inexplicable character which I have ever studied has been that of my friend Peterkin, whose eccentricities I have never been able fully to understand or account for. I have observed that, on first awaking in the mornings, he has been wont to exhibit several of his most eccentric and peculiar traits, so I resolved to feign myself asleep and watch him.

"Heigh-ho!" he exclaimed, after the yawn I have just referred to. Having said this, he stretched out both arms to the utmost above his head, and then flung himself back at full length on his couch, where he lay still for about half a minute. Then he started up suddenly into a sitting posture and looked slowly from one to another of the recumbent forms around him. Satisfied, apparently, that they were asleep, he gave vent to a long yawn which terminated in a gasp, and then he looked up contemplatively at the sky, which was at that hour beginning to warm with the red rays of the rising sun. While thus engaged, he caressed with his right hand the very small scrap of whisker that grew on his right cheek. At first it seemed as if this were an unconscious action, but he suddenly appeared to become absorbed in it, and stared straight before him as one does when only half awake, mumbling the while in an undertone. I could not make out distinctly what he said, but I think I caught the words, "Yes, a little —a *very* little thicker-six new hairs, I think-umph! slow, very slow." Here he looked at Jack's bushy beard and sighed.

Suddenly he thrust both hands deep into his breeches pockets and stared at the black embers of the extinct fire; then as suddenly he pulled out his hands, and placing the forefinger of his right hand on the end of the thumb of his left, said slowly —

"Let me see —I'll recall it."

He spoke with intense gravity. Most persons do when talking to themselves.

"Yes, I remember now. There were two elephants and four-or three, was it? —no, it must have been four lions. The biggest elephant had on a false front of fair curls and a marriage-ring on its tail. Stay; was it not the other one had that? No, it was the biggest. I remember now, for it was just above the marriage-ring I grasped it when I pulled its tail out. I didn't pull it off, for it wouldn't come off; it came out like a telescope or a long piece of indiarubber. Ha! and I remember thinking how painful it must be. That was odd, now, to think of that. The other elephant had on crinoline. That was odder still; for of all animals in the world it least required it. Well, let me see. What did I do? Oh yes, I shot them both. Of course, that was natural; but it wasn't quite so natural that the big one should vomit up a live lion, which attacked me with incredible fury. But I killed it cleverly. Yes, it *was* a clever thing, undoubtedly, to split a lion in two, from the tip of its nose to the extremity of its tail, with one stroke of a penknife —"

At this climax I could contain myself no longer, and burst into a loud laugh as I perceived that Peterkin had spent the night, as I myself had done, in hunting-though, I confess, there was a considerable difference in the nature of our achievements, and in the manner of their accomplishment.

"Why, what are you laughing at?" said Jack, sitting up and gazing at me with a stupid stare.

"At Peterkin's dreams," said I.

"Ah!" said Jack, with a smiling yawn, "that's it, is it? Been hunting elephants and lions, eh?"

"Why, how did you guess that?" I asked, in surprise; "were you not asleep just now?"

"Of course I was, and dreaming too, like yourself, I make no doubt. I had just bagged my fifteenth elephant and my tenth lion when your laugh awoke me. And the best of it is that I was carrying the whole bagful on my back at once, and did not feel much oppressed by the weight."

"That beats my dream hollow," observed Peterkin; "so its my opinion we'd better have break-fast. —Makarooroo, hy! d'ye hear? rouse up, you junk of ebony."

"Yis, massa, comin'," said our guide, rising slowly from his lair on the opposite side of our fireplace.

"D'you hear?"

"Yis, massa."

"You're a nigger!"

"Dat am a fact."

"Well, being a nigger you're a brick, so look sharp with that splendid breakfast you promised us last night. I'll wager a million pounds that you had forgotten all about it."

"No, massa, me no forgit. Me up in centre ob de night and put 'im in de hole. Wat you call 'im-oben?"

"Ay, oven, that's it."

"Yis. Well, me git 'im d'rec'ly."

"And, I say, hold on," added Peterkin. "Don't you suppose I'm going to stand on ceremony with you. Your name's too long by half. Too many rooroos about it, so I'm going to call you Mak in future, d'ye understand?"

The negro nodded and grinned from ear to ear as he left us. Presently he returned with a huge round, or lump of meat, at which we looked inquisitively. The odour from it was delightful, and the tender, juicy appearance of the meat when Makarooroo, who carved it for us, cut the first slice, was quite appetising to behold.

"What is it?" inquired Peterkin.

"Elephant's foot," replied the guide.

"Gammon," remarked Peterkin.

"It's true, massa. Don't you see him's toe?"

"So it is," said Jack.

"And it's first-rate," cried I, tasting a morsel.

With that we fell to and made a hearty meal, after which we, along with the king and all his people, retraced our steps to the river and returned to the native town, where we spent another day in making preparations to continue our journey towards the land of the gorilla.

During the hunt which I have just described I was very much amused as well as amazed at the reckless manner in which the negroes loaded their rusty old trade-guns. They put in a whole handful of powder each time, and above that as much shot and bits of old iron of all kinds as they dared; some I saw charged thus to within a few inches of the muzzle, and the owners seemed actually afraid to put them to their shoulders, as well they might be, for the recoil was tremendous, and had the powder been good their guns must have been blown to pieces and themselves killed.

On our return to the village we found the people on the eve of one of those terrible outbursts of superstitious passion which rarely if ever pass away without some wretched human creature perishing under the hands of murderers.

"There is something wrong with the fetishman, I think," remarked Jack, as we disembarked at the landing. "He seems excited. Do you know what it can be at, Makarooroo?"

"Jack," interposed Peterkin, "I have changed his name to Mak, so you and Ralph will please to remember that. —Mak, my boy, what's wrong with your doctor?"

The negro looked very grave and shook his head as he replied, "Don' know, massa. Him's be goin' to rizz de peepil wid him norrible doin's. Dere will be death in the camp mos' bery quick—p'raps dis night."

"That is terrible," said I. "Are you sure of what you say?"

"Sartin sure," replied the negro, with another shake of the head.

"Then, Mak," said Jack, "it behoves us to look to ourselves. You look like an honest fellow, and I believe we may trust you. We cannot expect you to help us to fight against your own kith and kin, but I do expect that you will assist us to escape if any foul play is intended. Whatever betides, it is as well that you should know that white men are not easily conquered. Our guns are good-they never miss fire. We will sell our lives dearly, you may depend on it."

"Ay," added Peterkin, "it is well that you should know that; moreover, it is well that the rascally niggers of your tribe should know it too; so you can take occasion to give them a hint that we shall keep ourselves prepared for them, with my compliments."

"De mans ob my peepil," replied the negro, with some dignity of manner, "be not wuss dan oder mans. But dem is bad enuff. But you no hab need for be fraid. Dey no touch de white mans. Dem bery much glad you com' here. If any bodies be killed it be black mans or 'oomans."

We felt somewhat relieved on hearing this, for, to say truth, we knew well enough that three men, no matter how well-armed or resolute they might be, could not hope to defend themselves against a whole tribe of savages in their own country. Nevertheless we resolved to keep a sharp lookout, and be prepared for the worst. Meanwhile we did all in our power to expedite our departure.

That evening the trader started on his return journey to the coast, leaving us in charge of King Jambai, who promised earnestly to take good care of us. We immediately put his willingness to fulfil his promise to the test by begging him to furnish us with men to carry our goods into the interior. He tried very hard to induce us to change our minds and remain hunting with his tribe, telling us that the gorilla country was far far away from his lands; that we should never reach it alive, or that if we did we should certainly be killed by the natives, who, besides being cruel and warlike, were cannibals; and that if we did meet in with gorillas we should all be certainly slain, for no one could combat successfully with that ferocious giant of the monkey tribe.

To this we replied that we were quite aware of the dangers we should have to encounter in our travels, but added that we had come there for the very purpose of encountering such dangers, and especially to pay a visit to the giant monkeys in their native land, so that it was in vain his attempting to dissuade us, as we were resolved to go.

Seeing that we were immovable, the king eventually gave in, and ordered some of his best men to hold themselves in readiness to start with us on the following morning. We then proceeded to his majesty's house, where we had supper, and afterwards retired to our own hut to rest.

But we were destined to have little or no rest that night. The doctor or fetishman of the tribe had stirred up the passions of the people in a manner that was quite incomprehensible to us. King Jambai, it seems, had been for some weeks suffering from illness-possibly from indigestion, for he was fond of gorging himself-and the medicine-man had stated that his majesty was bewitched by some of the members of his own tribe, and that unless these sorcerers were slain there was no possibility of his getting well.

We never could ascertain why the fetishman should fix upon certain persons to be slain, unless it was that he had a personal enmity against them; but this seemed unlikely, for two of the persons selected were old female slaves, who could never, of course, have injured the doctor in any way. But the doings of Africans, especially in regard to religious superstitions, I afterwards found were so mysterious that no one could or would explain the meaning of them to us. And I am inclined to believe that in reference to the meaning of many things they were themselves utterly ignorant.

Towards midnight the people had wrought themselves up to a frenzied condition, and made so much noise that we could not sleep. In the midst of the uproar Makarooroo, who we observed had been very restless all the evening, rushed into our hut, exclaiming, "Massa! massa! come, save my Okandaga! come quick!"

The poor fellow was trembling with anxiety, and was actually pale in the face; for a distinctly discernible pallor overspreads the countenance of the negro when under the influence of excessive terror.

Okandaga we had previously heard of and seen. She was, according to African notions, an exceedingly pretty young girl, with whom our worthy guide had fallen desperately in love. Makarooroo's education had done much for him, and especially in regard to females. Having observed the kind, respectful consideration with which the missionaries treated their wives, and the happiness that seemed to be the result of that course of conduct, he resolved in his own mind to try the experiment with one of the girls of his own tribe, and soon after rejoining it paid his attentions to Okandaga, who seemed to him the most modest and lovable girl in the village.

Poor Okandaga was first amazed and then terrified at the strangely gentle conduct of her lover, and thought that he meant to bewitch her; for having never before been accustomed to other than harsh and contemptuous treatment from men, she could not believe that Makarooroo meant her any good. Gradually, however, she began to like this respectful wooer, and finally she agreed to elope with him to the sea-coast and live near the missionaries. It was necessary, however, to arrange their plans with great caution. There was no difficulty in their getting married. A handsome present to the girl's father was all that was necessary to effect that end, and a good hunter like Makarooroo knew he could speedily obtain possession of his bride, but to get her removed from her tribe and carried to the coast was quite a different affair. While the perplexed negro was pondering this subject and racking his brains to discover a way of getting over the difficulty, our arrival at the village occurred. At once he jumped to the conclusion that somehow or other he should accomplish his object through our assistance; and holding this in view, he the more willingly agreed to accompany us to the gorilla country, intending first to make our acquaintance, and afterwards to turn us to account in furthering his plans. All this we learned long afterwards. At the period of which I am now writing, we were profoundly ignorant of everything save the fact that Okandaga was his affianced bride, and that the poor fellow was now almost beside himself with horror because the fetishman had condemned her, among others, to drink the poisoned cup.

This drinking of the poisoned cup is an ordeal through which the unhappy victims to whom suspicion has been attached are compelled to pass. Each one drinks the poison, and several executioners stand by, with heavy knives, to watch the result. If the poison acts so as to cause the supposed criminal to fall down, he is hacked in pieces instantly; but if, through unusual strength or peculiarity of constitution, he is enabled to resist the effects of the poison, his life is spared, and he is declared innocent.

Jack and Peterkin and I seized our weapons, and hurrying out, followed our guide to the spot where this terrible tragedy was enacting.

"Don't fear, Mak," said Peterkin, as we ran along; "we'll save her somehow. I'm certain of that."

The negro made no reply, but I observed a more hopeful expression on his countenance after the remark. He evidently had immense faith in Peterkin; which I must say was more than I had, for when I considered our small numbers, my hope of influencing savages was very slight.

The scene that met our eyes was indescribably horrible. In the centre of a dense circle of negroes, who had wrought themselves up to a pitch of ferocity that caused them to look more like wild beasts than men, stood the king, and beside him the doctor or fetishman. This latter was ornamented with a towering headdress of feathers. His face was painted white, which had the effect of imparting to him an infinitely more hideous and ghastly aspect than is produced in the white man when he is painted black. A stripe of red passed round his head, and another down his forehead and nose. His naked body was decked with sundry fantastic ornaments, and altogether he looked more like a fiend than I had believed it possible for man to appear.

The ground all round him was saturated with blood and strewn with arms, fingers, cleft skulls, and masses of flesh that had been hewn from the victims who had already fallen, one of whom, we afterwards learned, had belonged to the royal family. Two still remained —a young female and an old man. The emaciated frame and white woolly head of the latter showed that in the course of nature his earthly career must soon terminate. It is probable that the poor old man had become a burden to his relations, and the doctor took this opportunity of ridding the tribe of him. The girl was Okandaga, who stood weeping and trembling as she gazed upon the butchery that had already taken place.

The old man had swallowed the poison shortly before we arrived, and he was now struggling to maintain an erect position. But he failed, his quivering limbs sank beneath him, and before we could interfere the bloody executioners had cut off his head, and then, in a transport of passion, they literally hacked his body to pieces.

We rushed hastily forward to the king, and Jack, in an earnest voice, implored him to spare the last victim.

"Surely," said he, "enough have been sacrificed already. —Tell him, Makarooroo, that I will quit his village and never see him more if he does not spare the life of that young girl."

The king appeared much perplexed by this unlooked-for interference on our part.

"I cannot check the spirits of my people now," he replied. "They are roused. The girl has bewitched me and many others. She must die. It is our custom. Let not my white men be offended. Let them go to their hut and sleep."

"We cannot sleep while injustice is done in the village," answered Jack, in a lofty tone. "Let not King Jambai do that which will make his visitors ashamed of him. Let the girl live till to-morrow at midnight. Let the case be investigated, and if she be proved guilty then let her die."

The king commenced a long reply in the same dignified manner and tone which Jack had assumed. While he was thus engaged Peterkin touched our guide on the shoulder and whispered —

"I say, Mak, tell the doctor to back up Jack's request, and I'll give him a gun."

The negro slipped at once to the side of the doctor, who had begun to frown fiercely on Jack, and whispered a few words in his ear. Instantly his face assumed a calmer aspect, and presently he stepped up to the king, and a whispering conversation ensued, in which the doctor, carefully refraining from making any mention of the gun, commended the wise advice of the white man, and suggested that the proposal should be agreed to, adding, however, that he knew for certain that the girl was a witch, but that the investigation would do good in the way of proving that he, the doctor, was correct, and thus the girl should perish on the following night, and the white men would be satisfied.

Having announced this to the multitude, the king ordered Okandaga to be conducted back to her prison and carefully guarded; and we returned to our hut-not, however, to sleep, but to consult as to what was to be done next.

"I knew that you wanted a respite for her," said Peterkin, as we sat round our fire, "that you might have time to consider how to act, and I backed up your request accordingly, as you know. But now, I confess, I'm very much at a loss what to suggest. It seems to me we have only purchased a brief delay."

"True," answered Jack. "The delay is not so brief, however, but that we may plan some method of getting the poor girl out of this scrape. —What say you, Mak?"

"If _you_ no can tink 'pon someting, I gib up all hope," replied our guide sorrowfully.

"Come, Mak, cheer up," cried Peterkin. "If the worst comes to the worst, you can, at any rate, fight for your bride."

"Fight!" exclaimed the negro, displaying his white teeth like a mastiff, rolling his eyes and clinching his fists convulsively. Then in a calmer tone he continued, "Ay, me can fight. Me could kill all de guards an' take Okandaga by de hand, an' run troo de bushes for eber. But guards no die widout hollerin' an' yellerin' like de gorilla; an' nigger mans can run fasterer dan womans. No, no, dat am dumpossobable."

"Nothing's 'dumpossobable' to brave hearts and stout arms," replied Jack. "There are only four guards put over her, I believe. Well, there are just four of us-not that we require to be equal, by any means. Peterkin and I could settle them easily; but we require to be equal in numbers, in order to do it quietly. I have a plan in my head, but there's one hitch in it that I cannot unravel."

"And what may that be?" If asked.

"Why, I don't see how, after getting clear off with Okandaga, we are to avoid being pursued on suspicion and captured."

"Dere is one cave," remarked the guide, "not far off to here. P'raps we be safe if we git into 'im. But I 'fraid it not do, cause him be peepiled by fiends an' dead man's spirits."

"That's a grave objection," said Peterkin, laughing.

"Yes, an' de tribe neber go near dere; dey is most drefful terrorfied to be cotched dere."

"Then, that will just do," cried Jack, with animation. "The very thing. And now I'll tell you what my plan is. To-morrow morning early we will tell the king that we wish to be off at once-that we have put off too much time already, and wish to make no further delay. Then we'll pack up and start. At night we will encamp in a quiet, out-of-the-way part of the woods, and slip back to the village in the dark a short time before midnight. The whole village will at that time be assembled, probably, at the spot where the execution is to take place; so we can rush in, overpower the guard, free Okandaga, and make our escape to the cave, where they will never think of looking for us."

Peterkin shook his head. "There are two difficulties in your plan, Jack. First, what if the natives are *not* assembled on the place of execution, and we find it impossible to make our entrance into or exit from the village quietly?"

"I propose," replied Jack, "that we shall undress ourselves, rub ourselves entirely over with charcoal and grease, so that they shall not recognise us, and dash in and carry the girl off by a *coup de main*. In which case it will, of course, be neck or nothing, and a tremendous race to the cave, where, if they follow us, we will keep them at bay with our rifles."

"Umph! dashing, no doubt, but risky," said Peterkin —"extremely risky. Yet it's worth trying. Well, my second difficulty is-what if they don't stick to their promise after we quit, and kill the poor thing before midnight?"

"We must take our chance of that. But I shall put the king on his honour before leaving, and say that I will make particular inquiry into the way in which the trial has been conducted on my return."

"Put the king on his honour!" observed Peterkin. "I'm afraid that you'll put his majesty on an extremely unstable foundation. However, I see nothing better that can be done."

"Have you any more difficulties?"

"Yes," said I. "There is one other. What do you propose to do with the men who are to be supplied us by the king during these extremely delicate and difficult manoeuvres?"

The countenances of my comrades fell at this question.

"I never thought of them," said Jack.

"Nor I," said Peterkin.

Makarooroo groaned.

"Well," said I, "if you will allow me to suggest, I would recommend that we should, towards the close of the day, send them on ahead of us, and bid them encamp at a certain place, saying that we shall spend the night in hunting, and return to them in the morning."

"The very thing," said Jack. "Now, comrades, to rest. I will occupy myself until I fall asleep in maturing my plans and thinking out the details. Do you the same, and if anything should occur to you let us consult over it in the morning."

We were all glad to agree to this, being wearied more perhaps by excitement than want of rest; so bidding each other good-night, we lay down side by side to meditate, and for my part to dream of the difficult and dangerous work that awaited us on the morrow.

CHAPTER SEVEN
We Circumvent the Natives.

We arose on the following morning with the dawn of day, and began to make preparation for our departure.

To our satisfaction we found the king quite willing that we should go; so embarking our goods in one of the native canoes, we ordered our negroes to embark, and commenced our journey amid the firing of guns and the good wishes of the natives. I must confess that I felt some probings of conscience at the thought of the double part we were compelled to play; but the recollection of the horrid fate that awaited the poor negro girl put to flight such feelings, and induced a longing for the time of action to arrive.

I have more than once referred to our goods. Perhaps it may be as well to explain that, when we first landed on the African coast, we made inquiries of those who were best acquainted with the nature and requirements of the country we were about to explore, as to what goods we ought to purchase of the traders, in order to be in a position to pay our way as we went along; for we could not, of course, expect the savages to feed us and lodge us and help us on our way for nothing. After mature consideration, we provided ourselves with a supply of such things as were most necessary and suitable-such as tobacco, powder, and shot, and ball, a few trade-guns, several pieces of brightly-coloured cloth, packages of beads (some white enamelled, others of coloured glass), coffee and tea, knives, scissors, rings, and a variety of other knick-knacks. These, with a little brandy to be used medicinally, our blankets and camp cooking utensils, formed a heavy load for ten men; but, of course, as we advanced, the load was lightened by the consumption of our provisions and the giving away of goods. The additions which I made, however, in the shape of stuffed specimens, began in the course of time to more than counterbalance this advantage.

Being resolved to impress the natives with a respect for our physical powers, we made a point of each carrying a pretty heavy load on our journeys-excepting, of course, when we went out a-hunting. But to return.

Our crew worked willingly and well, so that ere night closed in upon us we were a considerable distance away from the village. As the sun set we landed, and ordering our men to advance in the canoe to a certain bend in the river, and there encamp and await our return, we landed and went off into the woods as if to search for game.

"Now, Makarooroo, quick march, and don't draw rein till we reach the cave," said Jack when we were out of sight of the canoe.

Our guide obeyed in silence, and for the next two hours we travelled through the woods at a sort of half trot that must have carried us over the ground at the rate of five miles in hour. The pace was indeed tremendous, and I now reaped the benefit of those long pedestrian excursions which for years past I had been taking, with scientific ends in view, over the fields and hills of my native land. Jack and Peterkin seemed both to be made of iron, and incapable of suffering from fatigue. But I have no doubt that the exciting and hazardous nature of the expedition on which we had embarked had much to do with our powers of endurance.

After running and doubling, gliding and leaping through the dense woods, as I have said, for two hours, we arrived at a broken, rocky piece of ground, over which we passed, and eventually came upon a thick jungle that concealed a vast cliff almost entirely from view. The cracking of the bushes as we approached showed that we had disturbed the slumbers of more than one of the wild beasts that inhabited the spot. Here Makarooroo paused, and although it was intensely dark I could observe that he was trembling violently.

"Come, Mak," said I in a whisper, "surely you, who have received a Christian education, do not really believe that devils inhabit this spot?"

"Me don know, massa. Eber since me was be a pikaniny me 'fraid-horrobably 'fraid ob dat cave."

"Come, come," said Jack impatiently; "we have no time for fears of any kind this night. Think of Okandaga, Mak, and be a man."

This was sufficient. The guide pushed boldly forward, and led us to the mouth of a large cavern, at which he halted and pointed to the gloomy interior.

"You have the matches, Peterkin; quick, strike a light. It is getting late," said Jack.

In another moment a light was struck, and with it we kindled three goodly-sized torches with which we had provided ourselves. Holding these high over our heads, we entered the cavern-Jack first, Peterkin second, I next, and the terrified negro in rear.

We had scarcely entered, and were peering upwards at the black vault overhead, when an indescribable rushing sound filled the air of the cavern, and caused the flame of our torches to flicker with such violence that we could not see any object distinctly. We all came to a sudden pause, and I confess that at that moment a feeling of superstitious dread chilled the blood in my veins. Before we could discover the cause of this strange effect, several large black objects passed through the air near our heads with a peculiar muffled noise. Next instant the three torches were extinguished.

Unable to command himself any longer, the negro uttered a cry of terror and turned to fly; but Jack, whose wits seemed always prepared for any emergency, had foreseen the probability of this, and springing quickly after him, threw his arms round his neck and effectually prevented his running away.

The noise caused by the scuffle seemed to arouse the fury of all the evil spirits of the place, for a perfect hurricane of whirring sounds raged around us for a few seconds.

"It's only bats," cried Jack. —"Look alive, Peterkin; another light."

In a few seconds the torches were rekindled, and we advanced into the cavern; and Mak, after recovering from his fright and learning the cause thereof, became much bolder. The cave was about a hundred yards deep by about fifty wide; but we could not ascertain its height, for the light of our torches failed to penetrate the deep gloom overhead. It was divided into two natural chambers, the outer being large, the inner small —a mere recess, in fact. In this latter we planted our torches, and proceeded with our hasty preparations. Peterkin was ready first. We endeavoured to make ourselves as like to the natives in all respects as possible; and when I looked at my companions, I was obliged to confess that, except in the full blaze of the torch-light, I could not discern any point of difference between them and our guide.

"Now then, Jack," said Peterkin, "as you're not quite ready and I am, I shall employ myself in preparing a little plan of my own which I intend to put in force if the savages dare to venture into the cavern after us."

"Very good; but see that you finish it in less than five minutes, for I'll be ready in that time."

Peterkin immediately poured out a large quantity of powder on a flat rock, and mingling with it a little water from a pool near by, converted it into a semi-moist ball. This he divided into three parts, and forming each part into the shape of a tall cone, laid the whole carefully aside.

"There!" said he, "lie you there until you are wanted."

At this moment, while Jack and I were bending down fastening the latchet of our shoes, our ears were saluted with one of the most appalling yells I ever listened to. Makarooroo fell flat to the earth in his fright, and my own heart chilled with horror, while Jack sprang up and instinctively grasped the handle of his hunting-knife.

"Very good," said Peterkin, as he stood laughing at us quietly, and we immediately perceived that it was he who uttered the cry.

"Why, what mean you?" said Jack, almost angrily. "Surely this is no time for foolish jesting."

"I am anything but jesting, Jack. I'm only rehearsing another part of my plan."

"But you ought to give us warning when you are about to do such startling things," said I remonstratively.

"Nay, that would not have done at all, because then I should not have known what effect my cry is likely to produce on unexpectant ears."

"Well, now, are you all ready?" inquired Jack. "Then let us go."

Issuing forth armed only with our double-barrelled guns and heavy hunting-knives, we hastened towards the native village. When within a hundred yards of the edge of the wood that skirted it we stopped to pull off our shoes, for it was necessary that we should have nothing about our persons to tell who we were should any one chance to see us as we ran. We also left our rifles beside the shoes at a spot where we could find them in an instant in passing, and then slowly approached the outskirts of the village.

Presently we heard the hum of distant voices shouting, and the fear that the scene of bloodshed had already begun induced us to quicken our pace to a smart run. I never saw a man so deeply affected as was our poor guide, and when I looked at him I felt extremely anxious lest his state of mind should unfit him for acting with needful caution.

We gained the first cottages-they were empty. The village having been recently built, no stockade had yet been thrown round it, so our progress was unimpeded.

"We must be very cautious now," observed Jack in a whisper. —"Restrain yourself, Makarooroo; Okandaga's life depends on our coolness."

On reaching the back of the next hut, which was also empty. Jack motioned to us to halt, and coming close to us looked earnestly in each of our faces without saying a word. I supposed that, like a wise general, he was reviewing his troops-seeing whether the men he was about to lead into battle were fit for their work.

"Now," said he rapidly, "it's evident from the shouting that's going on that they won't waste much time with their palaver. The hut in which she is confined is not fifty yards off; I took care to ascertain its position before leaving this morning. What we have to do is simple. Spring on the guards and knock them down with our fists or the hilts of our hunting-knives, or with bits of stick, as suits us best. But *mind*" —here he looked pointedly at our guide —"no shedding of blood if it can be avoided. These men are not our enemies. Follow me in single file; when I halt, come up into line; let each single out the man nearest to him, and when I hold up my hand spring like wild-cats. If there happen to be five or six guards instead of four, leave the additional ones to me." We merely nodded assent, and in another minute were close upon the prison. Peterkin, Mak, and I had provided us with short heavy bludgeons on our way. These we held in our right hands; our left hands we kept free either to grasp our opponents with, or to draw our knives if necessary. Jack carried his long knife-it might almost have been termed a short sword-in his left hand, and from the manner in which he clinched his right I saw that he meant to make use of it as his principal weapon.

On gaining the back of the house we heard voices within, but could see nothing, so we moved softly round to the front, keeping, however, well behind the screen of bushes. Here Jack halted, and we ranged up alongside of him and peeped through the bushes. The hut was quite open in front and the interior was brightly lighted by a strong fire, round which the four guards-stout fellows all of them-were seated with their spears beside them on the ground. They were conversing in an excited tone, and taking no notice of Okandaga, who sat behind them, partially in the shade, with her face buried in her hands. She was not tied in any way, as the guards knew well enough that she could not hope to escape them by mere running way.

One rapid glance showed us all this, and enabled us to select our men. Then Jack gave the signal, and without an instant's hesitation we darted upon them. I know not in what manner my comrades acted their part. From the moment I set eyes on the negro nearest to me, my blood began to boil. Somehow or other I saw Jack give the signal without taking my eyes off my intended victim, then I sprang forward, and he had barely time to look up in alarm when I struck him with all my force on the right temple. He fell without a groan. I looked round instantly, and there lay the other three, with my companions standing over them. Our plan had been so well concerted and so promptly executed that the four men fell almost at the same instant, and without a cry.

Poor Okandaga leaped up and uttered a faint scream of alarm, but Makarooroo's voice instantly reassured her, and with an exclamation of joy she sprang into his arms. There was no time for delay. While the scene I have described was being enacted the shouts in the centre of the village had been increasing, and we guessed that in a few minutes more the bloodthirsty executioners would come for their helpless victim. We therefore left the hut at once, and ran as fast as we could towards the place where our guns and shoes had been left. Our guide seized Okandaga by the wrist and dragged her along; but indeed she was so nimble that at first she required no assistance. In a short time, however, we were obliged to slacken our pace in order to enable her to keep up. We reached the guns in safety; but while we were in the act of lifting them a burst of wild cries, that grew louder and fiercer as they approached, told that the natives were rushing tumultuously towards the prison.

"Now, lads," said Jack, "we must put on full speed. —Mak, take her right hand. —Here, Okandaga, your left."

At that instant there was a shout in the village, so loud that we knew the escape was discovered. An indescribable hubbub ensued, but we soon lost it in the crackling of the underwood as we burst through it in our headlong flight towards the cave. The poor girl, feeling that her life depended on it, exerted herself to the utmost, and with the aid of Jack and her lover kept well up.

"She'll never hold out to the end," said Peterkin, glancing over his shoulder as he ran.

The cries of the savages filled the woods in all directions, showing that they had instantly scattered themselves in the pursuit, in order to increase their chances of intercepting us. We had already traversed the greater part of the wood that lay between the village and the haunted cavern, when two negroes, who must have taken a shorter route, descried us. They instantly uttered a yell of triumph and followed us at full speed, while from the cries closing in upon us we could tell that the others had heard and understood the shout. Just then Okandaga's strength began to fail, and her extreme terror, as the pursuers gained on us, tended still further to increase her weakness. This was all the more unfortunate that we were now almost within a couple of hundred yards of the mouth of the cave.

Makarooroo spoke encouragingly to her, but she was unable to reply, and it became evident that she was about to sink down altogether. Jack glanced over his shoulder. The two negroes were within fifty yards of us, but no others were in sight.

"Hold my gun," said Jack to me sharply.

I seized it. He instantly stooped down, grasped Okandaga round the waist, and without stopping, swung her, with an exertion of strength that seemed to me incredible, into his arms. We gained the mouth of the cavern; Jack dropped Okandaga, who immediately ran in, while the rest of us stopped abruptly and faced about.

"Back, all of you," cried Jack, "else they will be afraid to come on."

The words had scarcely passed his lips when the two negroes came up, but halted a few yards from the mouth of the cave on seeing such a giant form guarding the entrance.

To let those men escape and reveal the place of our concealment was not to be thought of. Jack darted out upon them. They separated from each other as they turned to fly. I was peeping out of the cave, and saw that Jack could not secure them both; I therefore darted out, and quickly overtaking one, seized him by the hair of the head and dragged him into the cave with the aid of Peterkin. Jack lifted the other savage completely from the ground, and carried him in struggling in his gripe like a child in its nurse's arms.

This last episode was enacted so quickly that the two negroes were carried into the cavern and gagged before the other pursuers came up. At the cave's mouth the whole of the men of the village shortly assembled with the king at their head. Thus far the excitement of the chase had led them; but now that the first burst of their rage was over, and they found themselves on the threshold of that haunted cavern, the fear of which had been an element in their training from infancy, they felt, no doubt, overawed by superstitious dread, and hesitated to enter, although most of them must have been convinced that the fugitives were there. Their fears increased as their anger abated, and they crowded round King Jambai, who seemed loath to take upon himself the honour of leader.

"They must have sought shelter here," said the king, pointing to the cavern and looking round with an assumption of boldness which he was evidently far from feeling. "Who among my warriors will follow me?"

"Perhaps the evil spirits have carried them away," suggested one of the sable crew.

"That is the word of a coward," cried the king, who, although somewhat timorous about spirits, was in reality a bold, brave man, and felt nettled that any of his warriors should show the white feather. "If evil spirits are there, our fetishman will drive them away. Let the doctor stand forth."

At that moment the doctor, worthy knave, must have wished in his inmost soul that he had remained quietly at home and left to warriors the task of capturing the fugitives, but there was no resisting the mandate of the king; besides, his honour and credit as a fetishman was at stake; moreover, no doubt he felt somewhat emboldened by the presence of such a large number of men–there were certainly several hundreds on the ground–so, all things considered, he thought it best to accept the post of leader with a good grace. Stepping quickly forward, he cried, "Let torches be brought, and I will lead the way."

A murmur of approbation ran through the crowd of blacks, who, like a flock of sheep, felt bold enough to follow a leader blindly.

While the consultation was going on outside, we were making hasty preparation for defending ourselves to the last extremity. Peterkin, in particular, was extremely active, and, to say truth, his actions surprised us not a little. I once or twice fancied that excitement had turned his brain. He first dressed up his head in a species of wild turban made of dried grass and tall sedgy leaves; then he put several patches of red and white earth on his black face, as well as on his body in various places, and fastened a number of loose pieces of rag, torn from a handkerchief, and bits of tattered leaves to his arms and legs in such a manner as to give him an extremely wild and dishevelled appearance. I must say that when his hasty toilet was completed he seemed to me the most horrible-looking demon I had ever conceived of. He next poured out nearly a whole flask of gunpowder on a ledge of rock, the edge of which was visible from the entrance to the cave, while the rock itself concealed him from view. Last of all, he took up the three cones of moistened gunpowder which the reader will remember he had made before we left the cave to attack the village. One of these he placed among the grass and branches on his head, the other two he held in his hands.

"Now, boys," he said, when all was ready, "all I have to ask of you is that you will stand by with matches, and when I give the word light the points of those three cones of gunpowder simultaneously and instantly, and leave me to finish the remainder of my part. Of course you will be prepared to back me up with your rifles if need be, but keep well out of sight at first."

We now saw the drift of our eccentric friend's intention, but for my part I felt little confidence in his success. The plan seemed altogether too wild and absurd. But our danger was imminent. No way of escape seemed possible, and it is wonderful how readily men will grasp at anything in the shape of a ruse or stratagem, no matter how silly or wild, that affords the most distant chance of escape from danger. Jack, too, I could see from the look of his face, put little faith in the plan; and I observed an expression on the countenance of our negro guide which seemed to indicate that his respect for Peterkin's wisdom was on the wane.

We had not to wait long. The doctor, with several torch-bearers, suddenly darted in with a shout, followed closely by the warriors, who yelled furiously, in order, no doubt, to keep up their courage.

Alarmed by such an unusual hubbub in their usually quiet domain, the bats came swooping from their holes in the walls by hundreds, and the torches were extinguished almost instantly. The savages who were near the entrance drew back in haste; those who had entered stood rooted to the spot in terror.

"Now!" whispered Peterkin eagerly.

We struck our lights at once and applied them to the points of the gunpowder cones, which instantly began to spout forth a shower of sparks with great violence. Peterkin darted out from behind the rock with a yell so appalling that we ourselves were startled by it, having forgotten that it formed an element in his plan. In passing he allowed a few sparks to fall on the heap of powder, which exploded with so bright a flame that the whole cavern was illuminated for an instant. It also set fire to the ragged scraps with which Peterkin had decked himself out —a result which had neither been intended nor anticipated-so that he rushed towards the mouth of the cave howling with pain as well as with a desire to scare the savages.

The effect of this apparition was tremendous. The negroes turned and crushed through the narrow entrance screaming and shrieking with terror. The bats, no less alarmed than the men, and half suffocated with smoke, fled out of the cave like a whirlwind, flapping their wings on the heads of the negroes in their flight, and adding, if that were possible, to their consternation. The negroes ran as never men ran before, tumbling over each other in their mad haste, dashing against trees and crashing through bushes in their terror, while Peterkin stood leaping in the cave's mouth, smoking and blazing and spurting, and unable to contain himself, giving vent to prolonged peals of demoniacal laughter. Had the laugh been that of negroes it might have been recognised; but Peterkin's was the loud, violent, British guffaw, which, I make no doubt, was deemed by them worthy of the fiends of the haunted cave, and served to spur them on to still greater rapidity in their wild career.

Returning into the cave's innermost recess, we lighted one of the torches dropped by the savages, and placing it in a sort of natural niche, seated ourselves on several pieces of rock to rest.

Our first act was to look earnestly in each other's faces; our next to burst into peals of laughter.

"I say, comrades," I exclaimed, checking myself, "don't we run some risk in giving vent to our feelings so freely?"

"No fear," cried Peterkin, who was still smoking a little from unextinguished sparks. "There is not a man in the whole crew who will draw rein till he is sitting, with the teeth still chattering in his head, at his own fireside. I never saw men in such a fright since I was born. Depend upon it, we are safe enough here from this day forth. —Don't you think so, Mak?"

Our guide, who was now trying to reassure his trembling bride, turned, with a broad grin on his sable countenance, and said —

"Safe? ho! yis, massa. Dere not be a man as'll come to dis yere cuvern for de nix tree hun'r year or more. Massa Peterkin be de most horriboble ghost dey ever did saw, an' no mistake. But, massas, we mus' go 'way quick an' git to our camp, for de king sure to go dere an' see if you no hab someting to do wid it all. Him's a bery clebber king, am Jambai-bery clebber; him's no be bughummed bery easy."

"Humbugged, you mean," said Jack, laughing. "You're right, Mak; we must set off at once. But what *are* we to do with poor Okandaga, now that we have got her?"

This was indeed a puzzling question. It was impossible to take her to our camp and account to the negroes for her appearance in a satisfactory manner; besides, if Jambai took it into his head to pursue us, in order to ascertain whether we had had anything to do with the rescue, our case would be hopeless. It was equally impossible to leave her where she was, and to let her try to make her escape through the woods alone was not to be thought of. While we pondered this dilemma an idea occurred to me.

"It seems to me," said I, "that men are seldom, perhaps never, thrown into a danger or difficulty in this world without some way of escape being opened up, which, if they will but grasp at it promptly, will conduct them at last out of their perplexities. Now, it has just occurred to me that, since everything else seems to be impossible, we might send Okandaga into the woods, with Makarooroo to guide and defend her and to hunt for her. Let them travel in a line parallel with the river route which we intend to follow. Each night Mak will make a secure shelter for her, and then return to our camp as if he had come in from hunting. Each morning he will set off again into the woods as if to hunt, rejoin Okandaga; and thus we will journey together, as it were, and when we reach the next tribe of natives we will leave the girl in their charge until we return from the gorilla country. What do you think of that plan?"

"Not a bad one," replied Jack; "but if Mak is away all day, what are we to do for an interpreter?"

"Make him describe to us and to the men the day's route before leaving us," suggested Peterkin; "and as for the talking, we can manage that well enough for all needful purposes by a mixture of the few phrases we know with signs."

In the excitement of this whole affair we had totally forgotten our two prisoners, who lay not far from us on the ground, gagged and pinioned. We were now reminded of their presence rather abruptly. We must have secured their fastenings badly, for during the time we were conversing they managed to free themselves, and made a sudden dash past us. Jack's eye fortunately caught sight of them in time. He sprang up, rushed at the one nearest him, and throwing out his foot as he passed, tripped him up. It chanced that at that spot there was a deep hole in the floor of the cavern. Into this the poor wretch plunged head first, and he was killed on the spot. Meanwhile, the other gained the outlet of the cave, and had almost escaped into the forest, when Makarooroo darted after him with the speed of an antelope. In a few seconds we heard a cry, and shortly after our guide returned with his knife clotted with blood. He had overtaken and slain the other negro.

I cannot convey to the reader the horror that filled me and my two companions at this unexpected and melancholy termination of the affair. Yet we felt that we were guiltless of rashly spilling human blood, for Jack had no intention of killing the poor negro whom he tripped up; and as to the other, we could not have prevented our guide from doing what he did. He himself deemed it justifiable, and said that if that man had escaped to the village, and told who it was that frightened them out of the cave, they would certainly have come back and murdered us all. There was truth in this. Still we could not but feel overwhelmed with sadness at the incident.

We were now doubly anxious to get away from this cave, so we rapidly finished the discussion of our plan, and Jack arranged that he should accompany what may be termed the overland part of our expedition. This settled, we washed the charcoal off our persons, with the exception of that on our faces, having been advised by King Jambai himself to hunt with black faces, as wild animals were quicker to perceive our white skins than their black ones. Then we resumed our garments, and quitting the haunted cavern, set out on our return journey to the camp.

CHAPTER EIGHT
Peterkin distinguishes himself, and Okandaga is disposed of, etcetera.

When within about three miles of the place where our men had been ordered to haul the canoe out of the water and make the camp, we came to a halt and prepared a spot for Okandaga to spend an hour or two in sleep. The poor creature was terribly exhausted. We selected a very sequestered place in a rocky piece of ground, where the light of the small fire we kindled, in order to cook her some supper, could not be seen by any one who might chance to pass by that way.

Jack remained with her, but the guide went on with us, in order to give instructions to our men, who, when we arrived, seemed much surprised that we had made such a bad hunt during the night. Having pointed out our route, Makarooroo then left us, and we lay down to obtain a few hours' repose.

We had not lain more than an hour when one of our men awoke us, saying that it was time to start; so we rose, very unwillingly, and embarked.

"I say, Ralph," observed Peterkin, as we glided up the stream, which in this place was narrow and sluggish, "isn't it strange that mankind, as a rule, with very few exceptions, should so greatly dislike getting up in the morning?"

"It is rather curious, no doubt. But I suspect we have ourselves to thank for the disinclination. If we did not sit up so late at night we should not feel the indisposition to rise so strong upon us in the morning."

"There you are quite wrong, Ralph. I always find that the sooner I go to bed the later I am in getting up. The fact is, I've tried every method of rousing myself, and without success. And yet I can say conscientiously that I am desirous of improving; for when at sea I used to have my cot slung at the head with a block-tackle, and I got one of the middies to come when the watch was changed and lower me, so that my head lay on the deck below, and my feet pointed to the beams above. And would you believe it, I got so accustomed to this at last that, when desperately sleepy, I used to hold on in that position for a few minutes, and secure a short nap during the process of suffocation with blood to the head."

"You must indeed have been incorrigible," said I, laughing. "Nevertheless, I feel assured that the want of will lies at the root of the evil."

"Of course you do," retorted Peterkin testily; "people always say that when I try to defend myself."

"Is it not probable that people always say that just because they feel that there is truth in the remark?"

"Humph!" ejaculated my friend.

"Besides," I continued, "our success in battling with the evil tendencies of our natures depends often very much on the manner in which we make the attack. I have pondered this subject deeply, and have come to the conclusion that there is a certain moment in the awaking hour of each day which if seized and improved gains for us the victory. You know Shakespeare's judicious remark—'There is a tide in the affairs of men which, taken at the flood, leads on to fortune,' or something to that effect. I never feel quite sure of the literal correctness of my quotations, although I am generally certain as to the substance. Well, there is a tide also in the affair of getting up in the morning, and its flood-point is the precise instant when you recover consciousness. At that moment every one, I believe, has moral courage to leap violently out of bed; but let that moment pass, and you sink supinely back, if not to sleep, at least into a desperate condition of unconquerable lethargy."

"You may be very correct in your reasoning," returned Peterkin; "but not having pondered that subject quite so deeply as you seem to have done, I shall modestly refrain from discussing it. Meanwhile I will go ashore, and stalk yonder duck which floats so comfortably and lazily in the cove just beyond the point ahead of us, that I think it must be in the condition of one who, having missed the flood-tide you have just referred to, is revelling in the luxury of its second nap. —Ho, you ebony-faced scoundrel!" he added, turning to the negro who steered our canoe; "shove ashore, like a good fellow. —Come, Ralph, lend me your fowling-piece, and do you carry my big rifle. There is nothing so good for breakfast as a fat duck killed and roasted before it has had time to cool."

"And here is a capital spot on which to breakfast," said I, as we landed.

"First-rate. Now then, follow me, and mind your muzzle. Better put the rifle over your shoulder, Ralph, so that if it does go off it may hit the sun or one of the stars. A six-ounce ball in one's spine is not a pleasant companion in a hunting expedition."

"But," retorted I, "you forget that I am particularly careful. I always carry my piece on half-cock, and *never* put my finger on the trigger."

"Indeed: not even when you pull it?"

"Of course when I am about to fire; but you know well enough what I mean."

"Hush, Ralph! we must keep silence now and step lightly."

In a few minutes we had gained the clump of bushes close behind which the duck lay; and Peterkin, going down on all fours, crept forward to get a shot. I followed him in the same manner, and when he stopped to take a deliberate aim, I crept up alongside. The duck had heard our approach, and was swimming about in a somewhat agitated manner among the tall reeds, so that my companion made one or two unsuccessful attempts to take aim.

"What an aggravating thing!" exclaimed Peterkin in a whisper.

At that moment I happened to cast my eyes across the river, and the reader may judge of my surprise when I beheld two elephants standing among the trees. They stood so silently and so motionless, and were so like in colour to the surrounding foliage, that we had actually approached to within about thirty yards without observing them. I touched Peterkin on the shoulder, and pointed to them without saying a word. The expression of amazement that instantly overspread his features showed that he also saw them.

"The rifle, Ralph," he said, in a low, excited whisper.

I handed it to him. With careful deliberation he took aim, and fired at the animal nearest to us. The heavy ball entered its huge body just behind the shoulder. Both elephants tossed up their trunks, and elevating their great ears they dashed furiously into the bush; but the one that had been hit, after plunging head foremost down a low bank fell to the ground with a heavy crash, quite dead.

It was a splendid shot. The natives, who almost immediately after came up screaming with delight, could scarcely believe their eyes. They dashed across the river in the canoe, while some of them, regardless of the alligators that might be hidden there, sprang into the water and swam over.

"I'm sorry we did not get the duck, however," observed Peterkin, as we returned to the place where we had left the canoe. "Elephant meat is coarse, nasty stuff, and totally unfit for civilised mouths, though these niggers seem to relish it amazingly."

"You forget the baked foot," said I.

"Well, so I did. It was pretty good, certainly; but that's the only part o' the brute that's fit to eat."

Soon after this the canoe came back and took us over the river; and we breakfasted on the side where the elephant had fallen, in order to allow the natives to cut off such portions of the meat as they required, and to secure the tusks. Then we continued our journey, and at night encamped near a grove of palm-trees which Makarooroo had described to us, and where we were soon joined by him and Jack, who told us that he had got on well, during the day-that he had shot an antelope, and had seen a zebra and a rhinoceros, besides a variety of smaller game. He also told us that Okandaga was encamped in a place of safety a few miles to the right of our position, and that she had stood the journey well.

I was much interested by Jack's account of the zebra and the rhinoceros, specimens of both of which animals I had seen in menageries, and felt disposed to change places with him on the march; but reflecting that he was much more likely than I successfully to hunt anything he might pursue, I made up my mind to remain by the canoe.

Thus we travelled for several days without anything particular occurring, and at length arrived at a native village which lay on the banks of a noble stream.

Here Makarooroo introduced us to Mbango the chief, a fine-looking and good-natured negro, who received us most hospitably, supplied us with food, and urged us to remain and hunt with his people. This, however, we declined to do, telling our entertainer that we had come to his country for the purpose of shooting that wonderful animal the gorilla, but assuring him that we would come back without fail if we should be spared. We further assured him on this head by proposing to leave in his charge a woman for whom we had a great respect and love, and whom we made him promise faithfully to take care of till we returned.

Peterkin, who soon gave them a specimen of his powers as a marksman, and contrived in other ways to fill the minds of the chief and his people with a very exalted idea of his powers both of body and intellect, endeavoured to make assurance doubly sure by working on their superstitious fears.

"Tell Mbango," said he to our guide, "that though we be small in numbers we are very powerful; that we can do deeds" (here he became awfully solemn and mysterious) "such as no black man ever conceived of; and that if a hair of the head of Okandaga is hurt, we will on our return —"

Instead of completing the sentence, Peterkin started up, threw himself into violent contortions, rolled his eyes in a fearful manner, and, in short, gave the chief and his people to understand that something quite indescribable and unutterably terrible would be the result of their playing us false.

"Send for Njamie," said Mbango to one of his retainers.

Njamie, who was the chief's principal wife, soon appeared. She led a sturdy little boy by the hand. He was her only son, and a very fine little fellow, despite the blackness of his skin and his almost total want of clothing.

To this woman Mbango gave Okandaga in charge, directing her in our presence how to care for her, and assuring her of the most terrible punishment should anything befall the woman committed to her care.

Njamie was a mild, agreeable woman. She had more modesty of demeanour and humility of aspect than the most of the women of her tribe whom we happened to see, so that we felt disposed to believe that Okandaga was placed in as safe keeping as it was possible for us to provide for her in our circumstances. Even Makarooroo appeared to be quite at ease in his mind; and it was evidently with a relieved breast and a light heart that he bade adieu to his bride, and started along with us on the following day on our journey into the deeper recesses of the wilderness.

Before entering upon these transactions with the people of this village, we took care to keep our crew in total ignorance of what passed by sending them on in advance with the canoe under Jack's care, a few hours before we brought Okandaga into the village, or even made mention of her existence; and we secured their ready obedience to our orders, and total indifference as to our motives in these incomprehensible actions, by giving them each a few inches of tobacco —a gift which rendered them supremely happy.

One day, about a week after the events above narrated, we met with an adventure which well-nigh cost Jack his life, but which ultimately resulted in an important change in our manner of travelling. We were traversing an extremely beautiful country with the goods on our shoulders, having, in consequence of the increasing turbulence of the river as well as its change of direction, been compelled to abandon our canoe, and cut across the country in as straight a line as its nature would permit. But this was not easy, for the grass, which was bright green, was so long as to reach sometimes higher than our shoulders.

In this species of country Jack's towering height really became of great use, enabling him frequently to walk along with his head above the surrounding herbage, while we were compelled to grope along, ignorant of all that was around us save the tall grass at our sides. Occasionally, however, we came upon more open ground, where the grass was short, and then we enjoyed the lovely scenery to the full. We met with a great variety of new plants and trees in this region. Many of the latter were festooned with wild vines and other climbing plants. Among others, I saw several specimens of that curious and interesting tree the banyan, with its drop-shoots in every state of growth-some beginning to point towards the earth, in which they were ultimately destined to take root; some more than half-way down; while others were already fixed, forming stout pillars to their parent branches-thus, as it were, on reaching maturity, rendering that support which it is the glory as well as the privilege of youth to accord to age. Besides these, there were wild dates and palmyra trees, and many others too numerous to mention, but the peculiar characteristics of which I carefully jotted down in my note-book. Many small water-courses were crossed, in some of which Mak pointed out a number of holes, which he said were made by elephants wading in them. He also told us that several mud-pools, which seemed to have been recently and violently stirred up, were caused by the wallowing of the rhinoceros; so we kept at all times a sharp lookout for a shot.

Lions were also numerous in this neighbourhood, and we constantly heard them roaring at night, but seldom saw them during our march.

Well, as I have already remarked, one day we were travelling somewhat slowly through the long grass of this country, when, feeling oppressed by the heat, as well as somewhat fatigued with my load, I called to Jack, who was in advance, to stop for a few minutes to rest.

"Most willingly," he replied, throwing down his load, and wiping away the perspiration which stood in large drops on his brow. "I was on the point of calling a halt when you spoke. —How do you get on down there, Peterkin?"

Our friend, who had seated himself on the bale he had been carrying, and seemed to be excessively hot, looked up with a comical expression of countenance, and replied —

"Pretty well, thank'ee. How do *you* get on *up there?*"

"Oh, capitally. There's such a nice cool breeze blowing, I'm quite sorry that I cannot send a little of it down."

"Don't distress yourself, my dear fellow; I'll come up to snuff it."

So saying, Peterkin sprang nimbly upon Jack's shoulders, and began to gaze round him.

"I say, Peterkin," said Jack, "why are you a very clever fellow just now?"

"Don't know," replied Peterkin. "I give it up at once. Always do. Never could guess a riddle in all my life."

"Because," said Jack, "you're '*up to snuff.*'"

"Oh, oh! that certainly deserves a *pinch*; so there's for you."

Jack uttered a roar, and tossed Peterkin off his shoulders, on receiving the punishment.

"Shabby fellow!" cried Peterkin, rubbing his head. "But, I say, do let me up again. I thought, just as you dropped me, that I saw a place where the grass is short. Ay, there it is, fifty yards or so ahead of us, with a palmyra tree on it. Come, let us go rest there, for I confess that I feel somewhat smothered in this long grass."

We took up our packs immediately, and carried them to the spot indicated, which we found almost free from long grass. Here we lay down to enjoy the delightful shade of the tree, and the magnificent view of the country around us. Our negroes also seemed to enjoy the shade, but they were evidently not nearly so much oppressed with the heat as we were, which was very natural. They seemed to have no perception of the beautiful in nature, however, although they appreciated fully the agreeable influences by which they were surrounded.

While I lay at the foot of that tree, pondering this subject, I observed a very strange-looking insect engaged in a very curious kind of occupation. Peterkin's eye caught sight of it at the same instant with mine.

"Hollo! Jack, look here!" he cried in a whisper. "I declare, here's a beast been and shoved its head into a hole, and converted its tail into a trap!"

We all three lay down as quietly as possible, and I could not but smile when I thought of the literal correctness of my friend's quaint description of what we saw.

The insect was a species of ant-eater. It was about an inch and a quarter long, as thick as a crow-quill, and covered with black hair. It put its head into a little hole in the ground, and quivered its tail rapidly. The ants, which seemed to be filled with curiosity at this peculiar sight, went near to see what the strange thing could be; and no sooner did one come within the range of the forceps on the insect's tail, than it was snapped up.

"Now, that is the most original trapper I ever did see or hear of," remarked Peterkin, with a broad grin. "I've seen many things in my travels, but I never expected to meet with a beast that could catch others by merely wagging its tail."

"You forget the hunters of North America," said Jack, "who entice little antelopes towards them by merely wagging a bit of rag on the end of a ramrod."

"I forget nothing of the sort," retorted Peterkin. "Wagging a ramrod is not wagging a tail. Besides, I spoke of beasts doing it; men are not beasts."

"Then I hold you self-convicted, my boy," exclaimed Jack; "for you have often called *me* a beast."

"By no means, Jack. I am not self-convicted, but quite correct, as I can prove to the satisfaction of any one who isn't a philosopher. You never can prove anything to a philosopher."

"Prove it, then."

"I will. Isn't a monkey a beast?"

"Certainly."

"Isn't a gorilla a monkey?"

"No doubt it is."

"And aren't *you* a gorilla?"

"I say, lads, it's time to be going," cried Jack, with a laugh, as he rose and resumed his load.

At that moment Mak uttered an exclamation, and pointed towards a particular spot in the plain before us, where, close by a clump of trees, we saw the graceful head and neck and part of the shoulders of a giraffe. We were naturally much excited at the sight, this being the first we had fallen in with.

"You'd better go after it," said Jack to Peterkin, "and take Mak with you."

"I'd rather you'd go yourself," replied Peterkin; "for, to say truth, I'm pretty well knocked up to-day. I don't know how it is-one day one feels made of iron, as if nothing could tire one; and the next, one feels quite weak and spiritless."

"Well, I'll go; but I shall not take any one with me. —Take observation of the sun, Mak, and keep a straight course as you are now going until night. D'ye see yonder ridge?"

"Yes, massa."

"Then hold on direct for that, and encamp there. I'll not be long behind you, and hope to bring you a giraffe steak for supper."

We endeavoured to dissuade Jack from going out alone, but he said truly that his load distributed among us all was quite sufficient, without adding to it by taking away another member of the party. Thus we parted; but I felt a strange feeling of depression, a kind of foreboding of evil, which I could not shake off, despite my utmost efforts. Peterkin, too, was unusually silent, and I could not avoid seeing that he felt more anxiety on account of Jack's rashness than he was willing to allow. Our friend took with him one of our large-bore rifles, and a double-barrel of smaller bore slung at his back.

Shortly after parting with him, we descried an ostrich feeding in the plain before us. I had long desired to meet with a specimen of this gigantic bird in its native wilds, and Peterkin was equally anxious to get a shot at it; so we called a halt, and prepared to stalk it. We were aware that the ostrich is a very silly and very timid bird, but not being aware of the best method of hunting it, we asked Makarooroo to explain how he was in the habit of doing it.

"You mus' know," he began, "dat bird hims be a mos' ex'roroninary beast. When hims run hims go fasterer dan-oh! it be dumpossobable for say how much fast hims go. You no can see him's legs; dey go same as legs ob leetle bird. But hims be horrobably stupid. Suppose he see you far, far away, goin' to de wind'ard ob him, he no run 'way to leeward; hims tink you wants to get round him, so off him start to git past you, and before hims pass he sometimes come close 'nuff to be shooted or speared. Me hab spear him dat way, but him's awful difficult to git at for all dat."

"Well then, Mak, after that lucid explanation, what d'you propose that we should do?" inquired Peterkin, examining the locks of his rifle.

"Me pruppose dat you go far ober dere, Massa Ralph go not jist so far, and me go to de wind'ard and gib him fright."

Acting upon this advice, we proceeded cautiously to the several spots indicated, and our guide set off towards an exposed place, where he intended to show himself. In a few minutes we observed the gigantic bird look up in alarm, and then we saw Makarooroo running like a deer over the plain. The ostrich instantly rushed off madly at full speed, not, as might have been expected, in a contrary direction, or towards any place of shelter, but simply, as it appeared to me, with no other end in view than that of getting to windward of his supposed enemy. I observed that he took a direction which would quickly bring him within range of my companion's rifle, but I was so amazed at the speed with which he ran that I could think of nothing else.

Every one knows that the ostrich has nothing worthy of the name of wings-merely a small tuft of feathers at each side, with which he cannot make even an attempt to fly; but every one does not know, probably, that with his stout and long legs he can pass over the ground nearly at the ordinary speed of a locomotive engine. I proved this to my own satisfaction by taking accurate observation. On first observing the tremendous speed at which he was going, I seized my note-book, and pulling out my watch, endeavoured to count the number of steps he took in a minute. This, however, I found was totally impossible; for his legs, big though they were, went so fast that I could no more count them than I could count the spokes of a carriage-wheel. I observed, however, that there were two bushes on the plain in the direction of his flight, which he would soon have to pass. I therefore laid down my note-book and rifle, and stood with my watch in hand, ready to note the precise instants at which he should pass the first and second. By afterwards counting the number of footsteps on the ground between the bushes, and comparing the result with the time occupied in passing between the two, I thus proposed to myself to ascertain his rate of speed.

Scarcely had I conceived this idea when the bird passed the first bush, and I glanced at my watch; then he passed the second, and I glanced again. Thus I noted that he took exactly ten seconds to pass from one bush to the other. While I was in the act of jotting this down I heard the report of Peterkin's rifle, and looking up hastily, saw the tail-feathers of the ostrich knocked into the air, but the bird itself passed on uninjured. I was deeply mortified at this failure, and all the more so that, from past experience, I had been led to believe that my friend *never* missed his mark. Hurrying up, I exclaimed —

"Why, my dear fellow, what *can* have come over you?"

Poor Peterkin seemed really quite distressed; he looked quite humbled at first.

"Ah!" said he, "it's all very well for you to say, 'What has come over you?' but you ought to make allowance for a man who has carried a heavy load all the forenoon. Besides, he was almost beyond range. Moreover, although I have hunted a good deal, I really have not been in the habit of firing at animal locomotives under full steam. Did you ever see such a slapping pace and such an outrageous pair of legs, Ralph?"

"Never," said I. "But come with me to yonder bushes. I'm going to make a calculation."

"What's a calcoolashun?" inquired our guide, who came up at that moment, panting violently.

"It's a summation, case of counting up one, two, three, etcetera-and may be multiplying, subtracting, and dividing into the bargain."

"Ho! dat's what me been do at de missionary school."

"Exactly; but what sort of calculation Ralph means to undertake at present I know not. Perhaps he's going to try to find out whether, if we were to run at the rate of six miles an hour till doomsday, in the wrong direction, there would be any chance of our ever sticking that ostrich's tail again on his big body. But come along; we shall see."

On reaching the spot I could scarcely believe my eyes. Each step this bird had taken measured fourteen feet in length! I always carried a rolled-up yard-measure about with me, which I applied to the steps, so that I could make no mistake. There were exactly thirty of those gigantic paces between the two bushes. This multiplied by six gave 180 steps, or 2,520 feet in one minute, which resulted in 151,200 feet, or 50,400 yards, or very nearly thirty miles in the hour.

"No wonder I only knocked his tail off," said Peterkin.

"On the contrary," said I, "the wonder is that under the circumstances you hit the bird at all."

On further examination of the place where we had seen the ostrich before it was alarmed, we ascertained that his ordinary walking pace varied from twenty to twenty-six inches in length.

After this unsuccessful hunt we returned to our comrades, and proceeded to the rendezvous where we expected to find Jack; but as he was not there, we concluded that he must have wandered farther than he intended, so, throwing down our packs, we set about preparing the camp and a good supper against his return. Gradually the sun began to sink low on the horizon; then he dipped below it, and the short twilight of those latitudes was rapidly merging into night; but Jack did not return, and the uneasiness which we had all along felt in regard to him increased so much that we could not refrain from showing it.

"I'll tell you what it is, Ralph," cried Peterkin, starting up suddenly: "I'm not going to sit here wasting the time when Jack may be in some desperate fix. I'll go and hunt for him."

"Me tink you right," said our guide; "dere is ebery sort ob ting here-beasties and mans. P'raps Massa Jack am be kill."

I could not help shuddering at the bare idea of such a thing, so I at once seconded my companion's proposal, and resolved to accompany him.

"Take your double-barrel, Ralph, and I'll lend our spare big gun to Mak."

"But how are we to proceed? which way are we to go? I have not the most distant idea as to what direction we ought to go in our search."

"Leave that to Mak. He knows the ways o' the country best, and the probable route that Jack has taken. Are you ready?"

"Yes. Shall we take some brandy?"

"Ay; well thought of. He'll perhaps be the better of something of that sort if anything has befallen him. Now, then, let's go."

Leaving our men in charge of the camp, with strict injunctions to keep good watch and not allow the fires to go down, lest they should be attacked by lions, we three set forth on our nocturnal search. From time to time we stood still and shouted in a manner that would let our lost friend know that we were in search of him, should he be within earshot, but no answering cry came back to us; and we were beginning to despair, when we came upon the footprints of a man in the soft soil of a swampy spot we had to cross. It was a clear moonlight night, so that we could distinguish them perfectly.

"Ho!" exclaimed our guide, as he stooped to examine the marks.

"Well, Mak, what do you make of it?" inquired Peterkin anxiously.

Mak made no reply for a few seconds; then he rose, and said earnestly, "Dat am Massa Jack's foot."

I confess that I was somewhat surprised at the air of confidence with which our guide made this statement; for after a most careful examination of the prints, which were exceedingly indistinct, I could discern nothing to indicate that they had been made by Jack.

"Are you sure, Mak?" asked Peterkin.

"Sartin sure, massa."

"Then push on as fast as you can."

Presently we came to a spot where the ground was harder and the prints more distinct.

"Ha! you're wrong, Mak," cried Peterkin, in a voice of disappointment, as he stooped to examine the footsteps again. "Here we have the print of a naked foot; Jack wore shoes. And, what's this? blood!"

"Yis, massa, me know dat Massa Jack hab shoes. But dat be him's foot for all dat, and him's hurt somehow for certain."

The reader may imagine our state of mind on making this discovery. Without uttering another word, we quickened our pace into a smart run, keeping closely in the track of Jack's steps. Soon we observed that these deviated from side to side in an extraordinary manner, as if the person who made them had been unable to walk straight. In a few minutes more we came on the footprints of a rhinoceros —a sight which still further increased our alarm. On coming out from among a clump of low bushes that skirted the edge of a small plain, we observed a dark object lying on the ground about fifty yards distant from us. I almost sank down with an undefinable feeling of dread on beholding this.

We held our rifles in readiness as we approached it at a quick pace, for we knew not whether it was not a wild animal which might spring upon us the moment we came close enough. But a few seconds dispelled our dread of such an attack and confirmed our worst fears, for there, in a pool of blood, lay Jack's manly form. The face was upturned, and the moon, which shone full upon it, showed that it was pale as death and covered with blood. His clothes were rent and dishevelled and covered with dust, as if he had struggled hard with some powerful foe, and all round the spot were footprints of a rhinoceros, revealing too clearly the character of the terrible monster with which our friend had engaged in unequal conflict.

Peterkin darted forward, tore open Jack's shirt at the breast, and laid his hand upon his heart.

"Thank God," he muttered, in a low, subdued tone, "he's not dead! Quick, Ralph-the brandy-flask."

I instantly poured a little of the spirit into the silver cup attached to the flask, and handed it to Peterkin, who, after moistening Jack's lips, began assiduously to rub his chest and forehead with brandy. Kneeling down by his side I assisted him, while I applied some to his feet. While we were thus engaged we observed that our poor friend's arms and chest had received several severe bruises and some slight wounds, and we also discovered a terrible gash in his right thigh which had evidently been made by the formidable horn of the rhinoceros. This, and the other wounds which were still bleeding pretty freely, we stanched and bound up, and our exertions were at length rewarded by the sight of a faint tinge of colour returning to Jack's cheeks. Presently his eyes quivered, and heaving a short, broken sigh, he looked up.

"Where am I, eh? Why, what's wrong? what has happened?" he asked faintly, in a tone of surprise.

"All right, old boy. Here, take a swig of this, you abominable gorilla," said Peterkin, holding the brandy-flask to his mouth, while one or two tears of joy rolled down his cheeks.

Jack drank, and rallied a little.

"I've been ill, I see," he said gently. "Ah! I remember now. I've been hurt-the rhinoceros; eh, have you killed it? I gave it a good shot. It must have been mortal, I think."

"Whether you've killed it or not I cannot tell," said I, taking off my coat and putting it under Jack's head for a pillow, "but it has pretty nearly killed *you*. Do you feel worse, Jack?"

I asked this in some alarm, observing that he had turned deadly pale again.

"He's fainted, man; out o' the way!" cried Peterkin, as he applied the brandy again to his lips and temples.

In a few seconds Jack again rallied.

"Now, Mak, bestir yourself," cried Peterkin, throwing off his coat. "Cut down two stout poles, and we'll make some sort of litter to carry him on."

"I say, Ralph," whispered Jack faintly, "do look to my wounds and see that they are all tightly bound up. I can't afford to lose another drop of blood. It's almost all drained away, I believe."

While I examined my friend's wounds and readjusted the bandages, my companions cut down two poles. These we laid on the ground parallel to each other and about two feet apart, and across them laid our three coats, which we fastened in a rough fashion by means of some strong cords which I fortunately happened to have with me. On this rude litter we laid our companion, and raised him on our shoulders. Peterkin and I walked in rear, each supporting one of the poles; while Makarooroo, being the stoutest of the three, supported the entire weight of the other ends on his broad shoulders. Jack bore the moving better than we had expected, so that we entertained sanguine hopes that no bones were broken, but that loss of blood was all he had to suffer from.

Thus slowly and with much difficulty we bore our wounded comrade to the camp.

CHAPTER NINE
I discover a curious insect, and Peterkin takes a strange flight.

It happened most fortunately at this time that we were within a short day's journey of a native village, to which, after mature consideration, we determined to convey Jack, and remain there until he should be sufficiently recovered to permit of our resuming our journey. Hitherto we had studiously avoided the villages that lay in our route, feeling indisposed to encounter unnecessarily the risk of being inhospitably received-perhaps even robbed of our goods, if nothing worse should befall us. There was, however, no other alternative now; for Jack's wounds were very severe, and the amount of blood lost by him was so great that he was as weak as a child. Happily, no bones were broken, so we felt sanguine that by careful nursing for a few weeks we should get him set firmly upon his legs again.

On the following morning we set forth on our journey, and towards evening reached the village, which was situated on the banks of a small stream, in the midst of a beautiful country composed of mingled plain and woodland.

It chanced that the chief of this village was connected by marriage with King Jambai —a most fortunate circumstance for us, as it ensured our being hospitably received. The chief came out to meet us riding on the shoulders of a slave, who, although a much smaller man than his master, seemed to support his load with much case. Probably habit had strengthened him for his special work. A large hut was set apart for our accommodation; a dish of yams, a roast monkey, and a couple of fowls were sent to us soon after our arrival, and, in short, we experienced the kindest possible reception.

None of the natives of this village had ever seen a white face in their lives, and, as may well be imagined, their curiosity and amazement were unbounded. The people came constantly crowding round our hut, remaining, however, at a respectful distance, and gazed at us until I began to fear they would never go away.

Here we remained for three weeks, during which time Jack's wounds healed up, and his strength returned rapidly. Peterkin and I employed ourselves in alternately tending our comrade, and in scouring the neighbouring woods and plains in search of wild animals.

As we were now approaching the country of the gorilla-although, indeed, it was still far distant-our minds began to run more upon that terrible creature than used to be the case; and our desire to fall in with it was increased by the strange accounts of its habits and its tremendous power that we received from the natives of this village, some of whom had crossed the desert and actually met with the gorilla face to face. More than once, while out hunting, I have been so taken up with this subject that I have been on the point of shooting a native who appeared unexpectedly before me, under the impression that he was a specimen of the animal on which my thoughts had been fixed.

One day about a week after our arrival, as I was sitting at the side of Jack's couch relating to him the incidents of a hunt after a buffalo that Makarooroo and I had had the day before, Peterkin entered with a swaggering gait, and setting his rifle down in a corner, flung himself on the pile of skins that formed his couch.

"I'll tell you what it is," said he, with the look and tone of a man who feels that he has been unwarrantably misled —"I don't believe there's such a beast as a gorilla at all; *now*, that's a fact."

There was something so confident and emphatic in my comrade's manner that, despite my well-grounded belief on that point, I felt a sinking at the heart. The bare possibility that, after all our trouble and toil and suffering in penetrating thus far towards the land which he is said to inhabit, we should find that there really existed no such creature as the gorilla was too terrible to think upon.

"Peterkin," said I anxiously, "what do you mean?"

"I mean," replied he slowly, "that Jack is the only living specimen of the gorilla in Africa."

"Come, now, I see you are jesting."

"Am I?" cried Peterkin savagely—"jesting, eh? That means expressing thoughts and opinions which are not to be understood literally. Oh, I would that I were sure that I am jesting! Ralph, it's my belief, I tell you, that the gorilla is a regular sell—a great, big, unnatural hairy *do!*"

"But I saw the skeleton of one in London."

"I don't care for that. You may have been deceived, humbugged. Perhaps it was a compound of the bones of a buffalo and a chimpanzee."

"Nay, that were impossible," said I quickly; "for no one pretending to have any knowledge of natural history and comparative anatomy could be so grossly deceived."

"What like was the skeleton, Ralph?" inquired Jack, who seemed to be rather amused by our conversation.

"It was nearly as tall as that of a medium-sized man—I should think about five feet seven or eight inches; but the amazing part about it was the immense size and thickness of its bones. Its shoulders were much broader than yours, Jack, and your chest is a mere child's compared with that of the specimen of the gorilla that I saw. Its legs were very short-much shorter than those of a man; but its arms were tremendous-they were more than a foot longer than yours. In fact, if the brute's legs were in the same proportion to its body as are those of a man, it would be a giant of ten or eleven feet high. Or, to take another view of it, if you were to take a robust and properly proportioned giant of that height, and cut down his legs until he stood about the height of an ordinary man, *that* would be a gorilla."

"I don't believe it," cried Peterkin.

"Well, perhaps my simile is not quite so felicitous as—"

"I don't mean that," interrupted Peterkin; "I mean that I don't believe there's such a brute as a gorilla at all."

"Why, what has made you so sceptical?" inquired Jack.

"The nonsense that these niggers have been telling me, through the medium of Mak as an interpreter; that is what has made me sceptical. Only think, they say that a gorilla is so strong that he can lift a man by the nape of the neck clean off the ground with one of his hind feet! Yes, they say he is in the habit of sitting on the lower branches of trees in lonely dark parts of the wood watching for prey, and when a native chances to pass by close enough he puts down his hind foot, seizes the wretched man therewith, lifts him up into the tree, and quietly throttles him. They don't add whether or not he eats him afterwards, or whether he prefers him boiled or roasted. Now, I don't believe that."

"Neither do I," returned Jack; "nevertheless the fact that these fellows recount such wonderful stories at all, is, to some extent, evidence in favour of their existence: for in such a country as this, where so many wonderful and horrible animals exist, men are not naturally tempted to invent *new* creatures; it is sufficient to satisfy their craving for the marvellous that they should merely exaggerate what does already exist."

"Go to, you sophist! if what you say be true, and the gorilla turns out to be only an exaggerated chimpanzee or ring-tailed roarer, does not that come to the same thing as saying that there is no gorilla at all-always, of course, excepting yourself?"

"Credit yourself with a punched head," said Jack, "and the account shall be balanced when I am sufficiently recovered to pay you off. Meanwhile, continue your account of what the niggers say about the gorilla."

Peterkin assumed a look of offended dignity as he replied—

"Without deigning any rejoinder to the utterly absurd and totally irrelevant matter contained in the preliminary sentences of your last remark, I pass on to observe that the natives of these wilds hold the opinion that there is one species of the gorilla which is the residence of the spirits of defunct niggers, and that these fellows are known by their unusual size and ferocity."

"Hold," cried I, "until I get out my note-book. Now, Peterkin, no fibs."

"Honour bright," said he, "I'll give it you just as I got it. These *possessed* brutes are never caught, and can't be killed. (I only hope I may get the chance to try whether that be true or not.) They often carry off natives into the woods, where they pull out their toe and finger nails by the roots and then let them go; and they are said to be uncommonly fond of sugar-cane, which they steal from the fields of the natives sometimes in a very daring manner."

"Is that all?" said I.

"All!" exclaimed my comrade. "How much more would you have? Do you suppose that the gorilla can do anything it likes-hang by its tail from the moon, or sit down on its nose and run round on its chin?"

"Massa Jack," said Makarooroo, entering the hut and interrupting our conversation at this point, "de chief hims tell to me for to tell to you dat w'en you's be fit for go-hid agin hims gib you cottle for sit upon."

"Cottle, Mak! what's *cottle?*" inquired Jack, with a puzzled look.

"Ho, massa, you know bery well; jist cottle-hoxes, you know."

"Indeed, I don't know," replied Jack, still more puzzled.

"I've no doubt," interposed Peterkin, "that he means cuttle, which is the short name for cuttle-fish, which, in such an inland place as this, must of course be hoaxes! But what do you mean, Mak? Describe the thing to us."

Mak scratched his woolly pate, as if he were quite unable to explain himself.

"O massas, you be most stoopid dis yer day. Cottle not a ting; hims am a beast, wid two horn an' one tail. Dere," said he, pointing with animation to a herd of cattle that grazed near our hut, "dat's cottle, or hoxes."

We all laughed at this proposal.

"What!" cried Jack, "does he mean us to ride upon 'hoxes' as if they were horses?"

"Yis, massa, hims say dat. Hims hear long ago ob one missionary as hab do dat; so de chief he tink it bery good idea, an' hims try too, an' like it bery much; only hims fell off ebery tree steps an' a'most broke all de bones in him's body down to powder. But hims git up agin and fell hoff agin. Oh, hims like it bery much!"

"If we follow the chief's example," said I, laughing, "we shall scarcely be in a fit state to hunt gorillas at the end of our journey; but now I come to think of it, the plan seems to me not a bad one. You know a great part of our journey now lies over a comparatively desert country, where we shall be none the worse of a ride now and then on ox-back to relieve our limbs. I think the proposal merits consideration."

"Right, Ralph," said Jack. —"Go, Mak, and tell his majesty, or chieftainship, or his royal highness, with my compliments, that I am much obliged by the offer, and will consider it. Also give him this plug of tobacco; and see you don't curtail its dimensions before it leaves your hand, you rascal."

Our guide grinned as he left the hut to execute his mission, and we turned to converse on this new plan, which, the more we thought of it, seemed the more to grow in our estimation as most feasible.

"Now, lads, leave me," said Jack, with a sigh, after we had chatted for more than an hour. "If I am to go through all that our worthy host seems to have suffered, it behoves me to get my frame into a fit state to stand it. I shall therefore try to sleep."

So saying he turned round on his side, and we left him to his slumbers.

As it was still early in the afternoon, we two shouldered our rifles and strolled away into the woods, partly with the intention of taking a shot at anything that might chance to come in our way, but chiefly with the view of having a pleasant chat about our prospect of speedily reaching that goal of our ambition-the gorilla country.

"It seems to me," observed Peterkin, as we walked side by side over an open grassy and flower-speckled plain that lay about a couple of miles distant from the village —"it seems to me that we shall *never* reach this far-famed country."

"I have no doubt that we shall," said I; "but tell me, Peterkin, do you really doubt the existence of the gorilla?"

"Well, since you do put it to me so very seriously, I can scarce tell what I believe. The fact is, that I'm such a sceptical wretch by nature that I find it difficult to believe anything unless I see it."

I endeavoured to combat this very absurd state of mind in my companion by pointing out to him very clearly that if he were to act upon such a principle at all times, he would certainly disbelieve many of the commonest facts in nature, and give full credit, on the other hand, to the most outrageous absurdities.

"For instance," said I, "you would believe that every conjurer swallows fire, and smoke, and penknives, and rabbits, because you *see* him do it; and you would disbelieve the existence of the pyramids, because you don't happen to have seen them."

"Ralph," said my companion seriously, "don't go in too deep, else I shall be drowned!"

I was about to make some reply, when my attention was attracted by a very singular appearance of moisture at the foot of a fig-tree under which we were passing. Going up to it I found that there was a small puddle of clear water near the trunk. This occasioned me much surprise, for no rain had fallen in that district since our arrival, and probably there had been none for a long period before that. The ground everywhere, except in the large rivers and water-courses, was quite dry, insomuch that, as I have said, this little solitary pool (which was not much larger than my hand) occasioned us much surprise.

"How comes it there?" said I.

"That's more than I can tell," replied Peterkin. "Perhaps there's a small spring at the root of the tree."

"Perhaps there is," said I, searching carefully round the spot in all directions; but I found nothing to indicate the presence of a spring-and, indeed, when I came to think of it, if there had been a spring there would also certainly have been a water-course leading from it. But such was not the case. Presently I observed a drop of water fall into the pool, and looking up, discovered that it fell from a cluster of insects that clung to a branch close over our heads.

I at once recognised this water-distilling insect as an old acquaintance. I had seen it before in England, although of a considerably smaller size than this African one. My companion also seemed to be acquainted with it, for he exclaimed —

"Ho! I know the fellow. He's what we used at home to call a 'frog-hopper' after he got his wings, and a 'cuckoo-spit' before that time; but these ones are six times the size of ours."

I was aware that there was some doubt among naturalists as to whence these insects procured the water they distilled. My own opinion, founded on observations made at this time, led me to think the greater part of the moisture is derived from the atmosphere, though, possibly, some of it may be procured by suction from the trees. I afterwards paid several visits to this tree, and found, by placing a vessel beneath them, that these insects distilled during a single night as much as three or four pints of water!

Turning from this interesting discovery, we were about to continue our walk, when we observed a buffalo bull feeding in the open plain, not more than five or six hundred yards off from us.

"Ha! Ralph, my boy," cried Peterkin enthusiastically, "here is metal more attractive! Follow me; we must make a détour in order to get to leeward of him."

We set off at a brisk pace, and I freely confess that, although the contemplation of the curious processes of the water-distilling insect afforded me deeper and more lasting enjoyment, the gush of excitement and eagerness that instantly followed the discovery of the wild buffalo bull enabled me thoroughly to understand the feeling that leads men-especially the less contemplative among them-infinitely to prefer the pleasures of the chase to the calmer joys attendant upon the study of natural history.

At a later period that evening I had a discussion with my companions on that subject, when I stood up for the pursuit of scientific knowledge as being truly elevating and noble, while the pursuit of game was, to say the least of it, a species of pleasure more suited to the tastes and condition of the savage than of the civilised man.

To this Peterkin replied-having made a preliminary statement to the effect that I was a hum-bug-that a man's pluck was brought out and his nerves improved by the noble art of hunting, which was beautifully scientific in its details, and which had the effect of causing a man to act like a man and look like a man-not like a woman or a nincompoop, as was too often the case with scientific men.

Hereupon Jack announced it as his opinion that we were both wrong and both right; which elicited a cry of "Bravo!" from Peterkin. "For," said Jack, "what would the naturalist do without the hunter? His museums would be almost empty and his knowledge would be extremely lim-ited. On the other hand, if there were no naturalists, the hunter-instead of being the hero who dares every imaginable species of danger, in order to procure specimens and furnish information that will add to the sum of human knowledge-would degenerate into the mere butcher, who supplies himself and his men with meat; or into the semi-murderer, who delights in shedding the blood of inferior animals. The fact is, that the naturalist and the hunter are indispensably necessary to each other —'both are best,' to use an old expression; and when both are combined in one, as in the case of the great American ornithologist Audubon, that is best of all."

"Betterer than both," suggested Peterkin.

But to return from this digression.

In less than quarter of an hour we gained a position well to leeward of the buffalo, which grazed quietly near the edge of the bushes, little dreaming of the enemies who were so cautiously approaching to work its destruction.

"Keep well in rear of me, Ralph," said Peterkin, as we halted behind a bush to examine our rifles. "I'll creep as near to him as I can, and if by any chance I should not kill him at the first shot, do you run up and hand me your gun."

Without waiting for a reply, my companion threw himself on his breast, and began to creep over the plain like a snake in the grass. He did this so well and so patiently that he reached to within forty yards of the bull without being discovered. Then he ceased to advance, and I saw his head and shoulders slowly emerge from among the grass, and presently his rifle appeared, and was slowly levelled. It was one of our large-bore single-barrelled rifles.

He lay in this position for at least two minutes, which seemed to me a quarter of an hour, so eager was I to see the creature fall. Suddenly I heard a sharp snap or crack. The bull heard it too, for it raised its huge head with a start. The cap of Peterkin's rifle had snapped, and I saw by his motions that he was endeavouring, with as little motion as possible, to replace it with another. But the bull caught sight of him, and uttering a terrific roar charged in an instant.

It is all very well for those who dwell at home in security to think they know what the charge of an infuriated buffalo bull is. Did they see it in reality, as I saw it at that time, tearing madly over the grass, foaming at the mouth, flashing at the eyes, tossing its tail, and bellowing hideously, they would have a very different idea from what they now have of the trials to which hunters' nerves are frequently exposed.

Peterkin had not time to cap. He leaped up, turned round, and ran for the woods at the top of his speed; but the bull was upon him in an instant. Almost before I had time to realise what was occurring, I beheld my companion tossed high into the air. He turned a distinct somersault, and fell with a fearful crash into the centre of a small bush. I cannot recall my thoughts on witnessing this. I remember only experiencing a sharp pang of horror and feeling that Peterkin must certainly have been killed. But whatever my thoughts were they must have been rapid, for the time allowed me was short, as the bull turned sharp round after tossing Peterkin and rushed again towards the bush, evidently with the intention of completing the work of destruction.

Once again I experienced that strange and sudden change of feeling to which I have before referred. I felt a bounding sensation in my breast which tingled to my finger-ends. At the same time my head became clear and cool. I felt that Providence had placed the life of my friend in my hands. Darting forward in advance of the bush, I awaited the charge of the infuriated animal. On it came. I knew that I was not a sufficiently good shot to make sure of hitting it in the brain. I therefore allowed it to come within a yard of me, and then sprang lightly to one side. As it flew past, I never thought of taking aim or putting the piece to my shoulder, but I thrust the muzzle against its side and pulled both triggers at once.

From that moment consciousness forsook me, and I knew not what had occurred for some minutes after. The first object that met my confused vision when I again opened my eyes was Peterkin, who was seated close beside me on the body of the dead buffalo, examining some bloody scratches on the calf of his left leg. He had evidently been attempting to restore me to consciousness, for I observed that a wet handkerchief lay on my forehead. He muttered to himself as he examined his wounds —

"This comes of not looking to one's caps. Humph! I do believe that every bone in my body is—ah! here's another cut, two inches at least, and into the bone of course, to judge from the flow of blood. I wonder how much blood I can afford to lose without being floored altogether. Such a country! I wonder how high I went. I felt as if I'd got above the moon. Hollo, Ralph! better?"

I sat up as he said this, and looked at him earnestly.

"My dear Peterkin, then you're not killed after all."

"Not quite, but pretty near. If it had not been for that friendly bush I should have fared worse. It broke my fall completely, and I really believe that my worst hurts are a few scratches. But how are *you*, Ralph? Yours was a much more severe case than mine. You should hold your gun tighter, man, when you fire without putting it to your shoulder."

"How? why? what do you mean?"

"Simply this, that in consequence of your reckless manner of holding your rifle, it came back with such a slap on your chest that it floored you."

"This, then, accounts for the pain I feel in it. But come," said I, rising and shaking my limbs to make sure that no bones were broken; "we have reason to be very thankful we have escaped so easily. I made sure that you were killed when I saw you flying through the air."

"I always had a species of cat-luck about me," replied Peterkin, with a smile. "But now let us cut off a bit o' this fellow to take back with us for Jack's supper."

With some difficulty we succeeded in cutting out the buffalo's tongue by the root, and carried it back to the village, where, after displaying it as an evidence of our prowess, we had it cooked for supper.

The slight hurts that we had received at the time of this adventure were speedily cured, and about two weeks after that we were all well enough to resume our journey.

CHAPTER TEN
Water Appreciated-Destructive Files, Etcetera.

Our first start from the village where we had been entertained so hospitably and so long was productive of much amusement to ourselves and to the natives.

We had determined to accept of three oxen from the chief, and to ride these when we felt fatigued; but we thought it best to let our native porters carry our baggage on their shoulders, as they had hitherto done.

When the animals were led up to our hut, we could not refrain from laughing. They were three sturdy-looking dark-skinned oxen, with wicked-looking black eyes and very long horns.

"Now, Jack, do you get up first," said Peterkin, "and show us what we are to expect."

"Nay, lad; I am still entitled to be considered an invalid: so you must get up first, and not only so, but you must try them all, in order that I may be enabled to select the quietest."

"Upon my word, you are becoming despotic in your sickness, and you forget that it is but a short time since I came down from a journey to the sky, and that my poor bones are still tender. But here goes. I was born to be victimised, so I submit to the decrees of Fate."

Peterkin went up to one of the oxen and attempted to mount it; but the animal made a demonstration of an intention to gore him, and obstinately objected to this.

"Hold him tight, Mak," he cried, after several futile attempts to mount. "I was always good at leap-frog when a schoolboy; see if I don't bring my powers into play now."

So saying, he went behind the ox, took a short race and sprang with the agility of a monkey over its tail on to its back! The ox began to kick and sidle and plunge heavily on receiving this unexpected load; but its rider held on well, until it took it into its head to dart under a neighbouring tree, the lower branches of which swept him off and caused him to fall with a heavy plump to the ground.

"I told you so," he cried, rising with a rueful face, and rubbing himself as he limped forward. However, his pain was more than half affected, for the next minute he was on the back of another ox. This one also proved restive, but not so much so as the first. The third was a very quiet animal, so Jack appropriated it as his charger.

Having bade adieu to the chief and rubbed noses with him and with several of our friends in the village, we all three got upon our novel steeds and set forth. But we had not got away from the village more than a mile when the two restive oxen began to display a firm determination to get rid of their intolerable burden. Mine commenced to back and sidle, and Peterkin's made occasional darts forward, and then stopping suddenly, refused to budge a step. We lost all patience at last, and belaboured them soundly with twigs, the effect of which was to make them advance rather slowly, and evidently under protest.

"Look out for branches," cried Peterkin as we came up to a narrow belt of wood.

I had scarcely time to raise my head when I was swept off my seat and hurled to the ground by a large branch. Peterkin's attention was drawn to me, and his ox, as if aware of the fact, seized the opportunity to swerve violently to one side, thereby throwing its rider off. Both animals gave a bellow, as of triumph, erected their tails, and ran away. They were soon recaptured, however, by our negroes; and mounting once more, we belaboured them well and continued our journey. In course of time they became more reconciled to their duties; but I cannot say that I ever came to enjoy such riding, and all of us ultimately agreed that it was a most undesirable thing to journey on ox-back.

Thus we commenced our journey over this desert or plain of Africa, and at the end of many weeks found ourselves approaching that part of the country near the equator in which the gorilla is said to dwell. On the way we had many adventures, some of an amusing, some of a dangerous character, and I made many additions to my collection of animals, besides making a number of valuable and interesting notes in my journal; but all this I am constrained to pass over, in order to introduce my reader to those regions in which some of our most wonderful adventures occurred.

One or two things, however, I must not omit to mention.

In passing over the desert we suffered much from want of water. Frequently the poor oxen had to travel two or three days without tasting a drop, and their distress was so great that we more than once thought of turning them adrift at the first good watering-place we should come to, and proceed, as formerly, on foot; for we had all recovered our wonted vigour, and were quite capable of standing the fatigues of the journey as well as our men. But several times we had found the country destitute of game, and were reduced to the point of starvation; so we continued to keep the oxen, lest we should require them for food.

On one occasion we were wending our way slowly along the bed of what in the rainy season would become a large river, but which was now so thoroughly dry that we could not find even a small pool in which the oxen might slake their thirst. They had been several days absolutely without a drop of water, while we were reduced to a mouthful or two per man in the day. As we could not exist much longer without the life-giving fluid, Jack dismounted, and placing the load of one of the men on the ox's back, sent him off in advance to look for water. We had that morning seen the footprints of several animals which are so fond of water that they are never found at any great distance from some spot where it may be found. We therefore felt certain of falling in with it ere long.

About two hours afterwards our negro returned, saying that he had discovered a pool of rain-water, and showing the marks of mud on his knees in confirmation of the truth of what he said.

"Ask him if there's much of it, Mak," said Jack, as we crowded eagerly round the man.

"Hims say there be great plenty ob it —'nuff to tumble in."

Gladdened by this news we hastened forward. The oxen seemed to have scented the water from afar, for they gradually became more animated, and quickened their pace of their own accord, until they at last broke into a run. Peterkin and I soon outstripped our party, and quite enjoyed the gallop.

"There it is," cried my comrade joyfully, pointing to a gleaming pond in a hollow of the plain not two hundred yards off.

"Hurrah!" I shouted, unable to repress my delight at the sight.

The oxen rushed madly forward, and we found that they were away with us. No pulling at our rope-bridles had any effect on them. My companion, foreseeing what would happen, leaped nimbly off just as he reached the margin of the pond. I being unable to collect my thoughts for the emergency, held on. My steed rushed into the water up to the neck, and stumbling as he did so, threw me into the middle of the pond, out of which I scrambled amidst the laughter of the whole party, who came up almost as soon as the oxen, so eager were they to drink.

After appeasing our own thirst we stood looking at the oxen, and it really did our hearts good to see the poor thirsty creatures enjoy themselves so thoroughly. They stood sucking in the water as if they meant to drink up the whole pond, half shutting their eyes, which became mild and amiable in appearance under the influence of extreme satisfaction. Their sides, which had been for the last two days in a state of collapse, began to swell, and at last were distended to such an extent that they seemed as if ready to burst. In point of fact the creatures were actually as full as they could hold; and when at length they dragged themselves slowly, almost unwillingly, out of the pool, any sudden jerk or motion caused some of the water to run out of their mouths!

Some time after that we were compelled to part with our poor steeds, in consequence of their being bitten by an insect which caused their death.

This destructive fly, which is called tsetse, is a perfect scourge in some parts of Africa. Its bite is fatal to the horse, ox, and dog, yet, strange to say, it is not so to man or to wild animals. It is not much larger than the common house-fly, and sucks the blood in the same manner as the mosquito, by means of a proboscis with which it punctures the skin. When man is bitten by it, no more serious evil than slight itching of the part follows. When the ox is bitten no serious effect follows at first, but a few days afterwards a running takes place at the eyes and nose, swellings appear under the jaw and on other parts of the body, emaciation quickly follows, even although the animal may continue to graze, and after a long illness, sometimes of many weeks, it dies in a state of extreme exhaustion.

The tsetse inhabits certain localities in great numbers, while other places in the immediate neighbourhood are entirely free. Those natives, therefore, who have herds of cattle avoid the dangerous regions most carefully; yet, despite their utmost care, they sometimes come unexpectedly on the *habitat* of this poisonous fly, and lose the greater part of their cattle.

When our poor oxen were bitten and the fatal symptoms began to appear, we knew that their fate was sealed; so we conducted them into a pleasant valley on which we chanced to alight, where there was plenty of grass and water, and there we left them to die.

Another incident occurred to us in this part of our journey which is worthy of record.

One day Peterkin and I had started before our party with our rifles, and had gone a considerable distance in advance of them, when we unexpectedly came upon a band of natives who were travelling in an opposite direction. Before coming up with their main body, we met with one of their warriors, who came upon us suddenly in the midst of a wooded spot, and stood rooted to the earth with fear and amazement; at which, indeed, we were not much surprised, for as he had probably never seen white faces before, he must have naturally taken us for ghosts or phantoms of some sort.

He was armed with shield and spear, but his frame was paralysed with terror. He seemed to have no power to use his weapons. At first we also stood in silent wonder, and returned his stare with interest; but after a few seconds the comicality of the man's appearance tickled Peterkin so much that he burst into a fit of laughter, which had the effect of increasing the terror of the black warrior to such a degree that his teeth began to chatter in his head. He actually grew livid in the face. I never beheld a more ghastly countenance.

"I say, Ralph," observed my companion, after recovering his composure, "we must try to show this fellow that we don't mean him any harm, else he'll die of sheer fright."

Before I could reply, or any steps could be taken towards this end, his party came up, and we suddenly found ourselves face to face with at least a hundred men, all of whom were armed with spears or bows and arrows. Behind them came a large troop of women and children. They were all nearly naked, and I observed that they were blacker in the skin than most of the negroes we had yet met with.

"Here's a pretty mess," said Peterkin, looking at me.

"What is to be done?" said I.

"If we were to fire at them, I'd lay a bet they'd run away like the wind," replied my comrade; "but I can't bear to think of shedding human blood if it can possibly be avoided."

While we spoke, the negroes, who stood about fifty yards distant from us, were consulting with each other in eager voices, but never for a moment taking their eyes off us.

"What say you to fire over their heads?" I suggested.

"Ready, present, then," cried Peterkin, with a recklessness of manner that surprised me.

We threw forward our rifles, and discharged them simultaneously.

The effect was tremendous. The whole band-men, women, and children-uttered an overwhelming shriek, and turning round, fled in mad confusion from the spot. Some of the warriors turned, however, ere they had gone far, and sent a shower of spears at us, one of which went close past my cheek.

"We have acted rashly, I fear," said I, as we each sought shelter behind a tree.

No doubt the savages construed this act of ours into an admission that we did not consider ourselves invulnerable, and plucked up courage accordingly, for they began again to advance towards us, though with hesitation. I now saw that we should be compelled to fight for our lives, and deeply regretted my folly in advising Peterkin to fire over their heads; but happily, before blood was drawn on either side, Makarooroo and Jack came running towards us. The former shouted an explanation of who and what we were to our late enemies, and in less than ten minutes we were mingling together in the most amicable manner.

We found that these poor creatures were starving, having failed to procure any provisions for some time past, and they were then on their way to another region in search of game. We gave them as much of our provisions as we could spare, besides a little tobacco, which afforded them inexpressible delight. Then rubbing noses with the chief, we parted and went on our respective ways.

CHAPTER ELEVEN
How We Met With Our First Gorilla, And How We Served Him.

"It never rains but it pours," is a true proverb. I have often noticed, in the course of my observations on sublunary affairs, that events seldom come singly. I have often gone out fishing for trout in the rivers of my native land, day after day, and caught nothing, while at other times I have, day after day, returned home with my basket full.

As it was in England, so I found it in Africa. For many days after our arrival in the gorilla country, we wandered about without seeing a single creature of any kind. Lions, we ascertained, were never found in those regions, and we were told that this was in consequence of their having been beaten off the field by gorillas. But at last, after we had all, severally and collectively, given way to despair, we came upon the tracks of a gorilla, and from that hour we were kept constantly on the *qui vive*, and in the course of the few weeks we spent in that part of the country, we "bagged," as Peterkin expressed it, "no end of gorillas" —great and small, young and old.

I will never forget the powerful sensations of excitement and anxiety that filled our breasts when we came on the first gorilla footprint. We felt as no doubt Robinson Crusoe did when he discovered the footprint of a savage in the sand. Here at last was the indubitable evidence of the existence and presence of the terrible animal we had come so far to see. Here was the footstep of that creature about which we had heard so many wonderful stories, whose existence the civilised world had, up to within a very short time back, doubted exceedingly, and in regard to which, even now, we knew comparatively very little.

Makarooroo assured us that he had hunted this animal some years ago, and had seen one or two at a distance, though he had never killed one, and stated most emphatically that the footprint before us, which happened to be in a soft sandy spot, was undoubtedly caused by the foot of a gorilla.

Being satisfied on this head, we four sat down in a circle round the footprint to examine it, while our men stood round about us, looking on with deep interest expressed in their dark faces.

"At last!" said I, carefully brushing away some twigs that partly covered the impression.

"Ay, at last!" echoed Jack, while his eyes sparkled with enthusiasm.

"Ay," observed Peterkin, "and a pretty big *last* he must require, too. I shouldn't like to be his shoemaker. What a thumb, or a toe. One doesn't know very well which to call it."

"I wonder if it's old?" said I.

"As old as the hills," replied Peterkin; "at least 50 I would judge from its size."

"You mistake me. I mean that I wonder whether the footprint is old, or if it has been made recently."

"Him's quite noo," interposed our guide.

"How d'ye know, Mak?"

"'Cause me see."

"Ay; but what do you see that enables you to form such an opinion?"

"O Ralph, how can you expect a nigger to understand such a sentence as that?" said Jack, as he turned to Mak and added, "What do you see?"

"Me see one leetle stick brok in middel. If you look to him you see him white and clean. If hims was old, hims would be mark wid rain and dirt."

"There!" cried Peterkin, giving me a poke in the side, "see what it is to be a minute student of the small things in nature. Make a note of it, Ralph."

I did make a note of it mentally on the spot, and then proposed that we should go in search of the gorilla without further delay.

We were in the midst of a dark gloomy wood in the neighbourhood of a range of mountains whose blue serrated peaks rose up into the clouds. Their sides were partly clothed with wood. We were travelling-not hunting-at the time we fell in with the track above referred to, so we immediately ordered the men to encamp where they were, while we should go after the gorilla, accompanied only by Mak, whose nerves we could depend on.

Shouldering our trusty rifles, and buckling tight the belts of our heavy hunting-knives, we sallied forth after the manner of American Indians, in single file, keeping, as may well be supposed, a sharp lookout as we went along. The fact was that long delay, frequent disappointment, and now the near prospect of success, conspired together to fill us with a species of nervous excitement that caused us to start at every sound.

The woods here were pretty thick, but they varied in their character so frequently that we were at one time pushing slowly among dense, almost impenetrable underwood, at another walking briskly over small plains which were covered in many places with large boulders. It was altogether a gloomy, savage-looking country, and seemed to me well suited to be the home of so dreadful an animal. There were few animals to be seen here. Even birds were scarce, and a few chattering monkeys were almost the only creatures that broke the monotonous silence and solitude around us.

"What a dismal place!" said Peterkin, in a low tone. "I feel as if we had got to the fag-end of the world, as if we were about plunging into ancient chaos."

"It is, indeed," I replied, "a most dreary region. I think that the gorillas will not be disturbed by many hunters with white faces."

"There's no saying," interposed Jack. "I should not wonder, now, if you, Ralph, were to go home and write a book detailing our adventures in these parts, that at least half the sportsmen of England would be in Africa next year, and the race of gorillas would probably become extinct."

"If the sportsmen don't come out until I write a book about them, I fear the gorillas will remain undisturbed for all time to come."

At that time, reader, I was not aware of the extreme difficulty that travellers experience in resisting the urgent entreaties of admiring and too partial friends!

Presently we came to a part of the forest where the underwood became so dense that we could scarcely make our way through it at all, and here we began for the first time to have some clearer conception of the immense power of the creature we were in pursuit of; for in order to clear its way it had torn down great branches of the trees, and in one or two places had seized young trees as thick as a man's arm, and snapped them in two as one would snap a walking-cane.

Following the track with the utmost care for several miles, we at length came to a place where several huge rocks lay among the trees. Here, while we were walking along in silence, Makarooroo made a peculiar noise with his tongue, which we knew meant that he had discovered something worthy of special attention, so we came to an abrupt pause and looked at him.

"What is it, Mak?" inquired Jack.

The guide put his finger on his mouth to impose silence, and stood in a listening attitude with his eyes cast upon the ground, his nostrils distended, and every muscle of his dusky frame rigid, as if he were a statue of black marble. We also listened attentively, and presently heard a sound as of the breaking of twigs and branches.

"Dat am be gorilla," said the guide, in a low whisper.

We exchanged looks of eager satisfaction.

"How shall we proceed, Mak?" inquired Jack.

"We mus' go bery slow, dis way," said the guide, imitating the process of walking with extreme caution. "No break leetle stick. If you break leetle stick hims go right away."

Promising Mak that we would attend to his injunctions most carefully, we desired him to lead the way, and in a few minutes after came so near to where the sound of breaking sticks was going on that we all halted, fearing that we should scare the animal away before we could get a sight of it amongst the dense underwood.

"What can he be doing?" said I to the guide, as we stood looking at each other for a few seconds uncertain how to act.

"Him's breakin' down branches for git at him's feed, s'pose."

"Do you see that?" whispered Peterkin, as he pointed to an open space among the bushes. "Isn't that a bit o' the hairy brute?"

"It looks like it," replied Jack eagerly.

"Cluck!" ejaculated Makarooroo, making a peculiar noise with his tongue. "Dat him. Blaze away!"

"But it may not be a mortal part," objected Peterkin. "He might escape if only wounded."

"Nebber fear. Hims come at us if hims be wound. Only we mus' be ready for him."

"All ready," said Jack, cocking both barrels of his rifle. —"Now, Peterkin, a good aim. If he comes here he shall get a quietus."

All this was said in the lowest possible whispers. Peterkin took a steady aim at the part of the creature that was visible, and fired.

I have gone through many wild adventures since then. I have heard the roar of the lion and the tiger in all circumstances, and the laugh of the hyena, besides many other hideous sounds, but I never in all my life listened to anything that in any degree approached in thundering ferocity the appalling roar that burst upon our ears immediately after that shot was fired. I can compare it to nothing, for nothing I ever heard was like it. If the reader can conceive a human fiend endued with a voice far louder than that of the lion, yet retaining a little of the intonation both of the man's voice and of what we should suppose a fiend's voice to be, he may form some slight idea of what that roar was. It is impossible to describe it. Perhaps Mak's expression in regard to it is the most emphatic and truthful: it was absolutely "*horriboble!*" Every one has heard a sturdy, well-grown little boy, when being thrashed, howling at the very top of his bent. If one can conceive of a full-grown male giant twenty feet high pouring forth his whole soul and voice with similarly unrestrained fervour, he may approximate to a notion of it.

And it was not uttered once or twice, but again and again, until the whole woods trembled with it, and we felt as if our ears could not endure more of it without the tympanums being burst.

For several moments we stood motionless with our guns ready, expecting an immediate attack, and gazing with awe, not unmingled-at least on my part-with fear, at the turmoil of leaves and twigs and broken branches that was going on round the spot where the monster had been wounded.

"Come," cried Jack at length, losing patience and springing forward; "if he won't attack us we must attack him."

We followed close on his heels, and next moment emerged upon a small and comparatively open space, in the midst of which we found the gorilla seated on the ground, tearing up the earth with its hands, grinning horribly and beating its chest, which sent forth a loud hollow sound as if it were a large drum. We saw at once that both its thighs had been broken by Peterkin's shot.

Of all the hideous creatures I had ever seen or heard of, none came up in the least degree to this. Apart altogether from its gigantic size, this monster was calculated to strike terror into the hearts of beholders simply by the expression of its visage, which was quite satanic. I could scarcely persuade myself that I was awake. It seemed as if I were gazing on one of those hideous creatures one beholds when oppressed with nightmare.

But we had little time to indulge in contemplation, for the instant the brute beheld us it renewed its terrible roar, and attempted to spring up; but both its legs at once gave way, and it fell with a passionate growl, biting the earth, and twisting and tearing bunches of twigs and leaves in its fury. Suddenly it rushed upon us rapidly by means of its fore legs or arms.

"Look out, Jack!" we cried in alarm.

Jack stood like a rock and deliberately levelled his rifle. Even at this moment of intense excitement I could not help marvelling at the diminutive appearance of my friend when contrasted with the gorilla. In height, indeed, he was of course superior, and would have been so had the gorilla been able to stand erect, but his breadth of shoulder and chest, and his length and size of arm, were strikingly inferior. Just as the monster approached to within three yards of him, Jack sent a ball into its chest, and the king of the African woods fell dead at our feet!

It is impossible to convey in words an idea of the gush of mingled feelings that filled our breasts as we stood beside and gazed at the huge carcass of our victim. Pity at first predominated in my heart, then I felt like an accomplice to a murder, and then an exulting sensation of joy at having obtained a specimen of one of the rarest animals in the world overwhelmed every other feeling.

The size of this animal-and we measured him very carefully-was as follows: —

Height, 5 feet 6 inches; girth of the chest, 4 feet 2 inches; spread of its arms, 7 feet 2 inches. Perhaps the most extraordinary measurement was that of the great thumb of its hind foot, which was 5 and a half inches in circumference. When I looked at this and at the great bunches of hard muscles which composed its brawny chest and arms, I could almost believe in the stories told by the natives of the tremendous feats of strength performed by the gorilla. The body of this brute was covered with grey hair, but the chest was bare and covered with tough skin, and its face was intensely black. I shuddered as I looked upon it, for there was something terribly human-like about it, despite the brutishness of its aspect.

"Now, I'll tell you what we shall do," said Jack, after we had completed our examination of the gorilla. "We will encamp where we are for the night, and send Makarooroo back to bring our fellows up with the packs, so that you, Ralph, will be able to begin the work of skinning and cleaning the bones at once. What say you?"

"Agreed, with all my heart," I replied.

"Well, then," observed Peterkin, "here goes for a fire, to begin with, and then for victuals to continue with. By the way, what say you to a gorilla steak? I'm told the niggers eat him. —Don't they, Mak?"

"Yis, massa, dey does. More dan dat, de niggers in dis part ob country eat mans."

"Eat mans!" echoed Peterkin in horror.

"Yis, eat mans, and womins, an' childerdens."

"Oh, the brutes! But I don't believe you, Mak. What are the villains called?"

"Well, it not be easy for say what dem be called. Miss'naries calls dem canibobbles."

"Ho!" shouted Peterkin, "canibobbles? eh! well done. Mak, I must get you to write a new dictionary; I think it would pay!"

"It won't pay to go on talking like this, though," observed Jack. "Come, hand me the axe. I'll fell this tree while you strike a light, Peterkin. —Be off with you, Mak. —As for Ralph, we must leave him to his note-book; I see there is no chance of getting him away from his beloved gorilla till he has torn its skin from its flesh, and its flesh from its bones."

Jack was right. I had now several long hours' work before me, which I knew could not be delayed, and to which I applied myself forthwith most eagerly, while my comrades lit the fire and prepared the camp, and Makarooroo set off on his return journey to bring up the remainder of our party.

That night, while I sat by the light of the camp-fire toiling at my task, long after the others had retired to rest, I observed the features of Jack and Peterkin working convulsively, and their hands clutching nervously as they slept, and I smiled to think of the battles with gorillas which I felt assured they must be fighting, and the enormous "bags" they would be certain to tell of on returning from the realms of dreamland to the regions of reality.

CHAPTER TWELVE
Peterkin's Schoolday Reminiscences.

The day following that on which we shot our first gorilla was a great and memorable day in our hunting career in Africa, for on that day we saw no fewer than ten gorillas: two females, seven young ones-one of which was a mere baby gorilla in its mother's arms-and a huge lone male, or bachelor gorilla, as Peterkin called him. And of these we killed four-three young ones, and the old bachelor. I am happy to add that I saved the lives of the infant gorilla and its mother, as I shall presently relate.

The portion of country through which we travelled this day was not so thickly wooded as that through which we had passed the day before, so that we advanced more easily, and enjoyed ourselves much as we went along. About the middle of the day we came to a spot where there were a number of wild vines, the leaves of which are much liked by the gorilla, so we kept a sharp lookout for tracks.

Soon we came upon several, as well as broken branches and twigs, in which were observed the marks of teeth, showing that our game had been there. But we passed from the wood where these signs were discovered, out upon an open plain of considerable extent. Here we paused, undecided as to whether we should proceed onward or remain there to hunt.

"I vote for advancing," said Peterkin, "for I observe that on the other side of this plain the wood seems very dense, and it is probable that we may find Mister Gorilla there. —What think you, Mak?"

The guide nodded in reply.

"I move," said Jack, "that as the country just where we stand is well watered by this little brook, besides being picturesque and beautiful to look upon, we should encamp where we are, and leaving our men to guard the camp, cross this plain-we three take Mak along with us, and spend the remainder of the day in hunting."

"I vote for the amendment," said I.

"Then the amendment carries," cried Jack, "for in all civilised societies most votes always carry; and although we happen to be in an uncivilised region of the earth, we must not forget that we are civilised hunters. The vote of two hunters ought certainly to override that of one hunter."

Peterkin demurred to this at once, on the ground that it was unfair.

"How so?" said I.

"In the first place," replied he, looking uncommonly wise, and placing the point of his right finger in the palm of his left hand —"in the first place, I do not admit your premises, and therefore I object to your conclusion. I do not admit that in civilised societies most votes carry; on the contrary, it too frequently happens that, in civilised societies, motions are made, seconded, discussed, and carried without being put to the vote at all; often they are carried without being made, seconded, or discussed-as when a bottle-nosed old gentleman in office chooses to ignore the rights of men, and carry everything his own way. Neither do I admit that we three are civilised hunters; for although it is true that I am, it is well-known that you, Ralph, are a philosopher, and Jack is a gorilla. Therefore I object to your conclusion that your two votes should carry; for you cannot but admit that the vote of one hunter ought to override that of two such creatures, which would not be the case were there an equality existing between us."

"Peterkin," said I, "there is fallacy in your reasoning."

"Can you show it?" said he.

"No; the web is too much ravelled to disentangle."

"Not at all," cried Jack; "I can unravel it in a minute, and settle the whole question by proving that there does exist an equality between us; for it is well-known, and generally admitted by all his friends, and must be acknowledged by himself, that Peterkin is an ass."

"Even admitting that," rejoined Peterkin, "it still remains to be proved that a philosopher, a gorilla, and an ass are equal. Of course I believe the latter to be superior to both the former animals; but in consideration of the lateness of the hour, and the able manner in which you have discussed this subject, I beg to withdraw my motion, and to state that I am ready to accompany you over the plain as soon as you please."

At this point our conversation was interrupted by the shriek of a small monkey, which had been sitting all the time among the branches of the tree beneath which we stood.

"I declare it has been listening to us," cried Peterkin.

"Yes, and is shouting in triumph at your defeat," added Jack.

As he spoke, Makarooroo fired, and the monkey fell to the ground almost at our feet.

"Alas! it has paid a heavy price for its laugh," said Peterkin, in a tone of sadness.

The poor thing was mortally wounded; so much so that it could not even cry. It looked up with a very piteous expression in our faces. Placing its hand on its side, it coughed once or twice, then lying down on its back and stretching itself out quite straight, it closed its eyes and died.

I never could bear to shoot monkeys. There was something so terribly human-like in their sufferings, that I never could witness the death of one without feeling an almost irresistible inclination to weep. Sometimes, when short of provisions, I was compelled to shoot monkeys, but I did so as seldom as possible, and once I resolved to go supperless to bed rather than shoot one whose aspect was so sad and gentle that I had not the heart to kill it. My companions felt as I did in this matter, and we endeavoured to restrain Makarooroo as much as possible; but he could not understand our feelings, and when he got a chance of a shot, almost invariably forgot our injunctions to let monkeys alone unless we were absolutely ill off for food. To do him justice, however, I must add that we were at this particular time not overburdened with provisions, and the men were much pleased to have the prospect of a roast monkey for supper.

Having given our men a little tobacco, a gift which caused their black faces to beam with delight, we shouldered our rifles and set off across the plain towards the thick wood, which was not more than five miles distant, if so much.

It was a beautiful scene, this plain with its clumps of trees scattered over it like islands in a lake, and its profusion of wild flowers. The weather, too, was delightful-cooler than usual-and there was a freshness in the air which caused us to feel light of heart, while the comparative shortness of the grass enabled us to proceed on our way with light steps. As we walked along for some time in silence, I thought upon the goodness and the provident care of the Creator of our world; for during my brief sojourn in Africa I had observed many instances of the wonderful exactness with which things in nature were suited to the circumstances in which they were placed, and the bountiful provision that was made everywhere for man and beast. Yet I must confess I could not help wondering, and felt very much perplexed, when I thought of the beautiful scenes in the midst of which I moved being inhabited only by savage men, who seemed scarcely to appreciate the blessings by which they were surrounded, and who violated constantly all the laws of Him by whom they were created. My meditations were interrupted by Jack saying —

"I cannot help wondering why that poor monkey kept so still all the time we were talking. One would think that it should have been frightened away just as we came under the tree."

"I have no doubt," said I, "that although of course it could not understand what we said, yet it was listening to us."

"I'm not so certain that it did not understand," observed Peterkin. "You know that sailors believe that monkeys could speak if they chose, but they don't for fear that they should be made to work!"

"Well, whatever truth there may be in that, of this I am certain, they are the most deceptive creatures that exist."

"I don't agree with you," rejoined Peterkin. "It's my opinion that little boys are the greatest deceivers living."

"What! *all* little boys!" exclaimed Jack.

"No, not all. I have not so bad an opinion of the race as that. I've had a good deal to do with boys during my naval career, and among the middies of her Majesty's navy I have met with as fine little chaps as one would wish to see-regular bricks, afraid of nothing (except of doing anything that would be thought sneaking or shabby), ready to dare anything-to attack a seventy-four single-handed in a punt or a bumboat if need be; nevertheless, I've met boys, and a good many of them too, who would beat all the monkeys in Africa at sneaking and deceiving. I remember one rascal, who went to the same school with me, who was a wonderfully plausible deceiver. I can't help laughing yet when I think of the curious way he took to free himself of the restraint of school."

"How was it?" cried Jack; "tell us about it-do."

"Well, you must know," began Peterkin, "that this boy was what Jack tars would call a 'great, stupid, lubberly fellow.' He was a very fair-haired, white eyelashed sort of chap, that seemed to grow at such a rate that he was always too big for his clothes, and showed an unusual amount of wrist and ankle even for a boy. Most people who met him thought him a very stupid boy at first; but those who came to know him well found that he was rather a sharp, clever fellow, but a remarkably shy dog. We called him Doddle.

"His mother was a widow, and he was an only son, and had been spoiled, of course, so that he was not put to school till he was nearly twelve years of age. He had been at several schools before coming to ours, but had been deemed by each successive schoolmaster a hopeless imbecile. And he was so mischievous that they advised his poor mother to take him away and try if she could not instil a little knowledge into him herself. The old lady was a meek, simple body, and quite as stupid as her hopeful son appeared to be. Hearing that our master was a sharp fellow, and somewhat noted as a good manager of obstreperous boys, she brought him to our school as a last resource, and having introduced him to the master, went her way.

"It was near the end of play-hour when she brought him, so he was turned out into the playground, and stood there looking like a mongrel cur turned unexpectedly into a kennel of pointers.

"'Well, Doddle,' said one of the sixth-form boys, going up to him and addressing him for the first time by the name which stuck to him ever after, 'where did *you* grow; and who cut you down and tossed you in here?'

"'Eh?' said Doddle, looking sheepish.

"'What's your name, man, and where did you come from, and how old are you, and how far can you jump without a race? and in fact I want to know all about you.'

"'My name's Tommy Thompson,' replied the boy, 'and I —'

"At that moment the bell rang, and the remainder of his sentence was drowned in the rush of the rest of us to the classroom.

"When all was quiet the master called Doddle up, and said, 'Well, Thompson, my boy, your mother tells me you have learned a little grammar and a little arithmetic. I hope that we shall instil into you a good deal of those branches of learning, and of many others besides, ere long. Let me hear what you can do.'

"'I can play hockey and dumps,' began Doddle, in a sing-song tone, and with the most un-commonly innocent expression of visage; 'an' I can —'

"'Stay, boy,' interrupted the master, smiling; 'I do not want to know what you can *play* at. Keep silence until I put a few questions to you. What is English grammar?'

"'Eh?'

"'Don't say "Eh!" When you fail to understand me, say "Sir?" interrogatively. What is English grammar?'

"'It's a book.'

"The master looked over the top of his spectacles at Doddle in surprise.

"'English grammar,' said he, slowly, and with a slight touch of sternness, 'is indeed contained in a book; but I wish to know what it teaches.'

"'Eh? —a —I mean sir interrogatively.'

"'What does English grammar *teach*, boy?' cried the master angrily.

"Doddle laid hold of his chin with his right hand, and looked down at the floor with an air of profound thought, saying slowly, in an undertone to himself, 'What-does-English-grammar-teach-teach-grammar-teach? It-teaches —a —I don't know *what* it teaches. Perhaps you can tell me, sir?'

"He looked up, and uttered the last sentence with such an air of blank humility that we all had to cram our pocket handkerchiefs into our mouths to prevent a universal explosion. The master looked over his spectacles again at Doddle with an expression of unutterable amazement. We looked on with breathless interest, not unmingled with awe, for we expected some awful outbreak on the part of the master, who seemed quite unable to make up his mind what to do or say, but continued to stare for nearly a minute at the boy, who replied to the stare with a humble, idiotic smile.

"Suddenly the master said sharply, 'How much are seven times nine?'

"'Five hundred and forty-two and a half,' answered Doddle, without a moment's hesitation.

"The master did not look surprised this time, but he took Doddle by the shoulder, and drawing him towards his chair, looked earnestly into his face. Then he said quietly, 'That will do, Thompson; go to your seat.'

"This was all that occurred at that time. During a whole week the master tried by every means to get Doddle to learn something; but Doddle could learn nothing. Yet he seemed to try. He pored over his book, and muttered with his lips, and sometimes looked anxiously up at the ceiling, with an expression of agony on his face that seemed to indicate a tremendous mental effort. Every species of inducement was tried, and occasionally punishment was resorted to. He was kept in at play-hours, and put in a corner during school-hours; and once, the master having lost patience with him, he was flogged. But it was all one to Doddle. All the methods tried proved utterly unavailing. He could not be got to acquire a single lesson, and often gave such remarkable answers that we all believed him to be mad.

"On the Monday forenoon of his second week at the school, the master called him up again for examination.

"'Now, Thompson,' he began, 'you have been a long time over that lesson; let us see how much of it you have learned. What is etymology?'

"'Etymology,' answered Doddle, 'is-is-an irregular pronoun.'

"'Boy!' cried the master sternly.

"'Please, sir,' pleaded Doddle, with deprecatory air, 'I —I suppose I was thinkin' o' one o' the *other* mologies, not the etty one.'

"'Ha!' ejaculated the master; 'well, tell me, how many parts of speech are there?'

"'Nineteen,' answered the boy, quite confidently.

"'Oh!' exclaimed the master, with a good deal of sarcasm in his tone; 'pray, name them.'

"In a very sing-song voice, and with an air of anxious simplicity, Doddle began, 'Article, noun, adjective, pronoun, verb, adverb, preposition, conjunction, interjection, outerjection, beginning with *ies* in the plural-as, baby, babies; lady, ladies; hady, hadies. Please, sir, isn't that last one a *bad* word?'

"'The boy is a lunatic!' muttered the master.

"The boys in the class were far past laughing now; we were absolutely stunned. The master seemed perplexed, for Doddle was gazing at him with a look of mild self-satisfaction.

"'I say, Peterkin,' whispered the boy next to me, 'as sure as you're alive that boy's shamming stupid.'

"Presently the master, who had been turning over the leaves of the grammar in a way that showed he was not conscious of what he was about, looked up, and said abruptly, 'What is a proper noun?'

"'A well-behaved one,' replied Doddle.

"At this the whole school tittered violently.

"'Silence, boys,' cried the master, in a tone that produced the desired effect so thoroughly that you might have heard a pin drop. Then laying his hand on Doddle's shoulder, he looked him full in the face, and said solemnly, 'Thompson, *I have found you out.* Go, sir, to your seat, and remain behind when the other boys go to the playground.'

"We observed that Doddle grew very red in the face as he came back to his seat, and during the rest of the hour he never once looked up.

"During the whole of the play-hour the master and he remained shut up together in the schoolroom. We never discovered what took place there between them, for neither threats nor coaxing could induce Doddle afterwards to speak on the subject; but from that day forward he was a changed boy. He not only learned his lessons, but he learned them well, and in the course of time became one of the best scholars in the school; so that although he never would admit it, we all came to the conclusion he had been shamming stupid-attempting to deceive the master into the belief that he was incurable, and thus manage to get rid of lessons and school altogether."

"A most remarkable boy," observed Jack when Peterkin concluded. "Certainly he beat the monkeys hollow."

"I wonder," said I, "what the master said or did to him that wrought such a mighty change."

"Don't know," replied Peterkin; "I suppose he told him that now he had found him out, he would flay him alive if he didn't give in, or something of that sort."

We had now entered the dark forest that edged the plain over which we had been walking, and further conversation on this subject was stopped, and the subject itself banished utterly from our minds by the loud, startling cry of a gorilla at no great distance from us.

"Hist! that's him," whispered Peterkin.

Instantly throwing our rifles into a position of readiness we pushed rapidly through the underwood in the direction whence the cry had come.

CHAPTER THIRTEEN
We get into "The Thick of it" —Great Success.

In a few minutes we came upon a female gorilla, which, all unconscious of our approach, was sitting at the foot of a vine, eating the leaves. There were four young ones beside her, engaged in the same occupation. In order to approach within shot of these, we had to creep on all fours through the brushwood with the greatest caution; for gorillas are sharp-sighted, and they have a remarkably acute sense of hearing, so that sometimes the breaking of a dry twig under one's foot is sufficient to alarm them.

We did not venture to speak even in whispers as we advanced; but by a sign Jack told Peterkin to take the lead. Jack himself followed. Makarooroo went next, and I brought up the rear.

In all our hunting expeditions we usually maintained this arrangement, where it was necessary. Peterkin was assigned the post of honour, because he was the best shot; Jack, being next best, came second; and I came last, not because our guide was a better shot than I, but because he was apt to get excited and to act rashly, so that he required looking after. I was at all times ready to lay hold of him by the hair of his woolly head, which, as he was nearly naked, was the only part of him that one could grasp with any degree of firmness.

After creeping in this manner for some distance, we got within range. Peterkin and Jack took aim and fired together. The old gorilla and one of the young ones fell instantly, and from their not struggling it was evident that they were shot quite dead. The guide and I fired immediately after, but only the one that I fired at fell. The other two ran off as fast as they could. Sometimes they ran on all fours; and I observed that while running in this fashion the hind legs passed between the arms, or, as it were, overstepped them. Occasionally, however, they rose and ran on their hind legs, in a stooping position.

When they did this I was particularly struck with their grotesque yet strong resemblance to man, and I do not think that I could at that time have prevailed upon myself to fire at them. I should have felt like a murderer. In truth, my thoughts and sensations just then were anything but agreeable. Nevertheless I was so excited by the chase that I am quite certain no one, to look at me, could have guessed what was passing in my mind.

We ran as rapidly as was possible in such a tangled forest, but we had no chance with the young gorillas. Peterkin at last ran himself out of breath. Stopping suddenly, he said, pantingly —

"It's —o' —no use whatever. Ho! dear me, my bellows are about exploded."

"We've no chance in a race with these hairy men," responded Jack, as he wiped the perspiration from his forehead. —"Why did you miss, Mak?"

"'Cause me no could hit, s'pose, massa."

"Very justly and modestly said," remarked Peterkin, with an approving nod. "'Tis a pity that men are not more generally animated with your spirit, Mak. Most people, when they do wrong or make a mistake, are too apt to try to excuse themselves."

"Yes," I added, with a laugh; "particularly when they blow the tails out of ostriches."

Peterkin shook his head, and said solemnly, "Ralph, my boy, don't take to joking. It don't agree with your constitution. You'll get ill if you do; and we can't afford to have you laid up on our hands in these out-o'-the-way regions."

"Come, now, let us back to the gorillas and secure them, lest their comrades carry them away," said Jack, turning to retrace our steps.

I was anxious to shoot as many gorillas as possible, in order that I might study the peculiarities of, and differences existing between, the different species-if there should be such-and between various individuals of the same species in all stages of development. I had made an elaborate examination of our first gorilla, and had taken copious notes in regard to it. Being desirous of doing the same as far as possible with the female and the two young ones we had just killed, I hastened back with my companions, and we fastened them securely among the branches of a conspicuous tree, intending to send out some of our men for them on our return to camp.

After this we resumed our search for more, but wandered about for several hours without meeting with any, although we observed recently-made footprints in abundance. We went as nearly as possible in a direction parallel to our camp, so that although we walked far we did not increase our distance from it to any great extent.

Presently Makarooroo made a peculiar "cluck" with his tongue, and we all came to an abrupt stand.

"What is't, Mak?"

The negro did not speak, but pointed eagerly in front of him, while the whites of his eyes seemed to sparkle with animation, and raised his gun to shoot.

We came up at the moment, and through an opening in the bushes saw what he was about to fire at. It was a female gorilla, with a baby gorilla in her arms. Fierce and hairy though she was, there was a certain air of tenderness about this mother, as she stroked and pawed her little one, that went straight to my heart, and caused me almost involuntarily to raise my arm and strike up the muzzle of Makarooroo's gun, at the moment he pulled the trigger. The consequence of this act was that the ball passed close over their heads. The report of the piece was instantly followed by a roar of consternation, mingled with rage, from the mother, and a shriek of terror from the baby, which again was immediately followed by a burst of laughter from us, as we beheld the little baby clasp its arms tightly round its mother, while she scampered wildly away from us.

Mak looked at me in amazement.

"What for you be do dat, massa?"

"To prevent you from committing murder, you rascal," said I, laughing. "Have you no feelings of natural pity or tenderness, that you could coolly aim at such a loving pair as that?"

The guide seemed a little put out by this remark, and went on reloading his gun without making reply. He had received enough of moral education at the mission stations to appreciate to some extent the feelings by which I was actuated; yet he had been so long accustomed and so early inured to harsh, unfeeling deeds, that the only idea that probably occurred to him on seeing this mother and her baby was, how near he could get to them in order to make sure of his aim.

"Ah! Ralph," said Jack, as we resumed our march, "you're too tender-hearted, my boy, for a hunter in Africa. There you've lost a chance of getting a gorilla baby, which you have been desiring so much the last few days, and which you might have stuck in a bottle of spirits, and sent home to be held up to universal admiration in Piccadilly, who knows."

"Ay, who knows?" echoed Peterkin. "I think it more probable, however, that it would be held up to universal ridicule. Besides, you forget that we have no spirits to preserve it in, except our own, which I admit are pretty high —a good deal overproof, considering the circumstances in which we are placed, and the unheard-of trials we have to endure. I'm sure I don't know what ever induced me to come, as a Scotch cousin of mine once said, 'so far frae my ain fireside' to endure trials. I do believe I've had more trials since I came to this outrageous land than all the criminals of the last century in England put together have had."

"Peterkin," said I seriously, "trials are a decided benefit and blessing to mankind —"

"Oh, of course," interrupted Peterkin; "but then, as you have often retorted upon me that I am of the monkey kind, I think that I could get on pretty well without them."

"My opinion is that they are good both for man and monkey," said Jack. "Just consider, now: it must have been a terrible trial for yon gorilla-mamma to hear a bullet pass within an inch of her head, and have her sweet little darling frightened almost out of its wits. Well, but just think of the state of satisfaction and rejoicing that she must be in now at having escaped. Had it not been for that trial she would now have been in her ordinary humdrum condition. I quite agree with Ralph that trials are really a blessing to us."

"I declare it is quite refreshing to hear that you 'agree' with anybody, Jack," rejoined Peterkin, in a tone of sarcasm. —"Perhaps Mr Rover will kindly enlarge on this most interesting subject, and give us the benefit of his wisdom. —And, Mak, you lump of ebony, do you keep a sharp lookout for gorillas in the meantime."

The guide, whose appreciation of fun was very considerable, said, "Yis, massa," grinned from ear to ear, in doing which he displayed a double row of tremendous white teeth, and pretended to be gazing earnestly among the bushes on either side in search of game, as he followed us. The moment we began to talk, however, I observed that he came close up behind, and listened with all his ears. If eager expansion indicates anything, I may add that he listened with all his eyes too!

"I shall have much pleasure in obliging you, Peterkin," said I, with a smile. "And in the first place —"

"O Ralph, I entreat you," interrupted Peterkin, "do not begin with a 'first place.' When men begin a discourse with that, however many intermediate places they may have to roam about in and enlarge on, they never have a place of any kind to terminate in, but go skimming along with a couple of dozen 'lastlies,' like a stone thrown over the surface of a pond, which, after the first two or three big and promising bounds, spends itself in an endless succession of twittering ripples, and finally sinks, somehow or nohow, into oblivion."

"Ahem! Shakespeare?" said Jack.

"Not at all," retorted Peterkin. "If anybody gave utterance to the sentiment before, it was Shelley, and he must have been on the sea-shore at the time with a crotchet, if not a crab, inside of him. —But pray go on, Ralph."

"Well, then, in the *first place*," I repeated with emphasis, whereat Peterkin sighed, "trials, when endured in a proper spirit, improve our moral nature and strengthen our hearts; the result of which is, that we are incited to more vigorous mental, and, by consequence, physical exertion, so that our nervous system is strengthened and our muscular powers are increased."

"Very well put, indeed," cried Peterkin. "Now, Ralph, try to forget your 'secondly,' omit your 'thirdly,' throw your 'fourthly' to the winds, and let your 'first place' be your 'last place,' and I'll give you credit for being a wise and effective speaker."

I gave in to my volatile friend at that time, as I saw that he would not allow me to go on, and, to say truth, I thought that I had exhausted my subject. But, after all, Peterkin did not require to be incited either to good thoughts or good actions. With all his exuberant fun and jocularity, he was at bottom one of the most earnest and attached friends I ever possessed. I have lived to know that his superficial lightness of character overlaid as deeply earnest and sympathetic a spirit as ever existed.

While we were thus conversing and wandering through the forest, we again came upon the fresh tracks of a gorilla, and from their great size we conjectured them to be those of a solitary male. It is a remarkable fact that among several of the lower animals we find specimens of that unnatural class of creatures which among men are termed old bachelors! Among the gorillas these *solitaires* are usually very large, remarkably fierce, uncommonly ugly, desperately vindictive, and peculiarly courageous; so much so that the natives hold them in special dread. It is of these wild men of the woods that their most remarkable and incredible stories are related.

"I don't think it's a gorilla at all," said Jack, stooping down to examine the footprints, which in that place were not very distinct; "I think an elephant or a rhinoceros must have passed this way."

"No, massa, them's not deep 'nuff for dat. Hims be a gorilla —a bery big one, too."

"Don't let us talk then, lest we should scare it," whispered Peterkin. "Lead the way, Mak; and mind, when we come close enough, move your great carcass out of the way and let me to the front."

"No, no, lad," said Jack. "Fair play. It's my turn now."

"So be it, my boy. But get on."

The tracks led us a considerable distance deeper into the wood, where the trees became so thick that only a species of twilight penetrated through them. To add to our discomfort, the light, we knew, would soon fail us altogether, as evening was drawing on apace, so we quickened our pace to a smart run.

We had not proceeded far when we were brought to a sudden standstill by one of those awfully loud and savage roars which we at once recognised as being that of a gorilla. It sounded like what we might term barking thunder, and from its intensity we were assured that our conjectures as to the creature being a solitary male gorilla were correct.

"Dat him, massas!" cried our guide quickly, at the same time cocking both barrels of his rifle. "Look hout! we no hab go after him no more. Him's come to fight us. Most always doos dot-de big ole gorilla."

We saw from the deeply earnest expression of the negro's countenance that he felt himself now to be in a very serious position, which would demand all his nerve and coolness.

Again the roar was repeated with terrible loudness and ferocity, and we heard something like the beating of a huge bass drum, mingled with the cracking of branches, as though some heavy creature were forcing its way through the underwood towards us.

We were all much impressed with this beating sound, and, as is often the case when men are startled by sounds which they cannot account for, we were more filled with the dread of this incomprehensible sound than of the gorilla which we knew was approaching us. We might, indeed, have asked an explanation from Makarooroo, but we were all too much excited and anxious just then to speak.

We drew together in a group.

Jack, who stood a little in front of us, having claimed the first shot, was whispering something about its being a pity there was so little light, when his voice was drowned by a repetition of the roar, so appalling that we each started, feeling as though it had been uttered close to our ears. Next instant the bushes in front of us were torn aside, and the most horrible monster I ever saw, or hope to set eyes on, stood before us.

He was evidently one of the largest-sized gorillas. In the gloom of the forest he appeared to us to be above six feet high. His jet-black visage was working with an expression of rage that was fearfully satanic. His eyes glared horribly. The tuft of hair on the top of his head rose and fell with the working of his low wrinkled forehead in a manner that peculiarly enhanced the ferocity of his expression. His great hairy body seemed much too large for his misshapen legs, and his enormous arms much too long for the body. It was with the fists at the ends of those muscular arms that he beat upon his bulky chest, and produced the unaccountable sounds above referred to. As he stood there uttering roar upon roar-apparently with the view of screwing up his courage to attack us-displaying his great canine teeth, and advancing slowly, step by step, I felt a mingling of powerful emotions such as I had never felt before in all my life, and such as cannot by any possibility be adequately described.

I felt quite self-possessed, however, and stood beside my comrades with my rifle ready and my finger on the trigger.

"Now!" whispered Peterkin. But Jack did not move.

"Now!" said he again, more anxiously, as the immense brute advanced, beating its chest and roaring, to within eight yards of us. Still Jack did not move, and I observed that it was as much as Peterkin could do to restrain himself.

As it took the next step, and appeared about to spring, Jack pulled the trigger. The cap alone exploded! Like a flash of light the other trigger was pulled; it also failed! some moisture must have got into the nipples in loading. Almost as quick as thought Jack hurled his piece at the brute with a force that seemed to me irresistible. The butt struck it full in the chest, but the rifle was instantly caught in its iron gripe. At that moment Peterkin fired, and the gorilla dropped like a stone, uttering a heavy groan as it fell prone with its face to the earth-not, however, before it had broken Jack's rifle across, and twisted the barrel as if it had been merely a piece of wire!

"That was a narrow escape, Jack," said I seriously, after we had recovered from the state of agitation into which this scene had thrown us.

"Indeed it was; and thanks to Peterkin's ever-ready rifle that it was an escape at all. What a monstrous brute!"

"Much bigger than the first one," said Peterkin. —"Where is your measure, Ralph? Out with it."

I pulled out my measure, and applying it to the prostrate carcass, found that the gorilla we had now shot was five feet eight inches in height, and proportionately large round the chest. It seemed to be a mass of sinews and hard muscles, and as I gazed at its massive limbs I could well imagine that it had strength sufficient to perform many, at least, if not all of the wonderful feats ascribed to it by the natives.

Shortly after the death of the gorilla, night settled down upon the scene, so we hurried back towards our camp, where we arrived much exhausted, yet greatly elated, by our successful day's sport.

I spent a great part of that night making entries in my note-book, by the light of our camp-fires, while my companions slept. And, truly, I enjoyed such quiet hours after days of so great mental and physical excitement. I observed, also, that the negroes enjoyed those seasons exceedingly. They sat round the blaze, talking and laughing, and recounting, I have no doubt, their feats of daring by flood and field; then, when they began to grow sleepy, they sat there swaying to and fro, making an occasional remark, until they became too sleepy even for that, when they began to nod and wink and start, and almost fell into the fire, so unwilling did they seem to tear themselves away from it, even for the distance of the few feet they required to draw back in order to enable them to lie down. At last nature could hold out no longer, and one by one they dropped back in their places.

I, too, began to nod at last, and to make entries in my note-book which were too disjointed at last to be comprehensible; so I finally resigned myself to repose, and to dream, as a matter of course.

CHAPTER FOURTEEN
Our Plans are Suddenly Altered-Wicked Designs Discovered.

For several weeks after this we wandered about in the woods searching for gorillas. We were very successful, and shot so many that I had the satisfaction of making elaborate notes of specimens of nearly all ages and kinds.

But an event was looming in the future which we little thought of, and which ultimately compelled us to abandon the gorilla country and retrace our steps towards the southern part of the continent.

One day we set out, as was our wont, to hunt for gorillas, accompanied only by our faithful follower Makarooroo. It chanced to be a lovely day, and the country through which we were passing was exceedingly beautiful, so that we found more pleasure at that time in conversing together on the beauties of nature and on the wonderful works of nature's God than in contemplating our chances of falling in with game.

"It's a splendid country," said Jack, as we walked along under the shade of some magnificent ebony trees. "I wish that it were inhabited by a Christian people. Perhaps this may be the case one of these days, but I don't think we shall live to see it."

"There's no saying, Jack," observed Peterkin. "Does not the Bible speak of a 'nation being born in a day?' Of course that must be figurative language; nevertheless it must mean something, and I incline to think that it means that there shall be a time when men shall flock rapidly, and in unusually great numbers, to the Saviour."

"It may be so," observed I, "but I have made up my mind on this point, that Christian people are not sufficiently awake to the terrible condition of the natives of countries such as this, or to the fact that they have much in their power to do for the amelioration of both their temporal and spiritual welfare. I, for one, will, if spared to return home, contribute more largely than I have been wont to do to the cause of missions."

"Talking of that," said Peterkin, "do you think it right to support the missions of other churches besides your own?"

"Do I think it right?" I exclaimed in surprise. "Of course I do. I think it one of the greatest evils that can befall a Christian, that he should become so narrow-minded as to give only to his own church, and think *only* of his own church's missions. Why, surely a soul saved, if a matter of rejoicing in heaven, ought to be a matter of joy on earth, without reference to the particular church which was the instrument used by the Holy Spirit for that end. I feel very strongly that all Christians who love our Saviour with deep sincerity must of necessity have a warm feeling towards His people in *all* churches. At any rate we ought to cultivate such a feeling."

"Who can these be?" cried Jack, stopping and pointing to some figures that appeared to be approaching us in the distance.

"They are negroes, at any rate," said I; "for they seem to be black, and are evidently naked."

"Warriors, too, if I mistake not. They have not yet observed us. Shall we hide and let them pass?"

Jack hesitated a moment, then leaping behind a bush, cried —

"Ay, 'tis well to be cautious when nothing is to be gained by daring. These fellows outnumber us, and war-parties are not to be trusted-at least not if these of Africa resemble those of North America."

"Hollo! there's a white man with them," cried Peterkin, as he peeped over the bushes behind which we were hid.

"You don't say so, eh? So there is. Come; we have nothing to fear from the party of a traveller. —What, Mak, you shake your head! What mean you?"

Makarooroo increased the shaking of his head, and said, "Me no know *dat*, massa. P'raps hab more to fear dan you tink."

"Oh, stuff! come along. Why, Mak, it seems as if gorilla-hunting had failed to improve your courage."

As Jack said this he stepped out from among the bushes and advanced to meet the strangers. Of course we all followed, and although we carried our rifles in a careless manner, as if we expected no evil, yet we held ourselves in readiness to take instant action if necessary.

The moment the negroes perceived us, they set up a great shout and brandished their spears and guns, but the voice of their leader was instantly heard commanding them to halt. They obeyed at once, and the European stranger advanced alone to meet us. As he drew near we observed that he was a splendid-looking man, nearly as large as Jack himself, with a handsome figure and a free, off-hand gait. But on coming closer we saw that his countenance, though handsome, wore a forbidding, stern expression.

"Dat am a slabe-dealer," whispered our guide, as the stranger came up and saluted us in French.

Jack replied in the same language; but on learning that we were Englishmen, he began to talk in our own tongue, although he evidently understood very little of it.

"Do you travel alone with the natives?" inquired Jack, after a few preliminary remarks.

"Yaas, sair, I doos," replied the stranger, who was a Portuguese trader, according to his own account.

"You seem to carry little or no merchandise with you," said Jack, glancing towards the party of natives, who stood at some distance looking at us and conversing together eagerly.

"I has none wis me, true, bot I has moche not ver' far off. I bees go just now to seek for ivory, and ebony, and sl–a– — w'at you call him? barwood."

The man corrected himself quickly, but the slip confirmed Makarooroo's remark and our own suspicions that he was a slave-dealer.

"De day is far gone," he continued, putting as amiable a smile on his countenance as possible; "perhaps you vill stop and we have dine togedder."

Although we did not much like the appearance of our new friend or his party, we felt that it would be uncourteous in so wild a country, where we had so few chances of meeting with white faces, to refuse, so we agreed. A camp-fire was speedily kindled, and the two parties mingled together, and sat down amicably to discuss roast monkey and venison steaks together.

During the course of the meal the Portuguese trader became so communicative and agreeable that we all began to think we had judged him harshly. We observed, too, that Makarooroo and the negroes had fraternised heartily, and our guide was singing and laughing, and making himself agreeable at a very uncommon rate, so much so as to call forth our surprise.

"Mak seems to be mad to-day," observed Peterkin, as one of our guide's jovial laughs rang through the wood and was echoed by his new acquaintances.

"Bees him not always so?" inquired the Portuguese.

"He's always hearty enough," replied Jack, "but I must confess I never saw him in such high spirits as he seems to be in just now. It must be the effect of meeting with new faces, I suppose."

"Ah! s'pose so," remarked the trader.

I was struck with the manner in which this was said. There was a tone of affected indifference, such as one assumes when making a passing remark, but at the same time a dark frown rested for one moment on his brow, and he cast a piercing vindictive glance at our guide. Next moment he was smiling blandly and making some humorous remark to Peterkin.

I looked at my companions, but they had evidently not observed this little piece of by-play. It seemed to me so unaccountable, considering that the two men had never met before, that I resolved to watch them. I soon observed that Makarooroo's mirth was forced, that he was in fact acting a part, and I noticed once or twice that he also cast an occasional stealthy and piercing glance at the Portuguese. It afterwards turned out that both men had been acting the same part, and that each had suspected what the other was doing.

When our meal was concluded we prepared to resume our separate routes.

"I goes to de west," observed the Portuguese, in a casual way, as he buckled on the belt that supported his hunting-knife.

"Indeed! I had understood you to say that you were going south."

"No; you not have onderstand me. I goes to de west, ver' long way."

"Then, sir, I wish you a safe and pleasant journey," said Jack, lifting his cap.

"De same to you, sairs, an' goot plenty of gorillas to you. Farder nord dey be more plenty. Adieu!"

We took off our caps to each other, and saying farewell, we turned away, and soon lost sight of the party.

"Ho! de yaller-faced villain," exclaimed Makarooroo between his clinched teeth, after we were out of earshot.

"Why, what's wrong, Mak?" inquired Peterkin, in great surprise.

"Ho! noting porteekler," replied the guide, with an air and tone of sarcasm that quite amused us. "Hims not go sout', ho no! hims go west, ho yis! hims advise us to go nort', ho dear! dat bery clibber, bery mush clibber; but we is clibberer, we is, ho! ho! ho!"

Our worthy guide looked so terribly fierce as he uttered this fiendish laugh, that we all came to a stand and gazed at him in surprise; we fancied that something must have deranged his mind.

"Mak," said Peterkin, "you are mad. What mean you by such grimaces?"

Pursing his lips tightly, and looking at each of us for a few moments in silence, he finally crossed his arms on his chest, and turning eagerly to Jack, said with extreme volubility —

"Dat rascal! dat tief! Him's no trader, him's slabe-dealer; hims no go west, hims go south; an' w'at for hims go? W'at for hims carry guns so many, eh? Hims go" (here the guide dropped his voice into a whisper of intense bitterness) —"hims go for attack village an' take all peepils away for be slabes. No pay for 'em–tief! —take dem by force."

"Why, how did you come to know all this," said Jack, "or rather to suspect it? for you cannot be sure that you are right."

"W'at, no can be sure me right? ho, yis, me sartin sure. Me bery clibber. Stop, now. Did him–dat tief! —speak bery mush?"

"Certainly he did, a good deal."

"Yis, ho! An' did him make *you* speak bery mush?"

"I rather think he did," replied Peterkin, laughing at our guide's eagerness.

"Yis, ho! hims did. An' did him ax you plenty question, all 'bout where you go, an' where you come from, an' *de way back* to village where we be come from? An' did hims say, when him find you was come from *sout*, dat hims was go *west*, though before dat hims hab say dat hims be go *sout*, eh?"

"Certainly," said Jack, with a thoughtful look, "he did say all that, and a great deal more to that effect."

"Yis, ho! hims did. Me know bery well. Me see him. An' me also dood to de niggers what hims do to you. Me talk an' laugh an' sing, *den me ax dem questions.* But dey bery wise; dey no speak mush, but dey manage to speak 'nuff for me. Yis, me bam-bam-eh?"

"Boozle," suggested Peterkin.

"Vis, bamboozle dem altogidder, ho! ho!"

After a little further explanation we found that this Portuguese trader was a man-stealer, on his way to one of the smaller villages, with the intention of attacking it. Makarooroo ascertained that they meant to proceed direct to that of King Jambai, first, however, getting one of the neighbouring tribes to pick a quarrel with that monarch and go to war with him; and we now recollected, with deep regret, that in our ignorance of what the Portuguese was, we had given him a great deal of information regarding the village of our late hospitable entertainer which might prove very useful to him, and very hurtful to poor King Jambai, in the event of such a raid being carried out.

But, in addition to this, Makarooroo had ascertained that it was possible that, before going to King Jambai's village, they might perhaps make a descent on that of our friend Mbango, with whom we had left poor Okandaga. It was this that raised the wrath of our guide to such a pitch.

The instant we heard it Jack said —

"Then that settles the question of our future proceedings. We must bid adieu to the gorillas at once, and dog the steps of this marauding party, so as to prevent our good friends Mbango and Jambai being surprised and carried into slavery along with all their people. It seems to me that our path is clear in this matter. Even if we were not bound in honour to succour those who have treated us hospitably, we ought to do our best to undo the evil we have done in telling their enemies so much about them. Besides, we must save Okandaga, whatever happens. What say you, comrades?"

"Of course we must," said Peterkin. I also heartily concurred.

"You's a good man," said Makarooroo, his eyes glistening with emotion.

"If I did not stand by you at such a time as this," replied Jack, smiling, "I should certainly be a very bad man."

"But what are we to do about our goods?" inquired I, "We cannot hope to keep up with these robbers if we carry our goods with us; and yet it seems hard to leave them behind, for we should fare ill, I fear, in this country if we travel as beggars."

"We shall easily manage as to that," replied Jack. "I have observed that one of our niggers is a sensible, and, I am disposed to think, a trustworthy fellow —"

"D'you mean the man with the blind eye and the thumping big nose?" inquired Peterkin.

"The same. Well, I shall put him in charge, and tell him to follow us to Mbango's village; then we four shall start off light, and hunt our way south, travelling as fast as we can, and carrying as many strings of beads, by way of small change, as we can stuff into our pockets and fasten about our persons."

"The very thing," cried Peterkin. "So let's put it in practice at once."

"Ay, this very night," said Jack, as we hurried back to the spot where our goods had been left.

As we went along in silence I noticed that Peterkin sighed once or twice very heavily, and I asked him if he was quite well.

"Well? Ay, well enough in body, Ralph, but ill at ease in mind. How can it be otherwise when we are thus suddenly and unexpectedly about to take leave of our dear friends the gorillas? I declare my heart is fit to break."

"I sympathise with you, Peterkin," said I, "for I have not yet made nearly as many notes in regard to these monster-monkeys as I could have wished. However, I am thankful for what I have got, and perhaps we may come back here again one of these days."

"What bloodthirsty fellows!" cried Jack, laughing. "If you talk so, I fear that Mak and I shall have to cut your acquaintance; for, you see, he and I have got a *little* feeling left."

"Well, it's natural, I fancy," observed Peterkin, "that gorillas should feel for their kindred. However, I console myself with the thought that the country farther south is much better filled with other game, although the great puggy is not there. And then we shall come among lions again, which we can never find, I believe, in the gorilla country. I wonder if the gorilla has really driven them out of this part of Africa."

"Some think it probable," observed I, "but we cannot make sure of that point."

"Well, we can at all events make sure of this point," cried Peterkin, as we came in sight of our encampment, "that lions are thick enough in the country whither we are bound; so let's have a good supper, and hurrah for the south! It's a bright prospect before us. A fair lady to be saved; possibly a fight with the niggers, and lion, elephant, rhinoceros, alligator, hippopotamus, and buffalo shooting by way of relaxation in the intervals of the war!"

CHAPTER FIFTEEN

An unexpected meeting-We fly, and I make a narrow escape from an appalling fate.

During many days after the incidents narrated in the last chapter did Jack, and Peterkin, and Makarooroo, and I, push across the continent through bush and brake, over hill and dale, morass and plain, at our utmost possible speed. We did not, during the whole course of our journey, overtake the Portuguese slave-dealer; but we thought little of that, for it was not very probable that we should hit upon exactly the same route, and we entertained sanguine hopes that the energy and speed with which we kept steadily and undeviatingly on our way would enable us to reach the village of Mbango before the slave-dealer and his party.

When I look back upon that time now, and reflect calmly on the dangers we encountered and the hardships we endured, I confess that I am filled with amazement. I might easily fill several volumes such as this with anecdotes of our encounters with wild animals, and other adventures; but however interesting these might be in themselves, I must not forget that some of the main incidents of our sojourn in Africa have yet to be related, and that there is a limit to the patience of even youthful readers.

Our power of enduring fatigue and sustained active exertion, with comparatively short intervals of nightly repose, was much greater than I could have believed to be possible. I have no doubt that anxiety to save Okandaga from the terrible fate that hung over her enabled us to bear up under fatigues which would at other times have overcome us. I know not well how it was that I kept up with my strong and agile comrades. Oftentimes I felt ready to drop down as I walked, yet somehow I never thought of falling behind, but went doggedly on, and at nights found myself little worse in condition than they. Peterkin, although small, was tough and springy, and his spirits seemed rather to rise than otherwise as his strength abated. As for Jack, I never saw any one like him. He seemed like a lion roaming in his strength over his native deserts. So hardened had we all become during the course of our travels that we found ourselves not only equal to Makarooroo in pedestrian powers, but superior; for when occasion required we could almost knock him up, but I am free to admit that we never succeeded in doing this thoroughly. In short, we were all as nearly as possible equal to each other, with the exception of Jack, who seemed in every way invulnerable.

During this long and hurried but intensely interesting and delightful journey we came upon, at different times, almost every species of animal, plant, and tree peculiar to the African continent. Oftentimes we passed by droves and herds of elephants, deer, buffalo, giraffes, antelopes, and zebras; we saw rhinoceroses, alligators, leopards, lions, apes of several kinds, and smaller monkeys innumerable. We also saw great numbers of birds-some curious on account of their habits and form, others beautiful and bright as the rainbow.

Yet although, as I have said, this journey was very delightful, our feelings were at different times exceedingly varied, and not unfrequently pained; for while we saw around us much that was beautiful, innocent, and lovely, we also witnessed the conflicts of many wild creatures, and sometimes came across evidences of the savage and cruel dispositions of the human beings by whom the country was peopled. We always, however, carefully avoided native villages, being anxious not to be interrupted on our forced march. Neither did we turn aside to hunt, although we were much tempted so to do, but contented ourselves with killing such animals as we required for our daily subsistence; and of these we shot as many as we required without having to turn aside from our straight course.

Thus we went on day after day, and slept under the shade of the trees or under the wide canopy of heaven night after night, until we arrived one day at a beautiful valley, bordered by a plain, and traversed by a river, where Peterkin met with a sad accident, and our onward progress was for a short period arrested.

It happened thus: — The region through which we chanced to be passing was peopled by so many natives that we had the utmost difficulty in avoiding them, and more than once were compelled to halt during the daytime in some sequestered dell, and resume our journey during the night.

One day-it was, if I remember rightly, about two o'clock in the afternoon-we came suddenly in sight of a native village on the banks of the river whose course we were at that time following, and made a wide détour in order to avoid it. We had passed it several miles, and were gradually bending into our course again, when we came unexpectedly upon a band of natives who had been out hunting and were returning to their village with the spoils of the chase on their shoulders. Both parties at once came to an abrupt halt, and we stood for several minutes looking at each other-the natives in speechless amazement, while we conversed in whispers, uncertain what to do.

We knew that if we made friendly advances we should no doubt be welcomed, but then we should certainly be compelled to go back with them to their village and spend at least a day or two with them, as we could not hope to give them a satisfactory reason for our going on at once. We also knew that to go on in spite of them would produce a quarrel, and, of course, a fight, which, as it would certainly result in bloodshed, was by all means to be avoided for we could not bear to think that a mere caprice of ours in visiting Africa should be the means of causing the death of a single human being, if we could prevent it.

"What *is* to be done?" said Peterkin, looking at Jack in despair.

"I don't know," replied Jack. "It's very awkward. It will never do to go all the way back to the village with these stupid fellows, and we cannot tell them our real reason for going on; for, in the first place, they would perhaps not believe us, or, in the second place, they might offer to join us."

"Fight," said Makarooroo in a low tone, grinding his teeth together and clutching his rifle.

I felt deep sympathy with the poor fellow, for I knew well that in disposition he was naturally the reverse of quarrelsome, and that his present state of mind was the consequence of anxiety for the deliverance of his faithful bride.

"No, no," replied Jack quickly; "we shall not fight."

"Suppose we bolt!" whispered Peterkin, brightening up as the idea occurred to him—"regularly run away!"

We seized at the idea instantly. We were all of us hard of muscle and strong of wind now, and we knew that we could outstrip the savages.

"We'll do it!" said Jack hastily. "Let us scatter, too, so as to perplex them at the outset."

"Capital! Then here goes. I'm off," cried Peterkin.

"Stay!" said Jack.

"Why?" demanded Peterkin.

"Because we must appoint a place of rendezvous if we would hope to meet again."

"True; I forgot that."

"D'you all see yonder blue mountain-peak?"

"Let us meet there. If we miss each other at the base, let us proceed to the summit and wait. Away!"

As Jack uttered the last word we all turned right about and fled like the wind. The savages instantly set up a hideous yell, and darted after us; but we made for the thick woods, and scattering in all directions, as had been previously arranged, speedily threw them off the scent, and finally made our escape.

For the first time since landing on the continent of Africa, I now found myself totally alone in the wild forest. After separating from my companions, I ran at my utmost speed in the direction of a dense jungle, where I purposed taking shelter until the natives should pass by, and then come out and pursue my way leisurely. But I was prevented from adopting this course in consequence of two very fleet negroes discovering my intention, and, by taking a short cut, frustrating it. I was compelled, therefore, to keep in the more open part of the forest, and trust simply to speed and endurance for escape.

I should think that I ran nearly two miles at full speed, and kept well ahead of my pursuers. Indeed, I had distanced them considerably; but feeling that I could not hold out long at such a killing pace, I pulled up a little, and allowed them to gain on me slightly. I was just about to resume my full speed, and, if possible, throw them at once far behind, when my foot was caught by a thorny shrub, and I fell headlong to the ground. I was completely stunned for a moment or two, and lay quite motionless. But my consciousness suddenly returned, accompanied by a feeling of imminent danger, which caused me to spring up and renew my headlong career. Glancing over my shoulder, I saw that the two natives had gained so much on me that had I lain a few seconds longer I must inevitably have been captured.

I exerted myself now beyond my powers. My head, too, from the shock I had received, became confused, and I scarce knew whither I was going. Presently a loud, dull roar, as if of distant thunder, struck upon my ear, and I beheld what appeared to me to be a vast white plain covered with mist before. Next moment I found myself on the brink of a precipice of a hundred feet deep, over which, a little to my left, a large river fell, and thundered down into a dark abyss, whence issued those clouds of spray which I had taken for a white plain in the confusion of my brain and vision.

I made a desperate effort to check myself, but it was too late. My heels broke off the earthy edge of the cliff, and I obtained just one awful glance of the horrid turmoil directly below me as I fell over with a mass of débris. I uttered an involuntary shriek of agony, and flung my arms wildly out. My hand clutched the branch of an overhanging bush. This, slight though it was, was the means, under God, of saving my life. The branch broke off, but it checked my fall, and at the same time swung me into the centre of a tree which projected out from the cliff almost horizontally. Through this tree I went crashing with fearful violence, until I was arrested by my chest striking against a stout branch. This I clutched with the tenacity of despair, and wriggling myself, as it were, along it, wound my arms and legs round it, and held on for some time with the utmost fervour of muscular energy.

My position now was beyond conception horrible. I shut my eyes and prayed earnestly for help. Presently I opened them, and in the position in which I then lay, the first thing I saw was the boiling water of the fall more than a hundred feet below me. My agony was such that large drops of perspiration broke out all over my forehead. It was many minutes before I could summon up courage to turn my head so as to look upward, for I had a vague feeling that if I were to move the branch on which I lay would break off. When I did so, I observed that the branches over my head completely screened the sky from me, so that I knew I had escaped one danger; for the natives, believing, no doubt, that I had fallen down into the river, would at once give up their hopeless pursuit. The branch on which I lay was so slender that it swayed about with every motion that I made, and the longer I remained there the more nervous did I become.

At last I bethought me that unless I made a manful effort I should certainly perish, so I looked about me until I became accustomed to the giddy position. Then I perceived that, by creeping along the branch until I gained the trunk of the tree, I could descend by means of it to the face of the precipice from which it projected, and thus gain a narrow ledge of rock that overhung the abyss. In any other circumstances I would as soon have ventured to cross the Falls of Niagara on a tight-rope; but I had no other alternative, so I crept along the branch slowly and nervously, clinging to it, at the same time, with terrible tenacity. At last I gained the trunk of the tree and breathed more freely, for it was much steadier than the branch.

The trunk projected, as I have said, almost horizontally from the precipice, so I had to draw myself carefully along it, not daring to get on my hands and knees, and finally reached the ledge above referred to. Compared with my former position, this was a place of temporary safety, for it was three feet wide, and having a good head, I had no fear of falling over. But on looking up my heart sank within me, for the bare cliff offered no foothold whatever. I do not believe that a monkey could have climbed it. To descend the precipice was equally impossible, for it was like a wall. My only hope, therefore, lay in the ledge on which I stood, and which, I observed, ran along to the right and turned round a projecting rock that hid the remainder of it from view.

Hasting along it, I found, to my inexpressible relief, that it communicated with the top of the precipice. The ascent was difficult and dangerous; but at last I succeeded in passing the most serious part, and soon gained the summit of the cliff in safety, where I immediately fell on my knees and returned thanks for my deliverance.

I had passed nearly an hour in the trying adventure which I have just related, and feeling that my companions would naturally begin soon to be anxious about me, I started for our rendezvous, which I reached in little more than an hour and a half. Here I found Jack seated alone beside a stream of water, from which he occasionally lifted a little in the hollow of his hand and drank greedily.

"Ah, Ralph, my boy!" he exclaimed joyfully as I came up, "I'm glad you've come. I had begun to fear that you must have been captured. Ay, drink, lad! You seem warm enough, though I scarcely think you can be much more so than I am. What a run we have had, to be sure! But, what, Ralph-your clothes are much torn, and your face and hands are scratched. Why, you must have got among thorns. Not badly hurt, I trust?"

"Oh no; nothing to speak of. I have, however, had a narrow escape. But before I speak of that, what of Peterkin?"

"I don't know," replied Jack, with an anxious expression; "and to say truth, I begin to feel uneasy about him, for he ought to have been here almost as soon as myself."

"How so? Did you, then, run together?"

"Latterly we did. At first we separated, and I knew not what had become either of him or you. The fact is, I had enough to do to look out for myself, for a dozen of rascally niggers kept close upon my heels and tried my powers of running somewhat; so I took to the thick wood and made a détour, to throw them off the scent. All at once I heard a smashing of the bushes right in front of me, and before I knew what I was about, Peterkin bounced through the underwood and almost plunged into my arms. We both gave an involuntary yell of alarm.

"'There's two of 'em right on my heels,' said he in a gasp, as he dashed off again. 'Come along with me, Jack.'

"I followed as fast as I could, and we crossed an open plain together, when I looked over my shoulder, and saw that all the other fellows had given up the chase except the two mentioned by Peterkin. These kept on after us, and somehow or other we got separated again, just after re-entering the wood on the other side of the plain. Of course I ran on, expecting to see my companion every minute. Finally I came to the rendezvous, and here I found that the savages had given up all hope of overtaking me, for I could see nothing of them."

"How long ago is that?" I inquired quickly.

"About an hour."

"Then poor Peterkin must have been caught," said I, in a voice of despair.

"No, that is not likely," replied Jack; "for I climbed a high tree and saw the savages recrossing the plain alone. I think it probable he may have lost his way, and is afraid to climb trees or to fire off his gun to signal us, for fear of being heard or seen by the niggers. I have sent Mak, who came here soon after I did, to search for him."

"It may be as you say, Jack, but we must go at once to look for him."

"With all my heart, Ralph. I only waited until you had sufficiently rested."

"The body cannot rest when the mind is ill at ease. Come, let us start at once. I shall tell you of my little adventure as we go along."

We soon reached the edge of the plain where Jack had been separated from his companion, and here we proceeded to make a careful search. Being certain that the savages were now out of earshot, we began to halloo occasionally as we went along. But monkeys and parrots alone replied to us.

"This is the very spot where I last saw him," said Jack, leading me to a palm-tree which stood a little within the outer verge of the wood; "and here are his footsteps faintly indicated on the grass."

"Ah! then let us follow these up," said I eagerly.

"We might, if we were North American backwoodsmen or Red Indians; but I can scarcely follow. Stay, here they enter upon a piece of soft ground, and are more distinct. Now, then, we shall get on."

For nearly quarter of an hour we followed the footprints; then we came to dry ground again, and lost all traces of them. We wandered about perseveringly, nevertheless, and were rewarded by again discovering them about quarter of a mile farther on, leading down to the banks of the river on another part of which I had had such a narrow escape.

While we were advancing —I in front —I felt the ground beneath me suddenly begin to give way with a crackling sound. I instinctively threw up my arms and sprang back.

"Hollo, Ralph!" cried my companion, seizing me with one hand by the collar, and hauling, or rather lifting me back, as if I had been a poodle dog. "Why, you were as near as possible into a pitfall."

"Thanks to you, Jack, that I am not actually in," said I, putting my somewhat twisted costume to rights. "But, I say, does it not strike you that perhaps Peterkin has fallen into one of these?"

We both started and listened with breathless attention, for at that moment we heard a faint groan not far from us. It was repeated almost immediately, though so faintly that we could scarcely ascertain the direction whence it came. We advanced cautiously, however, a few paces, and discovered a hole in the ground, from which, at that very moment, the dishevelled head of poor Peterkin appeared, like Jack coming out of his box. His sudden appearance and serio-comic expression would have been at any other time sufficient to have set us off in fits of laughter; but joy at finding him, and anxiety lest he should prove to be seriously hurt, restrained us at that time effectually.

"My dear fellow!" cried Jack, hurrying forward.

"Keep back! avaunt ye. Oh dear me, Jack, my poor head!" said Peterkin with a sigh, pressing his hand to his forehead; "what an intolerable whack I have got on my miserable caput. There; don't come nearer, else you'll break through. Reach me your hand. That's it; thank'ee."

"There you are, all safe, my boy," cried Jack, as he drew Peterkin out of the hole. —"But hollo! I say, Ralph, run down for some water; I believe the poor fellow has fainted."

I sprang down the river-bank, and speedily returned with some water in the crown of my wide-awake. Peterkin had recovered before I came back, and a long draught quite restored him, so that in a few minutes he was able to relate how the accident had befallen him.

"You see," said he, in a jocular tone, for it was a most unusually severe accident indeed that could drive the fun out of our little friend —"you see, after I lost sight of Jack, I took a leaf out of the hare's book, and doubled on my course. This brought me, unhappily, to the banks of the river, where I came upon one of the pitfalls that are made by the niggers here to catch wild beasts, and in I went. I kept hold of the surface boughs, however, scrambled out again, and pushed on. But I had not gone ten yards when the ground began to crackle and sink. I made a desperate bound to clear it, but my foot caught in a branch, and down I went head foremost into the pit. And that's the whole of my story. How long I remained there I know not. If I had known what time it was when I dived in, and you were to tell me what o'clock it is now, we might arrive at a knowledge of the time I have spent at the bottom of that hole. All that I can positively affirm is, that I went in, and within in the last ten minutes I came out!"

We laughed at this free-and-easy manner of narrating the incident, and then prepared to return to our rendezvous; but on attempting to walk, Peterkin found that he had received a greater shake than at first he had imagined. Several times during our march he became giddy, and had to be supported; and after reaching our encampment, where we found Makarooroo waiting for us, he fainted. We were therefore obliged to make up our minds to encamp where we were for a few days.

CHAPTER SIXTEEN
An unfortunate delay, and a terrible visitor.

Only those who have been forcibly held back when filled with the deepest anxiety to go forward, can form any thing like a conception of our state of mind during the few days that succeeded that on which Peterkin met with his accident.

We felt like chained hounds when the huntsmen pass by. We knew that every hour increased the distance between us and the slave-dealer's party, who, unless we succeeded in passing them and reaching the villages first, would infallibly succeed in their villainous design. But Peterkin was unable to proceed without great risk, as whenever he attempted to walk steadily for any distance his head became giddy, and we were compelled to halt, so that a day or two's rest was absolutely necessary. Poor Makarooroo was nearly beside himself with impatience; but to do him justice, he endeavoured to conceal the state of his feelings when in Peterkin's presence.

During this period of forced inaction, although of course I had nothing to do, I found it impossible to apply my mind closely to the study of any of the strange and beautiful objects by which I was surrounded. Anxiety banished from me almost entirely the love of study, as well as the power of observation. Nevertheless, one or two things that I saw were so curious that they could not but make a deep impression on my memory.

I discovered a spider of a very remarkable kind, which was such an ingenious creature as to be capable of making a door to the entrance of its house. I came upon the animal one day while taking a stroll a short distance from our camp. It was as large as a shilling, reddish in colour, and from the fierce, rapid way in which it ran about hither and thither as if in search of prey, it had an exceedingly horrible and voracious aspect. The hole of this creature is visible only when its owner is absent from home. It is quite evident either that there are no thieves among the lower animals there, or that there is nothing in the hole to steal, for when he goes out he leaves the door open behind him. When he returns he shuts the door, and the hole becomes invisible, in consequence of the door being coated with earth on the outside. Its inside is lined with a pure white silky substance, which at once attracted my attention as I passed. On trying to pick up the door, I found that it was attached by a hinge to the hole, and on being shut it fitted exactly.

Perhaps the most singular discovery I made was a tree, the stem of which had been so completely surrounded by spiders' webs that it could not be seen, and I had to cut through the network with my knife in order to get at the tree. The lines of those webs were as thick as coarse threads, and pretty strong, as I had reason to know; for when walking back to camp the same evening, meditating deeply on our unfortunate detention, I ran my head into the middle of a spider's web, and was completely enveloped in it, so much so that it was with considerable difficulty I succeeded in clearing it away. I was as regularly netted as if a gauze veil had been thrown over me.

On our third morning after the accident we set forth again, and continued our journey by forced marches as Peterkin could bear it. Although the two past days and nights had been absolutely lost, and could not now be recalled, yet the moment we set out and left our camp behind us, the load of anxiety was at once lifted off our minds, and we hurried forward with an elasticity of step and spirit that was quite delightful. We felt like prisoners set free, and kept up a continual flow of conversation, sometimes in reference to the scenery and objects around us, at other times in regard to our future plans or our past experiences.

"It seems to me," said Jack, breaking silence at the end of a long pause which had succeeded an animated discussion as to whether it were better to spend one's life in the civilised world or among the wilds of Africa, in which discussion Peterkin, who advocated the wild life, was utterly, though not admittedly, beaten —"it seems to me that, notwithstanding the short time we stayed in the gorilla country, we have been pretty successful. Haven't we bagged thirty-three altogether?"

"Thirty-six, if you count the babies in arms," responded Peterkin.

"Of course we are entitled to count these."

"I think you are both out in your reckoning," said I, drawing out my note-book; "the last baby that I shot was our thirty-seventh."

"What!" cried Peterkin, "the one with the desperately black face and the horrible squint, that nearly tore all the hair out of Jack's head before he managed to strangle him? That wasn't a baby; it was a big boy, and I have no doubt a big rascal besides."

"That may be so," I rejoined; "but whatever he was, I have him down as number thirty-seven in my list."

"Pity we didn't make up the forty," observed Jack.

"Ah! yes indeed," said Peterkin. "But let me see: could we not manage to make it up to that yet?"

"Impossible," said I. "We are far away from the gorilla land now, I know; for, in addition to the fact that we have seen no traces of gorillas for a long time, we have, within the last few days, seen several lions, which, you are well aware, do not exist in the gorilla country."

"True; but you mistake me," rejoined Peterkin. "I do not mean to make up the number to forty by killing three more, but by proving, almost to demonstration, that we have already been the death of that number, in addition to those noted down."

"You'll find that rather difficult," said Jack, laughing.

"Not at all," cried Peterkin. "Let me think a minute. You remember that enormously big, hairy fellow, that looked so like an ugly old man that Ralph refused point-blank to fire at him, whereupon you fired at him point-blank and wounded him in the shoulder as he was running away?"

"We treated several big fellows in that way," replied Jack; "which of them do you allude to? —the one that roared so loud and terrified you so much that you nearly ran away?"

"No, no; you know well enough which one I mean. The one that ran along the edge of the stagnant pool into which you tumbled as we were coming back."

"Oh yes! I remember," said Jack, laughing.

"Well, that fellow flew into such a horrible rage when he was wounded," continued Peterkin, "that I am perfectly certain he went straight home and murdered his wife in a passion; which brings up the number to thirty-eight. Then there was that old woman-gorilla that I brought down when we were descending yon hill that was covered with such splendid vines. You remember? Well, I'm quite certain that the young man-gorilla beside her, who ran off and escaped, was her son, and that he went home straightway and died of grief. That makes thirty-nine. Then —"

"Oh, do be quiet, Peterkin, please," said I, with a shudder. "You put things in such a fearfully dark and murderous light that I feel quite as if I were a murderer. I feel quite uneasy, I assure you; and if it were not that we have killed all these creatures in the cause of science, I should be perfectly miserable."

"In the cause of science!" repeated Peterkin; "humph! I suspect that a good deal of wickedness is perpetrated under the wing of science."

"Come, come," said Jack; "don't you begin to grow sarcastic, Master Peterkin. I abominate sarcasm, and cannot tolerate sarcastic people. If you adopt that style, I shall revert to my natural habits as a gorilla, and tear you in pieces."

"There you exhibit your unnatural ignorance of your own natural habits," retorted Peterkin; "for you ought to know that gorillas never tear men in pieces-their usual mode being to knock you down with a blow of their huge paws."

"Well, I will knock you down if you prefer it."

"Thank you; I'd rather not. Besides, you have almost knocked me up already; so pray call a halt and let me rest a bit."

We were all very willing to agree to this request, having walked the last two or three miles at a very quick pace. Seating ourselves on the trunk of a fallen tree, we enjoyed the beautiful prospect before us. An open vista enabled us to see beyond the wood in which we were travelling into an extensive sweep of prairie-land on which the sinking sun was shedding a rich flood of light. It happened to be a deliciously cool evening, and the chattering of numerous parrots as well as the twittering songs of other birds-less gorgeous, perhaps, but more musical than they-refreshed our ears as the glories of the landscape did our eyes. While we were gazing dreamily before us in silent enjoyment, Jack suddenly interrupted our meditations by exclaiming —

"Hist! look yonder!"

He pointed as he spoke to a distant part of the plain on which the forest closely pressed.

"A zebra!" cried I, with delight; for besides the feeling of pleasure at seeing this splendid creature, I entertained a hope that we might shoot him and procure a steak for supper, of which at that time we stood much in need.

"I'm too tired to stalk it now," said Peterkin, with an air of chagrin. —"Are you up to it, Jack?"

"Quite; but I fear he's an animal that's very difficult to stalk in such an open country. —What say you, Mak?"

"Hims no be cotched dis yer night, massa; hims too far away an' too wide 'wake."

"What say you to a long shot, Peterkin? Your rifle is sighted for four hundred yards, and he seems to be little more than six hundred off."

"I'll try," said our friend, going down on one knee and adjusting the sight of his piece. Taking a long, steady aim, he fired, and in another instant the zebra lay dead on the plain. I need hardly add that our amazement was excessive. Even Peterkin himself could scarcely believe his eyes. Had his rifle been sighted for such a distance, the shot, although a splendid one, would not have amazed us so much, because we knew that our friend's aim was deadly; but as he had to elevate the muzzle above the object fired at and guess the amount of elevation, the shot was indeed wonderful. It was a long time before our guide could move, but when he did recover himself he danced and shouted like a madman with delight, and then, setting off with a bound, sped across the plain like a deer.

"Come along," cried Jack with a laugh —"let's follow; for Mak looked so rabid when he went off that I believe he'll eat the beast raw before we can claim our share, if we don't look sharp."

We all of us set off at a smart trot, and soon came to the spot where our prize lay. It was a splendid creature, and in prime condition. After examining it carefully, and descanting on the beauty of its striped skin, I sat down beside it and pulled out my note-book, while my comrades entered the forest to search for a suitable place on which to encamp, and to kindle a fire. A spot was quickly found, and I had scarcely finished making notes when they returned to carry the zebra into the encampment. We accomplished this with some difficulty, and laid it beside the fire. Then cutting four large steaks from its flanks we proceeded to sup, after which we made our arrangements for spending the night there. We little knew the startling surprise that was in store for us that night.

As the forest in that place happened to be swarming with wild animals of every kind, we deemed it prudent to set a watch as well as to keep up a blazing fire. Jack and I and the ne-gro kept watch by turns; Peterkin, being still sufficiently an invalid to claim exemption from laborious duties, was permitted to rest undisturbed.

About midnight I aroused Jack, and having made him sit up, in order to show that he was thoroughly awake, I lay down and went to sleep.

How long I slept I cannot tell, but I was suddenly awakened by one of the most tremendous roars I ever heard. It was so chose to me that, in the confusion of my sleepy brain, it seemed to be far more terrible than that even of the gorilla. I was mistaken in this, however, and no doubt my semi-somnolent condition tended to increase its awfulness.

Springing into a sitting posture, and by an involuntary impulse reaching out my hand for my gun which lay close to me, I beheld a sight that was calculated to appal the stoutest heart. A lion of the largest size was in the very act of springing over the bushes and alighting on the zebra, which, as I have said, lay on the other side of the fire and not four yards off from us. As the light glared in the brute's eyes, and, as it were, sparkled in gleams on its shaggy mane, which streamed out under the force of its majestic bound, it seemed to my bewildered gaze as though the animal were in the air almost above my head, and that he must inevitably alight upon myself. This, at least, is the impression left upon my mind now that I look back upon that terrific scene. But there was no time for thought. The roar was uttered, the bound was made, and the lion alighted on the carcass of the zebra almost in one and the same moment. I freely confess that my heart quailed within me. Yet that did not prevent my snatching up my gun; but before I had time to cock it the crashing report of Jack's elephant rifle almost split the drum of my ear, and I beheld the lion drop as if it had been a stone.

It lay without motion, completely dead, and we found, on examination, that the ball had smashed in the centre of its forehead and completely penetrated its brain.

Some time elapsed before we could find words to express our feelings. Our guide, who had so completely enveloped his head and shoulders in grass when he lay down to sleep that he was the last to spring up, looked at the huge carcass of the lion with an expression of utter bewilderment.

"What a magnificent fellow! And what a splendid shot!" exclaimed Peterkin at last. "Why, Jack, I don't believe there's a finer lion in Africa. It's lucky, though, that you were on the *qui vive*."

"Yes," said I; "had it not been for you we might have been all killed by this time."

"No fear o' dat," chimed in our guide, as he sat down on the lion's shoulder, and began to stroke its mane; "hims was want him's supper off de zebra, ho! ho! Hims got him's supper off a bullet!"

"'Tis well that he has," observed Jack, as he reloaded his rifle. "To say truth, comrades, I scarcely deserve credit for being guardian of the camp, for I'm ashamed to say that I was sound asleep at the moment the lion roared. How I ever managed to take so quick and so good an aim is more than I can tell. Luckily my rifle was handy, and I had fallen asleep in a sitting posture. Had it been otherwise, I could scarcely have been in time to prevent the brute springing on us, had he felt so disposed."

Here was now another subject for my note-book, so I sat down, and began a minute inspection of the noble-looking animal, while my comrades, heaping fresh logs on the fire, sat down in front of it, and for upwards of an hour, "fought their battles o'er again."

It was a matter of deep regret to us all that we could not afford to carry away with us the skin of this lion as a memorial; but circumstanced as we then were, that was out of the question, so we contented ourselves with extracting his largest teeth and all his claws, which we still preserve in our museum as trophies of the adventure.

CHAPTER SEVENTEEN
We visit a natural menagerie, see wonderful sights, and meet with strange adventures.

We observed, on this journey, that the elephants which we met with in our farthest north point were considerably smaller than those farther to the south, yet though smaller animals, their tusks were much larger then those of the south. The weight of those tusks varied from twenty to fifty pounds, and I saw one that was actually upwards of one hundred pounds in weight-equal, in fact, to the weight of a big boy or a little man. Such tusks, however, were rare.

At nights, when we encamped near to a river or pool of water, we saw immense numbers of elephants come down to drink and enjoy themselves. They seemed, in fact, to be intoxicated with delight, if not with water; for they screamed with joy, and filling their trunks with water, spurted it over themselves and each other in copious showers. Of course, we never disturbed them on such occasions, for we came to the conclusion that it would be the height of barbarity and selfishness to spoil the pleasure of so many creatures merely for the sake of a shot.

Frequently we were wont to go after our supper to one of those ponds, when we chanced to be in the immediate neighbourhood of one, and lying concealed among the bushes, watch by the light of the moon the strange habits and proceedings of the wild creatures that came there to drink. The hours thus passed were to me the most interesting by far that I spent in Africa. There was something so romantic in the kind of scenery, in the dim mysterious light, and in the grand troops of wild creatures that came there in all the pith and fire of untamed freedom to drink. It was like visiting a natural menagerie on the most magnificent scale; for in places where water is scarce any pool that may exist is the scene of constant and ever-changing visits during the entire night.

In fact, I used to find it almost impossible to tear myself away, although I knew that repose was absolutely needful, in order to enable me to continue the journey on the succeeding day, and I am quite certain that had not Peterkin and Jack often dragged me off in a jocular way by main force, I should have remained there all night, and have fallen asleep probably in my ambush.

One night of this kind that we passed I shall never forget. It was altogether a remarkable and tremendously exciting night; and as it is a good type of the style of night entertainment to be found in that wild country, I shall describe it.

It happened on a Saturday night. We were then travelling through a rather dry district, and had gone a whole day without tasting water. As evening approached we came, to our satisfaction, to a large pond of pretty good water, into which we ran knee-deep, and filling our caps with water, drank long and repeated draughts. Then we went into a piece of jungle about a quarter of a mile distant, and made our encampment, intending to rest there during the whole of the Sabbath.

I may mention here that it was our usual custom to rest on the Sabbath days. This we did because we thought it right, and we came ere long to know that it was absolutely needful; for on this journey southward we all agreed that as life and death might depend on the speed with which we travelled, we were quite justified in continuing our journey on the Sabbath. But we found ourselves at the end of the second week so terribly knocked up that we agreed to devote the whole of the next Sabbath to repose. This we did accordingly, and found the utmost benefit from it; and we could not avoid remarking, in reference to this on the care and tenderness of our heavenly Father, who has so arranged that obedience to His command should not only bring a peculiar blessing to our souls, but, so to speak, a natural and inevitable advantage to our bodies. These reflections seemed to me to throw some light on the passage, "The sabbath was made for man, and not man for the sabbath." But as this is not the place for theological disquisition, I shall not refer further to that subject.

Not having, then, to travel on the following day, we made up our minds to spend an hour or two in a place of concealment near the margin of this pond; and I secretly resolved that I would spend the *whole* night there with my note-book (for the moon, we knew, would be bright), and make a soft pillow of leaves on which I might drop and go to sleep when my eyes refused any longer to keep open.

The moon had just begun to rise when we finished our suppers and prepared to go to our post of observation. We took our rifles with us of course, for although we did not intend to shoot, having more than sufficient food already in camp, we could not tell but that at any moment those weapons might be required for the defence of our lives. Makarooroo had been too long accustomed to see wild animals to understand the pleasure we enjoyed in merely staring at them, so he was left in charge of our camp.

"Now, then," said Peterkin, as we left the encampment, "hurrah, for the menagerie!"

"You may well call it that," said Jack, "for there's no lack of variety."

"Are we to shoot?" inquired Peterkin.

"Better not, I think. We don't require meat, and there is no use in murdering the poor things. What a splendid scene!"

We halted to enjoy the view for a few seconds. The forest out of which we had emerged bordered an extensive plain, which was dotted here and there with scattered groups of trees, which gave to the country an exceedingly rich aspect. In the midst of these the pond lay glittering in the soft moonlight like a sheet of silver. It was surrounded on three sides by low bushes and a few trees. On the side next to us it was open and fully exposed to view. The moonlight was sufficiently bright to render every object distinctly visible, yet not so bright as to destroy the pleasant feeling of mysterious solemnity that pervaded the whole scene. It was wonderfully beautiful. I felt almost as if I had reached a new world.

Continuing our walk we quickly gained the bushes that fringed the margin of the pool, which was nowhere more than thirty yards broad, and on our arrival heard the hoofs of several animals that we had scared away clattering on the ground as they retreated.

"There they go already," cried Jack; "now let us look for a hillock of some kind on which to take up our position."

"We shall not have to look far," said I, "for here seems a suitable spot ready at our hand."

"Your eyes are sharp to-night, Ralph," observed Peterkin; "the place is splendid, so let's to work."

Laying down our rifles, we drew our hunting-knives, and began to cut down some of the underwood on the top of a small hillock that rose a little above the surrounding bushes, and commanded a clear view of the entire circumference of the pond. We selected this spot for the double reason that it was a good point of observation and a safe retreat, as animals coming to the pond to drink, from whatever quarter they might arrive, would never think of ascending a hillock covered with bushes, if they could pass round it.

Having cleared a space sufficiently large to hold us-leaving, however, a thin screen of shrubs in front through which we intended to peep-we strewed the ground with leaves, and lay down to watch with our loaded rifles close beside us. We felt certain of seeing a good many animals, for even during the process of preparing our unlace of retreat several arrived, and were scared away by the noise we made.

Presently we heard footsteps approaching.

"There's something," whispered Peterkin.

"Ay," returned Jack. "What I like about this sort o' thing is your uncertainty as to what may turn up. It's like deep-sea fishing. Hist! look out."

The steps were rapid. Sometimes they clattered over what appeared to be pebbly ground, then they became muffled as the animal crossed a grassy spot; at last it trotted out of the shade of the bushes directly opposite to us into the moonlight, and showed itself to be a beautiful little antelope of the long-horned kind, with a little fawn by its side. The two looked timidly round for a few seconds, and snuffed the air as if they feared concealed enemies, and then, trotting into the water, slaked their thirst together. I felt as great pleasure in seeing them take a long, satisfactory draught as if I had been swallowing it myself, and hoped they would continue there for some time; but they had barely finished when the rapid gallop of several animals was heard, and scared them away instantly.

The newcomers were evidently heavy brutes, for their tread was loud and quite distinct, as compared with the steps of the antelopes. A few seconds sufficed to disclose them to our expectant eyes. A large herd of giraffes trotted to the water's edge and began to drink. It was a splendid sight to behold these graceful creatures stooping to drink, and then raising their heads haughtily to a towering height as they looked about from side to side. In the course of a couple of hours we saw elands, springboks, gnus, leopards, and an immense variety of wild creatures, some of which fawned on and played with each other, while others fought and bellowed until the woods resounded with the din.

While we were silently enjoying the sight, and I attempting to make a few entries in my note-book, our attention was attracted to a cracking of the branches close to the right side of our hillock.

"Look out!" whispered Jack; but the warning was scarcely needed, for we instinctively seized our rifles. A moment after our hearts leaped violently as we heard a crashing step that betokened the approach of some huge creature.

"Are we safe here?" I whispered to Jack.

"Safe enough if we keep still. But we shall have to cut and run if an elephant chances to get sight of us."

I confess that at that moment I felt uneasy. The hillock on the summit of which we lay was only a place of comparative safety, because no animal was likely to ascend an elevated spot without an object in view, and as the purpose of all the nocturnal visitors to that pond was the procuring of water, we did not think it probable that any of them would approach unpleasantly near to our citadel; but if any wild beast should take a fancy to do so, there was nothing to prevent him, and the slight screen of bushes by which we were surrounded would certainly have been no obstacle in the way.

A hunter in the African wilds, however, has not much time to think. Danger is usually upon him in a moment. We had barely time to full-cock our rifles when the bushes near us were trodden down, and a huge black rhinoceros sauntered slowly up to us. So near was he that we could have sprung out from our hiding-place and have caught hold of him, had we chosen to do so.

This enormous unwieldy monster seemed to me so large that he resembled an elephant on short legs, and in the dim, mysterious moonlight I could almost fancy him to be one of those dreadful monsters of the antediluvian world of which we read so much in these days of geological research. I held my breath and glanced at my comrades. They lay perfectly motionless, with their eyes fixed on the animal, which hesitated on approaching our hillock. My blood almost stagnated in my veins. I thought that he must have observed us or smelt us, and was about to charge. He was only undecided as to which side of the hillock he should pass by on his way to the pond. Turning to the left, he went down to the water with a heavy, rolling gait, crushing the shrubs under his ponderous feet in a way that filled me with an exalted idea of his tremendous power.

I breathed freely again, and felt as if a mighty load had been lifted off me. From the suppressed sighs vented by my comrades, I judge that they also had experienced somewhat similar relief. We had not, however, had time to utter a whisper before our ears were assailed by the most tremendous noise that we had yet heard. It came from the opposite side of the pool, as if a great torrent were rushing towards us. Presently a black billow seemed to burst out of the jungle and roll down the sloping bank of the pond.

"Elephants!" exclaimed Jack.

"Impossible," said I; "they must be buffaloes."

At that instant they emerged into the full blaze of the moon, and showed themselves to be a herd of full-grown elephants, with a number of calves. There could not have been fewer than one hundred on the margin of the pond; but from the closeness of their ranks and their incessant movements I found it impossible to count their numbers accurately. This magnificent army began to drink and throw water about, waving their trunks and trumpeting shrilly at the same time with the utmost delight. The young ones especially seemed enjoy themselves immensely, and I observed that their mothers were very attentive to them, caressing them with their trunks and otherwise showing great fondness for their offspring.

"I say," whispered Peterkin, "what a regiment of cavalry these fellows would make, mounted by gorillas armed with scythe-blades for swords and Highland claymores for dirks!"

"Ay, and cannon-revolvers in their pockets!" added Jack. "But, look-that hideous old rhinoceros. He has been standing there for the last two minutes like a rock, staring intently across the water at the elephants."

"Hush!" said I. "Whisper softly. He may hear us."

"There goes something else on our side," whispered Peterkin, pointing to the right of our hillock. "Don't you see it? There, against the —I do believe it's another giraffe!"

"So it is! Keep still. His ears are sharp," muttered Jack, examining the lock of his rifle.

"Come, come!" said I; "no shooting, Jack. You know we came to see, not to shoot."

"Very true; but it's not every day one gets such a close shot at a giraffe. I *must* procure a specimen for you, Ralph."

Jack smiled as he said this, and raised his rifle. Peterkin at the same moment quietly raised his, saying, "If that's your game, my boy, then here goes at the rhinoceros. Don't hurry your aim; we've lots of time."

As I waited for the reports with breathless attention, I was much struck at that moment by the singularity of the circumstances in which we were placed. On our left stood the rhinoceros, not fifteen yards off; on our right the giraffe raised his long neck above the bushes, about twenty yards distant, apparently uncertain whether it was safe to advance to the water; while in front lay the lake, reflecting the soft, clear moonlight, and beyond that the phalanx of elephants, enjoying themselves vastly. I had but two moments to take it all in at a glance, for Jack said "Now!" in a low tone, and instantly the loud report of the two rifles thundered out upon the night air.

Words cannot convey, and the reader certainly cannot conceive, any idea of the trumpeting, roaring, crashing, shrieking, and general hubbub that succeeded to the noise of our firearms. It seemed as if the wild beasts of twenty menageries had simultaneously commenced to smash the woodwork of their cages, and to dash out upon each other in mingled fury and terror; for not only was the crashing of boughs and bushes and smaller trees quite terrific, but the thunderous tread of the large animals was absolutely awful.

We were thoroughly scared, for, in addition to all this, from the midst of the horrid turmoil there came forth a royal roar close behind us that told of a lion having been secretly engaged in watching our proceedings; and we shuddered to think that, but for our firing, he might have sprung upon us as we lay there, little dreaming of his presence.

Since our last adventure with the king of beasts, Makarooroo had entertained us with many anecdotes of the daring of lions, especially of those monsters that are termed man-eaters; so that when we heard the roar above referred to, we all three sprang to our feet and faced about with the utmost alacrity. So intent were we on looking out for this dreadful foe-for we had made up our minds that it must be a man-eating lion-that we were utterly indifferent to the other animals. But they were not indifferent to us; for the wounded rhinoceros, catching sight of us as we stood with our backs towards him, charged at once up the hillock.

To utter three simultaneous yet fearfully distinct yells of terror, spring over the low parapet of bushes, and fly like the wind in three different directions, was the work of a moment. In dashing madly down the slope my foot caught in a creeping shrub, and I fell heavily to the earth.

The fall probably saved my life, for before I could rise the rhinoceros sprang completely over me in its headlong charge. So narrow was my escape that the edge of one of its ponderous feet alighted on the first joint of the little finger of my left hand, and crushed it severely. Indeed, had the ground not been very soft, it must infallibly have bruised it off altogether. The moment it had passed I jumped up, and turning round, ran in the opposite direction. I had scarcely gone ten paces when a furious growl behind me, and the grappling sound as of two animals in deadly conflict, followed by a fierce howl, led me to conclude that the lion and the rhinoceros had unexpectedly met each other, and that in their brief conflict the former had come off second best.

But I gave little heed to that. My principal thought at that moment was my personal safety; so I ran on as fast as I could in the direction of our encampment, for which point, I had no doubt, my companions would also make.

I had not run far when the growl of a lion, apparently in front, caused me to stop abruptly. Uncertain of the exact position of the brute, I turned off to one side, and retreated cautiously and with as little noise as possible, yet with a feeling of anxiety lest he should spring upon me unawares. But my next step showed me that the lion was otherwise engaged. Pushing aside a few leaves that obstructed my vision, I suddenly beheld a lion in the midst of an open space, crouched as if for a spring. Instinctively I threw forward the muzzle of my rifle; but a single glance showed me that his tail, not his head, was towards me. On looking beyond, I observed the head and shoulders of Jack, who, like the lion, was also in a crouching position, staring fixedly in the face of his foe. They were both perfectly motionless, and there could not have been more than fifteen or twenty yards between them.

The true position of affairs at once flashed across me. Jack in his flight had unwittingly run almost into the jaws of the lion; and I now felt convinced that this must be a second lion, for it could not have been the one that was disturbed by the rhinoceros, as I had been running directly away from the spot where these two brutes had met. Jack had crouched at once. We had often talked, over our camp-fire, of such an event as unexpectedly meeting a lion face to face; and Peterkin, who knew a good deal about such matters, had said that in such a case a man's only chance was to crouch and stare the lion out of countenance. We laughed at this; but he assured us positively that he had himself seen it done to tigers in India, and added that if a man turned and ran his destruction would be certain. To fire straight in the face of a lion in such a position would be excessively dangerous; for while the bullet *might* kill, it was more than probable it would glance off the bone of the forehead, which would be presented at an angle to the hunter. The best thing to do, he said, was to stare steadily at the creature until it began to wince, which, if not a wounded beast, it would certainly do; and then, when it turned slowly round, to slink away, take aim at its heart, and fire instantly.

The moon was shining full in Jack's face, which wore an expression of intense ferocity I had never before witnessed, and had not believed it possible that such a look could have been called up by him. The lower part of his face, being shrouded in his black beard, was undiscernible; but his cheeks and forehead were like cold marble. His dark brows were compressed so tightly that they seemed knotted, and beneath them his eyes glittered with an intensity that seemed to me supernatural. Not a muscle moved; his gaze was fixed; and it was not difficult to fancy that he was actually, instead of apparently, petrified.

I could not, of course, observe the visage of the lion, and, to say truth, I had no curiosity on that point; for just then it occurred to me that I was directly in the line of fire, and that if my friend missed the lion there was every probability of his killing me. I was now in an agony of uncertainty. I knew not what to do. If I were to endeavour to get out of the way, I might perhaps cause Jack to glance aside, and so induce the lion to spring. If, on the other hand, I should remain where I was, I might be shot. In this dilemma it occurred to me that, as Jack was a good shot and the lion was very close, it was extremely unlikely that I should be hit; so I resolved to bide my chance, and offering up a silent prayer, awaited the issue.

It was not long of coming. The fixed gaze of a bold human eye cowed at last even the king of the woods. The lion slowly and almost imperceptibly rose, and sidled gently round, with the intention, doubtless, of bounding into the jungle. I saw that if it did so it would pass very close to me so I cocked both barrels and held my piece in readiness.

The click of my locks attracted the lion's attention; its head turned slightly round. At that instant Jack's rifle sprang to his shoulder, and the loud crack of its report was mingled with and drowned by the roar of the lion, as he sprang with a terrible bound, not past me, but straight towards me. I had no time to aim, but throwing the gun quickly to my shoulder, drew both triggers at once.

I had forgotten, in my perturbation, that I carried Peterkin's heavy elephant rifle, charged with an immense quantity of powder and a couple of six-ounce balls. My shoulder was almost dislocated by the recoil, and I was fairly knocked head over heels. A confused sound of yells and roars filled my ear for a moment. I struggled to collect my faculties.

"Hollo! Jack! —Ralph! where are you?" shouted a voice that I well knew to be that of Peterkin. "Hurrah I'm coming. Don't give in! I've killed him! The rhinoceros is dead as a door-nail! Where have you —"

I heard no more, having swooned away.

CHAPTER EIGHTEEN
Strange and terrible discoveries-Jack is made commander-in-chief of an army.

When my consciousness returned, I found myself lying on my back beside our camp-fire, with my head resting on Peterkin's knee; and the first sound I heard was his pleasant voice, as he said —

"All right, Jack; he's coming round. I'm quite certain that no serious damage is done. I know well what sort o' rap he must have got. It'll bother him a little at first, but it won't last long."

Comforted not a little by this assurance, I opened my eyes and looked up.

"What has happened?" I inquired faintly.

"Ah! that's right, Ralph. I'm glad to hear your voice again. D'you know, I thought at first it was all over with you?"

"Over with him!" echoed Peterkin; "it's only begun with him. Ralph's days of valorous deeds are but commencing. —Here, my boy; put this flask to your mouth. It's lucky I fetched it with us. Here, drink."

"No, not until you tell me what has occurred," said I, for I still felt confused in my brain.

"Then I *won't* tell you a word until you drink," repeated my friend, as he looked anxiously in my face and held the flask to my lips.

I sipped a mouthful, and felt much revived.

"Now," continued Peterkin, "I'll tell you what has happened. We've floored a rhinoceros and a giraffe and a lion, which, to my thinking, is a pretty fair bag to make after dusk of a Saturday night! And my big rifle has floored *you*, which is the least satisfactory part of the night's entertainment, but which wouldn't have occurred had you remembered my instructions, which you never do."

"Oh, I recollect now," said I, as the spirits revived me. "I'm all right. —But, Jack, I trust that you have not received damage?"

"Not a scratch, I'm thankful to say; though I must confess I was near catching an ugly wound."

"How so?" I inquired quickly, observing a peculiar smile on Jack's face as he spoke.

"Oh, make your mind easy," put in Peterkin; "it was just a small bit of an escape he made. When you let drive at the lion so effectively, one of the balls went in at his mouth and smashed its way out at the back of his skull. The other ball shaved his cheek, and lodged in a tree not two inches from Jack's nose."

"You don't mean it!" cried I, starting up, regardless of the pain occasioned to my injured shoulder by the movement, and gazing intently in Jack's face.

"Come, come," said he, smiling; "you must not be so reckless, Ralph. Lie down again, sir."

"Peterkin, you should not talk lightly of so narrow an escape," said I reproachfully. "The fact that such a terrible catastrophe has nearly occurred ought to solemnise one."

"Granted, my dear boy; but the fact that such a catastrophe did *not* occur, ought, I hold, to make us jolly. There's no managing a fellow like you, Ralph. I knew that if I told you of this gravely, you would get into such a state of consternational self-reproachativeness, so to speak, that you would infallibly make yourself worse. And now that I tell it to you 'lightly,' as you call it, you take to blowing me up."

I smiled as my friend said this, and held out my hand, which he grasped and squeezed. Feeling at the moment overcome with drowsiness, I unconsciously retained it in my grasp, and thus fell sound asleep.

Three days after this misadventure I was nearly as well as ever, and we were once more journeying by forced marches towards the south. Two days more, we calculated, would bring us to Mbango's village. As the end of our journey approached, we grew more desperately anxious to push forward, lest we should be too late to give them timely warning of the slave-dealer's approach. We also became more taciturn, and I could see plainly that the irrepressible forebodings that filled my own heart, were shared by my companions. Poor Makarooroo never spoke, save in reply to questions addressed pointedly to himself; and seeing the state of his mind, we forbore to trouble him with conversation.

Yet, even while in this anxious state, I could not avoid noticing the singular variety and beauty of both the animal and the vegetable kingdom in the regions through which we passed.

In one part of our journey we had to cross a portion of what is called desert country, but which, notwithstanding its name, was covered with grass, and in many places with bushes, and even trees. Its vegetation, however, as compared with other parts of the country, was light; and it was almost entirely destitute of water, there being no rivers or springs; only a few pools of rain-water were to be found in the hard beds of ancient river-courses. This desert land was inhabited by numbers of bushmen and other natives, as well as by large quantities of game of various kinds. But what struck me as being most singular was the great variety of tuberous roots with which the region was supplied, and which were evidently designed by our beneficent Creator to make up to the inhabitants in a great degree for the want of a full supply of water.

I also observed, with much interest, a species of plant which, like man, is capable of being, as it were, acclimatised. It is not by nature a tuber-bearing plant; yet here it had become so, in order to be able to retain a sufficiency of moisture during the dry season. Makarooroo also dug up for us several tuber-roots, which were the size of a large turnip, and filled with a most delicious juice, which, as we were much oppressed with thirst at the time, appeared to us like nectar. Besides these, we also procured water-melons in abundance at certain spots, which were a great treat, not only to us, but also to elephants, rhinoceroses, antelopes, and many other animals, whose footprints we found in great numbers, and whose depredations among the water-melons were very evident.

During the whole of this journey we made a point, as I have already remarked, of avoiding man; not that we were indifferent to him, but anxious not to be detained at that particular time. We were very fortunate in this matter, for we succeeded in eluding the observation of the natives of many villages that we passed, in escaping others by flight, and in conciliating those who caught us by making them liberal gifts of beads.

One day we came to a halt under the most magnificent tree I ever saw. It was a mowano tree, whose trunk consisted of six stems united in one. The circumference a yard or so from the ground was eighty-four feet-upwards of nine yards in diameter.

"What a tree for a nobleman's park!" said Jack, as we gazed at it, lost in admiration.

"Ay; and behold a gentleman worthy to take up his residence under it," said Peterkin, pointing as he spoke to a living creature that sat among the grass near its roots.

"What can it be?" I exclaimed.

"The original father of all frogs!" replied Peterkin, as he darted forward and killed the thing with a stick.

"I believe it *is* a frog," said Jack.

We all burst into a fit of laughter, for undoubtedly it *was* a frog, but certainly the largest by far that any of us had ever seen. It was quite as large as a chicken!

"What a shame to have killed it!" said I. "Why did you do it?"

"Shame! It was no shame. In the first place, I killed it because I wish you to make scientific inspection of it; and in the second place, I wanted to eat it. Why should not we as well as Frenchmen eat frogs? By the way, that reminds me that we might introduce this giant species into France, and thereby make our fortunes."

"You greedy fellow," cried Jack, who was busying himself in lighting the fire, "your fortune is made already. How many would you have?"

"D'ye know, Jack, I have been in possession of my fortune, as you call it, so short a time that I cannot realise the fact that I have it. —Hollo! Mak, what's wrong with you?"

Peterkin thus addressed our guide because he came into the camp at that moment with a very anxious expression of countenance.

"Dere hab bin fight go on here," said he, showing several broken arrows, stained with blood, which he had picked up near our encampment.

"Ha! so there has, unless these have been shot at wild beasts," said Jack, examining the weapons carefully.

"No, massa; no shot at wild beast. De wild beast hab bin here too, but dey come for to eat mans after he dead."

"Come, let us see the spot," said Jack.

Makarooroo at once led the way, and we all followed him to a place not a hundred yards distant, where there were evident traces of a fight having taken place. Jack seemed to be much distressed at the sight.

"There can be no question as to the fact," he remarked as we returned to our fire; "and at any other time or in any other place I would have thought nothing of it, for we know well enough that the natives here often go to war with each other; but just at *this* time, and so near to our friend Mbango —I fear, I fear much that that villain has been before us."

"No been long, massa," said Makarooroo earnestly. "If we go quick we ketch 'im."

"We *shall* go quick, Mak. But in order to do that, we must eat well, and sleep at least an hour or so. If we push on just now, after a hard day's journey, without food or rest, we shall make but slow progress; and even if we did come up with the slave-dealer, we should not be in a very fit state for a battle."

This was so obvious that we all felt the wisdom of Jack's remarks; so we ate a hearty supper, and then lay down to rest. Peterkin declared the frog to be excellent, but I could not at that time make up my mind to try it.

An hour and a half after lying down, our guide awakened us, and we set forth again with recruited energies.

That night the lions and hyenas roared around us more than was their wont, as if they were aware of our anxious condition, and were desirous of increasing our discomforts. We had to keep a sharp lookout, and once or twice discharged our rifles in the direction of the nearest sounds, not in the expectation of hitting any of the animals, but for the purpose of scaring them away.

Towards morning we came out upon an open plain, and left these evil prowlers of the night behind us.

About daybreak we came within sight of Mbango's village, but the light was not sufficient to enable us to distinguish any object clearly. Here again we came upon traces of war, in the shape of broken arrows and daggers, and human bones; for the poor wretches who had been slain had been at once devoured by wild beasts.

Hurrying forward with intense anxiety, we reached the outskirts of the village; and here a scene presented itself that was well calculated to fill our breasts with horror and with the deepest anxiety. Many of the houses had been set on fire, and were reduced to ashes. The mangled corpses of human beings were seen lying here and there amongst the embers-some partially devoured by wild beasts, others reduced to simple skeletons, and their bones left to whiten on the ruins of their old homes. In one place the form of a woman tied to a tree, and dreadfully mangled, showed that torture had been added to the other horrors of the attack.

With feelings of mingled rage, pity, and anxiety, we hastened towards the hut that had been the residence of Mbango, the chief. We found it, like the rest, in ruins, and among them discovered the remains of a child. Recollecting the little son of our friend Njamie, Okandaga's guardian, I turned the body over in some anxiety; but the features were too much mutilated to be recognisable.

"Alas! alas!" I exclaimed, as we collected in a group round this remnant of a little child, "what a dreadful sight! What an unhappy race of beings! Without doubt our friends have been slain, or carried into captivity."

Poor Makarooroo, who had been from the first going about among the ruins like a maniac, with a bewildered air of utter despair on his sable countenance, looked at me as if he hoped for a slight word that might reanimate hope in his bosom. But I could give him none, for I myself felt hopeless.

Not so, Jack. With that buoyancy of spirit that was peculiar to him, he suggested many ideas that consoled our guide not a little.

"You see," said he, "the rascally Portuguese trafficker in human flesh would naturally try to effect his object with as little bloodshed as possible. He would just fight until he had conquered, not longer; and then he would try to take as many prisoners as he could, in order to carry them away into slavery. Now, I cannot conceive it possible that he could catch the whole tribe."

"Of course not," interrupted Peterkin; "he had a comparatively small party. To take a whole tribe prisoners with such a band were impossible."

"Ay, but you forget," said I, "that he might easily prevail on some other tribe to go to war along with him, and thus capture nearly the whole. Yet some must have escaped into the woods, and it is probable that among these may have been the chief and his household. Okandaga may be safe, and not far off, for all we know."

The guide shook his head.

"At any rate," observed Jack, "if caught they would certainly be guarded with care from injury; so that if we could only find out which way they have gone, we might pursue and attack them."

"Four men attack forty or fifty!" said I despondingly.

"Ay, Ralph. Why not?" asked Peterkin.

"Oh, I doubt not our pluck to do it," I replied; "but I doubt very much our chances of success."

While we were yet speaking our attention was attracted by a low wail, and the appearance of some living object creeping amongst the ruins not far from us. At first we thought it must be a beast of prey lurking in the neighbourhood of the dead, and impatient at our having interrupted its hideous banquet; but presently the object sat up and proved to be a woman. Yet she was so covered with blood and dust, and so awfully haggard in appearance, that we could with difficulty believe her to be a human being.

At first she appeared to be in ignorance of our presence. And indeed so she actually was; for her whole soul was absorbed in the contemplation of the dead and mangled body of an infant which lay in her arms, and which she pressed ever and anon with frantic energy to her breast, uttering occasionally a wail of such heart-broken sadness that the tears sprang irresistibly into my eyes while I gazed upon her. There needed no explanation of her tale of woe. The poor mother had crept back to her hut after the fierce din of battle was over to search for her child, and she had found it; but ah, who can conceive the unutterable anguish of heart that its finding had occasioned!

"Speak to her, Mak," said Peterkin, in a husky voice; "she will be less afraid of you, no doubt, than of us."

Our guide advanced. The slight noise he made in doing so attracted the poor woman's attention, and caused her to look up with a wild, quick glance. The instant she saw us she leaped up with the agility of a leopard, clasped her dead child tightly to her breast, and uttering shriek upon shriek, rushed headlong into the jungle.

"After her!" cried Jack, bounding forward in pursuit. "She's our only chance of gaining information."

We all felt the truth of this, and joined in the chase at top speed. But although we ran fast and well, the affrighted creature at first outstripped us. Then, as we tired her out and drew near, she doubled on her track, and dived hither and thither among the thick underwood in a way that rendered it exceedingly difficult to catch her.

Peterkin was the first to come up with her. He gradually but perseveringly ran her down. When he came within a few yards of her, the poor creature sank with a low wail to the ground, and turning half round, glanced at her pursuer with a timid, imploring, yet despairing expression. Alas! despair mingled with it, because she knew too well the terrible cruelty of savage men when their blood is up, and she knew nothing yet of the hearts of Christians.

Peterkin, whose susceptible nature was ever easily touched, felt a thrill of self-reproach as the thought suddenly occurred that, however good his intentions might be, he was in reality running a helpless woman down like a bloodhound. He stopped short instantly, and acting, as on most occasions he did, impulsively, he threw his rifle away from him, unclasped his belt, and throwing it, with his hunting-knife, also away, sat down on the ground and held out both his hands.

There was something almost ludicrous in the act, but it had the effect of, to some extent, relieving the poor woman's fears. Seeing this, as we successively came up we all laid down our rifles, and stood before the crouching creature with our empty hands extended towards her, to show that we meant her no harm. Still, although she seemed less terrified, she trembled violently, and panted from her recent exertion, but never for a moment relaxed her hold of the dead child.

"Speak to her, Mak," said Jack, as the guide came up. "Tell her who and what we are at once, to relieve her feelings; and let her know especially that we are the bitter enemies of the villain who has done this deed."

While Makarooroo explained, the woman's countenance seemed to brighten up, and in a few minutes she began to tell with great volubility the events of the attack. The trader, she said, had come suddenly on them in the dead of night with a large band, and had at once routed the warriors of the village, who were completely taken by surprise. A few had escaped; but Mbango, with Okandaga and his household, had been taken prisoners, and carried away with many others.

"How long is it since this happened?" inquired Jack.

"She say two days, massa. Den dey go off to 'tack King Jambai."

"Ah! then it is too late to save him," returned Jack, in a tone of sadness.

Our hearts sank on learning this; but on questioning the woman further, we found that the marauding party, deeming themselves too weak to attack so large a village as that of King Jambai, had talked of turning aside to secure the assistance of another tribe not far distant, who, they knew, would be too glad to pick a quarrel with that chief.

"Then we shall do it yet!" cried Jack, springing up energetically. "We shall be in time to warn Jambai and to save Okandaga and her friends. Come, Mak, cheer up; things begin to look better."

The cheerful, confident voice in which our friend said this raised my hopes wonderfully, even although, on consideration, I could not see that our chances of success were very great. Our guide was visibly comforted, and we stepped aside to pick up our rifles with considerable alacrity.

During the brief period in which we were thus employed, the poor woman managed to creep away, and when we again looked round she was gone. Our first impulse was to give chase again, but the thought of the needless terror which that would occasion her deterred us, and before we could make up our minds what to do she was almost beyond our reach, and would certainly have cost us an hour of search, if not longer, to find her. Time pressed. To reach the village of King Jambai with the utmost possible speed was essential to the safety of the tribe, so we resolved to leave her, feeling as we did so that the poor creature could sustain herself on roots and berries without much difficulty or suffering until she reached the village of some neighbouring tribe.

We now pushed on again by forced marches, travelling by night and by day, shooting just enough game as we required for food, and taking no more rest than was absolutely necessary to enable us to hold on our way. In a short time we reached the village, which, to our great joy, we found in much the same state as it was when we left it.

King Jambai received us with great delight, and his people went into a state of immense rejoicing-firing guns, and shouting, and beating kettles and drums, in honour of the arrival of the "white faces;" which name was certainly a misnomer, seeing that our faces had by that time become the very reverse of white-indeed they were little lighter than the countenances of the good people by whom we were surrounded.

But the king's consternation was very great when we told him the reason of our unexpected visit, and related to him the details of the terrible calamity that had befallen poor Mbango and his people. He appeared sincerely grateful for the effort we had made to warn him of the impending attack, and seemed unable to express his thanks when we offered to aid him in the defence of his village.

We now deemed this a fitting moment to tell the king boldly of our having assisted in the escape of Okandaga from his village, and beg his forgiveness. He granted this at once, but strongly advised us to keep our secret quiet, and leave it to him to account to his warriors for the reappearance of the runaway maiden when retaken. Of course we could make no objection to this, so after thanking him we entered upon a discussion of the best method of frustrating the slave-dealer's designs.

"Tell the king," said Jack, addressing himself to our guide, "that if he will make me commander-in-chief of his forces, I will show him how white warriors manage to circumvent their enemies."

"I would like much," said Peterkin, laughing, "to know how Mak will translate the word 'circumvent.' Your style is rather flowery, Jack, for such an interpreter; and upon my word, now I think of it, your presumption is considerable. How do you know that *I* do not wish to be commander-in-chief myself?"

"I shall make over the command to you with all my heart, if you wish it," said Jack, smiling blandly.

"Nay, I'll none of it. However suited I may be to the work, the work is not suited to me, so I resign in your favour."

"Well, then," said Jack, "since you decline to accept the chief command, I'll make you my second. Mak shall be my *aide-de-camp*; you and Ralph shall be generals of divisions."

"I thank you much, my honoured and honourable generalissimo; but perhaps before being thus liberal of your favours, it were well to ascertain that your own services are accepted."

"That is soon done. —What says the king, Mak?"

"Hims say that him's delighted to git you, an' you may doos how you like."

"That's plain and explicit. You see, Peterkin, that I'm fairly installed; so you and I will take a short walk together, and hold a consultation as to our plans in the approaching campaign, while Ralph arranges our hut and makes things comfortable."

"A glorious campaign, truly, to serve in an army of baboons, led by a white gorilla! I would deem it almost comical, did I not see too sure a probability of bloodshed before its conclusion," remarked Peterkin.

"That you shall not see, if I can prevent it; and it is for the purpose of consulting you on that point, and claiming your services in an old and appropriate character, that I drag you along with me now," said Jack, as he rose, and, making a bow to the king, left the hut.

CHAPTER NINETEEN
Preparations for War, and Peculiar Drill.

The plan which Jack and Peterkin concocted, while I was engaged in making the interior of our old residence as comfortable as possible, was as follows: —

Scouts were, in the first place, to be sent out that night all over the country, to ascertain the whereabouts of the enemy. Then, when the enemy should be discovered, they were to send back one of their number to report; while the remainder should remain to dog their steps, if need be, in order to ascertain whether Mbango and Okandaga were in their possession, and if so, where they were kept-whether in the midst of the warriors or in their rear.

This settled, the remainder of the warriors of the village were to be collected together, and a speech to be made to them by Jack, who should explain to them that they were to be divided into two bands: all who carried guns to be under the immediate charge of Jack himself; the others, carrying bows and spears, to be placed under me. Peterkin was to act a peculiar part, which will appear in the course of narration.

Having partaken of a hearty supper, we assembled the scouts, and having, through Makarooroo, given them their instructions, sent them away just as the shades of night began to fall. We next caused a huge bonfire to be kindled, and round this all the men of the village assembled, to the extent of several hundreds. The king soon appeared, and mounting the trunk of a fallen tree, made a long speech to his warriors, telling them of the danger that threatened them, in such vivid and lively terms that the greater part of them began to exhibit expressions of considerable uneasiness on their countenances. He then told them of the trouble that we had taken, in order to give them timely warning-whereat they cast upon us looks of gratitude; and after that introduced Jack to them as their commander-in-chief, saying, that as a white man led the enemy, nothing could be better than that a white man should lead them to meet the enemy-whereat the sable warriors gave a shout of satisfaction and approval.

Having been thus introduced, Jack mounted the trunk of the fallen tree, and Makarooroo got up beside him to interpret. He began, like a wise diplomatist, by complimenting King Jambai, and spoke at some length on courage in general, and on the bravery of King Jambai's warriors in particular; which, of course, he took for granted. Then he came to particulars, and explained as much of his intended movements as he deemed it good for them to know; and wound up by saying that he had three words of command to teach them, which they must learn to understand and act upon that very night. They were, "Forward!" "Halt!" and "Fire!" By saying the first of these words very slow and in a drawling voice, thus, "Forw-a-a-a-a-rd!" and the second in a quick, sharp tone, and the third in a ferocious yell that caused the whole band to start, he actually got them to understand and distinguish the difference between the commands, and to act upon them in the course of half an hour.

The drill of his army being thus completed, Jack dismissed them with a caution to hold themselves in readiness to answer promptly the first call to arms; and the king enforced the caution by quietly assuring them that the man who did not attend to this order, and otherwise respect and obey Jack as if he were the king, should have his heart, eyes, and liver torn out, and the rest of his carcass cast to the dogs —a threat which seemed to us very horrible and uncalled for, but which, nevertheless, was received by the black warriors with perfect indifference.

"Now, Mak," said Jack, as he descended to the ground, "do you come with me, and help me to place sentries."

"W'at be dat, massa?"

"Men who are placed to guard the village from surprise during the night," explained Jack.

"Ho! dat be de ting; me know someting 'bout dat."

"No doubt you do, but I daresay you don't know the best way to place them; and perhaps you are not aware that the pretty little threat uttered by the king shall be *almost* carried out in the case of every man who shall be found asleep at his post or who shall desert it."

The guide grinned and followed his commander in silence, while I returned to our hut and busied myself in cleaning the rifles and making other preparations for the expected fight.

At an early hour on the following morning we were awakened by the arrival of one of the scouts, who reported that the Portuguese trader, with a strong and well-armed force, was encamped on the margin of a small pond about fifteen miles distant from the village. The scout had gone straight to the spot on being sent out, knowing that it was a likely place for them to encamp, if they should encamp at all. And here he found them making active preparations for an attack on the village. Creeping like a serpent through the grass, the scout approached near enough to overhear their arrangements, which were to the elect that the attack should take place at midnight of the following day. He observed that there were many prisoners in the camp-men, women, and children-and these were to be left behind, in charge of a small party of armed men; while the main body, under the immediate command of the Portuguese trader, should proceed to the attack of the village.

From the scout's description of the prisoners, we became convinced that they were none other than our friends Mbango and his people, and one woman answering to the description of Okandaga was among them.

"So, Mak, we shall save her yet," cried Jack heartily, slapping the shoulder of the guide, whose honest visage beamed with returning hope.

"Yis, massa. S'pose we go off dis hour and fight 'em?"

"Nay; that were somewhat too hasty a movement. 'Slow but sure' must be our motto until night. Then we shall pounce upon our foes like a leopard on his prey. But ask the scout if that is all he has got to tell us."

"Hims say, massa, dat hims find one leetle chile-one boy-when hims go away from de camp to come back to here."

"A boy!" repeated Jack; "where-how?"

"In de woods, where hims was trow'd to die; so de scout take him up and bring him to here."

"Ah, poor child!" said I; "no doubt it must have been sick, and being a burden, has been left behind. But stay. How could that be possible if it was found between the camp and this village?"

On further inquiry, we ascertained that the scout, after hearing what he thought enough of their arrangements, had travelled some distance beyond the encampment, in order to make sure that there were no other bands connected with the one he had left, and it was while thus engaged that he stumbled on the child, which seemed to be in a dying condition.

"Hims say, too," continued Makarooroo, after interpreting the above information, "that there be one poor woman in awfable sorrow, screechin' and hollerowin' like one lion."

"Eh?" exclaimed Peterkin. "Describe her to us."

The scout did so as well as he could.

"As sure as we live," cried Peterkin, "it is our friend Njamie, and the child must be her boy! Come, show us the little fellow."

We all ran out and followed the scout to his hut, where we found his wives-for he had three of them-nursing the child as tenderly as if it had been their own. It was very much wasted, evidently through want of food and over-fatigue; but we instantly recognised the once sturdy little son of Njamie in the faded little being before us. He, too, recognised us, for his bright spectral eyes opened wide when he saw us.

"I knew it," said I.

"I told you so," cried Peterkin. —"Now, Mak, pump him, and let's hear what he knows."

The poor child was far too much exhausted to undergo the pumping process referred to. He could merely answer that Njamie and Okandaga and Mbango were prisoners in the camp, and then turned languidly away, as if he desired rest.

"Poor boy!" said Peterkin tenderly, as he laid his hand gently on the child's woolly pate. — "Tell them, Mak, to look well after him here, and they shall be paid handsomely for-nay" (here he interrupted himself), "don't say that. 'Tis a bad thing to offer to pay for that which people are willing to do for love."

"Right, lad," said Jack: "we can easily make these poor folk happy by giving them something afterwards, without saying that it is bestowed because of their kindness to the boy. The proper reward of diligent successful labour is a prize, but the best reward of love and kindness is a warm, hearty recognition of their existence. —Just tell them, Mak, that we are glad to see them so good and attentive to the little chap. —And now, my generals, if it is consistent with your other engagements, I would be glad to have a little private consultation with you."

"Ready and willing, my lord," said Peterkin, as we followed Jack towards the king's palace. "But," he added seriously, "I don't like to be a general of *division* at all."

"Why not, Peterkin?"

"Why, you see, when I was at school I found division so uncommonly difficult, and suffered so much, mentally and physically, in the learning of it, that I have a species of morbid antipathy to the very name. I even intend to refuse a seat in parliament, when offered to me, because of the divisions that are constantly going on there. If you could only make me a general of subtraction now, or —"

"That," interrupted Jack, "were easily done, by deducting you from the force altogether, and commanding you to remain at home."

"In which case," rejoined Peterkin, "I should have to become general of addition, by revolunteering my services, in order to prevent the whole expedition from resolving itself into General Muddle, whose name and services are well-known in all branches of military and civil service."

"So that," added Jack, "it all comes to this, that you and Ralph and I must carry on the war by rule of three, each taking his just and appropriate proportion of the work to be done. Now, to change the subject, there's the sun getting up, and so is the king, if I may judge from the stir in his majesty's household."

Having begged the king to assemble his warriors together, Jack now proceeded to divide them into four companies, or bands, over which he appointed respective leaders. All the men who possessed guns were assembled together in one band, numbering about one hundred and fifty men. These Jack subdivided into two companies, one including a hundred, the other fifty men. The remainder, constituting the main army, were armed with bows and arrows, spears and knives. Of these a large force was told off to remain behind and guard the village.

This home-guard was placed under command of the king in person. The hundred musketeers were placed under Peterkin's command. The other fifty were given to me, along with a hundred spear and bow men. Jack himself took command of the main body of spearmen. As Peterkin had to act a special and independent part, besides commanding his hundred musketeers, Makarooroo was made over to him, to act as lieutenant.

All these arrangements and appointments were made in a cool, quiet, and arbitrary manner by Jack, to whom the natives, including the king, looked up with a species of awe amounting almost to veneration.

"Now," said our commander-in-chief to Lieutenant Mak, "tell the niggers I am going to make them a speech," (this was received with a grunt of satisfaction), "and that if they wish to have the smallest chance of overcoming their enemies, they had better give their closest attention to what I have to say."

Another grunt of acquiescence followed this announcement.

"Say that I am going to speak to them of things so mysterious that they shall not by any conceivable or possible effort understand them."

This being quite in accordance with the superstitions and tastes of the negroes, was received with eager acclamations of delight.

"Tell them," continued Jack, in a deep, solemn tone, and frowning darkly, "that we shall gain the victory *only* through *obedience*. Each man must keep his ears open and his eye on his leader, and must obey orders *at once*. If the order 'Halt' should be given, and any man should have his mouth open at the time, he must *keep* his mouth open, and shut it *after* he has halted."

Here Jack took occasion to revert to the three orders, "Forward," "Halt," and "Fire," and repeated the lesson several times, until his men were quite perfect. Then he put the various bodies under their respective commanders, and telling the musketeers to make believe to fire (but making sure that they should not really do it, by taking their guns from them), he made each of us give the various words separately, so that our men should become familiar with our voices.

This done, he called the generals of divisions to him, and said —

"Now, gentlemen, I am going to review my troops, and to give them their final lesson in military tactics, with the double view of seeing that they know what they have got to do, and of impressing them with a due sense of the great advantage of even a slight knowledge of drill."

He then directed us to take command of our several companies (Makarooroo being placed on this occasion over the king's band), and pointed out the separate directions in which we were ultimately to post our troops, so as to advance upon the spot on which the king stood when the signal should be given. We had already taught the men the necessity of attacking in a compact single line, and of forming up into this position from what is termed Indian file, with which latter they were already acquainted. Of course we could not hope to teach them the principles of wheeling in the short time at our command. To overcome this difficulty, we told each band to follow its leader, who should walk in front; to advance when he advanced, to retire when he retired, and to turn this way or that way, according to his movements.

At a signal we gave the word "Forward!" and the whole band defiled into the woods before the king, and disappeared like a vision, to the unutterable amazement of his majesty, who stood perfectly motionless, with eyes and mouth open to their fullest extent.

Having marched together for some distance, each leader detached his men and led them, as it were, to opposite directions of the compass, three of the bands making a considerable détour, in order to get the spot where the king stood in the centre of us. Then we halted and awaited the next signal. In about ten minutes it was given —a loud whistle-and we gave the word "Forward" again. I say "we," because the result proved that we had done so. Being out of sight of the other bands, of course I could not see how they acted.

On I rushed over brake and bush and morass, my men following me in a very good line, considering the nature of the ground. I had divided them into four lines, with an interval of about six yards between each. And it was really wonderful how well they kept in that position. The other companies had been ordered to act in the same way.

On bursting out of the woods I saw that we had outstripped the other companies, so I held my men in check by running somewhat slower; and they had been so deeply impressed with the fatal consequences of not doing exactly as I did, that they stared at me with all their eyes, to the no small risk of their lives; for one or two dashed against trees, and others tumbled head over heels into holes, in their anxiety to keep their eyes upon me.

In a few seconds I observed Peterkin spring out of the woods, followed by his men, so I went on again at full speed. As we entered the village, our ranks were sadly broken and confused by the huts; but on gaining the open space where Jack stood, I was pleased to observe that the negroes tried, of their own accord, to regain their original formation, and succeeded so well that we came on in four tolerably straight and compact lines. Each commander having been forewarned to hold his men in check, or to push forward, so as to arrive at the central point at the same moment, Jack, Peterkin, Makarooroo, and I ran in upon the king together, and unitedly gave the word "Halt!" whereupon we found ourselves in the centre of a solid square.

So deeply had the men been impressed with the necessity of obedience that they had scarcely observed each other's approach. They now stood rooted to the ground in every possible attitude of suddenly-arrested motion, and all with their eyes and mouths wide open. In another moment the result of their combined movement became evident to them, and they uttered a yell of delighted surprise.

"Very good, very good indeed," said Jack; "and that concluding yell was very effective-quite magnificent. —But you see," he added, turning to me, "although such a yell is sufficiently appalling to us, it will no doubt be a mere trifle to men who are used to it. What say you to teaching them a British cheer?"

"Absurd," said I; "they will never learn to give it properly."

"I don't know that," rejoined Jack, in a doubtful manner.

"Try," said Peterkin.

"So I will. —Mak, tell them now that I'm going to continue the speech which this little review interrupted."

"They's all ready for more, massa."

This was patent to the meanest capacity; for the negroes stood gazing at their commander-in-chief with eyes and mouths and ears open, and nostrils expanded, as if anxious to gulp in and swallow down his words through every organ.

"There is a cry," said Jack, "which the white man gives when he enters into battle —a terrible cry, which is quite different from that of the black man, and which is so awful that it strikes terror into the heart of the white man's enemies, and has even been known to make a whole army fly almost without a shot being fired. We shall let you hear it."

Thereupon Jack and I and Peterkin gave utterance to a cheer of the most vociferous description, which evidently filled the minds of the natives with admiration.

"Now," resumed Jack, "I wish my black warriors to try that cheer —"

Some of the black warriors, supposing that the expression of this wish was a direct invitation to them to begin, gave utterance to a terrific howl.

"Stay! stop!" cried Jack, holding up his hand.

Every mouth was closed instantly.

"You must cheer by command. I will say 'Hip, hip, hip!' three times; as soon as I say the third 'hip,' out with the cry. Now then. Hip, hip —"

"Popotamus," whispered Peterkin.

"Hip, hurrah!" shouted Jack.

"Hurl! ho! sh! kee! how!" yelled the savages, each man giving his own idea of our terror-inspiring British cheer.

"That will do," said Jack quietly; "it is quite evident that the war-cry of the white man is not suited to the throat of the black. You will utter your usual shout, my friends, when the signal is given; but *remember*, not before that.

"And now I come to the greatest mystery of all." (Every ear was eagerly attentive.) "The shot and bits of metal and little stones with which King Jambai's warriors are accustomed to kill will not do on this great and peculiar occasion. They will not answer the purpose-my purpose; therefore I have provided a kind of bullet which every one must use instead of his usual shot. No warriors ever used such bullets in the fight before. They are very precious, because I have only enough of them to give one to each man. But that will do. If the enemy does not fly at the first discharge, then you may load with your own shot."

So saying, Jack, with the utmost gravity, took from the pouch that hung at his side a handful of little balls of paper about the size of a musket bullet, which he began to distribute among the savages. We had observed Jack making several hundreds of these, the night previous to this memorable day, out of one or two newspapers we had carried along with us for wadding; but he would not at that time tell us what he was going to do with them. The negroes received this novel species of ammunition with deep interest and surprise. Never having seen printed paper before, or, in all probability, paper of any kind, they were much taken up with the mysterious characters imprinted thereon, and no doubt regarded these as the cause of the supernatural power which the bullets were supposed to possess.

"Remember," said Jack, "when these are discharged at the enemy, I do not say that they will kill, but I do say that they will cause the enemy to fly. Only, be assured that everything depends on your *obedience*. And if one single stone, or nail, or hard substance is put in along with these bullets, the chief part of my plans will be frustrated."

It was quite evident, from the expression of their sable countenances, that the idea of the bullets not killing was anything but agreeable. They were too deeply impressed, however, with

Jack's power, and too far committed in the enterprise, and generally too much overwhelmed with mingled surprise and perplexity, to offer any objection.

"Now," said Jack in conclusion, "you may go and eat well. To-night, when it grows dark, hold yourselves in readiness to go forth in *dead silence*. Mind that: not a sound to be uttered until the signal, 'Hip, hip, hip!' is given."

"And," added Peterkin, in an undertone to Makarooroo, "tell them that King Jambai expects that every man will do his duty."

This remark was received with a shout and a frightful display of white teeth, accompanied by a tremendous flourish of guns, bows, and spears.

There was something quite awful, not to say picturesque, in this displaying of teeth, which took place many times during the course of the above proceedings. You looked upon a sea of black ebony balls, each having two white dots with black centres near the top of it. Suddenly the ebony balls were gashed across, and a sort of storm, as it were, of deep red mingled with pure white swept over the dark cloud of heads before you, and vanished as quickly as it had appeared, only to reappear, however, at the next stroke of humour, or at some "touch of that nature" which is said on very high authority, to "make the whole world kin."

The proceedings eventually closed with a brief speech from the king, who referred to Peterkin's remark about each man doing his duty, and said that, "if each man did *not* do his duty —" Here his majesty paused for a minute, and wrought his countenance into horrible contortions, indicative of the most excruciating agony, and wound up with an emphatic repetition of that dire threat about the unnatural treatment of eyes, heart, liver, and carcass, which had on the previous evening sounded so awful in our ears, and had been treated with such profound indifference by those whom it was specially designed to affect.

"I didn't know, Jack," observed Peterkin gravely, as we returned to our hut, "that you were such an out-and-out humbug."

"You are severe, Peterkin. I scarcely deserve to be called a humbug for acting to the best of my judgment in peculiar circumstances."

"Peculiar circumstances!" responded Peterkin. "Truly they have received peculiar treatment!"

"That is as it should be," rejoined Jack; "at any rate, be they peculiar or be they otherwise, our plans are settled and our mode of action fixed, so we must e'en abide the issue."

CHAPTER TWENTY
A Warlike Expedition and a Victory.

It was excessively dark that night when we set forth on our expedition.

The scout from whom we had already ascertained so much about the intended movements of the enemy also told us that they meant to set out at a little before midnight and march on the village by a certain route. Indeed, it was very unlikely that they would approach by any other, as the jungle elsewhere was so thick as to render marching, especially at night, very difficult.

Jack therefore resolved to place the greater proportion of his troops in ambush at the mouth of a small gully or dell a few miles from the enemy's camp, where they were almost certain to pass. But with a degree of caution that I thought highly creditable in so young and inexperienced a general, he sent out a considerable number of the most trustworthy men in advance, with instructions to proceed with the stealth of leopards, and to bring back instant information of any change of route on the part of the foe.

The troops placed in ambush at the dell above referred to were Peterkin's hundred musketeers, supported by Jack's spear and bow men. I was ordered to advance by a circuitous route on the camp itself with my fifty musketeers, followed by my small company of spearmen. My instructions were, to conceal my men as near to the camp as possible, and there await the first discharge of firearms from the dell, when I was to rise, advance upon the camp, utter a terrific shout when within fifty yards, rush forward to within twenty-five yards, halt, pour in one withering volley of blank cartridge, and charge without giving my men time to load.

Of course I could not speak to my men; but this was a matter of little consequence, as they were now well acquainted with our three words of command, "Forward," "Halt," and "Fire," and fully understood that they must under all circumstances follow their leader. I knew well enough that there must be no little danger in this arrangement, because the leader would necessarily be always in front of the muzzles of the loaded guns. But there was no help for it, so I resolved to act upon my usual principle-namely, that when a thing is inevitable, the best thing to do is to treat it as being unavoidable.

Having conducted my men stealthily and successfully to the vicinity of the enemy's camp, though with some difficulty, owing to the almost impenetrable nature of the jungle through which we had to pass in making the détour necessary to avoid falling in with the attacking force, we proceeded to advance to within as short a distance of it as possible without running the risk of being discovered. This was not difficult, for the men left to guard the camp, supposing, no doubt, that their presence in that part of the country was not suspected, had taken no precautions in the way of placing sentries; so we quickly arrived at the foot of a small mound about sixty yards or so from the encampment. At the foot of this mound I caused my men to lie down, giving them to understand, by signs, that they were on no account to move until I should return. Then I crept alone to the brow of the mound, and obtained a clear view of the camp.

The men who should have guarded it were, I found, busily employed in cooking their supper. There were, perhaps, upwards of a hundred of them. To my great satisfaction, I observed the captives sitting near to the fire; and although at so considerable a distance from them, I felt certain that I recognised the figures of Mbango and Okandaga. Hastening back to my men, I endeavoured to give them as much information as possible by means of signs, and then lay down beside them to await the signal from Jack's party.

Although the attack of both our parties was to be simultaneous, the first shot was to be fired by our troops in the dell. I will therefore describe their part of the engagement first. Jack described it to me minutely after all was over.

On reaching the dell Jack disposed his forces so as to command the only approach to it. The hundred musketeers he placed in a double row directly across the deepest and darkest part. The spearmen he divided into two bodies, which he posted on the flanks of the musketeers among the bushes. He then showed the rear rank of the latter how to point their pieces over the shoulders of the men in the front rank at a given signal, but carefully reiterated the order not to touch a trigger until the word "Fire" should be given.

"Now, Peterkin," said Jack, when these dispositions had been made, "it is time for you to get ready. Makarooroo and I can manage these fellows, so you have my permission to go and play your own independent part. Only let me warn you to remember your last exploit in this way, and see that you don't do yourself a damage."

"Thanks, noble general, for the permission," answered Peterkin, "of which I shall avail myself. In reference to your advice, I may remark that it is exceedingly valuable-so much so, indeed, that I would advise you not to part with it until asked for."

With that Peterkin ran into the jungle, and was soon lost to view.

On gaining a sufficient distance from the men, he took off the greater part of his clothes, and wound round his person several pieces of light-coloured cotton that he chanced to have with him, and some pieces of old newspaper. Then he decked his head with leaves and ragged branches, as he had done before in the haunted cave, making himself, in short, as wild and fantastic a looking creature as possible-the only difference between his getting-up on this and the former occasion being that he was white instead of black. For he wisely judged that a white demon must naturally appear infinitely more appalling and horrible to a negro than one of his own colour.

The two cones of moistened powder, however, which he had prepared for this occasion, were very much larger than the former, and had been fitted into two wooden handles, or cups, for safety. With these in his hands, he crept to the top of a steep, sloping mound or hill near the entrance to the dell, and considerably in advance of the troops. Here he sat down to await the approach of the enemy.

There is something very eerie and awe-inspiring in a solitary night-watch, especially if it be kept in a wild, lonesome place. Peterkin afterwards told me that, while sitting that night on the top of the mound, looking out upon a plain, over which the enemy were expected to approach, on the one hand, and down into the dark dell where our troops were posted, on the other hand, his heart more than once misgave him; and he could not help asking himself the questions, "What if our plans miscarry? What if our united volley and cheer, and my demoniac display, should fail to intimidate the negroes?" Such questions he did not like to dwell upon, for he knew that in the event of failure a regular pitched battle would be fought, and much blood would certainly flow.

While indulging in such thoughts, he observed a dark form glide past the foot of the mound on which he lay, and vanish in the obscurity of the dell, which was so surrounded by crags and rocky places covered with underwood that no light could penetrate into it. At first he was startled, and thought of giving the alarm to his comrades; but on second thoughts he concluded the person must have been one of his own scouts returned with news; at all events, he felt that one man could do no harm worth speaking of to so large a party.

Presently he observed a large band of men coming over the plain towards the entrance of the dell. These, he felt assured, must be the enemy; and he was right. They came on in a large, compact body, and were well-armed; yet, from the quick and unguarded manner of their approach, he could perceive that they suspected no ambush.

They entered the dell in a confused though solid and silent body; and Peterkin could observe, by the dim light, that they were led by one man, who walked in advance, whom he rightly judged to be the Portuguese slave-dealer.

The time for action had now come. He examined the points of his powder-cones, to ascertain that they were dry, then held a match in readiness, and listened intently to the footsteps of the foe.

I have already explained that Jack had drawn his musketeers across the dell, and placed the spearmen in the jungle on both flanks. They were arranged in such a way as to form three sides of a square, into which the unsuspecting enemy now marched. Jack allowed them to approach to within thirty paces of his musketeers, and then gave, in a loud, deep, sonorous tone, the word —"Hip! hip! hip!"

The compound cheer and yell that instantly followed the last hip was so tremendous, coming, as it did, from all sides except the rear, that the enemy were absolutely paralysed. They stood rooted to the earth, as motionless as if they had been transformed into stone.

Jack raised his hand, in which he held a bunch of white grass that could be distinctly seen in the dark.

Every muzzle was pointed on the instant, but not a sound was heard save the click of a hundred locks.

The sound was familiar to the enemy, although never before heard at one moment in such numbers. They started; but before a step could be taken, the word "Fire" was given.

Instantly a sheet of flame swept across the entire dell, and the united crash of a hundred guns seemed to rend the very earth. The surrounding cliffs reverberated and multiplied the horrid din, while, led by Jack, cheer followed cheer, or rather howls and yells filled the air, and kept awake the echoes of the place.

The enemy turned and fled, and the shrieks to which they gave utterance as they ran betokened the extremity of their terror. It wanted but one touch to complete their consternation, and that touch was given when Peterkin, lighting his powder-cones, showed himself on the mound, dancing in a blaze of fire, and shrieking furiously as the horrified tide of men swept by.

In the midst of his wild orgies, Peterkin acted an impromptu and unintentional part by tripping over the brow of the hill, and rolling down the steep declivity like a fire-wheel into the very midst of the flying crew. Jumping hastily up, he charged through the ranks of the foe, flung the two hissing cones high into the air, and darting into the jungle, hid himself effectually from view.

Meanwhile Jack still held the bunch of white straw aloft. Every eye was fixed on it, but not a man moved, because it remained stationary. This absence of pursuit in the midst of such appalling sights and sounds must, undoubtedly, have added to the mystery and therefore to the terrors of the scene.

Suddenly the white bunch was seen to dart forward. Jack, who now considered the enemy almost beyond the chance of being overtaken, gave the word, "Forward!" in the voice of a Stentor, following it up with "Hip, hip, hurrah!" and the whole host, musketeers and spearmen in a mingled mass, rushed yelling out upon the plain, and gave chase to the foe.

"Not so badly done," said Jack, with a quiet laugh, as he laid his hand on Peterkin's shoulder.

"Why, Jack, how did you find me out?"

"Easily enough, when it is considered that I saw you go in. The flame of your wild-fire indicated your movements pretty plainly to me, although terror and amazement no doubt blinded the eyes of every one else. Even Mak's teeth began to chatter when he saw you perform that singular descent of the hill, and no wonder. I hope no bones have been broken?"

"No; all right as far as that goes," replied Peterkin within a laugh; "but I've lost a good deal of skin. However, it'll grow again. I'm glad it's no worse. But I say, Jack, do you think our fellows won't overtake these rascals?"

"No fear of that. I took care to give them a good start, and if there be any truth in the generally received idea that terror lends wings, I'm pretty sure that each man in the enemy's ranks must have obtained the loan of several pairs to-night. But have you heard the sound of Ralph's guns?"

"No; the din here was enough to drown anything so distant."

"Well, we must away to him as fast as we can. I expect that poor Mak is off before us."

"But you'll wait until I put on my clothes?" said Peterkin, hasting back towards the place where he had undressed.

"Certainly, lad; only look alive."

Soon afterwards they left the place together.

While this was going on at the dell, I, on hearing the first shot, gave the word "Forward!" in a low tone. My men instantly rose and followed me, and I could not, even at that anxious moment, help admiring the serpent-like facility with which they glided from bush to bush, without the slightest noise. We descended a hill, crossed a small brook, and approached to within thirty yards of the camp without being discovered.

Suddenly I leaped on the top of a hillock, and shouted at the utmost pitch of my voice the single word "Halt!"

On hearing it all the men in the camp sprang to their arms, and stood gazing round them with looks of consternation.

My next word was, "Fire!"

A firm, tremendous crash burst from among the bushes, and my single person, enveloped in smoke and flame, was, I believe, the only object visible to those in the camp.

"Hip, hip, hip, hurrah! forward!" I shouted; and with a ferocious yell we poured like a whirlwind upon the foe.

The same result that had occurred at the dell took place here. The enemy never awaited our charge. They fled instantly, and so great was their terror that they actually threw down their arms, in order to facilitate their flight.

On gaining the camp, however, I found, to my sorrow, that we had done the thing only too vigorously; for we had not only put the enemy to flight, but we had also frightened away those whom we had come to deliver!

At this point in the engagement I came to learn how incompetent I was to command men in cases of emergency, for here my presence of mind utterly forsook me. In my anxiety to capture Mbango and his friends I ordered an immediate pursuit. Then it occurred to me that, in the event of my men being successful in overtaking the fugitives, they would instantly murder them all, so I tried to call them back; but, alas! they did not understand my words, and they were by this time so excited as to be beyond all restraint. In a few minutes I found myself left alone in the enemy's camp, and heard the shouts of pursued and pursuers growing gradually fainter and more distant, as they scattered themselves through the jungle.

Seating myself by the fire in a state of mind bordering on despair, I buried my face in my hands, and endeavoured to collect myself, and consider what, under the circumstances, should be now done.

CHAPTER TWENTY ONE

Arrangements for pursuing the enemy, and sudden change of plans.

"You seem to be taking it easy, old boy," said a voice close to my elbow.

I started, and looked up hastily.

"Ah! Peterkin. You there?"

"Ay; and may I not reply, with some surprise, *you here?*"

"Truly you may, —but what could I do? The men ran away from me, whether I would or no; and you are aware I could not make myself understood, not being able to — But where is Jack?"

I asked this abruptly, because it occurred to me at that moment that he and Peterkin should have been together.

"Where is Jack?" echoed Peterkin; "I may ask that of you, for I am ignorant on the point. He and I got separated in endeavouring to escape from the scrimmage caused by your valiant attack. You seem to have scattered the whole force to the winds. Oh, here he is, and Mak along with him."

Jack and our guide came running into the camp at that moment.

"Well, Ralph, what of Okandaga?"

"Ah! what of her indeed?" said Peterkin. "I forgot her. You don't moan to say she was not in the camp?"

"Indeed she was," said I, "and so were Mbango, and his wife Njamie, and one or two others whom I did not know; but my men went at them with such ferocity that they fled along with our enemies."

"Fled!" cried Jack.

"Ay; and I fear much that it will fare ill with them if they are overtaken, for the men were wild with excitement and passion."

"Come, this must be looked to," cried Jack, seizing his rifle and tightening his belt; "we must follow, for if they escape our hands they will certainly be retaken by their former captors."

We followed our comrade, without further remark, in the direction of the fugitives; but although we ran fast and long, we failed to come up with them. For two hours did we dash through bush and brake, jungle and morass, led by Makarooroo, and lighted by the pale beams of the moon. Then we came to a halt, and sat down to consult.

"Dem be gone," said our wretched guide, whose cup of happiness was thus dashed from his hand just as he was about to raise it to his lips.

"Now, don't look so dismal, Mak," cried Peterkin, slapping the man on the shoulder. "You may depend upon it, we will hunt her up somehow or other. Only let us keep stout hearts, and we can do anything."

"Very easily said, Master Peterkin," observed Jack; "but what course do you propose we should follow just now?"

"Collect our scattered men; go back to the village; have a palaver with King Jambai and his chiefs; get up a pursuit, and run the foxes to earth."

"And suppose," said Jack, "that you don't know in which direction they have fled, how can we pursue them?"

"It is very easy to suppose all manner of difficulties," retorted Peterkin. "If you have a better plan, out with it."

"I have no better plan, but I have a slight addition to make to yours, which is, that when we collect a few of our men, I shall send them out to every point of the compass, to make tracks like the spokes of a wheel, of which the village shall be the centre; and by that means we shall be pretty certain to get information ere long as to the whereabouts of our fugitives. So now let us be up and doing; time is precious to-night."

In accordance with this plan, we rapidly retraced our steps to the dell, which had been appointed as our place of rendezvous. Here we found the greater part of our men assembled; and so well-timed had Jack's movements been, that not one of them all had been able to overtake or slay a single enemy. Thus, by able generalship, had Jack gained a complete and bloodless victory.

Having detached and sent off our scouts-who, besides being picked men, travelled without any other encumbrance than their arms-we resumed our journey homeward, and reached the village not long after sunrise, to the immense surprise of Jambai, who could scarcely believe that we had routed the enemy so completely, and whose scepticism was further increased by the total, and to him unaccountable, absence of prisoners, or of any other trophies of our success in the fight. But Jack made a public speech, of such an elaborate, deeply mysterious, and totally incomprehensible character, that even Makarooroo, who translated, listened and spoke with the deepest reverence and wonder; and when he had concluded, there was evidently a firm impression on the minds of the natives that this victory was-by some means or in some way or other quite inexplicable but highly satisfactory-the greatest they had ever achieved.

The king at once agreed to Jack's proposal that a grand pursuit should take place, to commence the instant news should be brought in by the scouts. But the news, when it did come, had the effect of totally altering our plans.

The first scout who returned told us that he had fallen in with a large body of the enemy encamped on the margin of a small pond. Creeping like a snake through the grass, he succeeded in getting near enough to overhear the conversation, from which he gathered two important pieces of information-namely, that they meant to return to their own lands in a north-easterly direction, and that their prisoners had escaped by means of a canoe which they found on the banks of the river that flowed past King Jambai's village.

The first piece of information decided the king to assemble his followers, and go off in pursuit of them at once; the second piece of news determined us to obtain a canoe and follow Mbango and his companions to the sea-coast, whither, from all that we heard, we concluded they must certainly have gone. As this, however, was a journey of many weeks, we had to take the matter into serious consideration.

"It is quite evident," said Jack, as we sat over our supper on the night after receiving the above news —"it is quite evident that they mean to go to the coast, for Mbango had often expressed to Mak a wish to go there; and the mere fact of their having been seen to escape and take down stream, is in itself pretty strong evidence that they did not mean to return to their now desolated village, seeing that the country behind them is swarming with enemies; and of course they cannot know that we have conquered the main body of these rascals. I therefore propose that we should procure a canoe and follow them: first, because we must at all hazards get hold of poor Okandaga, and relieve the anxiety of our faithful guide Makarooroo; and second, because it is just as well to go in that direction as in any other, in order to meet with wild animals, and see the wonders of this land."

"But what if King Jambai takes it into his black woolly head to decline to let us go?" said Peterkin.

"In that case we must take French leave of him."

"In which case," said I, in some alarm, "all my specimens of natural history will be lost."

Jack received this remark with a shake of his head and a look of great perplexity; and Peterkin said, "Ah, Ralph, I fear there's no help for it. You must make up your mind to say good-bye to your mummies-big puggies and all."

"But you do not know," said I energetically, "that Jambai will detain us against our will."

"Certainly not," replied Jack; "and for your sake I hope that he will not. At any rate I will go to see him about this point after supper. It's of no use presenting a petition either to king, lord, or common while his stomach is empty. But there is another thing that perplexes me: that poor sick child, Njamie's son, must not be left behind. The poor distracted mother has no doubt given him up for lost. It will be like getting him back from the grave."

"True," said I; "we must take him with us. Yet I fear he is too ill to travel, and we cannot await his recovery."

"He is not so ill as he seemed," observed Peterkin. "I went to see him only half an hour ago, and the little chap was quite hearty, and glad to see me. The fact is, he has been ill-used and ill-fed. The rest and good treatment he has received have, even in the short time he has been here, quite revived him."

"Good," said Jack; "then he shall go with us. I'll engage to take him on my back when he knocks up on the march-for we have a march before us, as I shall presently explain-and when we get into a canoe he will be able to rest."

"But what march do you refer to?" I asked.

"Simply this. Mak, with whom I have had a good deal of conversation on the subject, tells me that the river makes a considerable bend below this village, and that by taking a short cut of a day's journey or so over land we can save time, and will reach a small hamlet where canoes are to be had. The way, to be sure, is through rather a wild country; but that to us is an advantage, as we shall be the more likely to meet with game. I find, also, that the king has determined to follow the same route with his warriors in pursuit of the enemy, so that thus far we may travel together. At the hamlet we will diverge to the north-east, while we, if all goes well, embarking in our canoe, will proceed toward the west coast, where, if we do not overtake them on the way, we shall be certain to find them on our arrival. Okandaga has often longed to go to the mission station there, and as she knows it is in vain to urge Mbango to return to his destroyed village, she will doubtless advise him to go to the coast."

"What you say seems highly probable," said I; "and I think the best thing you can do is to go to the king at once and talk him over."

"Trust Jack for that," added Peterkin, who was at that moment deeply engaged with what he called the drumstick of a roast monkey. "Jack would talk over any creature with life, so persuasive is his eloquence. I say, Ralph," he added, holding the half-picked drumstick at arm's length, and regarding it with a critical gaze, "I wonder, now, how the drumstick of an ostrich would taste. Good, I have no doubt, though rather large for one man's dinner."

"It would be almost equal to gorilla ham, I should fancy," said Jack, as he left the hut on his errand to the king.

"O you cannibal, to think of such a thing!" cried Peterkin, throwing the bone of his drumstick after our retreating comrade. —"But 'tis always thus," he added, with a sigh: "man preys upon man, monkey upon monkey. Yet I had hoped better things of Jack. I had believed him to be at least a refined species of gorilla. I say, Ralph, what makes you look so lugubrious?"

"The difficulties, I suppose, that beset our path," said I sadly; for, to say truth, I did not feel in a jesting humour just then. I was forced, however, in spite of myself, to laugh at the expression of mingled disgust and surprise that overspread the mobile countenance of my friend on hearing my reply.

"'The difficulties,'" echoed he, "'that beset our path!' Really, Ralph, life will become insupportable to me if you and Jack go on in this fashion. A man of nerve and sanguine temperament might stand it, but to one like me, of a naturally timid and leaning nature, with the addition of low spirits, it is really crushing-quite crushing."

I laughed, and replied that he must just submit to be crushed, as it was impossible for Jack and me to change our dispositions to suit his convenience; whereupon he sighed, lighted his pipe, and began to smoke vehemently.

In the course of little more than an hour Jack returned, accompanied by Makarooroo, and from the satisfied expression of their faces I judged that they had been successful.

"Ah! I see; it's all right," said Peterkin, raising himself on one elbow as they entered the hut and seated themselves beside the fire. "Old Jambai has been 'talked over.'"

"Right; but he needed a deal of talk-he was horribly obstinate," said Jack.

"Ho, yis; ho! ho! horribubly obsterlate," added Makarooroo in corroboration, rubbing his hands and holding his nose slyly over the bowl of Peterkin's pipe, in order to enjoy, as it were, a second-hand whiff.

"Here, there's a bit for yourself, old boy. Sit down and enjoy yourself while Jack tells us all about his interview with royalty," said Peterkin, handing a lump of tobacco to our guide, whose eyes glistened and white teeth gleamed as he received the much-prized gift.

Jack now explained to us that he had found the king in a happy state of satiety, smoking in his very curious and uneasy-looking easy-chair; that he had at first begged and entreated him (Jack) to stay and take command of his warriors, and had followed up his entreaties with a hint that it was just possible he might adopt stronger measures if entreaty failed.

To this Jack replied in a long speech, in which he pointed out the impossibility of our complying with the king's request under present circumstances, and the absolute necessity of our returning at some period or other to our native land to tell our people of the wonders we had seen in the great country of King Jambai. Observing that his arguments did not make much impression on the king, he brought up his reserve force to the attack, and offered all the remainder of our goods as a free gift to his majesty, stipulating only that he (the king) should, in consideration thereof, carefully send our boxes of specimens down to the coast, where the messengers, on arriving, should be handsomely paid if everything should arrive safely and in good order.

These liberal offers had a visible influence on the sable monarch, whose pipe indicated the state of his mind pretty clearly-thin wreaths of smoke issuing therefrom when he did not sympathise with Jack's reasoning, and thick voluminous clouds revolving about his woolly head, and involving him, as it were, in a veil of gauze, when he became pleasantly impressed. When Jack made mention of the valuable gifts above referred to, his head and shoulders were indistinctly visible amid the white cloudlets; and when he further offered to supply him with a few hundreds of the magical paper balls that had so effectually defeated his enemies the day before, the upper part of his person was obliterated altogether in smoke.

This last offer of Jack's we deemed a great stroke of politic wisdom, for thereby he secured that the pending war should be marked by the shedding of less blood than is normal in such cases. He endeavoured further to secure this end by assuring the king that the balls would be useless for the purpose for which they were made if any other substance should be put into the gun along with them, and that they would only accomplish the great end of putting the enemy to flight if fired at them in one tremendous volley at a time when the foe had no idea of the presence of an enemy.

All things being thus amicably arranged, we retired to rest, and slept soundly until daybreak, when we were awakened by the busy sounds of preparation in the village for the intended pursuit.

We, too, made active arrangements for a start, and soon after were trooping over the plains and through the jungle in the rear of King Jambai's army, laden with such things as we required for our journey to the coast, and Jack, besides his proportion of our food, bedding, cooking utensils, etcetera, carrying Njamie's little sick boy on his broad shoulders.

CHAPTER TWENTY TWO
We Meet with a Ludicrously Awful Adventure.

The day following that on which we set out from King Jambai's village, as narrated in the last chapter, Jack, Peterkin, Makarooroo, Njamie's little boy, and I embarked in a small canoe, and bidding adieu to our hospitable friends, set out on our return journey to the coast.

We determined to proceed thither by another branch of the river which would take us through a totally new, and in some respects different, country from that in which we had already travelled, and which, in the course of a few weeks, would carry us again into the neighbourhood of the gorilla country.

One beautiful afternoon, about a week after parting from our friends, we met with an adventure in which the serious and the comic were strangely mingled. Feeling somewhat fatigued after a long spell at our paddles, and being anxious to procure a monkey or a deer, as we had run short of food, we put ashore, and made our encampment on the banks of the river. This done, we each sallied out in different directions, leaving Makarooroo in charge of the camp.

For some time I wandered about the woods in quest of game, but although I fired at many animals that were good for food, I missed them all, and was unwillingly compelled to return empty-handed. On my way back, and while yet several miles distant from the camp, I met Jack, who had several fat birds of the grouse species hanging at his girdle.

"I am glad to see that you have been more successful than I, Jack," said I, as we met.

"Yet I have not much to boast of," he replied. "It is to be hoped that Peterkin has had better luck. Have you seen him?"

"No; I have not even heard him fire a shot."

"Well, let us go on. Doubtless he will make his appearance in good time. What say you to following the course of this brook? I have no doubt it will guide us to the vicinity of our camp, and the ground immediately to the left of it seems pretty clear of jungle."

"Agreed," said I; and for the next ten minutes or so we walked beside each other in silence. Suddenly our footsteps were arrested by a low peculiar noise.

"Hark! is that a human voice?" whispered Jack, as he cocked his rifle.

"It sounds like it," said I.

At the same moment we heard some branches in an opposite direction crack, as if they had been broken by a heavy tread. Immediately after, the first sound became louder and more distinct. Jack looked at me in surprise, and gradually a peculiar smile overspread his face.

"It's Peterkin," said I, in a low whisper.

My companion nodded, and half-cocking our pieces, we advanced with slow and cautious steps towards the spot whence the sound had come. The gurgling noise of the brook prevented us from hearing as well as usual, so it was not until we were close upon the bushes that fringed the banks of the streamlet that we clearly discerned the tones of Peterkin's voice in conversation with some one, who, however, seemed to make no reply to his remarks. At first I thought he must be talking to himself, but in this I was mistaken.

"Let's listen for a minute or two," whispered my companion, with a broad grin.

I nodded assent, and advancing cautiously, we peeped over the bushes. The sight that met our eyes was so irresistibly comic that we could scarcely restrain our laughter.

On a soft grassy spot, close to the warbling stream, lay our friend Peterkin, on his breast, resting on his elbows, and the forefinger of his right hand raised. Before him, not more than six inches from his nose, sat the most gigantic frog I ever beheld, looking inordinately fat and intensely stupid. My memory instantly flew back to the scene on the coral island where Jack and I had caught our friend holding a quiet conversation with the old cat, and I laughed internally as I thought on the proverb, "The boy is the father of the man."

"Frog," said Peterkin, in a low, earnest voice, at the same time shaking his finger slowly and fixing his eyes on the plethoric creature before him —"frog, you may believe it or not as you please, but I do solemnly assure you that I never did behold such a great, big, fat monster as you are in all-my-life! What do you mean by it?"

As the frog made no reply to this question, but merely kept up an incessant puffing motion in its throat, Peterkin continued —

"Now, frog, answer me this one question-and mind that you don't tell lies-you may not be aware of it, but you can't plead ignorance, for I now tell you that it is exceedingly wicked to tell lies, whether you be a frog or only a boy. Now, tell me, did you ever read 'Aesop's Fables?'"

The frog continued to puff, but otherwise took no notice of its questioner. I could not help fancying that it was beginning to look sulky at being thus catechised.

"What, you won't speak! Well, I'll answer for you: you have *not* read 'Aesop's Fables;' if you had you would not go on blowing yourself up in that way. I'm only a little man, it's true-more's the pity-but if you imagine that by blowing and puffing like that you can ever come to blow up as big as me, you'll find yourself mistaken. You can't do it, so you needn't try. You'll only give yourself rheumatism. Now, *will* you stop? If you won't stop you'll burst-there."

Peterkin paused here, and for some time continued to gaze intently in the face of his new friend. Presently he began again —

"Frog, what are you thinking of? Do you ever think? I don't believe you do. Tightened up as you seem to be with wind or fat or conceit, if you were to attempt to think the effort would crack your skin, so you'd better not try. But, after all, you've some good points about you. If it were not that you would become vain I would tell you that you've got a very good pair of bright eyes, and a pretty mottled skin, and that you're at least the size of a big chicken-not a plucked but a full-fledged chicken. But, O frog, you've got a horribly ugly big mouth, and you're too fat —a great deal too fat for elegance; though I have no doubt it's comfortable. Most fat people are comfortable. Oh! you would, would you?"

This last exclamation was caused by the frog making a lazy leap to one side, tumbling heavily over on its back, and rolling clumsily on to its legs again, as if it wished to escape from its tormentor, but had scarcely vigour enough to make the effort. Peterkin quietly lifted it up and placed it deliberately before him again in the same attitude as before.

"Don't try that again, old boy," said he, shaking his finger threateningly and frowning severely, "else I'll be obliged to give you a poke in the nose. I wonder, now, Frog, if you ever had a mother, or if you only grew out of the earth like a plant. Tell me, were you ever dandled in a mother's arms? Do you know anything of maternal affection, eh? Humph! I suspect not. You would not look so besottedly stupid if you did. I tell you what it is, old fellow: you're uncommonly bad company, and I've a good mind to ram my knife through you, and carry you into camp to my friend Ralph Rover, who'll skin and stuff you to such an extent that your own mother wouldn't know you, and carry you to England, and place you in a museum under a glass case, to be gazed at by nurses, and stared at by children, and philosophised about by learned professors. Hollo! none o' that now. Come, poor beast; I didn't mean to frighten you. There, sit still, and don't oblige me to stick you up again, and I'll not take you to Ralph."

The poor frog, which had made another attempt to escape, gazed vacantly at Peterkin again without moving, except in regard to the puffing before referred to.

"Now, frog, I'll have to bid you good afternoon. I'm sorry that time and circumstance necessitate our separation, but I'm glad that I have had the pleasure of meeting with you. Glad and sorry, frog, in the same breath! Did you ever philosophise on that point, eh? Is it possible, think you, to be glad and sorry at one and the same moment? No doubt a creature like you, with such a very small intellect, if indeed you have any at all, will say that it is not possible. But I know better. Why, what do you call hysterics? Ain't that laughing and crying at once-sorrow and joy mixed? I don't believe you understand a word that I say. You great puffing blockhead, what are you staring at?"

The frog, as before, refused to make any reply; so our friend lay for some time chuckling and making faces at it. While thus engaged he happened to look up, and to our surprise as well as alarm we observed that he suddenly turned as pale as death.

To cock our rifles, and take a step forward so as to obtain a view in the direction in which he was gazing with a fixed and horrified stare, was our immediate impulse. The object that met our eyes on clearing the bushes was indeed well calculated to strike terror into the stoutest heart; for there, not three yards distant from the spot on which our friend lay, and partially concealed by foliage, stood a large black rhinoceros. It seemed to have just approached at that moment, and had been suddenly arrested, if not surprised, by the vision of Peterkin and the frog. There was something inexpressibly horrible in the sight of the great block of a head, with its mischievous-looking eyes, ungainly snout, and ponderous horn, in such close proximity to our friend. How it had got so near without its heavy tread being heard I cannot tell, unless it were that the noise of the turbulent brook had drowned the sound.

But we had no time either for speculation or contemplation. Both Jack and I instantly took aim-he at the shoulder, as he afterwards told me; I at the monster's eye, into which, with, I am bound to confess, my usual precipitancy, I discharged both barrels.

The report seemed to have the effect of arousing Peterkin out of his state of fascination, for he sprang up and darted towards us. At the same instant the wounded rhinoceros crossed the spot which he had left with a terrific rush, and bursting through the bushes as if it had been a great rock falling from a mountain cliff, went headlong into the rivulet.

Without moving from the spot on which we stood, we recharged our pieces with a degree of celerity that, I am persuaded, we never before equalled. Peterkin at the same time caught up his rifle, which leaned against a tree hard by, and only a few seconds elapsed after the fall of the monster into the river ere we were upon its banks ready for another shot.

The portion of the bank of the stream at this spot happened to be rather steep, so that the rhinoceros, on regaining his feet, experienced considerable difficulty in the attempts to clamber out, which he made repeatedly and violently on seeing us emerge from among the bushes.

"Let us separate," said Jack; "it will distract his attention."

"Stay; you have blown out his eye, Ralph, I do believe," said Peterkin.

On drawing near to the struggling monster we observed that this was really the case. Blood streamed from the eye into which I had fired, and poured down his hideous jaws, dyeing the water in which he floundered.

"Look out!" cried Jack, springing to the right, in order to get on the animal's blind side as it succeeded in effecting a landing.

Peterkin instantly sprang in the same direction, while I bounded to the opposite side. I have never been able satisfactorily to decide in my own mind whether this act on my part was performed in consequence of a sudden, almost involuntary, idea that by so doing I should help to distract the creature's attention, or was the result merely of an accidental impulse. But whatever the cause, the effect was most fortunate; for the rhinoceros at once turned towards me, and thus, being blind in the other eye, lost sight of Jack and Peterkin, who with the rapidity almost of thought leaped close up to its side, and took close aim at the most vulnerable parts of its body. As they were directly opposite to me, I felt that I ran some risk of receiving their fire. But before I had time either to reflect that they could not possibly miss so large an object at so short a distance, or to get out of the way, the report of both their heavy rifles rang through the forest, and the rhinoceros fell dead almost at my feet.

"Hurrah!" shouted Peterkin, throwing his cap into the air at this happy consummation, and sitting down on the haunch of our victim.

"Shame on you, Peterkin," said I, as I reloaded his rifle for him —"shame on you to crow thus over a fallen foe!"

"Ha, boy! it's all very well for you to say that now, but you know well enough that you would rather have lost your ears than have missed such a chance as this. But, I say, it'll puzzle you to stuff that fellow, won't it?"

"No doubt of it," answered Jack, as he drew a percussion cap from his pouch, and placed it carefully on the nipple of his rifle. "Ralph will not find it easy; and it's a pity, too, not to take it home with us, for under a glass case it would make such a pretty and appropriate *pendant*, in his museum, to that interesting frog with which you —"

"Oh, you sneaking eavesdropper!" cried Peterkin, laughing. "It is really too bad that a fellow can't have a little *tête-à-tête* with a friend but you and Ralph must be thrusting your impertinent noses in the way."

"Not to mention the rhinoceros," observed Jack.

"Ah! to be sure-the rhinoceros; yes, I might have expected to find you in such low company, for 'birds of a feather,' you know, are said to 'flock together.'"

"If there be any truth in that," said I, "you are bound, on the same ground, to identify yourself with the frog."

"By the way," cried Peterkin, starting up and looking around the spot on which his interesting *tête-à-tête* had taken place, "where is the frog? It was just here that-Ah! —oh! —oh! poor, poor frog!

> "'Your course is run, your days are o'er;
> We'll never have a chat no more,'

"As Shakespeare has it. Well, well, who would have thought that so conversable and intelligent a creature should have come to such a melancholy end?"

The poor frog had indeed come to a sad and sudden end, and I felt quite sorry for it, although I could not help smiling at my companion's quaint manner of announcing the fact.

Not being gifted with the activity of Peterkin, it had stood its ground when the rhinoceros charged, and had received an accidental kick from the great foot of that animal which had broken its back and killed it outright.

"There's one comfort, however," observed Jack, as we stood over the frog's body: "you have been saved the disagreeable necessity of killing it yourself, Ralph."

This was true, and I was not sorry that the rhinoceros had done me this service; for, to say truth, I have ever felt the necessity of killing animals in cold blood to be one of the few disagreeable points in the otherwise delightful life of a naturalist. To shoot animals in the heat and excitement of the chase I have never felt to be particularly repulsive or difficult; but the spearing of an insect, or the deliberate killing of an unresisting frog, are duties which I have ever performed with a feeling of deep self-abhorrence.

Carefully packing my frog in leaves, and placing it in my pouch, I turned with my companions to quit the scene of our late encounter and return to our camp, on arriving at which we purposed sending back Makarooroo to cut off the horn of the rhinoceros; for we agreed that, as it was impossible to carry away the entire carcass, we ought at least to secure the horn as a memorial of our adventure.

CHAPTER TWENTY THREE
We see strange things, and give our negro friends the slip.

During the two following days we passed through a country that was more thickly covered with the indiarubber vine than any place we had before met with in our African travels. I could not help feeling regret that such a splendid region should be almost, if not altogether, unknown and useless to civilised man. There seemed to be an unlimited supply of caoutchouc; but the natives practised a method of gathering it which had the effect of destroying the vine.

One day, some weeks after this, we came upon the habitation of a most remarkable species of monkey, named the Nshiego Mbouve, which we had often heard of, but had not up to that time been so fortunate as to see. Being exceedingly anxious to observe how this remarkable creature made use of its singular house, Peterkin and I lay down near the place, and secreting ourselves in the bushes, patiently awaited the arrival of the monkey, while Jack went off in another direction to procure something for supper.

"I don't believe he'll come home to-night," said Peterkin, after we had lain down. "People never do come in when any one chances to be waiting for them. The human race seems to be born to disappointment. Did you never notice, Ralph, how obstinately contrary and cross-grained things go when you want them to go otherwise?"

"I don't quite understand you," said I.

"Of course you don't. Yours seems to be a mind that can never take anything in unless it is hammered in by repetition."

"Come now, Peterkin, don't become, yourself, an illustration of your own remark in reference to cross-grained things."

"Well, I won't. But seriously, Ralph, have you not observed, in the course of your observant life, that when you have particular business with a man, and go to his house or office, you are *certain* to find him out, to use the common phrase? It would be more correct, however, to say 'you are certain not to find him in.'"

"You are uncommonly particular, Peterkin."

"Truly I had need to be so, with such an uncommonly stupid audience."

"Thank you. Well?"

"Well, have you never observed that if you have occasion to call at a house where you have never been before, the number of that particular house is not in its usual place, and you find it after a search quite away from where it ought to be? Has it never struck you that when you take out your umbrella, the day is certain to become hot and sunny; while, if you omit to carry it with you, it is sure to rain?"

"From all of which you conclude," said I, "that the Nshiego will not come home to-night?"

"Exactly so; that is my meaning precisely."

After Peterkin said this, we relapsed into silence; and it was well that we did so, for had we continued our conversation even in the whispering tones in which it had up to that time been conducted, we should have frightened away the ape which now came, as it were, to rebuke Peterkin for his unbelief.

Coming quickly forward, the Nshiego Mbouve chambered quickly up the tree where its nest was built. This nest was not a structure *into* which it clambered, but a shelter or canopy formed of boughs with their leaves, somewhat in shape like an umbrella, under which it sat. The construction of this shelter exhibited a good deal of intelligent ingenuity on the part of the ape; for it was tied to the tree by means of wild vines and creepers, and formed a neat, comfortable roof, that was quite capable of shedding the night dews or heavy rains, and thus protecting its occupant.

We were greatly amused by the manner in which the creature proceeded to make itself comfortable. Just below the canopy was a small branch which jutted out horizontally from the stem of the tree. On this branch the ape seated itself, its feet and haunches resting thereon. Then it threw one arm round the tree, and hugging that lovingly to its side, gave what appeared to me to be a small sigh of satisfaction, and prepared to go to sleep.

At this Peterkin chuckled audibly. The Nshiego's eyes opened at once. I cocked my gun and took aim. The desire to procure a specimen was very strong within me, but an unconquerable aversion to kill an animal in such cozy circumstances restrained me. The Nshiego got up in alarm. I pointed the gun, but could not fire. It began to descend. I pulled the trigger, and, I am happy to add, missed my aim altogether, to the intense delight of Peterkin, who filled the woods with laughter, while the Nshiego Mbouve, dropping to the ground, ran shrieking from the spot.

My forbearance at this time was afterwards repaid by my obtaining two much finer specimens of this shelter-building ape, both of which were killed by Peterkin.

On quitting this place we had a narrow escape, the recollection of which still fills me with horror. We were walking rapidly back towards our encampment, chatting as we went, when Peterkin suddenly put his foot on what appeared to be the dead branch of a tree. No sooner had he done so than the curling folds of a black snake fully ten feet long scattered the dry leaves into the air, and caused us both to dart aside with a yell of terror.

I have thought that in the complicated and wonderful mechanism of man there lies a species of almost involuntary muscular power which enables him to act in all cases of sudden danger with a degree of prompt celerity that he could not possibly call forth by a direct act of volition. At all events, on the present emergency, without in the least degree knowing what I was about, I brought my gun from my shoulder into a horizontal position, and blew the snake's head off almost in an instant.

I have pondered this subject, and from the fact that while at one time a man may be prompt and courageous in case of sudden danger, at another time the same man may become panic-stricken and helpless, I have come to the conclusion that the all-wise Creator would teach us-even the bravest among us-the lesson of our dependence upon each other, as well as our dependence upon Himself, and would have us know that while at one time we may prove a tower of strength and protection to our friends, at another time our friends may have to afford succour and protection to us.

I have often wondered, in reference to this, that many men seem to take pride in bold inde-pendence, when it is an obvious fact that *every* man is dependent on his fellow, and that this mutual dependence is one of the chief sources of human happiness.

The black snake which I had killed turned out to be one of a very venomous kind, whose bite is said to be fatal, so that we had good cause to be thankful, and to congratulate ourselves on our escape.

In this region of Africa we were particularly fortunate in what we saw and encountered, as the narrative of our experiences on the day following the above incidents will show.

We had scarcely advanced a few miles on our journey on the morning of that day, when we came upon a part of the country where the natives had constructed a curious sort of trap for catching wild animals; and it happened that a large band of natives were on the point of setting out for a grand hunt at that time.

We were greeted with immense delight on our arrival, for those natives, we soon discovered, had already heard of our exploits in the lands of the gorilla, and regarded us as the greatest hunters that had ever been born. After a short conversation with the chief, through the medium of Makarooroo, we arranged to rest there a day, and accompany them on their hunting expedi-tion; and the better to secure their good will, we presented some of the head men with a few of the beads which we still possessed. Then hauling our canoe out of the water, we prepared ourselves for the chase.

After a long and tedious march through somewhat dense jungle, we came upon the ground, which was partly open, partly clothed with trees and shrubs. Here the natives, who numbered several hundreds, spread themselves out in a long semicircular line, in order to drive the game into the trap.

As we followed them, or rather formed part of the line, I overheard the following conversation between Peterkin and Makarooroo, who chanced to be together.

"Now, Mak," said the former, examining the caps of his rifle, "explain to me what sort of trap this is that we're coming to, and what sort of brutes we may expect to find in it."

"De trap, massa," replied our faithful follower, drawing the back of his hand across his mouth —"de trap am be call *hopo* —"

"Called what-o?" inquired Peterkin.

"*Hopo.*"

"Oh! go on."

"An' hims be made ob great number oh sticks tumble down-an' hole at de end ob dat; an' de beasties dat goes in be zebros, elosphants, eelands, buff'los, gaffs, nocrices, noos, an' great more noders ob which me forgit de names."

"Oh! you forgit de names, do you?"

"Yis, massa."

"Ah! it wouldn't be a great loss, Mak, if you were to forget the names of those you remember."

The conversation was interrupted at this point by the appearance of a buffalo, which showed that we were drawing near to the scene of action. But as Makarooroo's description is not remarkable for lucidity, I may explain here that the hopo, or trap, consists of two parts; one part may be termed the conducting hedges, the other the pit at their termination, and into which the game is driven. The conducting hedges are formed in the shape of the letter V. At the narrow extremity there is a narrow lane, at the end of which is the terminating pit. This pit is about eight feet deep and fifteen feet broad, and its edges are made to overlap in such a way that once the animals are in it, they have no chance whatever of getting out again. The surface of the pit is concealed by a thin crust of green rushes, and the hedges are sometimes a mile long, and nearly the same width apart at the outer extremities.

We were still a considerable distance from the outer ends of the hedges, when the natives spread out as above described, and I am convinced that our line extended over at least four miles of ground. The circle, of course, narrowed as they advanced, shouting wildly, in order to drive the game into the enclosure.

That the country was teeming with game soon became apparent, for ever and anon as we advanced a herd of gnus or buffaloes or hartbeests would dart affrighted from their cover, and sweep over the open ground into another place of shelter, out of which they were again driven as the line advanced. In the course of half an hour we drove out hartbeests, zebras, gnus, buffaloes, giraffes, rhinoceroses, and many other kinds of smaller game, either singly or in herds.

"Now, lads," said Jack, approaching Peterkin and me as we walked together, "it is quite evident that if we wish to see this sport in perfection we must get outside the hedge, and run along towards the pit; for there, in the natural course of things, we may expect the grand climax. What say you? Shall we go?"

"Agreed," said I.

"Ditto," cried Peterkin.

So without more words we turned aside, followed by Makarooroo, leaped the hedge, and running down along it soon reached the edge of the pit.

Here we found a number of the natives assembled with spears, looking eagerly through the interstices of the hedges in expectation of the advancing herds. We took up our stand on a convenient spot, and prepared to wait patiently. But our patience was not severely tried. We had not been more than five minutes stationed when the noise of the closing line was heard, and a herd of buffaloes dashed wildly out from a small piece of jungle in which they had sought shelter, and galloped over the plain towards us. Suddenly they halted, and stood for a moment snuffing the air, as if uncertain what to do; while we could see, even at that distance, that every muscle of their bodies trembled with mingled rage and terror. Before they could decide, a herd of gnus burst from the same place; and presently a dozen zebras galloped out, tossing up their heels and heads in magnificent indignation. These last scattered, and approached the hedges; which caused several natives to dart into the enclosure, who from beneath the shelter of oval shields as large as themselves, threw their spears with unerring certainty into the sides of the terrified creatures.

At this moment there was a general rush from the scattered groups of trees and clumps of jungle, for the animals were now maddened with terror, not only at the shouts of their human persecutors, but at their own wild cries and the increasing thunder of their tread.

The shouting and tumult now became excessive. It was almost bewildering. I looked round upon the faces of the negroes nearest to me. They seemed to be almost insane with suppressed excitement, and their dark faces worked in a manner that was quite awful to witness.

Presently there was a general and indiscriminate rush of all kinds of wild animals towards the narrow end of the hopo. The natives pressed in upon them with wild cries. Spears flew in all directions. Ere long the plain was covered with wounded animals struggling and bellowing in their death-agonies. As the rushing multitude drew nearer to the fatal pit, they became crowded together, and now the men near us began to play their part.

"Look out, Jack!" I cried, as a buffalo bull with glaring eyes and foaming jaws made a desperate effort to leap over the barrier in our very faces.

Jack raised his rifle and fired; at the same instant a spear was sent into the buffalo's breast, and it fell back to form a stumbling-block in the way of the rushing mass.

The report of the rifle caused the whole herd to swerve from our side so violently that they bore down the other side, until I began to fear the hedge would give way altogether; but they were met by the spears and the furious yells of the natives there, and again swept on towards the narrow lane.

And now the head of the bellowing mass came to the edge of the pit. Those in front seemed to suspect danger, for they halted suddenly; but the rush of those behind forced them on. In another moment the thin covering gave way, and a literal cataract of huge living creatures went surging down into the abyss.

The scene that followed was terrible to witness; and I could not regard it with other than feelings of intense horror, despite my knowledge of the fact that a large tribe of natives depended on the game then slain for their necessary food. The maddened animals attempted to leap out of the pit, but the overlapping edges already referred to effectually prevented this until the falling torrent filled it up; then some of them succeeded in leaping out from off the backs of their smothered comrades. These, however, were quickly met and speared by the natives, while ever and anon the great mass was upheaved by the frantic struggles of some gigantic creature that was being smothered at the bottom.

While this scene of wholesale destruction was going on, Makarooroo came up to me and begged me, with mysterious looks, to follow him out of the crowd.

I obeyed, and when we had got away from the immediate neighbourhood of the turmoil, I said, —"Well, Mak, what's wrong?"

"De chief, massa, hims tell me few moments ago dat canoe wid Mbango and oomans hab pass dis way to-morrow."

"To-morrow!" I exclaimed.

"No, me forgit; hab pass yistumday."

"Indeed!"

"Yis, an' de chief hims say hims want us to stop wid him and go hunt for week or two. P'raps he no let us go 'way."

"That's just possible, Mak. Have you told Jack?"

"No, massa."

"Then go bring him and Peterkin hither at once."

In a few minutes my companions were with me, and we held a brief earnest consultation as to what we should do.

"I think we should tell the chief we are anxious to be off at once, and leave him on good terms," said I.

Peterkin objected to this. "No," said he; "we cannot easily explain why we are anxious to be off so hastily. I counsel flight. They won't find out that we are gone until it is too late to follow."

Jack agreed with this view, so of course I gave in, though I could not in my heart approve of such a method of sneaking away. But our guide seemed also to be exceedingly anxious to be off, so we decided; and slipping quietly away under the shelter of the hedge, while the natives were still busy with their bloody work, we soon gained the forest. Here we had no difficulty in retracing our steps to the village, where, having picked up our little companion, Njamie's son, who had been left to play with the little boys of the place, we embarked, swept down the stream, and were soon far beyond the chance of pursuit.

CHAPTER TWENTY FOUR
A Long Chase, and a Happy Termination Thereof.

Knowing that unless we advanced with more than ordinary speed we could not hope to overtake our friends for several days —a stern chase being proverbially a long one-we travelled a great part of the night as well as all day; and on our third day after quitting the scene of the curious hunt described in the last chapter, we descried the fugitives descending the river about a quarter of a mile ahead of us.

Unhappily we made a stupid mistake at this time. Instead of waiting until we were near enough to be recognised, we shouted to our friends the moment we saw their canoe. I cannot say that we knew them to be our friends, but we had every reason to suppose so. The result of our shout was that they supposed us to be enemies, and paddled away as if for their lives. It was in vain that we tried to show by signs that we were not enemies.

"Yell!" cried Peterkin, turning to Makarooroo, who sat close behind him.

Our guide opened his huge mouth, and gave utterance to a yell that might well have struck terror into the heart of Mars himself.

"Stop! stay!" cried Peterkin hastily. "I didn't mean a war-yell; I meant a yell of-of *peace*."

"Me no hab a yell ob peace," said Makarooroo, with a look of perplexity.

"I should not suppose you had," observed Jack, with a quiet laugh, as he dipped his paddle more energetically than ever into the stream. —"The fact is, Peterkin, that we shall have to go in for a long chase. There is no doubt about it. I see that there are at least four men in their canoe, and if one of them is Mbango, as we have reason to believe, a stout and expert arm guides them. But ho! give way! 'never venture, never win.'"

With that we all plied our paddles with our utmost might. The chase soon became very exciting. Ere long it became evident that the crews of the two canoes were pretty equally matched, for we did not, apparently, diminish the distance between us by a single inch during the next half-hour.

"What if it turns out not to be Mbango and his party after all?" suggested Peterkin, who wielded his light paddle with admirable effect.

Jack, who sat in the bow, replied that in that case we should have to make the best apology and explanation we could to the niggers, and console ourselves with the consciousness of having done our best.

For some time the rapid dip of our paddles and the rush of our canoe through the water were the only sounds that were heard. Then Peterkin spoke again. He could never keep silence for any great length of time.

"I say, Jack, we'll never do it. If we had only another man, or even a boy." (Peterkin glanced at Njamie's little son, who lay sound asleep at the bottom of the boat.) "No, he won't do; we might as well ask a mosquito to help us."

"I say, lads, isn't one of the crew of that canoe a woman?" said Jack, looking over his shoulder, but not ceasing for an instant to ply his paddle.

"Can't tell," answered Peterkin. —"What say you, Mak?"

"Ye-is, massa," replied the guide, with some hesitation. "Me tink dat am be one ooman's arm what wag de paddil. Oh! yis, me sartin sure now, dat am a ooman."

"That being the case," observed Jack, in a tone of satisfaction, "the chase won't last much longer, for a woman's muscles can't hold out long at such a pace. Ho! give way once more."

In less than five minutes the truth of Jack's remark became apparent, for we began rapidly to overhaul the fugitives. This result acted with a double effect: while it inspirited us to additional exertion, it depressed those whom we were pursuing, and so rendered them less capable than before of contending with us. There was evidently a good deal of excitement and gesticulation among them. Suddenly the man in the stern laid down his paddle, and stooping down seized a gun, with which, turning round, he took deliberate aim at us.

"That's rather awkward," observed Jack, in a cool, quiet way, as if the awkwardness of the case had no reference whatever to him personally.

We did not, however, check our advance. The man fired, and the ball came skipping over the water and passed us at a distance of about two yards.

"Hum! I expected as much," observed Jack. "When a bad shot points a bad gun at you, your best plan is to stand still and take your chance. In such a case the chance is not a bad one. Hollo! the rascal seems about to try it again. I say, boys, we must stop this."

We had now gained so much on the fugitives that we had reason to hope that we might by signs enable them to understand that we were not enemies. We had to make the attempt rather abruptly, for as Jack uttered his last remark, the man in the stern of the canoe we were chasing, having reloaded his gun, turned round to aim at us again. At the same time the rest of the crew suddenly ceased to paddle, in order to enable their comrade to take a steady aim. It was evident that they rested all their hopes upon that shot disabling one of our number, and so enabling them to escape. Seeing this, Makarooroo in desperation seized his rifle and levelled it.

"No, no," said Peterkin, hastily holding up his hand. "Give me your rifle, Mak; and yours, Ralph. Now then, stop paddling for a moment; I'll try an experiment."

So saying, he sprang to his feet, and grasping a rifle in each hand, held them high above his head, intending thus to show that we were well-armed, but that we did not intend to use our weapons.

The device was happily successful: the man in the other canoe lowered the gun with which he was in the act of taking aim at us.

"Now, boys, paddle slowly towards the bank," cried Peterkin, laying down the rifles quickly and standing erect again with his empty hands extended in the air, to confirm the fugitives in regard to our good intentions. They understood the sign, and also turned toward the bank, where in a few minutes both parties landed, at the distance of about two hundred yards from each other.

"Mak, you had better advance alone," said Jack. "If it is Mbango and his friends, they will know you at once. Don't carry your rifle; you won't need it."

"Nay, Jack," I interposed; "you do not act with your usual caution. Should it chance not to be Mbango, it were well that Mak should have his rifle and a companion to support him."

"O most sapient Ralph," said Peterkin, "don't you know that Jack and I have nothing to do but sit down on this bank, each with a double-barrel in his hand, and if anything like foul play should be attempted, four of the enemy should infallibly bite the dust at the same time? But you'd better go with Mak, since you're so careful of him. We will engage to defend you both. —Hollo, Puggy! take the line of our canoe here and fasten it to yonder bush."

The latter part of this remark was addressed to Njamie's little boy, whose name we had never learned, and who had been called Puggy by Peterkin-not, let me remark, in anything approaching to a contemptuous spirit. He evidently meant it as a title of endearment. We had tacitly accepted it, and so had the lad, who for some time past had answered to the name of Puggy, in utter ignorance, of course, as to its signification.

Mak and I now advanced unarmed towards the negroes, and in a few seconds we mutually recognised each other. I was overjoyed to observe the well-known face of Okandaga, who no sooner recognised her lover than she uttered a joyful shout and ran towards him. I at the same time advanced to Mbango, and grasping his hand shook it warmly; but that good-hearted chief was not satisfied with such a tame expression of good will. Seizing me by the shoulders, he put forward his great flat nose and rubbed mine heartily therewith. My first impulse was to draw back, but fortunately my better judgment came to my aid in time, and prevented me from running the risk of hurting the feelings of our black friend. And I had at that time lived long enough to know that there is nothing that sinks so bitterly into the human heart as the repulse, however slightly, of a voluntary demonstration of affection. I had made up my mind that if the dirtiest negro in all Africa should offer to rub noses with me, I would shut my eyes and submit.

I observed among the crew of Mbango's canoe a female figure who instantly attracted my attention and awakened my sympathy. She was seated on a rock, paying no attention whatever to the events that were occurring so near to her, and which, for aught she could tell, might be to her matter of life or death. Her hands hung idly by her side; her body was bowed forward; her head drooped on her breast; and her whole appearance indicated a depth of woe such as I have never before seen equalled.

I pointed to her and looked at Mbango in surprise. He looked first at the woman and then at me, and shook his head mournfully; but being unable to speak to me, or I to him, of course I could not gather much from his looks.

I was about to turn to our guide, when the woman raised her head a little, so that her face was exposed. I at once recognised the features of Njamie, Mbango's favourite wife, and I was now at no loss to divine the cause of her grief.

Starting up in haste, I ran away back at full speed towards the spot where our canoe lay. Jack and Peterkin, seeing how matters stood, were by that time advancing to meet us, and the little boy followed. I passed them without uttering a word, seized the boy by the wrist, and dragged him somewhat violently towards the place where his mother sat.

"Hollo, Ralph," shouted Peterkin as I passed, "see that you don't damage my Puggy, else you'll have to —"

I heard no more. The next instant I stood beside Njamie, and placed her boy before her. I have never in my life witnessed such a mingling of intense eagerness, surprise, and joy, as was expressed by the poor woman when her eyes fell on the face of her child. For one moment she gazed at him, and the expressions I have referred to flitted, or rather flashed, across her dusky countenance; then giving utterance to a piercing shriek, she sprang forward and clasped her son to her bosom.

I would not have missed that sight for the world. I know not very well what my thoughts were at the time, but the memory of that scene has often since, in my musings, filled me with inexpressible gladness; and in pondering the subject, I have felt that the witnessing of that meeting has given additional force to the line in Scripture wherein the word "love" alone is deemed sufficiently comprehensive to describe the whole character of the Almighty.

Here, on the one hand, I beheld unutterable, indescribable woe; on the other hand, unutterable, inconceivable joy-both, I should suppose, in their extremest degree, and both resulting from pure and simple *love*. I pondered this much at the time; I have pondered it often since. It is a subject of study which I recommend to all who chance to read this page.

CHAPTER TWENTY FIVE
I Have a Desperate Encounter and a Narrow Escape.

The happiness that now beamed in the faces of Makarooroo, Okandaga, and Njamie was a sufficient reward to us for all the trouble we had taken and all the risk we had run on their account. Poor Njamie was exceedingly grateful to us. She sought by every means in her power to show this, and among other things, hearing us call her son by the name of Puggy, she at once adopted it, to the immense amusement and delight of Peterkin.

After the first excitement of our meeting had subsided somewhat, we consulted together as to what we should now do. On the one hand, we were unwilling to quit the scene of our hunting triumphs and adventures; on the other hand, Makarooroo and his bride were anxious to reach the mission stations on the coast and get married in the Christian manner.

"Our opposing interests are indeed a little perplexing," said Jack, after some conversation had passed on the subject. —"No doubt, Mak, you and Mbango with his friends might reach the coast safely enough without us; but then what should we do without an interpreter?"

Our poor guide, whose troubles seemed as though they would never end, sighed deeply and glanced at his bride with a melancholy countenance as he replied —

"Me'll go wid you, massa, an' Okandaga'll go to coast an' wait dere for me come."

"Ha!" ejaculated Peterkin, "that's all very well, Mak, but you'll do nothing of the sort. That plan won't do, so we'll have to try again."

"I agree with you, Peterkin," observed Jack. "That plan certainly will not do; but I cannot think of any other that will, so we must just exercise a little self-denial for once, give up all further attacks on the wild beasts of Africa, and accompany Mak to the coast."

"Could we not manage a compromise?" said I.

"What be a cumprumoise?" asked Makarooroo, who had been glancing anxiously from one to the other as we conversed.

Peterkin laid hold of his chin, pursed up his mouth, and looked at me with a gleeful leer.

"There's a chance for you, Ralph," said he; "why don't you explain?"

"Because it's not easy to explain," said I, considering the best way in which to convey the meaning of such a word. —"A compromise, Mak, is-is a bargain, a compact-at least so Johnson puts it —"

"Yes," interposed Peterkin; "so you see, Mak, when you agree with a trader to get him an elephant-tusk, that's a cumprumoise, according to Johnson."

"No, no, Mak," said I quickly; "Peterkin is talking nonsense. It is not a bargain of that kind; it's a —a —You know every question has two sides?"

"Yis, massa."

"Well, suppose you took one side."

"Yis."

"And suppose I took the other side."

"Then suppose we were to agree to forsake our respective sides and meet, as it were, half-way, and thus hold the same middle course —"

"Ay, down the middle and up again; that's it, Mak," again interrupted Peterkin —"that's a cumprumoise. In short, to put it in another and a clearer light, suppose that I were to resolve to hit you an awful whack on one side of your head, and suppose that Ralph were to determine to hit you a frightful bang on the other side, then suppose that we were to agree to give up those amiable intentions, and instead thereof to give you, unitedly, one tremendous smash on the place where, if you had one, the bridge of your nose would be —*that* would be a cumprumoise."

"Ho! ha! ha! hi!" shouted our guide, rolling over on the grass and splitting himself with laughter; for Makarooroo, like the most of his race, was excessively fond of a joke, no matter how bad, and was always ready on the shortest notice to go off into fits of laughter, if he had only the remotest idea of what the jest meant. He had become so accustomed at last to expect something jocular from Peterkin, that he almost invariably opened his mouth to be ready whenever he observed our friend make any demonstration that gave indication of his being about to speak.

From the mere force of sympathy Mbango began to laugh also, and I know not how long the two would have gone on, had not Jack checked them by saying —

"I suspect we are not very well fitted to instruct the unenlightened mind," ("Ho-hi!" sighed Makarooroo, gathering himself up and settling down to listen), "and it seems to me that you'll have to try again, Peterkin, some other mode of explanation."

"Very good, by all means," said our friend. —"Now, Mak, look here. You want to go *there*" (pointing to the coast with his left hand), "and we want to go there" (pointing to the interior with his right hand). "Now if we both agree to go there," (pointing straight before him with his nose), "*that* will be a cumprumoise. D'ye understand?"

"Ho yis, massa, me compiperhend now."

"Exactly so," said I; "that's just it. There is a branch of this river that takes a great bend away to the north before it turns towards the sea, is there not? I think I have heard yourself say so before now."

"Yis, massa, hall right."

"Well, let us go by that branch. We shall be a good deal longer on the route, but we shall be always nearing the end of our journey, and at the same time shall pass through a good deal of new country, in which we may hope to see much game."

"Good," said Jack; "you have wisdom with you for once, Ralph-it seems feasible. —What say you, Mak? I think it a capital plan."

"Yis, massa, it am a copitle plan, sure 'nuff."

The plan being thus arranged and agreed to, we set about the execution of it at once, and ere long our two canoes were floating side by side down the smooth current of the river.

The route which we had chosen led us, as I had before suspected, into the neighbourhood of the gorilla country, and I was much gratified to learn from Mbango, who had travelled over an immense portion of south-western Africa, that it was not improbable we should meet with several of those monstrous apes before finally turning off towards the coast. I say that I was much gratified to learn this; but I little imagined that I was at that time hastening towards a conflict that well-nigh proved fatal to me, and the bare remembrance of which still makes me shudder.

It occurred several weeks after the events just related. We had gone ashore for the purpose of hunting, our supply of provisions chancing at that time to be rather low. Feeling a desire to wander through the woods in solitude for a short time, I separated from my companions. I soon came to regret this deeply, for about an hour afterwards I came upon the tracks of a gorilla. Being armed only with my small-bore double rifle, and not being by any means confident of my shooting powers, I hesitated some time before making up my mind to follow the tracks.

At first I thought of retracing my steps and acquainting my comrades with the discovery I had made; but the little probability there was of my finding them within several hours deterred me. Besides, I felt ashamed to confess that I had been afraid to prosecute the chase alone; so, after pondering the matter a little, I decided on advancing.

Before doing so, however, I carefully examined the caps of my rifle and loosened my long hunting-knife in its sheath. Then I cautiously followed up the track, making as little noise as possible, for I was well aware of the watchfulness of the animal I was pursuing.

The footprints at first were not very distinct, but ere long I came on a muddy place where they were deeply imprinted, and my anxiety was somewhat increased by observing that they were uncommonly large-the largest I had ever seen-and that, therefore, they had undoubtedly been made by one of those solitary and gigantic males, which are always found to be the most savage.

I had scarcely made this discovery when I came unexpectedly on the gorilla itself. It was seated at the foot of a tree about fifty yards from the spot where I stood, the space between us being comparatively clear of underwood. In an instant he observed me, and rose, at the same time giving utterance to one of those diabolical roars which I have before referred to as being so terrible.

I halted, and felt an irresistible inclination to fire at once; but remembering the oft-repeated warnings of my companions, I restrained myself. At that moment I almost wished, I freely confess, that the gorilla would run away. But the monster had no such intention. Again uttering his horrible roar, he began slowly to advance, at the same time beating his drum-like chest with his doubled fist.

I now felt that my hour of trial had come. I must face the gorilla boldly, and act with perfect coolness. The alternative was death. As the hideous creature came on, I observed that he was considerably larger than the biggest we had yet seen; but, strange to say, this fact made no deeper impression upon me. I suppose that my whole mental and nervous being was wound up to the utmost possible state of tension. I *felt* that I was steady and able to brave the onset. But I was not aware of the severity of the test to which I was destined to be subjected. Instead of coming quickly on and deciding my fate at once, the savage animal advanced slowly, sometimes a step or two at a time, and then pausing for a moment ere it again advanced. Sometimes it even sat down on its haunches for a second or two, as if the weight of its overgrown body were too much for its hind legs; but it did not cease all that time to beat its chest, and roar, and twist its features into the most indescribable contortions. I suppose it took nearly five minutes to advance to within twelve yards of me, but those five minutes seemed to me an hour. I cannot describe the mental agony I endured.

When within ten yards of me I could restrain myself no longer. I raised my rifle, aimed at its chest, and fired. With a terrible roar it advanced. Again I fired, but without effect, for the gorilla rushed upon me. In despair, I drew my hunting-knife and launched it full at the brute's chest with all my might. I saw the glittering blade enter it as the enormous paw was raised to beat me down. I threw up my rifle to ward off the fatal blow, and at the same moment sprang to one side, in the hope of evading it. The stock of the rifle was shattered to pieces in an instant, and the blow, which would otherwise have fallen full on my head or chest, was diverted slightly, and took effect on my shoulder, the blade of which was smashed as I was hurled with stunning violence to the ground. For one moment I felt as if I were falling headlong down a precipice; the next, I became unconscious.

On recovering, I found myself lying on my back at the bottom of what appeared to be a large pit. I must have lain there for a considerable time, for I felt cold and stiff; and when I attempted to move, my wounded shoulder caused me unutterable anguish. I knew, however, that I must certainly perish if I did not exert myself; so with much difficulty I crept out of the pit. The first object that met my eyes, on rising to my feet, was the carcass of my late antagonist; which, on examination, I found, though badly wounded by both bullets, had eventually been killed by the knife. It must have died almost immediately after giving me the blow that had hurled me into the pit. I had not observed this pit, owing to the screen of bushes that surrounded it, but I have now no doubt that it was the means of saving my life.

My recollections of what followed this terrible adventure are exceedingly confused. I remember that I wandered about in a state of dreamy uncertainty, endeavouring to retrace my steps to our encampment. I have a faint recollection of meeting, to my surprise, with Jack and Peterkin, and of their tender expressions of sympathy; and I have a very vivid remembrance of the agony I endured when Jack set my broken shoulder-blade and bandaged my right arm tightly to my side. After that, all was a confused dream, in which all the adventures I had ever had with wild beasts were enacted over again, and many others besides that had never taken place at all.

Under the influence of fever, I lay in a state of delirium for many days in the bottom of the canoe; and when my unclouded consciousness was at length restored to me, I found myself lying in a bed, under the hospitable roof of a missionary, the windows of whose house looked out upon the sea.

And now, reader, the record of our adventures is complete. During the few weeks that I spent with the kind missionary of the Cross, I gained strength rapidly, and amused myself penning the first chapters of this book. Makarooroo and Okandaga were married, and soon became useful members of the Christian community on that part of the African coast. Mbango and his friends also joined the missionary for a time, but ultimately returned to the interior, whither I have no doubt they carried some of the good influences that they had received on the coast along with them.

King Jambai proved faithful to his engagement. All our packages and boxes of specimens arrived safely at the coast; and when unpacked for examination, and displayed in the large schoolroom of the station, the gorillas, and other rare and wonderful animals, besides curious plants, altogether formed a magnificent collection, the like of which has not yet been seen in Great Britain, and probably never will be.

When I was sufficiently restored to stand the voyage, Jack and Peterkin and I embarked in a homeward-bound trading vessel, and taking leave of our kind friends of the coast, and of Makarooroo and Okandaga, who wept much at the prospect of separation from us, we set sail for Old England.

"Farewell," said I, as we leaned over the vessel's side and gazed sadly at the receding shore — "farewell to you, kind missionaries and faithful negro friends."

"Ay," added Peterkin, with a deep sigh, "and fare-you-well, ye monstrous apes; gorillas, fare-you-well!"

Manufactured by Amazon.ca
Bolton, ON

34389264R00162